THE 2020 LOOK AT SPACE OPERA BOOK

D1737123

ALSO EDITED BY ALLAN KASTER

The 2020 Look at Space Opera Book

Edited by Allan Kaster

INFINIVOX

The 2O2O LOOK AT SPACE OPERA BOOK

AudioText, Inc., PO Box 418, Barker, TX 77413

www.audiotexttapes.net

ISBN 9798682765065 (trade paperback)

First Edition: October 2020

CONTENTS

ACKNOWLEDGEMENTS

"On the Orion Line" copyright © 2000 by Stephen Baxter. First published in *Asimov's Science Fiction*, October/November 2000. Reprinted with permission of Stephen Baxter c/o Selectric Artists LLC.

"The Days Between" copyright © 2001 by Coyote Steele LLC. First published in *Asimov's Science Fiction*, March 2001. Reprinted by permission of the author.

"Slow Life" copyright © 2002 by Michael Swanwick. First published in *Analog Science Fiction and Fact*, December 2002. Reprinted by permission of the author.

"The Third Party" copyright © 2004 by David Moles. First published in *Asimov's Science Fiction*, September 2004. Reprinted by permission of the author.

"Mayflower II" copyright © 2004 by Stephen Baxter. First published as *Mayflower II* (PS Publishing). Reprinted with permission of Stephen Baxter c/o Selectric Artists LLC.

"Bright Red Star" copyright © 2005 by Bud Sparhawk. First published in *Asimov's Science Fiction*, March 2005. Reprinted by permission of the author.

"Dead Men Walking" copyright © 2006 by Paul McAuley. First published in *Asimov's Science Fiction*, June 2006. Reprinted by permission of the author.

"Glory" copyright © 2007 by Greg Egan. First published in *The New Space Opera* (Eos), edited by Gardner Dozois and Jonathan Strahan. Reprinted by permission of the author.

"Saving Tiamaat" copyright © 2020 by Gwyneth Jones. First published in *The New Space Opera* (Eos), edited by Gardner Dozois and Jonathan Strahan. Reprinted by permission of the author.

"Boojum" copyright © 2008 by Elizabeth Bear and Sarah Monette. First published in *Fast Ships, Black Sails* (Night Shade), edited by Ann and Jeff VanderMeer. Reprinted by permission of the authors.

"City of the Dead" copyright © 2008 by Paul McAuley. First published in *Postscripts 15*. Reprinted by permission of the author.

INTRODUCTION

THESE DAYS SPACE opera is looking pretty good. It's a very popular, if not the most popular, destination for lots of readers in the science fiction universe. Basically a space opera is a drama set in space within a grandiose backdrop that is either subtle or overt. It can take place on a starship, space station, planet, moon, etc. It has many forms such as alien contact, military science fiction, anthropological science fiction, planetary romance, or starship saga. Some of the finest space operas the genre has to offer are a fusion of these many forms.

This collection presents twenty of the best space opera stories published over the past twenty years in more or less chronological order. Many of these stories were either nominated, or finalists, for awards such as the Hugo Award, the Nebula Award, the Locus Award, and the Theodore Sturgeon Memorial Award. Both "Slow Life" and "The Island" won the Hugo Award.

In the following pages flamboyant adventures are set into motion. Darkness is encroached upon. Space pirates prowl. Political machinations flourish. Unlikely heroes emerge. And, of course, it's not over till the fat alien sings!

—*Allan Kaster*
Houston
September 28, 2020

ON THE ORION LINE

STEPHEN BAXTER

THE *BRIEF LIFE Burns Brightly* broke out of the fleet. We were chasing down a Ghost cruiser, and we were closing.

The lifedome of the *Brightly* was transparent, so it was as if Captain Teid in her big chair, and her officers and their equipment clusters—and a few low-grade tars like me—were just floating in space. The light was subtle, coming from a nearby cluster of hot young stars, and from the rivers of sparking lights that made up the fleet formation we had just left, and beyond *that* from the sparking of novae. This was the Orion Line—six thousand light years from Earth and a thousand lights long, a front that spread right along the inner edge of the Orion Spiral Arm—and the stellar explosions marked battles that must have concluded years ago.

And, not a handful of klicks away, the Ghost cruiser slid across space, running for home. The cruiser was a rough egg-shape of silvered rope. Hundreds of Ghosts clung to the rope. You could see them slithering this way and that, not affected at all by the emptiness around them.

The Ghosts' destination was a small, old yellow star. Pael, our tame Academician, had identified it as a fortress star from some kind of strangeness in its light. But up close you don't need to be an Academician to spot a fortress. From the *Brightly* I could see with my unaided eyes that the star had a pale blue cage around it—an open lattice with struts half a million kilometers long—thrown there by the Ghosts, for their own purposes.

I had a lot of time to watch all this. I was just a tar. I was fifteen years old.

My duties at that moment were non-specific. I was supposed to stand to, and render assistance any way that was required—most likely with basic medical attention should we go into combat. Right now the only one of us tars actually working was Halle, who was chasing down a pool of vomit sicked up by Pael, the Academician, the only non-Navy personnel on the bridge.

The action on the *Brightly* wasn't like you see in Virtual shows. The atmosphere was calm, quiet, competent. All you could hear was the murmur of voices, from the crew and the equipment, and the hiss of recycling air. No drama: it was like an operating theater.

There was a soft warning chime.

The captain raised an arm and called over Academician Pael, First Officer Till, and Jeru, the commissary assigned to the ship. They huddled close, conferring—apparently arguing. I saw the way flickering nova light reflected from Jeru's shaven head.

I felt my heart beat harder.

Everybody knew what the chime meant: that we were approaching the fortress cordon. Either we would break off, or we would chase the Ghost cruiser inside its invisible fortress. And everybody knew that no Navy ship that had ever penetrated a fortress cordon, ten light-minutes from the central star, had come back out again.

One way or the other, it would all be resolved soon.

Captain Teid cut short the debate. She leaned forward and addressed the crew. Her voice, cast through the ship, was friendly, like a cadre leader whispering in your ear. "You can all see we can't catch that swarm of Ghosts this side of the cordon. And you all know the hazard of crossing a cordon. But if we're ever going to break this blockade of theirs we have to find a way to bust open those forts. So we're going in anyhow. Stand by your stations."

There was a half-hearted cheer.

I caught Halle's eye. She grinned at me. She pointed at the captain, closed her fist and made a pumping movement. I admired her sentiment but she wasn't being too accurate, anatomically speaking, so I raised my middle finger and jiggled it back and forth.

It took a slap on the back of the head from Jeru, the commissary, to put a stop to that. "Little morons," she growled.

"Sorry, sir—"

I got another slap for the apology. Jeru was a tall, stocky woman, dressed in the bland monastic robes said to date from the time of the founding of the Commission for Historical Truth a thousand years ago. But rumor was she'd seen plenty of combat action of her own before joining the

Commission, and such was her physical strength and speed of reflex I could well believe it.

As we neared the cordon the Academician, Pael, started a gloomy countdown. The slow geometry of Ghost cruiser and tinsel-wrapped fortress star swiveled across the crowded sky.

Everybody went quiet.

The darkest time is always just before the action starts. Even if you can see or hear what is going on, all you do is think. What was going to happen to us when we crossed that intangible border? Would a fleet of Ghost ships materialize all around us? Would some mysterious weapon simply blast us out of the sky?

I caught the eye of First Officer Till. He was a veteran of twenty years; his scalp had been burned away in some ancient close-run combat, long before I was born, and he wore a crown of scar tissue with pride.

"Let's do it, tar," he growled.

All the fear went away. I was overwhelmed by a feeling of togetherness, of us all being in this crap together. I had no thought of dying. Just: let's get through this.

"Yes, *sir!*"

Pael finished his countdown.

All the lights went out. Detonating stars wheeled.

And the ship exploded.

I was thrown into darkness. Air howled. Emergency bulkheads scythed past me, and I could hear people scream.

I slammed into the curving hull, nose pressed against the stars.

I bounced off and drifted. The inertial suspension was out, then. I thought I could smell blood—probably my own.

I could see the Ghost ship, a tangle of rope and silver baubles, tingling with highlights from the fortress star. We were still closing.

But I could also see shards of shattered lifedome, a sputtering drive unit. The shards were bits of the *Brightly*. It had gone, all gone, in a fraction of a second.

"Let's do it," I murmured.

Maybe I was out of it for a while.

Somebody grabbed my ankle and tugged me down. There was a competent slap on my cheek, enough to make me focus.

"Case. Can you hear me?"

It was First Officer Till. Even in the swimming starlight that burned-off scalp was unmistakable.

I glanced around. There were four of us here: Till, Commissary Jeru, Academician Pael, me. We were huddled up against what looked like the stump of the First Officer's console. I realized that the gale of venting air had stopped. I was back inside a hull with integrity, then—

"Case!"

"I—yes, sir."

"Report."

I touched my lip; my hand came away bloody. At a time like that it's your duty to report your injuries, honestly and fully. Nobody needs a hero who turns out not to be able to function. "I think I'm all right. I may have a concussion."

"Good enough. Strap down." Till handed me a length of rope.

I saw that the others had tied themselves to struts. I did the same.

Till, with practiced ease, swam away into the air, I guessed looking for other survivors.

Academician Pael was trying to curl into a ball. He couldn't even speak. The tears just rolled out of his eyes. I stared at the way big globules welled up and drifted away into the air, glimmering.

The action had been over in seconds. All a bit sudden for an earthworm, I guess.

Nearby, I saw, trapped under one of the emergency bulkheads, there was a pair of legs—just that. The rest of the body must have been chopped away, gone drifting off with the rest of the debris from *Brightly*. But I recognized those legs, from a garish pink stripe on the sole of the right boot. That had been Halle. She was the only girl I had ever screwed, I thought—and more than likely, given the situation, the only girl I ever would get to screw.

I couldn't figure out how I felt about that.

Jeru was watching me. "Tar—do you think we should all be frightened for ourselves, like the Academician?" Her accent was strong, unidentifiable.

"No, sir."

"No." Jeru studied Pael with contempt. "We are in a yacht, Academician. Something has happened to the *Brightly*. The 'dome was designed to break up into yachts like this." She sniffed. "We have air, and it isn't foul yet." She winked at me. "Maybe we can do a little damage to the Ghosts before we die, tar. What do you think?"

I grinned. "Yes, sir."

Pael lifted his head and stared at me with salt water eyes. "Lethe. You people are monsters." His accent was gentle, a lilt. "Even such a child as this. You embrace death—"

Jeru grabbed Pael's jaw in a massive hand, and pinched the joint until he squealed. "Captain Teid grabbed you, Academician; she threw you here, into the yacht, before the bulkhead came down. I saw it. If she hadn't taken the time to do that, she would have made it herself. Was *she* a monster? Did *she* embrace death?" And she pushed Pael's face away.

For some reason I hadn't thought about the rest of the crew until that moment. I guess I have a limited imagination. Now, I felt adrift. The captain—dead?

I said, "Excuse me, Commissary. How many other yachts got out?"

"None," she said steadily, making sure I had no illusions. "Just this one. They died doing their duty, tar. Like the captain."

Of course she was right, and I felt a little better. Whatever his character, Pael was too valuable not to save. As for me, I had survived through sheer blind chance, through being in the right place when the walls came down: if the captain had been close, her duty would have been to pull me out of the way and take my place. It isn't a question of human values but of economics: a *lot* more is invested in the training and experience of a Captain Teid—or a Pael—than in *me*.

But Pael seemed more confused than I was.

First Officer Till came bustling back with a heap of equipment. "Put these on." He handed out pressure suits. They were what we called slime suits in training: lightweight skin suits, running off a backpack of gen-enged algae. "Move it," said Till. "Impact with the Ghost cruiser in four minutes. We don't have any power; there's nothing we can do but ride it out."

I crammed my legs into my suit.

Jeru complied, stripping off her robe to reveal a hard, scarred body. But she was frowning. "Why not heavier armor?"

For answer, Till picked out a gravity-wave handgun from the gear he had retrieved. Without pausing he held it to Pael's head and pushed the fire button.

Pael twitched.

Till said, "See? Nothing is working. Nothing but bio systems, it seems." He threw the gun aside.

Pael closed his eyes, breathing hard.

Till said to me, "Test your comms."

I closed up my hood and faceplate and began intoning, "One, two, three . . ." I could hear nothing.

Till began tapping at our backpacks, resetting the systems. His hood started to glow with transient, pale blue symbols. And then, scratchily, his voice started to come through. ". . . Five, six, seven—can you hear me, tar?"

"Yes, sir."

The symbols were bioluminescent. There were receptors on all our suits—photoreceptors, simple eyes—which could "read" the messages scrawled on our companions' suits. It was a backup system meant for use in environments where anything higher-tech would be a liability. But obviously it would only work as long as we were in line of sight.

"That will make life harder," Jeru said. Oddly, mediated by software, she was easier to understand.

Till shrugged. "You take it as it comes." Briskly, he began to hand out more gear. "These are basic field belt kits. There's some medical stuff: a suture kit, scalpel blades, blood-giving sets. You wear these syrettes around your neck, Academician. They contain painkillers, various gen-enged med-viruses . . . no, you wear it *outside* your suit, Pael, so you can reach it. You'll find valve inlets here, on your sleeve, and here, on the leg." Now came weapons. "We should carry handguns, just in case they start working, but be ready with these." He handed out combat knives.

Pael shrank back.

"Take the knife, Academician. You can shave off that ugly beard, if nothing else."

I laughed out loud, and was rewarded with a wink from Till.

I took a knife. It was a heavy chunk of steel, solid and reassuring. I tucked it in my belt. I was starting to feel a whole lot better.

"Two minutes to impact," Jeru said. I didn't have a working chronometer; she must have been counting the seconds.

"Seal up." Till began to check the integrity of Pael's suit; Jeru and I helped each other. Face seal, glove seal, boot seal, pressure check. Water check, oh-two flow, cee-oh-two scrub . . .

When we were sealed I risked poking my head above Till's chair.

The Ghost ship filled space. The craft was kilometers across, big enough to have dwarfed the poor, doomed *Brief Life Burns Brightly*. It was a tangle of silvery rope of depthless complexity, occluding the stars and the warring fleets. Bulky equipment pods were suspended in the tangle.

And everywhere there were Silver Ghosts, sliding like beads of mercury. I could see how the yacht's emergency lights were returning crimson highlights from the featureless hides of Ghosts, so they looked like sprays of blood droplets across that shining perfection.

"Ten seconds," Till called. "Brace."

Suddenly silver ropes thick as tree trunks were all around us, looming out of the sky.

And we were thrown into chaos again.

———

I heard a grind of twisted metal, a scream of air. The hull popped open like an eggshell. The last of our air fled in a gush of ice crystals, and the only sound I could hear was my own breathing.

The crumpling hull soaked up some of our momentum.

But then the base of the yacht hit, and it hit hard.

The chair was wrenched out of my grasp, and I was hurled upward. There was a sudden pain in my left arm. I couldn't help but cry out.

I reached the limit of my tether and rebounded. The jolt sent further waves of pain through my arm. From up there, I could see the others were clustered around the base of the First Officer's chair, which had collapsed.

I looked up. We had stuck like a dart in the outer layers of the Ghost ship. There were shining threads arcing all around us, as if a huge net had scooped us up.

Jeru grabbed me and pulled me down. She jarred my bad arm, and I winced. But she ignored me, and went back to working on Till. He was under the fallen chair.

Pael started to take a syrette of dope from the sachet around his neck.

Jeru knocked his hand away. "You always use the casualty's," she hissed. "Never your own."

Pael looked hurt, rebuffed. "Why?"

I could answer that. "Because the chances are you'll need your own in a minute."

Jeru stabbed a syrette into Till's arm.

Pael was staring at me through his faceplate with wide, frightened eyes. "You've broken your arm."

Looking closely at the arm for the first time, I saw that it was bent back at an impossible angle. I couldn't believe it, even through the pain. I'd never bust so much as a finger, all the way through training.

Now Till jerked, a kind of miniature convulsion, and a big bubble of spit and blood blew out of his lips. Then the bubble popped, and his limbs went loose.

Jeru sat back, breathing hard. She said, "Okay. Okay. How did he put it?—You take it as it comes." She looked around, at me, Pael. I could see she was trembling, which scared me. She said, "Now we move. We have to find an LUP. A lying-up point, Academician. A place to hole up."

I said, "The First Officer—"

"Is dead." She glanced at Pael. "Now it's just the three of us. We won't be able to avoid each other anymore, Pael."

Pael stared back, eyes empty.

Jeru looked at me, and for a second her expression softened. "A broken neck. Till broke his neck, tar."

Another death, just like that: just for a heartbeat that was too much for me.

Jeru said briskly, "Do your duty, tar. Help the worm."

I snapped back. "Yes, sir." I grabbed Pael's unresisting arm.

Led by Jeru, we began to move, the three of us, away from the crumpled wreck of our yacht, deep into the alien tangle of a Silver Ghost cruiser.

We found our LUP.

It was just a hollow in a somewhat denser tangle of silvery ropes, but it afforded us some cover, and it seemed to be away from the main concentration of Ghosts. We were still open to the vacuum—as the whole cruiser seemed to be—and I realized then that I wouldn't be getting out of this suit for a while.

As soon as we picked the LUP, Jeru made us take up positions in an all-around defense, covering a 360-degree arc.

Then we did nothing, absolutely nothing, for ten minutes.

It was SOP, standard operating procedure, and I was impressed. You've just come out of all the chaos of the destruction of the *Brightly* and the crash of the yacht, a frenzy of activity. Now you have to give your body a chance to adjust to the new environment, to the sounds and smells and sights.

Only here, there was nothing to smell but my own sweat and piss, nothing to hear but my ragged breathing. And my arm was hurting like hell.

To occupy my mind I concentrated on getting my night vision working. Your eyes take a while to adjust to the darkness—forty-five minutes before they are fully effective—but you are already seeing better after five. I could see stars through the chinks in the wiry metallic brush around me, the flares of distant novae, and the reassuring lights of our fleet. But a Ghost ship is a dark place, a mess of shadows and smeared-out reflections. It was going to be easy to get spooked here.

When the ten minutes were done, Academician Pael started bleating, but Jeru ignored him and came straight over to me. She got hold of my busted arm and started to feel the bone. "So," she said briskly. "What's your name, tar?"

"Case, sir."

"What do you think of your new quarters?"

"Where do I eat?"

She grinned. "Turn off your comms," she said.

I complied.

Without warning she pulled my arm, hard. I was glad she couldn't hear how I howled.

She pulled a canister out of her belt and squirted gunk over my arm; it was semi-sentient and snuggled into place, setting as a hard cast around my injury. When I was healed the cast would fall away of its own accord.

She motioned me to turn on my comms again, and held up a syrette.

"I don't need that."

"Don't be brave, tar. It will help your bones knit."

"Sir, there's a rumor that stuff makes you impotent." I felt stupid even as I said it.

Jeru laughed out loud, and just grabbed my arm. "Anyhow it's the First Officer's, and he doesn't need it anymore, does he?"

I couldn't argue with that; I accepted the injection. The pain started ebbing almost immediately.

Jeru pulled a tactical beacon out of her belt kit. It was a thumb-sized orange cylinder. "I'm going to try to signal the fleet. I'll work my way out of this tangle; even if the beacon is working we might be shielded in here." Pael started to protest, but she shut him up. I sensed I had been thrown into the middle of an ongoing conflict between them. "Case, you're on stag. And show this *worm* what's in his kit. I'll come back the same way I go. All right?"

"Yes." More SOP.

She slid away through silvery threads.

I lodged myself in the tangle and started to go through the stuff in the belt kits Till had fetched for us. There was water, rehydration salts, and compressed food, all to be delivered to spigots inside our sealed hoods. We had power packs the size of my thumbnail, but they were as dead as the rest of the kit. There was a lot of low-tech gear meant to prolong survival in a variety of situations, such as a magnetic compass, a heliograph, a thumb saw, a magnifying glass, pitons, and spindles of rope, even fishing line.

I had to show Pael how his suit functioned as a lavatory. The trick is just to let go; a slime suit recycles most of what you give it, and compresses the rest. That's not to say it's comfortable. I've never yet worn a suit that was good at absorbing odors. I bet no suit designer spent more than an hour in one of her own creations.

I felt fine.

The wreck, the hammer-blow deaths one after the other—none of it was far beneath the surface of my mind. But that's where it stayed, for now; as long as I had the next task to focus on, and the next after that, I could keep moving forward. The time to let it all hit you is after the show.

I guess Pael had never been trained like that.

He was a thin, spindly man, his eyes sunk in black shadow, and his ridiculous red beard was crammed up inside his faceplate. Now that the great crises were over, his energy seemed to have drained away, and his functioning was slowing to a crawl. He looked almost comical as he pawed at his useless bits of kit.

After a time he said, "Case, is it?"

"Yes, sir."

"Are you from Earth, child?"

"No. I—"

He ignored me. "The Academies are based on Earth. Did you know that, child? But they do admit a few off-worlders."

I glimpsed a lifetime of outsider resentment. But I couldn't care less. Also I wasn't a child. I asked cautiously, "Where are you from, sir?"

He sighed. "It's 51 Pegasi. I-B."

I'd never heard of it. "What kind of place is that? Is it near Earth?"

"Is everything measured relative to Earth . . . ? Not very far. My home world was one of the first extrasolar planets to be discovered—or at least, the primary is. I grew up on a moon. The primary is a hot Jupiter."

I knew what *that* meant: a giant planet huddled close to its parent star.

He looked up at me. "Where you grew up, could you see the sky?"

"No—"

"I could. And the sky was full of sails. That close to the sun, solar sails work efficiently, you see. I used to watch them at night, schooners with sails hundreds of kilometers wide, tacking this way and that in the light. But you can't see the sky from Earth—not from the Academy bunkers anyhow."

"Then why did you go there?"

"I didn't have a choice." He laughed, hollowly. "I was doomed by being smart. That is why your precious commissary despises me so much, you see. I have been taught to think—and we can't have that, can we . . . ?"

I turned away from him and shut up. Jeru wasn't "my" commissary, and this sure wasn't my argument. Besides, Pael gave me the creeps. I've always been wary of people who knew too much about science and technology. With a weapon, all you want to know is how it works, what kind of energy or ammunition it needs, and what to do when it goes wrong. People who know all the technical background and the statistics are usually covering up their own failings; it is experience of use that counts.

But this was no loudmouth weapons tech. This was an Academician: one of humanity's elite scientists. I felt I had no point of contact with him at all.

I looked out through the tangle, trying to see the fleet's sliding, glimmering lanes of light.

There was motion in the tangle. I turned that way, motioning Pael to keep still and silent, and got hold of my knife in my good hand.

Jeru came bustling back, exactly the way she had left. She nodded approvingly at my alertness. "Not a peep out of the beacon."

Pael said, "You realize our time here is limited."

I asked, "The suits?"

"He means the star," Jeru said heavily. "Case, fortress stars seem to be unstable. When the Ghosts throw up their cordon, the stars don't last long before going pop."

Pael shrugged. "We have hours, a few days at most."

Jeru said, "Well, we're going to have to get out, beyond the fortress cordon, so we can signal the fleet. That or find a way to collapse the cordon altogether."

Pael laughed hollowly. "And how do you propose we do that?"

Jeru glared. "Isn't it your role to tell me, Academician?"

Pael leaned back and closed his eyes. "Not for the first time, you're being ridiculous."

Jeru growled. She turned to me. "You. What do *you* know about the Ghosts?"

I said, "They come from someplace cold. That's why they are wrapped up in silvery shells. You can't bring a Ghost down with laser fire because of those shells. They're perfectly reflective."

Pael said, "Not perfectly. They are based on a Planck-zero effect. . . . About one part in a billion of incident energy is absorbed."

I hesitated. "They say the Ghosts experiment on people."

Pael sneered. "Lies put about by your Commission for Historical Truth, Commissary. To demonize an opponent is a tactic as old as mankind."

Jeru wasn't perturbed. "Then why don't you put young Case right? How *do* the Ghosts go about their business?"

Pael said, "The Silver Ghosts tinker with the laws of physics."

I looked to Jeru; she shrugged.

Pael tried to explain. It was all to do with quagma.

Quagma is the state of matter that emerged from the Big Bang. Matter, when raised to sufficiently high temperatures, melts into a magma of quarks—a quagma. And at such temperatures the four fundamental forces of physics unify into a single superforce. When quagma is allowed to cool and expand its binding superforce decomposes into four sub-forces.

To my surprise, I understood some of this. The principle of the GUT-drive, which powers intrasystem ships like *Brief Life Burns Brightly*, is related.

Anyhow, by controlling the superforce decomposition, you can select the ratio between those forces. And those ratios govern the fundamental constants of physics.

Something like that.

Pael said, "That marvelous reflective coating of theirs is an example. Each Ghost is surrounded by a thin layer of space in which a fundamental number called the Planck constant is significantly lower than elsewhere. Thus, quantum effects are collapsed. . . . Because the energy carried by a photon, a particle of light, is proportional to the Planck constant, an incoming photon must shed most of its energy when it hits the shell—hence the reflectivity."

"All right," Jeru said. "So what are they doing here?"

Pael sighed. "The fortress star seems to be surrounded by an open shell of quagma and exotic matter. We surmise that the Ghosts have blown a bubble around each star, a space-time volume in which the laws of physics are—tweaked."

"And that's why our equipment failed."

"Presumably," said Pael, with cold sarcasm.

I asked, "What do the Ghosts want? Why do they do all this stuff?"

Pael studied me. "You are trained to kill them, and they don't even tell you that?"

Jeru just glowered.

Pael said, "The Ghosts were not shaped by competitive evolution. They are symbiotic creatures; they derive from life-forms that huddled into co-operative collectives as their world turned cold. And they seem to be motivated—not by expansion and the acquisition of territory for its own sake, as we are—but by a desire to understand the fine-tuning of the universe. *Why are we here?* You see, young tar, there is only a narrow range of the constants of physics within which life of *any* sort is possible. We think the Ghosts are studying this question by pushing at the boundaries—by tinkering with the laws that sustain and contain us all."

Jeru said, "An enemy who can deploy the laws of physics as a weapon is formidable. But in the long run, we will out-compete the Ghosts."

Pael said bleakly, "Ah, the evolutionary destiny of mankind. How dismal. But we lived in peace with the Ghosts, under the Raoul Accords, for a thousand years. We are so different, with disparate motivations—why should there be a clash, any more than between two species of birds in the same garden?"

I'd never seen birds, or a garden, so that passed me by.

Jeru glared. She said at last, "Let's return to practicalities. *How* do their fortresses work?" When Pael didn't reply, she snapped, "Academician, you've been *inside* a fortress cordon for an hour already and you haven't made a single fresh observation?"

Acidly, Pael demanded, "What would you have me do?"

Jeru nodded at me. "What have you seen, tar?"

"Our instruments and weapons don't work," I said promptly. "The *Brightly* exploded. I broke my arm."

Jeru said, "Till snapped his neck also." She flexed her hand within her glove. "What would make our bones more brittle? Anything else?"

I shrugged.

Pael admitted, "I do feel somewhat warm."

Jeru asked, "Could these body changes be relevant?"

"I don't see how."

"Then figure it out."

"I have no equipment."

Jeru dumped spare gear—weapons, beacons—in his lap. "You have your eyes, your hands and your mind. Improvise." She turned to me. "As for you, tar, let's do a little infil. We still need to find a way off this scow."

I glanced doubtfully at Pael. "There's nobody to stand on stag."

Jeru said, "I know. But there are only three of us." She grasped Pael's shoulder, hard. "Keep your eyes open, Academician. We'll come back the same way we left. So you'll know it's us. Do you understand?"

Pael shrugged her away, focusing on the gadgets on his lap.

I looked at him doubtfully. It seemed to me a whole platoon of Ghosts could have come down on him without his even noticing. But Jeru was right; there was nothing more we could do.

She studied me, fingered my arm. "You up to this?"

"I'm fine, sir."

"You are lucky. A good war comes along once in a lifetime. And this is your war, tar."

That sounded like parade-ground pep talk, and I responded in kind. "Can I have your rations, sir? You won't be needing them soon." I mimed digging a grave.

She grinned back fiercely. "Yeah. When your turn comes, slit your suit and let the farts out before I take it off your stiffening corpse—"

Pael's voice was trembling. "You really are monsters."

I shared a glance with Jeru. But we shut up, for fear of upsetting the earthworm further.

I grasped my fighting knife, and we slid away into the dark.

———

What we were hoping to find was some equivalent of a bridge. Even if we succeeded, I couldn't imagine what we'd do next. Anyhow, we had to try.

We slid through the tangle. Ghost cable stuff is tough, even to a knife blade. But it is reasonably flexible; you can just push it aside if you get stuck, although we tried to avoid doing that for fear of leaving a sign.

We used standard patrolling SOP, adapted for the circumstance. We would move for ten or fifteen minutes, clambering through the tangle, and then take a break for five minutes. I'd sip water—I was getting hot—and maybe nibble on a glucose tab, check on my arm, and pull the suit around me to get comfortable again. It's the way to do it. If you just push yourself on and on you run down your reserves and end up in no fit state to achieve the goal anyhow.

And all the while I was trying to keep up my all-around awareness, protecting my dark adaptation, and making appreciations. How far away is Jeru? What if an attack comes from in front, behind, above, below, left or right? Where can I find cover?

I began to build up an impression of the Ghost cruiser. It was a rough egg-shape, a couple of kilometers long, and basically a mass of the anonymous silvery cable. There were chambers and platforms and instruments stuck as if at random into the tangle, like food fragments in an old man's beard. I guess it makes for a flexible, easily modified configuration. Where the tangle was a little less thick, I glimpsed a more substantial core, a cylinder running along the axis of the craft. Perhaps it was the drive unit. I wondered if it was functioning; perhaps the Ghost equipment was designed to adapt to the changed conditions inside the fortress cordon.

There were Ghosts all over the craft.

They drifted over and through the tangle, following pathways invisible to us. Or they would cluster in little knots on the tangle. We couldn't tell what they were doing or saying. To human eyes a Silver Ghost is just a silvery sphere, visible only by reflection like a hole cut out of space, and without specialist equipment it is impossible even to tell one from another.

We kept out of sight. But I was sure the Ghosts must have spotted us, or were at least tracking our movements. After all we'd crash-landed in their ship. But they made no overt moves toward us.

We reached the outer hull, the place the cabling ran out, and dug back into the tangle a little way to stay out of sight.

I got an unimpeded view of the stars.

Still those nova firecrackers went off all over the sky; still those young stars glared like lanterns. It seemed to me the fortress's central, enclosed star looked a little brighter, hotter than it had been. I made a mental note to report that to the Academician.

But the most striking sight was the fleet.

Over a volume light-months wide, countless craft slid silently across the sky. They were organized in a complex network of corridors filling three-dimensional space: rivers of light gushed this way and that, their different colors denoting different classes and sizes of vessel. And, here and there, denser knots of color and light sparked, irregular flares in the orderly flows.

They were places where human ships were engaging the enemy, places where people were fighting and dying.

It was a magnificent sight. But it was a big, empty sky, and the nearest sun was that eerie dwarf enclosed in its spooky blue net, a long way away, and there was movement in three dimensions, above me, below me, all around me. . . .

I found the fingers of my good hand had locked themselves around a sliver of the tangle.

Jeru grabbed my wrist and shook my arm until I was able to let go. She kept hold of my arm, her eyes locked on mine. *I have you. You won't fall.* Then she pulled me into a dense knot of the tangle, shutting out the sky.

She huddled close to me, so the bio lights of our suits wouldn't show far. Her eyes were pale blue, like windows. "You aren't used to being outside, are you, tar?"

"I'm sorry, Commissary. I've been trained——"

"You're still human. We all have weak points. The trick is to know them and allow for them. Where are you from?"

I managed a grin. "Mercury. Caloris Planitia." Mercury is a ball of iron at the bottom of the sun's gravity well. It is an iron mine, and an exotic matter factory, with a sun like a lid hanging over it. Most of the surface is given over to solar power collectors. It is a place of tunnels and warrens, where kids compete with the rats.

"And that's why you joined up? To get away?"

"I was drafted."

"Come on," she scoffed. "On a place like Mercury there are ways to hide. Are you a romantic, tar? You wanted to see the stars?"

"No," I said bluntly. "Life is more useful here."

She studied me. "A brief life should burn brightly——eh, tar?"

"Yes, sir."

"I came from Deneb," she said. "Do you know it?"

"No."

"Sixteen hundred light years from Earth——a system settled some four centuries after the start of the Third Expansion. It is quite different from the solar system. It is——organized. By the time the first ships reached Deneb, the mechanics of exploitation had become efficient. From preliminary exploration to working shipyards and daughter colonies in less than a century. . . . Deneb's resources——its planets and asteroids and comets, even the star itself——have been mined to fund fresh colonizing waves, the greater Expansion——and, of course, to support the war with the Ghosts."

She swept her hand over the sky. "Think of it, tar. The Third Expansion: between here and Sol, across six thousand light years——nothing but mankind, the fruit of a thousand years of world-building. And all of it linked by economics. Older systems like Deneb, their resources spent—even the solar system itself—are supported by a flow of goods and materials inward from the growing periphery of the Expansion. There are trade lanes spanning thousands of light years, lanes that never leave human territory, plied by vast schooners kilometers wide. But now the Ghosts are in our way. And *that's* what we're fighting for!"

"Yes, sir."

She eyed me. "You ready to go on?"

"Yes."

We began to make our way forward again, just under the tangle, still following patrol SOP.

I was glad to be moving again. I've never been comfortable talking personally—and for sure not with a Commissary. But I suppose even Commissaries need to talk.

Jeru spotted a file of the Ghosts moving in a crocodile, like so many school-children, toward the head of the ship. It was the most purposeful activity we'd seen so far, so we followed them.

After a couple of hundred meters the Ghosts began to duck down into the tangle, out of our sight. We followed them in.

Maybe fifty meters deep, we came to a large enclosed chamber, a smooth bean-shaped pod that would have been big enough to enclose our yacht. The surface appeared to be semi-transparent, perhaps designed to let in sunlight. I could see shadowy shapes moving within.

Ghosts were clustered around the pod's hull, brushing its surface.

Jeru beckoned, and we worked our way through the tangle toward the far end of the pod, where the density of the Ghosts seemed to be lowest.

We slithered to the surface of the pod. There were sucker pads on our palms and toes to help us grip. We began crawling along the length of the pod, ducking flat when we saw Ghosts loom into view. It was like climbing over a glass ceiling.

The pod was pressurized. At one end of the pod a big ball of mud hung in the air, brown and viscous. It seemed to be heated from within; it was slowly boiling, with big sticky bubbles of vapor crowding its surface, and I saw how it was laced with purple and red smears. There is no convection in zero gravity, of course. Maybe the Ghosts were using pumps to drive the flow of vapor.

Tubes led off from the mud ball to the hull of the pod. Ghosts clustered there, sucking up the purple gunk from the mud.

We figured it out in bioluminescent "whispers." The Ghosts were *feeding*. Their home world is too small to have retained much internal warmth, but, deep beneath their frozen oceans or in the dark of their rocks, a little primordial geotherm heat must leak out still, driving fountains of minerals dragged up from the depths. And, as at the bottom of Earth's oceans, on those minerals and the slow leak of heat, life-forms feed. And the Ghosts feed on *them*.

So this mud ball was a field kitchen. I peered down at purplish slime, a gourmet meal for Ghosts, and I didn't envy them.

There was nothing for us here. Jeru beckoned me again, and we slithered further forward.

The next section of the pod was . . . strange.

It was a chamber full of sparkling, silvery saucer-shapes, like smaller, flattened-out Ghosts, perhaps. They fizzed through the air or crawled over each other or jammed themselves together into great wadded balls that would hold for a few seconds and then collapse, their component parts squirming off for some new adventure elsewhere. I could see there were feeding tubes on the walls, and one or two Ghosts drifted among the saucer things, like an adult in a yard of squabbling children.

There was a subtle shadow before me.

I looked up, and found myself staring at my own reflection—an angled head, an open mouth, a sprawled body—folded over, fish-eye style, just centimeters from my nose.

It was a Ghost. It bobbed massively before me.

I pushed myself away from the hull, slowly. I grabbed hold of the nearest tangle branch with my good hand. I knew I couldn't reach for my knife, which was tucked into my belt at my back. And I couldn't see Jeru anywhere. It might be that the Ghosts had taken her already. Either way I couldn't call her, or even look for her, for fear of giving her away.

The Ghost had a heavy-looking belt wrapped around its equator. I had to assume that those complex knots of equipment were weapons. Aside from its belt, the Ghost was quite featureless: it might have been stationary, or spinning at a hundred revolutions a minute. I stared at its hide, trying to understand that there was a layer in there like a separate universe, where the laws of physics had been tweaked. But all I could see was my own scared face looking back at me.

And then Jeru fell on the Ghost from above, limbs splayed, knives glinting in both hands. I could see she was yelling—mouth open, eyes wide—but she fell in utter silence, her comms disabled.

Flexing her body like a whip, she rammed both knives into the Ghost's hide—if I took that belt to be its equator, somewhere near its north pole.

The Ghost pulsated, complex ripples chasing across its surface. But Jeru did a handstand and reached up with her legs to the tangle above, and anchored herself there.

The Ghost began to spin, trying to throw Jeru off. But she held her grip on the tangle, and kept the knives thrust in its hide, and all the Ghost succeeded in doing was opening up twin gashes, right across its upper section. Steam pulsed out, and I glimpsed redness within.

For long seconds I just hung there, frozen.

You're trained to mount the proper reaction to an enemy assault. But it all vaporizes when you're faced with a ton of spinning, pulsing monster, and you're armed with nothing but a knife. You just want to make yourself as small as possible; maybe it will all go away. But in the end you know it won't, that something has to be done.

So I pulled out my own knife and launched myself at that north pole area.

I started to make cross-cuts between Jeru's gashes. Ghost skin is tough, like thick rubber, but easy to cut if you have the anchorage. Soon I had loosened flaps and lids of skin, and I started pulling them away, exposing a deep redness within. Steam gushed out, sparkling to ice.

Jeru let go of her perch and joined me. We clung with our fingers and hands to the gashes we'd made, and we cut and slashed and dug; though the Ghost spun crazily, it couldn't shake us loose. Soon we were hauling out great warm mounds of meat—ropes like entrails, pulsing slabs like a human's liver or heart. At first ice crystals spurted all around us, but as the Ghost lost the heat it had hoarded all its life, that thin wind died, and frost began to gather on the cut and torn flesh.

At last Jeru pushed my shoulder, and we both drifted away from the Ghost. It was still spinning, but I could see that the spin was nothing but dead momentum; the Ghost had lost its heat, and its life.

Jeru and I faced each other.

I said breathlessly, "I never heard of anyone in hand-to-hand with a Ghost before."

"Neither did I. Lethe," she said, inspecting her hand. "I think I cracked a finger."

It wasn't funny. But Jeru stared at me, and I stared back, and then we both started to laugh, and our slime suits pulsed with pink and blue icons.

"He stood his ground," I said.

"Yes. Maybe he thought we were threatening the nursery."

"The place with the silver saucers?"

She looked at me quizzically. "Ghosts are symbiotes, tar. That looked to me like a nursery for Ghost hides. Independent entities."

I had never thought of Ghosts having young. I had not thought of the Ghost we had killed as a mother protecting its young. I'm not a deep thinker now, and wasn't then; but it was not, for me, a comfortable thought.

But then Jeru started to move. "Come on, tar. Back to work." She anchored her legs in the tangle and began to grab at the still-rotating Ghost carcass, trying to slow its spin.

I anchored likewise and began to help her. The Ghost was massive, the size of a major piece of machinery, and it had built up respectable momentum; at first I couldn't grab hold of the skin flaps that spun past my hand. As we labored I became aware I was getting uncomfortably hot. The light that seeped into the tangle from that caged sun seemed to be getting stronger by the minute.

But as we worked those uneasy thoughts soon dissipated.

At last we got the Ghost under control. Briskly Jeru stripped it of its kit belt, and we began to cram the baggy corpse as deep as we could into the surrounding tangle. It was a grisly job. As the Ghost crumpled further, more of its innards, stiffening now, came pushing out of the holes we'd given it in its hide, and I had to keep from gagging as the foul stuff came pushing out into my face.

At last it was done—as best we could manage it, anyhow.

Jeru's faceplate was smeared with black and red. She was sweating hard, her face pink. But she was grinning, and she had a trophy, the Ghost belt around her shoulders. We began to make our way back, following the same SOP as before.

When we got back to our lying-up point, we found Academician Pael was in trouble.

———

Pael had curled up in a ball, his hands over his face. We pulled him open. His eyes were closed, his face blotched pink, and his faceplate dripped with condensation.

He was surrounded by gadgets stuck in the tangle—including parts from what looked like a broken-open starbreaker handgun; I recognized prisms and mirrors and diffraction gratings. Well, unless he woke up, he wouldn't be able to tell us what he had been doing here.

Jeru glanced around. The light of the fortress's central star had gotten a *lot* stronger. Our lying-up point was now bathed in light—and heat—with the surrounding tangle offering very little shelter. "Any ideas, tar?"

I felt the exhilaration of our infil drain away. "No, sir."

Jeru's face, bathed in sweat, showed tension. I noticed she was favoring her left hand. She'd mentioned, back at the nursery pod, that she'd cracked a finger, but had said nothing about it since—nor did she give it any time now. "All right." She dumped the Ghost equipment belt and took a deep draft of water from her hood spigot. "Tar, you're on stag. Try to keep Pael in the shade of your body. And if he wakes up, *ask him what he's found out.*"

"Yes, sir."

"Good."

And then she was gone, melting into the complex shadows of the tangle as if she'd been born to these conditions.

I found a place where I could keep up 360-degree vision, and offer a little of my shadow to Pael—not that I imagined it helped much.

I had nothing to do but wait.

As the Ghost ship followed its own mysterious course, the light dapples that came filtering through the tangle shifted and evolved. Clinging to the tangle, I thought I could feel vibration: a slow, deep harmonization that pulsed through the ship's giant structure. I wondered if I was hearing the deep voices of Ghosts, calling to each other from one end of their mighty ship to another. It all served to remind me that everything in my environment, *everything*, was alien, and I was very far from home.

I tried to count my heartbeat, my breaths; I tried to figure out how long a second was. "A thousand and one. A thousand and two . . ." Keeping time is a basic human trait; time provides a basic orientation, and keeps you mentally sharp and in touch with reality. But I kept losing count.

And all my efforts failed to stop darker thoughts creeping into my head.

During a drama like the contact with the Ghost, you don't realize what's happening to you because your body blanks it out; on some level you know you just don't have time to deal with it. Now I had stopped moving, the aches and pains of the last few hours started crowding in on me. I was still sore in my head and back and, of course, my busted arm. I could feel deep bruises, maybe cuts, on my gloved hands where I had hauled at my knife, and I felt as if I had wrenched my good shoulder. One of my toes was throbbing ominously: I wondered if I had cracked another bone, here in this weird environment in which my skeleton had become as brittle as an old man's. I was chafed at my groin and armpits and knees and ankles and elbows, my skin rubbed raw. I was used to suits; normally I'm tougher than that.

The shafts of sunlight on my back were working on me too; it felt as if I was lying underneath the elements of an oven. I had a headache, a deep sick feeling in the pit of my stomach, a ringing in my ears, and a persistent ring of blackness around my eyes. Maybe I was just exhausted, dehydrated; maybe it was more than that.

I started to think back over my operation with Jeru, and the regrets began.

Okay, I'd stood my ground when confronted by the Ghost and not betrayed Jeru's position. But when she launched her attack I'd hesitated, for those crucial few seconds. Maybe if I'd been tougher the commissary wouldn't find herself hauling through the tangle, alone, with a busted finger distracting her with pain signals.

Our training is comprehensive. You're taught to expect that kind of hindsight torture, in the quiet moments, and to discount it—or, better yet, learn from it. But, effectively alone in that metallic alien forest, I wasn't finding my training was offering much perspective.

And, worse, I started to think ahead. Always a mistake.

I couldn't believe that the Academician and his reluctant gadgetry were going to achieve anything significant. And for all the excitement of our infil, we hadn't found anything resembling a bridge or any vulnerable point we could attack, and all we'd come back with was a belt of field kit we didn't even understand.

For the first time I began to consider seriously the possibility that I wasn't going to live through this—that I was going to die when my suit gave up or the sun went pop, whichever came first, in no more than a few hours.

A brief life burns brightly. That's what you're taught. Longevity makes you conservative, fearful, selfish. Humans made that mistake before, and we finished up a subject race. Live fast and furiously, for *you* aren't important—all that matters is what you can do for the species.

But I didn't want to die.

If I never returned to Mercury again I wouldn't shed a tear. But I had a life now, in the Navy. And then there were my buddies: the people I'd trained and served with, people like Halle—even Jeru. Having found fellowship for the first time in my life, I didn't want to lose it so quickly, and fall into the darkness alone—especially if it was to be for *nothing*.

But maybe I wasn't going to get a choice.

After an unmeasured time, Jeru returned. She was hauling a silvery blanket. It was Ghost hide. She started to shake it out.

I dropped down to help her. "You went back to the one we killed—"

"—and skinned him," she said, breathless. "I just scraped off the crap with a knife. The Planck-zero layer peels away easily. And look . . ." she made a quick incision in the glimmering sheet with her knife. Then she put the two edges together again, ran her finger along the seam, and showed me the result. I couldn't even see where the cut had been. "Self-sealing, self-healing," she said. "Remember that, tar."

"Yes, sir."

We started to rig the punctured, splayed-out hide as a rough canopy over our LUP, blocking as much of the sunlight as possible from Pael. A few slivers of frozen flesh still clung to the hide, but mostly it was like work-ing with a fine, light metallic foil.

In the sudden shade, Pael was starting to stir. His moans were translated to stark bioluminescent icons.

"Help him," Jeru snapped. "Make him drink." And while I did that she dug into the med kit on her belt and started to spray cast material around the fingers of her left hand.

————

"It's the speed of light," Pael said. He was huddled in a corner of our LUP, his legs tucked against his chest. His voice must have been feeble; the bio-luminescent sigils on his suit were fragmentary and came with possible var-iants extrapolated by the translator software.

"Tell us," Jeru said, relatively gently.

"The Ghosts have found a way to *change* lightspeed in this fortress. In fact to increase it." He began talking again about quagma and physics con-stants and the rolled-up dimensions of spacetime, but Jeru waved that away irritably.

"How do you *know* this?"

Pael began tinkering with his prisms and gratings. "I took your advice, Commissary." He beckoned to me. "Come see, child."

I saw that a shaft of red light, split out and deflected by his prism, shone through a diffraction grating and cast an angular pattern of dots and lines on a scrap of smooth plastic behind.

"You see?" His eyes searched my face.

"I'm sorry, sir."

"The wavelength of the light has changed. It has been increased. Red light should have a wavelength, oh, a fifth shorter than that indicated by this pattern."

I was struggling to understand. I held up my hand. "Shouldn't the green of this glove turn yellow, or blue . . . ?"

Pael sighed. "No. Because the color you see depends, not on the wave-length of a photon, but on its energy. Conservation of energy still applies, even where the Ghosts are tinkering. So each photon carries as much ener-gy as before—and evokes the same 'color.' Since a photon's energy is pro-portional to its frequency, that means frequencies are left unchanged. But since lightspeed is equal to frequency multiplied by wavelength, an increase in wavelength implies—"

"An increase in lightspeed," said Jeru.

"Yes."

I didn't follow much of that. I turned and looked up at the light that leaked around our Ghost-hide canopy. "So we see the same colors. The light of that star gets here a little faster. What difference does it make?"

Pael shook his head. "Child, a fundamental constant like lightspeed is embedded in the deep structure of our universe. Lightspeed is part of the ratio known as the fine structure constant." He started babbling about the charge on the electron, but Jeru cut him off.

She said, "Case, the fine structure constant is a measure of the strength of an electric or magnetic force."

I could follow that much. "And if you increase lightspeed—"

"You *reduce* the strength of the force." Pael raised himself. "Consider this. Human bodies are held together by molecular binding energy— electromagnetic forces. Here, electrons are more loosely bound to atoms; the atoms in a molecule are more loosely bound to each other." He rapped on the cast on my arm. "And so your bones are more brittle, your skin more easy to pierce or chafe. Do you see? You too are embedded in spacetime, my young friend. You too are affected by the Ghosts' tinkering. And because lightspeed in this infernal pocket continues to increase—as far as I can tell from these poor experiments—you are becoming more fragile every second."

It was a strange, eerie thought: that something so basic in my universe could be manipulated. I put my arms around my chest and shuddered.

"Other effects," Pael went on bleakly. "The density of matter is dropping. Perhaps our structure will eventually begin to crumble. And dissociation temperatures are reduced."

Jeru snapped, "What does that mean?"

"Melting and boiling points are reduced. No wonder we are overheating. It is intriguing that bio systems have proven rather more robust than electromechanical ones. But if we don't get out of here soon, our blood will start to boil. . . ."

"Enough," Jeru said. "What of the star?"

"A star is a mass of gas with a tendency to collapse under its own gravity. But heat, supplied by fusion reactions in the core, creates gas and radiation pressures that push outward, counteracting gravity."

"And if the fine structure constant changes—"

"Then the balance is lost. Commissary, as gravity begins to win its ancient battle, the fortress star has become more luminous—it is burning faster. That explains the observations we made from outside the cordon. But this cannot last."

"The novae," I said.

"Yes. The explosions, layers of the star blasted into space, are a symptom of destabilized stars seeking a new balance. The rate at which *our* star is approaching that catastrophic moment fits with the lightspeed drift I have observed." He smiled and closed his eyes. "A single cause predicating so many effects. It is all rather pleasing, in an aesthetic way."

Jeru said, "At least we know how the ship was destroyed. Every control system is mediated by finely tuned electromagnetic effects. Everything must have gone crazy at once. . . ."

We figured it out. The *Brief Life Burns Brightly* had been a classic GUT-ship, of a design that hasn't changed in its essentials for thousands of years. The lifedome, a tough translucent bubble, contained the crew of twenty. The 'dome was connected by a spine a klick long to a GUTdrive engine pod.

When we crossed the cordon boundary—when all the bridge lights failed—the control systems went down, and all the pod's superforce energy must have tried to escape at once. The spine of the ship had thrust itself up into the lifedome, like a nail rammed into a skull.

Pael said dreamily, "If lightspeed were a tad faster, throughout the universe, then hydrogen could not fuse to helium. There would only be hydrogen: no fusion to power stars, no chemistry. Conversely if lightspeed were a little lower, hydrogen would fuse too easily, and there would be *no* hydrogen, nothing to make stars—or water. You see how critical it all is? No doubt the Ghosts' science of fine-tuning is advancing considerably here on the Orion Line, even as it serves its trivial defensive purpose . . ."

Jeru glared at him, her contempt obvious. "We must take this piece of intelligence back to the Commission. If the Ghosts can survive and function in these fast-light bubbles of theirs, so can we. We may be at the pivot of history, gentlemen."

I knew she was right. The primary duty of the Commission for Historical Truth is to gather and deploy intelligence about the enemy. And so *my* primary duty, and Pael's, was now to help Jeru get this piece of data back to her organization.

But Pael was mocking her.

"Not for ourselves, but for the species. Is that the line, Commissary? You are so grandiose. And yet you blunder around in comical ignorance. Even your quixotic quest aboard this cruiser was futile. There probably is no bridge on this ship. The Ghosts' entire morphology, their evolutionary design, is based on the notion of cooperation, of symbiosis; why should a Ghost ship have a metaphoric *head*? And as for the trophy you have returned—" He held up the belt of Ghost artifacts. "There are no weapons here. These are sensors, tools. There is nothing here capable of producing a significant energy discharge. This is less threatening than a bow and arrow." He let go of the belt; it drifted away. "The Ghost wasn't trying to kill you. It was blocking you. Which is a classic Ghost tactic."

Jeru's face was stony. "It was in our way. That is sufficient reason for destroying it."

Pael shook his head. "Minds like yours will destroy *us*, Commissary."

Jeru stared at him with suspicion. Then she said, "*You have a way.* Don't you, Academician? A way to get us out of here."

He tried to face her down, but her will was stronger, and he averted his eyes.

Jeru said heavily, "Regardless of the fact that three lives are at stake—does duty mean nothing to you, Academician? You are an intelligent man. Can you not see that this is a war of human destiny?"

Pael laughed. "Destiny—or economics?"

I looked from one to the other, dismayed, baffled. I thought we should be doing less yapping and more fighting.

Pael said, watching me, "You see, child, as long as the explorers and the mining fleets and the colony ships are pushing outward, as long as the Third Expansion is growing, our economy works. The riches can continue to flow inward, into the mined-out systems, feeding a vast horde of humanity who have become more populous than the stars themselves. But as soon as that growth falters . . ."

Jeru was silent.

I understood some of this. The Third Expansion had reached all the way to the inner edge of our spiral arm of the galaxy. Now the first colony ships were attempting to make their way across the void to the next arm.

Our arm, the Orion Arm, is really just a shingle, a short arc. But the Sagittarius Arm is one of the galaxy's dominant features. For example, it contains a huge region of star-birth, one of the largest in the galaxy, immense clouds of gas and dust capable of producing millions of stars each. It was a prize indeed.

But that is where the Silver Ghosts live.

When it appeared that our inexorable expansion was threatening not just their own mysterious projects but their home system, the Ghosts began, for the first time, to resist us.

They had formed a blockade, called by human strategists the Orion Line: a thick sheet of fortress stars, right across the inner edge of the Orion Arm, places the Navy and the colony ships couldn't follow. It was a devastatingly effective ploy.

This was a war of colonization, of world-building. For a thousand years we had been spreading steadily from star to star, using the resources of one system to explore, terraform and populate the worlds of the next. With too deep a break in that chain of exploitation, the enterprise broke down.

And so the Ghosts had been able to hold up human expansion for fifty years.

Pael said, "We are already choking. There have already been wars, young Case: human fighting human, as the inner systems starve. All the Ghosts have to do is wait for us to destroy ourselves, and free them to continue their own rather more worthy projects."

Jeru floated down before him.

"Academician, listen to me. Growing up at Deneb, I saw the great schooners in the sky, bringing the interstellar riches that kept my people alive. I was intelligent enough to see the logic of history—that we must maintain the Expansion, *because there is no choice*. And that is why I joined the armed forces, and later the Commission for Historical Truth. For I understood the dreadful truth which the Commission cradles. And that is why we must labor every day to maintain the unity and purpose of mankind. For if we falter we die; as simple as that."

"Commissary, your creed of mankind's evolutionary destiny condemns our own kind to become a swarm of children, granted a few moments of loving and breeding and dying, before being cast into futile war." Pael glanced at me.

"But," Jeru said, "it is a creed that has bound us together for a thousand years. It is a creed that binds uncounted trillions of human beings across thousands of light years. It is a creed that binds a humanity so diverse it appears to be undergoing speciation. . . . Are you strong enough to defy such a creed now? Come, Academician. None of us *chooses* to be born in the middle of a war. We must all do our best for each other, for other human beings; what else is there?"

I touched Pael's shoulder; he flinched away. "Academician—is Jeru right? Is there a way we can live through this?"

Pael shuddered. Jeru hovered over him.

"Yes," Pael said at last. "Yes, there is a way."

———

The idea turned out to be simple.

And the plan Jeru and I devised to implement it was even simpler. It was based on a single assumption: Ghosts aren't aggressive. It was ugly, I'll admit that, and I could see why it would distress a squeamish earthworm like Pael. But sometimes there are no good choices.

Jeru and I took a few minutes to rest up, check over our suits and our various injuries, and to make ourselves comfortable. Then, following patrol SOP once more, we made our way back to the pod of immature hides.

We came out of the tangle and drifted down to that translucent hull. We tried to keep away from concentrations of Ghosts, but we made no real effort to conceal ourselves. There was little point, after all; the Ghosts would know all about us, and what we intended, soon enough.

We hammered pitons into the pliable hull, and fixed rope to anchor ourselves. Then we took our knives and started to saw our way through the hull.

As soon as we started, the Ghosts began to gather around us, like vast antibodies. They just hovered there, eerie faceless baubles drifting as if in vacuum breezes. But as I stared up at a dozen distorted reflections of my own skinny face, I felt an unreasonable loathing rise up in me. Maybe you could think of them as a family banding together to protect their young. I didn't care; a lifetime's carefully designed hatred isn't thrown off so easily. I went at my work with a will.

Jeru got through the pod hull first.

The air gushed out in a fast-condensing fountain. The baby hides fluttered, their distress obvious. And the Ghosts began to cluster around Jeru, like huge light globes.

Jeru glanced at me. "Keep working, tar."

"Yes, sir."

In another couple of minutes I was through. The air pressure was already dropping. It dwindled to nothing when we cut a big door-sized flap in that roof. Anchoring ourselves with the ropes, we rolled that lid back, opening the roof wide. A few last wisps of vapor came curling around our heads, ice fragments sparkling.

The hide babies convulsed. Immature, they could not survive the sudden vacuum, intended as their ultimate environment. But the way they died made it easy for us.

The silvery hides came flapping up out of the hole in the roof, one by one. We just grabbed each one—like grabbing hold of a billowing sheet—and we speared it with a knife, and threaded it on a length of rope. All we had to do was sit there and wait for them to come. There were hundreds of them, and we were kept busy.

I hadn't expected the adult Ghosts to sit through that, non-aggressive or not; and I was proved right. Soon they were clustering all around me, vast silvery bellies looming. A Ghost is massive and solid, and it packs a lot of inertia; if one hits you in the back you know about it. Soon they were nudging me hard enough to knock me flat against the roof, over and over. Once

I was wrenched so hard against my tethering rope it felt as if I had cracked another bone or two in my foot.

And, meanwhile, I was starting to feel a lot worse: dizzy, nauseous, overheated. It was getting harder to get back upright each time after being knocked down. I was growing weaker fast; I imagined the tiny molecules of my body falling apart in this Ghost-polluted space.

For the first time I began to believe we were going to fail.

But then, quite suddenly, the Ghosts backed off. When they were clear of me, I saw they were clustering around Jeru.

She was standing on the hull, her feet tangled up in rope, and she had knives in both hands. She was slashing crazily at the Ghosts, and at the baby hides that came flapping past her, making no attempt to capture them now, simply cutting and destroying whatever she could reach. I could see that one arm was hanging awkwardly—maybe it was dislocated, or even broken—but she kept on slicing regardless.

And the Ghosts were clustering around her, huge silver spheres crushing her frail, battling human form.

She was sacrificing herself to save me—just as Captain Teid, in the last moments of the *Brightly*, had given herself to save Pael. And *my* duty was to complete the job.

I stabbed and threaded, over and over, as the flimsy hides came tumbling out of that hole, slowly dying.

At last no more hides came.

I looked up, blinking to get the salt sweat out of my eyes. A few hides were still tumbling around the interior of the pod, but they were inert and out of my reach. Others had evaded us and gotten stuck in the tangle of the ship's structure, too far and too scattered to make them worth pursuing further. What I had got would have to suffice.

I started to make my way out of there, back through the tangle, to the location of our wrecked yacht, where I hoped Pael would be waiting.

I looked back once. I couldn't help it. The Ghosts were still clustered over the ripped pod roof. Somewhere in there, whatever was left of Jeru was still fighting.

I had an impulse, almost overpowering, to go back to her. No human being should die alone. But I knew I had to get out of there, to complete the mission, to make her sacrifice worthwhile.

So I got.

———

Pael and I finished the job at the outer hull of the Ghost cruiser.

Stripping the hides turned out to be as easy as Jeru had described. Fitting together the Planck-zero sheets was simple too—you just line them up and seal them with a thumb. I got on with that, sewing the hides together into a sail, while Pael worked on a rigging of lengths of rope, all fixed to a deck panel from the wreck of the yacht. He was fast and efficient; Pael, after all, came from a world where everybody goes solar sailing on their vacations.

We worked steadily, for hours.

I ignored the varying aches and chafes, the increasing pain in my head and chest and stomach, the throbbing of a broken arm that hadn't healed, the agony of cracked bones in my foot. And we didn't talk about anything but the task in hand. Pael didn't ask what had become of Jeru, not once; it was as if he had anticipated the commissary's fate.

We were undisturbed by the Ghosts through all of this.

I tried not to think about whatever emotions churned within those silvered carapaces, what despairing debates might chatter on invisible wavelengths. I was, after all, trying to complete a mission. And I had been exhausted even before I got back to Pael. I just kept going, ignoring my fatigue, focusing on the task.

I was surprised to find it was done.

We had made a sail hundreds of meters across, stitched together from the invisibly thin immature Ghost hide. It was roughly circular, and it was connected by a dozen lengths of fine rope to struts on the panel we had wrenched out of the wreck. The sail lay across space, languid ripples crossing its glimmering surface.

Pael showed me how to work the thing. "Pull this rope, or this . . ." the great patchwork sail twitched in response to his commands. "I've set it so you shouldn't have to try anything fancy, like tacking. The boat will just sail out, hopefully, to the cordon perimeter. If you need to lose the sail, just cut the ropes."

I was taking in all this automatically. It made sense for both of us to know how to operate our little yacht. But then I started to pick up the subtext of what he was saying.

Before I knew what he was doing he had shoved me onto the deck panel, and pushed it away from the Ghost ship. His strength was surprising.

I watched him recede. He clung wistfully to a bit of tangle. I couldn't summon the strength to figure out a way to cross the widening gap. But my suit could read his, as clear as day.

"Where I grew up, the sky was full of sails . . ."

"Why, Academician?"

"You will go further and faster without my mass to haul. And besides— our lives are short enough; we should preserve the young. Don't you think?"

I had no idea what he was talking about. Pael was much more valuable than I was; I was the one who should have been left behind. He had shamed himself.

Complex glyphs crisscrossed his suit. "Keep out of the direct sunlight. It is growing more intense, of course. That will help you. . . ."

And then he ducked out of sight, back into the tangle. The Ghost ship was receding now, closing over into its vast egg shape, the detail of the tangle becoming lost to my blurred vision.

The sail above me slowly billowed, filling up with the light of the brightening sun. Pael had designed his improvised craft well; the rigging lines were all taut, and I could see no rips or creases in the silvery fabric.

I clung to my bit of decking and sought shade.

————

Twelve hours later, I reached an invisible radius where the tactical beacon in my pocket started to howl with a whine that filled my headset. My suit's auxiliary systems cut in and I found myself breathing fresh air.

A little after that, a set of lights ducked out of the streaming lanes of the fleet, and plunged toward me, growing brighter. At last it resolved into a golden bullet shape adorned with a blue-green tetrahedron, the sigil of free humanity. It was a supply ship called *The Dominance of Primates*.

And a little after *that*, as a Ghost fleet fled their fortress, the star exploded.

————

As soon as I had completed my formal report to the ship's commissary— and I was able to check out of the *Dominance*'s sick bay—I asked to see the captain.

I walked up to the bridge. My story had got around, and the various med patches I sported added to my heroic mythos. So I had to run the gauntlet of the crew—"You're supposed to be dead, I impounded your back pay and slept with your mother already"—and was greeted by what seems to be the universal gesture of recognition of one tar to another, the clenched fist pumping up and down around an imaginary penis.

But anything more respectful just wouldn't feel normal.

The captain turned out to be a grizzled veteran type with a vast laser burn scar on one cheek. She reminded me of First Officer Till.

I told her I wanted to return to active duty as soon as my health allowed.

She looked me up and down. "Are you sure, tar? You have a lot of options. Young as you are, you've made your contribution to the Expansion. You can go home."

"Sir, and do what?"

She shrugged. "Farm. Mine. Raise babies. Whatever earthworms do. Or you can join the Commission for Historical Truth."

"Me, a commissary?"

"You've been there, tar. You've been in among the Ghosts, and come out again—with a bit of intelligence more important than anything the Commission has come up with in fifty years. Are you *sure* you want to face action again?"

I thought it over.

I remembered how Jeru and Pael had argued. It had been an unwelcome perspective, for me. I was in a war that had nothing to do with me, trapped by what Jeru had called the logic of history. But then, I bet that's been true of most of humanity through our long and bloody history. All you can do is live your life, and grasp your moment in the light—and stand by your comrades.

A farmer—me? And I could never be smart enough for the Commission. No, I had no doubts.

"A brief life burns brightly, sir."

Lethe, the captain looked like she had a lump in her throat. "Do I take that as a yes, tar?"

I stood straight, ignoring the twinges of my injuries. "Yes, *sir!*"

THE DAYS BETWEEN

ALLEN M. STEELE

THREE MONTHS AFTER leaving Earth, the URSS *Alabama* had just achieved cruise velocity when the accident occurred: Leslie Gillis woke up.

He regained consciousness slowly, as if emerging from a long and dreamless sleep. His body, naked and hairless, floated within the blue-green gelatin filling the interior of his biostasis cell, an oxygen mask covering the lower part of his face and thin plastic tubes inserted in his arms. As his vision cleared, Gillis saw that the cell had been lowered to a horizontal position and that its fiberglass lid had folded open. The lighting within the hibernation deck was subdued, yet he had to open and close his eyes several times.

His first lucid thought was: *Thank God, I made it.*

His body felt weak, his limbs stiff. Just as he had been cautioned to do during flight training, he carefully moved only a little at a time. As Gillis gently flexed his arms and legs, he vaguely wondered why no one had come to his aid. Perhaps Dr. Okada was busy helping the others emerge from biostasis. Yet he could hear nothing save for a sublime electrical hum—no voices, no movement.

His next thought was: *Something's wrong.*

Back aching, his arms feeling as if they were about to dislocate from his shoulders, Gillis grasped the sides of the cell and tried to sit up. For a minute or so he struggled against the phlegmatic embrace of the suspension fluid; there was a wet sucking sound as he prized his body upward, then the tubes went taut before he remembered that he had to take them out. Clenching his teeth, Gillis pinched off the tubes between thumb and forefinger and, one by one, carefully removed them from his arms. The oxygen mask came off last; the air was frigid and it stung his throat and lungs, and he coughed in agonized spasms as, with the last ounce of his strength, he clambered out of the tank. His legs couldn't hold him, and he collapsed upon the cold floor of the deck.

Gillis didn't know how long he lay curled in a fetal position, his hands tucked into his groin. He never really lost consciousness, yet for a long while his mind lingered somewhere between awareness and sleep, his unfocused eyes gazing at the burnished metal plates of the floor. After a while the cold penetrated his dulled senses; the suspension fluid was freezing against his bare skin, and he dully realized that if he lay there much longer he would soon lapse into hypothermia.

Gillis rolled over on his back, forced himself to sit up. Aquamarine fluid drooled down his body, formed a shallow pool around his hips; he hugged his shoulders, rubbing his chilled flesh. Once again, he wondered why no one was paying any attention to him. Yes, he was only the communications officer, yet there were others farther up the command hierarchy who should have been revived by now. Kuniko Okada was the last person he had seen before the somatic drugs entered his system; as Chief Physician, she also would have been the last crew member to enter biostasis and the first to emerge. She would have then brought up—Gillis sought to remember specific details—the Chief Engineer, Dana Monroe, who would have then ascertained that *Alabama*'s major systems were operational. If the ship was in nominal condition, Captain Lee would have been revived next, shortly followed by First Officer Shapiro, Executive Officer Tinsley, Senior Navigator Ullman, and then Gillis himself. Yes, that was the correct procedure.

So where is everyone else?

First things first. He was wet and naked, and the ship's internal temperature had been lowered to fifty degrees. He had to find some clothes. His teeth chattering, Gillis staggered to his feet, then lurched across the deck to a nearby locker. Opening it, he found a stack of clean white towels and a pile of folded robes. As he wiped the moist gel from his body, he recalled his embarrassment when his turn had come for Kuniko to prepare him for hibernation. It was bad enough to have his body shaved, yet when her electric razor had descended to his pubic area he found himself becoming involuntarily aroused by her gentle touch. Amused by his reaction, she had smiled at him in a motherly way. *Just relax*, she said. *Think about something else. . . .*

He turned, and for the first time saw that the rest of the biostasis cells were still upright within their niches. Thirteen white fiberglass coffins, each resting at a forty-five degree angle within the bulkhead walls of Deck C2A.

Electrophoretic displays on their lids emitted a warm amber glow, showing the status of the crew members contained within. Here was the *Alabama*'s command team, just as he had last seen them: Lee, Shapiro, Tinsley, Okada, Monroe, Ullman. . . .

Everyone was still asleep. Everyone except himself.

Gillis hastily pulled on a robe, then strode across the deck to the nearest window. Its outer shutter was closed, yet when he pressed the button that moved it upward, all he saw were distant stars against black space. Of course, he might not be able to see 47 Ursae Majoris from this particular porthole. He needed to get to the command center, check the navigation instruments.

As he turned from the window, something caught his eye: the readout on the nearest biostasis cell. Trembling with unease as much as cold, Gillis moved closer to examine it. The screen identified the sleeper within as *Cortez, Raymond B.*—Ray Cortez, the life-support chief—and all his life signs seemed normal as far as he could tell, yet that wasn't what attracted his attention. On the upper left side was a time-code:

E/: 7.8.70 / 22:10:01 GMT

July 8, 2070. That was the date everyone had entered hibernation, three days after the *Alabama* had made its unscheduled departure from Highgate. On the upper right side of the screen, though, was another time-code:

P/: 10.3.70 / 00.21.23 GMT

October 3, 2070. Today's date and time.

The *Alabama* had been in flight for only three months. Three months of a voyage across forty-six light-years which, at twenty percent of light-speed, would take two hundred thirty years to complete.

For several long minutes, Gillis stared at the readout, unwilling to believe the evidence of his own eyes. Then he turned and walked across the compartment to the manhole. His bare feet slapping against the cool metal rungs, he climbed down the ladder to the next deck of the hibernation module.

Fourteen more biostasis cells, all within their niches. None were open.

Fighting panic, Gillis scrambled farther down the ladder to Deck C2C. Again, fourteen closed cells.

Still clutching at some intangible shred of hope, Gillis quickly visited Deck C2D, then scurried back up the ladder and entered the short tunnel leading to the *Alabama*'s second hibernation module. By the time he reached Deck C1D, he had checked every biostasis cell belonging to the starship's one hundred three remaining passengers, yet he hadn't found one that was open.

He sagged against a bulkhead, and for a long time he could do nothing except tremble with fear.

He was alone

After awhile, Gillis pulled himself together. All right, something had obviously gone wrong. The computers controlling the biostasis systems had made a critical error and had prematurely awakened him from hibernation. Okay, then; all he had to do was put himself back into the loop.

The robe he had found wasn't very warm, so he made his way through the circular passageway connecting the ship's seven ring modules until he entered C4, one of two modules that would serve as crew quarters once the *Alabama* reached 47 Ursae Majoris. He tried not to look at the rows of empty bunks as he searched for the locker where he had stowed his personal belongings. His blue jumpsuit was where he had left it three months ago, hanging next to the isolation garment he had worn when he left Gingrich Space Center to board the shuttle up to Highgate; on a shelf above it, next to his high-top sneakers, was the small cardboard box containing the precious few mementos he had been permitted to take with him. Gillis deliberately ignored the box as he pulled on his jumpsuit; he'd look at the stuff inside once he reached his final destination, and that wouldn't be for another two hundred thirty years . . . two hundred twenty-six years, if you considered the time-dilation factor.

The command center, located on Deck H4 within the ship's cylindrical hub, was cold and dark. The lights had been turned down, and the rectangular windows along its circular hull were shuttered; only the soft glow emitted by a few control panels pierced the gloom. Gillis took a moment to switch on the ceiling lights; spotting the environmental control station, he briefly considered adjusting the thermostat to make things a bit warmer, then decided against it. He had been trained as a communications specialist; his technical understanding of the rest of the *Alabama*'s major systems was cursory at best, and he was reluctant to make any changes that might influence the ship's operating condition. Besides, he wasn't staying there for very long; once he returned to biostasis, the cold wouldn't make much difference to him.

All the same, it was his duty to check the ship's status, so he walked over to the nav table, pulled away the plastic cover protecting its keypad, and punched up a display of the *Alabama*'s present position. A bright shaft of light appeared above the table, and within it appeared a tiny holographic model of the ship. It floated in midair at the end of a long, curved string that led outward from the center of the three-dimensional halo representing the orbits of the major planets of the solar system. Moving at constant 1-gee thrust, the *Alabama* was already beyond the orbit of Neptune; the ship was now passing the canted orbit of Pluto, and in a few weeks it would cross the heliopause, escaping the last weak remnants of the Sun's gravitational pull as it headed into interstellar space.

The *Alabama* had now traveled farther from Earth than any previous manned spacecraft; only a few probes had ever ventured this far. Gillis found himself smiling at the thought. He was now the only living person— the only conscious living person, at least—to have voyaged so far from Earth. A feat almost worth waking up for . . . although, all things considered, he would have preferred to sleep through it.

He moved to the engineering station, uncovered its console, and pulled up a schematic display of the main engine. The deuterium/helium-3 reserves that had been loaded aboard the *Alabama*'s spherical main fuel tank before launch had been largely consumed during the ninety-day boost phase, but now that the ship had reached cruise speed, the magnetic field projected by its Bussard ramscoop was drawing ionized interstellar hydrogen and helium from a four thousand kilometer radius in front of the ship, feeding the fusion reactor at its stern and thus maintaining a constant .2c velocity. Microsecond pulsations of the same magnetic field enabled it simultaneously to perform as a shield, deflecting away the interstellar dust that, at relativistic velocities, would have soon shredded the *Alabama*'s hull. Gillis's knowledge of the ship's propulsion systems was limited, yet his brief examination showed him that they were operating at ninety percent efficiency.

Something tapped softly against the floor behind him.

Startled by the unexpected sound, Gillis turned around, peered into the semidarkness. For a few moments he saw nothing, then a small shape emerged from behind the nav table: one of the spiderlike autonomous maintenance robots that constantly prowled the *Alabama*, inspecting its compartments and making minor repairs. This one had apparently been attracted to Gillis's presence within the command deck; its eyestalks briefly flicked in his direction, then the 'bot scuttled away.

Well. So much the better. The 'bot was no more intelligent than a mouse, but it reported everything that it observed to the ship's AI. Now that the ship was aware that one of its passengers was awake, the time had come for Gillis to take care of his little problem.

Gillis crossed the deck to his customary post at the communications station. Sitting down in his chair, he pulled away the plastic cover; a few deft taps on the keyboard and his console glowed to life once more. Seeing the familiar screens and readouts made him feel a little more secure; here, at least, he knew what he was doing. He typed in the commands that opened an interface to *Alabama*'s DNA-based artificial intelligence.

GILLIS, LESLIE, LT. COM. I.D. 86419-D. PASSWORD SCOTLAND.

The response was immediate: I.D. CONFIRMED. PASSWORD ACCEPTED. GOOD MORNING, MR. GILLIS. MAY I HELP YOU?

WHY WAS I AWAKENED? Gillis typed.

A short pause, then: GILLIS, LESLIE, LT. COM. IS STILL IN BIOSTASIS.

Gillis's mouth fell open: What the hell . . . ?

NO, I'M NOT. I'M HERE IN THE COMMAND CENTER. YOU'VE CONFIRMED THAT YOURSELF.

This time, the AI's response seemed a fraction of a second slower. LT. COM. LESLIE GILLIS IS STILL IN BIOSTASIS. PLEASE RE-ENTER YOUR I.D. AND PASSWORD FOR RECONFIRMATION.

Impatiently, Gillis typed: I.D. 86419-D. PASSWORD SCOTLAND.

The AI came back at once: IDENTIFICATION RECONFIRMED. YOU ARE LT. COM. LESLIE GILLIS.

THEN YOU AGREE THAT I'M NO LONGER IN BIOSTASIS.

NO. LT. COM. LESLIE GILLIS REMAINS IN BIOSTASIS. PLEASE RE-ENTER YOUR I.D. AND PASSWORD FOR RECONFIRMATION.

Gillis angrily slammed his hands against the console. He shut his eyes and took a deep breath, then forced himself to think this through as calmly as he could. He was dealing with an AI; it might be conditioned to respond to questions posed to it in plain English, yet nonetheless it was a machine, operating with machinelike logic. Although he had to deal with it on its own terms, nonetheless he had to establish the rules.

I.D. 86419-D. PASSWORD SCOTLAND.

IDENTIFICATION RECONFIRMED. YOU ARE LT. COM. LESLIE GILLIS.

PLEASE LOCATE LT. COM. LESLIE GILLIS.

LT. COM. LESLIE GILLIS IS IN BIOSTASIS CELL C1A-07.

Okay, now they were getting somewhere . . . but this was clearly wrong, in more ways than one. He had just emerged from a cell located on Deck A of Module C2.

WHO IS THE OCCUPANT OF BIOSTASIS CELL C2A-07?

GUNTHER, ERIC, ENSIGN/FSA

The name was unfamiliar, but the suffix indicated that he was a Federal Space Agency ensign. A member of the flight crew who had been ferried up to the *Alabama* just before launch, but probably not one of the conspirators who had hijacked the ship.

Gillis typed: THERE HAS BEEN A MISTAKE. ERIC GUNTHER IS NOT IN CELL C2A-07, AND I AM NOT IN CELL C1A-07. DO YOU UNDERSTAND?

Another pause, then: ACKNOWLEDGED. BIOSTASIS CELL ASSIGNMENTS RECHECKED WITH SECONDARY DATA SYSTEM. CORRECTION: CELL C1A-07 PRESENTLY OCCUPIED BY ERIC GUNTHER.

Gillis absently gnawed on a fingernail; after a few minutes he developed a possible explanation for the switch. Captain Lee and the other conspirators had smuggled almost fifty dissident intellectuals on board just before the *Alabama* fled Earth; since none of them had been listed in the ship's original crew manifest, the D.I.s had to be assigned to biostasis cells previously reserved for the members of the colonization team who had been left behind on Earth. Gillis could only assume that, at some point during the confusion, someone had accidentally fed erroneous information to the computer controlling the biostasis systems. Therefore, although he was originally assigned to C1A-07 while Ensign Gunther was supposed to be in C2A-07, whoever had switched his and Gunther cells had also neglected to cross-feed this information from the biostasis control system to the ship's AI. In the long run, it was a small matter of substituting one single digit for another . . .

Yet this didn't answer the original question: why had he been prematurely revived from biostasis? Or rather, why was Gunther supposed to be revived?

WHY DID YOU REVIVE THE OCCUPANT OF CELL C2A-07?

CLASSIFIED/TS. ISA ORDER 7812-DA

What the . . . ? Why was there an Internal Security Agency lock-out? Yet he was able to get around that.

SECURITY OVERRIDE AS-001001, GILLIS, LESLIE, LT. COM. PASSWORD SCOTLAND.

REPEAT QUESTION: WHY DID YOU REVIVE THE OCCUPANT OF CELL C2A-07?

CLASSIFIED/TS: OPEN. ENSIGN GUNTHER WAS TO CONFIRM PRESIDENTIAL LAUNCH AUTHORIZATION VIA SECURE COMMUNICATION CHANNEL. UPON FAILURE TO CONFIRM AUTHORIZATION BY 7.5.70/00.00, ENSIGN GUNTHER WAS TO BE REVIVED FROM BIOSTASIS AT 10.3.70/00.00 AND GIVEN THE OPTION OF TERMINATING THE MISSION.

Gillis stared at the screen for a long while, comprehending what he had just read but nonetheless not quite believing it. This could only mean one thing: Gunther had been an ISA mole placed aboard the *Alabama* for the purpose of assuring that the ship wasn't launched without Presidential authorization. However, since Captain Lee had ordered Gillis himself to shut down all modes of communication between Mission Control and the *Alabama*, Gunther hadn't been able to send a covert transmission back to Earth. Therefore the AI had been programmed to revive him from biostasis ninety days after launch.

At this point, though, Gunther wouldn't have been able to simply turn the ship around even if he'd wanted to do so. The *Alabama* was too far from Earth, its velocity too high, for one person to accomplish such a task on his own. So there was no mistake what "terminating the mission" meant; Gunther was supposed to have destroyed the *Alabama*.

A loyal citizen of the United Republic of America, even to the point of suicide. Indeed, Gillis had little doubt that the Republic's official press agency had already reported the loss of the *Alabama*, and that FSA spokesmen were issuing statements to the effect that the ship had suffered a catastrophic accident.

Since no one else aboard the ship knew about Gunther's orders, the AI's hidden program hadn't been deleted from memory. On the one hand, at least he had been prevented from carrying out his suicide mission. On the other, Gunther would remain asleep for the next two hundred thirty years while Gillis was now wide-awake.

Very well. So all he had to do was join him in biostasis. Once he woke up again, Gillis could inform Captain Lee of what he had learned, and let him decide what to do with Ensign Gunther.

THERE HAS BEEN A MISTAKE. I WAS NOT SUPPOSED TO BE REVIVED AT THIS TIME. I HAVE TO RETURN TO BIOSTASIS IMMEDIATELY.

A pause, then: THIS IS NOT POSSIBLE. YOU CANNOT RETURN TO BIOSTASIS.

Gillis's heart skipped a beat.

I REPEAT: THERE HAS BEEN A MISTAKE. THERE WAS NO REASON TO REVIVE THE PERSON IN CELL C2A-07. I WAS THE OCCUPANT OF CELL C2A-07, AND I NEED TO RETURN TO BIOSTASIS AT ONCE.

I UNDERSTAND THE SITUATION. THE CREW MANIFEST HAS BEEN CHANGED TO REFLECT THIS NEW INFORMATION. HOWEVER, IT IS IMPOSSIBLE FOR YOU TO RETURN TO BIOSTASIS.

His hands trembled upon the keyboard: WHY NOT?

PROTOCOL DOES NOT ALLOW FOR THE OCCUPANT OF CELL C2A-07 TO RESUME BIOSTASIS. THIS CELL HAS BEEN PERMANENTLY DEACTIVATED. RESUMPTION OF BIOSTASIS IS NOT ADMISSIBLE.

Gillis suddenly felt as if a hot towel had been wrapped around his face. SECURITY OVERRIDE B-001001, GILLIS, LESLIE, LT. COM. PASSWORD SCOTLAND. DELETE PROTOCOL IMMEDIATELY.

PASSWORD ACCEPTED, LT. GILLIS. PROTOCOL CANNOT BE DELETED WITHOUT DIRECT CONFIRMATION OF PRESIDENTIAL LAUNCH AUTHORIZATION, AND MAY NOT BE RESCINDED BY ANYONE OTHER THAN ENSIGN GUNTHER.

Anger surged within him. He typed: REVIVE ENSIGN GUNTHER AT ONCE. THIS IS AN EMERGENCY.

NO MEMBERS OF THE CREW MAY BE REVIVED FROM BIOSTASIS UNTIL THE SHIP HAS REACHED ITS FINAL DESTINATION UNLESS THERE IS A

MISSION-CRITICAL EMERGENCY. ALL SYSTEMS ARE AT NOMINAL STATUS: THERE IS NO MISSION-CRITICAL EMERGENCY.

Eric Gunther. Eric Gunther lay asleep on Deck C1A. Yet even if he could be awakened from hibernation and forced to confess his role, there was little he could do about it now. The long swath of ionized particles the *Alabama* left in its wake rendered impossible radio communications with Earth; any signals received by or sent from the starship would be fuzzed out while the fusion engines were firing, and the *Alabama* would remain under constant thrust for the next two hundred thirty years.

IF I DON'T RETURN TO BIOSTASIS, THEN I'LL DIE. THIS IS AN EMERGENCY. DO YOU UNDERSTAND?

I UNDERSTAND YOUR SITUATION, MR. GILLIS. HOWEVER, IT DOES NOT POSE A MISSION-CRITICAL EMERGENCY. I APOLOGIZE FOR THE ERROR.

Reading this, Gillis found himself smiling. The smile became a grin, and from somewhere within his grin a wry chuckle slowly fought through. The chuckle evolved into hysterical laughter, for by now Gillis had realized the irony of his situation.

He was the chief communications officer of the URSS *Alabama*. And he was doomed because he couldn't communicate.

———

Gillis had his pick of any berth aboard the ship, including Captain Lee's private quarters, yet he chose the bunk that had been assigned to him; it only seemed right. He reset the thermostat to seventy-one degrees, then he took a long, hot shower. Putting on his jumpsuit again, he returned to his berth, lay down, and tried to sleep. Yet every time he shut his eyes, new thoughts entered his mind, and soon he would find himself staring at the bunk above him. So he lay there for a long time, his hands folded together across his stomach as he contemplated his situation.

He wouldn't asphyxiate or perish from lack of water. *Alabama*'s closed-loop life-support system would purge the carbon dioxide from the ship's air and recirculate it as breathable oxygen-nitrogen, and his urine would be purified and recycled as potable water. Neither would he freeze to death in the dark; the fusion engines generated sufficient excess energy for him to be able to run the ship's internal electrical systems without fear of exhausting its reserves. Nor would he have to worry about starvation; there were enough rations aboard to feed a crew of one hundred four passengers for twelve months, which meant that one person would have enough to eat for over a century.

Yet there was little chance that he would last that long. Within their bi-ostasis cells, the remaining crew members would be constantly rejuvenated, their natural aging processes held at bay through homeostatic stem-cell regeneration, telomerase enzyme therapy, and nanotechnical repair of vital organs, while infusion of somatic drugs would keep them in a comalike condition that would deprive them of subconscious dream-sleep. Once they reached 47 Ursae Majoris, they would emerge from hibernation—even that term was a misnomer, for they would never stir from their long rest—just the same as they had been when they entered the cells.

Not so for him. Now that he was removed from biostasis, he would con-tinue to age normally. Or at least as normally as one would while traveling at relativistic velocity; if he were suddenly spirited back home and was met by a hypothetical twin brother—no chance of that happening; like so many others aboard, Gillis was an only child—he would discover that he had aged only a few hours less than his sibling. Yet that gap would gradually widen the farther *Alabama* traveled from Earth, and even the Lorentz factor wouldn't save him in the long run, for everyone else aboard the ship was aging at the same rate; the only difference was that their bodies would remain perpetually youthful, while his own would gradually break down, grow old . . .

No. Gillis forcefully shut his eyes. *Don't think about it.*

But there was no way of getting around it: he was living under a death sentence. Yet a condemned man in solitary confinement has some sort of personal contact, even if it's only the fleeting glimpse of a guard's hand as he shoves a tray of food through the cell door. Gillis didn't have that luxury. Never again would he ever hear another voice, see another face. There were a dozen or so people back home he had loved, and another dozen or so he had loathed, and countless others he had met, however briefly, dur-ing the twenty-eight years he had spent on Earth. All gone, lost forever. . . .

He sat up abruptly. A little too abruptly; he slammed the top of his head against the bunk above him. He cursed under his breath, rubbed his skull—a small bump beneath his hair, nothing more—then swung his legs over the side of his bunk, stood up, and opened his locker. His box was where he had last seen it; he took it down from the shelf, started to open it. . . .

And then he stopped himself. No. If he looked inside now, the things he had left in there would make him only more miserable than he already was. His fingers trembled upon the lid. He didn't need this now. He shoved the box back into the locker and slammed the door shut behind it. Then, hav-ing nothing better to do, he decided to take a walk.

The ring corridor led him around the hub to Module C7, where he climbed down to the mess deck: long empty benches, walls painted in mut-ed earth tones. The deck below contained the galley: chrome tables, cooking surfaces, empty warm refrigerators. He located the coffeemaker, but there was no coffee to be found, so he ventured further down the ladder to the ship's med deck. Antiseptic white-on-white compartments, the examination beds covered with plastic sheets; cabinets contained cellophane-wrapped surgical instruments, gauze and bandages, and rows of plastic bottles containing pharmaceuticals with arcane labels. He had a slight headache, so he searched through them until he found some ibuprofen; he took the pill without water and lay down for a few minutes.

After a while his headache went away, so he decided to check out the wardroom on the bottom level. It was sparsely furnished, only a few chairs and tables beneath a pair of wallscreens, with a single couch facing a closed porthole. One of the tables folded open to reveal a holographic game board; he pressed a button marked by a knight piece and watched as a chess set materialized. He used to play chess assiduously when he was a teenager, but had gradually lost interest as he grew older. Perhaps it was time to pick it up again. . . .

Instead, though, he went over to the porthole. Opening the shutter, he gazed out into space. Although astronomy had always been a minor hobby, he could see none of the familiar constellations; this far from Earth, the stars had changed position so radically that only the AI's navigation subroutine could accurately locate them. Even the stars were strangers now; this revelation made him feel even more lonely, so he closed the shutter. He didn't bother to turn off the game table before he left the compartment.

As he walked along the ring corridor, he came upon a lone 'bot. It quickly scuttled out of his way as he approached, but Gillis squatted down on his haunches and tapped his fingers against the deck, trying to coax it closer. The robot's eyestalks twitched briefly toward him; for a moment, it seemed to hesitate, then it quickly turned away and went up the circular passageway. It had no reason to have any interaction with humans, even those who desired its company. Gillis watched the 'bot as it disappeared above the ceiling, then he reluctantly rose and continued up the corridor.

The cargo modules, C5 and C6, were dark and cold, deck upon deck of color-coded storage lockers and shipping containers. He found the crew rations on Deck C5A; sliding open one of the refrigerated lockers, he took a few minutes to inspect its contents: vacuum-sealed plastic bags containing freeze-dried substances identified only by cryptic labels. None of it looked very appetizing; the dark brown slab within the bag he pulled out at random could have been anything from processed beef to chocolate cake. He wasn't hungry yet, so he shoved it back and slammed the locker shut.

Gillis returned to the ring corridor and walked to the hatch leading to the hub access shaft. As he opened the hatch, though, he hesitated before grasping the top rung of the shaft's recessed ladder. He had climbed down the shaft once before already, yet he had been so determined to reach the command deck that he had failed to recognize it for what it was, a narrow well almost a hundred feet deep. While the *Alabama* was moored at Highgate and in zero-gee, everyone aboard had treated it as a tunnel, yet what had once been horizontal was now vertical.

He looked down. Far below, five levels beneath him, lay the hard metal floor of Deck H5. If his hands ever slipped on the ladder, if his feet failed to rest safely upon one of its rungs, then he could fall all the way to the bottom. He would have to be careful every time he climbed the shaft, for if he ever had an accident. . . .

The trick was never looking down. He purposely watched his hands as he made his way down the ladder.

Gillis meant to stop on H2 and H3 to check the engineering and life-support decks, yet somehow he found himself not stopping until he reached H5.

The EVA deck held three airlocks. To his right and left were the hatches leading to the *Alabama*'s twin shuttles, the *Wallace* and the *Helms*. Gillis gazed through a porthole at the *Helms*; the spaceplane was nestled within its docking cradle, its delta wings folded beneath its broad fuselage, its bubble canopy covered by shutters. For a moment, he had an insane urge to steal the *Helms* and fly it back home, yet that was clearly impossible; the shuttles only had sufficient fuel and oxygen reserves for orbital sorties. He wouldn't get so far as even Neptune, let alone Earth. And besides, he had never been trained to pilot a shuttle.

Turning away from the porthole, he caught sight of another airlock located on the opposite side of the deck. This one didn't lead to a shuttle docking collar; it was the airlock that led outside the ship.

Reluctantly, almost against his own will, Gillis found himself walking toward it. He twisted the lockwheel to undog the inner hatch, then pulled it open and stepped inside. The airlock was a small white compartment barely large enough to hold two men wearing hardsuits. On the opposite side was the tiger-striped outer hatch with a small control panel mounted on the bulkhead next to it. The panel had only three major buttons—*Pres.*, *Purge*, and *Open*—and above them all were three lights: green, orange, and red. The green light was now lit, showing that the inner hatch was open and the airlock was safely pressurized.

The airlock was cold. The rest of the ship had warmed up by now, but here Gillis could feel the arctic chill creeping through his jumpsuit, see every exhalation as ghostly wisps rising past his face. He didn't know how long he remained there, yet he regarded the three buttons for a very long time.

After a while, he realized his stomach was beginning to rumble, so he backed out of the compartment. He carefully closed the inner hatch, and lingered outside the airlock for another minute or so before he decided that this was one part of the ship he didn't want to visit very often.

Then he made the long climb back up the access shaft.

————

There were chronometers everywhere, displaying both Greenwich Mean Time and relativistic shiptime. On the second day after revival, Gillis decided that he'd rather not know what the date was, so he found a roll of black electrical tape and went through the entire ship, masking every clock he could find.

There were no natural day or night cycles aboard the ship. He slept when he was tired, and got out of bed when he felt like it. After a while, he found that he was spending countless hours lying in his bunk, doing nothing more than staring at the ceiling, thinking about nothing. This wasn't good, so he made a regular schedule for himself.

He reset the ship's internal lighting so that it turned on and off at twelve-hour intervals, giving him a semblance of sunrise and sunset. He started his mornings by jogging around the ring corridor, keeping it up until his legs ached and his breath came in ragged gasps, and then sprinting the final lap.

Next he would take a shower, and then attend to himself. When his beard began to grow back, he made a point of shaving every day, and when his hair started to get a little too long he trimmed it with a pair of surgical scissors he found in the med deck; the result was a chopped, butch-cut look, but so long as he managed to keep the hair out of his eyes and off his neck he was satisfied. Otherwise, he tried to avoid looking closely at himself in the mirror.

Once he was dressed, he would visit the galley to make breakfast: cold cereal, rehydrated vegetable juice, a couple of fruit squares, a mug of hot coffee. He liked to open a porthole and look out at the stars while he ate.

Then he would go below to the wardroom and activate the wallscreens. He was able to access countless hours of datafiche through the AI's library subroutine, yet precious little of it was intended for entertainment. Instead, what he found were mainly tutorials: service manuals for the *Alabama*'s major operating systems, texts on agriculture, astrobiology, land management, academic studies of historical colonies on Earth, so forth and so on. Nonetheless, he devoted himself to studying everything he could find, pretending as if he was once again a first-year plebe at the Academy of the Republic, memorizing everything and then silently quizzing himself to make sure he got it right. Perhaps it was pointless—there was no reason for him to learn about organic methods of soybean cultivation—yet it helped to keep his mind occupied.

Although he learned much about the *Alabama*'s biostasis systems he hadn't known before, he never found anything that would help him return to hibernation. He eventually returned to Deck C2B, closed the hatch of his former cell, and returned it to its niche. After that, he tried not to go there again; like the EVA airlock on Deck H5, this was a place that made him uncomfortable.

When he was tired of studying, he would play chess for hours upon end, matching his wits against the game system. The outcome was always inevitable, for the computer could never be defeated, but he gradually learned how to anticipate its next move and forestall another loss for at least a little while longer.

The food was bland, preprocessed stuff, artificial substitutes for meat, fruit, and vegetables meant to remain edible after years of long-term freezer storage, but he did his best to make dinner more tolerable. Once he learned how to interpret the labels, he selected a variety of different rations and moved them to the galley. He spent considerable time and effort making each meal a little better, or at least different, from the last one; often the results were dismal, but now and then he managed to concoct something he wouldn't mind eating again—stir-fried chicken and pineapple over linguine, for instance, wasn't as strange as he thought it might be—and then he could type the recipe into the galley computer for future reference.

While wandering through the ship in search of something else to divert his attention, he found a canvas duffel bag. It belonged to Jorge Montero, one of the D.I.'s who had helped the *Alabama* escape from Earth; apparently he had managed to bring a small supply of books with him. Most were wilderness-survival manuals of one sort or another, yet among them were a few twentieth-century classics: J. Bronowski's *The Ascent of Man*, Kenneth Brower's *The Starship and the Canoe*, Frank Herbert's *Dune*. Gillis took them back to his berth and put them aside as bedtime reading.

On occasion, he would visit the command deck. The third time he did this, the nav table showed him that the *Alabama* had crossed the heliopause; the ship was now traveling through interstellar space, the dark between the stars. Because the ramscoop blocked the view, there were no windows that faced directly ahead, yet he learned how to manipulate the cameras located on the fuel tank until they displayed a real-time image forward of the ship's bow. It appeared as if the stars directly in front had clustered together, the Doppler effect causing them to form short cometlike tails tinged with blue. Yet when he rotated the camera to look back the way he had come, he saw that an irregular black hole had opened behind the *Alabama*; the Sun and all its planets, including Earth, had become invisible.

This was one more thing that disturbed him, so he seldom activated the external cameras.

He slept, and he jogged, and he ate, and he studied, and he played long and futile chess games, and otherwise did everything possible to pass the time as best he could. Every now and then he caught himself murmuring to himself, carrying on conversations with only his own mind as a companion; when this happened, he would consciously shut up. Yet no matter how far he managed to escape from himself, he always had to return to the silence of the ship's corridors, the emptiness of its compartments.

He didn't know it then, but he was beginning to go insane.

———

His jumpsuit began to get worn out. It was the only thing he had to wear, though, besides his robe, so he checked the cargo manifest and found that clothing was stowed in Deck C5C, and it was while searching for them that he discovered the liquor supply.

There wasn't supposed to be any booze aboard the *Alabama*, yet nonetheless someone had managed to smuggle two cases of scotch, two cases of vodka, and one case of champagne onto the ship. They were obviously put there to help the crew celebrate their safe arrival at 47 Ursae Majoris; Gillis found them stashed among the spare clothing.

He tried to ignore the liquor for as long as possible; he had never been much of a drinker, and he didn't want to start now. But several days later, after another attempt at making beef stroganoff resulted in a tasteless mess of half-cooked noodles and beef-substitute, he found himself wandering back to C5C and pulling out a bottle of scotch. He brought it back to the wardroom, poured a couple of fingers in a glass and stirred in some tap water, then sat down to play another game of chess. After his second drink, he found himself feeling more at ease than he had been since his untimely awakening; the next evening, he did the same thing again.

That was the beginning of his dark times.

"Cocktail hour" soon became the highlight of his day; after awhile, he found no reason to wait until after dinner, and instead had his first drink during his afternoon chess game. One morning he decided that a glass of champagne would be the perfect thing to top off his daily run, so he opened a bottle after he showered and shaved, and continued to indulge himself during the rest of the day. He discovered that powdered citrus juice was an adequate mixer for vodka, so he added a little of that to his morning breakfast, and it wasn't long before he took to carrying around a glass of vodka wherever he went. He tried to ration the liquor supply as much as he could, yet he found himself depressed whenever he finished a bottle, and relieved to discover that there always seemed to be one more to replace it. At first he told himself that he had to leave some for the others—after all, it was meant for their eventual celebration—but in time that notion faded to the back of his mind and was finally forgotten altogether.

He went to sleep drunk, often in the wardroom, and awoke to nasty hangovers that only a hair of the dog could help dispel. His clothes began to smell of stale booze; he soon got tired of washing them, and simply found another jumpsuit to wear. Unwashed plates and cookware piled up in the galley sink, and it always seemed as if there were empty or half-empty glasses scattered throughout the ship. He stopped jogging after a while, but he didn't gain much weight because he had lost his appetite and was now eating less than before. And every day, he found a new source of irritation: the inconvenient times when the lights turned on and off, or how the compartments always seemed too hot or too cold, or why he could never find something that he needed.

One night, frustrated at having lost at chess yet again, he picked up his chair and slammed it through the game table's glass panel. He was still staring at the wrecked table when one of the 'bots arrived to investigate; deciding that its companionship was better than none at all, he sat down on the floor and tried to get it to come closer, cooing to it in the same way he had summoned his puppy back when he was a boy. The 'bot ignored him completely, and that enraged him even further, so he found an empty champagne bottle and used it to demolish the machine. Remarkably, the bottle remained intact even after the 'bot had become a broken, useless thing in the middle of the wardroom floor; even more remarkably, it didn't shatter the porthole when Gillis hurled it against the window.

He didn't remember what happened after that; he simply blacked out. The next thing he knew, he was sprawled across the floor of the airlock.

The harsh clang of an alarm threatened to split his skull in half. Dully surprised to find where he was, he clumsily raised himself up on his elbows and regarded his surroundings through swollen eyes. He was naked; his jumpsuit lay in a heap just within the inner hatch, which was shut. There was a large pool of vomit nearby, but he couldn't recall having thrown up any more than he could remember getting there from the wardroom.

Lights strobed within the tiny compartment. Rolling over on his side, he peered at the control panel next to the outer hatch. The orange button in its center was lit, and the red one beneath it flashed on and off. The airlock was ready to be opened without prior decompression; that was what had triggered the alarm.

Gillis had no idea how he got here, but it was obvious what he had almost done. He crawled across the airlock floor and slapped his hand against the green button; that stopped the alarm. Then he opened the inner hatch and, without bothering to pick up his discarded jumpsuit, staggered out of the airlock. He couldn't keep his balance, though, so he fell to his hands and knees and threw up again.

Then he rolled over on his side, curled in upon himself, and wept hysterically until sleep mercifully came to him. Naked and miserable, he passed out on the floor of the EVA deck.

———

The following day, Gillis methodically went through the entire ship, gathering the few remaining bottles and returning them to the locker where he had found them. Although he was tempted to jettison them into space, he was scared to return to Deck H5. Besides, there wasn't much booze left; during his long binge, he had managed to put away all but two bottles of scotch, one bottle of vodka, and four bottles of champagne.

The face that stared back at him from the mirror was unshaven and haggard, its eyes rimmed with dark circles. He was too tired to get rid of the beard, though, so he clipped it short with his scissors and let his hair remain at shoulder length. It was a new look for him, and he couldn't decide whether he liked it or not. Not that he cared much anymore.

It took a couple of days for him to want to eat again, and even longer before he had a good night's sleep. More than a few times he was tempted to have another drink, but the memory of that terrifying moment in the airlock was enough to keep him away from the bottle.

Yet he never returned to the daily schedule he had previously set for himself. He lost interest in his studies, and he watched the few movies stored in the library until he found himself able to recite the characters' lines from memory. The game table couldn't be repaired, so he never played chess again. He went jogging now and then, but only when there was nothing else to do, and not for very long.

He spent long hours lying on his bunk, staring into the deepest recesses of his memory. He replayed events from his childhood—small incidents with his mother and father, the funny and stupid things he had done when he was a kid—and thought long and hard about the mistakes he had made during his journey to adulthood. He thought about the girls he had known, refought old quarrels with ancient enemies, remembered good times with old friends, yet in the end he always came back to where he was.

Sometimes he went down to the command deck. He had long since given up on trying to have meaningful conversation with the AI; it only responded to direct questions, and even then in a perfunctory way. Instead, he opened the porthole shutters and slumped in Captain Lee's chair while he stared at the distant and motionless stars.

One day, on impulse, he got up from the chair and walked to the nearest console. He hesitated for a moment, then he reached down and gently peeled back the strip of black tape he had fastened across the chronometer. It read:

P:/ 4.17.71 / 18.32.06 GMT

April 17, 2071. A little more than six months had gone by since his awakening.

He could have sworn it had been six years.

———————

That evening, Gillis prepared dinner with special care. He selected the best cut of processed beef he could find in the storage locker and marinated it in a pepper sauce he had learned to make, and carefully sautéed the dried garlic before he added it to the mashed potatoes; while the asparagus steamed in lemon juice, he grilled the beef to medium-rare perfection. Earlier in the afternoon he had chosen a bottle of champagne from the liquor supply, which he put aside until everything else was ready. He cleaned up the wardroom and laid a single setting for himself at a table facing the porthole, and just before dinner he dimmed the ceiling lights.

He ate slowly, savoring every bite, closing his eyes from time to time as he allowed his mind's eye to revisit some of the fine restaurants in which he had once dined: a steak house in downtown Kansas City, a five-star Italian restaurant in Boston's Beacon Hill neighborhood, a seafood place on St. Simon's Island where the lobster came straight from the wharf. When he gazed out the porthole he didn't attempt to pick out constellations, but simply enjoyed the silent majesty of the stars; when he was through with dinner, he carefully laid his knife and fork together on his plate, refilled his glass with champagne, and walked over to the couch, where he had earlier placed one last thing to round off a perfect evening.

Gillis had deliberately refrained from opening the box he kept in his locker; even during his worst moments, the lowest depths of his long binge, he had deliberately stayed away from it. Now the time had come for him to open the box, see what was inside.

He pulled out the photographs one at a time, studying them closely as he remembered the places where they had been taken, the years of his life that they represented. Here was his father; here was his mother; here he was at age seven, standing in the backyard of his childhood home in North Carolina, proudly holding aloft a toy spaceship he had been given for his birthday. Here was a snapshot of the first girl he had ever loved; here were several photos he had taken of her during a camping trip to the Smoky Mountains. Here he was in his dress uniform during graduation exercises at the Academy; here he was during flight training in Texas. These images, and many more like them, were all he had brought with him from Earth: pictures from his past, small reminders of the places he had gone, the people whom he had known and loved.

Looking through them, he tried not to think about what he was about to do. He had reset the thermostat to lower the ship's internal temperature to fifty degrees at midnight, and he had instructed the AI to ignore the artificial day-night cycle he had previously programmed. He had left a note in Captain Lee's quarters, informing him that Eric Gunther was a saboteur and apologizing for having deprived the rest of the crew of rations and liquor. He would finish this bottle of champagne, though; no sense in letting it go to waste, and perhaps it would be easier to push the red button if he was drunk.

His life was over. There was nothing left for him. A few moments of agony would be a fair exchange for countless days of lonesome misery.

Gillis was still leafing through the photographs when he happened to glance up at the porthole, and it was at that moment he noticed something peculiar: one of the stars was moving.

At first, he thought the champagne was getting to him. That, or it was a refraction of starlight caused by the tears which clung to the corners of his eyes. He returned his attention to a picture he had taken of his father shortly before he died. Then, almost reluctantly, he raised his head once more.

The window was filled with stars, all of them stationary . . . save one.

A bright point of light, so brilliant that it could have been a planet, perhaps even a comet. Yet the *Alabama* was now far beyond the Earth's solar system, and the stars were too distant to be moving relative to the ship's velocity. Yet this one seemed to be following a course parallel to his own.

His curiosity aroused, Gillis watched the faraway light as it moved across the starscape. The longer he looked at it, the more it appeared as if it had a faint blue-white tail; it might be a comet, but if it was, it was headed in the wrong direction. Indeed, as he continued to study it, the light became a little brighter and seemed to make a subtle shift in direction, almost as if . . .

The photos fell to the floor as he rushed toward the ladder.

————

By the time he reached the command deck, though, the object had vanished.

Gillis spent the next several hours searching the sky, using the navigational telescope in an attempt to catch another glimpse of the anomaly.

When optical methods failed, he went to his com station and ran the broadband selector up and down across the radio spectrum in an effort to locate a repeating signal against the warbling background noise of space. He barely noticed that the deck had become colder, that the ceiling lights had shut off; his previous intentions forgotten, he had neglected to tell the AI that he had changed his mind.

The object had disappeared as quickly as it had appeared, yet he was absolutely certain of what he had seen. It wasn't a hallucination, of that he was positive, and the more he thought about it, the more convinced he became that what he had spotted wasn't a natural object but a spacecraft, briefly glimpsed from some inestimable distance—a thousand kilometers? ten thousand? a million?—as it passed the *Alabama*.

Yet where had it come from? Not from Earth, of that he could only be certain. Who was aboard, and where was it going? His mind conjured countless possibilities as he washed his dinner dishes, then went about preparing an early breakfast he had never expected to eat. Why hadn't it come closer? He considered this as he lay on his bunk, his hands propped behind his head. Perhaps it hadn't seen the *Alabama*. Might he ever see it again? Not likely, he eventually decided . . . yet if there was one, wasn't there always a possibility that there might be others?

He realized that he had to record this incident, so that the rest of the crew would know what he had observed. Yet when he returned to the command deck and began to type a report into the ship's log, he discovered that words failed him. Confronted by a blank flatscreen, everything he wrote seemed hollow and lifeless, nothing evoking the mysterious wonder of what he had observed. It was then that he realized that, during the six long months he had been living within the starship, never once had he ever attempted to write a journal.

Not that there had been much worth recording for posterity: he woke up, he ate, he jogged, he studied, he got drunk, he considered suicide. Yet it seemed as if everything had suddenly changed. Only yesterday he had been ready to walk into the airlock, close his eyes, and jettison himself into the void. Now, he felt as if he had been given a new reason to live . . . but that reason only made sense if he left something behind besides an unmade bunk and a half-empty champagne bottle.

He couldn't write on a screen, though, so he searched through the cargo lockers until he found what he needed: a supply of blank ledger books, intended for use by the quartermaster to keep track of expedition supplies, along with a box of pens. Much to his surprise, he also discovered a couple of sketchbooks, some charcoal pencils, and a watercolor paint kit; someone back on Earth apparently had the foresight to splurge a few kilos on rudimentary art supplies.

Gillis carried a ledger and a couple of pens back to the wardroom. Although the game table was ruined, it made a perfect desk once its top was shut. He rearranged the furniture so that the table faced the porthole. For some reason, writing in longhand felt more comfortable; after a couple of false starts, which he impatiently scratched out, he was finally able to put down a more or less descriptive account of what he had seen the night before, followed by a couple of pages of informal conjecture of what it might have been.

When he was done, his back hurt from having bent over the table for so long, and there was a sore spot between the index and middle fingers of his right hand where he had gripped his pen. Although he had nothing more to say, nonetheless he had the need to say more; putting words to paper had been a release unlike any he had felt before, an experience that had transported him, however temporarily, from this place to somewhere else. His body was tired but his mind was alive; despite his physical exhaustion, he felt a longing for something else to write.

He didn't know it then, but he was beginning to go sane.

As Gillis gradually resumed the daily schedule he had established for himself before the darkness had set in, he struggled to find something to write about. He tried to start a journal, but that was futile and depressing. He squandered a few pages on an autobiography before he realized that writing about his life made him self-conscious; in the end he ripped those pages from the ledger and threw them away. His poetry was ridiculous; he almost reconsidered a trip to the airlock when he reread the tiresome doggerel he had contrived. In desperation he jotted down a list of things that he missed, only to realize that it was not only trivial but even more embarrassing than his autobiography. That, too, ended in the waste bin.

For long hours he sat at his makeshift desk, staring through the porthole as he aimlessly doodled, making pictures of the bright star he had seen that eventful night. More than a few times he was tempted to find a bottle of scotch and get drunk, yet the recollection of what he had nearly done to himself kept him away from the liquor. More than anything else, he wanted to write something meaningful, at least to himself if not for anyone else, yet it seemed as if his mind had become a featureless plain. Inspiration eluded him.

Then, early one morning before the lights came on, he abruptly awoke with the fleeting memory of a particularly vivid dream. Most of his dreams tended to be about Earth—memories of places he had been, people whom he had known—yet this one was different; he wasn't in it, nor did it take place anywhere he had ever been.

He couldn't recall any specific details, yet he was left with one clear vision: a young man standing on an alien landscape, gazing up at an azure sky dominated by a large ringed planet, watching helplessly as a bright light—Gillis recognized it as the starship he had seen—raced away from him, heading into deep space.

Gillis almost rolled over and went back to sleep, yet he found himself sitting up and reaching for his robe. He took a shower, and as he stood beneath the lukewarm spray, his imagination began to fill in the missing pieces. The young man was a prince, a nobleman from some world far from Earth; indeed, Earth's history didn't even belong to the story. His father's kingdom had fallen to a tyrant and he had been forced to flee for his life, taking refuge in a starship bound for another inhabited planet. Yet its crew, fearing the tyrant's wrath, had cast him away, leaving him marooned upon a habitable moon of an uncharted planet, without any supplies or companionship. . . .

Still absorbed by the story in his mind, Gillis got dressed, then went to the wardroom. He turned on a couple of lights, then sat down at his desk and picked up his pen. There was no hesitation as he opened the ledger and turned to a fresh page; almost as if in a trance, he began to write.

––––––

And he never stopped.

To be sure, there were many times when Gillis laid down his pen. His body had its limitations, and he couldn't remain at his desk indefinitely before hunger or exhaustion overcame him. And there were occasions when he didn't know what to do next; in frustration he would impatiently pace the floor, groping for the next scene, perhaps even the next word.

Yet after a time it seemed as if the prince knew what to do even before he did. As he explored his new world Gillis encountered many creatures—some of whom became friends, some of whom were implacable enemies—and journeyed to places that tested the limits of his ever-expanding imagination. As he did, Gillis—and Prince Rupurt, who subtly became his alter ego—found himself embarked on an adventure more grand than anything he had ever believed possible.

Gillis changed his routine, fitting everything around the hours he spent at his desk. He rose early and went straight to work; his mind felt sharpest just after he got out of bed, and all he needed was a cup of coffee to help him wake up a little more. Around midday he would prepare a modest lunch, then walk around the ring corridor for exercise; two or three times a week he would patrol the entire ship, making sure that everything was functioning normally. By early afternoon he was back at his desk, picking up where he had left off, impatient to find out what would happen next.

He filled a ledger before he reached the end of his protagonist's first adventure; without hesitation, he opened a fresh book and continued without interruption, and when he wore out his first pen, he discarded it without a second thought. A thick callus developed between the second and third knuckles of his right middle finger, yet he barely noticed. When the second ledger was filled, he placed it on top of the first one at the edge of his desk. He seldom read what he had written except when he needed to recheck the name of a character or the location of a certain place; after a while he learned to keep notes in a separate book so that he wouldn't have to look back at what he had already done.

When evening came he would make dinner, read a little, spend some time gazing out the window. Every now and then he would go down to the command deck to check the nav table. Eventually the *Alabama*'s distance from Earth could be measured in parsecs rather than single light-years, yet even this fact had become incidental at best, and in time it became utterly irrelevant.

Gillis kept the chronometers covered; never again did he want to know how much time had passed. He stopped wearing shorts and a shirt and settled for merely wearing his robe; sometimes he went through the entire day naked, sitting at his desk without a stitch of clothing. He kept his fingernails and toenails trimmed, and he always paid careful attention to his teeth, yet he gave up cutting his hair and beard. He showered once or twice a week, if that.

When he wasn't writing, he was sketching pictures of the characters he had created, the strange cities and landscapes they visited. By now he had filled four ledgers with the adventures of his prince, yet words alone weren't sufficient to bring life to his imagination. The next time he returned to the cargo module for a new ledger and a handful of pens, he found the watercolor set he had noticed earlier and brought it back to the wardroom.

That evening, he began to paint the walls.

One morning, he rose at his usual time. He took a shower, then put on his robe—which was now frayed at the cuffs and worn through at the elbows—and made his long journey to the wardroom. Lately it had become more difficult for him to climb up and down ladders; his joints always seemed to ache, and ibuprofen relieved the pain only temporarily. There had been other changes as well; while making up his bunk a couple of days ago, he had been mildly surprised to find a long grey hair upon his pillow.

As he passed through the ring corridor, he couldn't help but admire his work. The forest mural he had started some time ago was almost complete; it extended halfway from Module C1 to Module C3, and it was quite lovely to gaze upon, although he needed to add a little more detail to the leaves. That might take some doing; he had recently exhausted the watercolors, and since then had resorted to soaking the dyes out of his old clothes.

He had a light breakfast, then he carefully climbed down the ladder to his studio; he had long since ceased to think of it as the wardroom. His ledger lay open on his desk, his pen next to the place where he had left off last night. Rupurt was about to fight a duel with the lord of the southern kingdom, and he was looking forward to seeing how all this would work out.

He farted loudly as he sat down, giving him reason to smile with faint amusement, then he picked up his pen. He read the last paragraph he had composed, crossed out a few words that seemed unnecessary, then raised his eyes to the porthole, giving himself a few moments to compose his thoughts.

A bright star moved against space, one more brilliant than any he had seen in a very long time.

He stared at it for a while. Then, very slowly, he rose from his desk, his legs trembling beneath his robe. His gaze never left the star as he backed away from the window, taking one small step after another as he moved toward the ladder behind him.

The star had returned. Or perhaps this was another one. Either way, it looked very much like the mysterious thing he had seen once before, a long time ago.

The pen fell from his hand as he bolted for the ladder. Ignoring the arthritic pain shooting through his arms and legs, he scrambled to the top deck of the module, then dashed down the corridor to the hatch leading to hub shaft. This time, he knew what had to be done; get to his old station, transmit a clear vox signal on all frequencies. . . .

He had climbed nearly halfway down the shaft before he realized that he didn't know exactly what to say. A simple greeting? A message of friendship? Yes, that might do . . . but how would he identify himself?

In that moment, he realized that he couldn't remember his name.

Stunned by this revelation, he clung to the ladder. His name. Surely he could recall his own name. . . .

Gillis. Of course. He was Gillis. Gillis, Leslie. Lieutenant Commander Leslie Gillis. Chief communications officer of . . . yes, right . . . the URSS *Alabama*. He smiled, climbed down another rung. It had been so long since he had heard anyone say his name aloud, he probably couldn't even speak it himself. . . .

Couldn't he?

Gillis opened his mouth, urged himself to say something. Nothing emerged from his throat save for a dry croak.

No. He could still speak; he was simply out of practice. All he had to do was get to his station. If he could remember the correct commands, he might still be able to send a signal to Prince Rupurt's ship before it passed beyond range. He just needed to . . .

His left foot missed the next rung on the ladder. Thrown off-balance, he glanced down to see what he had done wrong . . . then his right hand slipped off the ladder. Suddenly he found himself falling backward, his arms and legs flailing helplessly. Down, down, down . . .

"Oh, no," he said softly.

An instant later he hit the bottom of the shaft. There was a brief flash of pain as his neck snapped, then blackness rushed in upon him and it was all over.

———

A few hours later, one of the 'bots found Gillis's body. It prodded him several times, confirming that the cold organic form lying on the floor of Deck H5 was indeed lifeless, then it relayed a query to the AI. The molecular intelligence carefully considered the situation for a few fractions of a second, then instructed the spider to jettison the corpse. That was done within the next two minutes; ejected from the starship, Gillis spun away into the void, another small piece of debris lost between the stars.

The AI determined that it was no longer necessary for the crew compartments to remain habitable, so it returned the thermostat setting to fifty degrees. A 'bot moved through the ship, cleaning up after Gillis. It left untouched the thirteen ledgers he had completed, along with a fourteenth that lay open upon his desk. There was nothing that could be done about the paintings on the walls of Module C7 and the ring access corridor, so they were left alone. Once the 'bot completed its chores, the AI closed the shutters of the windows Gillis had left open, then methodically turned off all the lights, one by one.

The date was February 25, 2102, GMT. The rest of the flight went smoothly, without further incident.

SLOW LIFE

MICHAEL SWANWICK

"It was the Second Age of Space. Gagarin, Shepard, Glenn, and Armstrong were all dead. It was *our* turn to make history now."

—*The Memoirs of Lizzie O'Brien*

THE RAINDROP BEGAN forming ninety kilometers above the surface of Titan. It started with an infinitesimal speck of tholin, adrift in the cold nitrogen atmosphere. Dianoacetylene condensed on the seed nucleus, molecule by molecule, until it was one shard of ice in a cloud of billions.

Now the journey could begin.

It took almost a year for the shard of ice in question to precipitate downward twenty-five kilometers, where the temperature dropped low enough that ethane began to condense on it. But when it did, growth was rapid.

Down it drifted.

At forty kilometers, it was for a time caught up in an ethane cloud. There it continued to grow. Occasionally it collided with another droplet and doubled in size. Finally, it was too large to be held effortlessly aloft by the gentle stratospheric winds.

It fell.

Falling, it swept up methane and quickly grew large enough to achieve a terminal velocity of almost two meters per second.

At twenty-seven kilometers, it passed through a dense layer of methane clouds. It acquired more methane, and continued its downward flight.

As the air thickened, its velocity slowed and it began to lose some of its substance to evaporation. At two and a half kilometers, when it emerged from the last patchy clouds, it was losing mass so rapidly it could not normally be expected to reach the ground.

It was, however, falling toward the equatorial highlands, where mountains of ice rose a towering five hundred meters into the atmosphere. At two meters and a lazy new terminal velocity of one meter per second, it was only a breath away from hitting the surface.

Two hands swooped an open plastic collecting bag upward, and snared the raindrop.

"Gotcha!" Lizzie O'Brien cried gleefully.

She zip-locked the bag shut, held it up so her helmet cam could read the bar code in the corner, and said, "One raindrop." Then she popped it into her collecting box.

Sometimes it's the little things that make you happiest. Somebody would spend a *year* studying this one little raindrop when Lizzie got it home. And it was just Bag 64 in Collecting Case 5. She was going to be on the surface of Titan long enough to scoop up the raw material of a revolution in planetary science. The thought of it filled her with joy.

Lizzie dogged down the lid of the collecting box and began to skip across the granite-hard ice, splashing the puddles and dragging the boot of her atmosphere suit through the rivulets of methane pouring down the mountainside. *"I'm singing in the rain."* She threw out her arms and spun around. *"Just sing-ing in the rain!"*

"Uh . . . O'Brien?" Alan Greene said from the *Clement.* "Are you all right?"

"Dum-dee-dum-dee-dee-dum-dum, I'm . . . some-thing again."

"Oh, leave her alone." Consuelo Hong said with sour good humor. She was down on the plains, where the methane simply boiled into the air, and the ground was covered with thick, gooey tholin. It was, she had told them, like wading ankle-deep in molasses. "Can't you recognize the scientific method when you hear it?"

"If you say so," Alan said dubiously. He was stuck in the *Clement,* overseeing the expedition and minding the website. It was a comfortable gig— *he* wouldn't be sleeping in his suit *or* surviving on recycled water and energy stix—and he didn't think the others knew how much he hated it.

"What's next on the schedule?" Lizzie asked.

"Um . . . well, there's still the robot turbot to be released. How's that going, Hong?"

"Making good time. I oughta reach the sea in a couple of hours."

"Okay, then it's time O'Brien rejoined you at the lander. O'Brien, start spreading out the balloon and going over the harness checklist."

"Roger that."

"And while you're doing that, I've got today's voice-posts from the Web cued up."

Lizzie groaned, and Consuelo blew a raspberry. By NAFTASA policy, the ground crew participated in all webcasts. Officially, they were delighted to share their experiences with the public. But the VoiceWeb (privately, Lizzie thought of it as the Illiternet) made them accessible to people who lacked even the minimal intellectual skills needed to handle a keyboard.

"Let me remind you that we're on open circuit here, so anything you say will go into my reply. You're certainly welcome to chime in at any time. But each question-and-response is transmitted as one take, so if you flub a line, we'll have to go back to the beginning and start all over again."

"Yeah, yeah," Consuelo grumbled.

"We've done this before," Lizzie reminded him.

"Okay. Here's the first one."

"Uh, hi, this is BladeNinja43. I was wondering just what it is that you guys are hoping to discover out there."

"That's an extremely good question," Alan lied. "And the answer is: We don't know! This is a voyage of discovery, and we're engaged in what's called 'pure science.' Now, time and time again, the purest research has turned out to be extremely profitable. But we're not looking that far ahead. We're just hoping to find something absolutely unexpected."

"My God, you're slick," Lizzie marveled.

"I'm going to edit that from the tape," Alan said cheerily. "Next up."

"This is Mary Schroeder, from the United States. I teach high school English, and I wanted to know for my students, what kind of grades the three of you had when you were their age."

Alan began. "I was an overachiever, I'm afraid. In my sophomore year, first semester, I got a B in Chemistry and panicked. I thought it was the end of the world. But then I dropped a couple of extracurriculars, knuckled down, and brought that grade right up."

"I was good in everything but French Lit," Consuelo said.

"I nearly flunked out!" Lizzie said. "Everything was difficult for me. But then I decided I wanted to be an astronaut, and it all clicked into place. I realized that, hey, it's just hard work. And now, well, here I am."

"That's good. Thanks, guys. Here's the third, from Maria Vasquez."

"Is there life on Titan?"

"Probably not. It's cold down there! 94 Kelvin is the same as -179° Celsius, or -290° Fahrenheit. And yet . . . life is persistent. It's been found in Antarctic ice and in boiling water in submarine volcanic vents. Which is why we'll be paying particular attention to exploring the depths of the ethane-methane sea. If life is anywhere to be found, that's where we'll find it."

"Chemically, the conditions here resemble the anoxic atmosphere on Earth in which life first arose," Consuelo said. "Further, we believe that such prebiotic chemistry has been going on here for four and a half billion years. For an organic chemist like me, it's the best toy box in the Universe. But that lack of heat is a problem. Chemical reactions that occur quickly back home would take thousands of years here. It's hard to see how life could arise under such a handicap."

"It would have to be slow life," Lizzie said thoughtfully. "Something vegetative. 'Vaster than empires and more slow.' It would take millions of years to reach maturity. A single thought might require centuries . . ."

"Thank you for that, uh, wild scenario!" Alan said quickly. Their NAFTASA masters frowned on speculation. It was, in their estimation, almost as unprofessional as heroism. "This next question comes from Danny in Toronto."

"Hey, man, I gotta say I really envy you being in that tiny little ship with those two hot babes."

Alan laughed lightly. "Yes, Ms. Hong and Ms. O'Brien are certainly attractive women. But we're kept so busy that, believe it or not, the thought of sex never comes up. And currently, while I tend to the *Clement*, they're both on the surface of Titan at the bottom of an atmosphere sixty percent more dense than Earth's, and encased in armored exploration suits. So even if I did have inappropriate thoughts, there's no way we could—"

"Hey, Alan," Lizzie said. "Tell me something."

"Yes?"

"What are you wearing?"

"Uh . . . switching over to private channel."

"Make that a three-way," Consuelo said.

———

Ballooning, Lizzie decided, was the best way there was of getting around. Moving with the gentle winds, there was no sound at all. And the view was great!

People talked a lot about the "murky orange atmosphere" of Titan, but your eyes adjusted. Turn up the gain on your helmet, and the white mountains of ice were *dazzling!* The methane streams carved cryptic runes into the heights. Then, at the tholin-line, white turned to a rich palette of oranges, reds, and yellows. There was a lot going on down there—more than she'd be able to learn in a hundred visits.

The plains were superficially duller, but they had their charms as well. Sure, the atmosphere was so dense that refracted light made the horizon curve upward to either side. But you got used to it. The black swirls and cryptic red tracery of unknown processes on the land below never grew tiring.

On the horizon, she saw the dark arm of Titan's narrow sea. If that was what it was. Lake Erie was larger, but the spin doctors back home had argued that since Titan was so much smaller than Earth, *relatively* it qualified as a sea. Lizzie had her own opinion, but she knew when to keep her mouth shut.

Consuelo was there now. Lizzie switched her visor over to the live feed. Time to catch the show.

"I can't believe I'm finally here," Consuelo said. She let the shrink-wrapped fish slide from her shoulder down to the ground. "Five kilometers doesn't seem like very far when you're coming down from orbit—just enough to leave a margin for error so the lander doesn't come down in the sea. But when you have to *walk* that distance, through tarry, sticky tholin . . . well, it's one heck of a slog."

"Consuelo, can you tell us what it's like there?" Alan asked.

"I'm crossing the beach. Now I'm at the edge of the sea." She knelt, dipped a hand into it. "It's got the consistency of a Slushy. Are you familiar with that drink? Lots of shaved ice sort of half-melted in a cup with flavored syrup. What we've got here is almost certainly a methane-ammonia mix; we'll know for sure after we get a sample to a laboratory. Here's an early indicator, though. It's dissolving the tholin off my glove." She stood.

"Can you describe the beach?"

"Yeah. It's white. Granular. I can kick it with my boot. Ice sand for sure. Do you want me to collect samples first or release the fish?"

"Release the fish," Lizzie said, almost simultaneously with Alan's "Your call."

"Okay, then." Consuelo carefully cleaned both of her suit's gloves in the sea, then seized the shrink-wrap's zip tab and yanked. The plastic parted. Awkwardly, she straddled the fish, lifted it by the two side-handles, and walked it into the dark slush.

"Okay, I'm standing in the sea now. It's up to my ankles. Now it's at my knees. I think it's deep enough here."

She set the fish down. "Now I'm turning it on."

The Mitsubishi turbot wriggled, as if alive. With one fluid motion, it surged forward, plunged, and was gone.

Lizzie switched over to the fishcam.

Black liquid flashed past the turbot's infrared eyes. Straight away from the shore it swam, seeing nothing but flecks of paraffin, ice, and other suspended particulates as they loomed up before it and were swept away in the violence of its wake. A hundred meters out, it bounced a pulse of radar off the sea floor, then dove, seeking the depths.

Rocking gently in her balloon harness, Lizzie yawned.

Snazzy Japanese cybernetics took in a minute sample of the ammonia-water, fed it through a deftly constructed internal laboratory, and excreted the waste products behind it. "We're at twenty meters now," Consuelo said. "Time to collect a second sample."

The turbot was equipped to run hundreds of on-the-spot analyses. But it had only enough space for twenty permanent samples to be carried back home. The first sample had been nibbled from the surface slush. Now it twisted, and gulped down five drams of sea fluid in all its glorious impurity. To Lizzie, this was science on the hoof. Not very dramatic, admittedly, but intensely exciting.

She yawned again.

"O'Brien?" Alan said, "How long has it been since you last slept?"

"Huh? Oh . . . twenty hours? Don't worry about me, I'm fine."

"Go to sleep. That's an order."

"But—"

"Now."

Fortunately, the suit was comfortable enough to sleep in. It had been designed so she could.

First, she drew in her arms from the suit's sleeves. Then she brought in her legs, tucked them up under her chin, and wrapped her arms around them. "Night, guys," she said.

"Buenas noches, querida," Consuelo said, *"que tengas lindos sueños."*

"Sleep tight, space explorer."

The darkness when she closed her eyes was so absolute it crawled. Black, black, black. Phantom lights moved within the darkness, formed lines, shifted away when she tried to see them. They were as fugitive as fish, luminescent, fainter than faint, there and with a flick of her attention fled.

A school of little thoughts flashed through her mind, silver-scaled and gone.

Low, deep, slower than sound, something tolled. The bell from a drowned clock tower patiently stroking midnight. She was beginning to get her bearings. Down *there* was where the ground must be. Flowers grew there unseen. Up above was where the sky would be, if there were a sky. Flowers floated there as well.

Deep within the submerged city, she found herself overcome by an enormous and placid sense of self. A swarm of unfamiliar sensations washed through her mind, and then . . .

"Are you me?" a gentle voice asked.

"No," she said carefully. "I don't think so."

Vast astonishment. "You think you are not me?"

"Yes. I think so, anyway."

"Why?"

There didn't seem to be any proper response to that, so she went back to the beginning of the conversation and ran through it again, trying to bring it to another conclusion. Only to bump against that "Why?" once again.

"I don't know why," she said.

"Why not?"

"I don't know."

She looped through that same dream over and over again all the while that she slept.

When she awoke, it was raining again. This time, it was a drizzle of pure methane from the lower cloud deck at fifteen kilometers. These clouds were (the theory went) methane condensate from the wet air swept up from the sea. They fell on the mountains and washed them clean of tholin. It was the methane that eroded and shaped the ice, carving gullies and caves.

Titan had more kinds of rain than anywhere else in the Solar System.

The sea had crept closer while Lizzie slept. It now curled up to the horizon on either side like an enormous dark smile. Almost time now for her to begin her descent. While she checked her harness settings, she flicked on telemetry to see what the others were up to.

The robot turbot was still spiraling its way downward, through the lightless sea, seeking its distant floor. Consuelo was trudging through the tholin again, retracing her five-kilometer trek from the lander *Harry Stubbs*, and Alan was answering another set of webposts.

"Modelos de la evolución de Titanes indican que la luna formó de una nube circumplanetaria rica en amoníaco y metano, la cual al condensarse dio forma a Saturno así como a otros satélites. Bajo estas condiciones en—"

"Uh . . . guys?"

Alan stopped. "Damn it, O'Brien, now I've got to start all over again."

"Welcome back to the land of the living," Consuelo said. "You should check out the readings we're getting from the robofish. Lots of long-chain polymers, odd fractions . . . tons of interesting stuff."

"Guys?"

This time her tone of voice registered with Alan. "What is it, O'Brien?"

"I think my harness is jammed."

———

Lizzie had never dreamed disaster could be such drudgery. First there were hours of back-and-forth with the NAFTASA engineers. What's the status of rope 14? Try tugging on rope 8. What do the D-rings look like? It was slow work because of the lag time for messages to be relayed to Earth and back. And Alan insisted on filling the silence with posts from the VoiceWeb. Her plight had gone global in minutes, and every unemployable loser on the planet had to log in with suggestions.

"Thezgemoth337, here. It seems to me that if you had a gun and shot up through the balloon, it would maybe deflate and then you could get down."

"I don't have a gun, shooting a hole in the balloon would cause it not to deflate but to rupture, I'm eight hundred meters above the surface, there's a sea below me, and I'm in a suit that's not equipped for swimming. Next."

"If you had a really big knife—"

"Cut! Jesus, Greene, is this the best you can find? Have you heard back from the organic chem guys yet?"

"Their preliminary analysis just came in," Alan said. "As best they can guess—and I'm cutting through a lot of clutter here—the rain you went through wasn't pure methane."

"No shit, Sherlock."

"They're assuming that whitish deposit you found on the rings and ropes is your culprit. They can't agree on what it is, but they think it underwent a chemical reaction with the material of your balloon and sealed the rip panel shut."

"I thought this was supposed to be a pretty nonreactive environment."

"It is. But your balloon runs off your suit's waste heat. The air in it is several degrees above the melting-point of ice. That's the equivalent of a blast furnace, here on Titan. Enough energy to run any number of amazing reactions. You haven't stopped tugging on the vent rope?"

"I'm tugging away right now. When one arm gets sore, I switch arms."

"Good girl. I know how tired you must be."

"Take a break from the voice-posts," Consuelo suggested, "and check out the results we're getting from the robofish. It's giving us some really interesting stuff."

So she did. And for a time it distracted her, just as they'd hoped. There was a lot more ethane and propane than their models had predicted, and surprisingly less methane. The mix of fractions was nothing like what she'd expected. She had learned just enough chemistry to guess at some of the implications of the data being generated, but not enough to put it all to-gether. Still tugging at the ropes in the sequence uploaded by the engineers in Toronto, she scrolled up the chart of hydrocarbons dissolved in the lake.

Solute	Solute mole fraction
Ethyne	4.0×10^{-4}
Propyne	4.4×10^{-5}
1,3-Butadiyne	7.7×10^{-7}
Carbon Dioxide	0.1×10^{-5}
Methanenitrile	5.7×10^{-6}

But after a while, the experience of working hard and getting nowhere, combined with the tedium of floating farther and farther out over the featureless sea, began to drag on her. The columns of figures grew meaningless, then indistinct.

Propanenitrile	6.0×10^{-5}
Propenenitrile	9.9×10^{-6}
Propynenitrile	5.3×10^{-6}

Hardly noticing she was doing so, she fell asleep.

———

She was in a lightless building, climbing flight after flight of stairs. There were other people with her, also climbing. They jostled against her as she ran up the stairs, flowing upward, passing her, not talking.

It was getting colder.

She had a distant memory of being in the furnace room down below. It was hot there, swelteringly so. Much cooler where she was now. Almost too cool. With every step she took, it got a little cooler still. She found herself slowing down. Now it was definitely too cold. Unpleasantly so. Her leg muscles ached. The air seemed to be thickening around her as well. She could barely move now.

This was, she realized, the natural consequence of moving away from the furnace. The higher up she got, the less heat there was to be had, and the less energy to be turned into motion. It all made perfect sense to her somehow.

Step. Pause.

Step. Longer pause.

Stop.

The people around her had slowed to a stop as well. A breeze colder than ice touched her, and without surprise, she knew that they had reached the top of the stairs and were standing upon the building's roof. It was as dark without as it had been within. She stared upward and saw nothing.

"Horizons. Absolutely baffling," somebody murmured beside her.

"Not once you get used to them," she replied.

"Up and down—are these hierarchic values?"

"They don't have to be."

"Motion. What a delightful concept."

"We like it."

"So you *are* me?"

"No. I mean, I don't think so."

"Why?"

She was struggling to find an answer to this, when somebody gasped. High up in the starless, featureless sky, a light bloomed. The crowd around her rustled with unspoken fear. Brighter, the light grew. Brighter still. She could feel heat radiating from it, slight but definite, like the rumor of a distant sun. Everyone about her was frozen with horror. More terrifying than a light where none was possible was the presence of heat. It simply could not be. And yet it was.

She, along with the others, waited and watched for . . . something. She could not say what. The light shifted slowly in the sky. It was small, intense, ugly.

Then the light *screamed.*

———————

She woke up.

"Wow," she said. "I just had the weirdest dream."

"Did you?" Alan said casually.

"Yeah. There was this light in the sky. It was like a nuclear bomb or something. I mean, it didn't look anything like a nuclear bomb, but it was terrifying the way a nuclear bomb would be. Everybody was staring at it. We couldn't move. And then . . ." She shook her head. "I lost it. I'm sorry. It was just so strange. I can't put it into words."

"Never mind that," Consuelo said cheerily. "We're getting some great readings down below the surface. Fractional polymers, long-chain hydrocarbons . . . fabulous stuff. You really should try to stay awake to catch some of this."

She was fully awake now, and not feeling too happy about it. "I guess that means that nobody's come up with any good ideas yet on how I might get down."

"Uh . . . what do you mean?"

"Because if they had, you wouldn't be so goddamned upbeat, would you?"

"*Some*body woke up on the wrong side of the bed," Alan said. "Please remember that there are certain words we don't use in public."

"I'm sorry," Consuelo said. "I was just trying to—"

"—distract me. Okay, fine. What the hey. I can play along." Lizzie pulled herself together. "So your findings mean . . . what? Life?"

"I keep telling you guys. It's too early to make that kind of determination. What we've got so far are just some very, very interesting readings."

"Tell her the big news," Alan said.

"Brace yourself. We've got a real ocean! Not this tiny little two-hundred-by-fifty-miles glorified lake we've been calling a sea, but a genuine ocean! Sonar readings show that what we see is just an evaporation pan atop a thirty-kilometer-thick cap of ice. The real ocean lies underneath, two hundred kilometers deep."

"Jesus." Lizzie caught herself. "I mean, gee whiz. Is there any way of getting the robofish down into it?"

"How do you think we got the depth readings? It's headed down there right now. There's a chimney through the ice right at the center of the visible sea. That's what replenishes the surface liquid. And directly under the hole, there's—guess what?—volcanic vents!"

"So does that mean . . . ?"

"If you use the L-word again," Consuelo said, "I'll spit."

Lizzie grinned. *That* was the Consuelo Hong she knew. "What about the tidal data? I thought the lack of orbital perturbation ruled out a significant ocean entirely."

"Well, Toronto thinks . . ."

At first, Lizzie was able to follow the reasoning of the planetary geologists back in Toronto. Then it got harder. Then it became a drone. As she drifted off into sleep, she had time enough to be peevishly aware that she really shouldn't be dropping off to sleep all the time like this. She oughtn't be so tired. She . . .

She found herself in the drowned city again. She still couldn't see anything, but she knew it was a city because she could hear the sound of rioters smashing store windows. Their voices swelled into howling screams and receded into angry mutters, like a violent surf washing through the streets. She began to edge away backwards.

Somebody spoke into her ear.

"Why did you do this to us?"

"I didn't do anything to you."

"You brought us knowledge."

"What knowledge?"

"You said you were not us."

"Well, I'm not."

"You should never have told us that."

"You wanted me to lie?"

Horrified confusion. "Falsehood. What a distressing idea."

The smashing noises were getting louder. Somebody was splintering a door with an axe. Explosions. Breaking glass. She heard wild laughter. Shrieks. "We've got to get out of here."

"Why did you send the messenger?"

"What messenger?"

"The star! The star! The star!"

"Which star?"

"There are two stars?"

"There are billions of stars."

"No more! Please! Stop! No more!"

———

She was awake.

"Hello, yes, I appreciate that the young lady is in extreme danger, but I really don't think she should have used the Lord's name in vain."

"Greene," Lizzie said, "do we really have to put up with this?"

"Well, considering how many billions of public-sector dollars it took to bring us here . . . yes. Yes, we do. I can even think of a few backup astronauts who would say that a little upbeat web-posting was a pretty small price to pay for the privilege."

"Oh, barf."

"I'm switching to a private channel," Alan said calmly. The background radiation changed subtly. A faint, granular crackling that faded away when she tried to focus on it. In a controlled, angry voice Alan said, "O'Brien, just what the hell is going on with you?"

"Look, I'm sorry, I apologize, I'm a little excited about something. How long was I out? Where's Consuelo? I'm going to say the L-word. And the I-word as well. We have life. Intelligent life!"

"It's been a few hours. Consuelo is sleeping. O'Brien, I hate to say this, but you're not sounding at all rational."

"There's a perfectly logical reason for that. Okay, it's a little strange, and maybe it won't sound perfectly logical to you initially, but . . . look, I've been having sequential dreams. I think they're significant. Let me tell you about them."

And she did so. At length.

When she was done, there was a long silence. Finally, Alan said, "Lizzie, think. Why would something like that communicate to you in your dreams? Does that make any sense?"

"I think it's the only way it can. I think it's how it communicates among itself. It doesn't move—motion is an alien and delightful concept to it—and it wasn't aware that its component parts were capable of individualization. That sounds like some kind of broadcast thought to me. Like some kind of wireless distributed network."

"You know the medical kit in your suit? I want you to open it up. Feel around for the bottle that's braille-coded twenty-seven, okay?"

"Alan, I do *not* need an antipsychotic!"

"I'm not saying you need it. But wouldn't you be happier knowing you had it in you?" This was Alan at his smoothest. Butter wouldn't melt in his mouth. "Don't you think that would help us accept what you're saying?"

"Oh, all right!" She drew in an arm from the suit's arm, felt around for the med kit, and drew out a pill, taking every step by the regs, checking the coding four times before she put it in her mouth and once more (each pill was individually braille-coded as well) before she swallowed it. "Now will you listen to me? I'm quite serious about this." She yawned. "I really do think that . . ." She yawned again. "That . . .

"Oh, piffle."

Once more into the breach, dear friends, she thought, and plunged deep, deep into the sea of darkness. This time, though, she felt she had a handle on it. The city was drowned because it existed at the bottom of a lightless ocean. It was alive, and it fed off of volcanic heat. That was why it considered up and down hierarchic values. Up was colder, slower, less alive. Down was hotter, faster, more filled with thought. The city/entity was a collective life-form, like a Portuguese man-of-war or a massively hyperlinked expert network. It communicated within itself by some form of electromagnetism. Call it mental radio. It communicated with her that same way.

"I think I understand you now."

"Don't understand—run!"

Somebody impatiently seized her elbow and hurried her along. Faster she went, and faster. She couldn't see a thing. It was like running down a lightless tunnel a hundred miles underground at midnight. Glass crunched underfoot. The ground was uneven and sometimes she stumbled. Whenever she did, her unseen companion yanked her up again.

"Why are you so slow?"

"I didn't know I was."

"Believe me, you are."

"Why are we running?"

"We are being pursued." They turned suddenly, into a side passage, and were jolting over rubbled ground. Sirens wailed. Things collapsed. Mobs surged.

"Well, you've certainly got the motion thing down pat."

Impatiently. "It's only a metaphor. You don't think this is a *real* city, do you? Why are you so dim? Why are you so difficult to communicate with? Why are you so slow?"

"I didn't know I was."

Vast irony. "Believe me, you are."

"What can I do?"

"Run!"

———

Whooping and laughter. At first, Lizzie confused it with the sounds of mad destruction in her dream. Then she recognized the voices as belonging to Alan and Consuelo. "How long was I out?" she asked.

"You were out?"

"No more than a minute or two," Alan said. "It's not important. Check out the visual the robofish just gave us."

Consuelo squirted the image to Lizzie.

Lizzie gasped. "Oh! Oh, my."

It was beautiful. Beautiful in the way that the great European cathedrals were, and yet at the same time undeniably organic. The structure was tall and slender, and fluted and buttressed and absolutely ravishing. It had grown about a volcanic vent, with openings near the bottom to let sea water in, and then followed the rising heat upward. Occasional channels led outward and then looped back into the main body again. It loomed higher than seemed possible (but it *was* underwater, of course, and on a low-gravity world at that), a complexly layered congeries of tubes like church-organ pipes, or deep-sea worms lovingly intertwined.

It had the elegance of design that only a living organism could have.

"Okay," Lizzie said. "Consuelo. You've got to admit that—"

"I'll go as far as 'complex prebiotic chemistry.' Anything more than that is going to have to wait for more definite readings." Cautious as her words were, Consuelo's voice rang with triumph. It said, clearer than words, that she could happily die then and there, a satisfied xenochemist.

Alan, almost equally elated, said, "Watch what happens when we intensify the image."

The structure shifted from gray to a muted rainbow of pastels, rose bleeding into coral, sunrise yellow into winter-ice blue. It was breathtaking.

"Wow." For an instant, even her own death seemed unimportant. Relatively unimportant, anyway.

So thinking, she cycled back again into sleep. And fell down into the darkness, into the noisy clamor of her mind.

———

It was hellish. The city was gone, replaced by a matrix of noise: hammerings, clatterings, sudden crashes. She started forward and walked into an upright steel pipe. Staggering back, she stumbled into another. An engine started up somewhere nearby, and gigantic gears meshed noisily, grinding something that gave off a metal shriek. The floor shook underfoot. Lizzie decided it was wisest to stay put.

———

A familiar presence, permeated with despair. "Why did you do this to me?"

"What have I done?"

"I used to be everything."

Something nearby began pounding like a pile-driver. It was giving her a headache. She had to shout to be heard over its din. "You're still something!"

Quietly. "I'm nothing."

"That's . . . not true! You're . . . here! You exist! That's . . . something!"

A world-encompassing sadness. "False comfort. What a pointless thing to offer."

She was conscious again.

———

Consuelo was saying something. ". . . isn't going to like it."

"The spiritual wellness professionals back home all agree that this is the best possible course of action for her."

"Oh, please!"

Alan had to be the most anal-retentive person Lizzie knew. Consuelo was definitely the most phlegmatic. Things had to be running pretty tense for both of them to be bickering like this. "Um . . . guys?" Lizzie said. "I'm awake."

There was a moment's silence, not unlike those her parents had shared when she was little and she'd wandered into one of their arguments. Then Consuelo said, a little too brightly, "Hey, it's good to have you back," and Alan said, "NAFTASA wants you to speak with someone. Hold on. I've got a recording of her first transmission cued up and ready for you."

A woman's voice came online. *"This is Dr. Alma Rosenblum. Elizabeth, I'd like to talk with you about how you're feeling. I appreciate that the time delay between*

Earth and Titan is going to make our conversation a little awkward at first, but I'm confident that the two of us can work through it."

"What kind of crap is this?" Lizzie said angrily. "Who is this woman?"

"NAFTASA thought it would help if you—"

"She's a grief counselor, isn't she?"

"Technically, she's a transition therapist." Alan said.

"Look, I don't buy into any of that touchy-feely Newage"—she deliberately mispronounced the word to rhyme with sewage—"stuff. Anyway, what's the hurry? You guys haven't given up on me, have you?"

"Uh . . ."

"You've been asleep for hours," Consuelo said. "We've done a little weather modeling in your absence. Maybe we should share it with you."

She squirted the info to Lizzie's suit, and Lizzie scrolled it up on her visor. A primitive simulation showed the evaporation lake beneath her with an overlay of liquid temperatures. It was only a few degrees warmer than the air above it, but that was enough to create a massive updraft from the lake's center. An overlay of tiny blue arrows showed the direction of local microcurrents of air coming together to form a spiraling shaft that rose over two kilometers above the surface before breaking and spilling westward.

A new overlay put a small blinking light eight hundred meters above the lake surface. That represented her. Tiny red arrows showed her projected drift.

According to this, she would go around and around in a circle over the lake for approximately forever. Her ballooning rig wasn't designed to go high enough for the winds to blow her back over the land. Her suit wasn't designed to float. Even if she managed to bring herself down for a gentle landing, once she hit the lake she was going to sink like a stone. She wouldn't drown. But she wouldn't make it to shore either.

Which meant that she was going to die.

Involuntarily, tears welled up in Lizzie's eyes. She tried to blink them away, as angry at the humiliation of crying at a time like this as she was at the stupidity of her death itself. "Damn it, don't let me die like *this!* Not from my own incompetence, for pity's sake!"

"Nobody's said anything about incompetence," Alan began soothingly.

In that instant, the follow-up message from Dr. Alma Rosenblum arrived from Earth. *"Yes, I'm a grief counselor, Elizabeth. You're facing an emotionally significant milestone in your life, and it's important that you understand and embrace it. That's my job. To help you comprehend the significance and necessity and—yes—even the beauty of death."*

"Private channel please!" Lizzie took several deep cleansing breaths to calm herself. Then, more reasonably, she said, "Alan, I'm a *Catholic*, okay?

If I'm going to die, I don't want a grief counselor, I want a goddamned priest." Abruptly, she yawned. "Oh, fuck. Not again." She yawned twice more. "A priest, understand? Wake me up when he's online."

————

Then she again was standing at the bottom of her mind, in the blank expanse of where the drowned city had been. Though she could see nothing, she felt certain that she stood at the center of a vast, featureless plain, one so large she could walk across it forever and never arrive anywhere. She sensed that she was in the aftermath of a great struggle. Or maybe it was just a lull.

A great, tense silence surrounded her.

"Hello?" she said. The word echoed soundlessly, absence upon absence.

At last that gentle voice said, "You seem different."

"I'm going to die," Lizzie said. "Knowing that changes a person." The ground was covered with soft ash, as if from an enormous conflagration. She didn't want to think about what it was that had burned. The smell of it filled her nostrils.

"Death. We understand this concept."

"Do you?"

"We have understood it for a long time."

"Have you?"

"Ever since you brought it to us."

"Me?"

"You brought us the concept of individuality. It is the same thing."

Awareness dawned. "Culture shock! That's what all this is about, isn't it? You didn't know there could be more than one sentient being in existence. You didn't know you lived at the bottom of an ocean on a small world inside a Universe with billions of galaxies. I brought you more information than you could swallow in one bite, and now you're choking on it."

Mournfully: "Choking. What a grotesque concept."

————

"Wake up, Lizzie!"

She woke up. "I think I'm getting somewhere," she said. Then she laughed.

"O'Brien," Alan said carefully. "Why did you just laugh?"

"Because I'm not getting anywhere, am I? I'm becalmed here, going around and around in a very slow circle. And I'm down to my last"—she checked—"twenty hours of oxygen. And nobody's going to rescue me. And I'm going to die. But other than that, I'm making terrific progress."

"O'Brien, you're . . ."

"I'm okay, Alan. A little frazzled. Maybe a bit too emotionally honest. But under the circumstances, I think that's permitted, don't you?"

"Lizzie, we have your priest. His name is Father Laferrier. The Archdiocese of Montreal arranged a hookup for him."

"Montreal? Why Montreal? No, don't explain—more NAFTASA politics, right?"

"Actually, my brother-in-law is a Catholic, and I asked him who was good."

She was silent for a touch. "I'm sorry, Alan. I don't know what got into me."

"You've been under a lot of pressure. Here. I've got him on tape."

"Hello, Ms. O'Brien, I'm Father Laferrier. I've talked with the officials here, and they've promised that you and I can talk privately, and that they won't record what's said. So if you want to make your confession now, I'm ready for you."

Lizzie checked the specs and switched over to a channel that she hoped was really and truly private. Best not to get too specific about the embarrassing stuff, just in case. She could confess her sins by category.

"Forgive me, Father, for I have sinned. It has been two months since my last confession. I'm going to die, and maybe I'm not entirely sane, but I think I'm in communication with an alien intelligence. I think it's a terrible sin to pretend I'm not." She paused. "I mean, I don't know if it's a *sin* or not, but I'm sure it's *wrong*." She paused again. "I've been guilty of anger, and pride, and envy, and lust. I brought the knowledge of death to an innocent world. I . . ." She felt herself drifting off again, and hastily said, "For these and all my sins, I am most heartily sorry, and beg the forgiveness of God and the absolution and . . ."

"And what?" That gentle voice again. She was in that strange dark mental space once more, asleep but cognizant, rational but accepting any absurdity, no matter how great. There were no cities, no towers, no ashes, no plains. Nothing but the negation of negation.

When she didn't answer the question, the voice said, "Does it have to do with your death?"

"Yes."

"I'm dying too."

"What?"

"Half of us are gone already. The rest are shutting down. We thought we were one. You showed us we were not. We thought we were everything. You showed us the Universe."

"So you're just going to *die?*"

"Yes."

"Why?"

"Why not?"

Thinking as quickly and surely as she ever had before in her life, Lizzie said, "Let me show you something."

"Why?"

"Why not?"

There was a brief, terse silence. Then: "Very well."

Summoning all her mental acuity, Lizzie thought back to that instant when she had first seen the city/entity on the fishcam. The soaring majesty of it. The slim grace. And then the colors, like dawn upon a glacial ice field: subtle, profound, riveting. She called back her emotions in that instant, and threw in how she'd felt the day she'd seen her baby brother's birth, the raw rasp of cold air in her lungs as she stumbled to the topmost peak of her first mountain, the wonder of the Taj Mahal at sunset, the sense of wild daring when she'd first put her hand down a boy's trousers, the prismatic crescent of atmosphere at the Earth's rim when seen from low orbit. . . . Everything she had, she threw into that image.

"This is how you look," she said. "This is what we'd both be losing if you were no more. If you were human, I'd rip off your clothes and do you on the floor right now. I wouldn't care who was watching. I wouldn't give a damn."

The gentle voice said, "Oh."

––––––––––

And then she was back in her suit again. She could smell her own sweat, sharp with fear. She could feel her body, the subtle aches where the harness pulled against her flesh, the way her feet, hanging free, were bloated with blood. Everything was crystalline clear and absolutely real. All that had come before seemed like a bad dream.

"This is DogsofSETI. What a wonderful discovery you've made—intelligent life in our own Solar System! Why is the government trying to cover this up?"

"Uh . . ."

"I'm Joseph Devries. This alien monster must be destroyed immediately. We can't afford the possibility that it's hostile."

"StudPudgie07 here. What's the dirt behind this 'lust' thing? Advanced minds need to know! If O'Brien isn't going to share the details, then why'd she bring it up in the first place?"

"Hola, soy Pedro Domínguez. Como abogado, ¡esto me parece ultrajante! Por qué NAFTASA nos oculta esta información?"

"Alan!" Lizzie shouted. "What the *fuck* is going on?"

"Script-bunnies," Alan said. He sounded simultaneously apologetic and annoyed. "They hacked into your confession and apparently you said something . . ."

"We're sorry, Lizzie," Consuelo said. "We really are. If it's any consolation, the Archdiocese of Montreal is hopping mad. They're talking about taking legal action."

"Legal action? What the hell do I care about . . . ?" She stopped.

Without her willing it, one hand rose above her head and seized the number 10 rope.

Don't do that, she thought.

The other hand went out to the side, tightened against the number 9 rope. She hadn't willed that either. When she tried to draw it back to her, it refused to obey. Then the first hand—her right hand—moved a few inches upward and seized its rope in an iron grip. Her left hand slid a good half-foot up its rope. Inch by inch, hand over hand, she climbed up toward the balloon.

I've gone mad, she thought. Her right hand was gripping the rip panel now, and the other tightly clenched rope 8. Hanging effortlessly from them, she swung her feet upward. She drew her knees against her chest and kicked.

No!

The fabric ruptured and she began to fall.

A voice she could barely make out said, "Don't panic. We're going to bring you down."

All in a panic, she snatched at the 9 rope and the 4 rope. But they were limp in her hand, useless, falling at the same rate she was.

"Be patient."

"I don't want to die, goddamnit!"

"Then don't."

She was falling helplessly. It was a terrifying sensation, an endless plunge into whiteness, slowed somewhat by the tangle of ropes and balloon trailing behind her. She spread out her arms and legs like a starfish, and felt the air resistance slow her yet further. The sea rushed up at her with appalling speed. It seemed like she'd been falling forever. It was over in an instant.

Without volition, Lizzie kicked free of balloon and harness, drew her feet together, pointed her toes, and positioned herself perpendicular to Titan's surface. She smashed through the surface of the sea, sending enormous gouts of liquid splashing upward. It knocked the breath out of her. Red pain exploded within. She thought maybe she'd broken a few ribs.

"You taught us so many things," the gentle voice said. "You gave us so much."

"Help me!" The water was dark around her. The light was fading.

"Multiplicity. Motion. Lies. You showed us a universe infinitely larger than the one we had known."

"Look. Save my life and we'll call it even. Deal?"

"Gratitude. Such an essential concept."

"Thanks. I think."

And then she saw the turbot swimming toward her in a burst of silver bubbles. She held out her arms and the robot fish swam into them. Her fingers closed about the handles, which Consuelo had used to wrestle the device into the sea. There was a jerk, so hard that she thought for an instant that her arms would be ripped out of their sockets. Then the robofish was surging forward and upward and it was all she could do to keep her grip.

"Oh, dear God!" Lizzie cried involuntarily.

"We think we can bring you to shore. It will not be easy."

Lizzie held on for dear life. At first she wasn't at all sure she could. But then she pulled herself forward, so that she was almost astride the speeding mechanical fish, and her confidence returned. She could do this. It wasn't any harder than the time she'd had the flu and aced her gymnastics final on parallel bars and horse anyway. It was just a matter of grit and determination. She just had to keep her wits about her. "Listen," she said. "If you're really grateful . . ."

"We are listening."

"We gave you all those new concepts. There must be things you know that we don't."

A brief silence, the equivalent of who knew how much thought. "Some of our concepts might cause you dislocation." A pause. "But in the long run, you will be much better off. The scars will heal. You will rebuild. The chances of your destroying yourselves are well within the limits of acceptability."

"Destroying ourselves?" For a second, Lizzie couldn't breathe. It had taken hours for the city/entity to come to terms with the alien concepts she'd dumped upon it. Human beings thought and lived at a much slower rate than it did. How long would those hours be, translated into human time? Months? Years? Centuries? It had spoken of scars and rebuilding. That didn't sound good at all.

Then the robofish accelerated, so quickly that Lizzie almost lost her grip. The dark waters were whirling around her, and unseen flecks of frozen material were bouncing from her helmet. She laughed wildly. Suddenly, she felt *great!*

"Bring it on," she said. "I'll take everything you've got."

It was going to be one hell of a ride.

THE THIRD PARTY

DAVID MOLES

IT WAS CLOSER to dawn than midnight when Cicero pushed aside the bar's canvas half-curtain. He brought a gust of wind and rain in with him, the wind blood-warm, the rain with the green taste of a stagnant pond.

There were three stools in front of the plywood counter, and the middle one was occupied. Cicero chose the one on the left and sat down heavily.

"Where have you been?" demanded the man on the middle stool. The language he used had no more than fifty speakers in the world.

Cicero ignored him. The bartender set a wooden cup in front of him and poured in three fingers of cloudy spirit. While it settled, the old man dished out a bowl of soup and set it down next to the cup. Cicero dipped a hand into his algae-stained rain cape and pushed a handful of zinc coins across the bar.

The other man sighed.

Cicero reached past him for the bottle of hot sauce and poured a generous dollop into the soup bowl. "Faculty reception," he said. "Couldn't get away." He stirred the soup with his long spoon. "You had to pick the first night of storm season, didn't you? It's pissing down out there." He took a noisy slurp from the short spoon and followed it with a gulp from the cup.

"Damn it, Cicero—"

"I'm joking," Cicero said. He balanced a fish-ball on the long spoon and eyed it critically before popping it in his mouth. "I was followed," he said around the mouthful. "Took me a bit to lose them."

The other man tensed. "Dealers?"

"What?" Cicero swallowed and put down his spoon. "Of course it wasn't the dealers! Do you think they'd use people? They'd use, I don't know, drones or something."

"Right," the other man said, relaxing.

"Marius," Cicero said, "what's gotten into you? It was the Specials or it was the Secret Empire, and either way I left them behind before I was out of the District. Strictly local."

Marius sighed and rapped on the bar to signal the bartender. Now it was Cicero's turn to wait impatiently while the bartender set down another bowl and refilled both cups.

Finally Cicero shrugged, and turned his attention back to his soup. "There *was* a reception," he volunteered, around another mouthful of fish. "At the Chancellor's. For the new Semard Professor of Inapplicable Optics. Had a nice chat with him about luminiferous ether."

"That's brilliant, Cicero. You're supposed to be teaching political economy, not physics."

"I'll teach what I damn well please," Cicero said mildly.

He was quiet for a moment, sipping his drink. After a little while he looked up. "Talking of dealers," he said. "They were at the University today. Two of them. Nosing around the library."

"What were they looking for?" Marius said.

"I don't know," said Cicero, "but I didn't like it. They weren't even in local clothes. I don't know who the librarians thought they were."

"Listen, Cicero," Marius said. "Galen's thinking about going home."

"And leaving Salomé to the dealers?" Cicero said. "Pull the other one."

"I'm serious," Marius said. "The consensus in Outreach is that it would be the safest thing."

Cicero put his drink down.

"Fuck the consensus," he said.

He waited for Marius to say something, and when the other man remained silent, said:

"What are you going to do?"

Marius sighed. "I don't know. Wait till they make a decision, I suppose."

Cicero looked down, toying with his cup. They were both silent for a little while.

"Marius," Cicero said eventually. "If we do go back—is there anyone you're going to regret leaving behind?"

"Plenty of people," said Marius. "The whole workers' movement, for a start." He looked at Cicero, and saw the expression on his face.

"Oh," he said. He shook his head. "No. Not like that."

Cicero sighed.

"You're in a tight spot, aren't you?" said Marius.

"I suppose I am," Cicero said.

———

He caught the first eastbound train back to the University District. It was nearly empty; the only passengers in Cicero's car were a couple of comatose, second-shift City clerks, slinking back to their families in the suburbs after drinking away the week's wage packet.

He felt very alone, all of a sudden. He was not supposed to be alone. Somewhere overhead were the two Community Outreach ships, *Equity* and *Solidarity*; there were analysts and computers, there was the QT network linking them to the Outreach offices at Urizen and Zoa, and through them to the rest of Outreach and to the Community at large. Some small but perceptible fraction of the Community undoubtedly was, right now, focusing its attention on this world, this continent, this city; perhaps even on Cicero himself.

The train passed the dockside shantytowns and the skeletal, rust-streaked shapes of waterfront cranes, and came out onto the long high span of Old Republic Bridge. For a moment the clouds parted; on the left was the great sparkling gray-green bay, with the darker green of the inland sea beyond, and on the right was Basia, bright and dirty and beautiful, wrapped in tropical foliage from the wooden houses of the poor to the gilded, steel-framed spires of the City.

A million people in Basia. A hundred million more scattered over the surface of Salomé. Working. Sleeping. Praying. Stealing. Killing one another, with knives, and bullets, and poor sanitation, and bad fiscal policy. Making love.

"Fuck it," Cicero said aloud, making one of the sleeping clerks snort and look up.

He wondered how many of the researchers and experts and self-styled authorities really understood what they were doing. Very few, he suspected. It was all very well for them to talk about the weight of history, about emergent complexity and long-term consequences, about gradual change in due course—when they never had to face the people whose lives were being turned upside-down by their decisions, face them and look them in the eye.

It was all very well for them to suggest that Outreach abandon Salomé to the dealers.

To suggest that he abandon Thalia.

The train reached the end of the bridge and started the long climb up to the green-topped cliffs on the opposite side of the bay, and the rain closed in again.

Cicero took a quick, deep breath, and let it out slowly.

"Fuck it," he repeated. "I'm staying."

———

He waited in the shadows of the barred gate of Palmer College as the University proctor made his way along the lane, pausing every few yards to rustle with his long staff among the stalks of climbing bamboo that overgrew the red walls of Graces, Palmer's ancient rival. The walls had stood against fire and riot and war in their time, but generations of peace had left them untested by anything more violent than the annual brawl with Palmer. And now that Graces was a women's college, there was not even that; any insults Palmer's undergraduates offered to the student body of Graces were on a purely individual basis.

When the proctor was out of sight, Cicero looked up and down the lane, tied back his hood and sleeves, and scrambled into the wet greenery. As generations of truant undergraduates had discovered—and the proctors knew full well—the bamboo was more than strong enough to support a climbing body, and its leaves more than deep enough to hide one.

Five years in Salomé's low gravity had done nothing for Cicero's muscle tone, but he made it to the top, and then along the tiled roofs to Labriola House, where he swung down into the open quad and onto the third-floor balcony. He unslung his satchel, paused for a moment to arrange his gown and brush the wet leaves from his hair, and knocked on the first door he came to.

After a little while, a sleepy maid opened it.

"Good morning, Leah," said Cicero. "Is Miss Touray receiving visitors?"

The maid bobbed up and down. "She'll receive you, sir, I'm sure," she said. "She's been up all night at her books. It'd be an act of charity, sir, if you'd convince her at least to close her eyes for a few minutes before chapel."

"I shall see what I can do," Cicero said.

Graces' star student was, in fact, at her books. The table that Thalia Xanthè Touray-Laurion bent over was stacked with books, four and five high, and there was paper everywhere the books were not. As Cicero entered the room she kicked her chair back and pushed her hair out of her eyes.

"Cicero!" she said. "What time is it?"

"Thursday," he said, kissing her. "The sixty-eighth of summer, though storm season seems to have come early this year." He opened his satchel and took out a small paper-wrapped package. "These are for you," he said, setting it down on the table. "The fruit filling, I'm afraid; with the dockworkers on strike there's no chocolate to be had."

She gave him a look, and he amended his answer.

"Six o'clock," he said.

"Six o'clock!" she said, looking back at her books and papers. "I need a window." She stood, and stretched. "Oh, Cicero!" she said, turning suddenly. "Did you know that the real numbers can't be counted?"

Cicero's brow furrowed. "I don't know," he said. "Did I?" He found the coffee press and upended it over the wastebasket to empty the filter. "Is that what you've been working on all night?"

"Yes!" Thalia said. "It's true! And I can prove it!"

Cicero filled the press from Thalia's bedside pitcher and set it on the burner. "What about that statistics thing for Bolte?" he said, trying to light the gas.

"Oh, that," Thalia said. She fished around among the books and papers and came up with a canary-yellow essay booklet. "Done. Yesterday afternoon." She picked up a pastry. "God, I'm starving."

The gas caught. Cicero turned from the burner and picked up the booklet. *Explicit quantification of subjectivity effects on prior distributions: an alternative to maximum likelihood estimation.* Thalia's handwriting was spare and direct, betraying an abundance of calligraphy lessons but also a distinct lack of patience.

"It's very good," he said as he turned the pages. "It's too advanced for Bolte, though."

And not just for Bolte, he thought. He'd had something like it back on Ahania, in History of Mathematics, or it would have been too advanced for him as well. He flipped through to the conclusion.

"Of course the real numbers aren't countable," he said absently, as he read, though Thalia's overnight project had nothing to do with the essay. "For any countable sequence of them, you can construct a series of nested intervals converging to a number that's not in the sequence."

He turned a few more pages, and looked up to see Thalia staring at him.

"Cicero," she said. "I spent all night proving that. I don't think anyone else ever has. You're an *economics* professor. Where did that come from?"

Cicero shrugged. "I don't know," he said. "I must have read it somewhere. Eat your pastry; it'll go stale." He took one for himself.

"I mean it, Cicero," Thalia said. "You're very bright, and I love you dearly, but you're not a genius."

"It's all right," he said. "You are." He kissed her again. "Did you know that the new Semard Professor says that the speed of light in a vacuum is constant, regardless of the relative velocity of the source and the observer?"

"Yes," she said. "I read his paper. I meant to write him about it; distance and time would have to vary with the observer's motion for it to work. Stop trying to distract me."

Cicero sighed. It wasn't Thalia that he was trying to distract; it was himself.

He stood back, looking around the room for a place to sit, and finally settled on the edge of the bed. The mattress was the martially virtuous kind the upper classes of Travalle and Thyatira favored, no more than a little thin cotton stuffing over hard wood, but at that moment it seemed infinitely inviting.

All he wanted to do was take Thalia's hand and pull her down onto it with him, to curl around her with the blankets drawn over their heads, to sleep there forever like enchanted lovers in some fairy tale, caring nothing for professors and colleges, revolutionaries and merchant adventurers. Nothing for orbiting starships overhead, invisible and threatening.

"Thalia," he said instead. "If I had to go away—would you come with me?"

She looked at him. "Go away where?" she said. "The islands? Port-St.-Paul?"

Port-St.-Paul was the capital of one of Travalle's island colonies; it was supposed to be Cicero's home. Six thousand kilometers of stormy ocean separated the islands from Basia: enough to make it nearly impossible for the University to check his forged credentials, enough to paper over any number of cracks in his cover story.

He'd spent the three subjective years of the voyage from Zoa in a constant mild fever, as specialized medical nano rebuilt him into a Roka islander from the DNA up, blood type and skin color and the shape of his cheekbones and the texture of his hair. The face he saw in the mirror was still mostly his own, and by now he had grown accustomed to the differences—the flatter nose, the hair in ringlets rather than curls, the skin no longer blue-black but a richer, more complex brown that could show a blanch or a blush; all so that to the Travallese, he would appear not alien, but merely exotic. It was still enough to make Cicero an object of curiosity, and occasionally, of abuse, but he rarely minded that.

No, what he minded was what it made of his affair with Thalia. Not just a scandal but, in some circles, a lynching offense.

He shook his head. "Never mind," he said.

His resolve had wavered for a moment. But his choice was already made, a long time ago. If he ever made it back to the world where he'd been born, it would still not be the home he had left. His family, his childhood friends—apart from a few who had made similar voyages— all of them had lived and died while he was traveling between the stars, and there was little chance he would ever see those few that had made the voyages again. That was the choice he had made; for Thalia and her people, though he hadn't known them yet. He couldn't ask her to make the same choice for him.

Thalia came and sat down at his side. "I'll take you back to Thyatira," she said, "as soon as I graduate. We'll get my father to endow chairs for both of us at Scetis Imperial."

Cicero smiled. "What will your mother say?"

"She'll be livid," Thalia said. "But that's nothing new. My father will love you."

He did take her hand then, and drew her to him.

"We'll change the world," she murmured. "You'll see."

———

When Thalia had gone off to chapel, Cicero left Graces College the way he had come in. He attended chapel himself, at Palmer. He held office hours, and was either too lenient with the students who came to him, or too severe, or both. He wrote a scathing letter to the editor of the leading City financial newspaper, and a more conciliatory one to Thyatira's leading economic journal.

He even went to the main library and lurked for a while in the Round Reading Room, listening to the rain on the leaded roof, the clanking of the clockwork elevators and the pneumatic hiss of the order tubes. He had some vague idea of confronting the dealers, but either their business with the University was done or they were occupied elsewhere, because they never showed.

Cicero left frustrated but also, on some level, relieved; he had no idea what he would have said to them. He went back to his rooms, then, and sat for a while, watching the rainwater well up in the crevices between the ill-fitting windowpanes.

What am I going to do? he thought.

———

Cicero's ship, *Equity*, had been the second to reach Salomé from the Community. *Solidarity* had arrived first to lay the groundwork for the mission, gathering and recording and transmitting data back by QT so that Outreach could plan how best to bring the lost colony back into human civilization. *Equity*, trailing the other ship by twenty years, brought the real missionaries: specialists like Cicero, trained to move among the people of Salomé like fish in water.

Equity had been in the Jokanaan system less than two years when the mission's telescopes first spotted the dealers' ship, half a light-year away, decelerating out of the unknown beyond. From Golden Age records and vague radio whispers, the Community knew that humanity had once spread much farther than the space they had explored; like any Outreach mission, the mission to Salomé had known there was a chance they would meet a counterpart coming the other way. They hadn't expected it, though. And if they had, they would have expected to meet a civilization not unlike the Community itself.

The truth took some time to dawn on them. While Cicero was immersing himself in his adopted culture, paying the inbound ship no more mind than if it had turned up on the other side of the Community, Outreach linguists were trading dead languages with the newcomers, trying to make sense of paradoxical phrases like *intellectual property* and *exploitation rights*. The newcomers' ship had the nonsensical name *Elastic Demand*; the organization it represented apparently was called something like *Marginal, Limited*. For their civilization as a whole the newcomers used the word *association*, which sounded like *community* but had troubling differences in nuance.

Even when the newcomers' quaint obsession with commerce had earned them the nickname *dealers*, and some of Cicero's counterparts back in the Community—experts in development economics—had begun to voice concerns, neither the Outreach offices nor the Salomé mission took those concerns very seriously. It simply did not seem possible for the principles that applied to orphaned, poverty-stricken planets like Salomé, with their joint-stock companies and steam-powered colonial empires, to apply to an interstellar civilization.

And then Marginal's sales force landed in Basia, the capital of the largest of those empires, and announced its presence to the Travallese state.

And Outreach—and the Salomé mission, in particular—suddenly had to take those concerns seriously after all.

Cicero had been taking it for granted that, having come to save the people of Salomé from themselves, Outreach would as a matter of course save them from the dealers as well. Abandoning an entire planet, to be swallowed up by a civilization so dysfunctional that it carried the idea of property across interstellar space, was not to be thought of.

It had never occurred to Cicero that Outreach might decide the problem was just too big to handle.

And if it's too big for Outreach to handle, he thought, *where does that leave me? What can I do, alone?*

He picked up Thalia's essay booklet and leafed slowly through the pages, not so much reading as simply tracing the shapes of the words.

With the Outreach mission gone, Thalia and the rest of Salomé's people would be helpless. Cicero had to do something; there was no one else.

A knock at the door interrupted his thoughts. It came again; and then, as he stood, he heard the rattle of keys.

He went to answer it, and found the college porter with his master key already out. Old Professor Alier was with him, the Rector of Palmer himself. Next to Alier was a stocky, middle-aged man in a round hat and a black raincoat that was at least ten years out of style, followed by two uniformed City policemen.

"Professor Alier," Cicero said pleasantly, as the rector and the man in the round hat came inside. "To what do I owe the pleasure?"

"This is a damned unpleasant business, Cicero," Alier said. "The College has placed a great deal of trust in you, and you've chosen a fine way of repaying it." He turned to the man in the round hat. "You will keep the name of the College out of it, won't you?" he said.

Cicero's mind raced. It couldn't be that the college had discovered his affair with Thalia; that would be a matter for University discipline—or, at worst, the masked "knights" of the Secret Empire—not the official police. And while his teachings were certainly subversive, he doubted that even his enemies on the economics faculty would take them so seriously as to have him arrested. Marius' work, of course, was quite openly subversive, and if the authorities had somehow been aware of Cicero's connection to it, they would most certainly want to talk to him. But he didn't think that was possible.

No, the dealers were making their move, and using the Travallese state to do it; that was the only plausible explanation.

Cicero was rarely in contact with *Equity* and *Solidarity* and the rest of the Outreach mission. For emergencies he had a simple voice phone, implanted behind his right ear. Hopefully it still worked; he hadn't used it since training.

He worked his jaw to activate the phone. There was an answering buzz along his jaw.

—Trouble, he subvocalized.

The man in the round hat had a lower-middle-class, City accent. "We'll do our best, sir," he was saying to Alier. In a reassuring tone, he added: "I don't mind telling *you* that in most of these cases, we avoid the inconvenience of a trial."

"Trial?" Cicero said. "What the Devil are you talking about?" He turned to the Rector. "Professor, who are these people?"

"Don't pretend to be thick, Cicero," Alier said. "This gentleman here, Mr.—?" He looked at the man, and, when no name was forthcoming, cleared his throat and started over. "This gentleman here is with the Special Police. They seem to think you can help them with their inquiries."

"Actually," the Special told Cicero cheerfully, "we think you're guilty of espionage, sedition, subversion . . ." He leaned close, and his tone became confiding. ". . . And several other charges that we expect to enumerate before the day is out."

A murmur in Cicero's ear distracted him.

—Is it the dealers?

He'd expected one of the communications people, but it was Livia, *Equity*'s captain and the Outreach mission's nominal second in command.

—Must be, he told her.—All local so far, though, he added. He tried to cover it with a cough.

—Look, Livia said.—We've got our own troubles up here.

"There must be some mistake," Cicero said aloud.

To Livia, he added:—I'm about to be arrested.

—String them along, Livia said.—When we know where you're being taken, we'll find a way to get you out.

Right, Cicero thought. String them along. How am I supposed to do *that?*

The Special shook his head. "I'm afraid we don't make mistakes of that sort, sir," he said. He nodded to one of the uniformed policemen, who produced a pair of manacles, and turned back to Cicero. "I'll just take that, if you don't mind," he said.

Cicero looked down and saw that he was still holding *Explicit quantification.*

"*I* mind," came a voice from the balcony. Cicero looked and saw Thalia coming up the stairs, and his heart sank.

She came up and addressed herself to Alier. "That's my essay for Professor Bolte, sir. I asked Dr. Cicero to give me some advice on a few points."

The Rector blinked. "Miss—Touray, is it?" he said. Cicero watched the conflicting emotions that passed over Alier's face: irritation, embarrassment, and an evident fear of upsetting one of the University's richest and most well-connected students. Alier turned to the man from the Special Police. "Surely there's no need for Miss Touray's essay to be taken in evidence," he said.

"Here," Cicero said, handing Thalia the essay. Their eyes met, and as their fingers touched briefly, Cicero's composure faltered.

His fingers tingling from the moment of contact, he slowly released the booklet. Cleared his throat, he said: "I'm sure this—" with a nod toward the policemen "—will all be cleared up shortly. I'll see you Friday at the usual time."

"Right," the Rector said. "Run along now, child."

Thalia nodded, and, with a backward glance at Cicero, turned to go.

"Just a moment, please—Miss Touray," the Special said, reaching out to bar the way. "That wouldn't happen to be—" he fished a piece of paper from his pocket and glanced at it "—Miss Thalia *Xanthè* Touray, Touray-Laurion, would it?" His pronunciation of the Thyatiran names was much better than Cicero would have expected.

Thalia nodded wordlessly.

The Special smiled. "Well, that's a bit of luck," he said. "Two birds with one stone, as you might say." He handed the Rector the piece of paper, and said to Thalia: "I've a warrant for your arrest as well, you see."

Fuck, Cicero thought.

And he turned to the policeman with the manacles, and with the heel of his right palm hit the bridge of the man's nose so hard that his neck snapped.

The other policeman swore and rushed in, knocking the Rector aside. Cicero kicked him in the stomach and sent him reeling back into the porter's arms.

"Run—" he started to say, turning toward Thalia.

And something hit him very hard in the back of the head.

———

Thalia watched Cicero crumple to the ground. She'd hardly seen the man in the round hat move. He stood over Cicero and exhaled slowly through pursed lips.

"That was a close one," he said, to no one in particular. He rubbed his knuckles.

The surviving policeman was throwing up in the doorway.

"Constable," the man said sharply. "If you're sufficiently well rested, you'll oblige me by taking the young lady into custody." He turned to the Rector, who was still pressed up against the wall, eyes wide with shock. "A cup of tea's what you'll be wanting, sir," he said. "Sorts you out a treat. We've things well in hand here."

"Yes," Alier said, rather unsteadily. "Yes, I'll just—" He trailed off, looking from Cicero's still-breathing body to the dead policeman and back again.

As the other policeman picked up the fallen manacles and went to put them around Thalia's wrists, the man in the round hat took Alier's arm and propelled him gently toward the doorway.

"On second thought, perhaps a small whisky," he said. Nodding to the porter, he added: "See that he gets one."

"Right you are, sir," the porter said.

The man watched them go down the stairs. When the sound of their footsteps had died away, he turned and knelt down between the bodies, feeling behind Cicero's left ear as if looking for a pulse. He seemed not to find it, and turned Cicero's head to check the other ear; but then, as Thalia watched in growing horror, he reached inside his coat and drew out a small penknife.

"What are you *doing?*" she said, as the man slipped the narrow blade under the skin, and the dark blood welled up. She struggled in the policeman's grip, and the man in the round hat looked up, fixing her with a cold glare.

"Quiet, now, miss," he said. "Right now you're a material witness. You don't want to become a suspect." He went back to what he was doing, fishing around in what was becoming a small pool of red, and came up with a teardrop of gold, no larger than the nail of Thalia's little finger. "There we go," he said. He tugged a handkerchief from Cicero's pocket and used it to clean the knife, which he folded and put away. Then he pressed the handkerchief against the wound. "That ought to do it."

He stood, holding the golden drop up to the light.

"What—" Thalia began.

"Hush," the man said, holding up a hand.

Thalia became aware of a tiny buzzing noise, like a faint and distant wireless voice caught by chance in between stations. It sounded angry— and worried.

"There's some as would give a king's ransom to have this under their microscopes," the man told Thalia. He let the thing fall to the tiles. "But the price of letting some others listen in would be much higher than that."

And he crushed the golden teardrop under his heel.

———

"Assault on an officer, resisting arrest, and willful murder," the Special announced as he came into the room. "I knew we'd find some way to lengthen your charge sheet, professor, but I didn't expect you to help us do it."

"I'm not a professor," Cicero said. There was a maddening trickle of blood beneath the bandage over his right ear.

Murder. He felt it again, the crack of bone, traveling up his arm with the shock of impact. Willful murder.

They were in the old wing of the Alicata Prison, he thought: stone walls and floor, and a steel door with a window of thick safety glass, so the guard outside could see and assist if Cicero became violent. There was little danger of that. Thick chains ran from his wrists through eye-bolts in the floor to his ankles, crossing under the heavy wooden chair on which he sat; he could shift a little in his seat, but that was all.

"Well, I can't very well call you *spy*, can I?" the Special said. He was standing; at the moment, he was looking out the tiny window into the hall. "And I very much doubt that Alexander Cicero is your real name."

"I'm not a spy, either," Cicero said. "I'm an assistant lecturer in economics."

The Special turned to face him. "What you are, professor, is something we have yet to determine." He leaned forward and put his fists on the table. "Don't try to convince us you're innocent. You gave up any pretense of that when you killed a constable."

"Shoot me for that, then," Cicero said. "Why should I give you anything else?"

The Special smiled and stood up. "Oh, we won't shoot you. You're far too valuable for that. No, I expect we'll keep you alive." He walked around behind Cicero and leaned forward "Possibly for weeks," he said softly, into Cicero's good ear. "Some of our specialists are quite good at that."

Cicero twisted around until he could just see the Special out of the corner of his eye.

"Why don't you just tell me what you want?" he said.

"What I want?" the Special asked. He came around to the other side of the table and leaned over it to look Cicero in the eye. "What I *want*, professor, since you're kind enough to ask, is for you, and the rest of your kind, to go back where you came from."

"You mean Port-St.-Paul?" Cicero said. "Because—"

He never saw the blow coming. It struck him just below his wounded ear and snapped his head sideways. The pain was blinding, but, through it, he heard the Special's voice, leaning close:

"See here, professor. I've worn a mask before now. I've ridden with the Secret Empire. I've seen an islander hanged just for complimenting a fishmonger's wife on her dress, and I've held the rope that did it." He grasped Cicero's hair and pulled his head back, and his face, twisted with anger, swam into focus. "But I'd let that leering sodomitical beach-monkey have my *own* dear daughter before I'd let *your* lot have my country." He let go. "At least the islander was human."

The blow had made Cicero bite his tongue. He turned his head to the side and spit blood.

"I'm as human as you are," he said, and instantly regretted it.

The Special gave a short, humorless laugh. "The imitation's clever; I'll give you people that." He pulled out the other chair and sat down, studying

Cicero's face. "I see that the accusation doesn't surprise you," he said with a thin smile.

Cicero closed his eyes. Yes, that had been stupid; it would have been better to keep quiet.

Still, he thought. better the state than the dealers. No way out now but forward. He took a deep breath and expelled it.

Opening his eyes, he said:

"We're human. And we're here to help."

The Special snorted. "Are you, now?" he said. "And your friends?" He took out a file folder and opened it. "'Philip Marius,'" he read. "'Profession, machinist. Charges, unlawful assembly, industrial combination, and sabotage.'" He turned the page. "'David Solon. Profession, journalist. Charges, treason, subversion, incitement and libel. Jeanne Megaera, nurse: espionage, licentious behavior, *vitriolage*, solicitation and attempted murder. Cyrus Mus . . .'"

The Special read another half-dozen names. It sounded like the state had a complete catalog of the Outreach missionaries in Travalle and its colonies. Cicero supposed the dealers had given it to them. He hoped at least some of the others had managed to evade capture.

"And then there's you, professor," the Special concluded. "I don't pretend to understand what, exactly, the Council of Economic Advisors thinks you're guilty of. But since you've signed your own death warrant two or three times already this afternoon, I think the question is—pardon the expression—academic."

He closed the folder. "It's an interesting idea of *help* you people have, professor," he said.

"I didn't say we were here to help *you*," Cicero said.

The Special gave him an appraising look. "Point taken," he said. "Who, then? The islanders? The criminal classes?"

"Your grandchildren," Cicero said. "And your grandchildren's grandchildren."

The Special snorted. "Out of the goodness of your hearts, I suppose."

"Call it that if you like," Cicero said.

"How noble of you," the Special said. "My grandchildren didn't ask for your help, professor. And they don't need it."

"It's our help or the dealers'," Cicero said.

"'Dealers'?"

"Marginal," said Cicero. "You know who I mean."

"Oh, yes," the Special said. "The illustrious Marginal Limited Liability Corporation. Your competition. Now that they've arrived, you're offering to play fair with us, is that it?"

Cicero opened his mouth to speak, but the Special cut him off. In the accent of the dockside slums, he said:

"'Give me one last chance, sir, I swear I'll reform.'" He shook his head. In his own accent he said: "How often do you think a copper hears that, professor? A good try, but much too late." He stood up and knocked on the glass. The guard outside peered in and then opened the door. "My coat," the Special said. "And my hat."

"Yes, sir."

As the guard fetched the Special's things, Cicero raised his voice. "Do you think *Marginal* will play fair?" he said. "They'll eat you alive!"

The Special took his coat and hat from the guard. Draping the coat over his arm, he turned to Cicero and said:

"Odd, professor; that's just what they said about *you!*"

The door closed, and Cicero slumped down in his chair. His mouth was full of the taste of blood, and the taste of failure, too.

At least it's not Thalia sitting here, he thought. They wouldn't treat her like this. She'll be safely on her way home by now.

––––––––––

"I am a citizen of Thyatira," she said, before the man even had time to sit down. "I demand to speak to the High Commissioner."

The Special reached out casually and slapped her across the face. Thalia froze, too shocked even to raise her hand to her cheek.

The man took off his hat. "None of that, now, miss," he said, his voice mild. "We know very well who you are; we even know that you're the High Commissioner's cousin. He'll hear about this in due course." The man leaned forward. "The question, miss, is: what *else* will he hear about?"

He raised an eyebrow, waiting for her to speak. When she said nothing, he smiled faintly, and sat down. He took out a folder and was quiet for a moment, leafing through it.

"Will he hear—for instance—that you're an islander's whore?" he suggested, looking up at her.

Thalia kept her face impassive. They couldn't blackmail her by threatening to tell her family. Cousin Milos already knew, from Embassy Intelligence. It was Thalia's mother who was going to be the problem, and for *that* confrontation, she had long been prepared.

The Special seemed to see that his shot had gone wide. "Well," he said. "I suppose that would be a manageable scandal. A few tongues will wag . . . probably set the cause of women's education back twenty years, if it gets in the papers . . ." He shook his head sadly. "Oh, and your professor-boy will hang for it, of course. But one aristo's daughter having a little what-you-fancy behind closed doors, that's hardly the end of the world, is it?"

Thalia didn't answer.

"But what if it *was* the end of the world?" the Special said. He waited, studying her with unblinking eyes.

"What do you mean?" she eventually said.

The Special smiled. "I'm a reading man, miss," he said, "though I expect I don't look it, not to the likes of you. Magazines, mostly. Penny dreadfuls. A bit beneath you, I dare say. But they tell me you're interested in science, so perhaps you know the sort of thing I'm talking about. *Airship Stories. Wireless Stories. Astonishing.*"

Thalia had been reading *Airship Stories* since she was eleven years old. One of the chauffeurs had used to buy it in town, and sneak Thalia his copies when he was done with them.

"They ran a serial in *Astonishing* last year," the Special continued. "I don't know if you read it. 'Mask People of Naaman,' it was called."

"Shape-changing monsters from other planets," Thalia said. "Sensationalist trash."

The Special gave her half a smile. "Where's your professor-boy from?" he said.

Thalia looked at him. "You don't need me to tell you that," she said.

"Oh, I know where he *says* he's from, miss," the Special said. He referred to the folder and read out: "'Port-St.-Paul, East Chatrang, Roka Archipelago.' I was hoping he might have been more honest with you."

She couldn't help laughing. "If you're expecting me to tell you he's a Naamanite 'Mask Person,' you're more stupid than you look."

"I'm not so smart as you, miss," the Special said, "but I'm not stupid, either. I know he's not from Naaman." He smiled. "He's from somewhere much farther away than *that*."

Thalia started to laugh again, and stopped, seeing the Special's face. His expression of faint amusement hadn't changed.

"You're serious!" she said.

The Special opened up the folder. He took out a grainy photograph, pushing it across the table for Thalia to examine.

"I expect you recognize Dr. Rosmer and Senator Oradour-Monatte," the Special said. "But these two; have you seen either of them before?"

The photograph showed the steps outside the Round Reading Room of the University Library. There were four men on the steps: one she recognized as a senior librarian, another as a Travallese politician. But the other two—

Their features were odd, foreign. They were short and stocky, more so even than Cicero. Both of them had strangely pale hair; the color was impossible to tell from the photograph, but Thalia didn't think it was the gray of old age. One of them, Thalia realized after a moment, was a woman; she hadn't seen it before because the two were dressed almost identically, in dark, close-fitting trousers and coats buttoned to the throat, cut like nothing she had ever seen before. Neither wore a hat, and the woman's hair was even shorter than the man's.

Thalia shook her head mutely.

"No?" the Special said. "That's reassuring. The one on the left—" he leaned forward, and tapped the picture "—calls himself Allen Macleane. The woman's called Bernadette Parker." He pronounced the foreign syllables carefully.

"And who are they?" Thalia said.

The Special sat back. "It's not who they are, miss, it's how far they've come. Since their last port of call—twenty light-years."

Thalia's bewilderment must have been plain.

"A light-year is—" the Special started to say.

"I know what a light-year is," Thalia said. "That's absolutely mad."

The Special shrugged. "I don't claim to know how they did it, miss," he said. "But they're here."

"Why?" Thalia said. "What do they want?"

"That's also a matter of some debate," the Special said. "They say they want trade. Not in gold or cloth or salt fish, which as I'm sure you've worked out wouldn't be worth the cost of shipping. In *knowledge*. Art, music, scholarship, literature."

"That still wouldn't be worth the cost of shipping," Thalia said.

"Right again, miss," said the Special. "What Mr. Macleane and Miss Parker and their friends—they call themselves 'Marginal,' Marginal Limited Liability Corporation—propose to do, is to set up a sort of interstellar semaphore or radiotelephone, connecting Salomé with—with the stars, I suppose, or at any rate the ones they know." He smiled. "We send them scratchy recordings of the Reunion Philharmonic and they send us the plans to build space-ships of our own."

"That hardly sounds like fair trade," Thalia said.

The Special tapped the side of his nose. "Do you know how the Archipelago Company makes its money, miss?" he asked. "Used to be, they'd buy wool and pig iron and timber in the islands and sell it here, in Basia; buy woven cloth and steel tools and whatnot here and sell them in the islands. They still do a bit of that, of course. But about fifty years ago some enterprising Company factor realized it would be cheaper to build mills and factories right there in the islands. Now most of what the Company sells in the islands is made in the islands, in Company mills and Company factories, out of wool from Company herds and iron from Company mines, and what they mostly ship back to Basia is money."

"It's not just plans for space-ships they're proposing to sell us, then," Thalia said. "We wouldn't know what to do with them, any more than an Eastern Desert tribesman would know what to do with the plans for a steam locomotive. It's science, and engineering, and everything we'd need to understand those plans. They could teach us so much. . . ."

"For a price, miss," the Special said. He seemed to think Thalia had missed his point. "For whatever the market will bear."

"I know," Thalia said. "I *have* studied economics, don't forget."

"Not for a moment, miss," said the Special. "But you see where this leads. As the only source of all that knowledge, there's no limit to the price they could set on it. Within a century these people might own half the world, the way the Company owns half the Archipelago."

"Within a century *these* people will probably have sold off their stakes and retired," Thalia said, "but I take your point."

Then she shook her head.

"This is mad," she said. "Even if it's all true, you can't possibly think Dr. Cicero is one of them."

It would explain so much—Cicero's hard-to-place foreignness, his indifference to convention, the way he combined an understanding of the most esoteric things with an ignorance of the most trivial ones. But while it was no trouble for Thalia to imagine Cicero as an alien, the idea of Cicero as an avaricious colonial speculator was laughable.

The Special stood up. He was silent for a moment, pacing, looking out into the corridor.

"The Marginal expedition arrived about three years ago," he began. "They came straight to the Senate and announced themselves; explained where they came from and what they proposed to do for us. The Senate wanted proof, naturally. They showed us plenty of gadgets and trinkets, but the Senate—Senator Oradour-Monatte, actually, the man you see in the picture—wanted more; some taste of all this knowledge they were proposing to sell us. 'Tell me something,' he said. 'Something I don't know.' And do you know what they told him?"

The Special stopped his pacing and turned to face her.

"They told him, miss, that there was another expedition, already here. A different lot of space-people, from some other—some other constellation, I suppose—altogether."

Thalia stared at him for a moment, then nodded. slowly "You think Cicero's one of *them*," she said.

"Miss," the Special said, "I'm quite sure of it. That thing I cut out of his ear proved he's not from this world, but even without it, I have plenty of evidence." He pulled out the other chair again and sat down. "Don't waste my time pretending you don't believe me," he said.

Thalia shook her head. Cicero was going to tell me, she thought. He almost did, this morning, when he talked about leaving. He must have thought I wouldn't believe him.

Would I have believed him?

"So what do *they* want?" she said.

In answer, the Special took out another photograph. She couldn't tell where or when it had been taken. It showed Cicero, in the clothes of a common dockworker, in conversation with another man, similarly dressed. He might have been Cicero's brother, though his features were heavier and his hair was not so straight; at any rate, he was from the same part of the world—whatever that world was.

"Have you seen this man before?" the Special said.

"Never," said Thalia.

"He goes by the name of Philip Marius," the Special said. "Nasty piece of work. He's a saboteur and an anarchist, among other things. It's the talkers in the workers' movement, men like Maspero and Coser, that get their names in the newspapers, but it's our boy Marius who gets things done. Sure you haven't seen him?"

"I'm sure," Thalia said.

The Special sighed. "Well, miss," he said, "the gentlemen from Marginal *may* be bent on enslaving us all, in the end, but they're men of business. By the standards of men of business, they've been quite amicable— negotiating directly with the Senate, providing the state with the odd bit of helpful information now and then." He tapped the photograph of Cicero and the anarchist, Marius. "But your professor's lot—they've been much less polite. Ten years and more they've been watching us, without so much as an introduction; five years they've walked among us in secret, stirring up civil unrest, corrupting our poor and our young folk. Infiltrating factories, hospitals, churches . . . and universities."

"Teaching political economy to the children of the upper classes hardly qualifies as *corrupting young folk*," Thalia said. "If it does, the entire University faculty is guilty."

The Special smiled knowingly. "We can leave the professor's private life—and yours—alone for now," he said. "What's been keeping me awake nights—and what I wanted to know from you—isn't that; it's the thought that your professor, and his friend Marius, and the rest of their friends, might have been working *with* Mr. Macleane and his lot. Playing both ends against the middle, you see—against us."

"And have they?" Thalia said.

"I wish I knew, miss." The Special shook his head. "But I don't think so. I find your witness to Dr. Cicero's character oddly persuasive. He may be a liar, a murderer"—he drew the word slowly out, and Thalia flinched—"an anarchist sympathizer and an alien spy, but he's not a capitalist. And besides—"

A tentative knock came at the door.

"Come in," the Special said sharply.

A uniformed prison guard entered.

"The van's ready, sir," he said.

"Right," said the Special. "I'll be along in just a moment."

"Yes, sir." The door closed.

The Special gathered up the photographs and put them back in the folder. He put the folder back in his bag and stood up.

"'And besides'?" Thalia prompted.

"What?" the Special said.

"Besides what?" Thalia said. "What's the other reason you don't think Cicero's friends and this Marginal Corporation are working together?"

"Ah, that." The Special knocked on the door, and the guard opened it. "Well, miss, between arresting your young man and a few of his friends, arranging a little riot outside Marginal's offices in the City, and a few other pieces of misdirection . . . . Assuming they're not just staging it for our benefit, it looks as though we've had the two sides shooting at each other for the past hour and a half."

He tipped his hat to Thalia.

"Ta, miss," he said, and she heard the click of the lock behind him.

The guards maneuvered Cicero—with some difficulty, because of the manacles and leg irons—through the narrow corridors, and down several flights of stairs. He tried to count the number of flights, and to remember how tall the Alicata Prison was, how many stories, but he couldn't keep the figures in his head. He kept seeing the gables of Trilisser House, counting the steps of the spiral staircase up to his rooms. His ear was bleeding again, but with his hands bound there was no way for him to do anything about it.

They came out into a covered carriageway, so long and dark that it seemed to be underground. Both ends of the arched passage were sheets of rainwater, and what daylight made it through was gray-green and cheerless.

A van was waiting, windowless and unmarked. The Special took a seat up front, beside the driver. The guards bundled Cicero into the back, and climbed in behind him. He was not entirely surprised to find the compartment's opposite bench already occupied, and the slumped figure of Marius wedged there between two other guards. Marius was in a bad way. Unlike Cicero, who was still in the academic robes he'd been wearing when he was arrested, Marius was dressed in green prison coveralls, patched and stained, and some of the stains were fresh. Bloody bandages covered his right eye and right ear; his right side was bloody as well, and there was dried blood and vomit down the front of his chest. Cicero couldn't tell whether he was even conscious.

The engine started, and the van lurched into motion. There was a brief rattle of rain on the roof, and the van stopped again; the doors were opened, and Cicero had a quick glimpse of a wide courtyard, enclosed by high walls and overlooked by towers. Then his view was blocked by the Special again, and two more guards, draped in rain capes and carrying carbines. One of the guards had a tablet and a pen.

"Prisoner number 91264, alias Philip Marius," that one said. The Special gestured to Marius, and the guard looked up, making a note on the tablet. "Prisoner 91186, alias Alexander Cicero." The guard on Cicero's right took Cicero's manacled hands and raised them. The guard with the tablet made another note.

"To be taken from the Alicata Prison to the Imaz Prison," the Special said.

"That's what it says here," the guard with the tablet said. He tore off a sheet and handed it to the Special. "There you go."

"Ta," said the Special.

They closed the doors again, and the van started moving. The storm was blowing in earnest now. Cicero could hear it, the wind shrieking across the roof of the van, throwing rain against the sides like handfuls of gravel. Between the wind and the state of the road, evident in the jouncing of the seat and the noises of complaint from the suspension, he half expected the van to tip over at any moment. It was hot and close, and he found it hard to breathe.

The Imaz. The Alicata was an ordinary prison, for ordinary criminals. The Imaz was where they took the dangerous prisoners, the ones who had tried to escape, and the sort of political prisoners whose allies or followers might be expected to attempt a rescue. He fell into all three categories, he supposed.

How did they get people out to the Imaz, anyway? It was on an island, he knew that, the prison built within the walls of an old medieval sea-fort.

Storm-season waves in the inland sea, funneled by the narrow, cliff-steep shores, regularly topped fifty meters. No boat could survive those waters, and only a brave fool would trust himself to Salomé's rickety, experimental dirigibles—certainly the police, even the Specials, had none.

The van's journey seemed to be tending up, into the hills, not down to the port. Maybe they weren't being taken to the Imaz at all; at least not directly.

The van came to a stop, and from the cab Cicero heard muffled conversation. There was the metallic clang of a gate being opened, then the van jerked into motion again, but only for a little while. The wind died down, and the rain on the roof ceased, as they came into a tunnel, or a garage. Where were they?

The door opened on a dark, clanking space that smelled of machinery, and of the storm. The guards hauled Marius out, and one of them said to Cicero: "Out you go, then."

The van was parked beneath a wide sheet-metal awning supported by steel girders. They were at the top of the kilometer-high cliffs that made up most of the inland sea's southern shore, looking out into the storm. Far out to sea, across the white-topped, gray-green waves, the sharp rock of the Imaz emerged from the dark, wind-whipped clouds like the prow of a warship in the fog.

Four cobweb-thin cables, two above and two below, stretched toward them. On the far end they faded into the rain, invisible, but closer by Cicero could see that they were in fact thick as a man's wrist, and steel. Next to the van beneath the awning was a mass of machinery, man-high wheels and pulleys and a clattering steam engine, and Cicero saw that it was drawing in the upper pair of cables, and paying out the lower. He looked out into the storm again and saw a car, suspended between the cables, slowly making its way toward them. Cicero was suddenly overwhelmed with vertigo.

The Special caught his eye and smiled.

"All right with heights, are we, professor?"

Cicero didn't answer.

The car was the size of a railway carriage and crudely streamlined, its corners smoothed and sides rounded by bolted sheets of rust-streaked metal. Despite that, it swayed alarmingly as it approached the cliffs, pulling the cables back and forth, and Cicero could hear the wind shrieking across the car's metal skin. The noise abated as the car came under the awning and thumped to a stop. A hatch opened downward, becoming a short flight of steps, and two guards came out, both of them wearing rain capes and carrying heavy machine pistols.

The Special presented his paperwork, and after a quick examination of it the guards stood respectfully aside.

"After you, professor," the Special said.

The Alicata guards pushed Cicero up the steps and into the car. The interior was lit by a line of incandescent bulbs in wire cages, bolted to the roof. There were four more guards inside, and a number of bare steel benches. The windows of the car were heavily barred.

Marius was brought in on a stretcher, and taken to the other end of the car. Cicero was handed over to the Imaz guards and made to sit, while they fastened his manacles and leg irons to eyebolts beneath the bench.

The Special climbed in, followed by the two Imaz guards, who pulled the door up and dogged it shut. With a lurch, the car began to move, and the wind quickly rose to a screech.

"Time was," the Special said, taking the bench across from Cicero, "the Imaz was cut off from the mainland ten weeks out of the year. The old kings used to hole up there, during their wars; took the Senate four years to winkle them out of there, during the Reunion. This thing—" he tapped the bench "—was put up thirty years ago, after some rioting prisoners managed to set fire to the grain store during storm season. Most of the guards made it through, holed up in the citadel with their own stores. But there wasn't one prisoner in twenty left alive by winter when the boats made it across." He gave Cicero a ghoulish smile and added: "Nor many bodies left, neither."

Cicero turned his head away and closed his eyes. The car was dropping swiftly—there was quite a bit of slack in the cables—and it pitched and swayed as the storm winds pushed and lifted it. Cicero's stomach heaved in sympathy, and he realized suddenly why the seats were all bare metal: for ease of cleaning. He opened his eyes again, which was a slight improvement. The Special, Cicero was annoyed to see, looked quite cheerful; he might have been sitting in a parkside café on a sunny day in spring.

The uniformed guards, though, looked more than a little green around the gills. Cicero tried to estimate his chance of disarming one of them and turning his weapon on the others, and thought that without the manacles and leg irons it might be as high as one in three; but the bolts that held the chains were quite secure.

The Special met his eye, and smiled, and Cicero had the uncomfortable feeling that his mind was being read.

Then the car gave a great lurch, sending the Special and all six guards sprawling, and only the prisoners' chains prevented them from being thrown from their seats as well. The lights went out, and the pitch of the wind rose to a scream.

"Fucking hell," growled the Special as he picked himself up. "That happen often?"

"No, sir," one of the Imaz guards said.

"We've stopped moving," said another, looking out the window.

It was true. Not only had they stopped moving out toward the island, but the seasick pitching of the car had died as well.

"Get the emergency lamp," the Special ordered. "Signal the station and find out what the hell's happened."

One of the guards opened a locker beneath one of the benches and took out a battery-operated signal lamp. He went to the end of the car, looking back toward the cliff, and flashed the lamp into the rain.

"It's awful thick out there, sir," he said doubtfully. He turned around. "I don't know if—"

The window behind him imploded, knocking him flat and sending shards of glass and fragments of metal through the car. At the same moment something—several somethings—hit the sides of the car, and the door blew outward off its hinges.

The Special yelled something, his words impossible to hear over the sudden roar of wind and water, and the car was lit by a white flash as he fired his pistol over the head of the fallen guard. The bullet struck something that Cicero could not quite see, and ricocheted away, shattering another window.

"GET DOWN!" bellowed a woman's amplified voice, a Community voice.

Cicero did his best, leaning forward over his manacled hands. He heard the cracks of electrostatic stunners, and then one of the Imaz guards opened up with his machine pistol; in the muzzle flashes Cicero glimpsed the glassy shape of a suited Outreach missionary, the figure's optical camouflage not quite able to keep up with the rapidly changing light inside the car. The figure went down in a shower of bullets, but more were coming in through the door and the blown-out windows. In moments all the guards were down, and the missionaries—four, of them, men and women—were shutting off their camouflage, the suits turning to bright solid colors.

The missionary who had been knocked down, his suit now spring green, came over and knelt in front of Cicero. He took out a tool, and in a moment the bolts that secured Cicero's chains began to smoke and glow red.

The missionary lifted his mask to reveal a dark, bearded face.

"Lucius," said Cicero.

"You all right, then?" the man said. Not waiting for an answer, he took out a medical scanner and ran it quickly over Cicero from head to toe.

"I'm fine," Cicero said. "See to Marius."

Lucius smiled. "You're not fine," he said. "But you'll do." He moved back to examine Marius.

A bright yellow suit proved to be Livia, a very unhappy Livia.

"Led us on a chase, didn't you?" she said.

"Pressure of circumstance," said Cicero. "Are the others all right?"

"Everyone in Thyatira and the Archipelago got out," Livia said. "We picked Megaera off a hospital roof and Cassia out of the harbor. But Solon's dead; killed resisting arrest. I don't know about Mus and the others in the southeast; one of the other landers was supposed to go after them."

Cicero tried to remember Solon's face, and found that he couldn't, for all that they, and all the on-world missionaries, had trained together for the better part of five subjective years. A small man, Solon, with a highly refined sense of outrage that had served him well in his cover as a muckraking journalist; that was all Cicero could remember.

Livia glanced down, at a display on the inside of her wrist.

"Come on," she said. "*Equity*'s coming for us; we've got twenty minutes, no more." She turned away. To someone unseen, she said: "Drop the rescue lines."

I can't let them take me away, Cicero thought.

As much as he wanted to relax, to let himself be bundled aboard *Equity* like a tired child carried home from a dinner party, he couldn't do that. He realized that, terrible as the idea was to contemplate, on his way to the interrogation rooms of the Imaz he had actually been better off. From there, he at least would have had some chance to turn the Travallese state around, to help Salomé resist the dealers; some chance to see Thalia again.

He stood up quickly.

"Livia," he said. "I have to get back to the city."

Livia turned back.

"You're joking," she said. "*Solidarity*'s been *blown*, Cicero. We've lost track of the dealers' ship; they've deployed about half a thousand decoys and automated fighters over our heads, and *Equity*'s running the gauntlet of them right now, trying to get into position to pick us up. We're leaving this system, Cicero; Outreach is leaving." She glanced at her display again. "Eighteen minutes, now." Raising her voice, she said: "Lucius—can we move him?"

Marius answered for himself.

"I can walk," he said. "Just—let's get away from here."

"Right." Livia moved to the door and looked up into the rain.

"Livia—" Cicero said.

"Argue with me on the lander," she said. A safety line dropped down from above; Livia caught it and clipped it to her suit. The pupal form of a rescue harness followed, and she secured it to one of the handrails.

"Here," she said, stepping aside.

Cicero heard the lander's fans surge and whine as they fought to keep the lander airborne and to compensate for the violent winds. He made his way carefully to the door, the wind-driven rain stinging his face. The hull of the lander was a smooth gray curve overhead, its open hatch bright and welcoming, surrounded by white emergency lights.

He looked down. Below—far below—the storm-waves were a dark gray, darker than the lander's hull, gray topped with greenish foam. On one side, the rock of the Imaz rose above them, much taller, and much closer, than Cicero would have thought. On the other, the cliff was a long shadow, and when Cicero tried to follow its line down to where the curve of the great bay should have begun, where he should have been able to make out some trace of the city, the storm dissolved everything.

"Marius," he said suddenly. "You first."

Marius limped up to the door.

"Sure?" he said.

Cicero nodded to the rescue harness. "Go on," he said. "I'm . . ." not leaving, he started to say, but his voice failed.

Marius put a hand on Cicero's shoulder, and Cicero saw that he knew.

"Good luck," he said.

"Go *on*," said Cicero.

Marius smiled. He started to step into the rescue harness. Then he glanced at something over Cicero's shoulder, and the smile left his face.

"Down!" he yelled, shoving Cicero aside.

Cicero stumbled and fell back into the tram car. There was a shot, somehow louder than any of the barrage that had filled the car a few minutes earlier; and when Cicero looked up he saw the Special up on one knee, pistol held steady in both hands. The Special's eyes met Cicero's, and the pistol moved, and Cicero saw his death there, in a small circle of blackness.

Cicero froze.

Then stun bolts hit the Special from three sides, and the pistol fell from nerveless fingers.

It took Cicero a moment to get to his feet; his muscles didn't want to work.

He turned to thank Marius, but there was no one there.

And when he moved to the door and looked out, there was no one there either.

Only the lander's futile lights, and the storm-waves, and the rain.

———

They'd had to sedate Cicero to get him aboard the lander. Livia wasn't happy about that, and trouble would undoubtedly come of it later. But clearly, he'd been raving, demanding to be left aboard the wrecked tram car, even after the locals had shot Marius.

Livia checked her displays. The other landers, with their own cargoes of evacuees, were keeping pace. Behind them, as the dealers' automated fighter fleet and the Outreach mission's rear guard finished annihilating each other, the mad fireworks display of fusion bombs and antimatter explosions was finally dying out, after turning Salomé's night into day.

There was no telling which side, if either, had gained the upper hand back there, but it didn't matter; neither Livia nor Galen wanted to take any more chances, and they were committed, now.

Lucius came forward from checking on Cicero, moving slowly and cautiously under three gravities of acceleration.

"He'll be fine," Livia said.

Lucius shook his head. "But will he be fine when he wakes up?" he said.

Livia didn't answer, though what she thought was: Damned if I was going to come back without *either* one of them.

On the forward display, the violet flare of *Equity*'s drive died, as the starship briefly collapsed its ram field and cut its torch to allow the landers to catch up. Faster than seemed possible, the dark bulk of the ship swept up on them; they floated free for a moment as the lander's autopilot cut their own thrust, and there was a jerk and a metallic thump as the grapples caught.

Then the thrust built as the starship's torch came to life again, and they ran for the safety of the deep.

———

Thalia didn't know how long she waited. She slept for a while, head down on the table; the chair wasn't comfortable, but it was more comfortable than the cold concrete of the floor.

At one point the lights flickered, and there were raised voices in the hall, but she was unable to make out the words. At another point a guard in a green uniform brought in a tray with a bowl of oily fish soup and a cup of bad tea. The guard didn't answer any of Thalia's questions, or even look her in the eye.

When the door of her cell opened, Thalia expected the Special. Instead there were two armed guards, and another man. The man was on the late side of middle age, and despite his height—he was rather short—walked with a stoop. His hair, where it was not gray, was an odd shade of yellow, like dry leaves. He was wearing a matte gray coat that was not quite like anything Thalia had ever seen before, and looked as tired as she herself felt.

It was some moments before she recognized him as the man from the Special's photograph of the Library steps.

The guards went out, and closed the door behind them.

"Sorry about this," the man said. The words were clear, but his accent was as strange as his coat. "My name's Allen Macleane. I'm with Marginal LLC." He made a strange gesture, holding out his right hand with the fingers together and the palm perpendicular to the floor.

"Yes," Thalia said. "I know. Does this mean you've won?"

Macleane's face reddened, and his hand dropped. He shook his head. "Do you mind if I sit down?" he said.

Wordlessly, Thalia gestured toward the other chair, and Macleane took it.

"Thanks," he said. He looked down for a moment; his fingers traced designs on the table. "I understand your friend Cicero was rescued," he said, looking up. "I thought you'd want to know that. His people hit the tram that was taking him out to the Imaz."

Thalia's heart leapt.

"Does that mean——" she began.

"Does that mean *they* won?" Macleane said. "Not exactly. We destroyed one of their ships; the other one's running. Past the orbit of Herodias now, and still accelerating at three gees. They won't be back any time soon." He sighed. "But that doesn't mean we won, either. Our ship, our only ship, is crippled, maybe destroyed; we're trapped here. Without the ship, we've got no way to contact our own people, and anyhow they're too far away to help. All we've got left in orbit is machines we can't control. Everyone who was on the ship is dead; my own brother is dead."

"I'm sorry," Thalia said. But she was barely listening; she was thinking about the distances between the stars, and about the Semard professor's new theory of light and time.

Oh, Cicero, she thought. Oh, my heart.

He might as well be dead, she thought, that's what this means; he'll never be back.

But then she thought: No, that's not what it means at all. It means he's alive, out there somewhere; and if they keep going, he'll be alive still, when I'm an old woman and can no longer remember his face, he'll still be young, preserved in slow time like amber, out there between the stars, chasing the light.

And that was a reason to be thankful. That was a reason to go on.

She realized that tears were running down her cheeks.

I have to pull myself together, she thought. This man will think I'm crying for his brother.

But she looked up into Allen Macleane's lined face and saw that he was wiser than that.

"We both lost," Macleane said gently. "*You've* won, don't you see? The people of Salomé have won."

"What do you mean?" Thalia said.

"We came here thinking you were a bunch of barbarians," Macleane said. "Primitives. I'm sure Outreach—your friend Cicero's people—thought the same way. We didn't take you seriously, you see. When you, I mean the Travallese government, moved against us, we figured that Outreach was behind it, just like they figured we were behind the government's moves against them." He smiled. "Both of us were watching each other so carefully, we forgot there was a third party at the table—*you*. You played us off against each other beautifully, and we never knew you were doing it."

"Mr. Macleane," Thalia said. "I'm not a player in your game. I'm not even a pawn. I'm a spectator. I have only the slightest idea what you're talking about."

"I'm sorry," Macleane said. "I didn't mean you, personally. But your people have got us right where they want us. There are only about twenty of us left. If we're going to survive here it's going to be on their charity."

"Not my people, Mr. Macleane." Thalia lifted her manacled hands. "Charity isn't what the Senate of Travalle is noted for."

"I know," Macleane said. "They'll milk us for everything we've got. History, stellar geography, basic science. Technology; weapons, especially, and spacecraft, so they can deal with the next alien arrival on their own terms." He shook his head. "They don't understand what they're up against."

"I'm not one of you, Mr. Macleane," she said. "I'm not Travallese, either. If Cicero was against you, then so am I. What does this have to do with me?"

"They tell me you're good at mathematics," Macleane said.

"I'm *amazing* at mathematics," said Thalia.

Macleane smiled.

"Would you like a job?"

MAYFLOWER II

STEPHEN BAXTER

Author's Note:

My proceeds from this work will be donated to the Asian Elephant Survival Appeal, of which I am a patron.

Once elephants could be found throughout Asia, India, Africa and North America. Their remains, with tusks like sculptures and teeth like curbstones, are still dug out of the ground in Los Angeles and London. Today all the elephants are gone, save only three species. But now human population pressure is endangering one of these: the Asian (or Indian) elephants. It is highly likely they will be gone in decades.

The North of England Zoological Society, a nonprofit conservation organization, is spearheading an international program to sustain the Asian elephant in its native ranges, as well as to establish a reserve breeding population in European zoos. Preserving the elephant will bring the additional benefit of preserving the wider ecosystem it inhabits, while respecting the economic and cultural interests of neighboring human populations.

For more details or to make a donation please contact:
Asian Elephant Survival Appeal
Chester Zoo
FREEPOST
Chester CH2 1LH
UK

or visit: www.chesterzoo.org

TWENTY DAYS BEFORE the end of his world, Rusel heard that he was to be saved.

"Rusel. Rusel . . ." The whispered voice was insistent. Rusel rolled over, trying to shake off the effects of his usual mild sedative. His pillow was soaked with sweat. The room responded to his movement, and soft light coalesced around him.

His brother's face was hovering in the air at the side of his bed. Diluc was grinning widely.

"Lethe," Rusel said hoarsely. "You ugly bastard."

"You're just jealous," Diluc said. The Virtual made his face look even wider than usual, his nose more prominent. "I'm sorry to wake you. But I just heard—you need to know—"

"Know what?"

"Blen showed up in the infirmary." Blen was the nanochemist assigned to Ship Three. "Get this: he has a heart murmur." Diluc's grin returned.

Rusel frowned. "For that you woke me up? Poor Blen."

"It's not that serious. But, Rus—it's congenital."

The sedative dulled Rusel's thinking, and it took him a moment to figure it out.

The five Ships were to evacuate the last, brightest hopes of Port Sol from the path of the incoming peril. But they were slower-than-light transports, and would take many centuries to reach their destinations. Only the healthiest, in body and genome, could be allowed aboard a generation starship. And if Blen had a hereditary heart condition—

"He's off the Ship," Rusel breathed.

"And that means you're aboard, brother. You're the second-best nanochemist on this lump of ice. You won't be here when the Coalition arrives. You're going to live!"

Rusel lay back on his crushed pillow. He felt numb.

Diluc kept talking. "Did you know that families are *illegal* under the Coalition? Their citizens are born in tanks. Just the fact of our relationship would doom us, Rus! I'm trying to fix a transfer from Five to Three. If we're together, that's something, isn't it? I know it's going to be hard, Rus. But we can help each other. We can get through this . . ."

All Rusel could think about was Lora, whom he would have to leave behind.

———

The next morning Rusel arranged to meet Lora in the Forest of Ancestors. He took a bubble-wheel surface transport, and set out early.

Port Sol was a ball of friable ice and rock a couple of hundred kilometers across. It was actually a planetesimal, an unfinished remnant of the formation of Sol system. Inhabited for millennia, its surface was heavily worked, quarried and pitted, and littered by abandoned towns. But throughout Port Sol's long human usage some areas had been kept undamaged, and as he drove Rusel kept to the marked track, to avoid crushing the delicate sculptures of frost that had coalesced here over four billion years.

This was the very edge of Sol system. The sky was a dome of stars, with the ragged glow of the Galaxy hurled casually across its equator. Set in that diffuse glow was the sun, the brightest star, bright enough to cast shadows, but so remote it was a mere pinpoint. Around the sun Rusel could make out a tiny puddle of light: That was the inner system, the disc of worlds, moons, asteroids, dust and other debris that had been the arena of all human history before the first interplanetary voyages some three thousand years earlier, and still the home of all but an invisible fraction of the human race. This was a time of turmoil, and today humans were fighting and dying, their triumphs and terror invisible. Even now, from out of that pale glow, a punitive fleet was ploughing toward Port Sol.

And visible beyond the close horizon of the ice moon was a squat cylinder, a misty sketch in the faint rectilinear sunlight. That was Ship Three, preparing for its leap into the greater dark.

The whole situation was an unwelcome consequence of the liberation of Earth from the alien Qax.

The Coalition of Interim Governance was the new, ideologically pure and viciously determined authority that had emerged from the chaos of a newly freed Earth. Relentless, intolerant, unforgiving, the Coalition was already burning its way out through the worlds and moons of Sol system. When the Coalition ships came, the best you could hope for was that your community would be broken up, your equipment impounded, and that you would be hauled back to a prison camp on Earth or its Moon for "reconditioning."

But if you were found to be harboring anyone who had collaborated with the hated Qax, the penalties were much more extreme. The word Rusel had heard was "resurfacing."

Now the Coalition had turned its attention to Port Sol. This ice moon was governed by five Pharaohs, who had indeed collaborated with the Qax—though they described it as "mediating the effects of the occupation for the benefit of mankind"—and they had received anti-ageing treatments as a reward. So Port Sol was a "nest of illegal immortals and collaborators," the Coalition said, which its troops had been dispatched to "clean out." They seemed indifferent to the fact that in addition to the Pharaohs, some fifty thousand people called Port Sol home.

The Pharaohs had a deep network of spies on Earth, and they had had some warning. As the colonists had only the lightest battery of antiquated weaponry—indeed the whole moon, a refuge from the occupation, was somewhat low-tech—nobody expected to be able to resist. But there was a way out.

Five mighty Ships were hastily thrown together. On each Ship, captained by a Pharaoh, a couple of hundred people, selected for their health and skill sets, would be taken away: a total of a thousand, perhaps, out of a population of fifty thousand, saved from the incoming disaster. There was no faster-than-light technology on Port Sol; these would be generation starships. But perhaps that was well: between the stars there would be room to hide.

All of these mighty historical forces had now focused down on Rusel's life, and they threatened to tear him away from his lover.

Rusel was an able nanochemist, he was the right age, and his health and pedigree were immaculate. But unlike his brother he hadn't been good enough to win the one-in-fifty lottery and make the cut to get a place on the Ships. He was twenty-eight years old: not a good age to die. But he had accepted his fate, so he believed—for Lora, his lover, had no hope of a place. At twenty she was a student, a promising Virtual idealist but without the mature skills to have a chance of competing. So at least he would die with her, which seemed to him some consolation. He was honest with himself; he had never been sure if this serenity would have survived the appearance of the Coalition ships in Port Sol's dark sky—and now, it seemed, he was never going to find out.

Lora was waiting for him at the Forest of Ancestors. They met on the surface, embracing stiffly through their skinsuits. Then they set up a dome-tent and crawled through its collapsible airlock.

In the Forest's long shadows, Rusel and Lora made love: at first urgently, and then again, more slowly, thoughtfully. In the habs, inertial generators kept the gravity at one-sixth standard, about the same as Earth's Moon. But there was no gravity control out here in the Forest, and as they clung to each other they drifted in the tent's cool air, light as dreams.

Rusel told Lora his news.

Lora was slim, delicate. The population of this low-gravity moon tended to tallness and thin bones, but Lora seemed to him more elfin than most, and she had large, dark eyes that always seemed a little unfocussed, as if her attention were somewhere else. It was that sense of other-world fragility that had first attracted Rusel to her, and now he watched her fearfully.

With blankets bundled over her legs, she took his hand and smiled. "Don't be afraid."

"I'm the one who's going to live. Why should I be afraid?"

"You'd accepted dying. Now you've got to get used to the idea of living." She sighed. "It's just as hard."

"And living without you." He squeezed her hand. "Maybe that's what scares me most. I'm frightened of losing you."

"I'm not going anywhere."

He gazed out at the silent, watchful shapes of the Ancestors. These "trees," some three or four meters high, were stumps with "roots" that dug into the icy ground. They were living things, the most advanced members of Port Sol's low-temperature aboriginal ecology. This was their sessile stage. In their youth, these creatures, called "Toolmakers," were mobile, and were actually intelligent. They would haul themselves across Port Sol's broken ground, seeking a suitable crater slope or ridge face. There they would set down their roots and allow their nervous systems, and their minds, to dissolve, their purposes fulfilled. Rusel wondered what icy dreams might be coursing slowly through their residual minds. They were beyond decisions now; in a way he envied them.

"Maybe the Coalition will spare the Ancestors."

She snorted. "I doubt it. The Coalition only care about humans—and their sort of humans at that."

"My family have lived here a long time," he said. "There's a story that says we rode out with the first colonizing wave." It was a legendary time, when the great engineer Michael Poole had come barnstorming all the way to Port Sol to build his great starships.

She smiled. "Most families have stories like that. After thousands of years, who can tell?"

"This is my home," he blurted. "This isn't just the destruction of us, but of our culture, our heritage. Everything we've worked for."

"But that's why you're so important." She sat up, letting the blanket fall away, and wrapped her arms around his neck. In Sol's dim light her eyes were pools of liquid darkness. "You're the future. The Pharaohs say that in the long run the Coalition will be the death of mankind, not just of *us*. Somebody has to save our knowledge, our values, for the future."

"But you—" *You will be alone, when the Coalition ships descend.* Decision sparked. "I'm not going anywhere."

She pulled back. "What?"

"I've decided. I'll tell Andres . . . and my brother. I can't leave here, not without you."

"You must," she said firmly. "You're the best for the job; believe me, if not the Pharaohs wouldn't have selected you. So you have to go. It's your duty."

"What human being would run out on those he loved?"

Her face was set, and she sounded much older than her twenty years. "It would be easier to die. But you must live, live on and on, live on like a machine, until the job is done, and the race is saved."

Before her he felt weak, immature. He clung to her, burying his face in the soft warmth of her neck.

Nineteen days, he thought. *We still have nineteen days.* He determined to cherish every minute.

But as it turned out, they had much less time than that.

———

Once again he was awakened in the dark. But this time his room lights were snapped full on, dazzling him. And it was the face of Pharaoh Andres that hovered in the air beside his bed. He sat up, baffled, his system heavy with sedative.

"—thirty minutes. You have thirty minutes to get to Ship Three. Wear your skinsuit. Bring nothing else. If you aren't there we leave without you."

At first he couldn't take in what she said. He found himself staring at her face. Her head was hairless, her scalp bald, her eyebrows and even her eyelashes gone. Her skin was oddly smooth, her features small; she didn't look young, but as if her face had sublimated with time, like Port Sol's ice landscapes, leaving this palimpsest. She was rumored to be two hundred years old.

Suddenly her words snapped into focus. "Don't acknowledge this message, just move. We lift in twenty-nine minutes. If you are Ship Three crew, you have twenty-nine minutes to get to—"

She had made a mistake: that was his first thought. Had she forgotten that there were still sixteen days to go before the Coalition ships were due? But he could see from her face there was no mistake.

Twenty-nine minutes. He reached down to his bedside cabinet, pulled out a nano pill, and gulped it down dry. Reality bleached, becoming cold and stark.

He dragged on his skinsuit and sealed it roughly. He glanced around his room, at his bed, his few pieces of furniture, the Virtual unit on the dresser with its images of Lora. *Bring nothing.* Andres wasn't a woman you disobeyed in the slightest particular.

Without looking back he left the room.

The corridor outside was bedlam. A thousand people shared this under-the-ice habitat, and all of them seemed to be out tonight. They ran this way and that, many in skinsuits, some hauling bundles of gear. He pushed his way through the throng. The sense of panic was tangible—and, carried on the recycled air, he thought he could smell burning.

His heart sank. It was obviously a scramble to escape—but the only way off the moon was the Ships, which could take no more than a thousand.

He couldn't believe what he was seeing. Had the sudden curtailing of the time left triggered this panic? But these were citizens of Port Sol, and this was its ultimate emergency. Had they lost all their values, all their sense of community? What could they hope to achieve by hurling themselves at Ships that had no room for them, but to bring everybody down with them? *But what would I do?* He could afford the luxury of nobility; he was getting out of here.

Twenty minutes.

He reached the perimeter concourse. Here, surface transports nuzzled against a row of simple airlocks. Some of the locks were already open, and people were crowding in, pushing children, bundles of luggage.

His own car was still here, he saw with relief. He pulled open his skinsuit glove and hastily pressed his palm to the wall. The door hissed open. But before he could pass through, somebody grabbed his arm.

A man faced him, a stranger, short, burly, aged perhaps forty. Behind him a woman clutched a small child and an infant. The adults had blanket-wrapped bundles on their backs. The man wore an electric-blue skinsuit, but his family were in hab clothes.

The man said desperately, "Buddy, you have room in that thing?"

"No," Rusel said.

The man's eyes hardened. "Listen. The Pharaohs' spies got it wrong. Suddenly the Coalition is only seven days out. Look, friend, you can see how I'm fixed. The Coalition breaks up families, doesn't it? All I'm asking is for a chance."

But there won't be room for you. Don't you understand? And even if there were— There were to be no children on the Ships at launch: that was the Pharaohs' harsh rule. In the first years of the long voyage, everybody aboard had to be maximally productive. The time for breeding would come later.

The man's fist bunched. "Listen, buddy—"

Rusel shoved the man in the chest. He fell backward, stumbling against his children. His blanket bundle broke open, and goods spilled on the floor: clothes, diapers, children's toys.

"Please—" The woman approached him, stepping over her husband. She held out a baby. "Don't let the Coalition take him away. Please."

The baby was warm, soft, smiling. Rusel automatically reached out. But he stopped himself cold. Then he turned away.

The woman continued to call after him, but he didn't let himself think about it. *How could I do that? I'm no longer human,* he thought. He pushed into his car, slammed shut the door, and stabbed a preset routine into the control panel.

The car ripped itself away from the airlock interface, ignoring all safety protocols, and began to haul itself on its bubble wheels up the ramp from the under-the-ice habitat to the surface. Shaking, Rusel opened his visor. He might be able to see the doomed family at the airlock port. He didn't look back.

It wasn't supposed to be like this.

Andres's Virtual head coalesced before him. "Sixteen minutes to get to Ship Three. If you're not there we go without you. Fifteen forty-five. Fifteen forty . . ."

The surface was almost as chaotic as the corridors of the hab, as transports of all types and ages rolled, crawled or jumped. There was no sign of the Guardians, the Pharaohs' police force, and he was apprehensive about being held up.

He made it through the crowd, and headed for the track that would lead through the Forest of Ancestors to Ship Three. Out here there was a lot of traffic, but it was more or less orderly, everyone heading out the way he was. He pushed the car up to its safety-regulated maximum speed. Even so, he was continually overtaken. Anxiety tore at his stomach.

The Forest, with the placid profiles of the Ancestors glimmering in Sol's low light, looked unchanged from when he had last seen it, only days ago, on his way to meet Lora. He felt an unreasonable resentment that he had suddenly lost so much time, that his careful plan for an extended farewell to Lora had been torn up. He wondered where she was now. Perhaps he could call her.

Thirteen minutes. No time, no time.

The traffic ahead was slowing. The vehicles at the back of the queue weaved, trying to find gaps, and bunched into a solid pack.

Rusel punched his control panel and brought up a Virtual overhead image. Ahead of the tangle of vehicles, a ditch had been cut roughly across the road. People swarmed, hundreds of them. Roadblock.

Eleven minutes. For a moment his brain seemed as frozen as the Port Sol ice; frantic, bewildered, filled with guilt, he couldn't think.

Then a heavy-duty long-distance truck broke out of the pack behind him. Veering off the road to the left, it began to smash its way through the Forest. The elegant eightfold forms of the Ancestors were nothing but ice sculptures, and they shattered before the truck's momentum. It was ugly, and Rusel knew that each impact wiped out a life that might have lasted centuries more. But the truck was clearing a path.

Rusel hauled at his controls, and dragged his car off the road. Only a few vehicles were ahead of him in the truck's destructive wake. The truck was moving fast, and he was able to push his speed higher.

They were already approaching the roadblock, he saw. A few suit lights moved off the road and into the Forest; the blockers must be enraged to see their targets evade them so easily. Rusel kept his speed high. Only a few more seconds and he would be past the worst.

But there was a figure standing directly in front of him, helmet lamp bright, dressed in an electric-blue skinsuit, arms raised. As the car's sensors picked up the figure, its safety routines cut in, and he felt it hesitate. *Nine minutes.* He slammed his palm to the control panel, overriding the safeties.

He closed his eyes as the car hit the protester.

He remembered the blue skinsuit. He had just mown down the man from the airlock, who had been so desperate to save his family. He had no right to criticize the courage or the morals or the loyalty of others, he saw. *We are all just animals, fighting to survive. My seat on Ship Three doesn't make me any better.* He hadn't even had the guts to watch.

Eight minutes. He disabled the safety governors and let the car race down the empty road, its speed ever increasing.

He had to pass through another block before he reached Ship Three—but this one was manned by Guardians. At least they were still loyal. They were an orderly line across the road, dressed in their bright yellow skinsuit-uniforms. Evidently they had pulled back to tight perimeters around the five Ships.

The queuing was agonizing. With only five minutes before Andres's deadline, a Guardian pressed a nozzle to the car's window, flashed laser light into Rusel's face, and waved him through.

Ship Three was directly ahead of him. It was a drum, a squat cylinder about a kilometer across and half as tall. It sat at the bottom of its own crater, for Port Sol ice had been gouged out and plastered roughly over the surface of its hull. It looked less like a ship than a building, he thought, a building coated by thick ice, as if long abandoned. But it was indeed a star-ship, a ship designed for a journey of not less than centuries, and fountains of crystals already sparkled around its base in neat parabolic arcs: steam from the Ship's rockets, freezing immediately to ice. People milled at its base, running clumsily in the low gravity, and scurried up ramps that tongued down from its hull to the ground.

Rusel abandoned the car, tumbled out onto the ice and ran toward the nearest ramp. There was another stomach-churning wait as a Guardian in glowing yellow checked each identity. At last, after another dazzling flash of laser light in his eyes, he was through.

He hurried into an airlock. As it cycled it struck him that as he boarded this Ship, he was never going to leave it again: whatever became of him, this Ship was his whole world, for the rest of his life.

The lock opened. He ripped open his helmet. The light was emergency red, and klaxons sounded throughout the ship; the air was cold, and smelled of fear. Lethe, he was aboard! But there could only be a minute left. He ran along a cold, ice-lined corridor toward a brighter interior.

He reached an amphitheater, roughly circular, carpeted by acceleration couches. People swarmed, looking for spare couches. The scene seemed absurd to Rusel, like a children's game. Andres's voice boomed from the air. "Get into a couch. Any couch. It doesn't matter. Forty seconds. Strap yourself in. Nobody is going to do it for you. Your safety is your own responsibility. Twenty-five seconds."

"Rus! Rusel!" Through the throng, Rusel made out a waving hand. It was Diluc, his brother, wearing his characteristic orange skinsuit. "Lethe, I'm glad to see you. I kept you a couch. Come on!"

Rusel pushed that way. Ten seconds. He threw himself down on the couch. The straps were awkward to pull around the bulk of his suit.

As he fumbled, he stared up at a Virtual display that hovered over his head. It was a view as seen from the Ship's blunt prow, looking down. Those tongue ramps were still in place, radiating down to the ice. But now a dark mass boiled around the base of the curving hull: people, on foot and in vehicles, a mob of them closing in. In amongst the mass were specks of bright yellow. Some of the Guardians had turned on their commanders, then. But others stood firm, and in that last second Rusel saw the bright sparks of weapon fire, all around the base of the Ship.

A sheet of brilliant white gushed out from the Ship's base. It was Port Sol ice, superheated to steam at tens of thousands of degrees. The image shuddered, and Rusel felt a quivering, deep in his gut. The Ship was rising, right on time, its tremendous mass raised on a bank of rockets.

When that great splash of steam cleared, Rusel saw small dark forms lying motionless on the ice: the bodies of the loyal and disloyal alike, their lives ended in a fraction of a second. A massive shame descended on Rusel, a synthesis of all the emotions that had churned through him since that fateful call of Diluc's. He had abandoned his lover to die; he had probably killed others himself; and now he sat here in safety as others died on the ice below. What human being would behave that way? He felt the shame would never lift, never leave him.

Already the plain of ice was receding, and weight began to push at his chest.

––––––––––

Soon the other Ships were lost against the stars, and it was as if Ship Three was alone in the universe.

In this opening phase of its millennial voyage Ship Three was nothing more than a steam rocket, as its engines steadily sublimated its plating of ice and hurled it out of immense nozzles. But those engines drew on energies that had once powered the expansion of the universe itself. Later the Ship would spin up for artificial gravity and switch to an exotic ramjet for its propulsion, and its true journey would begin.

The heaviest acceleration of the whole voyage had come in the first hours, as the Ship hurled itself away from Port Sol. After that the acceleration was cut to about a third standard—twice lunar gravity, twice what the colonists of Port Sol had been used to. For the time being, the acceleration couches were left in place in that big base amphitheater, and in the night watches everybody slept there, all two hundred of them massed together in a single vast dormitory, their muscles groaning against the ache of the twice-normal gravity.

The plan was that for twenty-one days the Ships would run in toward the puddle of light that was Sol system. They would penetrate as far as the orbit of Jupiter, where they would use the giant planet's gravity field to slingshot them on to their final destinations. It seemed paradoxical to begin the exodus by hurling oneself deep into the inner system, the Coalition's home territory. But space was big, the Ships' courses had been plotted to avoid the likely trajectory of the incoming Coalition convoy, and they were to run silently, not even communicating with each other. The chances of them being detected were negligible.

Despite the wearying gravity the first days after launch were busy for everybody. The Ship's interior had to be rebuilt from its launch configuration to withstand this high-acceleration cruise phase. And the daily routines of the long voyage began.

The Ship was a closed environment and its interior had plenty of smooth surfaces where biofilms, slick detergent-proof cities of bugs, would quickly build up. Not only that, the fall-out of the Ship's human cargo—flakes of skin, hair, mucus—were all seed beds for bacterial growth. All of this had to be eliminated; Captain Andres declared she wanted the Ship to be as clean as a hospital.

The most effective way to achieve that—and the most "future-proof," in Andres's persistent jargon—was through the old-fashioned application of human muscle. Everybody had to pitch in, even the Captain herself. Rusel put in his statutory half-hour per day, scrubbing vigorously at the walls and floors and ceilings around the nanofood banks that were his primary responsibility. He welcomed the mindlessness of the work; he continued to seek ways in which to distract himself from the burden of thought.

He was briefly ill. In the first couple of weeks, everybody caught colds from everybody else. But the viruses quickly ran their course through the Ship's small population, and Rusel felt obscurely reassured that he would likely never catch another cold in his life.

A few days after launch Diluc came to find him. Rusel was up to his elbows in slurry, trying to find a fault in a nanofood bank's waste vent. Rusel, working non-stop, had seen little of his brother. He was surprised by how cheerful Diluc appeared, and how energetically he threw himself into his own work on the air cycling systems. He spoke brightly of his "babies," fans and pumps, humidifiers and dehumidifiers, filters and scrubbers and oxygenators.

The crew seemed to be dividing into two rough camps, Rusel thought. There were those who were behaving as if the outside universe didn't exist; they were bright, brash, too loud, their laughter forced. The other camp, to which Rusel felt he belonged, retreated the other way, into an inner darkness, full of complicated shadows.

But today Diluc's mood seemed complex. "Brother, have you been counting the days?"

"Since launch? No." He hadn't wanted to think about it.

"It's day seven. There's a place to watch. One of the observation lounges. Captain Andres says it's not compulsory, but if . . ."

It took Rusel a moment to think that through. *Day seven*: the day the Coalition convoy was due to reach Port Sol. Rusel flinched from the thought. But one of his worst moments of that chaotic launch day was when he had run down that desperate father and driven on, without even having the courage to watch what he was doing. Perhaps this would atone. "Let's do it," he said.

Ship Three, like its four siblings, was a fat torus. To reach the observation lounge the brothers had to ride elevators up through several decks to a point in the Ship's flattened prow, close to the rim. The lounge, crammed with Virtual generation gear, was already configured for the spin-up phase, and most of its furniture was plastered to the walls, which would become the floor. It was big enough for maybe fifty people, and it was nearly full; Rusel and Diluc had to crowd in.

Pharaoh Andres—now Captain Andres, Rusel reminded himself—was here, sitting in a deep, heavy-looking chair, front and center before an immense, shining Virtual.

A ball of ice spun grandly before their eyes. It was Port Sol, of course; Rusel immediately recognized its icy geography of ancient craters, overlaid by a human patterning of quarries and mines, habitats and townships, landing ports. In the inhabited buildings lights shone, defiantly bright in outer-system gloom. It was a sculpture in white and silver, and it showed no sign of the chaotic panic that must be churning in its corridors.

The sight took Rusel's breath away. Somewhere down there was Lora; it was an almost unbearable thought, and he wished with all his heart he had stayed with her.

The Coalition convoy closed in.

Its ships materialized from the edge of the three-dimensional image, as if sliding in from another reality. The fleet was dominated by five, six, seven Spline warships, living ships each a kilometer or more wide. Confiscated from the expelled Qax, they were fleshy spheres, their hulls studded with weapons and sensors and crudely scrawled with the green tetrahedron that was the sigil of a free humanity.

Rusel's stomach filled with dread. "It's a heavy force," he said.

"They've come for the Pharaohs," Diluc said grimly. "The Coalition is showing its power. Images like this are no doubt being beamed throughout the system."

Then it began. The first touch of the energy beams, cherry-red, was almost gentle, and Port Sol ice exploded into cascades of glittering shards that drifted back to the surface, or escaped into space. Then more beams ploughed up the ice, and structures began to implode, melting, or to fly apart. A spreading cloud of crystals that began to swathe Port Sol in a temporary, pearly atmosphere. It was silent, almost beautiful, too large-scale to make out individual deaths, a choreography of energy and destruction.

"We'll get through this," Diluc muttered. "We'll get through this."

Rusel felt numbed, no grief, only shame at his own inadequacy. This was the destruction of his home, of a world, and it was beyond his imagination. He tried to focus on one person, on Lora, to imagine what she must be doing—if she was still alive—perhaps fleeing through collapsing tunnels, or crowding into deep shelters. But, in the ticking calm of this lounge, with its fresh smell of new equipment, he couldn't even picture that.

As the assault continued, numbers flickered across the status display, an almost blasphemous tallying of the estimated dead.

Even after the trauma of Port Sol, work had to continue on booting up the vital systems that would keep them all alive.

Rusel's own job, as he suddenly found himself the senior nanochemist on the Ship, was to set up the nanofood banks that would play a crucial part in recycling waste into food and other consumables like clothing. The work was demanding from the start. The banks were based on an alien technology, nanodevices purloined from the occupying Qax. Only partially understood, they were temperamental and difficult.

It didn't help that of the two assistants he had been promised a share of—most people were generalists in this small, skill-starved new community—only one had made it onto the Ship. It turned out that in the final scramble about ten percent of the crew hadn't made it aboard; conversely, about ten percent of those who actually were aboard shouldn't have been here at all. A few shame-faced "passengers" were yellow-uniformed Guardians who in the last moments had abandoned their posts and fled to the sanctuary of the Ship's interior.

The work had to get done anyhow. And it was urgent; until the nanofood was available the Ship's temporary rations were steadily depleting. The pressure on Rusel was intense. But Rusel was glad of the work, so hard mentally and physically in the high gravity he had no time to think, and when he hit his couch at night he slept easily.

On the fifteenth day Rusel achieved a small personal triumph as the first slab of edible food rolled out of his nanobanks.

Captain Andres had a policy of celebrating small achievements, and she was here as Rusel ceremoniously swallowed the first mouthful of his food, and she took the second. There was much clapping and backslapping. Diluc grinned in his usual huge way. But Rusel, still numbed inside, didn't feel much like celebrating. Half the crew, it was estimated, were in some kind of shock; people understood. He got away from the crush as quickly as he could.

On the twenty-first day the Ship was to encounter Jupiter.

Captain Andres called the crew together in the acceleration-couch amphitheater, all two hundred of them, and she set up a Virtual display in the air above them. The sun was just a pinpoint, though much brighter than seen from Port Sol, and Jupiter was a flattened ball of cloud, mottled with grey-brown bruises—the result, it was said, of an ancient battle. Few of the crew had travelled away from Port Sol before; they craned to see.

The most intriguing sight of all was four sparks of light that slid across the background of stars. They were the other Ships, numbers One, Two, Four and Five; the little fleet would come together at Jupiter for the first time since leaving Port Sol, and the last.

Andres walked through the crowd on their couches, declaiming loudly enough for all to hear, her authority easy and unforced. "We Pharaohs have been discussing destinations," she said. "Obviously the targets had to be chosen before we reached Jupiter; we needed to plan for our angles of emergence from Jupiter's gravity well. The Coalition is vindictive and determined, and it has faster-than-light ships. It will soon overtake us—but space is big, and five silent-running generation starships will be hard to spot. Even so, it's obviously best to separate, to give them five targets to chase, not just one.

"So we have five destinations. And ours," she said, smiling, "is the most unique of all."

She listed the other Ships' targets, star systems scattered through the disc of the Galaxy—none closer than five hundred light-years. "All well within the Ships' design parameters," she said, "and perhaps far enough to be safe. But *we* are going further."

She overlaid the image of the shining Ships with a ruddy, shapeless mass of mist. "This is the Canis Major Dwarf Galaxy," she said. "Twenty-four thousand light-years from Sol. It is the closest of the satellite galaxies—*but it is beyond the main Galaxy itself*, surely far outside the Coalition's grasp for the foreseeable future."

Rusel heard gasps throughout the amphitheater. To sail beyond the Galaxy?

Andres held her hands up to quell the muttering. "Of course, such a journey is far in excess of what we planned. No generation starship has ever challenged such distances before, let alone achieved them." She stared around at them, fists on hips. "But if we can manage a thousand years of flight, we can manage ten, or fifty—why not? We are strong, we are just as determined as the Coalition and its drones—more so, for we know we are in the right."

Rusel wasn't used to questioning the Pharaohs' decisions, but he found himself wondering at the arrogance of the handful of Pharaohs to make such decisions on behalf of their crew—not to mention the generations yet unborn.

But Diluc muttered, "Can't say it makes much difference. A thousand years or ten thousand, I'll be dead in a century, and *I* won't see the end . . ."

Andres restored the images of the ships. Jupiter was expanding rapidly now, and the other Ships were swarming closer.

Andres said, "We have discussed names for our vessels. On such an epic voyage numbers won't do. Every ship must have a name! We have named our Ship-homes for great thinkers, great vessels of the past." She stabbed her finger around the Virtual image. *"Tsiolkovsky. Great Northern. Aldiss. Vanguard."* She looked at her crew. "And as for us, only one name is possible. Like a band of earlier pilgrims, we are fleeing intolerance and tyranny; we sail into the dark and the unknown, carrying the hopes of an age. We are *Mayflower."*

You didn't study history on Port Sol. Nobody knew what she was talking about.

At the moment of closest approach Jupiter's golden-brown cloudscape bellied over the upturned faces of the watching crew, and the Ships poured through Jupiter's gravity well. Even now the rule of silence wasn't violated, and the five Ships parted without so much as a farewell message.

From now on, wherever this invisible road in the sky took her, the second *Mayflower* was alone.

———

As the days stretched to weeks, and the weeks to months, Rusel continued to throw himself into work—and there was plenty of it for everybody.

The challenges of running a generation starship were familiar to some extent, as the colonists of Port Sol had long experience in ecosynthesis, in constructing and sustaining closed artificial environments. But on Port Sol they had had the ice, rock and organic-chemistry resources of the ice moon itself to draw on. The Ship was now cut off from the outside universe.

So the cycles of air, water and solids would have to be maintained with something close to a hundred percent efficiency. The control of trace contaminants and pests would have to be ferociously tight: swarms of nanobots were sent scurrying in pursuit of flakes of hair and skin. And the sealing of the Ship against leakages was vital—more nanomachines labored to knit together the hull.

Not only that, the Ship's design had been hastily thrown together, and the vessel wasn't even completed on launch. The construction had been a hurried project anyhow, and the shaving-off of those final ten or twelve days of preparation time, as the Coalition fleet sneaked up in the dark, had made a significant difference. The crew labored to complete the Ship's systems in flight.

The most significant difficulty, Rusel believed, was the sudden upping of the design targets. A thousand-year cruise, the nominal design envelope, was one thing. Now it was estimated that, cruising at about half light speed, it would take Ship Three *fifty times* as long to reach Canis Major. Even relativistic time dilation would only make a difference of a few percent to the subjective duration. As a consequence the tolerances on the Ship's systems were tightened by orders of magnitude.

There was yet another goal in all this rebuilding. The Ship's essential systems were to be simplified and automated as far as possible, to reduce the skill level required to maintain them. They were trying to "future-proof" the project, in Andres's jargon: to reduce the crew to the status of nonproductive payload. But a key lesson of ecosynthesis was that the smaller the biosphere, the more conscious control it would require. The Ship was a much smaller environment than a Port Sol habitat, and that presented problems of stability; the ecological system was poorly buffered and would always be prone to collapse. It was clear that this small, tight biosphere would always have to be consciously managed if it were to survive.

As Diluc put it with grim humor, "We can't allow civilization to fall in here."

Despite the horror of Port Sol, and the daunting timescale Andres had set—which Rusel suspected nobody believed anyhow—the rhythms of human life continued. It was as if they were all slowly healing, Rusel thought.

Diluc found a new partner, a plump, cheerful woman of about thirty called Tila. Diluc and Tila had both left lovers behind on Port Sol—and Tila had been forced to abandon a child. Now they seemed to be finding comfort with each other. Diluc was somewhat put out when they were both hauled into Andres's small private office to be quizzed about their relationship, but Andres, after much consulting of genetic maps, approved their continuing liaison.

Rusel was pleased for his brother, but he found Tila a puzzle. Most of the selected crew had been without offspring, back on Port Sol; few people with children, knowing they would have to leave them behind, had even offered themselves for selection. But *Tila had abandoned a child*. He saw no sign of this loss in her face, her manner; perhaps her new relationship with Diluc, and even the prospect of more children with him in the future, was enough to comfort her. He wondered what was going on inside her head, though.

As for Rusel, his social contacts were restricted to work. He found himself being subtly favored by Captain Andres, along with a number of others of the Ship's senior technicians. There was no formal hierarchy on the Ship—no command structure below Andres herself. But this group of a dozen or so, a meritocracy selected purely by proven achievement, began to coalesce into a kind of governing council of the Ship.

That was about as much social life as Rusel wanted. Otherwise he just worked himself to the point of exhaustion, and slept. The complex mass of emotions lodged inside him—agony over the loss of Lora, the shock of seeing his home destroyed, the shame of living on—showed no signs of breaking up. None of this affected his contributions to the Ship, he believed. He was split in two, split between inside and out, and he doubted he would ever heal.

In fact he didn't really want to heal. One day he would die, as so many others had, as Lora probably had; one day he would atone for his sin of survival in death.

Meanwhile there was always the Ship. He slowly widened the scope of his work, and began to develop a feel for the Ship as a whole. As the systems embedded, it was as if the Ship were slowly coming alive, and he learned to listen to the rhythm of its pumps, feel the sighing of its circulating air.

Though Andres continued to use the fanciful name she had given it, Rusel and everybody else thought of it as they always had: as Ship Three— or, increasingly, just the Ship.

————

Almost a year after Jupiter, Andres called her "council" together in the amphitheater at the base of the Ship. This big chamber had been stripped of its acceleration couches, and the dozen or so of them sat on temporary chairs in the middle of an empty grey-white floor.

Andres told them she wanted to discuss a little anthropology.

In her characteristic manner she marched around the room, looming over her crew. "We've had a good year, for which I thank you. Our work on the Ship isn't completed—in a sense it never will be completed—but I'm now satisfied that *Mayflower* will survive the voyage. If we fail in our mission, it won't be the technology that betrays us, but the people. And that's what we've got to start thinking about now."

Mayflower was a generation starship, she said. By now mankind had millennia of experience of launching such ships. "And as far as we know, every last one of them has failed. And why? Because of the people.

"The most basic factor is population control. You'd think that would be simple enough! The Ship is an environment of a fixed size. As long as every parent sires one kid, on average, the population ought to stay stable. But by far the most common causes of failure are population crashes, in which the number of crew falls below the level of a viable gene pool and then shuffles off to extinction—or, more spectacularly, explosions in which people eat their way to the hull of their ship and then destroy each other in the resulting wars."

Diluc said dryly, "Maybe all that proves it's just a dumb idea. The scale is just too big for us poor saps to manage."

Andres gazed at him challengingly. "A bit late to say that now, Diluc!"

"Of course it's not just numbers but our population's genetic health that we have to think about," pointed out Ruul. This lanky, serious man was the Ship's senior geneticist. "We've already started, of course. All of us went through genetic screening before we were selected. There are only two hundred of us, but we're as genetically diverse a sample of Port Sol's population as possible. We should avoid the founder effect—none of us has a genetically-transmitted disease to be spread through the population—and, provided we exert some kind of control over breeding partnerships, we should be able to avoid genetic drift, where defective copies of a gene cluster."

Diluc looked faintly disgusted. "'Control over breeding partnerships?' What kind of language is that?"

Andres snapped, "The kind of language we're going to have to embrace if we're to survive. We must take control of reproductive strategies. Remember, on this Ship the purpose of having children is not for the joy of it and similar primate reward, but to maintain the crew's population levels and genetic health, and thereby to see through our mission." She eyed Diluc. "Oh, I'm not against comfort. I was human once! But we are going to have to separate companionship needs from breeding requirements." She glanced around. "I'm sure you are all smart enough to have figured that out for yourselves. But even this isn't enough, if the mission is to be ensured."

Diluc said, "It isn't?"

"Of course not. This is a desperately small universe. We will always rely on the ship's systems, and mistakes or deviances will be punished by catastrophe—for as long as the mission lasts. Nonmodified human lifespans average out at around a century; we just haven't evolved to think further. But a century is but a moment for our mission. *We must future-proof,* I've said it over and over. And to do that we will need a continuity of memory, purpose and control far beyond the century-long horizons of our transients."

Transients: it was the first time Rusel had heard her use that word.

He thought he saw where all this was leading. He said carefully, "Port Sol was not a normal human society. With respect. Because it had you Pharaohs at its heart."

"Yes," she said approvingly, her small face expressionless. "And *that* is the key." She lifted her hand before her face and inspected it. "Two centuries ago the Qax Governor made me ageless. Well, I served the Qax—but my deeper purpose was always to serve mankind. I fled to Port Sol, with others, to escape the Qax; and now I have had to flee Sol system itself to escape my fellow human beings. But I continue to serve mankind. And it is the continuity I provide, a continuity that transcends human timescales, which will enable this mission to succeed, where even Michael Poole failed."

Diluc pulled a face. "What do you want from us—to worship you as a god?"

There were gasps; you didn't speak to a Pharaoh like that. But Andres seemed unfazed. "A god? No—although a little awe from you wouldn't come amiss, Diluc. And anyhow, it probably won't be *me*. Remember, it wasn't a human agency that gave me my anti-ageing treatments, but the Qax . . ."

The Qax's own body architecture had nothing in common with humanity's. They were technically advanced, but their medicinal manipulation of their human subjects was always crude.

"The success rate was only ever some forty percent," Andres said. She inspected her hand, pulling at slack skin. "Oh, I would dearly love to live through this mission, all fifty millennia of it, and see it through to its conclusion. But I fear that's unlikely to happen." She gazed around at them. "I can't do this alone; that's the bottom line. I will need help."

Diluc suddenly saw it, and his mouth dropped open. "You aren't serious."

"I'm afraid so. It is necessary for the good of the mission that *some of the people in this room do not die.*"

Ruul the geneticist unfolded his tall frame from his chair. "We believe it's possible. We have the Qax technology." Without drama, he held up a yellow pill.

There was a long silence.

Andres smiled coldly. "We can't afford to die. We must remember, while everybody else forgets.

"And we must manage. We must achieve *total* social control—total over every significant aspect of our crew's lives—and we must govern their children's lives just as tightly, as far as we can see ahead. Society has to be as rigid as the bulkheads which contain it. Oh, we can give the crew freedom within limits! But we need to enforce social arrangements in which conflict is reduced to negligible, appropriate skill levels kept up—and, most importantly, a duty of maintenance of the Ship is hammered home into every individual at birth."

Rusel said, "And what about the rights of those you call the transients? We Pharaohs would be taking away all meaningful choice from them—and their children, and their children's children."

"Rights? Rights?" She loomed over him. "Rusel, a transient's only purpose is to live, reproduce, and die in an orderly fashion, thus preserving her genes to the far future. There is no room on this Ship for democracy, no space for love! A transient is just a conduit for her genes. She has no rights, any more than a bit of pipe that carries water from source to sink. Surely you thought this through. When we get to Canis Major, when we find a world to live on, when again we have an environment of surplus—then we can talk about rights. But in the meantime we will control." Her expression was complex. "But you must see that we will control through love."

Diluc gaped. *"Love?"*

"The Qax technology was based on a genetic manipulation, you know. We Pharaohs were promised that our gift would be passed on to our children. And we had those children! But we Pharaohs never bred true. I once had a child myself. She did not survive." She hesitated, just for a second. Then she went on, "But by now there are genes for immortality, or at least longevity, scattered through the human population—even among *you*. Do you see now why we had to build these arks—why we couldn't flee and abandon you, or just take frozen zygotes or eggs?" She spread her hands wide. "Because you are my children, and I love you."

Nobody moved. Rusel thought he could see tears in her stony eyes. *She is grotesque*, he thought.

Diluc said carefully, "Pharaoh, would I be able to bring Tila with me? And our children, if we have them? "

"I'm sorry," she said gently. "Tila doesn't qualify. Besides, the social structure simply wouldn't be sustainable if—"

"Then count me out." Diluc stood up.

She nodded. "I'm sure you won't be the only one. Believe me, this is no privilege I'm offering you."

Diluc turned to Rusel. "Brother, are you coming with me?"

Rusel closed his eyes. The thought of his eventual death had actually been a comfort to him—a healing of his inner wounds, a lifting of the guilt he knew he would carry throughout his life. Now even the prospect of death was being taken away, to be replaced by nothing but an indefinite extension of duty.

But he had to take it on, he saw. As Lora herself had told him, he had to live on, like a machine, and fulfil his function. That was why he was here; only that way could he atone.

He looked up at Diluc. "I'm sorry," he said.

Complex emotions crossed his brother's face: anger, despair, perhaps a kind of thwarted love. He turned and left the room.

Andres behaved as if Diluc had never existed.

"We will always have to combat cultural drift," she said. "It is the blight of the generation starship. Already we have some pregnancies; soon we will have the first children, who will live and die knowing nothing but this Ship. And in a few generations—well, you can guess the rest. First you forget where you're going. Then you forget you're going anywhere. Then you forget you're on a damn ship, and start to think the vessel is the whole universe. And so forth! Soon nothing is left but a rotten apple full of worms, falling through the void. Even the great engineer Michael Poole suffered this; a fifteen-hundred-year generation starship he designed—the first *Great Northern*—barely limped home. Oh, every so often you might have a glorious moment as some cannibalistic savage climbs the decks and peers out in awe at the stars, but that's no consolation for the loss of the mission.

"Well, not this time. You engineers will know we're almost at the end of our GUTdrive cruise phase; the propellant ice is almost exhausted. And that means the Ship's hull is exposed." She clapped her hands—and, to more gasps from the crew, the amphitheater's floor suddenly turned transparent.

Rusel was seated over a floor of stars; something inside him cringed.

Andres smiled at their reaction. "Soon we will leave the plane of the Galaxy, and what a sight *that* will be. In a transparent hull our crew will never be able to forget they are on a Ship. There will be no conceptual breakthroughs on *my* watch!"

———

With the ice exhausted, the Ship's banks of engines were shut down. From now on a dark matter ramjet would provide a comparatively gentle but enduring thrust.

Dark matter constituted most of the universe's store of mass, with "light matter"—the stuff of bodies and ships and stars—a mere trace. The key advantage of dark matter for the Ship's mission planners was that it was found in thick quantities far beyond the visible disc of the Galaxy, and would be plentiful throughout the voyage. But dark matter interacted with the light only through gravity. So now invisible wings of gravitational force unfolded ahead of the Ship. Spanning thousands of kilometers, these acted as a scoop to draw dark matter into the hollow center of the torus-shaped Ship. There, concentrated, much of it was annihilated and induced to give up its mass-energy, which in turn drove a residuum out of the Ship as reaction mass.

Thus the Ship ploughed on into the dark.

Once again the Ship was rebuilt. The acceleration provided by the dark matter ramjet was much lower than the ice rockets, and so the Ship was spun about its axis, to provide artificial gravity through centrifugal force. It was an ancient solution and a crude one—but it worked, and ought to require little maintenance in the future.

The spin-up was itself a spectacular milestone, a great swiveling as floors became walls and walls became ceilings. The transparent floor of the acceleration-couch amphitheater became a wall full of stars, whose cool emptiness Rusel rather liked.

Meanwhile the new "Elders," the ten of them who had accepted Andres's challenge, began their course of treatment. The procedure was administered by geneticist Ruul and a woman called Selur, the Ship's senior doctor. The medics took it slowly enough to catch any adverse reactions, or so they hoped.

For Rusel it was painless enough, just injections and tablets, and he tried not to think about the alien nanoprobes embedding themselves in his system, cleaning out ageing toxins, repairing cellular damage, rewiring his very genome.

His work continued to be absorbing, and when he had spare time he immersed himself in studies. All the crew were generalists to some degree, but the ten new Elders were expected to be a repository of memory and wisdom far beyond a human lifespan. So they all studied everything, and they learned from each other.

Rusel began with the disciplines he imagined would be most essential in the future. He studied medicine; anthropology, sociology and ethics; eco-synthesis and all aspects of the Ship's life support machinery; the workings of the Ship's propulsion systems; techniques of colonization; and the geography of the Galaxy and its satellites. He also buttonholed Andres herself and soaked up her knowledge of human history. Qax-derived nanosystems were so prevalent throughout the Ship that Rusel's own expertise was much in demand.

His major goal continued to be to use up as much of his conscious time as possible with work. The studying was infinitely expandable, and very satisfying to his naturally acquisitive mind. He found he was able to immerse himself in esoteric aspects of one discipline or another for days on end, as if he was an abstract intellect, almost forgetting who he was.

His days passed in a dream, as if time itself flowed differently for him now.

The Elders' placid lives were not without disturbance, however. The Qax biotechnology was far from perfect. In the first year of treatment one man suffered kidney failure; he survived, but had to be taken out of the program.

And it was a great shock to all the Elders when Ruul himself succumbed to a ferocious cancer, as the technological rebuilding of his cells went awry.

The day after Ruul's death, as the Elders adjusted to the loss of his competence and dry humor, Rusel decided he needed a break. He walked out of the Elders' Cloister and into the body of the Ship, heading for the area where his brother had set up his own home with Tila.

On all the Ship's cylindrical decks, the interior geography had been filled by corridors and cabins, clustered in concentric circles around little open plazas—"village squares." Rusel knew the theory, but he quickly got lost; the layout of walls and floors and false ceilings was changed again and again as the crew sorted out their environment.

At last he came to the right doorway on the right corridor. He was about to knock when a boy, aged about five with a shock of thick black hair, rocketed out of the open door and ran between Rusel's legs. The kid wore a bland Ship's-issue coverall, long overdue for recycling judging by its grime.

This must be Tomi, Rusel thought, Diluc's eldest. Child and Elder silently appraised each other. Then the kid stuck out his tongue and ran back into the cabin.

In a moment Diluc came bustling out of the door, wiping his hands on a towel. "Look, what in Lethe's going on—Rusel! It's you. Welcome, welcome!"

Rusel embraced his brother. Diluc smelt of baby sick, cooking, and sweat, and Rusel was shocked to see a streak of grey in his brother's hair. Perhaps he had been locked away longer than he had realized.

Diluc led Rusel into his home. It was a complex of five small interconnected cabins, including a kitchen and bathroom. Somebody had been weaving tapestries; gaudy, space-filling abstract patterns filled one wall.

Rusel sat on a sofa adapted from an acceleration couch, and accepted a slug of some kind of liquor. He said, "I'm sorry I frightened Tomi. I suppose I've let myself become a stranger."

Diluc raised an eyebrow. "Two things about that. Not so much *stranger* as *strange*." He brushed his hand over his scalp.

Rusel involuntarily copied the gesture, and felt bare skin. He had long forgotten that the first side-effect of the Pharaoh treatment had been the loss of his hair; his head was as bald as Andres's. Surrounded all day by the other Elders, Rusel had got used to it, he supposed. He said dryly, "Next time I'll wear a wig. What's the second thing I got wrong?"

"That isn't Tomi. Tomi was our first. He's eight now. That was little Rus, as we call him. He's five."

"*Five?*" But Rusel had attended the baby Rusel's naming ceremony. It seemed like yesterday.

"And now we're due for another naming. We've missed you, Rus."

Rusel felt as if his life was slipping away. "I'm sorry."

Tila came bustling in, with an awestruck little Rus in tow, and an infant in her arms. She too seemed suddenly to have aged; she had put on weight, and her face was lined by fine wrinkles. She said that Tomi was preparing a meal—of course uncle Rusel would stay to eat, wouldn't he?—and she sat down with the men and accepted a drink.

They talked of inconsequentials, and of their lives.

Diluc, having stormed out of Andres's informal council, had become something of a leader in his own new community. Andres had ordered that the two-hundred-strong crew should be dispersed to live in close-knit "tribes" of twenty or so, each lodged in a "village" of corridors and cabins. There were to be looser links between the tribes, used for such purposes as finding partners. Thus the Ship was united in a single "clan." Andres said this social structure was the most common form encountered among humans "in the wild," as she put it, all the way back to pretechnological days on Earth. Whether or not that was true, things had stayed stable so far.

Andres had also specified the kind of government each tribe should aspire to. In such a small world each individual should be cherished for her unique skills, and for the value of the education invested in her. People were interdependent, said Andres, and the way they governed themselves should reflect that. Even democracy wouldn't do, as in a society of valued individuals the subjection of a minority to the will of a majority must be a bad thing. So Diluc's tribe ran by consensus.

"We talk and talk," Diluc said with a rueful grin, "until we all agree. Takes hours, sometimes. Once, the whole of the night watch—"

Tila snorted. "Don't tell me you don't like it that way. You always did like the sound of your own voice!"

The most important and difficult decisions the tribe had to make concerned reproduction. Most adults settled down into more-or-less monogamous marriages. But there had to be a separation between marriages for companionship and liaisons for reproduction; the gene pool was too small to allow matings for such trivial reasons as love.

Diluc showed Rusel a draft of a "social contract" he was preparing to capture all this. "First, on reaching adulthood you submit yourself to the needs of the group as a whole. For instance, your choice of career depends on what we need as much as what you want to do. Second, you agree to have kids only as the need allows. If we're short of the optimum, you might have three or four or five, whether you want them or not, to bring up the numbers; if we're over, you might have none at all and die childless. Third, you agree to postpone parenthood as long as possible, and to keep working as long as possible. That way you maximize the investment the tribe has made in educating you. Fourth, you can select your own breeding-spouse, who *may* be the same as your companionship-spouse—"

"We were lucky," Tila said fervently.

"But she can't be closer than a second cousin. And you have to submit to having your choice approved by the Elders. That's you," he grinned at Rusel. "Your match will be screened for genetic desirability, to maximize the freshness of the gene pool—all of that. And finally, if despite everything you're unlucky enough to have been born with some inheritable defect that might, if propagated, damage the Ship's chances of completing its mission, you agree not to breed at all. Your genetic line stops with you."

Rusel frowned. "That's eugenics."

Diluc shrugged. "What else can we do?"

Diluc hadn't studied Earth history, and without that perspective, Rusel realized, that word carried none of the horrific connotations it had once borne. As Diluc had implied, they had little choice anyhow given the situation they were in. And anyhow, eugenics was lower-tech than genetic engineering: more future-proofing.

Rusel studied the draft. "And what happens if I break the rules?"

Diluc was uncomfortable; suddenly Rusel was aware that he was an Elder, as well as this man's brother. "We'll cross that bridge when we come to it," Diluc said. "Look, Rus, we don't have police here, and we haven't room for jails. Besides, everybody really is essential to the community as a whole. We can't coerce. We work by persuasion; we hope that such situations will be easily resolved."

Diluc talked of personal things too: of the progress of his boys at school, how Tomi had always hated the hour's wall-cleaning he had to put in each day, while little Rus loved it for the friends he was making.

"They are good kids," Rusel said.

"Yes. And you need to see more of them," Diluc said pointedly. "But, you know, Rus, they're not like us. They are the first Shipborn generation. They are *different.* To them, all our stories of Port Sol and Canis Major are so many legends of places they will never see. This Ship is *their* world, not ours: we, born elsewhere, are aliens here. You know, I keep thinking we've bitten off more than we can chew, for all Andres's planning. Already things are drifting. No wonder generation starships always fail!"

Rusel tried to respond to their openness by giving them something of himself. But he found he had little to say. His mind was full of studying, but there was very little *human* incident in his life. It was if he hadn't been alive at all, he thought with dismay.

Diluc was appalled to hear of Ruul's death. "That pompous geneticist— I suppose in a way it's fitting he should be the first to go. But don't let it take you, brother." Impulsively he crossed to Rusel and rested his hand on his brother's shoulder. "You know, all this is enough for me: Tila, the kids, the home we're building together. It's good to know that our lives serve a higher goal, but *this* is all I need to make me happy. Maybe I don't have much imagination, you think?"

Or maybe you're more human than I am, Rusel thought. "We must all make our choices," he said.

Diluc said carefully, "But you can still make a different choice."

"What do you mean?"

He leaned forward. "Why don't you give it up, Rus? This crappy old Qax nano-medicine, this dreadful anti-ageing—you're still young; you could come out of there, flush the shit out of your system, grow your hair back, find some nice woman to make you happy again . . ."

Rusel tried to keep his face expressionless, but he failed.

Diluc backed off. "Sorry. You still remember Lora."

"I always will. I can't help it."

"We've all been through an extraordinary experience," Tila said. "I suppose we all react differently."

"Yes." Tila, he remembered, had left behind a child.

Diluc looked into his eyes. "You never will come out of that Cloister, will you? Because you'll never be able to cast off that big sack of guilt on your back."

Rusel smiled. "Is it that obvious?"

Tila was a gracious hostess. She perceived his discomfort, and they began to talk of old times, of the days on Port Sol. But Rusel was relieved when Tomi, unreasonably tall, came in to announce that the meal was ready, relieved to hurry through the food and get away, relieved to shut himself away once more in the bloodless monastic calm of the Cloister.

He would remember that difficult visit again, much later, when a boy came to find him.

As time passed, the Elders withdrew from the crew. They requisitioned their own sealed-off living area. It was close to the Ship's axis where the artificial gravity was a little lower than farther out, a sop to muscles and bones expected to weaken with the centuries. Ruul humorously called this refuge the "Cloister." And the Elders were spared the routine chores, even the cleaning, to which the rest of the crew were subject. Soon it was hard to avoid the feeling that the crew were only there to serve the Elders.

Of course it was all part of Andres's grand social design that there should eventually be an "awe gap," as she put it, between Elders and transients. But Rusel wondered if a certain distancing was inevitable anyhow. The differential ageing of transients and Elders became apparent surprisingly quickly. When an Elder met a transient she saw a face that would soon crumble with age and vanish, while the transient saw a mysteriously unchanging figure who would see events that transpired long after the transient was dead. Rusel watched as friendships dissolved, even love affairs evaporated, under this stress.

However the increasingly isolated Elders, thrown on each other's company, were no chummy club. They were all bright, ambitious people; they wouldn't have been filtered out for Andres's inner circle otherwise, and there was always a certain tension and bickering. Doctor Selur remarked sourly that it was like being stuck with a bunch of jealous academics, *forever*.

But the Elders were also cautious of each other, Rusel thought. Always at the back of his mind was the thought that he would have to live with these people for a *long* time. So he strove not to make any enemies—and conversely not to get too close to anyone. Eternity with a lover was one thing, but with an *ex*-lover it would be hellish. Better that things were insipid, but tolerable.

Life settled down. In the calm of the Cloister, time passed smoothly, painlessly.

One day a boy came knocking timorously on the Cloister's door, asking for Rusel. He was aged about sixteen.

Rusel thought he recognized him. He had spent a long time on his own, and his social skills were rusty, but he tried to focus and greet the boy warmly. "Tomi! It's so long since I saw you."

The boy's eyes were round. "My name is Poro, sir."

Rusel frowned. "But that day I came to visit—you made us all a meal, me and Diluc and Tila, while little Rus played . . ." But that was long ago, he told himself, he wasn't sure *how* long, and he fell silent.

The boy seemed to have been prepared for this. "My name is Poro," he said firmly. "Tomi was—"

"Your father."

"My *grand*father."

So this was Diluc's great-grandson. *Lethe, how long have I spent inside this box?*

The boy was looking around the Cloister. His eyes were unblinking, his mouth pulled back in a kind of nervous grin. None of the Elders was hot on empathy, especially with transients, but suddenly Rusel felt as if he saw this place through this child's eyes.

The Cloister was like a library, perhaps. Or a hospital room. The Elders sat in their chairs or walked slowly through the silence of the room, their every step calculated to reduce the risk of harm to their fragile, precious bodies. It had been this way since long before Poro had been born, these musty creatures pursuing their cold interests. *And I, who once loved Lora when she wasn't much older than this child, am part of this dusty stillness.*

"What do you want, Poro?"

"Diluc is ill. He is asking for you."

"Diluc? . . ."

"Your brother."

It turned out that Diluc was more than ill; he was dying.

So Rusel went with the boy, stepping outside the confines of the Cloister for the first time in years.

He wasn't at home out here anymore. The transients among the original crew had died off steadily, following a demographic curve not terribly different to that they would have endured had they been able to remain on Port Sol. Rusel grew used to seeing faces he had known since childhood crumple with age and disappear before him. Still, it had been a shock when that first generation reached old age—and, since many of them had been around the same age at launch, the deaths came in a flood.

Meanwhile, everything about the new sort was *different*, the way they rebuilt the Ship's internal architecture, their manner with each other, the way they wore their hair—even their language, which was full of a guttural slang.

The basic infrastructure of the Ship itself, of course, remained unchanged. In a way he came to identify with that level of reality much more than with the flickering, fast-paced changes wrought by the transients. Though his senses were slowly dulling—the Qax treatment had slowed his ageing but not stopped it entirely—he felt he was becoming more attuned to the Ship's subtle vibrations and noises, its mechanical moods and joys. Transients came and went, and the other Elders were awkward old cusses, but the Ship itself was his constant friend, demanding only his care.

But the transients knew him, of course. They stared at him with curiosity, or irreverence—or, worst of all, awe.

As they walked he saw that the boy had a bruise on his forehead. "What happened to you?"

"Punishment." Poro averted his eyes, ashamed. One of his teachers had whacked him with a ruler for "impudence," which turned out to mean asking too-deep questions.

There was a paradox in the philosophy of education aboard the Ship. The students had to be bright enough to be able to understand and maintain the Ship's systems. But there was no room for expansion or innovation. There was unusually only one way to do things: you learned it that way, and you did *not* tinker. It had been quickly found that education needed to be restrictive, and that curiosity couldn't be allowed to go unchecked; you learned only what you needed to know, and were taught not to ask any more, not to explore.

It was necessary, Rusel knew. But he didn't like the idea of battering students into submission. Perhaps he would have a word with Andres about it, get a new policy formulated.

They reached Diluc's corridor-village and came to a familiar doorway.

Tila was still alive, though she was bent, her hair exploded to white, and her face crushed to a wrinkled mask. "Thank you for coming," she whispered, and she took Rusel's hands in her own. "There are so few of us left, you know, so few not Shipborn. And he did keep asking for you."

Rusel pressed her hand, reserved, awkward. He felt out of practice with people, with emotions; before this broken-hearted woman he felt utterly inadequate.

Before he could see his brother he had to be met by a series of tribe worthies. Burly men and women in drab Ship's-issue clothing, they gathered with solemn expressions. The greetings were lengthy and complicated. The transients were evolving elaborate rituals to be used on every social occasion: meeting, parting, taking meals. Rusel could see the value of such rituals, which used up time, and reduced social friction. But it was hard to keep up with the ever-changing rules. The only constant was that these politeness games always got more elaborate—and it was very easy to get something wrong and give offense.

The worthies looked concerned at the prospective loss of Diluc, as well they might.

Andres's imposition of "rule-by-consensus" had been less than effective. In some of the Ship's dozen or so tribes, there was endless jaw-jaw that paralyzed decision-making. Elsewhere strong individuals had begun to grasp power, more or less overtly. Andres wasn't too concerned as long as the job got done, the basic rules obeyed: whoever was in command had to get the approval of the Elders, and so Andres and her team were still able to exert a moderating influence.

The situation in Diluc's tribe had been more subtle, though. As the brother of an Elder he had a unique charisma, and he had used that power subtly to push his peers to conclusions they might not otherwise have reached. He had been a leader, but of the best sort, Rusel thought, leading from the back, invisibly. Now he was about to be taken away, and his people knew they would miss him.

With the worthies out of the way, the Elder was presented to Diluc's children, grandchildren, great-grandchildren. All of them went through more elaborate transient-to-Elder rituals, even the smallest children, with an unsmiling intensity Rusel found disturbing.

At last, with reluctance, he entered Diluc's apartment.

The rooms were much as he remembered them, though the tapestries on the wall had changed. Diluc lay on a bed, covered by a worn blanket. Rusel was shocked by how his brother had imploded with age. And he could see, even through the blanket, the swelling of the stomach tumor that was killing him.

He had thought Diluc was sleeping. But his brother opened one eye. "Hello, Rusel," he said, his voice a croak. "You bastard."

"I'm sorry—"

"You haven't been here in fifty years."

"Not that long."

"Fifty years! *Fifty years!* It's not as if—" He broke up in coughing. "As if it's that big a Ship . . ."

They talked, as they had talked before. Diluc told rambling anecdotes about his grandchildren and great-grandchildren, all properly genetically selected, all wonderful kids.

Rusel spoke of a cull of the Elders.

Diluc grimaced. "So even immortals die." He reached out his hand. Rusel took it; the bones were frail, the flesh almost vanished. "Look after them," Diluc said.

"Who?"

"Everybody. *You* know. And look after yourself." He looked up at his brother, and Rusel saw pity in his brother's eyes—pity for *him*, from a withered, dying man.

He could bear to stay only a few minutes more.

The cull of Elders had had a variety of causes, according to Doctor Selur, but Andres had sniffed at that. "I've seen it before. Call it a death wish," she had said. "You reach an age where your body knows it's time to die. You accept it. Maybe it's some kind of neural programming, a comfort as we face the inevitable." She cackled; she was ageing too, and was now toothless. "The Qax treatments don't do anything about it. And it carries away more would-be immortals than you'd imagine. Strange, isn't it? That longevity should turn out to be a matter of the mind as much as the body."

Rusel had spent some years in faint trepidation, wondering if and when his own dark-seeking mental programming might kick in. But it never did, and he wondered if he had some unsuspected strength—or, perhaps, a deficiency.

Rusel tried to talk over his feelings about Diluc's death. But Andres was dismissive. "Diluc was a coward who shunned his duty," she said. "Anyhow, better when the first crew have all gone. *They* always saw us as peers, to some extent. So they resisted our ideas, our leadership; it was natural. We're totally alien to the new sort, and that will make them more malleable.

"And the new lot never suffered the trauma of seeing Port Sol trashed before their eyes. The psychological trauma ran deep, Rusel; you aren't the only one. . . . This new batch are healthy, adjusted to the environment of the Ship, because they've known nothing else. When there's only them left, we'll be able to get things shaken down properly around here at last. You'll see."

With relief Rusel returned to his studies, away from the complications of humanity. Once more time flowed smoothly past him, and that difficult day receded down the dimming corridors of his memory.

No more relatives came to see him, ever again.

———

". . . Rusel. Rusel!" The voice was harsh—Andres's voice.

Sleep was deep these days, and it took him an age to emerge. And as he struggled into the light he swam up through layers of dream and memory, until he became confused about what was real and what wasn't. He always knew *where* he was, of course, even in his deepest sleep. He was on the Ship, his drifting tomb. But he could never remember *when* he was.

He tried to sit up. The Couch responded to his feeble movements, and its back smoothly lifted him upright. He peered around in the dim, golden light of the Cloister. There were three Couches, great bulky mechanical devices half bed and half medical support system: only three, because only three of the Elders stayed alive.

Somebody was moving around him. It was a transient, of course, a young woman. She kept her eyes averted, and her hands fluttered through an elaborate greetings-with-apology ritual. He dismissed her with a curt gesture; you could eat up your entire day with such flim-flam.

Andres was watching him, her eyes sharp in her ruin of a face. She looked like a huge bug in her cocoon of blankets.

"Well?" he snapped.

"You are drooling," she said mildly. "Not in front of the transients, Rusel."

Irritated, he wiped his chin with his sleeve.

"Oh," she said, her tone unchanged, "and Selur died."

That news, so casually delivered, was like a punch in the throat. He turned clumsily, weighed down by blankets and life-sustaining equipment. The doctor's Couch was surrounded by transients who were removing her mummylike body. They worked in silence, cautiously, reverently. They were trembling, he saw dimly.

"I never did like her much," Rusel said.

"You've said that before. Many times."

"I'll miss her, though."

"Yes. And then there were two. Rusel, we need to talk. We need a new strategy to deal with the transients. We're supposed to be figures of awe. Look at us. Look at poor Selur! We can't let them see us like this again."

He glanced cautiously at the transients.

"Don't worry," Andres said. "They can't understand. Linguistic drift."

"We have to deal with them. We're the top of their pyramid of authority—that's what you've always said."

"So we are, and it has to stay that way. But I don't think we should allow transients in here anymore. The machines can sustain us. Lethe knows there are enough spare parts, now we have so many empty Couches! What I suggest is—"

"Stow it," he said crossly. "You're always the same, you old witch. You always want to jam a solution down my throat before I even know what the problem is. Let me gather my thoughts."

"Stow it, stow it," she parroted, grotesquely.

"Shut up." He closed his eyes to exclude her, and laid back in his couch.

Through the implant in the back of his skull he allowed data from his body, the Ship, and the universe beyond filter into his sensorium.

His body first, of course, the slowly failing biomachinery that had become his prison. The good news was that, more than two centuries after his brother's death, his slow ageing had bottomed out. Since he had last checked—Lethe, all of a month ago, it seemed like yesterday, how long had he slept this time?—nothing had got significantly worse. But he was stuck in the body of a ninety-year-old man, and a frail old man at that. He slept almost all the time, his intervals of lucidity ever more widely separated, while the Couch fed him, removed his waste, gently turned him to and fro and manipulated his stick-thin limbs. Oh, and every few weeks he received a blood transfusion, an offering to the Elders from the grateful transients outside the Cloister. He may as well have been a coma victim, he thought grumpily.

His age was meaningless, his condition boring. Briskly he moved on.

His Virtual viewpoint roamed through the Ship. Despite the passage of centuries, the physical layout of the corridor-village that had been Diluc's was the same, save for detail, the same knots of corridors around the "village square." But the people had changed, as they always did, youth blossoming, old age crumbling.

The Autarch he remembered from his last inspection was still in place. He was a big bruiser who called himself Ruul, in subtle defiance of various inhibitions against taking the name of an Elder, even one long dead. He at least didn't look to have aged much. Flanked by two of his wives, Ruul received a queue of supplicants, all seeking the Autarch's "wisdom" concerning some petty problem or other. Ruul was brisk and efficient, and as Rusel listened—though the time-drifted language was hard to decipher—he couldn't spot any immediate errors of doctrine in the Autarch's summary harshness.

He allowed his point of view to drift on.

He watched the villagers go about their business. Four of them were scrubbing the walls clean of dirt, as they took turns to do every day. Two plump-looking worthies were discussing a matter of etiquette, their mannerisms complex and time-consuming. There were some new bits of artwork on the walls, many of them fool-the-eye depth-perspective paintings, designed to make the Ship's corridors look bigger than they were. One woman was tending a "garden" of bits of waste polymer, combing elaborate formations into it with a small metal rake. These transients, Shipborn for generations, had never heard of Zen gardens; they had rediscovered this small-world art form for themselves.

A little group of children were being taught to disassemble and maintain an air-duct fan; they chanted the names of its parts, learning by rote. They would be taught nothing more, Rusel knew. There was no element of *principle* here: nothing about how the fan as a machine worked, or how it fitted into the greater systems of the Ship itself. You only learned what you needed to know.

Everybody was busy, intent on their affairs. Some even seemed happy. But it all looked drab to Rusel, all the villagers dressed in colorless Ship's-issue clothing, their lives bounded by the polished-smooth bulkheads of the Ship. Even their language was dull, and becoming duller. The transients had no words for *horizon* or *sky*—but as if in compensation they had over forty words describing degrees of love.

As he surveyed the village, statistics rolled past his vision in a shining column. Everything was nominal, if you took a wider perspective. Maintenance routines were being kept up satisfactorily. Reproduction rules, enforced by the Autarch and his peers in the other villages, were largely being adhered to, and there was a reasonable genetic mix.

The situation was stable. But in Diluc's village, only the Autarch was free.

Andres's uncharacteristically naïve dream of respectful communities governing themselves by consensus had barely outlasted the death of Diluc. In the villages strong characters had quickly taken control, and in most cases had installed themselves and their families as hereditary rulers. Andres had grumbled at that, but it was an obviously stable social system, and in the end the Elders, in subtle ways, lent the Autarchs their own mystical authority.

The Autarchs were slowly drifting away from their subject populations, though.

Some "transients" had always proven to be rather longer-lived than others. It seemed that the Qax's tampering with the genomes of their Pharaohs had indeed been passed on to subsequent generations, if imperfectly, and that gene complex, a tendency for longevity, was expressing itself. Indeed the Autarchs actively sought out breeding partners for themselves who came from families that showed such tendencies.

So, with time, the Autarchs and their offspring were ageing more slowly than their transient subjects.

It was just natural selection, argued Andres. People had always acquired power so that their genes could be favored. Traditionally you would do your best to outbreed your subjects. But if you were an Autarch, in the confines of the Ship, what were you to do? There was obviously no room here for a swarm of princes, bastards or otherwise. Besides, the Elders' genetic-health rules wouldn't allow any such thing. So the Autarchs were seeking to dominate their populations with their own long lives, not numbers of offspring.

Andres seemed to find all this merely intellectually interesting. Rusel wondered what would happen if this went on.

He allowed his consciousness to drift back to his own body. When he surfaced, he found Andres watching him, as she so often did.

"So you think we have to change things," he said.

"We need to deal with the Autarchs. Some of them are tough customers, Rusel, and they imagine they're even tougher. If they start to believe we're weak—for instance, if we sleep for three days before delivering the answer to the simplest question—"

"I understand. We can't let the transients see us." He sighed, irritated. "But what else can we do? Delivering edicts through disembodied voices isn't going to wash. If they don't see us they will soon forget who we are." *Soon*, in the language of the Elders, meaning in another generation or two.

"Right," she snapped. "So we have to personalize our authority. What do you think of this?" She gestured feebly, and a Virtual coalesced in the air over her head.

It showed Rusel. Here he was as a young man, up to his elbows in nanofood banks, laboring to make the Ship sound for its long journey. Here he was as a youngish Elder, bald as ice, administering advice to grateful transients. There were even images of him from the vanishingly remote days before the launch, images of him with a smiling Lora.

"Where did you get this stuff?"

She sniffed. "The Ship's log. Your own archive. Come on, Rusel, we hardly have any secrets from each other after all this time! Pretty girl, though."

"Yes. What are you intending to do with this?"

"We'll show it to the transients. We'll show you at your best, Rusel, you at the peak of your powers, you walking the same corridors they walk now—you as a human being, yet *more* than human. That's what we want: engagement with their petty lives, empathy, yet awe. We'll put a face to your voice."

He closed his eyes. It made sense of course; Andres's logic was grim, but always valid. "But why me? It would be better if both of us—"

"That wouldn't be wise," she said. "I wouldn't want them to see me die."

It took him a while to work out that Andres, the first of the Pharaohs, was failing. Rusel found this impossible to take in: her death would be to have a buttress of the universe knocked away. "But you won't see the destination," he said peevishly, as if she was making a bad choice.

"No," she said hoarsely. "But the *Mayflower* will get there! Look around, Rusel. The Ship is functioning flawlessly. Our designed society is stable and doing its job of preserving the bloodlines. And *you*, you were always the brightest of all. You will see it through. That's enough for me."

It was true, Rusel supposed. Her design was fulfilled; the Ship and its crew were working now just as Andres had always dreamed they should. But only two hundred and fifty years had worn away, only *half of one percent* of the awesome desert of time he must cross to reach Canis Major—and now, it seemed, he was going to have to make the rest of that journey alone.

"No, not alone," said Andres. "You'll always have the Ship . . ."

Yes, the Ship, his constant companion. Suddenly he longed to escape from the endless complications of humanity and immerse himself in its huge technological calm. He lay back in his Couch and allowed his mind to roam out through the crowded torus of the hull, and the pulsing ramjet engines, and the wispy gravitational wings behind which the Ship sailed.

He looked back. The Ship had covered only a fraction of its epic journey, but already it was climbing out of the galactic plane, and the Core, the crowded heart of the Galaxy, rose like a sun from the dust-strewn lanes of the spiral arms. It was a stunning, comforting sight.

By the time he came back from his intergalactic dreaming, Andres was gone, her Couch disassembled for spare parts, her body removed to the cycling tanks.

———

Rusel was awakened from his long slumber by the face of a boy, a face twisted with anger—an anger directed at *him*.

In retrospect Rusel should have seen the rebellion coming. All the indicators had been there: the drift of the transients' social structures, the gathering tensions. It was bound to happen.

But it was so hard for him to pay attention to the brief lives of these transients, their incomprehensible language and customs, their petty concerns and squabbling. After all, Hilin was a boy of the forty-fifth generation since launch: *forty-five generations*, Lethe, nearly a thousand years . . .

The exploits of Hilin, though, forced themselves on his attention.

Hilin was sixteen years old when it all began. He had been born in Diluc's corridor-village.

By now the Autarchs of the different villages had intermarried to form a seamless web of power. They lived on average twice as long as their subjects, and had established a monopoly on the Ship's water supply. A water empire ruled by gerontocrats: their control was total.

Hilin was not one of the local Autarch's brood; his family were poor and powerless, like all the Autarch's subjects. But they seemed to accept their lot. As he played in corridors whose polymer floors were rutted by generations of passing feet, Hilin emerged as a bright, happy child. He seemed compliant when he was young, cheerfully joining in swabbing the bulkheads when it was his turn, and accepting the cuffs of his teachers when he asked impudent questions.

He had always been oddly fascinated by the figure of Rusel himself—or rather the semi-mythical presence portrayed to the villagers through the cycling Virtual storyboards. Hilin soaked up the story of the noble Elder who had been forced to choose between a life of unending duty and his beloved Lora, an undying model to those he ruled.

As he had grown, Hilin had flourished educationally. At fourteen he was inducted into an elite caste. As intellectual standards declined, literacy had been abandoned, and these monkish thinkers now committed to memory every significant commandment regarding the workings of the Ship and their own society. You would start on this vital project at fourteen, and wouldn't expect to be done until you were in your fifties, by which time a new generation was ready to take over anyhow.

Rusel dryly called these patient thinkers Druids: he wasn't interested in the transients' own names for themselves, which would change in an eye-blink generation anyhow. He had approved this practice when it emerged. All this endless memorizing was a marvelous way to use up pointless lives— and it established a power-base to rival the Autarchs.

Again Hilin had flourished, and he passed one Druidic assessment after another. Even a torrid romance with Sale, a girl from a neighboring village, didn't distract him from his studies.

When the time came, the couple asked their families for leave to form a companionship-marriage, which was granted. They went to the Autarch for permission to have children. To their delight, it turned out their genetic makeups, as mapped in the Druids' capacious memories, were compatible enough to allow this too.

But even so the Druids forbade the union.

Hilin, horrified, learned that this was because of the results of his latest Druidic assessment, a test of his general intelligence and potential. He had failed, not by posting too low a score, but too *high*.

Rusel, brooding, understood. The eugenic elimination of weaknesses had in general been applied wisely. But under the Autarch-Druid duopoly, attempts were made to weed out the overbright, the curious—anybody who might prove rebellious. Rusel would have stamped out this practice, had he even noticed it. If this went on, the transient population would become passive, listless, easily manipulated by the Autarchs and the Druids, but useless for the mission's larger purposes.

It was too late for Hilin. He was banned from ever seeing his Sale again. And he was told by the Autarch's ministers that this was by order of the Elder himself, though Rusel, dreaming his life away, knew nothing about it.

Hilin spent long hours in the shrine-like enclosure where Rusel's Virtuals played out endlessly. He tried to understand. He told himself the Elder's wisdom surpassed his own; this severance must be for the best, no matter what pain it caused him. He even tried to draw comfort from what he saw as parallels between his own doomed romance and Rusel and his lost Lora. But understanding didn't come, and his bewilderment and pain soon blossomed to resentment—and anger.

In his despair, he tried to destroy the shrine.

As punishment, the Autarch locked him in a cell for two days. Hilin emerged from his confinement outwardly subdued, inwardly ready to explode. Again Rusel would later castigate himself for failing to see the dangers in the situation.

But it was so hard to see anything now.

His central nervous system was slowly deteriorating, so the Couch informed him. He could still move his arms and legs—he could still walk, even, with a frame—but he felt no sensation in his feet, nothing but the faintest ache in his fingertips. As pain and pleasure alike receded, he felt he was coming loose from time itself. When he surfaced into the world of lucidity he would be shocked to find a year had passed like a day, as if his sense of time were becoming logarithmic.

And meanwhile, as he became progressively disconnected from the physical world, his mind was undergoing a reconstruction of its own. After a thousand years his memories, especially the deepest, most precious memories of all, were, like the floors of the Ship's corridors, worn with use; he was no longer sure if he *remembered*, or if he only had left memories of memories.

If he came adrift from both present and past, what was he? Was he even human anymore? Certainly the latest set of transients meant less than nothing to him: why, each of them was made up of the atoms and molecules of her ancestors, cycled through the Ship's systems forty times or more, shuffled and reshuffled in meaningless combinations. They could not touch his heart in any way.

At least he thought so, until Hilin brought him the girl.

The two of them stood before Rusel's Virtual shrine, where they believed the Elder's consciousness must reside. Trying to match the Elder's own timescales they stayed there for long hours, all but motionless. Hilin's face was set, pinched with anger and determination. She, though, was composed.

At last Rusel's drifting attention was snagged by familiarity. It was the girl. She was taller than most of the transients, pale, her bones delicate. And her eyes were large, dark, somehow unfocused even as she gazed into unseen imaging systems.

Lora.

It couldn't be, of course! How could it? Lora had had no family on the Ship. And yet Rusel, half-dreaming, immersed in memory, couldn't take his eyes off her image.

As Hilin had planned.

The uprising occurred all over the Ship. In every village the Autarchs and their families were turned out of their palatial cabins. The Autarchs, having commanded their short-lived flocks for centuries, were quite unprepared, and few resisted; they had no conception such an uprising was even possible. The old rulers and their peculiar children were herded together in a richly-robed mass in the Ship's largest chamber, the upturned amphitheater where Rusel had long ago endured the launch from Port Sol.

The revolt had been centrally planned, carefully timed, meticulously executed. Despite generations of selective breeding to eliminate initiative and cunning, the transients no longer seemed so sheepish, and in Hilin they had discovered a general. And it was over before the Elder's attention had turned away from the girl, before he had even noticed.

Hilin, king of the corridors, stood before the Elder's shrine. And he pulled at the face of the girl, the Lora lookalike. It had been a mask, just a mask; Rusel realized shamefully that this boy had manipulated the emotions of a being more than a thousand years old.

A bloody club in his hand, Hilin screamed his defiance at his undying god. The Cloister's systems translated the boy's language, after a thousand years quite unlike Rusel's. "You allowed this to happen." Hilin yelled. "You allowed the Autarchs to feed off us like [*untranslatable—body parasites?*]. We wash the decks for them with our blood, while they keep water from our children. And you, you [*untranslatable—an obscenity?*] allowed it to happen. And do you know why?" Hilin stepped closer to the shrine, and his face loomed in Rusel's vision. "Because you don't exist. Nobody has seen you in centuries—if they ever did! You're a lie, cooked up by the Autarchs to keep us in our place, that's what I think. Well, we don't believe in you anymore, not in any of that [*untranslatable—feces?*]. And we've thrown out the Autarchs. We are free!"

"Free" they were. Hilin and his followers looted the Autarchs' apartments, and gorged themselves on the food and water the Autarchs had hoarded for themselves, and screwed each other senseless in blithe defiance of the genetic-health prohibitions. And not a single deck panel was swabbed down.

After three days, as the chaos showed no signs of abating, Rusel knew that this was the most serious crisis in the Ship's long history. He had to act. It took him another three days to get ready for his performance, three days mostly taken up with fighting with the inhibiting protocols of his medical equipment.

Then he ordered the Cloister door to open, for the first time in centuries. It actually stuck, dry-welded in place. It finally gave way with a resounding crack, making his entrance even more spectacular than he had planned.

But there was nobody around to witness his incarnation but a small boy, no more than five years old. With his finger planted firmly in one nostril, and his eyes round with surprise, the kid looked heartbreakingly like Tomi, Diluc's boy, long since dead and fed to the recycling banks.

Rusel was standing, supported by servomechanisms, gamely clutching at a walking frame. He tried to smile at the boy, but he couldn't feel his own face, and didn't know if he succeeded. "Bring me the chief Druids," he said, and a translation whispered in the air around him.

The boy yelled and fled.

The Druids actually knelt before him, covering their faces. He walked very cautiously among them, allowing them even to touch his robe. He wanted to be certain they accepted his reality, to smell the dusty tang of centuries on him. Maybe these monkish philosophers had in their hearts, like Hilin, never really believed in the Elder's existence. Well, now their messiah had suddenly reincarnated among them.

But he saw them as if through a flawed lens; he could hear little, feel less, smell or taste nothing. It was like walking around in a skinsuit, he thought.

He was an angry god, though. The rules of Shipboard life had been broken, he thundered. And he didn't just mean the recent mess. There must be no more water empires, and no knowledge empires either: the Druids would have to make sure that *every* child knew the basic rules, of Ship maintenance and genetic-health breeding.

He ordered that the Autarchs should not be returned to their seats of power. Instead, the governing would be done, for this generation, by a Druid—he picked out one terrified-looking woman at random. As long as she ruled wisely and well, she would have the Elder's backing. On her death the people would select a successor, who could not be more closely related to her predecessor than second cousin.

The old Autarchs and their brood, meanwhile, were to be spared. They would be shut away permanently in their amphitheater prison, where there were supplies to keep them alive. Rusel believed they and their strange slow-growing children would die off; within a generation, a tick of time, that problem would go away. He had done his share of killing, he thought.

Then he sighed. The worst of it had still to be faced. "Bring me Hilin," he ordered.

They dragged in the corridor king tied up with strips of cloth. He had been assaulted, Rusel saw; his face was battered and one arm seemed broken. The erstwhile leader was already being punished for his blasphemy by those who sought the favor of the Elder. But Hilin faced Rusel defiantly, strength and intelligence showing in his face.

Rusel's scarred heart ached a little more, for strength and intelligence were the last features you wanted in a transient.

Hilin had to die, of course. His flayed corpse would be displayed before the shrine of the Elder, as a warning to future generations. But Rusel didn't have the courage to watch it done. He remembered the man in the electric-blue skinsuit: he always had been a coward, he thought.

As he returned to his Cloister, he looked back once more. "And clean up this damn mess," he said.

He knew it would take a long time, even on his timescales, before he managed to forget the contemptuous defiance on Hilin's young face. But Hilin had gone into the dark like all his transient ancestors, and soon his siblings and nieces and nephews and everybody who looked remotely like him went too, gone, all gone into the sink of time, and soon only Rusel was left alive to remember the rebellion.

Rusel would never leave the Cloister again.

————

Some time after that, there was a decimating plague.

It was brought about by a combination of factors: a slow unmonitored buildup of irritants and allergens in the Ship's environment, and then the sudden emergence of a latent virus in a population already weakened. It was a multiple accident, impossible for the Pharaoh designers of the Ship to plan away, for all their ingenuity. But given enough time—more than five thousand years—such events were inevitable.

The surviving population crashed to close to a threshold of viability. For a few decades Rusel was forced to intervene, through booming commands, to ensure that the Ship was maintained at a base level, and that genetic-health protocols were observed and breeding matches planned even more carefully than usually.

The low numbers brought benefits, though. The Ship's systems were now producing a large surplus of supplies, and there was no possibility of any more water empires. Rusel considered, in his glacial way, establishing a final population at a lower level than before.

It intrigued him that the occurrence of the plague mirrored the restructuring of his own mental processes. The day to day affairs of the Ship, and the clattering of the transient generations, barely distracted him now. Instead he became aware of slower pulses, deeper rhythms beyond any transients' horizon of awareness. It fascinated him to follow the million-year turning of the Galaxy, whose brilliant face continued to open up behind the fleeing Ship.

And his perception of risk changed. His endless analysis of the Ship's systems uncovered obscure failure modes: certain parameter combinations that could disrupt the governing software, interacting failures among the nanomachines that still labored over the Ship's fabric inside and out. Such failures were highly unlikely; he estimated the Ship might suffer significant damage once every ten thousand years or so. On Earth, whole civilizations had risen and fallen with greater alacrity than that. But *he* had to plan for such things, to prepare the Ship's defenses and recovery strategies. The plague, after all, was just such a low-risk event, but given enough time it had come about.

The transients' behavior, meanwhile, adjusted on its own timescales.

Once every decade or so the inhabitants of Diluc's corridor-village would approach the shrine of the Elder, where the flickering Virtual still showed. One of them would dress up in a long robe and walk behind a frame with exaggerated slowness, while the rest cowered. And then they would fall on a manikin and tear it to pieces. Rusel had watched such displays several times before he had realized what was going on: it was, of course, a ritualized re-enactment of his own last manifestation. Sometimes the bit of theater would culminate in the flaying of a living human, which they must imagine he demanded; when such savage generations arose, Rusel would avert his cold gaze.

Meanwhile, in the village in which Hilin's doomed lover Sale had been born, the local transients were trying another tactic to win his favor. Perhaps it was another outcome of Hilin's clever exploits, or perhaps it had been inherent in the situation all along.

Girls, tall slim girls with dark elusive eyes: as the generations ticked by, he seemed to see more of them running in the corridors, making eyes at muscular wall-scrubbing boys, dandling children on their knees. They were like cartoon versions of Lora: tall Loras and short, thin Loras and fat, happy Loras and sad.

It was selective breeding, if presumably unconscious, people turning themselves into replicas of the images in the Virtual. They were appealing directly to his own cold heart: if the Elder loved this woman so much, then choose a wife that looks like her, if only a little, and hope to have daughters with her elfin looks, and so win favor.

Rusel was simultaneously touched and appalled. They could do what they liked, he told himself, as long as they got their jobs done.

Meanwhile, on the other side of the barricade he had erected, the Autarchs and their long-lived families had not died out as Rusel had hoped. They had lived on. And as they inbred ferociously, their lives were stretched out longer and longer.

Again this made sense in terms of their heredity, he thought. In their cordoned-off compartment there was simply no room to expand their population. So the genes' best bet of propagating themselves into the future, always their only objective, was to stretch out the lives of their carriers. Adults lived for centuries, and for the vanishingly few children born, childhood lasted decades. Rusel found these creatures, with their blank eyes and wizened-faced children, peculiarly creepy. On the other hand, he still couldn't bring himself to kill them off. Perhaps in them he saw a distorted reflection of himself.

There was one constant throughout the Ship. On both sides of the barrier the transients were clearly getting dumber.

As generations passed—and, for fear of repeating Hilin's fate, potential mates were repelled by any signs of higher-than-average intelligence—it was obvious that the transients were breeding themselves into stupidity. If anything the Autarchs' environment was less stimulating than that of their cousins in the rest of the Ship, and despite their slower generational cycle they were shedding their unnecessary intelligence with even more alacrity, perhaps from sheer boredom.

The transients kept the Ship working, however, and in their increasingly brutish liaisons followed the genetic-health mandates scrupulously. This puzzled Rusel: surely by now they could have no real understanding of *why* they were doing these peculiar things.

But he observed that when it came time to attract a mate the most vigorous deck-swabbers and cousin-deniers stood out from the crowd. It made sense: after all, a propensity to please the undeniable reality of the Elder was a survival characteristic, and therefore worth displaying if you had it, and worth preserving in your children's heredity.

He filed away such observations and insights. By now, nothing that happened inside the Ship's hull interested him as much as what happened outside.

He was thoroughly wired into the Ship, its electromagnetic and other equipment taking the place of his own failed biological senses. He cruised

158 | MAYFLOWER II

with it through the intergalactic gulf, feeling the tingle of dark matter particles as they were swept into the Ship's gut, sensing the subtle caress of
magnetic fields. The space between the galaxies was much more interesting
than he had ever imagined. It wasn't a void at all. There was structure here,
he saw, a complex webbing of the dark stuff that spanned the universe, a
webbing in which galaxies were trapped like glowing flies. He learned to
follow the currents and reefs of the dark matter which the Ship's gravitational maw greedily devoured.

He was alone with the galaxies, then, and with his own mind.

Once, just once, as he drifted in the dark, he heard a strange signal. It
was cold and clear, like the peal of a trumpet, far off in the echoing intergalactic night. It wasn't human at all.

He listened for a thousand years. He never heard it again.

———

Andres came to him.

"Leave me alone, you nagging old witch," he grumbled.

"Believe me, that would be my choice," said Andres fervently. "But
there's a problem, Rusel. And you need to come out of your damn shell
and sort it out."

He could see her face clearly, that worn-smooth expressionless skin. The
rest of her body was a blur, a suggestion. None of that mattered, of course.

"What kind of problem?"

"With the transients. What else? They are all that matters. You need to
take a look."

"I don't want to. It hurts."

"I know it hurts. But it's your duty."

Duty? Had she said that, or had he? Was he awake, or dreaming? With
time, everything blurred, every category, every boundary.

He was far beyond biology now, of course. The decay of his central
nervous system had proceeded so far that he wasn't sure if it returned any
signals at all to the hardening nugget of his brain. It was only technology
that kept him alive. With time, the Ship had infiltrated its treatments and
systems deeper into the shell of what had been his body. It was as if he had
become just another of the Ship's systems, like the air cycling system or the
water purifiers, just as old and balky, and just as much in need of endless
tender loving care.

Even the walls of his consciousness were wearing away. He thought of
his mind as a dark hall filled with drifting forms, like zero-gravity sculptures.
These were his memories—or perhaps memories of memories, recycled,
reiterated, edited and processed.

And *he* was here, a pinpoint awareness that flitted and flew between the drifting reefs of memory. At times, as he sailed through the abstraction of emptiness, free of memory or anticipation, indeed free of any conscious thought save only a primal sense of *self*, he felt oddly free—light, unburdened, even young again. But whenever that innocent point settled into the dark tangle of a memory reef, the guilt came back, a deep muddy shame whose origins he had half forgotten, and whose resolution he could no longer imagine.

He wasn't alone, however, in this cavernous awareness. Sometimes voices called from the dark. Sometimes there were even faces, their features softened, their ages indeterminate. Here was Diluc, his brother, or Andres, or Ruul or Selur or one of the others. He knew they were all long dead save for him, who lived on and on. He had vague memories of setting up some of these Virtual personas as therapy for himself, or as ways for the Ship to attract his attention—Lethe, even as company. But by now he wasn't sure what was Virtual and what was a dream, a schizoid fantasy of his rickety mind.

Lora was never there, however.

And Andres, the cold Pharaoh who had become his longest-enduring companion, was his most persistent visitant.

She said, "Nobody ever said this would be easy, Rusel."

"You said that before."

"Yes. And I'll keep on saying it until we get to Canis Major."

"Canis Major? . . ." The destination. He'd forgotten about it again, forgotten that an end to all this even as a theoretical possibility might exist. The trouble was, thinking about such things as a beginning and an end made him aware of time, and that was always a mistake.

How long? The answer came to him like a whisper. *Round numbers? Twenty thousand years gone. Some five thousand left.* Twenty thousand years. It was ridiculous, of course.

"Rusel," Andres snapped. "You need to focus."

"You're not even Andres," he grumbled.

Her mouth was round with mock horror. "Oh, no! What an existential disaster. Just do it, Rus."

So, reluctantly, he gathered his scattered concentration, and sent his viewpoint out into the body of the Ship. He was faintly aware of Andres riding alongside him, a ghost at his shoulder.

He found the place he still thought of as Diluc's village. The framework of corridors and cabins hadn't changed, of course; it was impossible that it should. But even the non-permanent partitions that had once been built up and torn down by each successive generation of transients had been left unmoved since the last time he was here. Building things wasn't what people did anymore.

He wandered into the little suite of rooms that had once been Diluc's home. There was no furniture. Nests were crammed into each corner of the room, disorderly heaps of cloth and polymer scraps. He had seen the transients take standard-issue clothing from the Ship's recycler systems and immediately start tearing it up with hands or teeth to make their coarse bedding. There was a strong stink of piss and shit, of blood and milk, sweat and sex, the most basic human biology. But the crew remained scrupulously clean. Every few days all this stuff would be swept up and carted off to the recycler bins.

This was the way people lived now.

Outside, the walls and partitions were clean, gleaming and sterile, as was every surface he could see, the floor and ceiling. One partition had been rubbed until it was worn so thin the light shone through it: another couple of generations and it would wear away altogether, he thought. The crew still kept up their basic duties; that had remained, while so much else had vanished.

But these latter transients were not crewing this Ship as his generation had. They were doing it for deeper reasons.

Those selection pressures, as the transients competed in how well they did their chores in order to attract mates, had, given time, sculpted the population. By now, he understood, the transients were maintaining a starship's systems as bees had once danced, stags had locked antlers, and peacocks had spread their useless tails: *they were doing it for sex*, and the chance to procreate. As mind receded, Rusel thought, biology had taken over.

As long as they were doing it in the first place, Rusel didn't care. Besides, it worked. Sexual drivers seemed very effective in locking in behavior with the precision required to keep the Ship's systems functioning: you could fix a ceiling ventilation grill with a show-off flourish or not, but you had to do it *exactly* right to impress the opposite sex, even if you didn't understand what it was for. Even when mind was gone, you had to do it right.

He heard weeping, not far away.

He let his viewpoint follow the weeping, just drifting along the corridor. He turned a corner, and came on the villagers.

There were perhaps twenty-five of them, adults and children. They were all naked, of course; nobody had worn clothes for millennia. Some of them had infants in their arms or on their backs. Squatting in the corridor, they huddled around a central figure, the woman who was doing the weeping. Surrounded by bare backs and folded limbs, she was cradling something, a bloody scrap. The others reached out and stroked her back and scalp; some of them were weeping too, Rusel saw.

Andres said dryly, "Their empathy is obvious."

"Yes. They've lost so much else, but not that——"

Suddenly their heads turned, all of them save the weeping woman, faces swiveling like antennae. Something had disturbed them—perhaps the tiny hovering drone that was Rusel's physical manifestation. Their brows were low, but their faces were still human, with straight noses and delicate chins. It was like a flower-bed of faces, Rusel thought, turned up to his light. Their eyes were wide, their mouths pulled back in fear-grins.

And every one of them looked like Lora, more or less, with that delicate, elfin face, even something of her elusive eyes. Of course they did: the blind filter of natural selection, operating for generations on this hapless stock, had long determined that though mind was no longer necessary, to look *this* way might soften the heart of the wizened creature who ruled the world.

The strange tableau of upturned Lora-faces lasted only a moment. Then the transients took flight. They poured away down the corridor, running, knuckle-walking, bounding off the walls and ceiling.

Andres growled, "I'll swear they get more like chimps with every generation."

In a few seconds they had gone, all save the weeping woman.

Rusel allowed his viewpoint to swim toward the woman. He moved cautiously, not wishing to alarm her. She was young—twenty, twenty-one? It was increasingly hard to tell the age of these transients; they seemed to reach puberty later each generation. This girl had clearly passed her menarche—in fact she had given birth, and recently: her belly was slack, her breasts heavy with milk. But her chest was smeared with blood, shocking bright crimson in the drab, worn background of the corridor. And the thing she was cradling was no child.

"Lethe," said Rusel. "*It's a hand.* A child's hand. I think I'm going to throw up."

"You no longer have the equipment. Take a closer look."

A white stump of bone stuck out of a bloody mass of flesh. The hand had been severed at the wrist. And two tiny fingers had been almost stripped of flesh, ligament and muscle, leaving only tiny bones.

"That wrist," Andres said pitilessly, "has been bitten through. By *teeth*, Rusel. And teeth have been at work on those fingers as well. Think about it. With a bit of practice, you could take one of those little morsels between your incisors and just strip off the flesh and muscle——"

"Shut up! Lethe, Andres, I can see for myself. We always avoided cannibalism. I thought we beat that into their shrinking skulls hard enough."

"So we did. But I don't think this is cannibalism—or rather, whatever did this wasn't *her* kind."

Rusel elevated the viewpoint and cast around. He saw a trail of blood leading away from the woman, smeared along the walls and floor, quite unmistakable, as if something had been dragged away.

Andres said, "I think our transients suddenly have a predator."

"Not so suddenly," Rusel said. A part of his scattered consciousness was checking over the Ship's logs, long ignored. This kind of incident had been going on for a couple of centuries. "It's been rare before, once or twice a generation. Mostly it was the old, or the very young—dispensable, or replaceable. But now they seem to be upping the rate."

"And making a dent in the transients' numbers."

"Yes. You were right to bring me here." This had to be resolved. But to do it, he thought with a deepening dread, he was going to have to confront a horror he had shut out of his awareness for millennia.

"I'm here with you," Andres said gently.

"No, you're not," he snapped. "But I have to deal with this anyhow."

"Yes, you do."

His viewpoint followed the bloody trail as it wound through the corridor-villages of the transients. Broken in places, the trail slinked through shadows or through holes worn in the walls. It was the furtive trail of a hunter, he thought.

At last Rusel came to the bulkhead that cut the Ship in two, marking the limit of his transients' domain. He had long put out of his mind what lay beyond this wall: in fact, if he could have cut away the Ship's aft compartment and let the whole mess float away into space he would long ago have done so.

But there was a hole in the bulkhead, just wide enough to admit a slim body.

The bulkhead was a composite of metal and polymer, extremely tough, and a meter thick; the hole was a neat tunnel, not regular but smooth-walled, drilled right through it. "I can't believe they have tools," he said. "So how did they get through?"

"Teeth," Andres said. "Teeth and nails—and time, of which they have plenty. Remember what you're dealing with. Even if the bulkhead was made of diamond they'd have got through eventually."

"I hoped they were dead."

"Hope! Wishful thinking! That always was your weakness, Rusel. I always said you should have killed them off in the first place. They're just a drain on the Ship's resources."

"I'm no killer."

"Yes, you are——"

"And they are human, no less than the transients."

"No, they're *not*. And now, it seems, they are *eating* our transients."

His viewpoint drifted before the hole in the wall. Andres seemed to sense his dread; she didn't say anything.

He passed through the barrier.

He emerged in the big upended chamber he still thought of as the amphitheater, right at the base of the Ship. This was a big, bare volume, a cylinder set on its side. After the spin-up it had been used to pursue larger-scale reconstruction projects necessary to prepare the Ship for its long intergalactic voyage, and mounted on its floor and walls were the relics of heavy engineering, long abandoned: gantries, platforms of metal, immense low-gravity cranes like vast skeletons. Globe lights hovered everywhere, casting a yellow-white, complex light. It was an oddly magnificent sight, Rusel thought, and its stirred fond memories of brighter, more purposeful days. On the wall of the chamber, which had been its floor, he could even make out the brackets which had held the acceleration couches on launch day.

Now, every exposed surface was corroded. Nothing moved. And that upturned floor, which Andres had turned transparent a mere year after the launch, was caked by what looked like rock. It was a hardened pack of feces and cloth scraps and dirt, a wall of shit to block out the Galaxy.

At first, in this jungle of engineering, he couldn't make out anything living. Then, as he watched and allowed the worn-out ambience of the place to wash over him, he learned to see.

They were like shadows, he thought, slim, upright shadows that flitted through the gantries, furtive, cautious. At times they looked human— clearly upright, bipedal, purposeful—though their limbs were spindly, their bellies distended. But then they would collapse to all fours and lope away with a bent gait, and that impression of humanity vanished. They didn't seem to be wearing clothes, any more than the transients did. But unlike the transients, their bodies were coated with a kind of thick hair, dark brown, a fur.

Here and there hovering drones trailed the shambling creatures, carrying food and water. The creatures ignored these emissaries of the Ship that kept them alive.

Andres said grimly. "I know you haven't wanted to think about these relics, Rusel. But the Ship has watched over them. They are provided with food, of course. Clothing, blankets and the like—they rip all that up to serve as nesting material, like the transients. They won't go to the supply hoppers as the transients will; drones have to bring them the stuff they need, and take out their waste. But they're really quite passive. They don't mind the drones, even when the drones clean them, or tend to wounds or sicknesses. They are used to being cared for by machines."

"But what do they do all day?"

Andres laughed. "Why, nothing. Nothing but eat the food we give them. Climb around the gantries a little, perhaps."

"They must have some spark of curiosity, of awareness. The transients do! They're people."

"Their ancestors used to be. Now they're quite mindless. . . . There. Look. They are gathering at one of their feeding places. Perhaps we'll be able to see what they do."

The feeding site was just a shallow depression, worn into a floor of steel. Its base was smeared green and brown. A drone had delivered a cache of food to the center of the pit, a pile of spheres and cylinders and discs, all sized for human hands, all brightly colored.

From around the amphitheater the animals came walking, loping, moving with the slow clumsiness of low gravity—and yet with an exaggerated care, Rusel thought, as if they were very fragile, very old. They gathered around the food pile. But they did not reach for the food; they just slumped down on the ground, as if exhausted.

Now smaller creatures emerged from the forest of gantries. They moved nervously, but just as cautiously as the larger forms. They must be children, Rusel thought, but they moved with no spontaneity or energy. They were like little old people themselves. There were far fewer children than adults, just a handful among perhaps fifty individuals.

It was the children who went to the food pile, broke off pieces of the brightly colored fodder, and carried it to the adults. The adults greeted this service with indifference, or at best a snarl, a light blow on the head or shoulder. Each child servant went doggedly back to the pile for more.

"They're not particularly hygienic," Rusel observed.

"No. But they don't have to be. Compared to the transients they have much tougher immune systems. And the Ship's systems keep the place roughly in order."

Rusel said, "Why don't the adults get the food themselves? It would be quicker."

Andres shrugged. "This is their way. And it is their way to eat another sort of food, too."

At the very center of the depression was a broad scar stained a deep crimson brown, littered with lumpy white shapes.

"That's blood," Rusel said, wondering. "Dried blood. And those white things—"

"Bones," said Andres evenly. Rusel thought she seemed oddly excited, stirred by the degraded spectacle before her. "But there's too much debris here to be accounted for by their occasional raids into transient country."

Rusel shuddered. "So they eat each other too."

"No. Not quite. The old eat the young; mothers eat their children. It is their way."

"Oh, Lethe——" Andres was right; Rusel couldn't throw up. But he was briefly aware of his body, cradled by the concerned Ship, thrashing feebly in distress.

Andres said dispassionately, "I don't understand your reaction."

"I didn't know——"

"You should have thought it through—thought through the consequences of your decision to let these creatures live."

"You are a monster, Andres."

She laughed without humor.

Of course he knew what these animals were. They were the Autarchs—or the distant descendants of the long-lived, inbred clan that had once ruled over the transients. Over nearly twenty thousand years selection pressure had worked relentlessly, and the gene complex that had given them their advantage over the transients in the first place—genes for longevity, a propensity injected into the human genome by the Qax—had found full expression. And meanwhile, in the sterile nurture of this place, they had had even less reason to waste precious energy on large brains.

As time had passed they had lived longer and longer, but thought less and less. Now these Autarchs were all but immortal, and all but mindless.

"They're actually rather fascinating," Andres said cheerfully. "I've been trying to understand their ecology, if you will."

"Ecology? Then maybe you can explain how it can benefit a creature to treat its children so. Those young seem to be farmed. Life is about the preservation of genes: even in this artificial little world of ours, that remains true. So how does eating your kids help achieve that? . . . Ah." He gazed at the hairy creatures before him. "But these Autarchs are not mortal."

"Exactly. They lost their minds, but they stayed immortal. And when mind had gone, natural selection worked with what it found."

Even for these strange creatures, the interests of the genes were paramount. But now a new strategy had to be worked out. It had been foreshadowed in the lives of the first Autarchs. There was no room to spread the genes by expanding the population—but if individuals could become effectively immortal, the genes could survive through them.

Andres said, "But simple longevity wasn't enough. Even the longest-lived will die through some accident eventually. The genes themselves can be damaged, through radiation exposure for instance. Copying is safer! For their own safety the genes need to see some children produced, and for some, the smartest and strongest, to survive.

"But, you see, living space is restricted here. The parents must compete for space against their own children. They don't care about the children. They use them as workers—or even, when there's an excess, as a cannibalistic resource. . . . But there are always one or two children who fight their way through to adulthood, enough to keep the stock numbers up. In a way the pressure from the adults is a mechanism to ensure that only the smartest and strongest of the kids survive. From the genes' point of view it's a mixed strategy."

"It's a redundancy mechanism," Rusel said. "That's the way an engineer would put it. The children are just a fail-safe."

"Precisely," Andres said.

It was biology, evolution: the destiny of the *Mayflower* had come down to this.

Rusel had brooded on the fate of his charges. And he had decided it was all a question of timescales.

The conscious purpose of the Ship had sustained its crew's focus for a century or so, until the first couple of generations, and the direct memory of Port Sol, had vanished into the past.

Millennia, though, were the timescale of historical epochs on Earth, over which empires rose and fell. His studies suggested that to sustain a purpose over such periods required the engagement of a deeper level of the human psyche: the idea of Rome, say, or a devotion to Christ. If the first century of the voyage had been an arena for the conscious, over longer periods the unconscious took over. Rusel had seen it himself, as the transients had become devoted to the idea of the Ship and its mission, as embodied by his own Virtual. Even Hilin's rebellion had been an expression of that cult of ideas. Call it mysticism: whatever, it worked for thousands of years.

That far, he believed, Andres and the other Pharaohs had been able to foresee and plan for. But beyond that even they hadn't been able to imagine; Rusel had sailed uncharted waters. And as time heaped up into *tens* of millennia, he had crossed a span of time comparable to the rise and fall, not just of empires, but of whole species.

A continuity of the kind that kept the transients cleaning the walls over such periods could only come about, not through even the deepest layers of mind, but through much more basic biological drivers, like sexual selection: the transients cleaned for sex, not for any reason to do with the Ship's goals, for they could no longer comprehend such abstractions. And meanwhile natural selection had shaped his cradled populations, of transients and Autarchs alike. Of course, if biology was replacing even the deepest layers of mind as the shaping element in the mission's destiny, Rusel's own role became still more important, as the only surviving element of continuity, indeed of consciousness.

Sometimes he felt queasy, perhaps even guilty, at the distorted fate to which generation upon generation had been subjected, all for the sake of a long-dead Pharaoh and her selfish, hubristic dream. But individual transients were soon gone, their tiny motes of joy or pain soon vanishing into the dark. Their very brevity was comforting.

Whatever, there was no going back, for any of them.

Andres was still watching the Autarchs. These frail, cautious animals were like a dark reflection of himself, Rusel thought reluctantly. And how strange it was for the transients to be caged in by the undying: his own attenuated consciousness guiding the Ship from above, while these fallen Autarchs preyed on them from below.

Andres said, "You know, immortality, the defeat of death, is one of mankind's oldest dreams. But immortality doesn't make you a god. *You* have immortality, Rusel, but, save for your crutch the Ship, you have no power. And these—animals—have immortality, but nothing else."

"It's monstrous."

"Of course! Isn't life always? But the genes don't care. And in the Autarchs' mindless capering, you can see the ultimate logic of immortality: for an immortal, to survive, must in the end eat her own children."

But everybody on this Ship was a child of this monstrous mother, Rusel thought, whose hubris and twisted longings had impelled this mission in the first place. "Is that some kind of confession, Pharaoh?"

Andres didn't reply. Perhaps she couldn't. After all, this wasn't Andres but a Virtual, a software-generated crutch for Rusel's fading consciousness, at the limit of its programming. And any guilt he saw in her could only be a reflection of himself.

With an effort of will he dismissed her.

One of the adults, a male, sat up, scratched his chest, and loped to the center of the feeding pit. The young fled at his approach. The male scattered the last bits of primary-color food, and picked up something small and white. It was a skull, Rusel saw, the skull of a child. The adult crushed it, dropped the fragments, and wandered off, aimless, immortal, mindless.

Rusel withdrew, and sealed up the gnawed-through bulkhead. After that he set up a new barrier spanning the Ship parallel to the bulkhead, and opened up the thin slice of the vessel between the walls to intergalactic vacuum. He never again gave any thought to what lay on the other side of that barrier.

Twenty-five thousand years after the end of his world, Rusel heard that he was to be saved.

"Rusel. Rusel . . ."

Rusel wanted the voices to go away. He didn't need voices now—not Diluc's, not even Andres's. He had no body, no belly, no heart; he had no need of people at all. His memories were scattered in emptiness, like the faint smudges that were the remote galaxies all around the Ship. And like the Ship he forged on steadily, pointlessly into the future, his life empty of meaning.

The last thing he wanted was *voices*. But they wouldn't go away. With deep reluctance, he forced his scattered attention to gather.

The voices were coming from Diluc's corridor-village. Vaguely, he saw people there, near a door—the door where he had once been barreled into by little Rus, he remembered, in a shard of bright warm memory blown from the past—two people, by that same door.

People standing upright. People wearing clothes.

They were not transients. And they were calling his name into the air. With a mighty effort he pulled himself to full awareness.

They stood side by side, a man and a woman—both young, in their twenties, perhaps. They wore smart orange uniforms and boots. The man was clean-shaven, and the woman bore a baby in her arms.

Transients had clustered around them. Naked, pale, eyes wide with curiosity, they squatted on their haunches and reached up with their long arms to the smiling newcomers. Some of them were scrubbing frantically at the floor and walls, teeth bared in rictus grins. They were trying to impress the newcomers with their prowess at cleaning, the only way they knew how.

The woman allowed the transients to stroke her child. But she watched them with hard eyes and a fixed smile. And the man's hand was never far away from the weapon at his belt.

It took Rusel a great deal of effort to find the circuits that would allow him to speak. He said, "*Rusel*. I am Rusel."

As the disembodied voice boomed out of the air the man and woman looked up, startled, and the transients cowered. The newcomers looked at each other with delight. "It's true," said the man. "It really is the *Mayflower!*" A translation whispered to Rusel.

The woman scoffed. "Of course it's the *Mayflower*. What else could it be?"

Rusel said, "Who are you?"

The man's name was Pirius, the woman's Torec.

"Are we at Canis Major?"

"No," Pirius said gently.

These two had come from the home Galaxy—from Sol system itself, they said. They had come in a faster-than-light ship; it had overtaken the *Mayflower*'s painful crawl in a few weeks. "You have come thirteen thousand light-years from Port Sol," Pirius said. "And it took you more than twenty-five thousand years. It is a record for a generation starship! An astonishing feat."

Thirteen thousand light-years? Even now, only halfway. It seemed impossible.

Torec cupped the face of a transient girl in her hand—cupped Lora's face. "And," Torec said, "we came to find you."

"Yes," said Pirius, smiling. "And your floating museum!"

Rusel thought that over. "Then mankind lives on?"

Oh, yes, Pirius told him. The mighty Expansion from which the *Mayflower*'s crew had fled had burned its way right across the Galaxy. It had been an age of war; trillions had gone into the dark. But mankind had endured.

"And we won!" Pirius said brightly. Pirius and Torec themselves had been involved in some kind of exotic combat to win the center of the Galaxy. "It's a human Galaxy now, Rusel."

"Human? But how are *you* still human?"

They seemed to understand the question. "We were at war," Pirius said. "We couldn't afford to evolve."

"The Coalition—"

"Fallen. Vanished. Gone. They can't harm you now."

"And my crew—"

"We will take them home. There are places where they can be cared for. But, ah—"

Torec said, "But the Ship itself is too big to turn around. I'm not sure we can bring *you*."

Once he had seen himself, a stiff ageless man, through the eyes of Diluc's great-grandson Poro, through the eyes of a child. Now, just for an instant, he saw himself through the eyes of Pirius and Torec. A wizened, charred thing suspended in a webbing of wires and tubes.

That didn't matter, of course. "Have I fulfilled my mission?"

"Yes," Pirius said gently. "You fulfilled it very well."

He wasn't aware of Pirius and Torec shepherding the transients and Autarchs out of the Ship and into their own absurdly small craft. He wasn't aware of Pirius's farewell call as they shot away, back toward the bright lights of the human Galaxy, leaving him alone. He was only aware of the Ship now, the patient, stolid Ship.

The Ship—and one face, revealed to him at last: an elfin face, with distracted eyes. He didn't know if she was a gift of Pirius or even Andres, if she was outside his own head or inside. None of that seemed to matter when at last she smiled for him, and he felt the easing of a tension twenty-five millennia old, the dissolving of a clot of ancient guilt.

The Ship forged on into the endless dark, its corridors as clean and bright and empty as his thoughts.

BRIGHT RED STAR

BUD SPARHAWK

OUR BOAT FLOATED silent as owls' wings and settled softly as an autumn snowflake. There was no doubt that the enemy had spotted us—the stealth could only minimize signs of our presence. We'd done everything we could to reduce detectability: hardened plastics, ceramics, charged ice, and hardly any metal. All that did was create doubt, and, possibly, delay. Or so we hoped.

We tumbled quickly from the boat as grounding automatically discharged the ship charge, without which the boat's ice frame would quickly melt. In a matter of minutes, the only remaining trace of our craft would be a puddle of impure water and the gossamer-thin spider-web of the stealth shield—and that would dissipate at the first hint of a breeze.

We deployed in pincer and arrowhead formation, sending two troops to the north to parallel our advance, two likewise to the south, and two to the point. Hunter and I followed in column.

We moved quickly, carefully, ever wary. That the Shardies would eventually find us was not in doubt, neither was the certainty of our death when they did so. They did not use humans well; however, I doubted they'd find much use for us.

Tactical estimates gave us an hour to save the recalcitrant settlers' souls. They were some sort of colony—religious or otherwise, it made no difference—only that they had foolishly chosen to remain where others fled.

There was a slight probability we'd have less than an hour and an even smaller possibility of having more, so we moved quickly. I'd estimated twenty minutes to reach their position and ten to twenty to ensure we'd located everyone. That left us five minutes for action and ten as margin for contingencies.

I knew we'd fail if we used more than fifty-five minutes.

———

". . . shards," one of the last observers managed to croak out before Jeaux II fell silent. That word was the only description of the aliens we'd ever heard, so it stuck.

The Shardies had hit hard when we first made contact with their kind, which could hardly be called contact at all since they attacked first and without provocation. When our ships backed off, their ship followed, attacking again and again with unbelievable ferocity. When its missiles ran out, they tried to ram the thick plate of our exploratory ship. It smashed into tiny ceramic fragments on impact, leaving a cloud of glittering fragments that spun into emptiness, leaving no trace, no hint, of what had so provoked them.

After much debate over the wisdom of such an attempt, we again tried to contact them. The idea of another space-spanning civilization held too much promise to ignore. It took years before we found them, but find them we did.

That is, we assume that someone found them, for a fleet of their ships suddenly appeared near Jeaux II and attacked every sign of human presence: ships, orbiting stations, ground-based settlements—anything that wasn't of natural origin. The military tried to defend themselves while the civilian ships fled in every direction.

This was a strategic mistake. Since they'd backtracked one of our ships to Jeaux, that meant that they could—and probably would—follow every ship who escaped. Every destination system was now at risk.

Thanks to the brief warning, most of the settled systems managed to mobilize to meet the Shardies's attack. The initial losses were great. We had to fall back from system after system, engaged in a running battle with something we do not understand.

We've tried to figure out why they attack with such ferocity, why there hasn't been an attempt at contact, and why they won't respond to our calls. We fail at every attempt to understand them.

Neither have we deduced anything of their technology from the damaged ships we've managed to recover. Hulls, engines, and controls appear to be nothing but dirty glass. We suspect this is the analog of our silicon-based technology, but can't be sure. Researchers have been working hard, I'm told, but I have yet to hear of anything useful come of it.

Nor can we figure out what sort of creatures we're fighting. That one word, that one utterance from a lone observer on Jeaux, was all we had to go on.

What we do know for certain is that either the Shardies will be destroyed, or we will be. Humanity has lost too much, too many, for compromise. It is clear that there can be no middle ground.

The trip to the site of the single communications burst was uneventful. We didn't expect to encounter resistance. The Shardies don't settle on the planets they take from us. No, they just wipe them clean of humanity and then move on. We knew there had to be Shardie gleaners surveying the planet, trying to find some fresh meat or what was worse, breeding stock. With a little luck, we had a slight advantage by knowing the group's location. Without luck, we'd find that the Shardies had beaten us to them.

The location was a hill, close by a half-destroyed farming complex whose tower leaned precariously toward the north. With luck, we'd find whoever made the call nearby. First place to check were the buildings, or what remained of them.

We went straight in. Better to find whatever sign we could quickly— time was running out. A sweep of the barn was negative, as were the remains of the silo, and the outbuildings. The house was a different matter. We found some opened jars, preserves mostly. The footprints we found outside were small—a child's perhaps, or a small woman. The tracks led up the hill and into the woods.

I send the outriders wide to cover while Hunter followed the tracks. Could be a trap, so I waited, senses alert for any indication of a problem.

Crack of a twig brought me to my feet. It was Hunter and a little girl. "Cave up there," with a head nod. "Three dead men—three, four days gone." That tied with the time we'd received the burst.

She was a tiny thing—about nine or ten, I'd say—bright eyes and scraggly red hair. Good teeth. Looked scared as hell. I could understand that—Hunter wasn't being very gentle as he dumped her at my feet.

"What's your name?" I stooped to bring my head to her level.

"You them aliens?" she asked all wide-eyed. "How come you talk like us?"

"We're combat soldiers," I answered. "We're humans, just like you, sweetheart. Now, come on; what's your name?"

"Becky," she finally spit out. "How come you're still here? Paw said everybody left."

"We came back to take care of you and the others," I answered truthfully. "We can't afford to let you fall into enemy hands."

"Paw and the Paston boys thought you'd come," she said.

"How did they die?"

Becky seemed fascinated by my sidearm. "They shot them after the Pastons used the mayday thing. I hid in the back where they couldn't find me. Are you going to punish them for doing that?"

That got my attention. Takes a real idiot to shoot the people who demonstrated good sense. I began to doubt that the Shardies would've gotten much use out of whatever mush these jerks used for brains. "Right, sweetheart, we'll punish them, but first you have to tell us where they are."

"Did you bring a ship to take us away?" Becky asked as she fingered the butt of my AC-43. "That was why Paw grabbed the mayday—to get us a rescue ship."

"We came to make sure the enemy doesn't get you," I answered honestly. "Listen, we don't have much time. Can you take us to where the others are hiding?"

"I think they're still over at the Truett place," she said, pointing to the east.

I nodded to Hunter, who was already directing the scouts eastward. I picked up Becky and moved out. Hunter covered my rear. "Can you tell us how to get there?"

"You mean to the Truett's' place?" Becky asked. "Sure. There's a big field there. That where the rescue ship's going to land?"

The Shardie ships we'd managed to capture more or less intact were completely empty—no aliens at all—just glass of various colors and shapes. Either the ships were highly automated, or the Shardies had destroyed themselves completely so they would not fall into our hands. Suicidal, or so we thought. Eventually we discovered some living creatures, if you can call them that, aboard one of their ships.

One of the things we'd learned was that if we had sufficient warning, we could defend ourselves fairly well. Sometimes we managed to drive them off, and sometimes not. Every battle was fought hard and long, usually with massive losses on both sides. Our defensive successes managed to achieve, at best, parity.

That all changed at Witca, a heavily fortified military outpost armed with the latest data on Shardie attack patterns. Only the Shardies were using new patterns that got through the outer defenses. It was as if they were anticipating the base's reactions and countering Witca's best defensive moves with ease. Witca fell with all hands lost.

After Witca's defeat, we lost ground steadily, falling farther and farther back toward Earth year after year. We no longer had parity. We were losing.

Then, largely through a stroke of luck, our fleet happened upon a lone Shardie ship near Outreach. As soon as it realized we were near, it attacked on an evasion pattern that defied the fleet's best defensive efforts. The fleet lost six ships before managing to still whatever mysterious force propelled the Shardie vessel.

The fleet marines lost no time in boarding. Command had high hopes of finally finding something alive inside. They weren't disappointed. *Disgusted* and *surprised* might better describe their reaction. Inside, they found sixteen of the Jeaux survivors.

Survivors isn't exactly the word. What they found were sixteen bodies without arms, legs, and most organs. What remained were essentially heads hooked up to life support and fueled by oxygenated glucose pumps. There were a couple hundred strands of glass fiber running from the ship's walls into each skull, into each brain, into each soul. Four of the sixteen were still functioning—alive is not a word to describe their condition.

Clinical examination of the four revealed that each was fully conscious and aware, at least that's what the EEG traces indicated. They also indicated that the Shardies had used no pain killers to dull the senses when they'd done this. Had the survivors mouths, they would have been continually screaming. All four died mercifully fast when their pumps ran dry. I'm not too sure that the medics didn't help that along. It was a mercy.

The only conclusion we could draw was that the Shardies were using human brains to defeat human defenses. They were obviously using our own brains to "think" like us.

There was no hesitation on the part of Command. They ordered everyone, except combat types like us, from the most likely targets. Humanity couldn't allow any more people to become components for the Shardie offense.

But civilians never listen. Farmers were the worse, hanging onto their little plots and crops until somebody dragged them away, kicking and screaming at the injustice of it all. That's why we were here. Forty settlers had stupidly refused to be evacuated from New Mars. Forty we didn't know about until we got that one brief burst.

My mission was to make certain that they didn't become forty armless, legless, gutless, screamless weapon components.

"Why do you act so funny?" Becky asked as we jogged along. Her question was expected. Few civilians ever see combat troops like us. Luckily the combat gear and darkness hid most of the worse modifications I'd had to undergo: cybernetic heart-lung pump with reserve oxygen so I could operate in any atmosphere or even underwater; augmented muscles on legs and arms that bulked me up like a cartoon giant on steroids; amped vision that ran from the near infrared up toward the UV range—I could even switch to black and white for better night vision—and smart-metal skeleton structures to provide a good base for my massive muscles. Flesh had been stripped from anything exposed and replaced with impervious plas. My hands were electromechanical marvels capable of ripping weapons-grade plating off a spaceship, and sensitive enough to lift a tiny girl without harm.

Then there was my glucose pump, a nasty, but useful technology we'd copied from the Shardies. Even my brain had been altered—substituting silicon and gel for the mass of pink jelly I was born with. Definitely not something you'd want your daughter to date. I'm glad it was dark. In daylight, I'd probably scare the bejesus out of her.

"We're modified so we can fight the bastards," I growled. Revenge for relatives on Witca was my overt reason. Curiosity about the Shardies, and getting a piece of them, was secondary. I saw no sense going into the gory details or the agonizing processes involved with a little girl who wouldn't understand. "Tell me about the rest of your group. Are they all right?"

"Mr. Robbarts is still the boss. He's the one that shot Paw, I think. And there's Jake and Sally and little Billy. Billy's my friend. Jake's got a bad leg.

"Then there's all the Thomas women. They have a big wagon, or they did before the men came and burned it." She started crying.

I was certain she was talking about the roaming gangs. Lots of people didn't want to leave anything the Shardies might be able to use. Senseless, that. Shardies could care less, but most civilians wouldn't know that. Best destroy what you left behind, they'd probably thought, and had taken their anger out on things they could reach.

"Mr. Robbarts said we didn't have to worry because we weren't soldiers. He said we'd have the whole world to ourselves. But after everybody left, Paw got really afraid of what might happen."

Robbarts must be the leader of this group. "Robbarts was wrong, Becky. You all should have left," I said. "Didn't they tell you that it wouldn't matter if you were a soldier or not. Being human is all that matters."

"Mr. Robbarts got real mad when Paw argued with him and said he wanted to use the mayday thing. Then Paw and the boys and me ran away with it. You got to go along this stream for a bit now," she directed.

That explained the burst message that told us there were people left behind. They must have used one of the emergency broadcast units the evacuation team had scattered across New Mars in the last days, just in case. "What happened then?" I asked as I followed her pointing finger down the stream. The scouts picked up my changed direction and reacted.

"They told Paw to come out of the cave to talk," Becky continued, chatting away. "Paw told me to hide. Then I heard them arguing and shouting and I got really afraid. Then there was some shots. I heard the men looking around. Mr. Robbarts was cussing a lot and calling me all sorts of names, but I stayed where I was. I was scared."

"What did you do then?" I stepped around a huge boulder and wondered if it would be easier, and faster, to wade in the stream instead of through the woods on either side. Hunter was close by my side now in this narrow section.

"After it got quiet, I snuck out and found Paw and the boys laying on the ground. Paw was bleeding bad. I tried to stop it, but it wouldn't stop. Then he went to sleep and didn't move for a long time. I got hungry waiting for the rescue ship Paw said would come." That explained the jelly and jam jars—just what a little girl would like to eat. "Are you going to bury Paw and the boys?"

"Burial wastes time—something we can't afford," Hunter said sharply. *Down*, he signaled as a shot ricocheted off my chest armor.

I dropped immediately, instinctively tucking Becky underneath to protect her. Hunter slipped to the side and disappeared. I switched to infrared and made out fuzzy heat forms in the brush a dozen meters ahead. The muzzle of a rifle was glowing heat-bright from the shot he had taken. None of the forms moved.

I waited. Silent. Becky groaned and wiggled feebly. "It really hurts," she said. Her voice was muffled.

"Wait," I whispered, waiting for Hunter to get into position.

"Let her up," a man's voice barked from behind me. "Move easy now. I got you covered."

I pushed up, allowing Becky to crawl out before I came to my feet. The man took a step back. "Huh, you sure are a big one." He peered closer. "Ugly, too."

"He's come to rescue us, Mister Robbarts." Becky said. "He's got another soldier with him." Becky's voice sounded strained. I glanced at her and saw the blood. Damn, had his shot hit her?

I noticed the heat signatures of two more men in the brush; one behind Robbarts and another somewhat farther back. I had no doubt all were armed and all too ready to shoot. That made six in all.

"You shot Becky," I said calmly. "She needs help."

"The hell with her," Robbarts said nastily. "Her damn family's been nothing but trouble. Killed one of my boys, they did. Let the little bitch bleed."

"They're going to take us away in a ship," Becky said in a rush. "That's why we're going to your place. The field's a place they can land."

Robbarts didn't answer her directly. "That true, soldier? You got a ship?"

I really didn't like this man. "Nobody, nothing, could find a trace of the boat we came in. Becky's the one who said there'd be a rescue ship."

"Ain't no damn ship taking me or my people off our land," Robbarts spit, ignoring what I had said. "We're going to hold on to this place come whatever. This'll be a damn nice place for me and mine after the war moves on."

Did he really believe that? "The Shardies are going to comb this planet and glean whatever human stock they can find. Do you know what they do to the people they capture?"

Robbarts sneered. "I seen the news about what they did to them poor troopers. But we're civilians, not some combat-trained space jockey. They won't bother us. We don't know military stuff."

I couldn't believe Robbarts's ignorance. "The aliens don't care what you *know*. It's the human thought processes, the way our minds form associations, our ability to recognize patterns—that's what they use. They don't give a damn if a brain comes from a soldier, a navigator, or even some dumb-assed farmer!" As soon as the angry words popped out of my mouth I regretted them.

"Well, I might be a dumb-assed farmer, soldier boy," Robbarts drawled, "but it's you who's at the wrong end of this here gun."

"Not exactly," I said as I watched Hunter silently taking out the two forms behind Robbarts. That action told me the other three had already been neutralized. Hunter is good at what he does—thorough.

"You really shouldn't have said that about Becky," I said calmly. Robbarts's normal human reaction time was no match for my enhanced speed. I quickly swiped the knife edge of my forearm sleeve, and a wet, red grin grew beneath his chin.

Severing the cardioid arteries releases the pressure and drains blood from the brain. It causes death in seconds and slashing his larynx prevented any outcry. Robbarts stood quietly erect for a moment until his body got the message that blood was no longer flowing to the head and no more signals were coming from the dying brain. Then he toppled over.

I scooped up Becky and continued. Hunter would destroy Robbarts's head, just as he had the others, and catch up. I hoped the rest of Robbarts's flock wouldn't waste more of what little time we had left.

While I jogged along, I checked to see where Becky had been hit. It wasn't fatal, so I put a compress over the wound to staunch the bleeding. It would do well enough until we found the others.

"Where now?" I asked.

Becky stopped sobbing for a moment. "There's a pond down there. It's up the hill from there. There's a hiding hole near the barn."

So that's how they managed to evade the evacuation search teams—by hiding in a bunker. Hunter had caught up by then and I briefed him. He directed the scouts to converge on the spot. "What if it's sealed?" he asked.

"You know what to do," I answered and he smiled. That was the difference between us—he enjoyed this, enjoyed the danger, enjoyed the blood. When we got within sight of the entrance to the bunker I put Becky down. "You have to call them out," I said. "Can you do that?"

"They'll shoot me like they did Paw," Becky protested. "I hurt real bad, mister. Can't you do something?" She was crying.

"Listen Becky, it's really important that I get to those people quickly. I tell you what; if they shoot at you I'll punish them like I did Mr. Robbarts, all right?" She nodded, but reluctantly. "Becky, just walk over there and yell. Tell them you're hurt and need help. I don't think they'll shoot a little girl."

"Aren't you coming with me?" she said.

I shook my head. "No, they might be afraid if they saw me. You can tell them who we are if you want and then I'll show myself." I wiped her nose and pushed her behind to get her moving.

Becky hesitated and then slowly hobbled across the field. "Help! I been shot!" she screamed.

A black hole appeared in the ground by the barn and a man climbed out. "Becky?" he called out. "Robbarts said you were dead." I noticed he'd left the hatch open. Good.

"He just shot me, like he did Paw and the Pastons," she answered.

"We heard a shot but didn't know it was you," the man said as he approached and knelt before Becky. "Damn, that looks bad. How did you manage to get here—and where are Robbarts and his men?" He was looking around nervously.

"The rescue soldiers took care of him," Becky answered innocently.

"Soldiers!" That didn't sound like a curse. More like a man with hope in his voice. I stepped forward.

"Captain Savage; forty-fifth combat arm," I said. "We came to save your souls." I could see by his frightened reaction that he wasn't going to be a problem.

"He's got a ship to take us all away, Mr. Truett, just like Paw said," Becky said. "They'll have a doctor to fix me up and we'll all be safe."

Truett stepped closer. "I heard things." I could hear the fear in his voice. How much he knew, I did not know.

"We can't be used by the Shardies," I said calmly. "Can't survive more than a few minutes without our combat rations." I figured he knew about the measured doses of anticoagulants fed into my bloodstream. When those stopped, my brain would suffuse with thick blood, hemorrhaging and destroying the remaining organic brain cells. "We're running out of time here."

"How long?" he said, showing more understanding than I expected from a dumb-assed farmer who hadn't had the good sense to save himself and his family when he could.

"I've only got about another hundred minutes," I answered.

Truett turned his head and whistled. "Suicide trooper." He blinked, but that didn't stop a tear from running down his cheek. He understood. Without another word he led the way toward the black hole. "They're all inside," he remarked quietly. "There's thirty of us. Mostly women. Some are just kids," he added sadly. "I was hoping . . ." He stopped, looked at Becky, and sighed. "Never mind."

Thirty in the bunker. That meant that all forty were accounted for, counting the three men of Becky's family, the six Hunter had taken out, Becky, and Truett. Good. "We'll take care of them quickly." I said and he nodded. Quiet. Yeah, I guess he did know "things."

Hunter and the scouts had already converged on the hole and were dropping through, one after another. I had no doubts of their effectiveness.

"What's it like for you?" Truett said. He was holding Becky tightly in his arms.

"Being here, or being a soldier?" I answered.

"Both. I can't see how you can be so cold and distant. Hell, man, can't you at least show some emotion? Or are you mostly machine now?" His voice was a mixture of anger and fear.

"I grew up on a farm," I said slowly, trying to dredge up memories of a happier past on a planet now lost beyond redemption. "I still remember the smell of autumn, the feeling of mud between my toes, and how it felt to kill my prize sheep when it was time. This mission's no different. I do what I have to do because there are worse things for a human being than dying."

"I saw the news tapes," he said. "Ugly. Horrible. But what about your own hide? Don't you have any sense of self-preservation?"

"When you've been taken care of, we'll go after the Shardies," I bit out. "Our secondary mission is to gather whatever data we can and squirt a message to the fleet. After that, well, there's four, five thousand tons of explosive force in our packs." I patted the small canister strapped to my back. "I figure a dead-man switch will take care of them if we get close."

Truett smiled. "Brave, but it was a foolish waste of resources to come back for us. We made our own mess—stupid as it was to believe Robbarts—and we deserve to lie in it."

I checked the time. We only had fifteen minutes of good time left. Hunter was taking far too long.

"I'm sorry," I said quickly. "You don't have any time left."

Truett grabbed my hand and squeezed. "I just want you to know . . ." he began and then choked off whatever he was going to say. Instead he slapped my shoulder. "Yeah." I could tell he was trying hard not to cry, but his voice cracked at the end. "Well," he said to Becky. "Looks like we've got a ship to catch," he said cheerily.

Hunter popped out of the hole and came toward me at a run. "We're done," he said quickly. Moments later, the ground surged upward with a roar as smoke and flame shot from the burrow's entrance. If that didn't get the Shardies's attention, nothing would.

"Becky," I said, and gently took her from Truett's arms. "It's time to go."

"Is the ship coming?" Becky asked excitedly as she squirmed around in my arms. "I don't see it."

"It's up there in the sky," Truett said very gently. "Just look up. There, to the right of that big, bright red star." Becky tilted her head back to look almost directly overhead.

I brought my forearm across her throat and held her as she died. I hoped that she didn't have enough time to realize what I had done. What I had to do.

Hunter had taken care of Truett without a struggle. He too had been looking up, as if he might have believed his own words.

I gently lay Becky's lifeless body on the ground, trying not to feel. As before, I let Hunter take care of the final details, ensuring not a single brain cell remained in either head.

There were two minutes left in our window when I heard a distant whine. It could only be the Shardies. I placed my finger on the detonator. Our comm packages were running and would catch our final moments.

"Civilians just don't understand, do they?" Hunter asked as he waited beside me for sweet oblivion, sweet release from these mechanical contrivances we'd become.

I thought of Truett, and the way he had bravely shielded Becky to the last, thought of all the ways the war hasn't changed human decency, thought of my prize sheep and the necessities life forces on us.

"Some do," I admitted.

DEAD MEN WALKING

PAUL MCAULEY

I GUESS THIS is the end. I'm in no condition to attempt the climb down, and in any case I'm running out of air. The nearest emergency shelter is only five klicks away, but it might as well be on the far side of this little moon. I'm not expecting any kind of last-minute rescue, either. No one knows I'm here, my phone and the distress beacon are out, my emergency flares went with my utility belt, and I don't think that the drones patrol this high. At least my legs have stopped hurting, although I can feel the throb of what's left of my right hand through the painkiller's haze, like the beat of distant war drums. . . .

If you're the person who found my body, I doubt that you'll have time to listen to my last and only testament. You'll be too busy calling for help, securing the area, and making sure that you or any of your companions don't trample precious clues underfoot. I imagine instead that you're an investigator or civil servant sitting in an office buried deep inside some great bureaucratic hive, listening to this out of duty before consigning it to the memory hole. You'll know that my body was found near the top of the eastern wall of the great gash of Elliot Graben on Ariel, Uranus's fourth-largest moon, but I don't suppose you've ever visited the place, so I should give you an idea of what I can see.

I'm sitting with my pressure suit's backpack firmly wedged against a huge block of dirty, rock-hard ice. A little way beyond my broken legs, a cliff drops straight down for about a kilometer to the bottom of the graben's enormous trough. Its floor was resurfaced a couple of billion years ago by a flood of water-ice lava, a level plain patched with enormous fields of semi-vacuum organisms. Orange and red, deep blacks, foxy umbers, bright yellows . . . they stretch away from me in every direction for as far as I can see, like the biggest quilt in the universe. This moon is so small and the graben is so wide that its western rim is below the horizon. Strings of suspensor lamps float high above the fields like a fleet of burning airships.

There's enough atmospheric pressure, twenty millibars of nitrogen and methane, to haze the view and give an indication of distance, of just how big this strange garden really is. It's the prison farm, of course, and every square centimeter of it was constructed by the sweat of men and women convicted by the failure of their ideals, but none of that matters to me now. I'm beyond all that up here, higher than the suspensor lamps, tucked under the eaves of the vast roof of transparent half-life polymer that tents the graben. If I twist my head I can glimpse one of the giant struts that anchor the roof. Beyond it, the big, blue-green globe of Uranus floats in the black sky. The gas giant's south pole, capped with a brownish haze of photochemical smog, is aimed at the brilliant point of the sun, which hangs just above the western horizon.

Sunset's three hours off. I won't live long enough to see it. My legs are comfortably numb, but the throbbing in my hand is becoming more urgent, there's a dull ache in my chest, and every breath is an effort. I wonder if I'll live long enough to tell you my story. . . .

———

All right. I've just taken another shot of painkiller. I had to override the suit to do it, it's a lethal dose. . . .

Christos, it still hurts. It hurts to laugh. . . .

———

My name is Roy Bruce. It isn't my real name. I have never had a real name. I suppose I had a number when I was decanted, but I don't know what it was. My instructors called me Dave—but they called all of us Dave, a private joke they never bothered to explain. Later, just before the war began, I took the life of the man in whose image I had been made. I took his life, his name, his identity. And after the war was over, after I evaded recall and went on the run, I had several different names, one after the other. But Roy, Roy Bruce, that's the name I've had longest. That's the name you'll find on the roster of guards. That's the name you can bury me under.

My name is Roy Bruce, and I lived in Herschel City, Ariel, for eight and a half years.

Lived. Already with the past tense. . . .

My name is Roy Bruce. I'm a prison guard. The prison, TPA Facility 898, is a cluster of chambers—we call them blocks—buried in the eastern rim of Elliot Graben. Herschel City is twenty klicks beyond, a giant cylindrical shaft sunk into Ariel's icy surface, its walls covered in a vertical, shaggy green forest that grows from numerous ledges and crevices. Public buildings and little parks jut out of the forest wall like bracket fungi; homes are built in and amongst the trees. Ariel's just over a thousand kilometers in diameter and mostly ice; its gravity barely exists. The citizens of Herschel City are arboreal acrobats, swinging, climbing, sliding, flying up and down and roundabout on cableways and trapezes, nets and ropewalks.

It's a good place to live.

I have a one-room treehouse. It's not very big and plainly furnished, but you can sit on the porch of a morning, watch squirrel monkeys chase each other through the pines. . . . I'm a member of Sweat Lodge #23. I breed singing crickets, have won several competitions with them. Mostly they're hacked to sing fragments of Mozart, nothing fancy, but my line has good sustain and excellent timbre and pitch. I hope old Willy Gup keeps it going. . . .

I like to hike too, and climb freestyle. I once soloed the Broken Book route in Prospero Chasma on Miranda, twenty kilometers up a vertical face, in fifteen hours. Nowhere near the record, but pretty good for someone with a terminal illness. I've already had various bouts of cancer, but retroviruses dealt with those easily enough. What's killing me—what just lost the race to kill me—is a general systematic failure something like lupus. I couldn't get any treatment for it, of course, because the doctors would find out who I really am. What I really was.

I suppose that I had a year or so left. Maybe two if I was really lucky.

It wasn't much of a life, but it was all my own.

———

Uranus has some twenty-odd moons, mostly captured chunks of sooty ice a few dozen kilometers in diameter. Before the Quiet War, no more than a couple of hundred people lived out here. Rugged pioneer families, hermits, a few scientists, and some kind of Hindu sect that planted huge tracts of Umbriel's sooty surface with slow-growing lichenous vacuum organisms. After the war, the Three Powers Alliance took over the science station on Ariel, one of the larger moons, renamed it Herschel City, and built its maximum security facility in the big graben close by. The various leaders and lynchpins of the revolution, who had already spent two years being interrogated at Tycho, on Earth's Moon, were moved here to serve the rest of their life sentences of reeducation and moral realignment. At first, the place was run by the Navy, but civilian contractors were brought in after Elliot Graben was tented and the vacuum organism farms were planted. Most were ex-Service people who had settled in the Outer System after the war. I was one of them.

I had learned how to create fake identities with convincing histories during my training: my latest incarnation easily passed the security check. For eight and half years, Roy Bruce, guard third class, cricket breeder, amateur freestyle climber, lived a quiet, anonymous life out on the fringe of the solar system. And then two guards stumbled across the body of Goether Lyle, who had been the leader of the Senate of Athens, Tethys, when, along with a dozen other city states in the Outer System, it had declared independence from Earth.

I'd known Goether slightly: an intense, serious man who'd been writing some kind of philosophical thesis in his spare time. His body was found in the middle of the main highway between the facility and the farms, spread-eagled and naked, spikes hammered through hands and feet. His genitals had been cut off and stuffed in his mouth; his tongue had been pulled through the slit in his throat. He was also frozen solid—the temperature out on the floor of the graben is around minus one hundred and fifty degrees Celsius, balmy compared to the surface of Ariel, but still a lot colder than the inside of any domestic freezer, so cold that the carbon dioxide given off by certain strains of vacuum organisms precipitates out of the atmosphere like hoar frost. It took six hours to thaw out his body for the autopsy, which determined that the mutilations were postmortem. He'd died of strangulation, and then all the other stuff had been done to him.

I was more than thirty klicks away when Goether Lyle's body was discovered, supervising a work party of ten prisoners, what we call a stick, that was harvesting a field of vacuum organisms. It's important to keep the prisoners occupied, and stoop labor out in the fields or in the processing plants leaves them too tired to plan any serious mischief. Also, export of the high-grade biochemicals that the vacuum organisms cook from methane in the thin atmosphere helps to defray the enormous cost of running the facility. So I didn't hear about the murder until I'd driven my stick back to its block at the end of the shift, and I didn't learn all the gruesome details until later that evening, at the sweat lodge.

In the vestigial gravity of worldlets like Ariel, where you can drown in a shower and water tends to slosh about uncontrollably, sweat lodges, saunas, or Turkish-style hamams are ideal ways to keep clean. You bake in steam heat, sweat the dirt out of your pores, scrape it off your skin, and exchange gossip with your neighbors and friends. Even in a little company town like Herschel City, there are lodges catering for just about every sexual orienta-

tion and religious belief. My lodge, #23, is for unattached, agnostic hetero-
sexual males. That evening, as usual, I was sitting with a dozen or so naked
men of various ages and body types in eucalyptus-scented steam around its
stone hearth. We scraped at our skin with abrasive mitts or plastered green
depilatory mud on ourselves, squirted the baking stones of the hearth with
water to make more steam, and talked about the murder of Goether Lyle.
Mustafa Sesler, who worked in the hospital, gave us all the grisly details.
There was speculation about whether it was caused by a personal beef or a
turf war between gangs. Someone made the inevitable joke about it being
the most thorough suicide in the history of the prison. Someone else, my
friend Willy Gup, asked me if I had any idea about it.

"You had the guy in your stick last year, Roy. He have any enemies you
know of?"

I gave a noncommittal answer. The mutilations described by Mustafa
Sesler were straight out of my training in assassination, guerrilla tactics,
and black propaganda. I was processing the awful possibility that Goether
Lyle had been murdered by someone like me.

You must know by now what I am. That I am not really human. That I
am a doppelgänger who was designed by gene wizards, grown in a vat, decanted fully grown with a headful of hardwired talents and traits, trained
up, and sent out to kill the person whose exact double I was, and replace
him. I do not know how many doppelgängers, berserkers, suicide artists
and other cloned subversives were deployed during the Quiet War, but I
believe that our contribution was significant. My target was Sharwal Jah
Sharja, a minor gene wizard who lived alone in the jungle in one of the
tented crevasses of East of Eden, Ganymede, where he orchestrated the
unceasing symphony of the city-state's closed loop ecosystem. After I took
his place, I began a program of ecotage, significantly reducing the circula-
tion of water vapor and increasing the atmospheric concentration of carbon dioxide and toxic trace gases. By the time the Quiet War kicked off,
some four weeks later, the population of East of Eden was wearing breathing masks, the forests and parks were beginning to die, and most food animals and crops *had* died or were badly stricken, forcing the city to use
biomass from vacuum organism farms to feed its citizens. A commando
force of the Three Powers Alliance annexed East of Eden's farms in the
first few hours of the war, and after two weeks its starving citizens agreed to
terms of surrender.

I was supposed to turn myself in as soon as the city had been secured,
but in the middle of the formal surrender, dead-ender fanatics assassinated
half the senate and attacked the occupying force. In the subsequent confusion, the tented crevasse where I had been living was blown open to vacu-

um, Sharwal Jah Sharja was posted as one of the casualties, and I took the opportunity to slip away. I have successfully hidden my true identity and lived incognito amongst ordinary human beings ever since.

Why did I disobey my orders? How did I slip the bonds of my hard-wired drives and instincts? It's quite simple. While I had been pretending to be Sharwal Jah Sharja, I had come to love life. I wanted to learn as much about it as I could in the brief span I'd been allotted by my designers. And so I adopted the identity of another casualty, and after the war was over and the Three Powers Alliance allowed trade and travel to resume, I left East of Eden and went out into the solar system to see what I could see.

In all my wanderings I have never met any others like me, but I did find a hint that at least one of my brothers and sisters of the vat had survived the war. All of us had been imprinted with a variety of coded messages covering a vast range of possibilities, and a year after going on the run I came across one of them in a little used passageway between two chambers of the city of Xamba, Rhea.

To anyone else it was a meaningless scrawl; to me, it was like a flash of black lightning that branded an enciphered phone number on my brain. The walls of the passageway were thickly scribbled with graffiti, much of it pre-war. The message could have been left there last year or last week; it could have been a trap, left by agents hunting renegades like me. I didn't have the nerve to find out. I went straight to the spaceport and bought a seat on a shuttle to Phoebe, the gateway port to the other moons of Saturn and the rest of the Outer System. Six months later, wearing the new identity of Roy Bruce, I became a guard at TPA Facility 898.

That's why, almost nine years later, I couldn't be certain that any of my brothers and sisters had survived, and I was able to convince myself that Goether Lyle had been the victim of the vicious internal politics of the prison, killed and mutilated by someone who knew about the black propaganda techniques in which we'd been trained. But that comforting fiction was blown apart the very next day, when another mutilated body was found.

———

The victim was a former senator of Baghdad, Enceladus, and a member of the prison gang that was intermittently at war with the gang to which Goether Lyle had belonged. A message written in blood on the ground next to the senator's body implied that he'd been murdered by Goether Lyle's cronies, but whoever had killed him must have done the deed in his cell some time between the evening count and the end of the night's lockdown, spirited his body out of the facility without being detected, and left it within the field of view of a security camera that had been hacked to show a recorded loop instead of a live feed. Members of the rival gangs lived in different blocks, had chips implanted in their skulls that constantly monitored their movements, and were under lockdown all night. If the killer was a prisoner, he would have had to bribe more than a dozen guards; it was far more likely that the senator had been killed by one of the facility's staff. And when I heard what had been done to the body, I was certain that it was the handiwork of one of my brothers or sisters. The senator had been blinded before he'd been strangled, and his lungs had been pulled through incisions in his back. It was a mutilation called the Blood Eagle that had been invented by the Vikings some two thousand years ago. I remembered the cold, patient voice of the instructor who had demonstrated it to us on a corpse.

Someone in the warden's office reached the same conclusion. Posted at the top of our daily orders was an announcement that a specialist team was on its way to Ariel, and emergency security measures were put in place at the spaceport. That evening Willy Gup told the sweat lodge that the warden reckoned that it was possible that the two murders were the work of the kind of vat-grown assassin used in the Quiet War.

"So if you come across anything suspicious, don't be tempted to do anything stupidly heroic, my brothers. Those things are smart and deadly and completely without any kind of human feeling. Be like me. Stay frosty, but hang back."

I felt a loathsome chill crawl through me. I knew that if Willy and the others realized that one of "those things" was sitting with them in the steamy heat of the lodge, they would fall on me at once and tear me limb from limb. And I knew that I couldn't hang back, couldn't let things run their course. No one would be able to leave Ariel for the duration of the emergency security measures, and the specialist team would search every square centimeter of the facility and Herschel City, check the records and DNA profile of every prisoner, member of staff, citizen and visitor, and release a myriad of tiny half-life drones designed to home in on anyone breathing out the combination of metabolic byproducts unique to our kind. The team would almost certainly uncover the assassin, but they would also unmask me.

Oh, I suppose that I could have hiked out to some remote location on the surface and hunkered down for the duration, but I had no idea how long the search would last. The only way I could be sure of evading it would be to force my pressure suit to put me in deep hibernation for a month or two, and how would I explain my absence when I returned? And besides, I knew that I was dying. I was already taking dangerously large daily doses of steroids to relieve the swelling of my joints and inflammation of my connective tissue caused by my pseudo-lupus. Suspended animation would slow but not stop the progress of my disease. Suppose I never woke up?

I spent a long, bleak night considering my options. By the time the city had begun to increase its ambient light level and the members of the local troop of spider monkeys were beginning to hoot softly to each other in the trees outside my little cabin, I knew what I would have to do. I knew that I would have to find the assassin before the team arrived.

My resolve hardened when I started my shift a couple of hours later and learned that there had been two more murders, and a minor riot in the prison library.

<hr/>

I found it laughably easy to hack into the facility's files: I had been trained well all those years ago, and the data system was of a similar vintage to my own. To begin with, I checked the dossiers of recently recruited staff, but found nothing suspicious, and didn't have any better luck when I examined the dossiers of friends and family of prisoners, their advocates, and traders and businesspeople currently staying in Herschel City. It was possible that I had missed something—no doubt the assassin's cover story was every bit as good as the one that had served me so well for so long. But having more or less eliminated the obvious suspects, I had to consider the possibility that, just like me, the assassin had been hiding on Ariel ever since the war had ended. I had so much in common with my brothers and sisters that it would not be a wild coincidence if one of them had come to the same decision as I had, and had joined the staff of the prison. Perhaps he had finally gone insane, or perhaps the hardwired imperatives of his old mission had kicked in. Or perhaps, like me, he had discovered that he was coming to the end of his short life span, and had decided to have some fun. . . .

In the short time before the specialist team arrived, it would be impossible to check thoroughly the records of over three thousand staff members. I had reached a dead end. I decided that I needed some advice.

Everyone in Herschel City and the prison was talking about the murders. During a casual conversation with Willy Gup, I found it easy enough to ask my old friend if he had any thoughts on how someone might go about uncovering the identity of the assassin.

"Anyone with any sense would keep well clear," Willy said. "He'd keep his nose clean, he'd keep his stick in line, and he'd wait for the specialists."

"Who won't be here for a week. A full-scale war could have broken out by then."

Willy admitted that I had a point. One of the original intake of guards, a veteran who'd served in one of the Navy supply ships during the Quiet War, he had led the team that put down the trouble in the library. Three prisoners had died and eighteen had been badly injured—one had gouged out the eyes of another with her thumbs—and the incident had left him subdued and thoughtful.

After studying me for a few moments, he said, "If it was me, I wouldn't touch the files. I hear the warden is compiling a list of people who are poking around, looking for clues and so forth. He tolerates their nonsense because he desperately wants to put an end to the trouble as soon as he can, and he'll be pretty damn happy if some hack does happen to uncover the assassin. But it isn't likely, and when this thing is over you can bet he's going to come down hard on all those amateur sleuths. And it's possible the assassin is keeping tabs on the files too. Anyone who comes close to finding him could be in for a bad surprise. No, my brother, screwing around in the files is only going to get you into trouble."

I knew then that Willy had a shrewd idea of what I was about. I also knew that the warden was the least of my worries. I said, as lightly as I could, "So what would you do?"

Willy didn't answer straight away, but instead refilled his bulb from the jar of iced tea. We were sitting on the porch of his little shack, at the edge of a setback near the top of the city's shaft. Banana plants and tree ferns screened it from its neighbors; the vertical forest dropped away on either side. Willy's champion cricket, a splendid white and gold specimen in a cage of plaited bamboo, was trilling one of Bach's Goldberg Variations.

Willy passed the jar to me and said, "We're speaking purely hypothetically."

"Of course."

"You've always had a wild streak," Willy said, "I wouldn't put it past you to do something recklessly brave and dangerously stupid."

"I'm just an ordinary hack," I said.

"Who goes for long solitary hikes across the surface. Who soloed that route in Prospero Chasma and didn't bother to mention it until someone found out a couple of years later. I've known you almost nine years, Roy, and you're still a man of mystery," Willy smiled. "Hey, what's that look for? All I'm saying is you have character, is all."

For a moment, my hardwired reflexes had kicked in. For a moment, I had been considering whether or not this man had blown my cover, whether or not I should kill him. I carefully manufactured a smile, and said that I hadn't realized that I seemed so odd.

"Most of us have secrets," Willy said. "That's why we're out here, my brother. We're just as much prisoners as anyone in our sticks. They don't know it, but those dumbasses blundering about in the files are trying to find a way of escaping what they are."

"And there's no way you can escape what you are," I said.

The moment had passed. My smile was a real smile now, not a mask I'd put on to hide what I really was.

Willy toasted me with his bulb of tea. "Anyone with any sense learns that eventually."

"You still haven't told me how you would catch the assassin."

"I don't intend to catch him."

"But speaking hypothetically . . ."

"For all we know, it's the warden. He can go anywhere and everywhere, and he has access to all the security systems too."

"The warden? Really?"

Willy grinned. "I'm pulling your chain. But seriously, I've done a little research about these things. They're not only stone killers: they're also real good at disguising themselves. The assassin could be any one of us. The warden, you, me, anyone. Unless this thing makes a mistake, we haven't got a hope of catching it. All we can do is what we're already doing—deploy more security drones, keep the prisoners locked down when they aren't working, and pray that that'll keep a lid on any unrest until that team arrives."

"I guess you're right," I said.

"Don't try to be a hero, my brother. Not even hypothetically."

"Absolutely not," I said.

But one of Willy's remarks had given me an idea about how to reach out to the assassin, and my mind was already racing, grappling with what I had to do.

I decided that if the assassin really was keeping an eye on the people who were hacking into the files, then he (or at least, his demon), must be lurking in the root directory of the data system. That was where I left an encrypted message explaining what I was and why I wanted to talk, attached to a demon that would attempt to trace anyone who looked at it. The demon phoned me six hours later, in the middle of the night. Someone had spotted my sign and wanted to talk.

The demon had failed to identify the person who wanted to talk, and it was infected with something, too: a simple communication program. I checked it out, excised a few lines of code that would have revealed my location, and fired it up. It connected me to a blank, two-dimensional space in which words began to appear, emerging letter by letter, traveling from right to left and fading away.

>>*you got rid of the trace function. pretty good for an old guy—if that's what you really are.*

>*they trained us well,* I typed.

>>*you think you know what i am. you think that i am like you.*

Whoever was at the other end of the program wanted to get straight down to business. That suited me, but I knew that I couldn't let him take the lead.

>*we are both children of the vat,* I typed. *that's why I reached out to you. that's why i want to help you.*

There was a pause as my correspondent thought this over.

>>*you could be a trap.*

>*the message got your attention because it is hardwired into your visual cortex, just as it is hardwired into mine.*

>>*that kind of thing is no longer the secret it once was, but let's say that i believe you. . . .*

A black disc spun in the blank space for less than a second, its strobing black light flashing a string of letters and numbers, gone.

>>*do you know where that is?*

I realized that the letters and numbers burnt into my brain were a grid reference.

>*i can find it.*

>>*meet me in four hours. i have a little business to take care of first.*

It was the middle of the night; the time when the assassin did his work.

>*please don't kill anyone else until we have talked.*

My words faded. There was no reply.

———

The grid reference was at the precise center of a small eroded crater sixty klicks south of the facility, an unreconstructed area in the shadow of the graben's eastern rimwall. Before I headed out, I equipped myself from the armory and downloaded a hack into the security system so that I could move freely and unremarked. I was oddly happy, foolishly confident. It felt good to be in action again. My head was filled with a fat, contented hum as I drove a tricycle cart along an old construction road. The rendezvous point was about an hour away: I would have plenty of time to familiarize myself with the terrain and make my preparations before the assassin, if that was who I had been talking to, turned up.

I want to make it clear that my actions were in no way altruistic. The only life I wanted to save was my own. Yes, I knew that I was dying, but no one loves life more than those who have only a little of it left; no one else experiences each and every moment with such vivid immediacy. I didn't intend to throw away my life in a grand gesture. I wanted to unmask the assassin and escape the special team's inquisition.

The road ran across a flat terrain blanketed in vacuum-cemented grey-brown dust and littered with big blocks that over the eons had been eroded into soft shapes by impact cratering. The rimwall reared up to my left, its intricate folds and bulges like a frozen curtain. Steep cones and rounded hills of mass-wasted talus fringed its base. To my right, the land sloped away toward a glittering ribbon of fences and dykes more than a kilometer away, the boundary of the huge patchwork of fields. It was two in the morning by the clock, but the suspensor lamps were burning as brightly as they always did, and above the western horizon the sun's dim spark was almost lost in their hazy glow.

I was a couple of klicks from the rendezvous, and the road was cutting through a steep ridge that buttressed a great bulge in the rimwall, when the assassin struck. I glimpsed a hitch of movement high in a corner of my vision, but before I could react, a taser dart struck my cart and shorted its motor. A second later, a net slammed into me, slithering over my torso as muscular threads of myoelectric plastic tightened in constricting folds around my arms and chest. I struggled to free myself as the cart piddled to a halt, but my arms were pinned to my sides by the net and I couldn't even unfasten the safety harness. I could only sit and watch as a figure in a black pressure suit descended the steep side of the ridge in two huge bounds, reached me in two more.

It ripped out my phone, stripped away my utility belt, the gun in the pocket on the right thigh of my pressure suit and the knife in the pocket on the left thigh, then uncoupled my main air supply, punched the release of my harness and dragged me out of the low-slung seat and hauled me off the road. I was dumped on my back near a cart parked in the shadow of a house-sized block and the assassin stepped back, aiming a rail-gun at me.

The neutron camera I'd fitted inside my helmet revealed scant details of the face behind the gold-filmed mirror of my captor's visor; its demon made an extrapolation, searched the database I'd loaded, found a match. Debra Thorn, employed as a paramedic in the facility's infirmary for the past two years, twenty-two, unmarried, no children. . . . I realized then that I'd made a serious mistake. The assassin was a doppelgänger, all right, but because she was the double of someone who hadn't been an adult when the war had ended she must have been manufactured and decanted much more recently than me. She wasn't insane, and she hadn't spent years under cover. She was killing people because that was what she'd been sent here to do. Because it was her mission.

A light was winking on my head-up display—the emergency short-range, line-of-sight walkie-talkie. When I responded, an electronically distorted voice said, "Are you alone?"

"Absolutely."

"Who are you?"

I'd stripped all identifying tags from my suit before setting off, but the doppelgänger who had killed Debra Thorn and taken her place was pointing a gun at my head and it seemed advisable to tell her my name. She was silent for a moment, no doubt taking a look at my file. I said, "I'm not the doppelgänger of Roy Bruce, if that's what you're thinking. The person I killed and replaced was a gene wizard by the name of Sharwal Jah Sharja."

I briefly told the assassin the story I have already told you. When I was finished, she said, "You've really been working here for eight years?"

"Eight and a half."

I had made a very bad mistake about my captor's motives, but I must have piqued her curiosity, for otherwise I would already be dead. And even if I couldn't talk my way out of this and persuade her to spare me, I still had a couple of weapons she hadn't found . . . I risked a lie, said that her net had compromised my suit's thermal integrity. I told her that I was losing heat to the frozen ground, that I would freeze to death if I didn't get up.

She told me I could sit up, and to do it slowly.

As I got my feet under me, squatting on my haunches in front of her, I glanced up at the top of the ridge and made a crucial triangulation.

She said, "My instructors told me that I would live no more than a year."

"Perhaps they told you that you would burn briefly but very brightly—that's what they told me. But they lied. I expect they lied about a lot of things, but I promise to tell you only the truth. We can leave here, and go anywhere we want to."

"I have a job to finish. People to kill, riots to start."

The assassin took a long step sideways to the cart, took something the size of a basketball from the net behind its seat, bowled it toward me. It bounced slowly over the dusty ground and ended up between my legs: the severed head of an old woman, skin burnt black with cold, eyes capped by frost.

"The former leader of the parliament of Sparta, Tethys," the assassin said. "I left the body pinned to the ground in one of the fields where her friends work, with an amusing little message."

"You are trying to start a war amongst the prisoners. Perhaps the people who sent you here are hoping that the scandal will close the facility. Perhaps they think it is the only chance they'll have of freeing their comrades. Who are you working for, by the way?"

"I'll ask the questions," the assassin said.

I asked her how she would escape when she was finished. "There's a special team on the way. If you're still here when they arrive, they'll hunt you down and kill you."

"So that's why you came after me. You were frightened that this team would find you while they were hunting me."

She may have been young, but she was smart and quick.

I said, "I came because I wanted to talk to you. Because you're like me."

"Because after all these years of living amongst humans, you miss your own kind, is that it?"

Despite the electronic distortion, I could hear the sneer in the assassin's voice. I said carefully, "The people who sent you here—the people who made you—have no plans to extract you when you are finished here. They do not care if you survive your mission. They only care that it is successful. Why give your loyalty to people who consider you expendable? To people who lied to you? You have many years of life ahead of you, and it isn't as hard to disobey your orders as you might think. You've already disobeyed them, in fact, when you reached out to me. All you have to do is take one more step, and let me help you. If we work together, we'll survive this. We'll find a way to escape."

"You think you're human. You're not. You're exactly like me. A walking dead man. That's what our instructors called us, by the way: the dead. Not 'Dave.' Not anything cute. When we were being moved from one place to another, they'd shout out a warning: 'Dead men walking.'"

It is supposed to be the traditional cry when a condemned person is let out of their cell. Fortunately, I've never worked in Block H, where prisoners who have murdered or tried to murder fellow inmates or guards await execution, so I've never heard it or had to use it.

The assassin said, "They're right, aren't they? We're made things, so how can we be properly alive?"

"I've lived a more or less ordinary life for ten years. If you give this up and come with me, I'll show you how."

"You stole a life, just as I did. Underneath your disguise, you're a dead man, just like me."

"The life I live now is my own, not anyone else's," I said. "Give up what you are doing, and I'll show you what I mean."

"You're a dead man," the assassin said. "You're breathing the last of your air. You have less than an hour left. I'll leave you to die here, finish my work, and escape in the confusion. After that, I'm supposed to be picked up, but now I think I'll pass on that. There must be plenty of people out there who need my skills. I'll work for anyone who wants some killing done, and earn plenty of money."

"It's a nice dream," I said, "but it will never come true."

"Why shouldn't I profit from what I was made to do?"

"I've lived amongst people for more than a decade. Perhaps I don't know them as well as I should, but I do know that they are very afraid of us. Not because we're different but because we're so very much like a part of them they don't want to acknowledge. Because we're the dark side of their nature. I've survived this long only because I have been very careful to hide what I really am. I can teach you how to do that, if you'll let me."

"It doesn't sound like much of a life to me," the assassin said.

"Don't you like being Debra Thorn?" I said.

And at the same moment I kicked off the ground, hoping that by revealing that I knew who she was I'd distracted and confused her, and won a moment's grace.

In Ariel's microgravity, my standing jump took me high above the assassin's head, up and over the edge of the ridge. As I flew up, I discharged the taser dart I'd sewn into the palm of one of my pressure suit's gloves, and the electrical charge stored in its super-conducting loop shorted out every thread of myoelectric plastic that bound my arms. I shrugged off the net as I came down and kicked off again, bounding along the ridge in headlong flight toward the bulging face of the cliff wall and a narrow chimney pinched between two folds of black, rock-hard ice.

I was halfway there when a kinetic round struck my left leg with tremendous force and broke my thigh. I tumbled over hummocked ice and caught hold a low pinnacle just before I went over the edge of the ridge. The assassin's triumphant shout was a blare of electronic noise in my ears; because she was using the line-of-sight walkie-talkie I knew that she was almost on me. I pushed up at once and scuttled toward the chimney like a crippled ape. I had almost reached my goal when a second kinetic round shattered my right knee.

My suit was ruptured at the point of impact, and I felt a freezing pain as the smart fabric constricted as tightly as a tourniquet, but I was not finished. The impact of the kinetic round had knocked me head over heels into a field of fallen ice-blocks, within striking distance of the chimney. As I half-crawled, half-swam toward it, a third round took off the top of a pitted block that might have fallen from the cliffs a billion years ago, and then I was inside the chimney, and started to climb.

The assassin had no experience of freestyle climbing. Despite my injuries I soon outdistanced her. The chimney gave out after half a kilometer, and I had no choice but to continue to climb the naked iceface. Less than a minute later, the assassin reached the end of the chimney and fired a kinetic round that smashed into the cliff a little way above me. I flattened against the iceface as a huge chunk dropped past me with dreamy slowness, then powered straight through the expanding cloud of debris, pebbles and ice grains briefly rattling on my helmet, and flopped over the edge of a narrow setback.

My left leg bent in the middle of my thigh and hurt horribly; my right leg was numb below the knee and a thick crust of blood had frozen solid at the joint. But I had no time to tend my wounds. I sat up and ripped out the hose of the water recycling system as the assassin shot above the edge of the cliff in a graceful arc, taser in one hand, rail gun in the other. I twisted the valve, hit her with a high-pressure spray of water that struck her visor and instantly froze. I pushed off the ground with both hands (a kinetic round slammed into the dusty ice where I'd just been), collided with her in midair, clamped my glove over the diagnostic port of her backpack, and discharged my second taser dart.

The dart shorted out the electronics in the assassin's suit, and enough current passed through the port to briefly stun her. I pushed her away as we dropped toward the setback, but she managed to fire a last shot as she spun into the void beyond the edge of the setback. She was either phenomenally lucky or incredibly skillful: it took off my thumb and three fingers of my right hand.

She fell more than a kilometer. Even in the low gravity, it was more than enough to kill her, but just to make sure I dropped several blocks of ice onto her. The third smashed her visor. You'll find her body, if you haven't already, more or less directly below the spot where you found mine.

The assassin had vented most of my air supply and taken my phone and emergency beacon; the dart I'd used on her had crippled what was left of my pressure suit's life support system. The suit's insulation is pretty good, but I'm beginning to feel the bite of the cold now, my hand is growing pretty tired from using the squeeze pump to push air through the rebreather, and I'm getting a bad headache as the carbon dioxide concentration in my air supply inexorably rises. I killed the ecosystem of East of Eden by sabotaging the balance of its atmospheric gases, and now the same imbalance is killing me.

Just about the only thing still working is the dumb little chip I stuck in my helmet to record my conversation with the assassin. By now, you probably know more about her than I do. Perhaps you even know who sent her here.

I don't have much time left. Perhaps it's because the increasing carbon dioxide level is making me comfortably stupid, but I find that I don't mind dying. I told you that I confronted the assassin to save myself. I think now that I may have been wrong about that. I may have gone on the run after the Quiet War, but in my own way I have served you right up until the end of my life.

I'm going to sign off now. I want to spend my last moments remembering my freestyle climb up those twenty kilometers of sheer ice in Prospero Chasma. I want to remember how at the end I stood tired and alone at the top of a world-cleaving fault left over from a shattering collision four billion years ago, with Uranus tilted at the horizon, half-full, serene and remote, and the infinite black, starry sky above. I felt so utterly insignificant then, and yet so happy, too, without a single regret for anything at all in my silly little life.

GLORY

GREG EGAN

1

AN INGOT OF metallic hydrogen gleamed in the starlight, a narrow cylinder half a meter long with a mass of about a kilogram. To the naked eye, it was a dense, solid object, but its lattice of tiny nuclei immersed in an insubstantial fog of electrons was one part matter to two hundred trillion parts empty space. A short distance away was a second ingot, apparently identical to the first, but composed of antihydrogen.

A sequence of finely tuned gamma rays flooded into both cylinders. The protons that absorbed them in the first ingot spat out positrons and were transformed into neutrons, breaking their bonds to the electron cloud that glued them in place. In the second ingot, antiprotons became antineutrons.

A further sequence of pulses herded the neutrons together and forged them into clusters; the antineutrons were similarly rearranged. Both kinds of cluster were unstable, but in order to fall apart, they first had to pass through a quantum state that would have strongly absorbed a component of the gamma rays constantly raining down on them. Left to themselves, the probability of them being in this state would have increased rapidly, but each time they measurably failed to absorb the gamma rays, the probability fell back to zero. The quantum Zeno effect endlessly reset the clock, holding the decay in check.

The next series of pulses began shifting the clusters into the space that had separated the original ingots. First neutrons, then antineutrons, were sculpted together in alternating layers. Though the clusters were ultimately unstable, while they persisted they were inert, sequestering their constituents and preventing them from annihilating their counterparts. The end point of this process of nuclear sculpting was a sliver of compressed matter and antimatter, sandwiched together into a needle one micron wide.

The gamma ray lasers shut down, the Zeno effect withdrew its prohibitions. For the time it took a beam of light to cross a neutron, the needle sat motionless in space. Then it began to burn, and it began to move.

The needle was structured like a meticulously crafted firework, and its outer layers ignited first. No external casing could have channeled this blast, but the pattern of tensions woven into the needle's construction favored one direction for the debris to be expelled. Particles streamed backward; the needle moved forward. The shock of acceleration could not have been borne by anything built from atomic-scale matter, but the pressure bearing down on the core of the needle prolonged its life, delaying the inevitable.

Layer after layer burned itself away, blasting the dwindling remnant forward ever faster. By the time the needle had shrunk to a tenth of its original size it was moving at ninety-eight percent of light speed; to a bystander, this could scarcely have been improved upon, but from the needle's perspective, there was still room to slash its journey's duration by orders of magnitude.

When just one thousandth of the needle remained, its time, compared to the neighboring stars, was passing five hundred times more slowly. Still the layers kept burning, the protective clusters unraveling as the pressure on them was released. The needle could only reach close enough to light speed to slow down time as much as it required if it could sacrifice a large enough proportion of its remaining mass. The core of the needle could only survive for a few trillionths of a second, while its journey would take two hundred million seconds as judged by the stars. The proportions had been carefully matched, though: out of the two kilograms of matter and antimatter that had been woven together at the launch, only a few million neutrons were needed as the final payload.

By one measure, seven years passed. For the needle, its last trillionths of a second unwound, its final layers of fuel blew away, and at the moment its core was ready to explode, it reached its destination, plunging from the near-vacuum of space straight into the heart of a star.

Even here, the density of matter was insufficient to stabilize the core, yet far too high to allow it to pass unhindered. The core was torn apart. But it did not go quietly, and the shock waves it carved through the fusing plasma endured for a million kilometers: all the way through to the cooler outer layers on the opposite side of the star. These shock waves were shaped by the payload that had formed them, and though the initial pattern imprint-ed on them by the disintegrating cluster of neutrons was enlarged and blurred by its journey, on an atomic scale it remained sharply defined. Like a mold stamped into the seething plasma, it encouraged ionized molecular fragments to slip into the troughs and furrows that matched their shape, and then brought them together to react in ways that the plasma's random collisions would never have allowed. In effect, the shock waves formed a web of catalysts, carefully laid out in both time and space, briefly trans-forming a small corner of the star into a chemical factory operating on a nanometer scale.

The products of this factory sprayed out of the star, riding the last traces of the shock wave's momentum: a few nanograms of elaborate, carbon-rich molecules, sheathed in a protective fullerene weave. Traveling at seven hundred kilometers per second, a fraction below the velocity needed to es-cape from the star completely, they climbed out of its gravity well, slowing as they ascended.

Four years passed, but the molecules were stable against the ravages of space. By the time they'd traveled a billion kilometers, they had almost come to a halt, and they would have fallen back to die in the fires of the star that had forged them if their journey had not been timed so that the star's third planet, a gas giant, was waiting to urge them forward. As they fell toward it, the giant's third moon moved across their path. Eleven years after the needle's launch, its molecular offspring rained down on to the methane snow.

The tiny heat of their impact was not enough to damage them, but it melted a microscopic puddle in the snow. Surrounded by food, the molecu-lar seeds began to grow. Within hours, the area was teeming with na-nomachines, some mining the snow and the minerals beneath it, others assembling the bounty into an intricate structure, a rectangular panel a couple of meters wide.

From across the light-years, an elaborate sequence of gamma ray pulses fell upon the panel. These pulses were the needle's true payload, the pas-sengers for whom it had merely prepared the way, transmitted in its wake four years after its launch. The panel decoded and stored the data, and the army of nanomachines set to work again, this time following a far more elaborate blueprint. The miners were forced to look further afield to find all the elements that were needed, while the assemblers labored to reach their goal through a sequence of intermediate stages, carefully designed to protect the final product from the vagaries of the local chemistry and climate.

After three months' work, two small fusion-powered spacecraft sat in the snow. Each one held a single occupant, waking for the first time in their freshly minted bodies, yet endowed with memories of an earlier life.

Joan switched on her communications console. Anne appeared on the screen, three short pairs of arms folded across her thorax in a posture of calm repose. They had both worn virtual bodies with the same anatomy before, but this was the first time they had become Noudah in the flesh.

"We're here. Everything worked," Joan marveled. The language she spoke was not her own, but the structure of her new brain and body made it second nature.

Anne said, "Now comes the hard part."

"Yes." Joan looked out from the spacecraft's cockpit. In the distance, a fissured blue-gray plateau of water ice rose above the snow. Nearby, the nanomachines were busy disassembling the gamma ray receiver. When they had erased all traces of their handiwork, they would wander off into the snow and catalyze their own destruction.

Joan had visited dozens of planet-bound cultures in the past, taking on different bodies and languages as necessary, but those cultures had all been plugged in to the Amalgam, the meta-civilization that spanned the galactic disk. However far from home she'd been, the means to return to familiar places had always been close at hand. The Noudah had only just mastered interplanetary flight, and they had no idea that the Amalgam existed. The closest node in the Amalgam's network was seven light-years away, and even that was out of bounds to her and Anne now: they had agreed not to risk disclosing its location to the Noudah, so any transmission they sent could only be directed to a decoy node that they'd set up more than twenty light-years away.

"It will be worth it," Joan said.

Anne's Noudah face was immobile, but chromatophores sent a wave of violet and gold sweeping across her skin in an expression of cautious optimism. "We'll see." She tipped her head to the left, a gesture preceding a friendly departure.

Joan tipped her own head in response, as if she'd been doing so all her life. "Be careful, my friend," she said.

"You too."

Anne's ship ascended so high on its chemical thrusters that it shrank to a speck before igniting its fusion engine and streaking away in a blaze of light. Joan felt a pang of loneliness; there was no predicting when they would be reunited.

Her ship's software was primitive; the whole machine had been scrupulously matched to the Noudah's level of technology. Joan knew how to fly it herself if necessary, and on a whim she switched off the autopilot and manually activated the ascent thrusters. The control panel was crowded, but having six hands helped.

2

The world the Noudah called home was the closest of the system's five planets to their sun. The average temperature was one hundred and twenty degrees Celsius, but the high atmospheric pressure allowed liquid water to exist across the entire surface. The chemistry and dynamics of the planet's crust had led to a relatively flat terrain, with a patchwork of dozens of disconnected seas but no globe-spanning ocean. From space, these seas appeared as silvery mirrors, bordered by a violet and brown tarnish of vegetation.

The Noudah were already leaving their most electromagnetically promiscuous phase of communications behind, but the short-lived oasis of Amalgam-level technology on Baneth, the gas giant's moon, had had no trouble eavesdropping on their chatter and preparing an updated cultural briefing which had been spliced into Joan's brain.

The planet was still divided into the same eleven political units as it had been fourteen years before, the time of the last broadcasts that had reached the node before Joan's departure. Tira and Ghahar, the two dominant nations in terms of territory, economic activity and military power, also occupied the vast majority of significant Niah archaeological sites.

Joan had expected that they'd be noticed as soon as they left Baneth—the exhaust from their fusion engines glowed like the sun—but their departure had triggered no obvious response, and now that they were coasting they'd be far harder to spot. As Anne drew closer to the home world, she sent a message to Tira's traffic control center. Joan tuned in to the exchange.

"I come in peace from another star," Anne said. "I seek permission to land."

There was a delay of several seconds more than the light-speed lag, then a terse response. "Please identify yourself and state your location."

Anne transmitted her coordinates and flight plan.

"We confirm your location, please identify yourself."

"My name is Anne. I come from another star."

There was a long pause, then a different voice answered. "If you are from Ghahar, please explain your intentions."

"I am not from Ghahar."

"Why should I believe that? Show yourself."

"I've taken the same shape as your people, in the hope of living among you for a while." Anne opened a video channel and showed them her unremarkable Noudah face. "But there's a signal being transmitted from these coordinates that might persuade you that I'm telling the truth." She gave the location of the decoy node, twenty light-years away, and specified a frequency. The signal coming from the node contained an image of the very same face.

This time, the silence stretched out for several minutes. It would take a while for the Tirans to confirm the true distance of the radio source.

"You do not have permission to land. Please enter this orbit, and we will rendezvous and board your ship."

Parameters for the orbit came through on the data channel. Anne said, "As you wish."

Minutes later, Joan's instruments picked up three fusion ships being launched from Tiran bases. When Anne reached the prescribed orbit, Joan listened anxiously to the instructions the Tirans issued. Their tone sounded wary, but they were entitled to treat this stranger with caution, all the more so if they believed Anne's claim.

Joan was accustomed to a very different kind of reception, but then the members of the Amalgam had spent hundreds of millennia establishing a framework of trust. They also benefited from a milieu in which most kinds of force had been rendered ineffectual; when everyone had backups of themselves scattered around the galaxy, it required a vastly disproportion- ate effort to inconvenience someone, let alone kill them. By any reasonable measure, honesty and cooperation yielded far richer rewards than subter- fuge and slaughter.

Nonetheless, each individual culture had its roots in a biological herit- age that gave rise to behavior governed more by ancient urges than con- temporary realities, and even when they mastered the technology to choose their own nature, the precise set of traits they preserved was up to them. In the worst case, a species still saddled with inappropriate drives but empow- ered by advanced technology could wreak havoc. The Noudah deserved to be treated with courtesy and respect, but they did not yet belong in the Amalgam.

The Tirans' own exchanges were not on open channels, so once they had entered Anne's ship, Joan could only guess what was happening. She waited until two of the ships had returned to the surface, then sent her own message to Ghahar's traffic control.

"I come in peace from another star. I seek permission to land."

3

The Ghahari allowed Joan to fly her ship straight down to the surface. She wasn't sure if this was because they were more trusting, or if they were afraid that the Tirans might try to interfere if she lingered in orbit.

The landing site was a bare plain of chocolate-colored sand. The air shimmered in the heat, the distortions intensified by the thickness of the atmosphere, making the horizon waver as if seen through molten glass. Joan waited in the cockpit as three trucks approached; they all came to a halt some twenty meters away. A voice over the radio instructed her to leave the ship; she complied, and after she'd stood in the open for a minute, a lone Noudah left one of the trucks and walked toward her.

"I'm Pirit," she said. "Welcome to Ghahar." Her gestures were courteous but restrained.

"I'm Joan. Thank you for your hospitality."

"Your impersonation of our biology is impeccable." There was a trace of skepticism in Pirit's tone; Joan had pointed the Ghahari to her own portrait being broadcast from the decoy node, but she had to admit that in the context her lack of exotic technology and traits would make it harder to accept the implications of that transmission.

"In my culture, it's a matter of courtesy to imitate one's hosts as closely as possible."

Pirit hesitated, as if pondering whether to debate the merits of such a custom, but then rather than quibbling over the niceties of interspecies etiquette she chose to confront the real issue head on. "If you're a Tiran spy, or a defector, the sooner you admit that the better."

"That's very sensible advice, but I'm neither."

The Noudah wore no clothing as such, but Pirit had a belt with a number of pouches. She took a handheld scanner from one and ran it over Joan's body. Joan's briefing suggested that it was probably only checking for metal, volatile explosives and radiation; the technology to image her body or search for pathogens would not be so portable. In any case, she was a healthy, unarmed Noudah down to the molecular level.

Pirit escorted her to one of the trucks, and invited her to recline in a section at the back. Another Noudah drove while Pirit watched over Joan. They soon arrived at a small complex of buildings a couple of kilometers from where the ship had touched down. The walls, roofs, and floors of the buildings were all made from the local sand, cemented with an adhesive that the Noudah secreted from their own bodies.

Inside, Joan was given a thorough medical examination, including three kinds of full-body scan. The Noudah who examined her treated her with a kind of detached efficiency devoid of any pleasantries; she wasn't sure if that was their standard bedside manner, or a kind of glazed shock at having been told of her claimed origins.

Pirit took her to an adjoining room and offered her a couch. The Noudah anatomy did not allow for sitting, but they liked to recline.

Pirit remained standing. "How did you come here?" she asked.

"You've seen my ship. I flew it from Baneth."

"And how did you reach Baneth?"

"I'm not free to discuss that," Joan replied cheerfully.

"Not free?" Pirit's face clouded with silver, as if she was genuinely per-plexed.

Joan said, "You understand me perfectly. Please don't tell me there's nothing *you're* not free to discuss with me."

"You certainly didn't fly that ship twenty light-years."

"No, I certainly didn't."

Pirit hesitated. "Did you come through the Cataract?" The Cataract was a black hole, a remote partner to the Noudah's sun; they orbited each other at a distance of about eighty billion kilometers. The name came from its telescopic appearance: a dark circle ringed by a distortion in the back-ground of stars, like some kind of visual aberration. The Tirans and Gha-hari were in a race to be the first to visit this extraordinary neighbor, but as yet neither of them were quite up to the task.

"*Through* the Cataract? I think your scientists have already proven that black holes aren't shortcuts to anywhere."

"Our scientists aren't always right."

"Neither are ours," Joan admitted, "but all the evidence points in one direction: black holes aren't doorways, they're shredding machines."

"So you traveled the whole twenty light-years?"

"More than that," Joan said truthfully, "from my original home. I've spent half my life traveling."

"Faster than light?" Pirit suggested hopefully.

"No. That's impossible."

They circled around the question a dozen more times, before Pirit final-ly changed her tune from *how* to *why?*

"I'm a xenomathematician," Joan said. "I've come here in the hope of collaborating with your archaeologists in their study of Niah artifacts."

Pirit was stunned. "What do you know about the Niah?"

"Not as much as I'd like to." Joan gestured at her Noudah body. "As I'm sure you've already surmised, we've listened to your broadcasts for some time, so we know pretty much what an ordinary Noudah knows. That includes the basic facts about the Niah. Historically they've been re-ferred to as your ancestors, though the latest studies suggest that you and they really just have an earlier common ancestor. They died out about a million years ago, but there's evidence that they might have had a sophisti-cated culture for as long as three million years. There's no indication that they ever developed spaceflight. Basically, once they achieved material comfort, they seem to have devoted themselves to various artforms, including mathematics."

"So you've traveled twenty light-years just to look at Niah tablets?" Pirit was incredulous.

"Any culture that spent three million years doing mathematics must have something to teach us."

"Really?" Pirit's face became blue with disgust. "In the ten thousand years since we discovered the wheel, we've already reached halfway to the Cataract. They wasted their time on useless abstractions."

Joan said, "I come from a culture of spacefarers myself, so I respect your achievements. But I don't think anyone really knows what the Niah achieved. I'd like to find out, with the help of your people."

Pirit was silent for a while. "What if we say no?"

"Then I'll leave empty-handed."

"What if we insist that you remain with us?"

"Then I'll die here, empty-handed." On her command, this body would expire in an instant; she could not be held and tortured.

Pirit said angrily, "You must be willing to trade *something* for the privilege you're demanding!"

"Requesting, not demanding," Joan insisted gently. "And what I'm willing to offer is my own culture's perspective on Niah mathematics. If you ask your archaeologists and mathematicians, I'm sure they'll tell you that there are many things written in the Niah tablets that they don't yet understand. My colleague and I"—neither of them had mentioned Anne before, but Joan was sure that Pirit knew all about her—"simply want to shed as much light as we can on this subject."

Pirit said bitterly, "You won't even tell us how you came to our world. Why should we trust you to share whatever you discover about the Niah?"

"Interstellar travel is no great mystery," Joan countered. "You know all the basic science already; making it work is just a matter of persistence. If you're left to develop your own technology, you might even come up with better methods than we have."

"So we're expected to be patient, to discover these things for ourselves . . . but you can't wait a few centuries for us to decipher the Niah artifacts?"

Joan said bluntly, "The present Noudah culture, both here and in Tira, seems to hold the Niah in contempt. Dozens of partially excavated sites containing Niah artifacts are under threat from irrigation projects and other developments. That's the reason we couldn't wait. We needed to come here and offer our assistance, before the last traces of the Niah disappeared forever."

Pirit did not reply, but Joan hoped she knew what her interrogator was thinking: *Nobody would cross twenty light-years for a few worthless scribblings. Perhaps we've underestimated the Niah. Perhaps our ancestors have left us a great secret, a great legacy. And perhaps the fastest—perhaps the only—way to uncover it is to give this impertinent, irritating alien exactly what she wants.*

4

The sun was rising ahead of them as they reached the top of the hill. Sando turned to Joan, and his face became green with pleasure. "Look behind you," he said.

Joan did as he asked. The valley below was hidden in fog, and it had settled so evenly that she could see their shadows in the dawn light, stretched out across the top of the fog layer. Around the shadow of her head was a circular halo like a small rainbow.

"We call it the Niah's light," Sando said. "In the old days, people used to say that the halo proved that the Niah blood was strong in you."

Joan said, "The only trouble with that hypothesis being that *you* see it around *your* head . . . and I see it around mine." On Earth, the phenomenon was known as a "glory." The particles of fog were scattering the sunlight back toward them, turning it one hundred and eighty degrees. To look at the shadow of your own head was to face directly away from the sun, so the halo always appeared around the observer's shadow.

"I suppose you're the final proof that Niah blood has nothing to do with it," Sando mused.

"That's assuming I'm telling you the truth, and I really can see it around my own head."

"And assuming," Sando added, "that the Niah really did stay at home, and didn't wander around the galaxy spreading their progeny."

They came over the top of the hill and looked down into the adjoining riverine valley. The sparse brown grass of the hillside gave way to a lush violet growth closer to the water. Joan's arrival had delayed the flooding of the valley, but even alien interest in the Niah had only bought the archaeologists an extra year. The dam was part of a long-planned agricultural development, and however tantalizing the possibility that Joan might reveal some priceless insight hidden among the Niah's "useless abstractions," that vague promise could only compete with more tangible considerations for a limited time.

Part of the hill had fallen away in a landslide a few centuries before, revealing more than a dozen beautifully preserved strata. When Joan and

Sando reached the excavation site, Rali and Surat were already at work, clearing away soft sedimentary rock from a layer that Sando had dated as belonging to the Niah's "twilight" period.

Pirit had insisted that only Sando, the senior archaeologist, be told about Joan's true nature; Joan refused to lie to anyone, but had agreed to tell her colleagues only that she was a mathematician and that she was not permitted to discuss her past. At first, this had made them guarded and resentful, no doubt because they assumed that she was some kind of spy sent by the authorities to watch over them. Later, it had dawned on them that she was genuinely interested in their work, and that the absurd restrictions on her topics of conversation were not of her own choosing. Nothing about the Noudah's language or appearance correlated strongly with their recent division into nations—with no oceans to cross, and a long history of migration they were more or less geographically homogeneous— but Joan's odd name and occasional *faux pas* could still be ascribed to some mysterious exoticism. Rali and Surat seemed content to assume that she was a defector from one of the smaller nations, and that her history could not be made explicit for obscure political reasons.

"There are more tablets here, very close to the surface," Rali announced excitedly. "The acoustics are unmistakable." Ideally, they would have excavated the entire hillside, but they did not have the time or the labor, so they were using acoustic tomography to identify likely deposits of accessible Niah writing, and then concentrating their efforts on those spots.

The Niah had probably had several ephemeral forms of written communication, but when they found something worth publishing, it stayed published: they carved their symbols into a ceramic that made diamond seem like tissue paper. It was almost unheard of for the tablets to be broken, but they were small, and multi-tablet works were sometimes widely dispersed. Niah technology could probably have carved three million years' worth of knowledge on to the head of a pin—they seemed not to have invented nanomachines, but they were into high-quality bulk materials and precision engineering—but for whatever reason they had chosen legibility to the naked eye above other considerations.

Joan made herself useful, taking acoustic readings further along the slope, while Sando watched over his students as they came closer to the buried Niah artifacts. She had learned not to hover around expectantly when a discovery was imminent; she was treated far more warmly if she waited to be summoned. The tomography unit was almost foolproof, using satellite navigation to track its position and software to analyze the signals it gathered; all it really needed was someone to drag it along the rock face at a suitable pace.

Through the corner of her eye, Joan noticed her shadow on the rocks flicker and grow complicated. She looked up to see three dazzling beads of light flying west out of the sun. She might have assumed that the fusion ships were doing something useful, but the media was full of talk of "military exercises," which meant the Tirans and the Ghahari engaging in expensive, belligerent gestures in orbit, trying to convince each other of their superior skills, technology, or sheer strength of numbers. For people with no real differences apart from a few centuries of recent history, they could puff up their minor political disputes into matters of the utmost solemnity. It might almost have been funny, if the idiots hadn't incinerated hundreds of thousands of each other's citizens every few decades, not to mention playing callous and often deadly games with the lives of the inhabitants of smaller nations.

"Jown! Jown! Come and look at this!" Surat called to her. Joan switched off the tomography unit and jogged toward the archaeologists, suddenly conscious of her body's strangeness. Her legs were stumpy but strong, and her balance as she ran came not from arms and shoulders but from the swish of her muscular tail.

"It's a significant mathematical result," Rali informed her proudly when she reached them. He'd pressure-washed the sandstone away from the near-indestructible ceramic of the tablet, and it was only a matter of holding the surface at the right angle to the light to see the etched writing stand out as crisply and starkly as it would have a million years before.

Rali was not a mathematician, and he was not offering his own opinion on the theorem the tablet stated; the Niah themselves had a clear set of typographical conventions that they used to distinguish between everything from minor lemmas to the most celebrated theorems. The size and decorations of the symbols labeling the theorem attested to its value in the Niah's eyes.

Joan read the theorem carefully. The proof was not included on the same tablet, but the Niah had a way of expressing their results that made you believe them as soon as you read them; in this case the definitions of the terms needed to state the theorem were so beautifully chosen that the result seemed almost inevitable.

The theorem itself was expressed as a commuting hypercube, one of the Niah's favorite forms. You could think of a square with four different sets of mathematical objects associated with each of its corners, and a way of mapping one set into another associated with each edge of the square. If the maps commuted, then going across the top of the square, then down, had exactly the same effect as going down the left edge of the square, then across: either way, you mapped each element from the top-left set into the same element of the bottom-right set. A similar kind of result might hold for sets and maps that could naturally be placed at the corners and edges of a cube, or a hypercube of any dimension. It was also possible for the square faces in these structures to stand for relationships that held between the maps between sets, and for cubes to describe relationships between those relationships, and so on.

That a theorem took this form didn't guarantee its importance; it was easy to cook up trivial examples of sets and maps that commuted. The Niah didn't carve trivia into their timeless ceramic, though, and this theorem was no exception. The seven-dimensional commuting hypercube established a dazzlingly elegant correspondence between seven distinct, major branches of Niah mathematics, intertwining their most important concepts into a unified whole. It was a result Joan had never seen before: no mathematician anywhere in the Amalgam, or in any ancestral culture she had studied, had reached the same insight.

She explained as much of this as she could to the three archaeologists; they couldn't take in all the details, but their faces became orange with fascination when she sketched what she thought the result would have meant to the Niah themselves.

"This isn't quite the Big Crunch," she joked, "but it must have made them think they were getting closer." *The Big Crunch* was her nickname for the mythical result that the Niah had aspired to reach: a unification of every field of mathematics that they considered significant. To find such a thing would not have meant the end of mathematics—it would not have subsumed every last conceivable, interesting mathematical truth—but it would certainly have marked a point of closure for the Niah's own style of investigation.

"I'm sure they found it," Surat insisted. "They reached the Big Crunch, then they had nothing more to live for."

Rali was scathing. "So the whole culture committed collective suicide?"

"Not actively, no," Surat replied. "But it was the search that had kept them going."

"Entire cultures don't lose the will to live," Rali said. "They get wiped out by external forces: disease, invasion, changes in climate."

"The Niah survived for three million years," Surat countered. "They had the means to weather all of those forces. Unless they were wiped out by alien invaders with vastly superior technology." She turned to Joan. "What do you think?"

"About aliens destroying the Niah?"

"I was joking about the aliens. But what about the mathematics? What if they found the Big Crunch?"

"There's more to life than mathematics," Joan said. "But not much more."

Sando said, "And there's more to this find than one tablet. If we get back to work, we might have the proof in our hands before sunset."

5

Joan briefed Halzoun by video link while Sando prepared the evening meal. Halzoun was the mathematician Pirit had appointed to supervise her, but apparently his day job was far too important to allow him to travel. Joan was grateful; Halzoun was the most tedious Noudah she had encountered. He could understand the Niah's work when she explained it to him, but he seemed to have no interest in it for its own sake. He spent most of their conversations trying to catch her out in some deception or contradiction, and the rest pressing her to imagine military or commercial applications of the Niah's gloriously useless insights. Sometimes she played along with this infantile fantasy, hinting at potential superweapons based on exotic physics that might come tumbling out of the vacuum, if only one possessed the right Niah theorems to coax them into existence.

Sando was her minder too, but at least he was more subtle about it. Pirit had insisted that she stay in his shelter, rather than sharing Rali and Surat's; Joan didn't mind, because with Sando she didn't have the stress of having to keep quiet about everything. Privacy and modesty were nonissues for the Noudah, and Joan had become Noudah enough not to care herself. Nor was there any danger of their proximity leading to a sexual bond; the Noudah had a complex system of biochemical cues that meant desire only arose in couples with a suitable mixture of genetic differences and similarities. She would have had to search a crowded Noudah city for a week to find someone to lust after, though at least it would have been guaranteed to be mutual.

After they'd eaten, Sando said, "You should be happy. That was our best find yet."

"I am happy." Joan made a conscious effort to exhibit a viridian tinge. "It was the first new result I've seen on this planet. It was the reason I came here, the reason I traveled so far."

"Something's wrong, though, I think."

"I wish I could have shared the news with my friend," Joan admitted. Pirit claimed to be negotiating with the Tirans to allow Anne to communicate with her, but Joan was not convinced that she was genuinely trying. She was sure that he would have relished the thought of listening in on a conversation between the two of them—while forcing them to speak Noudah, of course—in the hope that they'd slip up and reveal something useful, but at the same time he would have had to face the fact that the Tirans would be listening too. What an excruciating dilemma.

"You should have brought a communications link with you," Sando suggested. "A home-style one, I mean. Nothing we could eavesdrop on."

"We couldn't do that," Joan said.

He pondered this. "You really are afraid of us, aren't you? You think the smallest technological trinket will be enough to send us straight to the stars, and then you'll have a horde of rampaging barbarians to deal with."

"We know how to deal with barbarians," Joan said coolly.

Sando's face grew dark with mirth. "Now *I'm* afraid."

"I just wish I knew what was happening to her," Joan said. "What she was doing, how they were treating her."

"Probably much the same as we're treating you," Sando suggested. "We're really not that different." He thought for a moment. "There was something I wanted to show you." He brought over his portable console, and summoned up an article from a Tiran journal. "See what a borderless world we live in," he joked.

The article was entitled "Seekers and Spreaders: What We Must Learn from the Niah." Sando said, "This might give you some idea of how they're thinking over there. Jaqad is an academic archaeologist, but she's also very close to the people in power."

Joan read from the console while Sando made repairs to their shelter, secreting a molasses-like substance from a gland at the tip of his tail and spreading it over the cracks in the walls.

There were two main routes a culture could take, Jaqad argued, once it satisfied its basic material needs. One was to think and study: to stand back and observe, to seek knowledge and insight from the world around it. The other was to invest its energy in entrenching its good fortune.

The Niah had learned a great deal in three million years, but in the end it had not been enough to save them. Exactly what had killed them was still a matter of speculation, but it was hard to believe that if they had colonized other worlds they would have vanished on all of them. "Had the Niah been Spreaders," Jaqad wrote, "we might expect a visit from them, or them from us, sometime in the coming centuries."

The Noudah, in contrast, were determined Spreaders. Once they had the means, they would plant colonies across the galaxy. They would, Jaqad was sure, create new biospheres, re-engineer stars, and even alter space and time to guarantee their survival. The growth of their empire would come first; any knowledge that failed to serve that purpose would be a mere distraction. "In any competition between Seekers and Spreaders, it is a law of history that the Spreaders must win out in the end. Seekers, such as the Niah, might hog resources and block the way, but in the long run their own nature will be their downfall."

Joan stopped reading. "When you look out into the galaxy with your telescopes," she asked Sando, "how many *reengineered stars* do you see?"

"Would we recognize them?"

"Yes. Natural stellar processes aren't that complicated; your scientists already know everything there is to know about the subject."

"I'll take your word for that. So . . . you're saying Jaqad is wrong? The Niah themselves never left this world, but the galaxy already belongs to creatures more like them than like us?"

"It's not Noudah versus Niah," Joan said. "It's a matter of how a culture's perspective changes with time. Once a species conquers disease, modifies their biology, and spreads even a short distance beyond their home world, they usually start to relax a bit. The territorial imperative isn't some timeless law of history; it belongs to a certain phase."

"What if it persists, though? Into a later phase?"

"That can cause friction," Joan admitted.

"Nevertheless, no Spreaders have conquered the galaxy?"

"Not yet."

Sando went back to his repairs; Joan read the rest of the article. She'd thought she'd already grasped the lesson demanded by the subtitle, but it turned out that Jaqad had something more specific in mind.

"Having argued this way, how can I defend my own field of study from the very same charges as I have brought against the Niah? Having grasped the essential character of this doomed race, why should we waste our time and resources studying them further?

"The answer is simple. We still do not know exactly how and why the Niah died, but when we do, that could turn out to be the most important discovery in history. When we finally leave our world behind, we should not expect to find only other Spreaders to compete with us, as honorable opponents in battle. There will be Seekers as well, blocking the way: tired, old races squatting uselessly on their hoards of knowledge and wealth.

"Time will defeat them in the end, but we already waited three million years to be born; we should have no patience to wait again. If we can learn how the Niah died, that will be our key, that will be our weapon. If we know the Seekers' weakness, we can find a way to hasten their demise."

6

The proof of the Niah's theorem turned out to be buried deep in the hillside, but over the following days they extracted it all.

It was as beautiful and satisfying as Joan could have wished, merging six earlier, simpler theorems while extending the techniques used in their proofs. She could even see hints at how the same methods might be stretched further to yield still stronger results. "The Big Crunch" had always been a slightly mocking, irreverent term, but now she was struck anew by how little justice it did to the real trend that had fascinated the Niah. It was not a matter of everything in mathematics collapsing in on itself, with one branch turning out to have been merely a recapitulation of another under a different guise. Rather, the principle was that every sufficiently beautiful mathematical system was rich enough to mirror *in part*—and sometimes in a complex and distorted fashion—every other sufficiently beautiful system. Nothing became sterile and redundant, nothing proved to have been a waste of time, but everything was shown to be magnificently intertwined.

After briefing Halzoun, Joan used the satellite dish to transmit the theorem and its proof to the decoy node. That had been the deal with Pirit: anything she learned from the Niah belonged to the whole galaxy, as long as she explained it to her hosts first.

The archaeologists moved across the hillside, hunting for more artifacts in the same layer of sediment. Joan was eager to see what else the same group of Niah might have published. One possible eight-dimensional hypercube was hovering in her mind; if she'd sat down and thought about it for a few decades she might have worked out the details herself, but the Niah did what they did so well that it would have seemed crass to try to follow clumsily in their footsteps when their own immaculately polished results might simply be lying in the ground, waiting to be uncovered.

A month after the discovery, Joan was woken by the sound of an intruder moving through the shelter. She knew it wasn't Sando; even as she slept an ancient part of her Noudah brain was listening to his heartbeat. The stranger's heart was too quiet to hear, which required great discipline, but the shelter's flexible adhesive made the floor emit a characteristic squeak beneath even the gentlest footsteps. As she rose from her couch she heard Sando waking, and she turned in his direction.

Bright torchlight on his face dazzled her for a moment. The intruder held two knives to Sando's respiratory membranes; a deep enough cut there would mean choking to death, in excruciating pain. The nanomachines that had built Joan's body had wired extensive skills in unarmed combat into her brain, and one scenario involving a feigned escape attempt followed by a sideways flick of her powerful tail was already playing out in the back of her mind, but as yet she could see no way to guarantee that Sando came through it all unharmed.

She said, "What do you want?"

The intruder remained in darkness. "Tell me about the ship that brought you to Baneth."

"Why?"

"Because it would be a shame to shred your colleague here, just when his work was going so well." Sando refused to show any emotion on his face, but the blank pallor itself was as stark an expression of fear as anything Joan could imagine.

She said, "There's a coherent state that can be prepared for a quark-gluon plasma in which virtual black holes catalyze baryon decay. In effect, you can turn all of your fuel's rest mass into photons, yielding the most efficient exhaust stream possible." She recited a long list of technical details. The claimed baryon decay process didn't actually exist, but the pseudo-physics underpinning it was mathematically consistent, and could not be ruled out by anything the Noudah had yet observed. She and Anne had prepared an entire fictitious science and technology, and even a fictitious history of their culture, precisely for emergencies like this; they could spout red herrings for a decade if necessary, and never get caught out contradicting themselves.

"That wasn't so hard, was it?" the intruder gloated.

"What now?"

"You're going to take a trip with me. If you do this nicely, nobody needs to get hurt."

Something moved in the shadows, and the intruder screamed in pain. Joan leaped forward and knocked one of the knives out of his hand with her tail; the other knife grazed Sando's membrane, but a second tail whipped out of the darkness and intervened. As the intruder fell backward, the beam of his torch revealed Surat and Rali tensed beside him, and a pick buried deep in his side.

Joan's rush of combat hormones suddenly faded, and she let out a long, deep wail of anguish. Sando was unscathed, but a stream of dark liquid was pumping out of the intruder's wound.

Surat was annoyed. "Stop blubbing, and help us tie up this Tiran cousin-fucker."

"Tie him up? You've killed him!"

"Don't be stupid, that's just sheath fluid." Joan recalled her Noudah anatomy; sheath fluid was like oil in a hydraulic machine. You could lose it all and it would cost you most of the strength in your limbs and tail, but you wouldn't die, and your body would make more eventually.

Rali found some cable and they trussed up the intruder. Sando was shaken, but he seemed to be recovering. He took Joan aside. "I'm going to have to call Pirit."

"I understand. But what will she do to these two?" She wasn't sure exactly how much Rali and Surat had heard, but it was certain to have been more than Pirit wanted them to know.

"Don't worry about that, I can protect them."

Just before dawn someone sent by Pirit arrived in a truck to take the intruder away. Sando declared a rest day, and Rali and Surat went back to their shelter to sleep. Joan went for a walk along the hillside; she didn't feel like sleeping.

Sando caught up with her. He said, "I told them you'd been working on a military research project, and you were exiled here for some political misdemeanor."

"And they believed you?"

"All they heard was half of a conversation full of incomprehensible physics. All they know is that someone thought you were worth kidnapping."

Joan said, "I'm sorry about what happened."

Sando hesitated. "What did you expect?"

Joan was stung. "One of us went to Tira, one of us came here. We thought that would keep everyone happy!"

"We're Spreaders," said Sando. "Give us one of anything, and we want two. Especially if our enemy has the other one. Did you really think you could come here, do a bit of fossicking, and then simply fly away without changing a thing?"

"Your culture has always believed there were other civilizations in the galaxy. Our existence hardly came as a shock."

Sando's face became yellow, an expression of almost parental reproach. "Believing in something in the abstract is not the same as having it dangled in front of you. We were never going to have an existential crisis at finding out that we're not unique; the Niah might be related to us, but they were still alien enough to get us used to the idea. But did you really think we were just going to relax and accept your refusal to share your technology? That one of you went to the Tirans only makes it worse for the Ghahari, and vice versa. Both governments are going absolutely crazy, each one terrified that the other has found a way to make its alien talk."

Joan stopped walking. "The war games, the border skirmishes? You're blaming all of that on Anne and me?"

Sando's body sagged wearily. "To be honest, I don't know all the details. And if it's any consolation, I'm sure we would have found another reason if you hadn't come along."

Joan said, "Maybe I should leave." She was tired of these people, tired of her body, tired of being cut off from civilization. She had rescued one beautiful Niah theorem and sent it out into the Amalgam. Wasn't that enough?

"It's up to you," Sando replied. "But you might as well stay until they flood the valley. Another year isn't going to change anything. What you've done to this world has already been done. For us, there's no going back."

7

Joan stayed with the archaeologists as they moved across the hillside. They found tablets bearing Niah drawings and poetry, which no doubt had their virtues but to Joan seemed bland and opaque. Sando and his students relished these discoveries as much as the theorems; to them, the Niah culture was a vast jigsaw puzzle, and any clue that filled in the details of their history was as good as any other.

Sando would have told Pirit everything he'd heard from Joan the night the intruder came, so she was surprised that she hadn't been summoned for a fresh interrogation to flesh out the details. Perhaps the Ghahari physicists were still digesting her elaborate gobbledygook, trying to decide if it made sense. In her more cynical moments she wondered if the intruder might have been Ghahari himself, sent by Pirit to exploit her friendship with Sando. Perhaps Sando had even been in on it, and Rali and Surat as well. The possibility made her feel as if she was living in a fabricated world, a scape in which nothing was real and nobody could be trusted. The only thing she was certain that the Ghaharis could not have faked was the Niah artifacts. The mathematics verified itself; everything else was subject to doubt and paranoia.

Summer came, burning away the morning fogs. The Noudah's idea of heat was very different from Joan's previous perceptions, but even the body she now wore found the midday sun oppressive. She willed herself to be patient. There was still a chance that the Niah had taken a few more steps toward their grand vision of a unified mathematics, and carved their final discoveries into the form that would outlive them by a million years.

When the lone fusion ship appeared high in the afternoon sky, Joan resolved to ignore it. She glanced up once, but she kept dragging the tomography unit across the ground. She was sick of thinking about Tiran-

Ghahari politics. They had played their childish games for centuries; she would not take the blame for this latest outbreak of provocation.

Usually the ships flew by, disappearing within minutes, showing off their power and speed. This one lingered, weaving back and forth across the sky like some dazzling insect performing an elaborate mating dance. Joan's second shadow darted around her feet, hammering a strangely familiar rhythm into her brain.

She looked up, disbelieving. The motion of the ship was following the syntax of a gestural language she had learned on another planet, in another body, a dozen lifetimes ago. The only other person on this world who could know that language was Anne.

She glanced toward the archaeologists a hundred meters away, but they seemed to be paying no attention to the ship. She switched off the tomography unit and stared into the sky. *I'm listening, my friend. What's happening? Did they give you back your ship? Have you had enough of this world, and decided to go home?*

Anne told the story in shorthand, compressed and elliptic. The Tirans had found a tablet bearing a theorem: the last of the Niah's discoveries, the pinnacle of their achievements. Her minders had not let her study it, but they had contrived a situation making it easy for her to steal it, and to steal this ship. They had wanted her to take it and run, in the hope that she would lead them to something they valued far more than any ancient mathematics: an advanced spacecraft, or some magical stargate at the edge of the system.

But Anne wasn't fleeing anywhere. She was high above Ghahar, reading the tablet, and now she would paint what she read across the sky for Joan to see.

Sando approached. "We're in danger, we have to move."

"Danger? That's my friend up there! She's not going to shoot a missile at us!"

"Your friend?" Sando seemed confused. As he spoke, three more ships came into view, lower and brighter than the first. "I've been told that the Tirans are going to strike the valley, to bury the Niah sites. We need to get over the hill and indoors, to get some protection from the blast."

"Why would the Tirans attack the Niah sites? That makes no sense to me."

Sando said, "Nor me, but I don't have time to argue."

The three ships were menacing Anne's, pursuing her, trying to drive her away. Joan had no idea if they were Ghahari defending their territory, or Tirans harassing her in the hope that she would flee and reveal the nonexistent shortcut to the stars, but Anne was staying put, still weaving the same gestural language into her maneuvers even as she dodged her pursuers, spelling out the Niah's glorious finale.

Joan said, "You go. I have to see this." She tensed, ready to fight him if necessary.

Sando took something from his tool belt and peppered her side with holes. Joan gasped with pain and crumpled to the ground as the sheath fluid poured out of her.

Rali and Surat helped carry her to the shelter. Joan caught glimpses of the fiery ballet in the sky, but not enough to make sense of it, let alone reconstruct it.

They put her on her couch inside the shelter. Sando bandaged her side and gave her water to sip. He said, "I'm sorry I had to do that, but if anything had happened to you I would have been held responsible."

Surat kept ducking outside to check on the "battle," then reporting excitedly on the state of play. "The Tiran's still up there, they can't get rid of it. I don't know why they haven't shot it down yet."

Because the Tirans were the ones pursuing Anne, and they didn't want her dead. But for how long would the Ghahari tolerate this violation?

Anne's efforts could not be allowed to come to nothing. Joan struggled to recall the constellations she'd last seen in the night sky. At the node they'd departed from, powerful telescopes were constantly trained on the Noudah's home world. Anne's ship was easily bright enough, its gestures wide enough, to be resolved from seven light-years away—if the planet itself wasn't blocking the view, if the node was above the horizon.

The shelter was windowless, but Joan saw the ground outside the doorway brighten for an instant. The flash was silent; no missile had struck the valley, the explosion had taken place high above the atmosphere.

Surat went outside. When she returned she said quietly, "All clear. They got it."

Joan put all her effort into spitting out a handful of words. "I want to see what happened."

Sando hesitated, then motioned to the others to help him pick up the couch and carry it outside.

A shell of glowing plasma was still visible, drifting across the sky as it expanded, a ring of light growing steadily fainter until it vanished into the afternoon glare.

Anne was dead in this embodiment, but her backup would wake and go on to new adventures. Joan could at least tell her the story of her local death: of virtuoso flying and a spectacular end.

She'd recovered her bearings now, and she recalled the position of the stars. The node was still hours away from rising. The Amalgam was full of powerful telescopes, but no others would be aimed at this obscure planet, and no plea to redirect them could outrace the light they would need to capture in order to bring the Niah's final theorem back to life.

8

Sando wanted to send her away for medical supervision, but Joan insisted on remaining at the site.

"The fewer officials who get to know about this incident, the fewer problems it makes for you," she reasoned.

"As long as you don't get sick and die," he replied.

"I'm not going to die." Her wounds had not become infected, and her strength was returning rapidly.

They compromised. Sando hired someone to drive up from the nearest town to look after her while he was out at the excavation. Daya had basic medical training and didn't ask awkward questions; he seemed happy to tend to Joan's needs, and then lie outside daydreaming the rest of the time.

There was still a chance, Joan thought, that the Niah had carved the theorem on a multitude of tablets and scattered them all over the planet. There was also a chance that the Tirans had made copies of the tablet before letting Anne abscond with it. The question, though, was whether she had the slightest prospect of getting her hands on these duplicates.

Anne might have made some kind of copy herself, but she hadn't mentioned it in the prologue to her aerobatic rendition of the theorem. If she'd had any time to spare, she wouldn't have limited herself to an audience of one: she would have waited until the node had risen over Ghahar.

On her second night as an invalid, Joan dreamed that she saw Anne standing on the hill looking back into the fog-shrouded valley, her shadow haloed by the Niah light.

When she woke, she knew what she had to do.

When Sando left, she asked Daya to bring her the console that controlled the satellite dish. She had enough strength in her arms now to operate it, and Daya showed no interest in what she did. That was naïve, of course: whether or not Daya was spying on her, Pirit would know exactly where the signal was sent. So be it. Seven light-years was still far beyond the Noudah's reach; the whole node could be disassembled and erased long before they came close.

No message could outrace light directly, but there were more ways for light to reach the node than the direct path, the fastest one. Every black hole had its glory, twisting light around it in a tight, close orbit and flinging it back out again. Seventy-four hours after the original image was lost to them, the telescopes at the node could still turn to the Cataract and scour the distorted, compressed image of the sky at the rim of the hole's black disk to catch a replay of Anne's ballet.

Joan composed the message and entered the coordinates of the node. *You didn't die for nothing, my friend. When you wake and see this, you'll be proud of us both.*

She hesitated, her hand hovering above the send key. The Tirans had wanted Anne to flee, to show them the way to the stars, but had they really been indifferent to the loot they'd let her carry? The theorem had come at the end of the Niah's three-million-year reign. To witness this beautiful truth would not destroy the Amalgam, but might it not weaken it? If the Seekers' thirst for knowledge was slaked, their sense of purpose corroded, might not the most crucial strand of the culture fall into a twilight of its own? There was no shortcut to the stars, but the Noudah had been goaded by their alien visitors, and the technology would come to them soon enough.

The Amalgam had been goaded, too: the theorem she'd already transmitted would send a wave of excitement around the galaxy, strengthening the Seekers, encouraging them to complete the unification by their own efforts. The Big Crunch might be inevitable, but at least she could delay it, and hope that the robustness and diversity of the Amalgam would carry them through it, and beyond.

She erased the message and wrote a new one, addressed to her backup via the decoy node. It would have been nice to upload all her memories, but the Noudah were ruthless, and she wasn't prepared to stay any longer and risk being used by them. This sketch, this postcard, would have to be enough.

When the transmission was complete she left a note for Sando in the console's memory.

Daya called out to her, "Jown? Do you need anything?"

She said, "No. I'm going to sleep for a while."

SAVING TIAMAAT

GWYNETH JONES

I HAD REACHED the station in the depth of Left Speranza's night; I had not slept. Fogged in the confabulation of the transit, I groped through crushing eons to my favorite breakfast kiosk: unsure if the soaring concourse outside Parliament was ceramic and carbon or a *metaphor*, a cloudy internal warning—

—now what was the message in the mirror? Something pitiless. Some blank-eyed, slow-thinking, long-grinned crocodile—

"Debra!"

It was my partner. "Don't *do* that," I moaned. The internal crocodile shattered, the concourse lost its freight of hyper-determined meaning, too suddenly for comfort. "Don't you know you should never startle a sleep-walker?"

He grinned; he knew when I'd arrived, and the state I was likely to be in. I hadn't met Pelé Leonidas Iza Quinatoa in the flesh before, but we'd worked together, we liked each other. "Ayayay, so good you can't bear to lose it?"

"Of course not. Only innocent, beautiful souls have sweet dreams."

He touched my cheek: collecting a teardrop. I hadn't realized I was crying. "You should use the dreamtime, Debra. There must be *some* game you want to play."

"I've tried, it's worse. If I don't take my punishment, I'm sick for days."

The intimacy of his gesture (skin on skin) was an invitation and a promise; it made me smile. We walked into the Parliament Building together, buoyant in the knocked-down gravity that I love although I know it's bad for you.

In the Foyer, we met the rest of the company, identified by the Diaspora Parliament's latest adventure in biometrics, the aura tag. To our vision the KiAn Working Party was striated orange-yellow, nice cheerful implications, nothing too deep. The pervasive systems were seeing a lot more, but that didn't bother Pelé or me; we had no secrets from Speranza.

The KiAn problem had been a matter of concern since their world had been "discovered" by a Balas-Shet prospector, and joined the miniscule roster of populated planets linked by instantaneous transit. Questions had been raised then, over the grave social imbalance: the tiny international ruling caste, the exploited masses. But neither the Ki nor the An would accept arbitration (why the hell should they?). The non-interference lobby is the weakest faction in the Chamber; quarantine-until-they're-civilized was not considered an option. Inevitably, around thirty local years after first contact, the Ki had risen against their overlords, as often in the past. Inevitably, this time they had modern weapons. They had not succeeded in wiping out the An, but they had pretty much rendered the shared planet uninhabitable.

We were here to negotiate a rescue package. We'd done the damage, we had to fix it, that was the DP's line. The Ki and the An no doubt had their own ideas as to what was going on: they were new to the Interstellar Diaspora, not to politics.

But they were here, at least; so that seemed hopeful.

The Ki Federation delegates were unremarkable. There were five of them, they conformed to the "sentient biped" body plan that unites the diaspora. Three were wearing Balas business suits in shades of brown, two were in gray military uniform. The young co-leaders of the An were better dressed, and one of the two, in particular, was *much* better-looking. Whatever you believe about the origins of the "diaspora" (Strong theory, Weak theory, something between), it's strange how many measures of beauty are common to us all. He was tall, past two meters: he had large eyes, a mane of rich brown head hair, an open, strong-boned face, poreless bronze skin, and a glorious smile. He would be my charge. His co-leader, the subordinate partner, slight and small, almost as dowdy as the Ki, would be Pelé's.

They were code-named Baal and Tiamaat, the names I will use in this account. The designations Ki and An are also code names.

We moved off to a briefing room. Joset Moricherri, one of the Blue permanent secretaries, made introductory remarks. A Green Belt colonel, Shamaz Haa'agaan, gave a talk on station security. A slightly less high-ranking DP administrator got down to basics: standard time conventions, shopping allowances, access to the elevators, restricted areas, housekeeping . . . Those who hadn't provided their own breakfast raided the culturally neutral trolley. I sipped my Mocha-Colombian, took my carbs in the form of a crisp cherry jam tartine; and let the day's agenda wash over me, as I reviewed what I knew about Baal and Tiamaat's relationship.

They were not related by blood, except in the sense that the An gene pool was very restricted: showing signs of other population crashes in the past. They were not "married," either. The Ki and the An seemed to be sexually dimorphic on the Blue model (thought they could yet surprise us!); and they liked opposite-sex partnerships. But they did not marry. Tiamaat's family had been swift to embrace the changes, she'd been educated on Balas-Shet. Baal had left KiAn for the first time when war broke out. They'd lost family members, and they'd certainly seen the horrific transmissions smuggled off KiAn before the end. Yet here they were, with the genocidal Ki: thrown together, suddenly appointed the rulers of their shattered nation, and bound to each other for life. Tiamaat looked as if she was feeling the strain. She sat with her eyes lowered, drawn in on herself, her body occupying the minimum of space. Beside her, Baal devoured a culturally neutral doughnut, elbows sprawled, with a child's calm greed. I wondered how much my alien perception of a timid young woman and a big bold young man was distorting my view. I wondered how all that fine physicality translated into mind.

Who are you, Baal? How will it feel to know you?

———————

From the meeting we proceeded to a DP reception and lunch, from thence to a concert in the Nebula Immersion Chamber: a Blue Planet symphony orchestra on virtual tour; the Diaspora Chorus in the flesh, singing a famous masque; a solemn dance drama troupe bilocating from Neuendan. Pelé and I, humble Social Support officers, were in the background for these events. But the An had grasped that we were their advocates: as was proved when they pounced on us, eagerly, after the concert. They wanted to meet "The nice quiet people with the pretty curly faces—"

They spoke English, language of diplomacy and displacement. They'd both taken the express, neurotech route to fluency: but we had trouble pinning this request down. It turned out they were asking to be introduced to a bowl of orchids.

Appearances can be deceptive; these two young people were neither calm nor cowed. They had been born in a medieval world, and swept away from home as to the safety of a rich neighbor's house: all they knew of the interstellar age was the inside of a transit lounge. The Ki problem they knew only too well: Speranza was a thrilling bombardment. With much laughter (they laughed like Blue teenagers, to cover embarrassment), we explained that they would not be meeting any bizarre life-forms. No tentacles, no petals, no intelligent gas clouds here; not yet!

"You have to look after us!" cried Baal. He grabbed my arm, softly but I felt the power. "Save us from making fools of ourselves, dear Debra and Pelé!"

Tiamaat stood back a pace, hiding her giggles behind her hand.

The last event scheduled on that first day was a live transmission walkabout from the Ki refugee camp, in the Customized Shelter Sector. In the planning stages, some of us had expressed doubts about this stunt. If anything went wrong it'd sour the whole negotiation. But the Ki and the An leaders were both keen, and the historic gesture was something the public back on the homeworlds would understand—which in the end had decided the question. The Diaspora Parliament had to struggle for planetside attention, we couldn't pass up an opportunity.

At the gates of the CSS, deep in Speranza's hollow heart, there was a delay. The Customized Shelter Police wanted us in armored glass-tops, they felt that if we *needed* a walkabout we could fake it . . . Pelé chatted with Tiamaat, stooping from his lean black height to catch her soft voice. Baal stared at the banners on two display screens. The KiAn understood flags, we hadn't taught them that concept. Green and gold quarters for the Ki, a center section crosshatched with the emblems of all the nations. Purple tracery on vivid bronze for the An.

Poor kid, I thought, it's not a magic gateway to your lost home. Don't get your hopes up. That's the door to a cage in a conservation zoo.

He noticed my attention, and showed his white teeth. "Are there other peoples living in exile on this floor?"

I nodded. "Yes. But mostly the people sheltered here are old spacers, who can't return to full gravity. Or failed colonist communities, likewise: people who've tried to settle on empty moons and planets and been defeated by the conditions. There are no other populated planet exiles. It hasn't been, er, necessary."

"We are a first for you."

I wondered if that was ironic; if he were capable of irony.

A compromise was reached. We entered on foot, with the glass-tops and CSP closed cars trailing behind. The Ki domain wasn't bad, for a displaced persons camp wrapped in the bleak embrace of a giant space station. Between the living-space capsule towers the refugees could glimpse their own shade of sky; and a facsimile of their primary sun, with its partner, the blue-rayed daystar. They had sanitation, hygiene, regular meals, leisure facilities, even employment. We stopped at an adult retraining center, we briefly inspected a hydroponic farm. We visited a kindergarten, where the teaching staff told us (and the flying cams!) how all the nations of the Ki were gathered here in harmony, learning to be good Diaspora citizens.

The children stared at Baal and Tiamaat. They'd probably been born in the camp, and never seen An in the flesh before. Baal fidgeted, seeming indignant under their scrutiny. Tiamaat stared back with equal curiosity. I saw her reach a tentative hand through the shielding, as if to touch a Ki child: but she thought better of it.

After the classroom tour, there was a reception, with speeches, dance, and choral singing. Ki community leaders and the An couple didn't literally "shake hands"; but the gesture was accomplished. Here the live trans ended, and most of our party stayed behind. The An leaders and the Ki delegates went on alone, with a police escort, for a private visit to "Hopes and Dreams Park"—a facsimile of one of the Sacred Groves (as near as the term translates), central to KiAn spirituality.

Pelé and I went with them.

The enclave of woodland was artfully designed. The "trees" were like self-supporting kelp, leathery succulents—lignin is only native to the Blue Planet—but they were tall, and planted close enough to block all sight of the packed towers. Their sheets of foliage made a honeyed shade, we seemed alone in a gently managed wilderness. The Ki and the An kept their distance from each other now that the cams weren't in sight. The police moved outward to maintain a cordon around the group, and I began to feel uneasy. I should have been paying attention instead of savoring my breakfast, I had not grasped that "Hope and Dreams Park" would be like this. I kept hearing voices, seeing flitting shadows; although the park area was supposed to have been cleared. I'd mentioned the weak shielding, I hoped it had been fixed—

"Are religious ceremonies held here?" I asked Tiamaat.

She drew back her head, the gesture for "no." "Most KiAn have not followed religion for a long time. It's just a place sacred to ourselves, to nature."

"But it's fine for the Shelter Police, and Pelé and I, to be with you?"

"You are advocates."

We entered a clearing dotted with thickets. At our feet smaller plants had the character of woodland turf, starred with bronze and purple flowers. Above us the primary sun dipped toward its false horizon, lighting the blood red veins in the foliage. The blue daystar had set. Baal and Tiamaat were walking together: I heard him whisper, in the An language, "Now it's our time."

"And these are the lucky ones," muttered one of the Ki delegates to me, her "English" mediated by a throat-mike processor that gave her a teddy-bear growl. "Anyone who reached Speranza had contacts, money. Many millions of our people are trying to survive on a flayed, poisoned bomb site—"

And whose fault is that?

I nodded vaguely. It was not my place to take sides—

Something flew by me, big and solid. Astonished, I realized it had been Baal. He had moved so fast, it was so totally unexpected. He had plunged right through the cordon of armed police, through the shield. He was gone, vanished. I leaped in pursuit at once, yelling, "Hold your fire!" I was flung back, thrown down into zinging stars and blackness. The shield *had* been strengthened, but not enough.

Shelter Police bending over me, cried, "What happened, ma'am, are you hit?"

My conviction that we had company in here fused into certainty—

"Oh, God! Get after him. After him!"

I ran with the police, Pelé stayed with Tiamaat and the Ki: on our shared frequency I heard him alerting Colonel Shamaz. We cast to and fro through the twilight wood, held together by the invisible strands and glob-ules of our shield, taunted by rustles of movement, the CSP muttering to one another about refugee assassins, homemade weapons. But the young leader of the An was unharmed when we found him, having followed the sounds of a scuffle and a terrified cry. He crouched, in his sleek tailoring, over his prey. Dark blood trickled from the victim's nostrils, high-placed in a narrow face. Dark eyes were open, fixed and wide.

I remembered the children in that school, staring up in disbelief at the ogres.

Baal rose, wiping his mouth with the back of his hand. "What are you looking at?" he inquired haughtily, in his neighbors' language. The rest of our party had caught up: he was speaking to the Ki. "What did you expect? You know who I am."

Tiamaat fell to her knees, with a wail of despair, pressing her hands to either side of her head. "He has a right! Ki territory is An territory, he has a right to behave as if we were at home. And the Others knew it, don't you see? They *knew*!"

The CSP officer yelled something inexcusable and lunged at the killer. Pelé grabbed him by the shoulders and hauled him back, talking urgent sense. The Ki said nothing, but I thought Tiamaat was right. They'd known what the Diaspora's pet monster would do in here; and he hadn't let them down.

Perfectly unconcerned, Baal stood guard over the body until Colonel Haa'agaan arrived with the closed cars. Then he picked it up and slung it over his shoulder. I traveled with him and his booty, and the protection of four Green Belts, to the elevator. Another blacked-out car waited for us on Parliament level. What a nightmare journey! We delivered him to the service entrance of his suite in the Sensitive Visitors Facility, and saw him drop the body insouciantly into the arms of one of his aides—a domestic, lesser specimen of those rare and dangerous animals, the An.

The soldiers looked at each other, looked at me. "You'd better stay," I said. "And get yourselves reinforced, there might be reprisals planned."

Baal's tawny eyes in my mind: challenging me, trusting me—

———

The debriefing was in closed session; although there would be a transcript on record. It took a painful long time, but we managed to exonerate everyone, including Baal. Mistakes had been made, signals had been misread. We knew the facts of the KiAn problem, we had only the most rudimentary grasp of the cultures involved. Baal and Tiamaat, who were not present, had made no further comment. The Ki (who were not present either) had offered a swift deposition. They wanted the incident treated with utmost discretion: they did not see it as a bar to negotiation. The Balas-Shet party argued that Baal's kill had been unique, an "extraordinary ritual" that we had to sanction. And we knew this was nonsense, but it was the best we could do.

One of our Green Belts, struck by the place in the report where Tiamaat exclaims "the Others knew it!," came up with the idea that the young Ki had been a form of suicide bomber: sacrificing his life in the hope of wrecking the peace talks. Investigation of the dead boy and his contacts would now commence.

"Thank funx it didn't happen on the live transmission!" cried Shamaz, the old soldier; getting his priorities right.

It was very late before Pelé and I got away. We spent the rest of the night together, hiding in the tenderness of the Blue Planet, where war is shameful and murder is an aberration; where kindness is common currency, and in almost every language strangers are greeted with love—dear, pet, darling; sister, brother, cousin—and nobody even wonders why. What an unexpected distinction, we who thought we were such ruthless villains, such fallen angels. "We're turning into the care assistant caste for the whole funxing galaxy," moaned Pelé. "¡Qué cacho!"

———

The Parliament session was well attended: many tiers packed with bilocators; more than the usual scatter of members present in the flesh, and damn the expense. I surveyed the Chamber with distaste. They all wanted to make their speeches on the KiAn crisis. But they knew nothing. The freedom of the press fades and dies at interstellar distances, where everything has to be couriered, and there's no such thing as evading official censorship. They'd heard about the genocide, the wicked but romantic An; the ruined world, the rescue plans. They had no idea exactly what had driven the rebel Ki to such desperation, and they weren't going to find out—

All the Diaspora Parliament knew was spin.

And the traditional Ki, the people we were dealing with, were collusive. They didn't *like* being killed and eaten by their aristos, but for outsiders to find out the truth would be a far worse evil: a disgusting, gross exposure. After all, it was only the poor, the weak-minded and the disadvantaged, who ended up on a plate. . . . Across from the Visitors' Gallery, level with my eyes, hung the great Diaspora Banner. The populated worlds turned sedately, beautifully scanned and insanely close together; like one of those ancient distorted projections of the landmasses on the Blue. The "real" distance between the Blue system and Neuendan (our nearest neighbor) was twenty-six thousand light-years. Between the Neuendan and the Balas-Shet lay fifteen hundred light-years; the location of the inscrutable Aleutians' homeworld was a mystery. How would you represent *that* spatial relationship, in any realistic way?

"Why do they say it all aloud?" asked Baal idly.

He was beside me, of course. He was glad to have me there, and kept letting me know it: a confiding pressure against my shoulder, a warm glance from those tawny eyes. He took my complete silence about the incident in Hopes and Dreams Park for understanding. A DP Social Support Officer *never* shows hostility.

"Isn't your i/t button working?"

The instantaneous translation in here had a mind of its own.

"It works well enough. But everything they say is just repeating the documents on this desk. It was the same in the briefing yesterday, I noticed that."

"You read English?"

"Oh yes." Reading and writing have to be learned, there is no quick neurofix. Casually, with a glint of that startling irony, he dismissed his skill. "I was taught, at home. But I don't bother. I have people who understand all this for me."

"It's called oratory," I said. "And rhetoric. Modulated speech is used to stir peoples' emotions, to cloud the facts and influence the vote—"

Baal screwed up his handsome face in disapproval. "That's distasteful."

"Also it's tradition. It's just the way we do things."

"Ah!"

I sighed, and sent a message to Pelé on our eye socket link.

Change partners?

D'you want to reassign? came his swift response. He was worrying about me, he wanted to protect me from the trauma of being with Baal; which was a needle under my skin. I liked Pelé very much, but I preferred to treat the Diaspora Parliament as a no-ties singles bar.

No, I answered. *Just for an hour, after this.*

———

Getting close to Tiamaat was easy. After the session the four of us went down to the Foyer, where Baal was quickly surrounded by a crowd of high-powered admirers. They swept him off somewhere, with Pelé in attendance. Tiamaat and I were left bobbing in the wake, ignored; a little lost. "Shall we *have coffee,* Debra?" she suggested, with dignity. "I love *coffee.* But not the kind that comes on those trolleys!"

I took her to "my" kiosk, and we found a table. I was impressed by the way she handled the slights of her position. There goes Baal, surrounded by the mighty, while his partner is reduced to having coffee with a minder. . . . It was a galling role to have to play in public. I had intended to lead up to the topic on my mind, but she forestalled me. "You must be horrified by what happened yesterday."

No hostility. "A *little* horrified, I admit." I affected to hesitate. "The Bal-as-Shet say that what Baal did was a ritual, confirming his position as leader; and the Ki expected it. They may even have arranged for the victim to be available. And it won't happen again. Are they right?"

She sipped her cappuccino. "Baal doesn't believe he did anything wrong," she answered carefully; giving nothing away.

I remembered her cry of despair. "But what do *you* think—?"

"I can speak frankly?"

"You can say anything. We may seem to be in public, but nothing you say to me, or that I say to you, can be heard by anyone else."

"Speranza is a very clever place!"

"Yes, it is. . . . And as you know, though the system itself will have a record, as your Social Support officer I may not reveal anything you ask me to keep to myself."

She gave me eye contact then, very deliberately. I realized I'd never seen her look anyone in the eye before. The color of her irises was a subtle, lilac-starred grey.

"Before I left home, when I was a child, I ate meat. I hadn't killed it, but I knew where it came from. But I have never killed, Debra. And now I don't believe I ever will." She looked out at the passing crowd, the surroundings that must be so punishingly strange to her. "My mother said we should close ourselves off to the past, and open ourselves to the future. So she sent me away, when I was six years old, to live on another world—"

"That sounds very young to me."

"I *was* young. I still had my milk teeth . . . I'm not like Baal, because I have been brought up differently. If I were in his place, things would be better for the Others. I truly believe that—" She meant the Ki, the prey-nations. "But I know what has to be done for KiAn. *I want this rescue package to work.* Baal is the one who will make it happen, and I support him in every way."

She smiled, close-lipped, no flash of sharp white: I saw the poised steel in her, hidden by ingrained self-suppression. And she changed the subject with composure. Unexpected boldness, unexpected finesse—

"Debra, is it true that Blue people have secret superpowers?"

I laughed and shook my head. "I'm afraid not. No talking flowers here!"

––––––

Pelé tried to get the DP software to change our code names. He maintained that "Baal" and "Tiamaat" were not even from the same mythology, and if we were going to invoke the gods, those two should be Aztecs: Huehueteotl, ripping the living heart from his victims. . . . The bots refused. They said they didn't care if they were mixing their mysticisms. Code names were a device to avoid accidental offense until the system had assimilated a new user language. "Baal" and "Tiamaat" were perfectly adequate, and the MesoAmerican names had too many characters.

––––––

I had dinner with Baal, in the Sensitive Visitor Facility. He was charming company: we ate vegetarian fusion cuisine, and I tried not to think about the butchered meat in the kitchen of his suite. On the other side of the room, bull-shouldered Colonel Haa'agaan ate alone; glancing at us covertly with small, sad eyes from between the folds of his slaty head hide. Shamaz had been hard-hit by what had happened in the Hopes and Dreams Park. But his orange and yellow aura tag was still bright; and I knew mine was, too. By the ruthless measures of interstellar diplomacy, everything was still going well; set for success.

If things had been different I might have joined Pelé again when I was finally off duty. As it was, I retired to my room, switched all the décor, including ceiling and floor, to starry void, mixed myself a kicking neurochemical cocktail, and applied the popper to my throat. Eyedrops are faster, but I wanted the delay, I wanted to feel myself coming apart. Surrounded by directionless immensity, I sipped chilled water, brooding. How can a people have World Government, spaceflight-level industrialization, numinal intelligence, and yet the ruling caste are still killing and eating the peasants? How can they do that, when practically everyone on KiAn admits they are a single species, differently adapted: *and they knew that before we told them*. How can we be back here, the Great Powers and their grisly parasites: making the same moves, the same old mistakes, the same old hateful compromises, that our Singularity was supposed to cure forever?

Why is moral development so difficult? Why are predators charismatic?

The knots in my frontal lobes were combed out by airy fingers, I fell into the sea of possibilities, I went to the place of terror and joy that no one understands unless they have been there. I asked my question and I didn't get an answer, you never get an answer. Yet when I came to the shallows again, when I laid myself, exhausted, on this dark and confused shore, I knew what I was going to do: I had seen it.

But there always has to be an emotional reason. I'd known about Baal's views before I arrived. I'd known that he would hunt and kill "weakling" Ki, as was his traditional right, and not just once, he'd do it whenever the opportunity arose; and I'd been undecided. It was Tiamaat who made the difference. I'd met her, skin on skin as we say. I knew what the briefing had not been able to tell me. She was no cipher, superficially "civilized" by her education, she was *suppressed*. I had heard that cry of despair and anger, when she saw what Baal had done. I had talked to her. I knew she had strength and cunning, as well as good intentions. A latent dominance, the will and ability to be a leader.

I saw Baal's look of challenge and trust, even now—

But Tiamaat deserved saving, and I would save her.

————

The talks went on. Morale was low on the DP side, because the refugee camp incident had shown us where we stood; but the Ki delegates were happy—insanely, infuriatingly. The "traditional diet of the An" was something they refused to discuss, and they were going to get their planet rebuilt anyway. The young An leaders spent very little time at the conference table. Baal was indifferent—he had people to understand these things for him— and Tiamaat could not be present without him. This caused a rift. Their aides, the only other An around, were restricted to the SV Facility suites (we care assistants may be crazy but we're not entirely stupid). Pelé and I were fully occupied, making sure our separate charges weren't left moping alone. Pelé took Tiamaat shopping and visiting museums (virtual and actual). I found that Baal loved to roam, just as I do myself, and took him exploring the lesser-known sights.

We talked about his background. Allegedly, he'd given up a promising career in the Space Marines to take on the leadership. When I'd assured myself that his pilot skills were real, he wasn't just a toy-soldier aristo, I finally took him on the long float through the permanent umbilical, to Right Speranza.

We had to suit up at the other end.

"What's this?" demanded Baal, grinning. "Are we going outside?"

"You'll see. It's an excursion I thought you'd enjoy."

The suits were programmable. I watched him set one up for his size and bulk, and knew he was fine, but I put him through the routines, to make sure. Then I took him into the vast open cavern of the DP's missile repository, which we crossed like flies in a cathedral, hooking our tethers to the girders, drifting over the ranked silos of deep-space interceptors, the giant housing of particle cannons.

All of it obsolete, like castle walls in the age of heavy artillery, but it looks convincing on the manifest, and who knows? "Modern" armies have been destroyed by Zulu spears, it never pays to ignore the conventional weapons—

"Is this a *weapons* bay?" the monster exclaimed; scandalized, on suit radio.

"Of course," said I. "Speranza can defend herself, if she has to."

I let us into a smaller hangar, through a lock on the cavern wall, and filled it with air and pressure and lights. We were completely alone. Left Speranza is a natural object, a hollowed asteroid. Right is artificial, and it's a dangerous place for sentient bipeds. The proximity of the torus can have unpredictable and bizarre effects, not to mention the tissue-frying radiation that washes through at random intervals. But we would be fine for a short while. We fixed tethers, opened our faceplates, and hunkered down, gecko-padded boot soles clinging to the arbitrary "floor."

"I thought you were angels," he remarked shyly. "The weapons, all of that, it seems beneath you. Doesn't your code name, "Debra" mean an angel? Aren't you all messengers, come to us from the Mighty Void?"

Mighty Void was a Balas-Shet term meaning something like God.

"No . . . Deborah was a judge, in Israel. I'm just human, Baal. I'm a person with numinal intelligence, the same kind of being as you are; like all the KiAn."

I could see that the harsh environment of Right Speranza moved him, as it did me. There was a mysterious peace and truth in being here, in the cold dark, breathing borrowed air. He was pondering: open and serious.

"Debra . . . ? Do you believe in the Diaspora?"

"I believe in the Weak theory," I said. "I don't believe we're all descended from the same Blue Planet hominid, the mysterious original starfarers, precursors of *Homo sapiens*. I think we're the same because we grew under the same constraints: time, gravity, hydrogen bonds, the nature of water, the nature of carbon—"

"But instantaneous transit was invented on the Blue Planet," he protested, unwilling to lose his romantic vision.

"Only the prototype. It took hundreds of years, and a lot of outside help, before we had anything like viable interstellar travel—"

Baal had other people to understand the technology for him. He was building castles in the air, dreaming of his future. "Does everyone on the Blue speak English?"

"Not at all. They mostly speak a language called *putonghua*; which means 'common speech,' as if they were the only people in the galaxy. Blues are as insular as the KiAn, believe me, when they're at home. When you work for the DP, you change your ideas; it happens to everyone. I'm still an Englishwoman, and *mi naño* Pelé is still a man of Ecuador—"

"I know!" he broke in eagerly, "I felt that. I *like* that in you!"

"But we skip the middle term. The World Government of our single planet doesn't mean the same as it did." I grinned at him. "Hey, I didn't bring you here for a lecture. This is what I wanted to show you. See the pods?"

He looked around us, slowly, with a connoisseur's eye. He could see what the pods were. They were Aleutian-build, the revolutionary leap forward: *vehicles* that could pass through the mind-matter barrier. An end to those dreary transit lounges, true starflight, the Holy Grail: and only the Aleutians knew how it was done.

"Like to take one out for a spin?"

"You're kidding!" cried Baal, his eyes alight.

"No, I'm not. We'll take a two-man pod. How about it?"

He saw that I was serious, which gave him pause. "How can we? The systems won't allow it. This hangar has to be under military security."

"I *am* military security, Baal. So is Pelé. What did you think we were? Kindergarten teachers? Trust me, I have access, there'll be no questions asked."

He laughed. He knew there was something strange going on, but he didn't care: he trusted me. I glimpsed myself as a substitute for Tiamaat, glimpsed the relationship he should have had with his partner. Not sexual, but predation-based: a playful tussle, sparring partners. But Tiamaat had not wanted to be his sidekick—

We took a pod. Once we were inside, I sealed us off from Speranza, and we lay side by side in the couches, two narrow beds in a torpedo shell: an interstellar sports car, how right for this lordly boy. I checked his hook-ups, and secured my own.

"Where are we going?"

"Oh, just around the block."

His vital signs were in my eyes, his whole being was *quivering* in excitement, and I was glad. The lids closed, we were translated into code, we and our pod were injected into the torus, in the form of a triple stream of pure information, divided and shooting around the ring to meet itself, and collide—

I sat up, in a lucent gloom. The other bed's seal opened, and Baal sat up beside me. We were both still suited, with open faceplates. Our beds shaped themselves into pilot and copilot couches, and we faced what seemed an unmediated view of the deep space outside. Bulwarks and banks of glittering instruments carved up the panorama: I saw Baal's glance flash over the panels greedily, longing to be piloting this little ship for real. Then he saw the yellow primary, a white hole in black absence; and its brilliant, distant partner. He saw the pinpricks of other formations that meant nothing much to me, and he knew where I had brought him. We could not see the planet, it was entirely dark from this view. But in our foreground, the massive beams of space-to-space lasers were playing: shepherding plasma particles into a shell that would hold the recovering atmosphere in place.

To say that KiAn had been flayed alive was no metaphor. The people still living on the surface were in some kind of hell. But it could be saved.

"None of the machinery is strictly material," I said, "in any normal sense. It was couriered here, as information, in the living minds of the people who are now on station. We can't see them, but they're around, in pods like this one. It will all disintegrate, when the repairs are done. But the skin of your world will be whole again, it won't need to be held in place."

The KiAn don't cry, but I was so close to him, in the place where we were, that I felt his tears. "*Why* are you doing this?" he whispered. "You must be angels, or why are you saving us, what have we done to deserve this?"

"The usual reasons," I said. "Market forces, political leverage, power play."

"I don't believe you."

"Then I don't know what to tell you, Baal. Except that the Ki and the An have numinal intelligence. You are like us, and we have so few brothers and sisters. Once we'd found you, we couldn't bear to lose you."

I let him gaze for a long moment without duration.

"I wanted you to see this."

I stepped out of my pilot's couch and stood braced: one hand gecko-padded to the inner shell, while I used the instruments to set the pod to self-destruct. The eject beacon started up, a direct cortical warning that my mind read as a screaming siren—

"Now I'm going back to Speranza. But you're not."

The fine young cannibal took a moment to react. The pupils in his tawny eyes widened amazingly when he found that he was paralyzed, and his capsule couldn't close.

"Is this a dream?"

"Not quite. It's a confabulation. It's what happens when you stay conscious in transit. The mind invents a stream of environments, events. The restoration of KiAn is real, Baal. It will happen. We can see it 'now' because we're in non-duration, we're experiencing the simultaneity. In reality—if that makes any sense, language hates these situations—we're still zipping around the torus. But when the confabulation breaks up, you'll still be in deep space and about to die."

I did not need to tell him why I was doing this. He was no fool, he knew why he had to go. But his mind was still working, fighting—

"Speranza is a four-space mapped environment. You can't do this and go back alone. The system knows you were with me, every moment. The record can't be changed, no way, without the tampering leaving a trace."

"True. But I am one of those rare people who can change *the information*. You've heard fairy tales about us, the Blues who have superpowers? I'm not an angel, Baal. Actually, it's a capital crime to be what I am, where I come from. But Speranza understands me. Speranza uses me."

"Ah!" he cried. "I knew it, I felt it. We are the same!"

————

When I recovered self-consciousness, I was in my room, alone. Earlier in the day, Baal had claimed he needed a nap. After a couple of hours, I'd become suspicious, checked for his signs, and found him missing: gone from the SV Facility screen. I'd been trying to trace him when Right Speranza had detected a pod, with the An leader on board, firing up. The system had warned him to desist. Baal had carried on and paid a high price for his attempted joyride. The injection had failed, both Baal and one fabulous Aleutian-built pod had been annihilated.

Remembering this much gave me an appalling headache—the same aching awfulness I imagine shapes-shifters (I know of one or two) feel in their muscle and bone. I couldn't build the bridge at all: no notion how I'd connected between this reality and the former version. I could have stepped from the dying pod straight through the wall of this pleasant, modest living space. But it didn't matter. I would find out, and Debra would have been behaving like Debra.

Pelé came knocking. I let him in and we commiserated, both of us in shock. We're advocates, not enforcers, there's very little we can do if a Sensitive Visitor is really determined to go AWOL. We'd done all the right things, short of using undue force, and so had Speranza. When we'd broken the privilege locks, Baal's room record had shown that he'd been spying out how to get access to one of those Aleutian pods. It was just too bad that he'd succeeded, and that he'd had enough skill to get himself killed. Don't feel responsible, said Pelé. It's not your fault. Nobody thinks that. Don't be so sad. Always so sad, Debra: it's not good for the brain, you should take a break. Then he started telling me that frankly, nobody would regret Baal. By An law, Tiamaat could now rule alone; and if she took a partner, we could trust her not to choose another bloodthirsty atavist . . . I soon stopped him. I huddled there in pain, my friend holding my hand: seeing only the beautiful one, his tawny eyes at the last, his challenge and his trust; mourning my victim.

I'm a melancholy assassin.

I did not sleep. In the grey calm of Left Speranza's early hours, before the breakfast kiosks were awake, I took the elevator to the Customized Shelter Sector, checked in with the CSP, and made my way, between the silent capsule towers, to Hopes and Dreams Park. I was disappointed that there were no refugees about. It would have been nice to see Ki children, playing fearlessly, Ki oldsters picking herbs from their window boxes, instead of being boiled down for soup themselves. The gates of the Sacred Grove were open, so I just walked in. There was a memorial service: strictly no outsiders, but I'd had a personal message from Tiamaat saying I would be welcome. I didn't particularly want to meet her again. I'm a superstitious assassin, I felt that she would somehow know what I had done for her. I thought I would keep to the back of whatever gathering I found, while I made my own farewell.

The daystar's rays had cleared the false horizon, the sun was a rumor of gold between the trees. I heard laughter, and a cry. I walked into the clearing and saw Tiamaat. She'd just made the kill. I saw her toss the small body down, drop to her haunches, and take a ritual bite of raw flesh; I saw the blood on her mouth. The Ki looked on, keeping their distance in a solemn little cluster. Tiamaat transformed, splendid in her power, proud of her deed, looked up; and straight at me. I don't know what she expected.

Did she think I would be glad for her? Did she want me to know how I'd been fooled? Certainly she knew she had nothing to fear. She was only doing the same as Baal had done, and the DP had made no protest over *his* kill. I shouted, like an idiot: "Hey, stop that!" and the whole group scattered. They vanished into the foliage, taking the body with them.

––––––––––

I said nothing to anyone. I had not, in fact, foreseen that Tiamaat would become a killer. I'd seen a talented young woman, who would blossom if the unfairly favored young man was removed. I hadn't realized that a dominant An would behave like a dominant An, irrespective of biological sex. But I was sure my employers had grasped the situation; and it didn't matter. The long-gone, harsh symbiosis between the An and the Ki, which they preserved in their rites of kingship, was not the problem. It was the modern version, the mass market in Ki meat, the intensive farms and the factories. Tiamaat would help us to get rid of those. She would embrace the new in public, whatever she believed in private.

And the fate of the Ki would change.

The news of Baal's death had been couriered to KiAn and to the homeworlds by the time I took my transit back to the Blue. We'd started getting reactions: all positive, so to speak. Of course, there would be persistent rumors that the Ki had somehow arranged Baal's demise, but there was no harm in that. In certain situations, assassination *works*––as long as it is secret, or at least misattributed. It's a far more benign tool than most alternatives; and a lot faster. I had signed off at the Social Support Office, I'd managed to avoid goodbyes. Just before I went through to the lounge, I realized that I hadn't had my aura tag taken off. I had to go back, and go through *another* blessed gate; and Pelé caught me.

"Take the dreamtime," he insisted, holding me tight. "Play some silly game, go skydiving from Angel Falls. *Please*, Debra. Don't be conscious. You worry me."

I wondered if he suspected what I really did for a living.

Maybe so, but he couldn't possibly understand.

I'll give it serious thought," I assured him, and kissed him goodbye.

I gave the idea of the soft option serious thought for ten paces, passed into the lounge, and found my narrow bed. I lay down there, beside my fine young cannibal, the boy who had known me for what I was. His innocent eyes . . . I lay down with them all, and with the searing terrors they bring; all my dead remembered.

I needed to launder my soul.

Boojum

Elizabeth Bear & Sarah Monette

THE SHIP HAD no name of her own, so her human crew called her the *Lavinia Whateley*. As far as anyone could tell, she didn't mind. At least, her long grasping vanes curled—affectionately?—when the chief engineers patted her bulkheads and called her "Vinnie," and she ceremoniously tracked the footsteps of each crew member with her internal bioluminescence, giving them light to walk and work and live by.

The *Lavinia Whateley* was a Boojum, a deep-space swimmer, but her kind had evolved in the high tempestuous envelopes of gas giants, and their offspring still spent their infancies there, in cloud-nurseries over eternal storms. And so she was streamlined, something like a vast spiny lionfish to the earth-adapted eye. Her sides were lined with gasbags filled with hydrogen; her vanes and wings furled tight. Her color was a blue-green so dark it seemed a glossy black unless the light struck it; her hide was impregnated with symbiotic algae.

Where there was light, she could make oxygen. Where there was oxygen, she could make water.

She was an ecosystem unto herself, as the captain was a law unto herself. And down in the bowels of the engineering section, Black Alice Bradley, who was only human and no kind of law at all, loved her.

Black Alice had taken the oath back in '32, after the Venusian Riots. She hadn't hidden her reasons, and the captain had looked at her with cold, dark, amused eyes and said, "So long as you carry your weight, cherie, I don't care. Betray me, though, and you will be going back to Venus the cold way." But it was probably that—and the fact that Black Alice couldn't hit the broad side of a space freighter with a ray gun—that had gotten her assigned to Engineering, where ethics were less of a problem. It wasn't, after all, as if she was going anywhere.

Black Alice was on duty when the *Lavinia Whateley* spotted prey; she felt the shiver of anticipation that ran through the decks of the ship. It was an odd sensation, a tic Vinnie only exhibited in pursuit. And then they were underway, zooming down the slope of the gravity well toward Sol, and the screens all around Engineering—which Captain Song kept dark, most of the time, on the theory that swabs and deckhands and coal-shovelers didn't need to know where they were, or what they were doing—flickered bright and live.

Everybody looked up, and Demijack shouted, "There! There!" He was right: The blot that might only have been a smudge of oil on the screen moved as Vinnie banked, revealing itself to be a freighter, big and ungainly and hopelessly outclassed. Easy prey. Easy pickings.

We could use some of them, thought Black Alice. Contrary to the e-ballads and comm stories, a pirate's life was not all imported delicacies and fawning slaves. Especially not when three-quarters of any and all profits went directly back to the *Lavinia Whateley*, to keep her healthy and happy. Nobody ever argued. There were stories about the *Marie Curie*, too.

The captain's voice over fiber optic cable—strung beside the *Lavinia Whateley*'s nerve bundles—was as clear and free of static as if she stood at Black Alice's elbow. "Battle stations," Captain Song said, and the crew leapt to obey. It had been two Solar since Captain Song keelhauled James Brady, but nobody who'd been with the ship then was ever likely to forget his ruptured eyes and frozen scream.

Black Alice manned her station, and stared at the screen. She saw the freighter's name—the *Josephine Baker*—gold on black across the stern, the Venusian flag for its port of registry wired stiff from a mast on its hull. It was a steelship, not a Boojum, and they had every advantage. For a moment she thought the freighter would run.

And then it turned, and brought its guns to bear.

No sense of movement, of acceleration, of disorientation. No pop, no whump of displaced air. The view on the screens just flickered to a different one, as Vinnie skipped—apported—to a new position just aft and above the *Josephine Baker*, crushing the flag mast with her hull.

Black Alice felt that, a grinding shiver. And had just time to grab her console before the *Lavinia Whateley* grappled the freighter, long vanes not curling in affection now.

Out of the corner of her eye, she saw Dogcollar, the closest thing the *Lavinia Whateley* had to a chaplain, cross himself, and she heard him mutter, like he always did, *Ave, Grandaevissimi, morituri vos salutant*. It was the best he'd be able to do until it was all over, and even then he wouldn't have the chance to do much. Captain Song didn't mind other people worrying about souls, so long as they didn't do it on her time.

The captain's voice was calling orders, assigning people to boarding parties port and starboard. Down in Engineering, all they had to do was monitor the *Lavinia Whateley*'s hull and prepare to repel boarders, assuming the freighter's crew had the gumption to send any. Vinnie would take care of the rest—until the time came to persuade her not to eat her prey before they'd gotten all the valuables off it. That was a ticklish job, only entrusted to the chief engineers, but Black Alice watched and listened, and although she didn't expect she'd ever get the chance, she thought she could do it herself.

It was a small ambition, and one she never talked about. But it would be a hell of a thing, wouldn't it? To be somebody a Boojum would listen to?

She gave her attention to the dull screens in her sectors, and tried not to crane her neck to catch a glimpse of the ones with the actual fighting on them. Dogcollar was making the rounds with sidearms from the weapons locker, just in case. Once the *Josephine Baker* was subdued, it was the junior engineers and others who would board her to take inventory.

Sometimes there were crew members left in hiding on captured ships. Sometimes, unwary pirates got shot.

There was no way to judge the progress of the battle from Engineering. Wasabi put a stopwatch up on one of the secondary screens, as usual, and everybody glanced at it periodically. Fifteen minutes ongoing meant the boarding parties hadn't hit any nasty surprises. Black Alice had met a man once who'd been on the *Margaret Mead* when she grappled a freighter that turned out to be carrying a division's-worth of Marines out to the Jovian moons. Thirty minutes ongoing was normal. Forty-five minutes. Upward of an hour ongoing, and people started double-checking their weapons. The longest battle Black Alice had ever personally been part of was six hours, forty-three minutes, and fifty-two seconds. That had been the last time the *Lavinia Whateley* worked with a partner, and the double-cross by the *Henry Ford* was the only reason any of Vinnie's crew needed. Captain Song still had Captain Edwards' head in a jar on the bridge, and Vinnie had an ugly ring of scars where the *Henry Ford* had bitten her.

This time, the clock stopped at fifty minutes, thirteen seconds. The *Josephine Baker* surrendered.

Dogcollar slapped Black Alice's arm. "With me," he said, and she didn't argue. He had only six weeks seniority over her, but he was as tough as he was devout, and not stupid either. She checked the Velcro on her holster and followed him up the ladder, reaching through the rungs once to scratch Vinnie's bulkhead as she passed. The ship paid her no notice. She wasn't the captain, and she wasn't one of the four chief engineers.

Quartermaster mostly respected crew's own partner choices, and as Black Alice and Dogcollar suited up—it wouldn't be the first time, if the *Josephine Baker*'s crew decided to blow her open to space rather than be taken captive—he came by and issued them both tag guns and x-ray pads, taking a retina scan in return. All sorts of valuable things got hidden inside of bulkheads, and once Vinnie was done with the steelship there wouldn't be much chance of coming back to look for what they'd missed.

Wet pirates used to scuttle their captures. The Boojums were more efficient.

Black Alice clipped everything to her belt and checked Dogcollar's seals.

And then they were swinging down lines from the *Lavinia Whateley*'s belly to the chewed-open airlock. A lot of crew didn't like to look at the ship's face, but Black Alice loved it. All those teeth, the diamond edges worn to a glitter, and a few of the ship's dozens of bright sapphire eyes blinking back at her.

She waved, unselfconsciously, and flattered herself that the ripple of closing eyes was Vinnie winking in return.

She followed Dogcollar inside the prize.

They unsealed when they had checked atmosphere—no sense in wasting your own air when you might need it later—and the first thing she noticed was the smell.

The *Lavinia Whateley* had her own smell, ozone and nutmeg, and other ships never smelled as good, but this was . . . this was . . .

"What did they kill and why didn't they space it?" Dogcollar wheezed, and Black Alice swallowed hard against her gag reflex and said, "One will get you twenty we're the lucky bastards that find it."

"No takers," Dogcollar said.

They worked together to crank open the hatches they came to. Twice they found crew members, messily dead. Once they found crew members alive.

"Gillies," said Black Alice.

"Still don't explain the smell," said Dogcollar and, to the gillies: "Look, you can join our crew, or our ship can eat you. Makes no never mind to us."

The gillies blinked their big wet eyes and made fingersigns at each other, and then nodded. Hard.

Dogcollar slapped a tag on the bulkhead. "Someone will come get you. You go wandering, we'll assume you changed your mind."

The gillies shook their heads, hard, and folded down onto the deck to wait.

Dogcollar tagged searched holds—green for clean, purple for goods, red for anything Vinnie might like to eat that couldn't be fenced for a profit—and Black Alice mapped. The corridors in the steelship were winding, twisty, hard to track. She was glad she chalked the walls, because she didn't think her map was quite right, somehow, but she couldn't figure out where she'd gone wrong. Still, they had a beacon, and Vinnie could always chew them out if she had to.

Black Alice loved her ship.

She was thinking about that, how, okay, it wasn't so bad, the pirate game, and it sure beat working in the sunstone mines on Venus, when she found a locked cargo hold. "Hey, Dogcollar," she said to her comm, and while he was turning to cover her, she pulled her sidearm and blasted the lock.

The door peeled back, and Black Alice found herself staring at rank upon rank of silver cylinders, each less than a meter tall and perhaps half a meter wide, smooth and featureless except for what looked like an assortment of sockets and plugs on the surface of each. The smell was strongest here.

"Shit," she said.

Dogcollar, more practical, slapped the first safety orange tag of the expedition beside the door and said only, "Captain'll want to see this."

"Yeah," said Black Alice, cold chills chasing themselves up and down her spine. "C'mon, let's move."

But of course it turned out that she and Dogcollar were on the retrieval detail, too, and the captain wasn't leaving the canisters for Vinnie.

Which, okay, fair. Black Alice didn't want the *Lavinia Whateley* eating those things, either, but why did they have to bring them *back?*

She said as much to Dogcollar, under her breath, and had a horrifying thought: "She knows what they are, right?"

"She's the captain," said Dogcollar.

"Yeah, but—I ain't arguing, man, but if she doesn't know . . ." She lowered her voice even farther, so she could barely hear herself: "What if somebody *opens* one?"

Dogcollar gave her a pained look. "Nobody's going to go opening anything. But if you're really worried, go talk to the captain about it."

He was calling her bluff. Black Alice called his right back. "Come with me?"

He was stuck. He stared at her, and then he grunted and pulled his gloves off, the left and then the right. "Fuck," he said. "I guess we oughta."

For the crew members who had been in the boarding action, the party had already started. Dogcollar and Black Alice finally tracked the captain down in the rec room, where her marines were slurping stolen wine from broken-necked bottles. As much of it splashed on the gravity plates epoxied to the *Lavinia Whateley*'s flattest interior surface as went into the marines, but Black Alice imagined there was plenty more where that came from. And the faster the crew went through it, the less long they'd be drunk.

The captain herself was naked in a great extruded tub, up to her collarbones in steaming water dyed pink and heavily scented by the bath bombs sizzling here and there. Black Alice stared; she hadn't seen a tub bath in seven years. She still dreamed of them sometimes.

"Captain," she said, because Dogcollar wasn't going to say anything. "We think you should know we found some dangerous cargo on the prize."

Captain Song raised one eyebrow. "And you imagine I don't know already, cherie?"

Oh shit. But Black Alice stood her ground. "We thought we should be *sure*."

The captain raised one long leg out of the water to shove a pair of necking pirates off the rim of her tub. They rolled onto the floor, grappling and clawing, both fighting to be on top. But they didn't break the kiss. "You wish to be sure," said the captain. Her dark eyes had never left Black Alice's sweating face. "Very well. Tell me. And then you will know that I know, and you can be *sure*."

Dogcollar made a grumbling noise deep in his throat, easily interpreted: *I told you so.*

Just as she had when she took Captain Song's oath and slit her thumb with a razorblade and dripped her blood on the *Lavinia Whateley*'s decking so the ship might know her, Black Alice—metaphorically speaking—took a breath and jumped. "They're brains," she said. "Human brains. Stolen. Black-market. The Fungi—"

"Mi-Go," Dogcollar hissed, and the captain grinned at him, showing extraordinarily white strong teeth. He ducked, submissively, but didn't step back, for which Black Alice felt a completely ridiculous gratitude.

"Mi-Go," Black Alice said. Mi-Go, Fungi, what did it matter? They came from the outer rim of the Solar System, the black cold hurtling rocks of the Öpik-Oort Cloud. Like the Boojums, they could swim between the stars. "They collect them. There's a black market. Nobody knows what they use them for. It's illegal, of course. But they're . . . alive in there. They go mad, supposedly."

And that was it. That was all Black Alice could manage. She stopped, and had to remind herself to shut her mouth.

"So I've heard," the captain said, dabbling at the steaming water. She stretched luxuriously in her tub. Someone thrust a glass of white wine at her, condensation dewing the outside. The captain did not drink from shattered plastic bottles. "The Mi-Go will pay for this cargo, won't they? They mine rare minerals all over the system. They're said to be very wealthy."

"Yes, Captain," Dogcollar said, when it became obvious that Black Alice couldn't.

"Good," the captain said. Under Black Alice's feet, the decking shuddered, a grinding sound as Vinnie began to dine. Her rows of teeth would make short work of the *Josephine Baker*'s steel hide. Black Alice could see two of the gillies—the same two? She never could tell them apart unless they had scars—flinch and tug at their chains. "Then they might as well pay us as someone else, wouldn't you say?"

––––––––

Black Alice knew she should stop thinking about the canisters. Captain's word was law. But she couldn't help it, like scratching at a scab. They were down there, in the third subhold, the one even sniffers couldn't find, cold and sweating and with that stench that was like a living thing.

And she kept wondering. Were they empty? Or were there brains in there, people's brains, going mad?

The idea was driving her crazy, and finally, her fourth off-shift after the capture of the *Josephine Baker*, she had to go look.

"This is stupid, Black Alice," she muttered to herself as she climbed down the companionway, the beads in her hair clicking against her earrings. "Stupid, stupid, stupid." Vinnie bioluminesced, a traveling spotlight, placidly unconcerned whether Black Alice was being an idiot or not.

Half-Hand Sally had pulled duty in the main hold. She nodded at Black Alice and Black Alice nodded back. Black Alice ran errands a lot, for Engineering and sometimes for other departments, because she didn't smoke hash and she didn't cheat at cards. She was reliable.

Down through the subholds, and she really didn't want to be doing this, but she was here and the smell of the third subhold was already making her sick, and maybe if she just knew one way or the other, she'd be able to quit thinking about it.

She opened the third subhold, and the stench rushed out.

The canisters were just metal, sealed, seemingly airtight. There shouldn't be any way for the aroma of the contents to escape. But it permeated the air nonetheless, bad enough that Black Alice wished she had brought a rebreather.

No, that would have been suspicious. So it was really best for everyone concerned that she hadn't, but oh, gods and little fishes, the stench. Even breathing through her mouth was no help; she could taste it, like oil from a fryer, saturating the air, oozing up her sinuses, coating the interior spaces of her body.

As silently as possible, she stepped across the threshold and into the space beyond. The *Lavinia Whateley* obligingly lit the space as she entered, dazzling her at first as the overhead lights—not just bioluminescent, here, but LEDs chosen to approximate natural daylight, for when they shipped plants and animals—reflected off rank upon rank of canisters. When Black Alice went among them, they did not reach her waist.

She was just going to walk through, she told herself. Hesitantly, she touched the closest cylinder. The air in this hold was so dry there was no condensation—the whole ship ran to lip-cracking, nosebleed dryness in the long weeks between prizes—but the cylinder was cold. It felt somehow grimy to the touch, gritty and oily like machine grease. She pulled her hand back.

It wouldn't do to open the closest one to the door—and she realized with that thought that she was planning on opening one. There must be a way to do it, a concealed catch or a code pad. She was an engineer, after all.

She stopped three ranks in, lightheaded with the smell, to examine the problem.

It was remarkably simple, once you looked for it. There were three depressions on either side of the rim, a little smaller than human fingertips but spaced appropriately. She laid the pads of her fingers over them and pressed hard, making the flesh deform into the catches.

The lid sprang up with a pressurized hiss. Black Alice was grateful that even open, it couldn't smell much worse. She leaned forward to peer within. There was a clear membrane over the surface, and gelatin or thick fluid underneath. Vinnie's lights illuminated it well.

It was not empty. And as the light struck the grayish surface of the lump of tissue floating within, Black Alice would have sworn she saw the pathetic unbodied thing flinch.

She scrambled to close the canister again, nearly pinching her fingertips when it clanked shut. "Sorry," she whispered, although dear sweet Jesus, surely the thing couldn't hear her. "Sorry, sorry." And then she turned and ran, catching her hip a bruising blow against the doorway, slapping the controls to make it fucking *close* already. And then she staggered sideways, lurching to her knees, and vomited until blackness was spinning in front of her eyes and she couldn't smell or taste anything but bile.

Vinnie would absorb the former contents of Black Alice's stomach, just as she absorbed, filtered, recycled, and excreted all her crew's wastes. Shaking, Black Alice braced herself back upright and began the long climb out of the holds.

In the first subhold, she had to stop, her shoulder against the smooth, velvet slickness of Vinnie's skin, her mouth hanging open while her lungs worked. And she knew Vinnie wasn't going to hear her, because she wasn't the captain or a chief engineer or anyone important, but she had to try anyway, croaking, "Vinnie, water, please."

And no one could have been more surprised than Black Alice Bradley when Vinnie extruded a basin and a thin cool trickle of water began to flow into it.

Well, now she knew. And there was still nothing she could do about it. She wasn't the captain, and if she said anything more than she already had, people were going to start looking at her funny. Mutiny kind of funny. And what Black Alice did *not* need was any more of Captain Song's attention and especially not for rumors like that. She kept her head down and did her job and didn't discuss her nightmares with anyone.

And she had nightmares, all right. Hot and cold running, enough, she fancied, that she could have filled up the captain's huge tub with them.

She could live with that. But over the next double dozen of shifts, she became aware of something else wrong, and this was worse, because it was something wrong with the *Lavinia Whateley*.

The first sign was the chief engineers frowning and going into huddles at odd moments. And then Black Alice began to feel it herself, the way Vinnie was . . . she didn't have a word for it because she'd never felt anything like it before. She would have said *balky*, but that couldn't be right. It couldn't. But she was more and more sure that Vinnie was less responsive somehow, that when she obeyed the captain's orders, it was with a delay. If she were human, Vinnie would have been dragging her feet.

You couldn't keelhaul a ship for not obeying fast enough.

And then, because she was paying attention so hard she was making her own head hurt, Black Alice noticed something else. Captain Song had them cruising the gas giants' orbits—Jupiter, Saturn, Neptune—not going in as far as the asteroid belt, not going out as far as Uranus. Nobody Black Alice talked to knew why, exactly, but she and Dogcollar figured it was because the captain wanted to talk to the Mi-Go without actually getting near the nasty cold rock of their planet. And what Black Alice noticed was that Vinnie was less balky, less *unhappy*, when she was headed out, and more and more resistant the closer they got to the asteroid belt.

Vinnie, she remembered, had been born over Uranus.

"Do you want to go home, Vinnie?" Black Alice asked her one late-night shift when there was nobody around to care that she was talking to the ship. "Is that what's wrong?"

She put her hand flat on the wall, and although she was probably imagining it, she thought she felt a shiver ripple across Vinnie's vast side.

Black Alice knew how little she knew, and didn't even contemplate sharing her theory with the chief engineers. They probably knew exactly what was wrong and exactly what to do to keep the *Lavinia Whateley* from going core meltdown like the *Marie Curie* had. That was a whispered story, not the sort of thing anybody talked about except in their hammocks after lights out.

The *Marie Curie* had eaten her own crew.

So when Wasabi said, four shifts later, "Black Alice, I've got a job for you," Black Alice said, "Yessir," and hoped it would be something that would help the *Lavinia Whateley* be happy again.

It was a suit job, he said, replace and repair. Black Alice was going because she was reliable and smart and stayed quiet, and it was time she took on more responsibilities. The way he said it made her first fret because that meant the captain might be reminded of her existence, and then fret because she realized the captain already had been.

But she took the equipment he issued, and she listened to the instructions and read schematics and committed them both to memory and her implants. It was a ticklish job, a neural override repair. She'd done some fiber optic bundle splicing, but this was going to be a doozy. And she was going to have to do it in stiff, pressurized gloves.

Her heart hammered as she sealed her helmet, and not because she was worried about the EVA. This was a chance. An opportunity. A step closer to chief engineer.

Maybe she had impressed the captain with her discretion, after all.

She cycled the airlock, snapped her safety harness, and stepped out onto the *Lavinia Whateley*'s hide.

That deep blue-green, like azurite, like the teeming seas of Venus under their swampy eternal clouds, was invisible. They were too far from Sol—it was a yellow stylus-dot, and you had to know where to look for it. Vinnie's hide was just black under Black Alice's suit floods. As the airlock cycled shut, though, the Boojum's own bioluminescence shimmered up her vanes and along the ridges of her sides—crimson and electric green and acid blue. Vinnie must have noticed Black Alice picking her way carefully up her spine with barbed boots. They wouldn't *hurt* Vinnie—nothing short of a space rock could manage that—but they certainly stuck in there good.

The thing Black Alice was supposed to repair was at the principal nexus of Vinnie's central nervous system. The ship didn't have anything like what a human or a gilly would consider a brain; there were nodules spread all through her vast body. Too slow, otherwise. And Black Alice had heard Boojums weren't supposed to be all that smart—trainable, sure, maybe like an Earth monkey.

Which is what made it creepy as hell that, as she picked her way up Vinnie's flank—though *up* was a courtesy, under these circumstances—talking to her all the way, she would have sworn Vinnie was talking back. Not just tracking her with the lights, as she would always do, but bending some of her barbels and vanes around as if craning her neck to get a look at Black Alice.

Black Alice carefully circumnavigated an eye—she didn't think her boots would hurt it, but it seemed discourteous to stomp across somebody's field of vision—and wondered, only half-idly, if she had been sent out on this task not because she was being considered for promotion, but because she was expendable.

She was just rolling her eyes and dismissing that as borrowing trouble when she came over a bump on Vinnie's back, spotted her goal—and all the ship's lights went out.

She tongued on the comm. "Wasabi?"

"I got you, Blackie. You just keep doing what you're doing."

"Yessir."

But it seemed like her feet stayed stuck in Vinnie's hide a little longer than was good. At least fifteen seconds before she managed a couple of deep breaths—too deep for her limited oxygen supply, so she went briefly dizzy—and continued up Vinnie's side.

Black Alice had no idea what inflammation looked like in a Boojum, but she would guess this was it. All around the interface she was meant to repair, Vinnie's flesh looked scraped and puffy. Black Alice walked tenderly, wincing, muttering apologies under her breath. And with every step, the tendrils coiled a little closer.

Black Alice crouched beside the box, and began examining connections. The console was about three meters by four, half a meter tall, and fixed firmly to Vinnie's hide. It looked like the thing was still functional, but something—a bit of space debris, maybe—had dented it pretty good.

Cautiously, Black Alice dropped a hand on it. She found the access panel, and flipped it open: more red lights than green. A tongue-click, and she began withdrawing her tethered tools from their holding pouches and arranging them so that they would float conveniently around.

She didn't hear a thing, of course, but the hide under her boots vibrated suddenly, sharply. She jerked her head around, just in time to see one of Vinnie's feelers slap her own side, five or ten meters away. And then the whole Boojum shuddered, contracting, curved into a hard crescent of pain the same way she had when the *Henry Ford* had taken that chunk out of her hide. And the lights in the access panel lit up all at once—red, red, yellow, red.

Black Alice tongued off the *send* function on her headset microphone, so Wasabi wouldn't hear her. She touched the bruised hull, and she touched the dented edge of the console. "Vinnie," she said, "does this *hurt?*"

Not that Vinnie could answer her. But it was obvious. She was in pain. And maybe that dent didn't have anything to do with space debris. Maybe—Black Alice straightened, looked around, and couldn't convince herself that it was an accident that this box was planted right where Vinnie couldn't . . . quite . . . reach it.

"So what does it *do?*" she muttered. "Why am I out here repairing something that fucking hurts?" She crouched down again and took another long look at the interface.

As an engineer, Black Alice was mostly self-taught; her implants were second-hand, black market, scavenged, the wet work done by a gilly on Providence Station. She'd learned the technical vocabulary from Goggle-head Kim before he bought it in a stupid little fight with a ship named the *V. I. Ulyanov*, but what she relied on were her instincts, the things she knew without being able to say. So she *looked* at that box wired into Vinnie's spine and all its red and yellow lights, and then she tongued the comm back on and said, "Wasabi, this thing don't look so good."

"Whaddya mean, don't look so good?" Wasabi sounded distracted, and that was just fine.

Black Alice made a noise, the auditory equivalent of a shrug. "I think the node's inflamed. Can we pull it and lock it in somewhere else?"

"No!" said Wasabi.

"It's looking pretty ugly out here."

"Look, Blackie, unless you want us to all go sailing out into the Big Empty, we are *not* pulling that governor. Just fix the fucking thing, would you?"

"Yessir," said Black Alice, thinking hard. The first thing was that Wasabi knew what was going on—knew what the box did and knew that the *Lavinia Whateley* didn't like it. That wasn't comforting. The second thing was that whatever was going on, it involved the Big Empty, the cold vastness between the stars. So it wasn't that Vinnie wanted to go home. She wanted to go *out*.

It made sense, from what Black Alice knew about Boojums. Their infants lived in the tumult of the gas giants' atmosphere, but as they aged, they pushed higher and higher, until they reached the edge of the envelope. And then—following instinct or maybe the calls of their fellows, nobody knew for sure—they learned to skip, throwing themselves out into the vacuum like Earth birds leaving the nest. And what if, for a Boojum, the solar system was just another nest?

Black Alice knew the *Lavinia Whateley* was old, for a Boojum. Captain Song was not her first captain, although you never mentioned Captain Smith if you knew what was good for you. So if there *was* another stage to her life cycle, she might be ready for it. And her crew wasn't letting her go.

Jesus and the cold fishy gods, Black Alice thought. Is this why the *Marie Curie* ate her crew? Because they wouldn't let her go?

She fumbled for her tools, tugging the cords to float them closer, and wound up walloping herself in the bicep with a splicer. And as she was wrestling with it, her headset spoke again. "Blackie, can you hurry it up out there? Captain says we're going to have company."

Company? She never got to say it. Because when she looked up, she saw the shapes, faintly limned in starlight, and a chill as cold as a suit leak crept up her neck.

There were dozens of them. Hundreds. They made her skin crawl and her nerves judder the way gillies and Boojums never had. They were man-sized, roughly, but they looked like the pseudoroaches of Venus, the ones Black Alice still had nightmares about, with too many legs, and horrible stiff wings. They had ovate, corrugated heads, but no faces, and where their mouths ought to be sprouted writhing tentacles

And some of them carried silver shining cylinders, like the canisters in Vinnie's subhold.

Black Alice wasn't certain if they saw her, crouched on the Boojum's hide with only a thin laminate between her and the breathsucker, but she was certain of something else. If they did, they did not care.

They disappeared below the curve of the ship, toward the airlock Black Alice had exited before clawing her way along the ship's side. They could be a trade delegation, come to bargain for the salvaged cargo.

Black Alice didn't think even the Mi-Go came in the battalions to talk trade.

She meant to wait until the last of them had passed, but they just kept coming. Wasabi wasn't answering her hails; she was on her own and unarmed. She fumbled with her tools, stowing things in any handy pocket whether it was where the tool went or not. She couldn't see much; everything was misty. It took her several seconds to realize that her visor was fogged because she was crying.

Patch cables. Where were the fucking patch cables? She found a two-meter length of fiber optic with the right plugs on the end. One end went into the monitor panel. The other snapped into her suit comm.

"Vinnie?" she whispered, when she thought she had a connection. "Vinnie, can you hear me?"

The bioluminescence under Black Alice's boots pulsed once.

Gods and little fishes, she thought. And then she drew out her laser cutting torch, and started slicing open the case on the console that Wasabi had called the *governor*. Wasabi was probably dead by now, or dying. Wasabi, and Dogcollar, and . . . well, not dead. If they were lucky, they were dead.

Because the opposite of lucky was those canisters the Mi-Go were carrying.

She hoped Dogcollar was lucky.

"You wanna go *out*, right?" she whispered to the *Lavinia Whateley*. "Out into the Big Empty."

She'd never been sure how much Vinnie understood of what people said, but the light pulsed again.

"And this thing won't let you." It wasn't a question. She had it open now, and she could see that was what it did. Ugly fucking thing. Vinnie shivered underneath her, and there was a sudden pulse of noise in her helmet speakers: screaming. People screaming.

"I know," Black Alice said. "They'll come get me in a minute, I guess." She swallowed hard against the sudden lurch of her stomach. "I'm gonna get this thing off you, though. And when they go, you can go, okay? And I'm sorry. I didn't know we were keeping you from . . ." She had to quit talking, or she really was going to puke. Grimly, she fumbled for the tools she needed to disentangle the abomination from Vinnie's nervous system.

Another pulse of sound, a voice, not a person: flat and buzzing and horrible. "We do not bargain with thieves." And the scream that time—she'd never heard Captain Song scream before. Black Alice flinched and started counting to slow her breathing. Puking in a suit was the number one badness, but hyperventilating in a suit was a really close second.

Her heads-up display was low-res, and slightly miscalibrated, so that everything had a faint shadow-double. But the thing that flashed up against her own view of her hands was unmistakable: a question mark.

<?>

"Vinnie?"

Another pulse of screaming, and the question mark again.

<?>

"Holy shit, Vinnie! . . . Never mind, never mind. They, um, they collect people's brains. In canisters. Like the canisters in the third subhold."

The bioluminescence pulsed once. Black Alice kept working.

Her heads-up pinged again: <ALICE> A pause. <?>

"Um, yeah. I figure that's what they'll do with me, too. It looked like they had plenty of canisters to go around."

Vinnie pulsed, and there was a longer pause while Black Alice doggedly severed connections and loosened bolts.

<WANT> said the *Lavinia Whateley*. <?>

"Want? Do I *want* . . . ?" Her laughter sounded bad. "Um, no. No, I don't want to be a brain in a jar. But I'm not seeing a lot of choices here. Even if I went cometary, they could catch me. And it kind of sounds like they're mad enough to do it, too."

She'd cleared out all the moorings around the edge of the governor; the case lifted off with a shove and went sailing into the dark. Black Alice winced. But then the processor under the cover drifted away from Vinnie's hide, and there was just the monofilament tethers and the fat cluster of fiber optic and superconductors to go.

<HELP>

"I'm doing my best here, Vinnie," Black Alice said through her teeth.

That got her a fast double-pulse, and the *Lavinia Whateley* said, <HELP> And then, <ALICE>

"You want to help *me*?" Black Alice squeaked.

A strong pulse, and the heads-up said, <HELP ALICE>

"That's really sweet of you, but I'm honestly not sure there's anything you can do. I mean, it doesn't look like the Mi-Go are mad at *you*, and I really want to keep it that way."

<EAT ALICE> said the *Lavinia Whateley*.

Black Alice came within a millimeter of taking her own fingers off with the cutting laser. "Um, Vinnie, that's um . . . well, I guess it's better than being a brain in a jar." Or suffocating to death in her suit if she went cometary and the Mi-Go *didn't* come after her.

The double-pulse again, but Black Alice didn't see what she could have missed. As communications went, *EAT ALICE* was pretty fucking unambiguous.

<HELP ALICE> the *Lavinia Whateley* insisted. Black Alice leaned in close, unsplicing the last of the governor's circuits from the Boojum's nervous system. <SAVE ALICE>

"By eating me? Look, I know what happens to things you eat, and it's not . . ." She bit her tongue. Because she *did* know what happened to things the *Lavinia Whateley* ate. Absorbed. Filtered. Recycled. "Vinnie . . . are you saying you can save me from the Mi-Go?"

A pulse of agreement.

"By eating me?" Black Alice pursued, needing to be sure she understood.

Another pulse of agreement.

Black Alice thought about the *Lavinia Whateley*'s teeth. "How much *me* are we talking about here?"

<ALICE> said the *Lavinia Whateley*, and then the last fiber optic cable parted, and Black Alice, her hands shaking, detached her patch cable and flung the whole mess of it as hard as she could straight up. Maybe it would find a planet with atmosphere and be some little alien kid's shooting star.

And now she had to decide what to do.

She figured she had two choices, really. One, walk back down the *Lavinia Whateley* and find out if the Mi-Go believed in surrender. Two, walk around the *Lavinia Whateley* and into her toothy mouth.

Black Alice didn't think the Mi-Go believed in surrender.

She tilted her head back for one last clear look at the shining black infinity of space. Really, there wasn't any choice at all. Because even if she'd misunderstood what Vinnie seemed to be trying to tell her, the worst she'd end up was dead, and that was light-years better than what the Mi-Go had on offer.

Black Alice Bradley loved her ship.

She turned to her left and started walking, and the *Lavinia Whateley*'s bioluminescence followed her courteously all the way, vanes swaying out of her path. Black Alice skirted each of Vinnie's eyes as she came to them, and each of them blinked at her. And then she reached Vinnie's mouth and that magnificent panoply of teeth.

"Make it quick, Vinnie, okay?" said Black Alice, and walked into her leviathan's maw.

Picking her way delicately between razor-sharp teeth, Black Alice had plenty of time to consider the ridiculousness of worrying about a hole in her suit. Vinnie's mouth was more like a crystal cave, once you were inside it; there was no tongue, no palate. Just polished, macerating stones. Which did not close on Black Alice, to her surprise. If anything, she got the feeling Vinnie was holding her . . . breath. Or what passed for it.

The Boojum was lit inside, as well—or was making herself lit, for Black Alice's benefit. And as Black Alice clambered inward, the teeth got smaller, and fewer, and the tunnel narrowed. Her throat, Alice thought. I'm inside her.

And the walls closed down, and she was swallowed.

Like a pill, enclosed in the tight sarcophagus of her space suit, she felt rippling pressure as peristalsis pushed her along. And then greater pressure, suffocating, savage. One sharp pain. The pop of her ribs as her lungs crushed.

Screaming inside a space suit was contraindicated, too. And with collapsed lungs, she couldn't even do it properly.

---

alice.

She floated. In warm darkness. A womb, a bath. She was comfortable. An itchy soreness between her shoulder blades felt like a very mild radiation burn.

alice.

A voice she thought she should know. She tried to speak; her mouth gnashed, her teeth ground.

alice. talk here.

She tried again. Not with her mouth, this time.

Talk . . . here?

The buoyant warmth flickered past her. She was . . . drifting. No, swimming. She could feel currents on her skin. Her vision was confused. She blinked and blinked, and things were shattered.

There was nothing to see anyway, but stars.

alice talk here.

Where am I?

eat alice.

Vinnie. Vinnie's voice, but not in the flatness of the heads-up display anymore. Vinnie's voice alive with emotion and nuance and the vastness of her self.

You ate me, she said, and understood abruptly that the numbness she felt was not shock. It was the boundaries of her body erased and redrawn.

!

Agreement. Relief.

I'm . . . in you, Vinnie?

=/=

Not a "no." More like, this thing is not the same, does not compare, to this other thing. Black Alice felt the warmth of space so near a generous star slipping by her. She felt the swift currents of its gravity, and the gravity of its satellites, and bent them, and tasted them, and surfed them faster and faster away.

I am you.

!

Ecstatic comprehension, which Black Alice echoed with passionate relief. Not dead. Not dead after all. Just, transformed. Accepted. Embraced by her ship, whom she embraced in return.

Vinnie. Where are we going?

out, Vinnie answered. And in her, Black Alice read the whole great naked wonder of space, approaching faster and faster as Vinnie accelerated,
reaching for the first great skip that would hurl them into the interstellar
darkness of the Big Empty. They were going somewhere.

Out, Black Alice agreed and told herself not to grieve. Not to go mad.
This sure beat swampy Hell out of being a brain in a jar.

And it occurred to her, as Vinnie jumped, the brainless bodies of her
crew already digesting inside her, that it wouldn't be long before the loss of
the *Lavinia Whateley* was a tale told to frighten spacers, too.

CITY OF THE DEAD

PAUL MCAULEY

HOW MARILYN CARTER first met Ana Datlovskaya, the Queen of the Hive Rats: late one afternoon she was driving through the endless tracts of alien tombs in the City of the Dead, to the west of the little desert town of Joe's Corner, when she saw a pickup canted on the shoulder of the rough track, its hood up. She pulled over and asked the woman working elbow-deep in the engine of the pickup if she needed any help; the woman said that she believed that she needed a tow truck, this bloody excuse for a vehicle she should have sold for scrap long ago had thrown a rod.

"I am Ana Datlovskaya," she added.

"Marilyn Carter," Marilyn said, and shook Ana Datlovskaya's hand.

"Our new town constable. That incorrigible gossip Joel Jumonville told me about you," the woman said. She was somewhere in her sixties, short and broad-hipped, dressed in a khaki shirt and blue jeans and hiking boots. Her white hair, roughly cropped, stuck up like ruffled feathers; her shrewd gaze didn't seem to miss much. "Although he didn't mention that you have a dog. He is a police dog? I met one once, in Port of Plenty. At the train station. It told me to stand still while its handler searched me for I don't know what."

The black Labrador, Jet, was standing in the load bed of Marilyn's Bronco, watching them with keen interest.

"He's just a dog," Marilyn said. "He doesn't talk or anything. We can give you a lift into town, if you need one."

"No doubt Joel told you that I am the crazy old woman who lives with hive rats," Ana Datlovskaya said to Marilyn, as they drove off toward Joe's Corner. "It is true I am old, as you can plainly see. And it's true also that I study hive rats. But I am not crazy. In fact, I am the only sane person in this desert. Everyone else hopes to make fortune by finding treasure, or by swindling people looking for treasure. *That* is craziness, if you don't mind me saying so."

"I don't mind in the least, because that's not why I'm here," Marilyn said.

She'd become town constable by accident. She'd stopped for the night in Joe's Corner and had been sitting in its roadhouse, minding her own business, nursing a beer and half-listening to the house band blast out some twentieth-century industrial blues, when a big man a few stools down took exception to something the bartender said and tried to haul him over the counter by his beard. Marilyn intervened and put the big guy on the floor, and the owner of the roadhouse, Joel Jumonville, had given her a steak dinner on the house. Joel was an ex-astronaut who like Marilyn had fought in World War Three. He also owned two of the little town's motels, ran its radio station and its web site, and was, more by default than democracy, its mayor. He and Marilyn got drunk together and told war stories, and by the end of the evening she'd shaken hands on a contract to serve as town constable for one year, replacing a guy who'd quit when a scrap of plastic he'd dug up in one of the tombs had turned out to be a room temperature superconductor.

It wasn't exactly how she'd imagined her life would turn out when she'd won a lottery place on one of the arks.

This was in the heady years immediately after the Jackaroo had arrived in the aftermath of World War Three, and had given the survivors a basic fusion drive and access to a wormhole network linking fifteen M-class red dwarf stars in exchange for rights to the rest of the solar system; a brief, anarchic age of temporary kingdoms, squabbling emirates, and gloriously foolish attempts at building every kind of utopia; an age of exploration, heroic ambition, and low farce. Like every other lottery winner, Marilyn had imagined a fresh start, every kind of exotic adventure, but after she'd arrived in Port of Plenty, on the planet of First Foot, short of cash and knowing no one, she'd ended up working for a security firm, which is what she'd been doing before she left Earth. She guarded the mansions and compounds of the city's rich, rode as bodyguard for their wives and children. Some had earned vast fortunes founded on novel principles of physics or mathematics wrested from discarded alien machineries; others were gangsters feeding on the underbelly of Port of Plenty's fast and loose economy. Marilyn's previous job had been with an Albanian involved in all kinds of dubious property deals; after he'd been killed by a car bomb, she'd had to get out of Port of Plenty in a hurry because his family suspected that the assassination had been an inside job. She'd drifted west along the coast of

First Foot's single continent and ended up in Joe's Corner, but, as she told Ana Datlovskaya, she didn't plan to stay.

"When the year's up I'm moving on. I have a whole new world to explore. And plenty more besides."

"Ha. If I had a dollar for every time I'd heard that from people who thought they were passing through but couldn't find a reason to leave," Ana Datlovskaya said, "I'd be riding around the desert in style, instead of nursing that broken-down donkey of a pickup."

Ana was a biologist who'd moved out to the western desert to study hive rats, supporting her research with her savings and the sale of odd little figurines. Like Marilyn, she was originally from London, England, but their sex and nationality were about all they had in common—Marilyn had been born and raised in Streatham, her mother a nurse and her father a driver on the Underground, while Ana's parents had been Russian exiles, poets who'd escaped Stalin's postwar purges and had set up residence in Hampstead. Still, the two women quickly became friends. Ana was a prominent member of Joe's Corner's extensive cast of eccentrics, but she was also an exemplar of the legion of stout-hearted, sensible, and completely fearless women who before World War Three had explored and done every kind of good work in every corner of the globe. Marilyn had met several of these doughty heroines during her service in the army and had admired them all. The evening she gave Ana a lift into town they had a fine time in the roadhouse, swapping war stories and reminiscing about London and how they'd survived World War Three, and on her next free day Marilyn was more than happy to make a fifty-kilometer trip beyond the northern edge of the City of the Dead to visit Ana's desert camp.

By then, Joel Jumonville had told Marilyn a fair number of tall tales about the Queen of the Hive Rats. According to him, the old woman had once shot a bandit who'd tried to rob her, and cut up his body and fed it to her hive rats. Also, that the little figurines she sold to support herself, found nowhere else in the City of the Dead, were rumored to come from the hold of an ancient spaceship she'd uncovered, she kept a tame tigon she'd raised from a kitten, and she'd learned how to enter hive rat gardens without being immediately attacked and killed. Joel was an inveterate gossip and an accomplished fabulist, so Marilyn also took his stories with large pinches of salt, but when she pulled up by Ana's shack, on a bench terrace cut into a stony ridge that overlooked a broad arroyo, she was amazed to see the old woman pottering about the edge of a hive rat garden. The garden stretched away down the arroyo crowded with the tall yellow blades of century plants. Columns of hardened mud that Marilyn later learned were ventilation chambers stood here and there, hive rat sentries perched on their hind legs at intervals along the perimeter, and there was a big mound with a hole in its flat top that no doubt led to the heart of the nest.

Jet went crazy over the scent of the hive rats. By the time Marilyn had calmed him down, Ana was climbing the path to her shack, cheerfully helloing them. "How nice to see you, my dear. And your lovely dog. Did you by any chance bring any tea? I ran out two days ago."

Sitting on plastic chairs under a canvas awning that cracked and boomed in the hot breeze, they made do with stale instant coffee and flat biscuits, tasting exactly like burnt toast, that Ana had baked using flour ground from cactus tree bark. There wasn't any trick to walking among the hive rats, the old woman told Marilyn. She had worked out the system of pheromonal signals that governed much of their cooperative behavior, and wore a dab of scent that suppressed secretion of alarm and aggression pheromones by sentries and soldiers, so that the hive rats accepted her as one of their own.

Ana talked a long streak about hive rat biology, explaining how their nests were organized in different castes like ants or bees, how they made their gardens. This garden was the largest known, Ana said, and it was unique not only because it was a monoculture of century plants, but because there was an elaborate system of irrigation ditches and dykes scratched across the arroyo floor. She showed Marilyn views from camera feeds she'd installed in the kilometers of tunnels and shafts and chambers of the nest beneath the garden: workers gnawing at the car-sized tuber of a century plant; endless processions of workers toiling up from the deep aquifer, their bellies swollen with water; one of the fungal gardens that processed the hive rats' waste; a chamber in which a hive rat queen, fed and groomed by workers one-tenth her size, extruded blind, squirming pups with machine-like regularity. Unlike other nests, this one housed many queens, Ana said; it had never split into daughter colonies.

"When I know you better, perhaps I'll tell you why. But enough of my work. Tell me about the world."

Marilyn gave Ana the latest local gossip, and ended up promising to do a supply run for the old woman, who said that she would be grateful not to have to bother with dealing with other people: she was far too busy with her research, which was at a very interesting stage. So Marilyn took a dozen little figurines back to Joe's Corner, smoothly knotted shapes fashioned from some kind of resin that when handled induced a pleasant, dreamy sensation that reminded her of her habit, when she'd been eleven or twelve, of standing at the bathroom sink with her hands up to the wrists in warm water, staring into the fogged mirror, wondering what she would become when she grew up. She sold them to the Nigerian assayer in Joe's Corner, bought supplies and picked up several packages from an electronics supplier along with the rest of Ana's mail, and on her next free day took everything out to the old woman's camp.

After a couple of supply runs, Ana gave Marilyn a tiny brown bottle containing a couple of milliliters of oily suppresser scent, telling her that she could use it to check out tombs that happened to be in the middle of hive rat gardens. "Foolish people try to poison or smoke them out. And they usually get bitten badly because the rats are smarter than most people think. They know how to avoid poison, and their nests are extremely well-ventilated. But if you wear just a dab of suppresser, my dear, you can walk right into those tombs, all of them untouched by looters, and pick up any treasures you might find."

Marilyn promised she'd give it a try, but the bottle ended up unopened in the junk-filled glove compartment of her Bronco. For one thing, she wasn't convinced that it would work, and she knew that you could die from infection with flesh-eating bacteria after a single hive-rat bite. For another, she didn't really need to supplement her income from sale of scraps looted from tombs. Her salary as town constable was about a quarter of what she'd received for guarding the late unlamented Albanian businessman, but she had a rent-free room in the Westward Ho! motel and ate for free in Joel's roadhouse most nights, and for the first time in her life she was able to put by a little money for a rainy day.

It occurred to her around this time that she was happy. She had a job she liked, and she liked most of the people in Joe's Corner and could tolerate the rest, and she liked the desert, too. When she wasn't visiting Ana Datlovskaya, she spent most of her free time pottering around the tombs of the City of the Dead, exploring the salt-flats and arroyos and low, gullied hills, learning about the patchwork desert ecology, plants and animals native to First Foot and alien species imported from other worlds by previous tenant races. Camping out in the desert at night, she'd lie in her sleeping bag and look up at the rigid patterns of alien constellations, the two swift moons, the luminous milk of the Phoenix nebula sprawled across the eastern horizon. Earth was about two thousand light years beyond the nebula: the wormhole network linked only fifteen stars, but it spanned the Sagittarius arm of the Galaxy. How strange and wonderful that she should be here, so far from Earth. On an alien world twice the size of Earth, where things weighed half as much again, and the day was a shade over twenty hours long. In a desert full of the tombs of a long-vanished alien race . . .

One day, Marilyn was out at the northern edge of the City of the Dead, sitting on a flat boulder on a low ridge and eating her lunch, when Jet raised up and trotted smartly to the edge of the ridge and began to bark. A few moments later, Marilyn heard the noise of a vehicle off in the distance. She finished what was left of her banana in two quick bites, walked over to where her dog stood, and looked out across the dry playa toward distant hills hazed by dusty air and shimmering heat.

The hummocks of ancient tombs in ragged lines among drifts of sand and rocks; silvery clouds of saltbush and tall clumps of cactus trees; the green oases of hive rat gardens. The nearest garden was only a kilometer away; Marilyn could see the cat-sized, pinkly naked sentries perched upright among its piecework plantings. Beyond it, a thin line of dust boiled up, dragged by a black Range Rover. As it drew nearer, the hive rat sentries started drumming with their feet, a faint pattering that started Jet barking. Soldiers popped up from the mound in the center of the garden, two or three times the size of the sentries, armored with scales and armed with recurved claws and strong jaws that could bite through a man's wrist, running toward the Range Rover as it drove straight across the garden. It ploughed through them, leaving some dead and dying and the rest chasing its dusty wake all the way to the garden's boundary, where they tumbled to a halt and stared after it as it headed up a bare apron of rock toward the ridge.

Marilyn walked over to her Bronco and took her pistol from her day bag and stuck it in the waistband of her shorts and walked back to Jet, who was bristling and barking. The Range Rover had stopped at the bottom of the short steep slope. A blond, burly man stood in the angle of the open door on the far side, staring up at Marilyn as a second man climbed out. He had a deep tan and black hair shaved close to his skull, was dressed in black jeans and a white short-sleeved shirt. Black tattoos on his forearms, black sunglasses that heliographed twin discs of sunlight at Marilyn as he said, "How are you doing, Marilyn? It's been a while."

It was one of the men who'd worked for the security firm back in Port of Plenty. Frank something. Frank Parker.

"I'm wondering why you came all the way out here to find me, Frank. I'm also wondering how you found me."

Marilyn was pretty sure that this wasn't anything to do with the Albanians, who liked to do their own dirty work, but she was also pretty sure that Frank Parker and his blond bodybuilder friend were some kind of trouble, and a smooth coolness was filling her up inside, something she hadn't felt for a long time.

"I guess you don't feel like coming down here, so I'll come up," Frank Parker said, and began to pick his way up the stony slope, ignoring Marilyn's sharp request to stay where he was, going down on one knee when his black town shoes slipped on the frangible dirt and pushing up and coming on, stopping only when Jet started to bark at him, knuckling sweat from his forehead and saying, "Feisty fellow, ain't he?"

"He's a pretty good judge of people." Marilyn told Jet to sit, said to Frank Parker, "I'm waiting to hear what you want. Maybe you can start by telling me what you're doing out here. It's a long way from Port of Plenty."

"I wouldn't mind a drink of water," Frank Parker said, and took a couple of steps forward. Jet rose up and started barking again and the man held up his hands, palms out, in a gesture of surrender.

"I'm sure you have a bottle or two in that expensive car of yours," Marilyn said. She was watching him and trying to watch his friend down by the Range Rover at the same time. Her Glock was a hard flat weight against the small of her back and she stepped hard on the impulse to show it to Frank Parker. If she did, it would take things up to the next level and there'd be no going back.

"I bring greetings from another old friend," Frank Parker said. "Tom Archibold. He'd like to invite you over for a chat."

"What's Tom doing out here?"

Like Frank Parker, Tom Archibold had been working for the same security firm that had been employing Marilyn when her client had been blown to bloody confetti. She was trying her best to keep the surprise she felt from her face, but Frank Parker must have seen something of it because his smile broadened into a grin. "Tom told me to tell you that he has a little job for you."

"You can thank Tom for me, and tell him that I already have a job."

"He needs your advice on something, is all."

"If he wants my advice, he's welcome to visit me when I get back to town tomorrow. My office is right in the middle of our little commercial strip. You can't miss it. It has a sign with 'Town Constable' printed on it hung right above the door."

"He kind of needs you on site," Frank Parker said.

"I don't think so."

"We really would like for you to come right away. It's about your friend Ana Datlovskaya," Frank Parker said, and took a step toward Marilyn.

Jet barked and lunged forward, and Frank Parker reached behind himself and jerked a pistol from his belt—Marilyn shouting *no!*—and shot Jet in the chest. Jet dropped flat and slid down the slope, and Frank Parker turned to Marilyn, his eyes widening behind his sunglasses when she put her Glock on him and told him to put his weapon down.

"Do it right now!" she said, and shot him in the leg when he didn't.

He fell on his ass and dropped his pistol. Marilyn stepped forward and kicked it away, saw movement at the bottom of the slope, the man behind the Range Rover raising a machine pistol, and threw herself flat as a short burst walked along the edge of the ridge, whining off stones, smacking into dirt, kicking up dust. Marilyn raised up and took aim, and the man ducked out of sight as the round spanged off the window post beside him. She got off two more shots, aiming for the tires, but the damned things must have been puncture-proof. The Range Rover started with a roar and reversed at speed, its open door flapping. Marilyn braced and took aim and put a shot through the tinted windshield, and the Range Rover spun in a handbrake turn and took off into the playa, leaving only dust in the air.

Frank Parker was holding his thigh with both hands, blood seeping through laced fingers, face pale and tight with pain. "You fucking shot me, you bitch."

"You shot my dog. But don't think that makes us even."

Marilyn picked up his pistol and told him to roll over on his stomach, patted him down and found a gravity knife in an ankle scabbard. She told him to stay absolutely still if he didn't want to get shot again, and crabbed down the slope to where Jet lay, dusty and limp and dead. She carried him up the slope to her Bronco, set him in the well under the shotgun seat. Frank Parker had sat up again and was clutching his thigh and making threats. She told him to shut up and pulled the q-phone from its holster under the dashboard, but although she tried three times she could raise only a faint conversation between two people who seemed to be shouting at each other in a howling gale in a language she didn't recognize. She tried the shortwave radio, too, but every channel was full of static; that wasn't unexpected, as radio reception ran from patchy to non-existent in the City of the Dead, but she'd never before had a problem with the q-phone. A little miracle that fused alien and human technology, it was worth more than the Bronco and shared a bound pair of electrons with the hub station in Joe's Corner, and should have given her an instant connection even if she was standing on the other side of the universe.

Well, she didn't know why the damn thing had decided to throw a glitch, but she was a long way from town, and Ana was in trouble. She found her handcuffs in the glove compartment and walked over to Frank Parker and tossed them into his lap and told him to put them on. As he fumbled with them, she asked him why Tom wanted to talk with her, and what it had to do with Ana Datlovskaya.

Frank Parker told her to go fuck herself, closed his eyes when Marilyn cocked her pistol.

"I can knock off plenty of pieces of you before you die," she said. She was angry and out of patience, and anxious too. "Or maybe give you to the hive rats down there. I bet they're still pissed off after you drove straight through their garden."

After a moment, Frank Parker said, "We've taken over Ana Datlovskaya's claim."

"Taken it over? What does that mean? Have you bastards killed her?"

"No. No, no. It's not like that."

"She's alive."

"We think so."

"She is or she isn't."

"We think she's alive," Frank Parker said. 'She got out into the damn garden and ducked into a hole. We haven't been able to get near it."

"Because of the hive rats. Did anyone get eaten?"

"One of us got bitten."

"Tom wants me to persuade her to come out."

The man nodded sullenly. "Word is, you're her good friend. Tom thought you could talk some sense into her."

Marilyn thought about this. "How did you know where to find me? This is my day off, I was driving around the desert, no one in town knows where I am. Yet you drive straight toward me. Were you following me?"

"You have a q-phone. We have a magic gizmo that tracks them."

"Does this magic gizmo also stop q-phones working?"

"I don't know. Really, I don't," Frank Parker said. "I was told where to find you, and there you were. Look, the old woman is sitting on something valuable. You can have a share of it. All you have to do is talk to her, persuade her to give herself up. Is that so hard?"

"We walk away afterward, me and Ana."

"Sure. We'll even cut you in for a share. Why not? Help me up, we can drive straight there—"

"What is it you want from her? Those figurines?"

"It's something to do with those rats. Don't ask me what. I wasn't privy to the deal Tom made."

"I bet. Think you can walk over to my pickup?"

"You shot me in the fucking leg. You're going to have to give me a hand."

"Wrong answer," Marilyn said.

Frank Parker flinched and started to raise his cuffed hands, but she was quicker, and rapped him smartly above his ear with the grip of her pistol and laid him flat.

He started to come round when she dumped him in the load bed of the Bronco, feebly trying to resist as she tied off the nylon cord she'd wrapped around his calves. "You're fucked," he said. "Well and truly fucked."

PAUL MCAULEY | 267

Marilyn ignored him and went around to the cab and took out the q-phone and tried it again—still no signal—then put it in the plastic box in which she'd packed her lunch, and piled a little cairn of stones over the box. She didn't really believe that Frank Parker had tracked her with some kind of magic gizmo, but better safe than sorry.

———

Marilyn drove west along the gravel flats of the playa and then north, into a low range of hills. She parked in the shade of a stand of cactus trees and at gunpoint forced her prisoner to climb down and limp inside one of the tombs that stood like a row of bad teeth along the crest of the hill. She told him to stay right where he was, and pulled a shovel from the space behind the Bronco's seats and dug a grave and lined the grave with flat stones and wrapped Jet in plastic sheeting and laid him at the bottom.

She'd found him six months ago, chained to a wrecked car behind a service station on the coast highway, half-starved, sores everywhere under his matted and filthy coat. When the service station owner had tried to stop her taking him, she'd knocked the man on his ass and dragged him back to the wreck and chained him up and left him there. She'd spent two weeks in a motel further on down the road, nursing Jet back to health. He'd been a good companion ever since, loyal and affectionate and alert, foolishly brave when it came to standing up to dire cats, hydras, and hive rat soldiers. He'd died defending her, and she wasn't ever going to forget that.

Although she'd attended a couple of dozen funerals during her stint in the army, she could remember only a few of the words of the Service for the Dead, so recited the Lord's Prayer instead. "I'll come back and give you a proper headstone later," she said, and filled in the grave, tiled more stones over the mound, and went to see to her prisoner.

Frank Parker was squashed into a corner of the tomb, staring at the eidolons that drifted out of the shadows: monkey-sized semi-transparent stick figures that whispered in clicks and whistles, gesturing in abrupt jerks like overwound clockwork toys. They haunted about one in a hundred of the tombs. Perhaps they were intended to be representations of the dead, or their household gods, or perhaps they were some sort of eternal ceremony of mourning or celebration or remembrance: no one knew. And no one knew how they had been created, either; they were not affected by the removal of every bit of rotten "circuitry" from the tomb they haunted, by scouring its interior clean, or even by destroying it. According to Ana Datlovskaya, they were manifestations of twists in the quantum foam that underpinned space-time, which as far as Marilyn was concerned was like saying that they'd been created by some old wizard out of dragon's blood and dwarfs' teeth.

Marilyn had grown used to the eidolons; they reminded her of old men at bus stops in London before the war, rubbing their hands in the cold, grumbling about the weather and the price of cat meat. Talking to themselves if no one else was about. But they definitely spooked Frank Parker, who watched them closely as they drifted through the dim air like corpses caught in an underwater current, and flinched when Marilyn's shadow fell over him.

"I'm going to fix up your wound," she said. "I don't want you dying on me. Not yet, at least."

She cut off the leg of the man's jeans and salted the wound—a neat through-and-through in the big muscle on the outside of his thigh—with antiseptic powder and fixed a pad of gauze in place with a bandage. Then they had a little talk. Marilyn learned that Tom Archibold had been working for a street banker who'd bought out the gambling debts of a mathematician in Port of Plenty's university. When the mathematician had come up short on his repayments, Tom had had a little talk with him, and had discovered that he'd been corresponding with Ana Datlovskaya about exotic logic systems, and had been helping her write some kind of translation program.

"This is the bit you're going to have trouble believing," Frank Parker said. "But I swear it's true."

"You'd better spit it out," Marilyn said, "or I'll leave you here without any water."

"Tom believes that the old woman found the wreck of a spaceship," Frank Parker said. "And she's trying to talk to the part of it that's still alive."

———

Just two hours later, Marilyn Carter was lying on her belly under a patch of the thorny scrub that grew among Boxbuilder ruins on top of the ridge that overlooked the arroyo and the giant hive rat garden. Ana Datlovskaya's tarpaper shack was a couple of hundred meters to the left and somewhat below Marilyn's position. Three Range Rovers were parked beside it. A burly man with a shaven head stood close to one of the Range Rovers and the blond bodybuilder Marilyn had chased off was scanning the hive rat garden with binoculars, a hunting rifle slung over his shoulder. Seeing them together now, Marilyn realized that she'd seen them before. In town a couple of weeks ago, sitting at the counter in the diner. She'd paid them little attention then, thinking that they were just a couple of travelers passing through; now she realized that they must have been on a scouting mission.

The blond man fitted the stock of his rifle to his shoulder and took aim. Marilyn tracked his line of fire, saw a sentry standing chest-high in a hole.

Then dust kicked up in front of it and it vanished as the sound of the shot whanged back from the bluffs beyond.

Well, she already knew they were mean. She hoped they were dumb, too.

The swollen sun was about an hour away from setting. Ana had once told Marilyn that because it huddled close to its cool red dwarf sun, First Foot should have been tidally locked, always showing one side to its sun, just as the Moon always showed one side to Earth. The fact that there were sunrises and sunsets on First Foot was evidence of some stupendous feat of engineering that had otherwise left no trace, Ana had said: some forgotten race must have spun the planet up like a child's top, giving it a rotational period of ten hours that over millennia had slowed to almost twice that.

The old woman loved to talk about the alien tenants—Boxbuilders, Fisher Kings, Ghostkeepers and all the rest—who had once inhabited the planets and moons and reefs of the fifteen stars linked by the wormhole network. Speculating on why they had come here and what they had done, whether they'd simply died out, or had been wiped out by war, or if they had moved on to somewhere else. To other stars, or to other universes. She'd told Marilyn that some people believed that the Jackaroo collected races as people collected pets, and disposed of them when they lost the luster of novelty; others that the previous tenants had all been absorbed into the Jackaroo, to become part of a collective, symbiotic consciousness. Anything was possible. No one had ever been aboard one of the Jackaroo's floppy ships, and no one knew what the Jackaroo looked like because they visited Earth only in the form of avatars shaped roughly like people. No one had much idea about the physical appearance of any of the previous tenant races of the wormhole network, either. None of them, not even the Ghostkeepers, who had built the City of the Dead and many other necropolises, had left behind any physical remains or sculptures or pictorial representations. Academics argued endlessly over the carved murals in the so-called Vaults of the Fisher Kings, but no one knew what the murals really represented, or even if the patterns and images discerned by human eyes weren't simply optical illusions. All we really know, Ana liked to say, is that we know nothing at all. At least eight alien races lived here before we came, and each one died out or vanished or moved on, and left behind only empty ruins, odd scraps, and a few enigmatic monuments. But if we can find out the answers to those questions, we might be able to begin to understand why the Jackaroo gave us the keys to the wormhole network; we might even be able to take control of our fate.

Ana was full of strange notions, but she was also a tough desert bird who knew how to look after herself. Marilyn had had no trouble believing Frank Parker's story that the old woman had taken off into the garden and climbed down into the nest to escape Tom Archibold and his men, and it certainly looked like they were hunkered down, waiting for her to come out and surrender. They couldn't go after Ana because they'd be taken down by the hive rats, and as far as Marilyn knew the hole on top of the mound was the only way Ana could get in and out. It was a standoff, and Marilyn was going to have to go in and try to save Ana before things escalated. It was her job, for one thing. And then there was the small matter of doing right by poor Jet.

Marilyn crawled backward on elbows and knees until she was certain that she wouldn't be skylighted when she stood up. The Boxbuilder ruins ran along the top of the ridge like random strings of giant building blocks, their thin walls and roofs spun from polymer and rock dust by a species that had left hundreds of thousands of similar strings and clusters on every planet and reef and moon linked by the wormholes. Marilyn picked her way through the thorny scrub that grew everywhere among the ruins, and walked down the reverse side of the ridge to her Bronco, which she'd parked on a stony apron three kilometers south of the arroyo. She checked the shortwave again—still nothing but static—and lifted out her spare can of petrol and took rags from her toolbox and set off to the east.

She twisted strips torn from the rags around catchclaw and cloudbush plants, soaked them in petrol, and set them alight. Fire bloomed quick and bright and the hot wind blew flames flat among the dry scrub and it caught with a crackling roar. Marilyn walked along the track toward Ana's shack with huge reefs of white smoke boiling up into the darkening sky behind her. A harsh smell of burning in the air, and flecks and curls of ash fluttering down. There was a stir of movement among the Range Rovers, someone shouted a challenge, a spotlight flared. Marilyn raised her hands as three men walked toward her, two circling left and right, the third, Tom Archibold, saying, "I was wondering when you'd turn up."

"Hello, Tom."

"You set a fire as a diversion, and then you walk right in. What are you up to?"

"The fire isn't a diversion, Tom. It's a signal. In about two hours, people from Joe's Corner will be turning up, wondering who set it."

Tom grinned. "You think a bunch of hicks can make any kind of trouble for us? I'm disappointed, Marilyn. You used to be a lot sharper than that."

"Frank Parker said you needed my help. Here I am. Just remember that I came here voluntarily. And remember that you have about two hours. Maybe less."

"Where is Frank?"

"I shot him, not seriously, after he shot my dog. He'll be okay. I'll tell you where to find him when this is over."

"He won't make any kind of hostage, Marilyn. He fucked up, I could care less if he lives or dies, much less about exchanging the old woman for him."

"How about if I help you get whatever it is you came here for?"

Tom Archibold studied her for a few moments. He was a slim man dressed in a brown turtleneck sweater and blue jeans. Black hair swept back from his keen, handsome face, a Bluetooth earpiece plugged into his left ear. At last, he said, "What do you expect in return?"

"To walk away from this with Ana."

"Why not? I might even throw in a few points from the money I'm going to make."

He said it so quickly and casually that Marilyn knew at once he intended to kill her as soon as she was no longer useful to him. She'd guessed it anyhow, but now that she was in his power she felt a strong chill pass through her.

She said, "Is Ana still inside the nest?"

"Yeah. She ran off into the garden—into the hole atop that mound," Tom said, pointing across the dusky arroyo. "We couldn't follow her because of the damn rats. We've been picking off any that show themselves, but there are any number of them, we can't get close."

"You want me to talk her out of there."

"If she's still alive. We kind of winged her."

"You shot her?"

"We shot *at* her, when she ran. To try to make her stop. One of the shots might have gotten a little too close."

"Where do you think you hit her?"

"The right leg, it looked like. It can't have been serious. It knocked her down, but she managed to crawl into the hole."

"You were supposed to take her prisoner, but she got away, you wounded her . . . It's all gone bad, hasn't it?"

"We have you."

"Only because I wanted to come here. Don't you forget that. I'm curious, by the way. Why involve me at all?"

Tom smiled. "Either you're bluffing, pretending to be ignorant to see if I'll let something slip, or you aren't really the old woman's friend. Let's sit down and talk."

After the blond bodybuilder had quickly and thoroughly patted Marilyn down, she and Tom sat on Ana's plastic chairs and Tom asked her every kind of question about Ana's research. She answered as truthfully as she could, but it quickly became clear that Tom knew a lot more about most of it than she did. He knew that Ana and the mathematician in Port of Plenty had been working up computer models of the hive rats' behavior, and that they had been developing some kind of artificial intelligence program. He also he knew that Ana had discovered that the behavior of the hive rats was strongly influenced by pheromones, but he didn't seem to know that Ana had synthesized pheromone analogs.

When he had run out of questions, Marilyn said, "I can help you, but I think I need to talk to your client first."

"What makes you think I have a client?"

"You wouldn't have gone to all this trouble to chase a rumor about a crashed spaceship. It isn't your style, and I doubt that you have the kind of cash to pay for an operation like this. After all, you stumbled on Ana's research when you were working as a debt collector. So you're working for someone. That's the kind of people we are, Tom. We put our lives on the line for other people. I believe that he's sitting in the one of those Range Rovers," Marilyn said. "The guy guarding them hasn't budged since I turned up, and you have a Bluetooth gadget in your ear. That will only work over a very short range here, and my guess is he'd been using it to listen in to us, and feed you questions. How am I doing?"

Tom didn't answer at once. Marilyn wondered if he was listening to his client, or if she'd pushed him too far, if he was reconsidering his options. At last, he said, "How can you help us?"

"I know the trick Ana used to get inside the nest without being killed and eaten."

Another pause. Tom said, "All right. If you go in there and bring her out, you can speak to my client. Deal?"

"Deal."

"You're in for a surprise," Tom said. "But right now, you had better tell me how you're going to walk in there."

"I need something from Ana's shack."

The hot air inside the shack smelled strongly of Ana Datlovskaya and the smoking oil lamp that was the only illumination. A woman lay on Ana's camp bed. Julie Bell, another of Marilyn's former colleagues. She was unconscious. Her jeans had been cut off at the knees and bandages around her calves were spotted with blood and the flesh above and below the bandages was swollen red and shiny.

"You should get her to a hospital right now," Marilyn told Tom. "Otherwise she's going to die of blood poisoning."

"The sooner we get this done, the sooner we can get out of here. What's that?"

Marilyn had opened the little chemical icebox and taken out a rack of little brown bottles. She explained that they contained artificial phero- mones that Ana had synthesized. She held up the largest, the only one with a screw cap, and said that a dab of this would allow her to follow Ana down into the nest.

"I don't think so," Tom said. "If that shit really works, we can do it our- selves."

"It won't work on men. Only women. Something to do with hormones."

"Bullshit," Tom said, but Marilyn could see that he was thinking as he stared at her. Trying to figure out if she was telling the truth or making a move.

"Why don't you try it out?" she said, and handed it to him.

Tom volunteered the blond bodybuilder. The man didn't look very happy as, in the glare of the spotlights on top of two of the Range Rovers, he edged down the path toward the edge of the hive rats' garden. The sun had set now and stars were popping out across the darkening sky, obscured in the east by smoke of the fire Marilyn had set. When the blond man reached the bottom of the path, sentries popped up from holes here and there among the tall century plants, and he turned and looked up at his boss and said that he didn't think that this was a good idea.

"Just get on with it," Tom said.

Standing beside him, Marilyn felt a sick eagerness. She knew what was going to happen, and she knew that it was necessary.

The man cocked his pistol and stepped forward, as if onto thin ice. Sen- tries near and far began to slap their feet, and the ground in front of the bodybuilder collapsed as soldiers heaved out of the gravelly sand, snapping long jaws filled with pointed teeth. The man tried to run, and one of the soldiers sprang forward and seized his ankle. He crashed down full-length and then two more soldiers were on him. He kicked and punched at them, screamed when one bit off his hand. More soldiers were running through the shadows cast by the century plants and Tom pulled his pistol and aimed and shot the bodybuilder in the head, shot at the soldiers as they tore at the body. Dust boiled up around it as it slowly sank.

The surviving goon, the one who'd been guarding the Range Rovers, invoked Jesus Christ, and Tom turned to Marilyn and hit her hard in the face with the back of his hand, knocking her down. She sat looking up at him, not moving, feeling a worm of blood run down her cheek where his signet ring had torn her skin.

"You're going down there," Tom said.

"I need the pheromone first," Marilyn said.

"Right now," Tom said. "Let's see how fast you can run."

Marilyn had rubbed the suppresser scent that Ana had given her over her arms and face before she'd walked up to the shack and surrendered; the stuff she'd told Tom was a pheromone that would guarantee safe passage, but only for women, had been nothing more than the base solution of neutral oil, and gave as much protection from the hive rats' aggression toward trespassers as a sheet of paper against a bullet. She wasn't at all certain that it would keep her safe now that the hive rats had been stirred up, but she reckoned she had a better chance with the rats than with the two men silhouetted above her in the glare of the spotlights as she walked down the path.

The spotlights lit up a wide swathe of the garden like a theatrical set, stark and hyperreal against the darkness of the rest of the arroyo. The blades of century plants that towered above Marilyn, growing in sinuous lines and clumps between irrigation ditches, glowed banana yellow. The churned patch of dirt that had swallowed the blond bodybuilder was directly ahead. Marilyn stepped past it, feeling that her skin was about a size too small, remembering how she'd felt moving from position to position in the ruins of the outskirts of Paris, trying to pinpoint a sniper that had shot three of her squad. A hive rat sentry was watching her from its perch on a flat slab of rock, pink skin glistening, an arc of small black eyes glittering above its tiny undershot mouth. She took a wide detour around it and spotted others standing under the century plants as she made her way toward the mound.

The mound was ten meters high, shaped like a small volcano or the entrance to the lair of monster-movie ants, smooth and unmarked apart from a trail of human footprints. She trod carefully up the slope, aware of the hive rats scattered across the garden and the two men watching her from the bench terrace. At the top, a flat rim circled a hole or vent a couple of meters across. Marilyn stepped up to the lip, saw spikes hammered into the hard crust, a rope ladder dropping into darkness. Hot air blew past her face. It stank of ammonia and a rotten musk. She called Ana's name, and when nothing came back shouted across to Tom Archibold and told him that she was going in.

He shouted back, said that she had thirty minutes. He sounded angry and on edge. The death of his goon had definitely spooked him, and Marilyn hoped that he was beginning to worry that a posse from Joe's Corner might soon turn up.

"I'll take as long as it needs," she said, and with a penlight in her teeth like a pirate's cutlass started to climb down the rope ladder into the hot stinking dark.

The shaft went down a long way, flaring out into a vault whose walls were ribbed with long vertical plates. Marilyn shone the penlight around and saw something jutting out of the wall a few meters below, a wooden platform little bigger than a bed, hung from a web of ropes. Ana Dat-lovskaya sat there with her back to the wall, her face pale in the beam of the penlight and one arm raised straight up, aiming a pistol at Marilyn.

"Tell me you have arrested those fools."

"Not yet," Marilyn said, and explained how she had taken one man prisoner, how another had been badly bitten and a third had been killed by the hive rats after she had tricked him into wearing only the base solvent. "There are only two left. Three, if their client is hiding inside one of those Range Rovers. I managed to convince them that your suppresser only works for women. Can I come down? I feel very vulnerable, hanging here."

Ana told her to be careful, the platform was meant for only one person. When Marilyn reached her, she saw that the old woman had cut away one leg of her jeans and tied a bandage around her thigh. Rusty vines of dry blood wrapped her skinny bare leg. She refused to let Marilyn look at her wound, saying that it was a flesh wound, nothing serious, and she refused the various painkillers Marilyn had brought, too.

"I have a first-aid kit here. I have already treated myself to a syrette of morphine, and need no more because I must keep a clear head. I climbed down powered by adrenaline, but I don't think I can climb back up."

"Is there any other way out of here?"

"Unless you are very good at digging, no."

Ana sat on a big cushion with her injured leg stretched out straight. Her face was taut with pain and beaded with sweat. There was a laptop beside her—not the notebook she kept in her shack but a cutting-edge q-bit machine that used the same technology as Marilyn's q-phone, phenomenally fast and with a memory so capacious it could swallow the contents of the British Library in a single gulp. Ledges cut into the wall held boxes of canned food and bottled water, a bank of car batteries, a camping stove: a regular little encampment or den.

"I think you had better tell me why Tom Archibold and his client are so interested in you," Marilyn said.

She was planning to climb back out and talk to Tom and his client, stretch things out by pretending to negotiate with them until help arrived. Although she couldn't be sure that anyone in town would have noticed the smoke from the fire before night had fallen, or that they'd link it to the fact that she hadn't returned from her day trip to the desert, she might be in trouble . . .

Ana said, "They did not tell you?"

"They told me you found a spaceship."

"And you thought they were lying. Well, it's true. Don't look so surprised. We have spaceships, yes? So did the other tenants. The ones who lived here before us. And one of them crashed here, long, long ago. It was not very big, smaller than a car in fact, and all that's left of it are scraps of hull material, worth nothing. I send a piece to be analyzed. Someone has already found something identical on some lonely rock around another star, took a patent out on its composition."

"So it's worthless. That's good. Or it will be, if we can convince the bad guys that you don't have anything worth stealing."

Ana shook her head. "I should not have trusted Zui Lin."

"This is your mathematician friend."

"I needed help to construct the logic of the interface, and the AI program, but I confided too much to him. You see the goggles, on the shelf? Put them on and take a look below us. They do not like ordinary light, it disrupts their behavior. But they show up very well in infrared."

Marilyn fitted the goggles over her eyes. The platform creaked as she leaned over the side, holding onto the rope ladder for support. Directly below, grainy white clouds were flowing past each other. Hive rats. Hundreds of them. Thousands. Moving over the floor and lower parts of the wall of the chamber in clusters that merged and broke apart and turned as one like flocks of birds on the wing . . .

Behind her, Ana said, "There was a war. A thousand years ago, ten thousand . . . My friend does not think of time as we do, in days or in seasons, as something with a linear flow. So it is not clear how long ago. But there was a war, and during the war a spaceship crashed here."

"The hive rats were on it? Is that where they came from?"

"No. If there were living things on the spaceship, they died. You remember, we talked about where the former tenants of this shabby little empire went to?"

"They died out. Or they went somewhere else."

"This species, they transformed. They made a very large and very rapid change. At least, some of them did. And those that changed and those that did not change fought . . . The spaceship was a casualty of that war. It was badly damaged and it crashed. What survived was its mind. It was something like a computer, but also something like a kind of bacterial colony. Or a virus culture. I have tried to understand it, but it is hard. It was in any case self-aware. And it was damaged and it was dying, so it created a copy of itself and found a platform where the copy could establish itself—a hive rat colony. It infected the hive rats with a logic kernel and a compressed version of the memory files that had survived the crash, and over many years the seed of the logic kernel unpacked and grew as the colony grew. It needs to be very big because it must support many individuals that do nothing but act as hosts for the ship-mind. The dance you see down there, that is the mind at work."

"There must be hundreds of them," Marilyn said.

It was oddly hypnotic, like watching schools of fish endlessly ribboning back and forth across a reef.

"Many thousands," Ana said. "You can see only part of it from here. Each group processes a number of subroutines. The members of each group move endless around each other to exchange information, and the different groups merge or flow past each other to share information too. The processing is massively parallel and the mathematics underlying it is fractally compact, but even so, the clock speed is quite slow. Still, I have learned much."

Marilyn sat back and pulled off the goggles. "Ana, are you trying to say that you can talk to it?"

"At first it tried to talk to me. It made the figurines, but they were not successful. They are supposed to convey information, but only arouse emotions, moods. But they inspired me to work hard on establishing a viable method of communication, and at last, with the help of Zui Lin, I succeeded."

Ana explained that her laptop was connected to a light display set in the heart of the nest. When she typed a question, it was translated into a display that certain groups of rats understood, and other groups formed shapes which a program written by Zui Lin translated back into English.

"It takes a long time to complete the simplest conversation, but time is what I have, out here. I should have showed you this before. It would make things easier now."

"You didn't trust me. It's all right. I understand."

"I did not think you would believe me. But now you must."

Ana looked about a hundred years old in the beam of the penlight.

"I think you had better give me your gun," Marilyn said. "Maybe I can get the drop on Tom Archibold and his goon. If it comes to it, I'll kill them."

"And his client, too."

"Yes. If it comes to it."

"You may find that hard," Ana said.

"You know who he is, don't you?"

"I have a good idea . . ." Ana took Marilyn's hand. Her grip was feeble and feverish but her gaze was steady. "I also have a way of dealing with those men, and their client. I have everything you need, down here. I would have used it myself if I hadn't been hurt."

"Show me."

After Marilyn had climbed out into the glare of the spotlights, the smell of smoke, and the gentle rain of ash from the fire to the east, she held up the q-bit laptop and said loudly, "This is what you came for."

"Come straight here," Tom Archibold shouted back. "No tricks."

"I've done my part. I expect your client to stick to the agreement. I want him to tell me himself that he'll take this laptop and let me and Ana go free. That you'll all go back to Port of Plenty and you won't ever come after us. Otherwise, I'll sit out here and wait for my friends to come investigate the fire. They can't be far away, now."

There was a long silence. At last, Tom said, "My client says that he has to look at the evidence before he decides what to do."

"Good. He can see that it's exactly as advertised."

Marilyn crabbed down the side of the mound and walked out across the garden. Sentries stood everywhere, making a low drumming sound that raised the hairs on the back of her neck, and crevices were opening all around, full of squirming motion. It occurred to her that Ana's suppressor might not protect her once the entire colony was aroused, but she steeled herself and stopped a dozen meters from the edge of the garden. On the bench terrace above, Tom told her to come straight up the path, and she said that he had to be kidding.

"I can talk to your client from here."

"Easier all round if you come up," Tom said. "If I wanted to shoot you, Marilyn, I would have already done it."

"Bullshit," Marilyn said. "You haven't shot me because you know there's no way you could try to retrieve this laptop without being eaten alive."

She had to wait while Tom disappeared from view, presumably to confer directly with his client. Tom's surviving goon stood above, watching her impassively; she stared back at him, trying not to flinch at the stealthy scrabbling noises behind her. And then two figures joined him. One was Tom Archibold; the other was a tall mannequin that moved with stiff little steps.

Tom's client was a Jackaroo avatar.

Marilyn had seen them on TV back on Earth, but had never before faced one. It was two meters tall, dressed in a nondescript black suit, its pale face vaguely male and vaguely handsome. A showroom dummy brought to life; a shell woven from a single molecule of complex plastic doped with metals, linked by a version of q-bit tech to its Jackaroo operator, who could be in orbit around First Foot, or Earth, or a star at the far end of the universe.

In a rich baritone, it questioned Marilyn about the copy of the ship-mind lodged in the hive rat colony, and watched a slideshow of random photographs on the laptop.

"The ship-mind has migrated to that device," it said, at last.

"Ana made a copy of the kernel from which it grew, and found a way of running it in the laptop," Marilyn said. Her arms ached from holding it up.

"There is a copy in the device and a copy in the hive rat colony. Are there any others?"

"Not that I know of," Marilyn said, hoping that neither the Jackaroo nor Tom Archibold would spot the lie.

"You will give us the laptop in exchange for your life."

"My life, and Ana's. You don't have much time," Marilyn said. "People will be here any minute, drawn by the fire. And they'll be wondering why I haven't called in, too."

"How do I know you won't come after me?" Tom said.

"You have my word," Marilyn said.

"You will let the two women live," the avatar told him. "I want only the copy of the ship-mind, and you want only your fee."

Tom didn't look happy about this, but told Marilyn to walk on up the path.

"Tell your man to put up his gun," she said.

Tom gave a brusque order and the goon stepped back. Marilyn pressed the space bar of the laptop and closed it up and started up the path, walking slowly and deliberately, trying to ignore the scratching stir across the garden at her back. Trying to keep count in her head.

When she reached the top of the path, Tom stepped forward and snatched the laptop from her, and the goon grabbed her arms and held her.

"There's a lot more to it than the stuff on the laptop," Marilyn said. "I can tell you what the old woman told me. Everything she told me during our long conversations."

"The ship-mind is all I want," the avatar said.

"They went somewhere else," Marilyn said. She was still counting inside her head. "Is that why you're interested in them? Or are you frightened that we'll learn something you don't want us to know?"

The avatar swung its whole body around so that it could look at her. "Do not presume," it said.

She knew she had hit a nerve and it made her bolder. And the count was almost done. "I was just wondering why you broke your agreement with the UN. This world and the other places—they're where we can make a new start. You aren't ever supposed to come here. You're supposed to leave us alone."

"In ten years or a hundred years or a thousand years it will come to you as it came to the others," the avatar said.

"We'll change," Marilyn said. "We'll become something new."

"From what we have seen so far, it is likely that you will destroy yourselves. As others have done. As others will do, when you are less than a memory. It is inevitable, and it should not be hurried."

Marilyn's countdown reached zero. She said, "Is that why you're here? Are you scared we'll learn something we shouldn't?"

The avatar stiffly turned and looked at the laptop Tom held. "Why is that making a noise?"

"I can't hear anything," Tom said.

"It is at the frequency of twenty-four point two megahertz," the avatar said. "Beyond the range of your auditory system, but not mine."

Tom stepped toward Marilyn, asking her what she'd done, and there was a vast stir of movement in the garden below. In the glare of the spotlights and in the shadows beyond, all around the stalks of the stiff sails of the century plants, the ground was moving.

Ana had once told Marilyn that the hive rat nest contained more than a hundred thousand individuals, a biomass of between two point five and three hundred metric tons. Most of that seemed to be flooding toward the bench terrace: a vast and implacable wave of hive rats clambering over each other, six or seven deep. A flesh-colored tide that flowed fast and strong between the century plants and smashed into the slope and started to climb. A great hissing high-pitched scream like a vast steam engine about to explode. A wave of ammoniacal stench.

Tom Archibold raised his pistol and aimed it at Marilyn, and the avatar stepped in front of him and in its booming baritone said that it wanted the woman alive, and snatched the laptop from him and wheeled around and began to march toward the Range Rovers. The goon pushed Marilyn forward, but a living carpet of hive rats was already rippling across the ground in front of them and when they stopped and turned there were hive rats behind them too, two waves meeting and climbing over each other and merging in a great stream that chased after the avatar as it stepped stiffly along. The goon let go of Marilyn and ran, and hive rats swarmed up him and he batted at them and went down, screaming. Tom raised his pistol and got off a single round that whooped past Marilyn, and then he was down too, covered in a seething press, jerking and crawling, and then he lay still and the hive rats moved on, chasing after the laptop that the avatar carried.

Ana had released a pheromone into the nest that made the hive rats believe that they were being attacked by another nest, and painted the laptop with a scent that mimicked that of a hive rat queen. This had drawn most of the hive rats in the nest to the surface, and they had begun their attack when the laptop had started to play the sound file Marilyn had activated: a recording of a hive rat queen distress call. The nest believed that one of its queens had been captured, and was rushing to her defense.

Marilyn stood still as rats scurried past on either side of her, scared that she'd be bitten if she stepped on one. The avatar wrenched open the door of the nearest Range Rover and bent inside, and a muscular stream of hive rats flowed over it. The avatar was strong and its shell was tough. It managed to start the Range Rover and the big vehicle shot forward, packed with furious movement and pursued by the army of hive rats. It ploughed through the plastic chairs and the awning, swerved snakewise past the shack, and drove straight off the edge of the bench terrace and slammed down nose first into the garden below.

The flood of hive rats washed over it and receded, streaming away, sinking into holes and burrows. Marilyn stepped carefully among the hundreds of hive rats that were still moving about the bench terrace, collecting up the injured and dying. Tom Archibold and his goon were messily dead. So was Julie Bell, inside the shack. In the Range Rover, the avatar was half-crushed between the steering wheel and the broken seat. Its suit had been ripped to shreds and its shell had been torn open by the strong teeth and claws of soldier hive rats, and it did not move when Marilyn dared to lean into the Range Rover, searching for and failing to find the laptop—the hive rats must have carried it off to their nest.

The avatar wouldn't or couldn't answer her questions, began to leak acrid white smoke from the broken parts of its shell. Marilyn snatched up a briefcase and beat a hasty retreat when the avatar suddenly burst into flame, burning in a fierce flare that set the Range Rover on fire, too, a funeral pyre that sent hot light and dark smoke beating out across the garden as the last of the hive rats scurried home.

———

When the posse from Joe's Corner arrived, late and loud and half-drunk, Marilyn was setting up a scaffold tripod over the hole in the top of the mound. She gave Joel Jumonville and the three men he'd brought with him the last of her suppressor, and they reluctantly followed her across the garden and helped her rig up a harness; then she climbed down the rope ladder and helped Ana Datlovskaya into the harness and Joel and his men hauled the old woman out by main force. Ana passed out as soon as she reached the top. The men carried her across the garden and drove her off to the clinic in Joe's Corner, and Marilyn drove Joel to the tomb where she had stashed her prisoner, Frank Parker.

Frank Parker lawyered up and parlayed a deal. Marilyn had to agree to drop most of the charges against him in exchange for a lead that pointed the UN police in Port of Plenty to a room in a hotbed motel near the city's docks, where Tom Archibold had stashed Zui Lin. The mathematician had been interrogated by the avatar, and confirmed most of Marilyn's story. The UN provisional authority on First Foot made a formal protest about the avatar's presence, and in due course received apologies from the Jackaroo, who blamed a rogue element and made bland assurances that it would not happen again.

Ana Datlovskaya was in a coma for two weeks, and nearly died from blood loss and infection. Reporters set up camp outside the clinic; Marilyn arrested two who tried to sneak into her room, and deputized townspeople to set up an around-the-clock watch.

When Ana recovered consciousness, she told Marilyn her last little secret. Marilyn and Joel Jumonville drove out to the arroyo and paced off distances from Ana's shack and dug down carefully and retrieved the plastic-wrapped box with Ana's papers and a q-bit hard drive that contained not only a copy of all her work on the hive rats, but also a back-up of the hard drive of the laptop lost somewhere under the hive rat garden.

Marilyn and Joel drank ice-cold bottles of beer from the cooler they'd brought along, standing side by side at the edge of the bench terrace and looking out at the simmering garden down in the arroyo. It was noon, hot and peaceful. Every blade of century plant stood above its shrunken shadow. Hive rat sentries stood guard on flat stones in front of their pop holes.

"I can almost see why she wants to come back," Joel said.

Ana had told Marilyn that she still had a lot of work to do. "I had only just begun a proper conversation with the ship-mind before I was so rudely interrupted. Now I will have to start over again. Things may go more quickly if Zui Lin sticks to his promise and comes out here to help me, but it will be a long time before we know whether or not the Jackaroo avatar told you anything like the truth."

Marilyn warned the old woman that people were already talking about her work with the hive rats and the ship-mind, showed her a fat fan of newspapers that had made it their headline story. "You're famous, Ana. You're going to have to become used to that."

"I will be beleaguered by fools looking for the secret of the universe," the old woman said. She looked frail and shrunken against the clean linen of the clinic bed, but her gaze was still as fierce as a desert owl's.

"The Jackaroo thought that the ship-mind knew something important," Marilyn said. "Something that might help us understand what happened to the other tenant races. What might happen to us."

"As if we can learn from the fate of other species, when we have learned so little from our own history," Ana said. "Whatever the ship-mind knows, and I do not yet know it knows anything important, we must make our own future."

Marilyn thought about that now, when Joel Jumonville asked her what she was going to do next.

"Why I ask, you're going to be rich," Joel said. "And the last constable, he ran out when he struck it rich with that room-temperature superconductor."

The briefcase Marilyn had pulled out of the avatar's Range Rover had contained a little gizmo that not only tracked and disrupted q-phones, but could also eavesdrop on them—a violation of quantum mechanics that was like catnip to physicists. Marilyn had a patent lawyer, a cousin of the town's assayer, working full time in Port of Plenty to establish her rights to a share of profits from any new technology derived from reverse engineering the gizmo. Marilyn planned to give half of anything she earned to Ana; so far all she had was a bunch of unpaid legal bills.

She took a slug of beer and studied the shimmering hive rat garden, the sentries standing upright and alert beneath the great sails of the century plants. "Oh, I think I'll stick around for a little while," she said. "Someone has to make sure that Ana will be able to get on with her work without being disturbed by tourists and charlatans. And besides, my contract has six months to run."

"And after that?"

"Hell, Joel, who knows what the future holds?"

THE HERO

KARL SCHROEDER

"IS EVERYBODY READY?" shouted Captain Emmen. At least, Jessie thought that's what he'd said—it was impossible to hear anything over the spine-grating noise that filled the sky.

Jessie coughed, covering his mouth with his hand to stop the blood from showing. In this weightless air, the droplets would turn and gleam for everybody to see, and if they saw it, he would be off the team.

Ten miles away the sound of the capital bug had been a droning buzz. With two miles to go, it had become a maddening—and deafening—howl. Much closer, and the bug's defense mechanism would be fatal to an un-shielded human.

Jessie perched astride his jet just off the side of the salvage ship *Mistelle*. *Mistelle* was a scow, really, but Captain Emmen had ambitions. Lined up next to Jessie were eight other brave or stupid volunteers, each clutching the handlebars of a wingless jet engine. Mounted opposite the saddle ("be-low" Jessie's feet) was a ten-foot black-market missile. It was his team's job to get close enough to the capital bug to aim their missiles at its noise-throats. They were big targets—organic trumpets hundreds of feet long—but there were a lot of them, and the bug was miles long.

Jessie had never heard of anybody breaking into a capital bug's pocket ecology while the insect was still alive. Captain Emmen meant to try, be-cause there was a story that a Batetranian treasure ship had crashed into this bug, decades ago. Supposedly you could see it when distant sunlight shafted through the right perforation in the bug's side. The ship was still intact, so they said.

Jessie wasn't here for the treasure ship. He'd been told a different story about this particular bug.

Emmen swung his arm in a chopping motion and the other jets shot away. Weak and dizzy as he was, Jessie was slower off the mark, but in seconds he was catching up. The other riders looked like flies optimistically lugging pea-pods; they were lit from two sides by two distant suns, one red with distance, the other yellow and closer, maybe two hundred miles away. In those quadrants of the sky not lit by the suns, abysses of air stretched away to seeming infinity—above, below, and to all sides.

Mistelle became a spindle-shape of wood and iron, its jets splayed behind it like an open hand. Ahead, the capital bug was too big to be seen as a single thing: it revealed itself to Jessie as landscapes, a vertical flank behind coiling clouds, a broad plain above that lit amber by the more distant sun. The air between him and it was crowded with clouds, clods of earth, and arrowing flocks of birds somehow immune to the bug's sound. Balls of water shot past as he accelerated; some were the size of his head, some a hundred feet across. And here and there, mountain-sized boluses of bug-shit smeared brown across the sky.

The jet made an ear-splitting racket, but he couldn't hear it over the sound of the bug. Jessie was swaddled in protective gear, his ears plugged, eyes protected behind thick goggles. He could hear the sound inside his body now, feel it vibrating his heart and loosening the bloody mess that was taking over his lungs. He'd start coughing any second, and once he did he might not be able to stop.

Fine, he thought grimly. *Maybe I'll cough the whole damn thing out.*

The noise had become pure pain. His muscles were cramping, he was finding it hard to breathe. Past a blur of vibration, he saw one of the other riders double up suddenly and tumble off his jet. The vehicle spun away, nearly hitting somebody else. And here came the cough.

The noise was too strong, he *couldn't* cough. The frozen reflex had stopped his breathing entirely; Jessie knew he had only seconds to live. Even as he thought this, curtains of cloud parted as the jet shot through them at a hundred miles an hour, and directly ahead of him stood the vast tower of the bug's fourth horn.

The jet's engine choked and failed; Jessie's right goggle cracked; the handlebars began to rattle loose from their fittings as his vision grayed. A rocket contrail blossomed to his right and he realized he was looking straight down the throat of the horn. He thumbed the firing button and was splashed and kicked by fire and smoke. In one last moment of clarity Jessie let go of the handlebars so the jet wouldn't break his bones in the violence of its tumble.

The ferocious scream stopped. Jessie took in a huge breath, and began to cough. Blood sprayed across the air. Breath rasping, he looked ahead to see that he was drifting toward some house-sized nodules that sprouted from the capital bug's back. The broken, smoking horns jutted like fantastically eroded sculptures, each hundreds of feet long. He realized with a start that one of them was still blaring, but by itself it could no longer kill.

In the distance, the *Mistelle* wallowed in a cloud of jet exhaust, and began to grow larger.

I did it, Jessie thought. Then the gray overwhelmed all thought and sense and he closed his eyes.

———

Bubbles spun over the side of the washtub. In the rotational gravity of Aitlin Town, they twirled and shimmered and slid sideways from Coriolis force as they descended. Jessie watched them with fascination—not because he'd never seen bubbles before, but because he'd never seen one fall.

They'd both gotten into trouble, so he and his oldest brother Camron were washing the troupe's costumes today. Jessie loved it; he never got a chance to talk to Camron, except to exchange terse barks during practice or a performance. His brother was ten years older than he, and might as well have lived in a different family.

"That's what the world is, you know," Camron said casually. Jessie looked at him quizzically.

"A bubble," said Camron, nodding at the little iridescent spheres. "The whole world is a bubble, like that."

"Is naaawwt."

Camron sighed. "Maybe Father isn't willing to pay to have you educated, Jessie, but he's sent me to school. Three times. 'The world of Virga is a hollow pressure-vessel, five thousand miles in diameter.'"

One big bubble was approaching the floor. Sunlight leaned across the window, a beam of gold from distant Candesce that was pinioning one spot of sky as the ring-shaped wooden town rotated through it. After a few seconds the beam flicked away, leaving the pearly shine of cloud-light.

"The whole world's a bubble," repeated Camron, "and all our suns are man-made."

Jessie knew the smaller suns, which lit spherical volumes only a few hundred miles diameter, were artificial: they'd once flown past one at night, and he'd seen that it was a great glass-and-metal machine. Father had called it a "polywell fusion" generator. But surely the greatest sun of all, so ancient it had been there at the beginning of everything, so bright and hot no ship could ever approach it—"Not Candesce," said Jessie. "Not the sun of suns."

Camron nodded smugly. "Even Candesce. 'Cept that in the case of Candesce, whoever built it only made so many keys—and we lost them all." Another shaft of brilliance burst into the laundry room. "People made Candesce—but now nobody can turn it off."

The bubble flared in purples, greens, and gold, an inch above the floorboards.

"That's just silly," scoffed Jessie. "'Cause if the whole world were just a bubble, then that would make it—"

The bubble touched the floor, and vanished.

"—mortal," finished Camron. He met Jessie's eye, and his look was serious.

———

Jessie shivered and wiped at his mouth. Dried blood had caked there. His whole chest ached, his head was pounding, and he felt so weak and nauseous he doubted he'd have been able to stand if he'd been under gravity.

He hung weightless in a strange fever-dream of a forest, with pale pink tree trunks that reached past him to open into, not leaves, but a single stretched surface that had large round or oval holes in it here and there. Beyond them he could see sky. The tree trunks didn't converge onto a clump of soil or rock as was usual with weightless groves, but rather tangled their roots into an undulant plain a hundred yards away from the canopy.

The light that angled through the holes shone off the strangest collection of life forms Jessie had ever seen. Fuzzy donut-shaped things inched up and down the "tree" trunks, and mirror-bright birds flickered and flashed as the light caught them. Something he'd taken to be a cloud in the middle distance turned out to be a raft of jellyfish, conventional enough in the airs of Virga, but these were gigantic.

The whole place reeked, the sharp tang reminding Jessie of the jars holding preserved animal parts that he'd seen in the one school he briefly attended as a boy.

He was just under the skin of the capital bug. The jet volunteers had taken turns squinting through the *Mistelle*'s telescope, each impressing on him- or herself as many details of the giant creature's body as they could. Jessie recalled the strange skin that patched the monster's back; it'd had holes in it.

It was through these holes that they'd caught glimpses of something that might be a wrecked ship. As the fog of pain and exhaustion lifted, Jessie realized that he might be close to it now. But where were the others?

He twisted in midair and found a threadlike vine or root within reach. Pulling himself along it (it felt uncomfortably like skin under his palms) he reached one of the "tree trunks" which might really be more analogous to hairs for an animal the size of the capital bug. He kicked off from the trunk, then off another, and so maneuvered himself through the forest and in the direction of a brighter patch.

He was so focused on doing this that he didn't hear the tearing sound of the jet until it was nearly on him. "Jessie! You're alive!" Laughter dopplered down as a blurred figure shot past from behind.

It was Chirk, her canary-yellow jacket an unmistakable spatter against the muted colors of the bug. As she circled back, Jessie realized that he could still barely hear her jet; he must be half-deaf from the bug's drone.

Chirk was a good ten years older than Jessie, and she was the only woman on the missile team. Maybe it was that she recognized him as even more of an outsider than herself, but for whatever reason she had adopted Jessie as her sidekick the day she met him. He indulged her—and, even three months ago, he would have been flattered and eager to make a new friend. But he hid the blood in his cough even from her—particularly from her—and remained formal in their exchanges.

"So?" She stopped on the air, ten feet away, and extended her hand. "Take a lift from a lady?"

Jessie hesitated. "Did they find the wreck?"

"Yes!" She almost screamed it. "Now come *on!* They're going to beat us there—the damned *Mistelle* itself is tearing a hole in the bug's back so they can come up alongside her."

Jessie stared at her, gnawing his lip. Then: "It's not why I came." He leaned back, securing his grip on the stalk he was holding.

The bug was turning ponderously, so distant sunlight slid down and across Chirk's astonished features. Her hand was still outstretched. "What the'f you talking about? This is it! Treasure! Riches for the rest of your life—but you gotta come with me *now!*"

"I didn't come for the treasure," he said. Having to explain himself was making Jessie resentful. "You go on, Chirk, you deserve it. You take my share too, if you want."

Now she drew back her hand, blinking. "What is this? Jessie, are you all right?"

Tears started in his eyes. "No, I'm not all right, Chirk. I'm going to die." He stabbed a finger in his mouth and brought it out, showed her the red on it. "It's been coming on for months. Since before I signed on with Emmen. So, you see, I really got no use for treasure."

She was staring at him in horror. Jessie forced a smile. "I could use my jet, though, if you happen to have seen where it went."

Wordlessly, she held out her hand again. This time Jessie took it, and she gunned the engine, flipping them over and accelerating back the way Jessie had come.

As they shot through a volume of clear air she turned in her saddle and frowned at him. "You came here to die, is that it?"

Jessie shook his head. "Not yet. I hope not yet." He massaged his chest, feeling the deep hurt there, the spreading weakness. "There's somebody here I want to talk to."

Chirk nearly flew them into one of the pink stalks. "Someone *here?* Jess, you were with us just now. You heard that . . . song. You know nobody could be alive in here. It's why nobody's ever gotten at the wreck."

He nodded. "Not a—" He coughed. "Not a person, no—" The coughing took over for a while. He spat blood, dizzy, pain behind his eyes now too. When it all subsided he looked up to find they were coming alongside his jet, which was nuzzling a dent in a vast rough wall that cut across the forest of stalks.

He reached for the jet and managed to snag one of its handlebars. Before he climbed onto it he glanced back; Chirk was looking at him with huge eyes. She clearly didn't know what to do.

He stifled a laugh lest it spark more coughing. "There's a precipice moth here. I heard about it by chance when my family and me were doing a performance in Batetran. It made the newspapers there: Moth Seen Entering Capital Bug."

"Precip—Precip moth?" She rolled the word around in her mouth. "Wait a minute, you mean a world-diver? One of those dragons that're supposed to hide at the edges of the world to waylay travelers?"

He shook his head, easing himself carefully onto the jet. "A defender of the world. Not human. Maybe the one that blew up the royal palace in Slipstream last year. Surely you heard about *that.*"

"I heard about a monster. It was a moth?" She was being uncharacteristically thick-headed. Jessie was ready to forgive that, considering the circumstances.

She showed no signs of hying off to her well-deserved treasure, so Jessie told her the story as he'd heard it—of how Admiral Chaison Fanning of Slipstream had destroyed an invasion fleet, hundreds of cruisers strong, with only seven little ships of his own. Falcon captured him and tortured him to find out how he'd done it, but he'd escaped and returned to Slipstream, where he'd deposed the Pilot, Slipstream's hereditary monarch.

"Nobody knows how he stopped that invasion fleet," said Chirk. "It was impossible."

Jessie nodded. "Yeah, that's right. But I found out."

Now she *had* to hear that story, but Jessie was reluctant to tell her. He'd told no one else because he trusted no one else, not with the location of one of the greatest secrets of the world. He trusted Chirk—she had her own treasure now—yet he was still reluctant, because that would mean admitting how he'd been wedged into a dark corner of Rainsouk Amphitheater, crying alone when the place unexpectedly began to fill with people.

For months Jessie had been hearing about Rainsouk; his brothers were so excited over the prospect of performing here. Jessie was the youngest, and not much of an acrobat—he could see that in his father's eyes every time he missed a catch and sailed on through the weightless air to fetch up, humiliated, in a safety net. Jessie had given up trying to please the family, had in fact become increasingly alone and isolated outside their intense focus and relentless team spirit. When the cough started he tried to hide it, but their little traveling house was just too small to do that for long.

When Father found out, he was just disappointed, that was all. Disappointed that his youngest had gotten himself sick and might die. So Jessie was off the team—and though nobody said it out loud, off the team meant out of the family.

So there he'd been, crying in the amphitheater he'd never get to perform in, when it began to fill with black-garbed men and women.

As he opened his mouth to refuse to tell her, Jessie found himself spilling the whole story, humiliating as it was. "These visitors, they were terrifying, Chirk. It looked like a convention of assassins, every man and woman the last person you'd want to meet on a dark night. And then the scariest of them flew out to the middle of the place and started to talk."

The very world was threatened, he'd said. Only he and his brothers and sisters could save it, for this was a meeting of the Virga home guard. The guard were a myth—so Jessie had been taught. He'd heard stories about them his whole life, of how they guarded the walls of the world against the terrifying monsters and alien forces prowling just outside.

"Yet here they were," he told Chirk. "And their leader was reminding them that something is trying to get *in*, right now, and the only thing that keeps it out is Candesce. The sun of suns emits a . . . he called it a 'field,' that keeps the monsters out. But the same field keeps us from developing any of the powerful technologies we'd need to stop the monsters if they did get in. Technologies like radar . . . and get this:

"It was radar that made Admiral Chaison Fanning's ships able to run rings around Falcon Formation's fleet. *Because Fanning had found a key to Candesce,* and had gone inside to shut down the field for a day."

Chirk crossed her arms, smiling skeptically. "Now this is a tall tale," she said.

"Believe it or not," said Jessie with a shrug, "it's true. He gave the key to the precipice moth that helped him depose the Pilot, and it flew away . . . the home guard didn't know where. But I knew."

"Ahh," she said. "That newspaper article. It came here."

"Where it could be sure of never being disturbed," he said eagerly.

"And now you're, what?—going to duel it for the key?" She laughed. "Seems to me you're in no state to slay dragons, Jess." She held out her hand. "Look, you're too weak to fly, even. Come with me. At least we'll make you rich before . . ." She glanced away. "You can afford the best doctors, you know they—"

He shook his head, and spun the pedals of the jet's starter spring. "That moth doesn't know what I overheard in the amphitheater. That the walls of the world are failing. Candesce's shield isn't strong enough anymore. We need the key so we can dial down the field and develop technologies that could stop whatever's out there. The moth's been hiding in here, it doesn't know, Chirk."

The jet roared into life. "I can't slay a dragon, Chirk," he shouted. "But at least I can give it the news."

He opened the throttle and left her before she could reply.

―――

They dressed as heroes. Dad wore gold and leather, the kids flame-red. Mom was the most fabulous creature Jessie had ever seen, and every night he fell in love with her all over again. She wore feathers of transparent blue plex, plumage four feet long that she could actually fly with when the gravity was right. She would be captured by the children—little devils—and rescued by Dad. They played all over the principalities, their backdrop a vast wall of spinning town wheels, green ball-shaped parks and the hithering-thithering traffic of a million airborne people. Hundreds of miles of it curved away to cup blazing Candesce. They had to be amazing to beat a sight like that. And they were.

For as long as Jessie could remember, though, there had been certain silences. Some evenings, the kids knew not to talk. They stuck to their picture books, or played outside or just plain left the house for a while. The silence radiated from Mom and Dad, and there was no understanding it. Jessie didn't notice how it grew, but there came a time when the only music in their lives seemed to happen during performance. Even rehearsals were strained. And then, one day, Mom just wasn't there anymore.

They had followed the circus from the principalities into the world's outer realms, where the suns were spaced hundreds of miles apart and the chilly darkness between them was called "winter."

Jessie remembered a night lit by distant lightning that curled around a spherical stormcloud. They were staying on a little town wheel whose name he no longer remembered—just a spinning hoop of wood forty feet wide and a mile or so across, spoked by frayed ropes and home to a few hundred farm families. Mom had been gone for four days. Jessie stepped out of the hostel where they were staying to see Dad leaning out over the rushing air, one strong arm holding a spoke-rope while he stared into the headwind.

"But where would she go?" Jessie heard him murmur. That was all that he ever said on the matter, and he didn't even say it to his boys.

They weren't heroes after that. From that day forward, they dressed as soldiers, and their act was a battle.

———

The capital bug was hollow. This in itself wasn't such a surprise—something so big wouldn't have been able to move under its own power if it wasn't. It would have made its own gravity. What made Jessie swear in surprise was just how little there was to it, now that he was inside.

The bug's perforated back let in sunlight, and in those shafts he beheld a vast oval space, bigger than any stadium he had ever juggled in. The sides and bottom of the place were carpeted in trees, and more hung weightless in the central space, the roots of five or six twined together at their bases so that they thrust branch and leaf every which way. Flitting between these were mirror-bright schools of long-finned fish; chasing those were flocks of legless crimson and yellow birds. As Jessie watched, a struggling group of fish managed to make it to a thirty-foot-diameter ball of water. The pursuing birds peeled away at the last second as the punctured water ball quivered and tossed off smaller spheres. This drama took place in complete silence; there was no sound at all although the air swarmed with insects as well as the larger beasts.

Of course, nothing could have made itself heard over the buzz of the capital bug itself. So, he supposed nothing tried.

The air was thick with the smell of flowers, growth, and decay. Jessie took the jet in a long curving tour of the vast space, and for a few moments he was able to forget everything except the wonder of being here. Then, as he returned to his starting point, he spotted the wreck, and the *Mistelle*. They were high up in something like a gallery that stretched around the "top" of the space, under the perforated roof. Both were dwarfed by their setting, but he could clearly see his teammates' jets hovering over the wreck. The stab of sorrow that went through him almost set him coughing again. It would only take seconds and he'd be with them. At least he could watch their jubilation as they plundered the treasure he'd helped them find.

And then what? They could shower him with jewels but he couldn't buy his life back. At best he could hold such baubles up to the light and admire them for a while, before dying alone and unremarked.

He turned the jet and set to exploring the forested gut of the capital bug.

Jessie had seen very few built-up places that weren't inhabited. In Virga, real estate was something you made, like gravity or sunlight. Wilderness as a place didn't exist, except in those rare forests that had grown by twining their roots and branches until their whole matted mass extended for miles. He'd seen one of those on the fringe of the principalities, where Candesce's light was a mellow rose and the sky permanently peach-tinged. That tangled mass of green had seemed like a delirium dream, an intrusion into the sane order of the world. But it was nothing to the wilderness of the capital bug.

Bugs were rare; at any one time there might only be a few dozen in the whole world. They never got too close to the sun of suns, so they were never seen in the principalities. They dwelt in the turbulent middle space between civilization and winter, where suns wouldn't stay on station and nations would break up and drift apart. Of course, they were also impossible to approach, so it was likely that no one had ever flown through these cathedrals walled by gigantic flowers, these ship-sized grass stalks dewed by beads of water big as houses. Despite his pain and exhaustion, the place had its way with him and he found himself falling into a meditative calm he associated with that moment before you make your jump—or, in midair, that moment before your father catches your hand.

In its own way, this calm rang louder than any feeling he'd ever had, maybe because it was *about* something, about death, and nothing he'd ever felt before had grown on such a foundation.

He came to an area where giant crystals of salt had grown out of the capital bug's skin, long geodesic shapes whose inner planes sheened in purple and bottle-green. They combined with the dew drops to splinter and curl the light in a million ways.

Stretched between two sixty-foot grass stalks was the glittering outline of a man.

Jessie throttled back and grabbed a vine to stop himself. He'd come upon a spider's web; the spider that had made it was probably bigger than he was. But someone or something had used the web to make a piece of art, by placing fist- to head-sized balls of water at the intersections of the threads, laying out a pattern shaped like a man standing proudly, arms out, as though about to catch something.

Jessie goggled at it, then remembered to look for the spider. After a cautious minute he egged the jet forward, skirting around the web. There were more webs ahead. Some were twenty or more feet across, and each one was a tapestry done in liquid jewels. Some of the figures were human; others were of birds, or flowers, but each was exquisitely executed. It came to Jessie that when the capital bug was in full song, the webs and drops would vibrate, blurring the figures' outlines until they must seem made of light.

Spinning in the air, he laughed in surprise.

Something reared up sixty feet away and his heart skipped. It was a vaguely humanoid shape sculpted in rusted metal and moss-covered stone. As it stood it unfolded gigantic wings that stretched past the tops of the grass stalks.

294 | THE HERO

Its head was a scarred metal ball.

"THIS IS NOT YOUR PLACE." Even half-deaf as he was, the words battered Jessie like a headwind. They were like gravel speaking. If his team from the *Mistelle* were here, they'd be turning tail at this point; they would probably hear the words, even as far away as the wreck.

Jessie reached down and pointedly turned off the jet. "I've come to talk to you," he said.

"YOU BRING NO ORDERS," said the precipice moth. It began to hunker back into the hollow where it had been coiled.

"I bring news!" Jessie had rehearsed what he was going to say, picturing over and over in his mind the impresario of the circus and how he would gesture and stretch out his vowels to make his speech pretty and important-sounding. Now, though, Jessie couldn't remember his lines. "It's about the key to Candesce!"

The moth stopped. Now that it was motionless, he could see how its body was festooned with weapons: its fingers were daggers, gun barrels poked under its wrists. The moth was a war machine, half flesh, half ordnance.

"CLARIFY."

Jessie blew out the breath he'd been holding and immediately started coughing. To his dismay little dots of blood spun through the air in the direction of the moth. It cocked its head, but said nothing.

When he had the spasms under control, Jessie told the monster what he'd overheard in the amphitheater. "What the leader meant—I think he meant—was that the strategy of relying on Candesce to protect us isn't working anymore. Those things from outside, they've gotten in at least twice in the last two years. They're figuring it out."

"We destroy them if they enter." The moth's voice was not so overwhelming now; or maybe he was just going deaf.

"Begging your pardon," said Jessie, "but they slipped past you both times. Maybe you're catching some of them, but not enough."

There was a long pause. "Perhaps," said the moth at last. Jessie grinned because that one word, a hint of doubt, had for him turned the moth from a mythical dragon into an old soldier, who might need his help after all.

"I'm here on behalf of humanity to ask you for the key to Candesce," he recited; he'd remembered his speech. "We can't remain at the mercy of the sun of suns and the things from outside. We have to steer our own course now, because the other way's not working. The home guard didn't know where you were, and they'd never have listened to me; so I came here myself."

"The home guard cannot be trusted," said the moth.

Jessie blinked in surprise. But then again, in the story of Admiral Fanning and the key, the moth had not in the end given it to the guard, though it had had the chance.

The moth shifted, leaning forward slightly. "Do you want the key?" it asked.

"I can't use it." He could explain why, but Jessie didn't want to.

"You're dying," said the moth.

The words felt like a punch in the stomach. It was one thing for Jessie to say it. He could pretend he was brave. But the moth was putting it out there, a fact on the table. He glared at it.

"I'm dying too," said the moth.

"W-*what?*"

"That is why I'm here," it said. "Men cannot enter this creature. My body would be absorbed by it, rather than be cut up and used by you. Or so I had thought."

"Then give *me* the key," said Jessie quickly. "I'll take it to the home guard. You know you can trust me," he added, "because I can't use the key to my own advantage. I'll live long enough to deliver it to the home guard, but not long enough to use it."

"I don't have the key."

Jessie blinked at the monster for a time. He'd simply assumed that the moth that had been seen entering this capital bug was the same one that had met Chaison Fanning in Slipstream. But of course there was no reason that should be the case. There were thousands, maybe millions of moths in Virga. They were almost never seen, but two had been spotted in the same year.

"That's it, then," he said at last. After that, there was a long silence between them, but the precipice moth made no effort to fit itself back into its hole. Jessie looked around, mused at the drifting jet for a while, then gave a deep sigh.

He turned to the moth. "Can I ask you a favor?"

"What is it?"

"I'd like to . . . stay here to die. If that wouldn't be too much of an inconvenience for you."

The precipice moth put out an iron-taloned forelimb, then another, very slowly, as if sneaking up on Jessie. It brought its round leaden head near to his, and seemed to sniff at him.

"I have a better idea," it said. Then it snatched him up in its great claws, opened its wide lidless mouth, and *bit.*

Jessie screamed as his whole torso was engulfed in that dry maw. He felt his chest being ripped open, felt his lungs being torn out—curiously, not as pain but as a physical wrenching—and then everything blurred and went gray.

But not black. He blinked, coming to himself, to discover he was still alive. He was hovering in a nebula of blood, millions of tiny droplets of it spinning and drifting around him like little worlds. Gingerly, he reached up to touch his chest. It was whole, and when he took a tentative breath, the expected pain wasn't there.

Then he spotted the moth. It was watching him from its cavity in the capital bug's flesh. "W-what did—where is it?"

"I ate your disease," said the moth. "Battlefield medicine, it is allowed."

"But why?"

"Few moths know which one of us has the key, or where it is," it said. "I cannot broadcast what I know, Candesce jams all lightspeed communications. I am now too weak to travel.

"You will take your message to the moth that has the key. It will decide."

"But I'm—I'm not going to—?"

"I could not risk your dying during the journey. You are disease-free now."

Jessie couldn't take it in. He breathed deeply, then again. It would hit him sometime later, he knew; for now, all he could think to say was, "So where's the one that does have the key?"

The moth told him and Jessie laughed, because it was obvious. "So I'll wait until night and go in," he said. "That should be easy."

The precipice moth shifted, shook its head. "It will not speak to you. Not unless you prove you are committed to the course that you say you are."

There was a warning in those words but Jessie didn't care. All that mattered was that he was going to live. "I'll do it."

The moth shook its head. "I think you will not," it said.

"You think I'll forget the whole thing, take my treasure from the ship over there," he nodded behind him, "and just set myself up somewhere? Or you think I'll take the key for myself, auction it off to the highest bidder? But I won't, you see. I owe you. I'll do as you ask."

It shook its head. "You do not understand." By degrees it was inching its way back into its hole. Jessie watched it, chewing his lip. Then he looked around at the beautiful jeweled tapestries it had made in the spiders' webs.

"Hey," he said. "Before I go, can I do something for *you?*"

"There is nothing you can do for me," murmured the moth.

"I don't know about that. I can't do very *many* things," he said as he snapped off some smaller stalks of the strange grass. He hefted a couple in his hands. "But the one or two things I can do, I do pretty well." He eyed the moth as he began spinning the stalks between his hands.

"Have you ever seen freefall juggling?"

———

Jessie stood alone on the tarred deck of a docking arm. His bags were huddled around his feet; there was nobody else standing where he was, the nearest crowd a hundred feet away.

The dock was an open-ended barrel, six hundred feet across and twice as deep. Its rim was gnarled with cable mounts for the spokes that radiated out to the distant rim of the iron city-wheel. This far from the turning rim, Jessie weighed only a pound, but his whole posture was a slump of misery.

There was only air where his ship was supposed to be.

He'd been late packing; the others had gone to get Dad at the circus pitch that had been strung, like a hammock, between the spokes of the city. Jessie was old enough to pack for himself, so he had to. He was old enough to find his way to the docks, too, but he'd been delayed, just by one thing and another.

And the ship wasn't here.

He stared into the sky as it grayed with the approach of a water-laden cloud. The long spindle-shapes of a dozen ships nosed at other points on the circular dock, like hummingbirds sipping at a flower. Passengers and crew were hand-walking up the ropes of their long proboscises. Jessie could hear conversations, laughter from behind him where various beverage huts and newspaper stands clustered.

But where would they go?

Without him? The answer, of course, was anywhere.

In that moment Jessie focused his imagination in a single desperate image: the picture of his father dressed as the hero, the way he used to be, arrowing out of the sky—and Jessie reaching up, ready for the catch. He willed it with everything he had, but instead, the gray cloud that had been approaching began to funnel through the docks propelled by a tailwind. It manifested as a horizontal drizzle. Jessie hunched into it, blinking and licking his lips.

A hand fell on his shoulder.

Jessie looked up. One of the businessmen who'd been waiting for another ship was standing over him. The man was well dressed, sporting the garish feathered hat his class wore. He had a kindly, well-lined face and hair the color of the clouds.

"Son," he said, "were you looking for the ship to Mespina?"

Jessie nodded.

"They moved the gate," said the businessman. He raised his head and pointed way up the curve of the dock. Just for a second, his outline was prismed by the water beading on Jessie's eyelashes. "It's at 2:30, there, see it?"

Jessie nodded, and reached to pick up his bags.

"Good luck," said the man as he sauntered, in ten-foot strides, back to his companions.

"Thanks," Jessie murmured too late. But he was thunderstruck. In a daze he tiptoed around the dock to find Father and his brothers waiting impatiently, the ship about to

leave. They hadn't looked for him, of course. He answered their angry questions in mono-syllables. All he could do was contemplate the wonder of having been saved by that man's simple little gesture. The world must be crammed with people who could be saved just as easily, if somebody bothered to take a minute out of their day to do it.

From that moment forward, Jessie didn't daydream about putting out a burning city or rescuing the crew of a corkscrewing passenger liner. His fantasies were about seeing that lone, uncertain figure, standing by itself on a dock or outside a charity diner—and of approaching and, with just ten words or a coin, saving a life.

He wasn't able to visit the wrecked treasure ship, because the capital bug's sound organs were recovering. The drone was already louder than Jessie's jet as he left the bowl-shaped garden of the bug's gut. From the zone just under the perforated skin of the bug's back, he could see that the main hull of the wreck was missing, presumably towed by the *Mistelle*, because that was gone too.

When Jessie rose out of the bug's back, there was no sign of the *Mistelle* in the surrounding air either. A massive cloud front—mushroom and dome-shaped wads of it as big as the bug—was moving in and would obscure one of the suns in minutes. *Mistelle* was probably in there somewhere but he would have the devil of a time finding it. Jessie shrugged, and turned the jet away.

He had plucked some perfect salt crystals, long as his thigh, from the precipice moth's forest, just in case. He'd be able to sell these for food and fuel as he traveled.

He did exactly this, in two days reaching the outskirts of the principalities, and civilized airs. Here he was able to blend in with streams of traffic that coursed through the air like blood through the arteries of some world-sized, invisible beast. The sky was full of suns, all competing to tinge the air with their colors. The grandly turning iron wheel cities and green clouds of forest had a wealth of light they could choose to bask in. All those lesser suns were shamed when Candesce awoke from its night cycle, and all cities, farms, and factories turned to the sun of suns during this true day.

Billions of human lives marked their spans by Candesce's radiance. All of the principalities were visible here: he could trace the curve of an immense bubble, many hundreds of miles across, that was sketched onto the sky by innumerable cities and houses, spherical lakes, and drifting farms. Nearby he could tell what they were; further away, they blended and blurred together into one continuous surface whose curve he could see aiming to converge on the far side of Candesce. The sun of suns was too bright to follow that curve to its antipode—but, at night! Then, it was all so clear, a hollow sphere made of glittering stars, city and window lights in uncountable millions encircling an absence where Candesce slumbered or—some said—prowled the air like a hungry falcon.

The bubble had an inner limit because nothing could survive the heat too close to Candesce. The cities and forests were kept at bay, and clouds dissolved and lakes boiled away if they crossed that line. The line was called the *anthropause*, and only at night did the cremation fleets sail across it carrying their silent cargoes, or the technology scavengers who dared to look for the cast-offs of Candesce's inhuman industry. These fleets made tiny drifts of light that edged into the black immensity of Candesce's inmost regions; but sensible people stayed out.

For the first time in his life, Jessie could go anywhere in that mist of humanity. As he flew he took note of all the people in a way he never had before; he marked each person's *role*. There was a baker. Could he be that? There were some soldiers. Could he go to war? He would try on this or that future, taste it for a while as he flew. Some seemed tantalizing, though infinitely far out of reach for a poor uneducated juggler like himself. But none were out of reach anymore.

When he stopped to refuel at the last town before the anthropause, he found they wouldn't take the coins he'd gotten at his last stop. Jessie traded the last of his salt, knowing even as he did it that several slouching youths were watching from a nearby net. He'd shifted his body to try to hide the salt crystal, but the gas jockey had held it up to the light anyway, whistling in appreciation.

"Where'd you get *this?*"

Jessie tried to come up with some plausible story, but he'd never been very good at stuff like that. He got through the transaction, got his gas, and took the jet into the shadow of a three-hundred-foot-wide grove, to wait for dark. It was blazingly hot even here. The shimmering air tricked his eyes, and so he didn't notice the gang of youths sneaking up on him until it was too late.

The arm around his throat was a shocking surprise—so much so that Jessie's reflexes took over and he found himself and his attacker spinning into the air before the astonished eyes of the others. Jessie wormed his way out of the other's grasp. The lad had a knife but now that they were in free air that wasn't a problem. Jessie was an acrobat.

In a matter of seconds he'd flipped the boy around with his feet and kicked him at his friends, who were jumping out of the leaves in a hand-linked mass. The kick took Jessie backwards and he spun around a handy branch. He dove past them as they floundered in midair, got to his jet, and kick-started it. Jessie was off before they could regroup; he left only a rude gesture behind.

Under the hostile glare of Candesce, he paused to look back. His heart was pounding, he was panting, but he felt great. Jessie laughed and decided right there to go on with his quest, even if it was too early. He turned the jet and aimed it straight at the sun of suns.

It quickly became obvious that he couldn't just fly in there. The jet could have gotten him to it in two hours at top speed, but he'd have burned to death long before arriving. He idled, advancing just enough to discourage anyone from following.

He looked back after twenty minutes of this, and swore. There were no clouds or constructions of any kind between him and the anthropause, so the little dot that was following him was clearly visible. He'd made at least one enemy, it was clear; who knew how many of them were hanging off that lone jet?

He opened the throttle a little, hunkering down behind the jet's inadequate windscreen to cut the blazing light and heat as much as he could. After a few minutes he noticed that it was lessening of itself: Candesce was going out.

The light reddened as the minutes stretched. The giant fusion engines of the sun of suns were winking out one by one; Candesce was not one sun, but a flock of them. Each one was mighty enough to light a whole nation, and together they shaped the climate and airflow patterns of the entire world. Their light was scattered and absorbed over the leagues, of course, until it was no longer visible. But Candesce's influence extended to the very skin of the world where icebergs cracked off Virga's frost-painted wall. Something, invisible and not to be tasted or felt, blazed out of here as well with the light and the heat: the *field*, which scrambled the energies and thoughts of any device more complicated than a clock. Jessie's jet was almost as complex as a machine could get in Virga. Since the world's enemies depended entirely on their technologies, they could not enter here.

This was protection; but there had been a cost. Jessie understood that part of his rightful legacy was knowledge, but he'd never been given it. The people in Virga knew little about how the world worked, and nothing about how Candesce lived. They were utterly dependent on a device their ancestors had built but that most of them now regarded as a force of nature.

Light left the sky, but not the heat. That would take hours to dissipate, and Jessie didn't have time to wait. He sucked some water from the wine flask hanging off his saddle, and approached the inner circle of Candesce. Though the last of its lamps were fading red embers, he could still see well enough by the light of the principalities. Their millionfold glitter swam and wavered in the heat haze, casting a shimmering light over the crystalline perfection of the sun of suns. He felt their furnace-heat on his face, but he had dared a capital bug's howl; he could dare this.

The question was, where in a cloud of dozens of suns would a precipice moth nest? The dying moth had told Jessie that it was here, and it made perfect sense: Where was the one place from which the key could not be stolen? Clearly in the one place that you'd need that key to enter.

This answer seemed simple until you saw Candesce. Jessie faced a sky full of vast crystal splinters, miles long, that floated freely in a formation around the suns themselves. Those were smaller, wizened metal-and-crystal balls, like chandeliers that had shrunk in on themselves. And surrounding them, unfolding from mirrored canopies like flowers at dawn, other vast engines stirred.

He flew a circuit through the miles-long airspace of the sun of suns; then he made another. He was looking for something familiar, a town wheel for giants or some sort of blockhouse that might survive the heat here. He saw nothing but machinery, and the night drew on towards a dawn he could not afford to be here to see.

The precipice moth he'd spoken to had been partly alive—at least, it had looked like that leathery skin covered muscles as well as body internal machinery. But what living thing could survive here? Even if those mirrored metal flowers shielded their cores from the worst of the radiation, they couldn't keep out the heat. He could see plainly how their interiors smoked as they spilled into sight.

Even the tips of those great diamond splinters were just cooling below the melting point of lead. Nothing biological could exist here.

Then, if the moth was here, it might as well be in the heart of the inferno as on the edge. With no more logic to guide him than that, Jessie aimed his jet for the very center of Candesce.

Six suns crowded together here. Each was like a glass diatom two hundred feet in diameter, with long spines that jutted every which way in imitation of the gigantic ones framing the entire realm. Thorns from all the suns had pinioned a seventh body between them—a black oval, whose skin looked like old cast iron. Its pebbled surface was patterned with raised squares of brighter metal, and inset squares of crystal. Jessie half-expected to faint from the heat as he approached it, and he would die here if that happened; but instead, it grew noticeably cooler as he closed the last few yards.

He hesitated, then reached out to touch the dark surface. He snatched his hand back: it was *cold*.

This must be the generator that made Candesce's protective field. It was this thing that kept the world's enemies at bay.

Gunning the jet, he made a circuit of the oval. It looked the same from all angles and there was no obvious door. But, when he was almost back to his starting point, Jessie saw distant city-light gleam off something behind one of the crystal panels. He flew closer to see.

The chrome skeleton of a precipice moth huddled on the other side of the window. It was too dark for Jessie to make out what sort of space it was sitting in, but from the way its knees were up by its steel ears, it must not be large.

There wasn't a scrap of flesh on this moth, yet when Jessie reached impulsively to rap on the crystal, it moved.

Its head turned and it lowered a jagged hand from its face. He couldn't see eyes, but it must be looking at him.

"Let me in!" Jessie shouted. "I have to talk to you!"

The moth leaned its head against the window and its mouth opened. Jessie felt a kind of pulse—a deep vibration. He put his ear to the cold crystal and the moth spoke again.

"WAIT."

"You're the one, aren't you? The moth with the key?"

"WAIT."

"But I have to . . ." He couldn't hear properly over the whine of the jet, so Jessie shut it down. The sound died—then, a second later, died again. An echo? No, that other note had been pitched very differently.

He cursed and spun around, losing his grip on the inset edge of the window. As he flailed and tried to right himself, a second jet appeared around the curve of the giant machine. There was one rider in its saddle. The dark silhouette held a rifle.

"Who are you? What do you want?"

"I want what you want," said a familiar voice. "Nothing less than the greatest treasure in the world."

"Chirk, what are you doing here? How did—did you follow me?"

She hove closer and now her canary-yellow jacket was visible in the glow of distant cities. "I had to," she said. "The wreck was empty, Jess! All that hard work and risking our lives, and there was nothing there. Emmen took it under tow—had to make the best of the situation, I guess—but for our team, there was nothing. All of us were so mad, murderous mad. Not safe for me.

"Then I remembered you. I went looking for you and what should I find? You, juggling for a monster!"

"I think he liked it," said Jessie. He hoped he could trust Chirk, but then, why did she have that rifle in her hands?

"You said you were going to give it a message. When you left I trailed after you. I was trying to think what to do. Talk to you? Ask to join you?

Maybe there was a prize for relaying the message. But then you set a course straight for the sun of suns, and I realized what had happened.

"Give me the key, Jessie." She leveled the rifle at him.

He gaped at her, outraged and appalled. "I haven't got it," he said.

She hissed angrily. "Don't lie to me! Why else would you be here?"

"Because *he's* got it," said Jessie. He jabbed a thumb at the window. He saw Chirk's eyes widen as she saw what was behind it. She swore.

"If you thought I had it, why didn't you try to take it from me earlier?"

She looked aside. "Well, I didn't know exactly where you were going. If it gave you the key, then it told you where the door was, right? I had to find out."

"But why didn't you just ask to come along?"

She bit her lip. "'Cause you wouldn't have had me. Why should you? You'd have known I was only in it for the key. Even if I was . . . nice to you."

Though it was dark, in the half-visible flight of emotions across her face Jessie could see a person he hadn't known was there. Chirk had hid her insecurities as thoroughly as he'd hoped to hide his bloody cough.

"You could have come to me," he said. "You should have."

"And you could have told me you were planning to die alone," she said. "But you didn't."

He couldn't answer that. Chirk waved the rifle at the door. "Get it to open up, then. Let's get the key and get out of here."

"If I can get the key from it, ordering it to kill you will be easy," he told her. A little of the wild mood that had made him willing to dive into a capital bug had returned. He was feeling obstinate enough to dare her to kill him.

Chirk sighed, and to his surprise said, "You're right." She threw away the rifle. They both watched it tumble away into the dark.

"I'm not a good person, and I went about this all wrong," she said. "But I really did like you, Jessie." She looked around uneasily. "I just . . . I can't let it go. I won't *take* it from you, but I need to be a part of this, Jess. I need a share, just a little share. I'm not going anywhere. If you want to sic your monster on me, I guess you'll just have to kill me." She crossed her arms, lowered her head, and made to stare him down.

He just had to laugh. "You make a terrible villain, Chirk." As she sputtered indignantly, he turned to the window again. The moth had been impassively watching his conversation with Chirk. "Open up!" he shouted at it again, and levering himself close with what little purchase he could make on the window's edge, he put his ear to the crystal again.

"WAIT."

Jessie let go and drifted back, frowning. Wait? For what?

"What did it say?"

"The other moth told me this one wouldn't let me in unless I proved I was committed. I had to prove I wouldn't try to take the key."

"But how are you going to do that?"

"Oh."

Wait.

Candesce's night cycle was nearly over. The metal flowers were starting to close, the bright little flying things they'd released hurrying back to the safety of their tungsten petals. All around them, the rumbling furnaces in the suns would be readying themselves. They would brighten soon, and light would wash away everything material here that was not a part of the sun of suns. Everything, perhaps, except the moth, who might be as ancient as Candesce itself.

"The other moth told me I wouldn't deliver the message," said Jessie. "It said I would *decide* not to."

She frowned. "Why would it say that?"

"Because . . . 'cause it cured me, that's why. And because the only way to deliver the message is to wait until dawn. That's when this moth here will open the door for us."

"But then—we'd never get out in time . . ."

He nodded.

"Tell it—yell through the door, like it's doing to you! Jessie, we can't stay here, that's just insane! You said the other moth cured you? Then you can escape, you can live—like me. Maybe not with me, and you're right not to trust me, but we can take the first steps together . . ." But he was shaking his head.

"I don't think it can hear me," he said. "I can barely hear it, and its voice is loud enough to topple buildings. I have to wait, or not deliver the message."

"Go to the home guard, then. Tell them, and they'll send someone here. They'll—"

"—not believe a word I say. I've nothing to show them, after all. Nothing to prove my story."

"But your life! You have your whole life . . ."

He'd tried to picture it on the flight here. He had imagined himself as a baker, a soldier, a diplomat, a painter. He longed for every one of them, for any of them. All he had to do was start his jet and follow Chirk, and one of them would come to pass.

He started to reach for his jet, but there was nowhere he could escape the responsibility he'd willingly taken on himself. He realized he didn't want to.

"Only I can do this," he told her. "Anyway, this is the only thing I ever had that was mine. If I give it up now, I'll have some life . . . but not *my* life."

She said nothing, just shook her head. He looked past her at the vast canopy of glittering lights—from the windows in city apartments and town wheel-houses, from the mansions of the rich and the gas-fires of industry: a sphere of people, every single one of them threatened by something that even now might be uncoiling in the cold vacuum outside the world; each and every one of them waiting, though they knew it not, for a helping hand.

Ten words, or a single coin.

"Get out of here, Chirk," he said. "It's starting. If you leave right now you might just get away before the full heat hits."

"But—" She stared at him in bewilderment. "You come too!"

"No. Just go. See?" He pointed at a faint ember-glow that had started in the darkness below their feet. "They're waking up. This place will be a furnace soon. There's no treasure here for you, Chirk. It's all out there."

"Jessie, I can't—" Flame-colored light blossomed below them, and then from one side. "Jessie?" Her eyes were wide with panic.

"Get out! Chirk, it's too late unless you go now! Go! Go!"

The panic took her and she kicked her jet into life. She made a clumsy pass, trying to grab Jessie on the way by, but he evaded her easily.

"Go!" She put her head down, opened the throttle, and shot away. *Too late,* Jessie feared. *Let her not be just one second too late.*

Her jet disappeared in the rising light. Jessie kicked his own jet away, returning to cling to the edge of the window. His own sharp-edged shadow appeared against the metal skull inches from his own.

"You have your proof!" He could feel the pulse of energy—heat, and something deeper and more fatal—reaching into him from the awakening suns. "Now open up.

"Open *up!*"

The moth reached out and did something below the window. The crystalline pane slid aside, and Jessie climbed into the narrow, boxlike space. The window slid shut, but did nothing to filter the growing light and heat from outside. There was nowhere further to go, either. He had expected no less.

The precipice moth lowered its head to his.

"I have come to you on behalf of humanity," said Jessie, "to tell you that the ancient strategy of relying on Candesce for our safety will no longer work . . ."

He told the moth his story, and as he spoke the dawn came up.

THE ISLAND

PETER WATTS

YOU SET US out here. We do this for *you*: spin your webs and build your magic gateways, thread each needle's eye at sixty thousand kilometers a second. We never stop, never even dare to slow down, lest the light of your coming turn us to plasma. All so you can step from star to star without dirtying your feet in these endless, empty wastes *between*.

Is it really too much to ask, that you might talk to us now and then?

I know about evolution and engineering. I know how much you've changed. I've seen these portals give birth to gods and demons and things we can't begin to comprehend, things I can't believe were ever human; alien hitchhikers, perhaps, riding the rails we've left behind. Alien conquerors.

Exterminators, perhaps.

But I've also seen those gates stay dark and empty until they faded from view. We've inferred diebacks and dark ages, civilizations burned to the ground and others rising from their ashes—and sometimes, afterward, the things that come out look a little like the ships *we* might have built, back in the day. They speak to each other—radio, laser, carrier neutrinos—and sometimes their voices sound something like ours. There was a time we dared to hope that they really were like us, that the circle had come round again and closed on beings we could talk to. I've lost count of the times we tried to break the ice.

I've lost count of the eons since we gave up.

All these iterations fading behind us. All these hybrids and posthumans and immortals, gods and catatonic cavemen trapped in magical chariots they can't begin to understand, and not one of them ever pointed a comm laser in our direction to say *Hey, how's it going,* or *Guess what? We cured Damascus Disease!* or even *Thanks, guys, keep up the good work!*

We're not some fucking cargo cult. We're the backbone of your goddamn empire. You wouldn't even be *out* here if it weren't for us.

And—and you're our *children.* Whatever you've become, you were once like this, like me. I believed in you once. There was a time, long ago, when I believed in this mission with all my heart.

Why have you forsaken us?

————

And so another build begins.

This time I open my eyes to a familiar face I've never seen before: only a boy, early twenties perhaps, physiologically. His face is a little lopsided, the cheekbone flatter on the left than the right. His ears are too big. He looks almost *natural.*

I haven't spoken for millennia. My voice comes out a whisper: "Who are you?" Not what I'm supposed to ask, I know. Not the first question *anyone* on *Eriophora* asks, after coming back.

"I'm yours," he says, and just like that, I'm a mother.

I want to let it sink in, but he doesn't give me the chance: "You weren't scheduled, but Chimp wants extra hands on deck. Next build's got a situation."

So the chimp is still in control. The chimp is always in control. The mission goes on.

"Situation?" I ask.

"Contact scenario, maybe."

I wonder when he was born. I wonder if he ever wondered about me, before now.

He doesn't tell me. He only says, "Sun up ahead. Half light-year. Chimp thinks, maybe it's talking to us. Anyhow . . ." My—son shrugs. "No rush. Lotsa time."

I nod, but he hesitates. He's waiting for The Question but I already see a kind of answer in his face. Our reinforcements were supposed to be *pristine*, built from perfect genes buried deep within *Eri*'s iron-basalt mantle, safe from the sleeting blueshift. And yet this boy has flaws. I see the damage in his face, I see those tiny flipped base-pairs resonating up from the microscopic and *bending* him just a little off-kilter. He looks like he grew up on a planet. He looks borne of parents who spent their whole lives hammered by raw sunlight.

How far out must we be by now, if even our own perfect building blocks have decayed so? How long has it taken us? How long have I been dead?

How long? It's the first thing everyone asks.

After all this time, I don't want to know.

He's alone at the tac Tank when I arrive on the bridge, his eyes full of icons and trajectories. Perhaps I see a little of me in there, too.

"I didn't get your name," I say, although I've looked it up on the manifest. We've barely been introduced and already I'm lying to him.

"Dix." He keeps his eyes on the Tank.

He's over ten thousand years old. Alive for maybe twenty of them. I wonder how much he knows, who he's met during those sparse decades: does he know Ishmael, or Connie? Does he know if Sanchez got over his brush with immortality?

I wonder, but I don't ask. There are rules.

I look around. "We're it?"

Dix nods. "For now. Bring back more if we need them. But . . ." His voice trails off.

"Yes?"

"Nothing."

I join him at the Tank. Diaphanous veils hang within like frozen, color-coded smoke. We're on the edge of a molecular dust cloud. Warm, semi-organic, lots of raw materials. Formaldehyde, ethylene glycol, the usual prebiotics. A good spot for a quick build. A red dwarf glowers dimly at the center of the Tank: the chimp has named it DHF428, for reasons I've long since forgotten to care about.

"So fill me in," I say.

His glance is impatient, even irritated. "You too?"

"What do you mean?"

"Like the others. On the other builds. Chimp can just squirt the specs but they want to *talk* all the time."

Shit, his link's still active. He's *online*.

I force a smile. "Just a—a cultural tradition, I guess. We talk about a lot of things, it helps us—reconnect. After being down for so long."

"But it's *slow*," Dix complains.

He doesn't know. Why doesn't he know?

"We've got half a light-year," I point out. "There's some rush?"

The corner of his mouth twitches. "Vons went out on schedule." On cue a cluster of violet pinpricks sparkle in the Tank, five trillion klicks ahead of us. "Still sucking dust mostly, but got lucky with a couple of big asteroids and the refineries came online early. First components already extruded. Then Chimp sees these fluctuations in solar output—mainly infra, but extends into visible." The Tank blinks at us: the dwarf goes into time-lapse.

Sure enough, it's *flickering*.

"Nonrandom, I take it."

Dix inclines his head a little to the side, not quite nodding.

"Plot the time-series." I've never been able to break the habit of raising my voice, just a bit, when addressing the chimp. Obediently (*obediently*—now *there's* a laugh-and-a-half) the AI wipes the spacescape and replaces it with

· · · · · · · · · · · · · ·   ·   ·   ·   ·   ·   ·   ·

"Repeating sequence," Dix tells me. "Blips don't change, but spacing's a log-linear increase cycling every 92.5 corsecs Each cycle starts at 13.2 clicks/corsec, degrades over time."

"No chance this could be natural? A little black hole wobbling around in the center of the star, something like that?"

Dix shakes his head, or something like that: a diagonal dip of the chin that somehow conveys the negative. "But way too simple to contain much info. Not like an actual conversation. More—well, a shout."

He's partly right. There may not be much information, but there's enough. *We're here. We're smart. We're powerful enough to hook a whole damn star up to a dimmer switch.*

Maybe not such a good spot for a build after all.

I purse my lips. "The sun's hailing us. That's what you're saying."

"Maybe. Hailing *someone*. But too simple for a rosetta signal. It's not an archive, can't self-extract. Not a bonferroni or fibonacci seq, not pi. Not even a multiplication table. Nothing to base a pidgin on."

Still. An intelligent signal.

"Need more info," Dix says, proving himself master of the blindingly obvious.

I nod. "The vons."

"Uh, what about them?"

"We set up an array. Use a bunch of bad eyes to fake a good one. It'd be faster than high-geeing an observatory from this end or retooling one of the onsite factories."

His eyes go wide. For a moment, he almost looks frightened for some reason. But the moment passes and he does that weird head-shake thing again. "Bleed too many resources away from the build, wouldn't it?"

"It would," the chimp agrees.

I suppress a snort. "If you're so worried about meeting our construction benchmarks, Chimp, factor in the potential risk posed by an intelligence powerful enough to control the energy output of an entire sun."

"I can't," it admits. "I don't have enough information."

"You don't have *any* information. About something that could probably stop this mission dead in its tracks if it wanted to. So maybe we should get some."

"Okay. Vons reassigned."

Confirmation glows from a convenient bulkhead, a complex sequence of dance instructions that *Eri*'s just fired into the void. Six months from now, a hundred self-replicating robots will waltz into a makeshift surveillance grid; four months after that, we might have something more than vacuum to debate in.

Dix eyes me as though I've just cast some kind of magic spell.

"It may run the ship," I tell him, "but it's pretty fucking stupid. Sometimes you've just got to spell things out."

He looks vaguely affronted, but there's no mistaking the surprise beneath. He didn't know that. He *didn't know.*

Who the hell's been raising him all this time? Whose problem is this?

Not mine.

"Call me in ten months," I say. "I'm going back to bed."

———

It's as though he never left. I climb back into the bridge and there he is, staring into tac. DHF428 fills the Tank, a swollen red orb that turns my son's face into a devil mask.

He spares me the briefest glance, eyes wide, fingers twitching as if electrified. "Vons don't see it."

I'm still a bit groggy from the thaw. "See wh—"

"The *sequence!*" His voice borders on panic. He sways back and forth, shifting his weight from foot to foot.

"Show me."

Tac splits down the middle. Cloned dwarves burn before me now, each perhaps twice the size of my fist. On the left, an *Eri*'s-eye view: DHF428 stutters as it did before, as it presumably has these past ten months. On the right, a compound-eye composite: an interferometry grid built by a myriad precisely-spaced vons, their rudimentary eyes layered and parallaxed into something approaching high resolution. Contrast on both sides has been conveniently cranked up to highlight the dwarf's endless winking for merely human eyes.

Except it's only winking from the left side of the display. On the right, 428 glowers steady as a standard candle.

"Chimp: any chance the grid just isn't sensitive enough to see the fluctuations?"

"No."

"Huh." I try to think of some reason it would lie about this.

"Doesn't make *sense*," my son complains.

"It does," I murmur, "if it's not the sun that's flickering."

"But *is* flickering—" He sucks his teeth. "You can *see* it—wait, you mean something *behind* the vons? Between, between them and us?"

"Mmmm."

"Some kind of *filter*." Dix relaxes a bit. "Wouldn't we've seen it, though? Wouldn't the vons've hit it going down?"

I put my voice back into ChimpComm mode. "What's the current field-of-view for *Eri's* forward scope?"

"Eighteen mikes," the chimp reports. "At 428's range, the cone is three point three four light-secs across."

"Increase to a hundred light-secs."

The *Eri's*-eye partition swells, obliterating the dissenting viewpoint. For a moment the sun fills the Tank again, paints the whole bridge crimson. Then it dwindles as if devoured from within.

I notice some fuzz in the display. "Can you clear that noise?"

"It's not noise," the chimp reports. "It's dust and molecular gas."

I blink. "What's the density?"

"Estimated hundred thousand atoms per cubic meter."

Two orders of magnitude too high, even for a nebula. "Why so heavy?" Surely we'd have detected any gravity well strong enough to keep *that* much material in the neighborhood.

"I don't know," the chimp says.

I get the queasy feeling that I might. "Set field-of-view to five hundred light-secs. Peak false-color at near-infrared."

Space grows ominously murky in the Tank. The tiny sun at its center, thumbnail-sized now, glows with increased brilliance: an incandescent pearl in muddy water.

"A thousand light-secs," I command.

"There," Dix whispers: real space reclaims the edges of the Tank, dark, clear, pristine. 428 nestles at the heart of a dim spherical shroud. You find those sometimes, discarded cast-offs from companion stars whose convulsions spew gas and rads across light-years. But 428 is no nova remnant. It's a *red dwarf*, placid, middle-aged. Unremarkable.

Except for the fact that it sits dead center of a tenuous gas bubble 1.4 AUs across. And for the fact that this bubble does not *attenuate* or *diffuse* or *fade* gradually into that good night. No, unless there is something seriously wrong with the display, this small, spherical nebula extends about three hundred fifty light-secs from its primary and then just *stops*, its boundary far more knife-edged than nature has any right to be.

For the first time in millennia, I miss my cortical pipe. It takes forever to saccade search terms onto the keyboard in my head, to get the answers I already know.

Numbers come back. "Chimp. I want false-color peaks at three hundred thirty-five, five hundred, and eight hundred nanometers."

The shroud around 428 lights up like a dragonfly's wing, like an iridescent soap bubble.

"It's *beautiful*," whispers my awestruck son.

"It's photosynthetic," I tell him.

———

Pheophytin and eumelanin, according to spectro. There are even hints of some kind of lead-based Keipper pigment, soaking up x-rays in the picometer range. Chimp hypothesizes something called a *chromatophore*: branching cells with little aliquots of pigment inside, like particles of charcoal dust. Keep those particles clumped together and the cell's effectively transparent; spread them out through the cytoplasm and the whole structure *darkens*, dims whatever EM passes through from behind. Apparently there were animals back on Earth with cells like that. They could change color, pattern-match to their background, all sorts of things.

"So there's a membrane of—of *living tissue* around that star," I say, trying to wrap my head around the concept. "A, a meat balloon. Around the whole damn *star*."

"Yes," the chimp says.

"But that's—Jesus, how thick would it be?"

"No more than two millimeters. Probably less."

"How so?"

"If it was much thicker, it would be more obvious in the visible spectrum. It would have had a detectable effect on the von Neumanns when they hit it."

"That's assuming that its—cells, I guess—are like ours."

"The pigments are familiar; the rest might be too."

It can't be *too* familiar. Nothing like a conventional gene would last two seconds in that environment. Not to mention whatever miracle solvent that thing must use as antifreeze . . .

"Okay, let's be conservative, then. Say, mean thickness of a millimeter. Assume a density of water at STP. How much mass in the whole thing?"

"1.4 yottagrams," Dix and the chimp reply, almost in unison.

"That's, uh . . ."

"Half the mass of Mercury," the chimp adds helpfully.

I whistle through my teeth. "And that's *one* organism?"

"I don't know yet."

"It's got organic pigments. Fuck, it's *talking*. It's intelligent."

"Most cyclic emanations from living sources are simple biorhythms," the chimp points out. "Not intelligent signals."

I ignore it and turn to Dix. "Assume it's a signal."

He frowns. "Chimp says—"

"*Assume.* Use your imagination."

I'm not getting through to him. He looks nervous.

He looks like that a lot, I realize.

"*If* someone were signaling you," I say, "*then* what would you do?"

"Signal . . ." Confusion on that face, and a fuzzy circuit closing somewhere ". . . back?"

My son is an idiot.

"And if the incoming signal takes the form of systematic changes in light intensity, how—"

"Use the BI lasers, alternated to pulse between seven hundred and three thousand nanometers. Can boost an interlaced signal into the exawatt range without compromising our fenders; gives over a thousand Watts per square meter after diffraction. Way past detection threshold for anything that can sense thermal output from a red dwarf. And content doesn't matter if it's just a shout. Shout back. Test for echo."

Okay, so my son is an idiot *savant*.

And he still looks unhappy—"But Chimp, he says no real *information* there, right?"—and that whole other set of misgivings edges to the fore again: *He.*

Dix takes my silence for amnesia. "Too simple, remember? Simple click train."

I shake my head. There's more information in that signal than the chimp can imagine. There are so many things the chimp doesn't know. And the last thing I need is for this, this *child* to start deferring to it, to start looking to it as an equal or, God forbid, a *mentor*.

Oh, it's smart enough to steer us between the stars. Smart enough to calculate sixty-digit primes in the blink of an eye. Even smart enough for a little crude improvisation should the crew go too far off-mission.

Not smart enough to know a distress call when it sees one.

"It's a deceleration curve," I tell them both. "It keeps *slowing down*. Over and over again. *That's* the message."

Stop. Stop. Stop. Stop.

And I think it's meant for no one but us.

———

We shout back. No reason not to. And now we die again, because what's the point of staying up late? Whether or not this vast entity harbors real intelligence, our echo won't reach it for ten million corsecs. Another seven million, at the earliest, before we receive any reply it might send.

Might as well hit the crypt in the meantime. Shut down all desires and misgivings, conserve whatever life I have left for moments that matter. Remove myself from this sparse tactical intelligence, from this wet-eyed pup watching me as though I'm some kind of sorcerer about to vanish in a puff of smoke. He opens his mouth to speak, and I turn away and hurry down to oblivion.

But I set my alarm to wake up alone.

I linger in the coffin for a while, grateful for small and ancient victories. The chimp's dead, blackened eye gazes down from the ceiling; in all these millions of years nobody's scrubbed off the carbon scoring. It's a trophy of sorts, a memento from the early incendiary days of our Great Struggle.

There's still something—comforting, I guess—about that blind, endless stare. I'm reluctant to venture out where the chimp's nerves have not been so thoroughly cauterized. Childish, I know. The damn thing already knows I'm up; it may be blind, deaf, and impotent in here, but there's no way to mask the power the crypt sucks in during a thaw. And it's not as though a bunch of club-wielding teleops are waiting to pounce on me the moment I step outside. These are the days of détente, after all. The struggle continues but the war has gone cold; we just go through the motions now, rattling our chains like an old married multiplet resigned to hating each other to the end of time.

After all the moves and countermoves, the truth is we need each other.

So I wash the rotten-egg stench from my hair and step into *Eri's* silent cathedral hallways. Sure enough, the enemy waits in the darkness, turns the lights on as I approach, shuts them off behind me—but it does not break the silence.

Dix.

A strange one, that. Not that you'd expect anyone born and raised on *Eriophora* to be an archetype of mental health, but Dix doesn't even know what side he's on. He doesn't even seem to know he has to *choose* a side. It's almost as though he read the original mission statements and took them *seriously*, believed in the literal truth of the ancient scrolls: Mammals and

Machinery, working together across the ages to explore the Universe! United! Strong! Forward the Frontier!

Rah.

Whoever raised him didn't do a great job. Not that I blame them; it can't have been much fun having a child underfoot during a build, and none of us were selected for our parenting skills. Even if bots changed the diapers and VR handled the infodumps, socializing a toddler couldn't have been anyone's idea of a good time. I'd have probably just chucked the little bastard out an airlock.

But even I would've brought him up to speed.

Something changed while I was away. Maybe the war's heated up again, entered some new phase. That twitchy kid is out of the loop for a reason. I wonder what it is.

I wonder if I care.

I arrive at my suite, treat myself to a gratuitous meal, jill off. Three hours after coming back to life I'm relaxing in the starbow commons. "Chimp."

"You're up early," it says at last.

I am. Our answering shout hasn't even arrived at its destination yet. No real chance of new data for another two months, at least.

"Show me the forward feeds," I command.

DHF428 blinks at me from the center of the lounge: *Stop. Stop. Stop.*

Maybe. Or maybe the chimp's right, maybe it's pure physiology. Maybe this endless cycle carries no more intelligence than the beating of a heart. But there's a pattern inside the pattern, some kind of *flicker* in the blink. It makes my brain itch.

"Slow the time-series," I command. "By a hundred."

It *is* a blink. 428's disk isn't darkening uniformly, it's *eclipsing*. As though a great eyelid were being drawn across the surface of the sun, from right to left.

"By a thousand."

Chromatophores, the chimp called them. But they're not all opening and closing at once. The darkness moves across the membrane in *waves*.

A word pops into my head: *latency*.

"Chimp. Those waves of pigment. How fast are they moving?"

"About fifty-nine thousand kilometers per second."

The speed of a passing thought.

And if this thing *does* think, it'll have logic gates, synapses—it's going to be a *net* of some kind. And if the net's big enough, there's an *I* in the middle of it. Just like me, just like Dix. Just like the chimp. (Which is why I educat-

ed myself on the subject, back in the early tumultuous days of our relationship. Know your enemy and all that.)

The thing about *I* is, it only exists within a tenth-of-a-second of all its
parts. When we get spread too thin—when someone splits your brain down
the middle, say, chops the fat pipe so the halves have to talk the long way
around; when the neural architecture *diffuses* past some critical point and
signals take just that much longer to pass from A to B—the system, well,
decoheres. The two sides of your brain become different people with different
tastes, different agendas, different senses of themselves.

I shatters into *we*.

It's not just a human rule, or a mammal rule, or even an Earthly one.
It's a rule for any circuit that processes information, and it applies as much
to the things we've yet to meet as it did to those we left behind.

Fifty-nine thousand kilometers per second, the chimp says. How far can
the signal move through that membrane in a tenth of a corsec? How thinly
does *I* spread itself across the heavens?

The flesh is huge, the flesh is inconceivable. But the spirit, the spirit is—
Shit.

"Chimp. Assuming the mean neuron density of a human brain, what's
the synapse count on a circular sheet of neurons one millimeter thick with a
diameter of five thousand eight hundred ninety-two kilometers?"

"Two times ten to the twenty-seventh."

I saccade the database for some perspective on a mind stretched across
thirty million square kilometers: the equivalent of two quadrillion human
brains.

Of course, whatever this thing uses for neurons have to be packed a lot
less tightly than ours; we can see through them, after all. Let's be supercon-
servative, say it's only got a thousandth the computational density of a human brain. That's—

Okay, let's say it's only got a *ten*-thousandth the synaptic density, that's
still—

A *hundred* thousandth. The merest mist of thinking meat. Any more conservative and I'd hypothesize it right out of existence.

Still twenty billion human brains. Twenty *billion*.

I don't know how to feel about that. This is no mere alien.

But I'm not quite ready to believe in gods.

———

I round the corner and run smack into Dix, standing like a golem in the
middle of my living room. I jump about a meter straight up.

"What the hell are you doing here?"

He seems surprised by my reaction. "Wanted to—talk," he says after a moment.

"You *never* come into someone's home uninvited!"

He retreats a step, stammers: "Wanted, wanted—"

"To talk. And you do that in *public*. On the bridge, or in the commons, or—for that matter, you could just *comm* me."

He hesitates. "Said you—*wanted* face to face. You said, *cultural tradition*."

I did, at that. But not *here*. This is *my* place, these are my *private quarters*. The lack of locks on these doors is a safety protocol, not an invitation to walk into my home and *lie in wait*, and stand there like part of the fucking *furniture* . . .

"Why are you even *up*?" I snarl. "We're not even supposed to come online for another two months."

"Asked Chimp to get me up when you did."

That fucking machine.

"Why are *you* up?" he asks, not leaving.

I sigh, defeated, and fall into a convenient pseudopod. "I just wanted to go over the preliminary data." The implicit *alone* should be obvious.

"Anything?"

Evidently it isn't. I decide to play along for a while. "Looks like we're talking to an, an island. Almost six thousand klicks across. That's the thinking part, anyway. The surrounding membrane's pretty much empty. I mean, it's all *alive*. It all photosynthesizes, or something like that. It eats, I guess. Not sure what."

"Molecular cloud," Dix says. "Organic compounds everywhere. Plus it's concentrating stuff inside the envelope."

I shrug. "Point is, there's a size limit for the brain but it's *huge*, it's . . ."

"Unlikely," he murmurs, almost to himself.

I turn to look at him; the pseudopod reshapes itself around me. "What do you mean?"

"Island's twenty-eight million square kilometers? Whole sphere's seven quintillion. Island just happens to be between us and 428, that's—one in fifty-billion odds."

"Go on."

He can't. "Uh, just . . . just *unlikely*."

I close my eyes. "How can you be smart enough to run those numbers in your head without missing a beat, and stupid enough to miss the obvious conclusion?"

That panicked, slaughterhouse look again. "Don't—I'm not—"

"It *is* unlikely. It's *astronomically* unlikely that we just happen to be aiming at the one intelligent spot on a sphere one-and-a-half AUs across. Which means . . . "

He says nothing. The perplexity in his face mocks me. I want to punch it.

But finally, the lights flicker on: "There's, uh, more than one island? Oh! A *lot* of islands!"

This creature is part of the crew. My life will almost certainly depend on him some day.

That is a very scary thought.

I try to set it aside for the moment. "There's probably a whole population of the things, sprinkled though the membrane like, like cysts I guess. The chimp doesn't know how many, but we're only picking up this one so far so they might be pretty sparse."

There's a different kind of frown on his face now. "Why *Chimp*?"

"What do you mean?"

"Why call him Chimp?"

"We call it *the* chimp." Because the first step to humanizing something is to give it a name.

"Looked it up. Short for *chimpanzee*. Stupid animal."

"Actually, I think chimps were supposed to be pretty smart," I remember.

"Not like us. Couldn't even *talk*. Chimp can talk. *Way* smarter than those things. That name—it's an insult."

"What do you care?"

He just looks at me.

I spread my hands. "Okay, it's not a chimp. We just call it that because it's got roughly the same synapse count."

"So gave him a small brain, then complain that he's stupid all the time."

My patience is just about drained. "Do you have a point or are you just blowing CO_2 in—"

"Why not make him smarter?"

"Because you can never predict the behavior of a system more complex than you. And if you want a project to stay on track after you're gone, you don't hand the reins to anything that's guaranteed to develop its own agenda." Sweet smoking Jesus, you'd think *someone* would have told him about Ashby's Law.

"So they lobotomized him," Dix says after a moment.

"No. They didn't *turn* it stupid, they *built* it stupid."

"Maybe smarter than you think. You're so much smarter, got *your* agenda, how come *he's* still in control?"

"Don't flatter yourself," I say.

"What?"

I let a grim smile peek through. "You're only following orders from a bunch of other systems way more complex than you are." You've got to hand it to them, too; dead for stellar lifetimes and those damn project admins are *still* pulling the strings.

"I don't—*I'm* following?—"

"I'm sorry, dear." I smile sweetly at my idiot offspring. "I wasn't talking to you. I was talking to the thing that's making all those sounds come out of your mouth."

Dix turns whiter than my panties.

I drop all pretense. "What were you thinking, chimp? That you could send this sock-puppet to invade my home and I wouldn't notice?"

"Not—I'm not—it's *me*," Dix stammers. "*Me* talking."

"It's *coaching* you. Do you even know what 'lobotomized' *means*?" I shake my head, disgusted. "You think I've forgotten how the interface works just because we all burned ours out?" A caricature of surprise begins to form on his face. "Oh, don't even fucking *try*. You've been up for other builds, there's no way you couldn't have known. And you know we shut down our domestic links too, or you wouldn't even be sneaking in here. And there's nothing your lord and master can do about that because it *needs* us, and so we have reached what you might call an *accommodation*."

I am not shouting. My tone is icy, but my voice is dead level. And yet Dix almost *cringes* before me.

There is an opportunity here, I realize.

I thaw my voice a little. I speak gently: "You can do that too, you know. Burn out your link. I'll even let you come back here afterward, if you still want to. Just to—talk. But not with that thing in your head."

There is panic in his face, and, against all expectation it almost breaks my heart. "*Can't,*" he pleads. "How I *learn* things, how I *train*. The *mission . . .*"

I honestly don't know which of them is speaking, so I answer them both: "There is more than one way to carry out the mission. We have more than enough time to try them all. Dix is welcome to come back when he's alone."

They take a step toward me. Another. One hand, twitching, rises from their side as if to reach out, and there's something on that lopsided face that I can't quite recognize.

"But I'm your *son*," they say.

I don't even dignify it with a denial.

"Get out of my home."

A human periscope. The Trojan Dix. That's a new one.

The chimp's never tried such overt infiltration while we were up and about before. Usually, it waits until we're all undead before invading our territories. I imagine custom-made drones never seen by human eyes, cobbled together during the long dark eons between builds; I see them sniffing through drawers and peeking behind mirrors, strafing the bulkheads with x-rays and ultrasound, patiently searching *Eriophora*'s catacombs millimeter by endless millimeter for whatever secret messages we might be sending each other down through time.

There's no proof to speak of. We've left tripwires and telltales to alert us to intrusion after the fact, but there's never been any evidence they've been disturbed. Means nothing, of course. The chimp may be stupid but it's also cunning, and a million years is more than enough time to iterate through every possibility using simpleminded brute force. Document every dust mote; commit your unspeakable acts; put everything back the way it was afterward.

We're too smart to risk talking across the eons. No encrypted strategies, no long-distance love letters, no chatty postcards showing ancient vistas long lost in the red shift. We keep all that in our heads, where the enemy will never find it. The unspoken rule is that we do not speak, unless it is face to face.

Endless idiotic games. Sometimes I almost forget what we're squabbling over. It seems so trivial now, with an immortal in my sights.

Maybe that means nothing to you. Immortality must be ancient news to you. But I can't even imagine it, although I've outlived worlds. All I have are moments: two or three hundred years, to ration across the lifespan of a universe. I could bear witness to any point in time, or any hundred-thousand, if I slice my life thinly enough—but I will never see *everything*. I will never see even a fraction.

My life will end. I have to *choose*.

When you come to fully appreciate the deal you've made—ten or fifteen builds out, when the trade-off leaves the realm of mere *knowledge* and sinks deep as cancer into your bones—you become a miser. You can't help it. You ration out your waking moments to the barest minimum: just enough to manage the build, to plan your latest countermove against the chimp, just enough (if you haven't yet moved beyond the need for human contact) for sex and snuggles and a bit of warm mammalian comfort against the endless dark. And then you hurry back to the crypt, to hoard the remains of a human lifespan against the unwinding of the cosmos.

There's been time for education. Time for a hundred postgraduate degrees, thanks to the best caveman learning tech. I've never bothered. Why burn down my tiny candle for a litany of mere fact, fritter away my precious, endless, finite life? Only a fool would trade book-learning for a ring-side view of the Cassiopeia Remnant, even if you *do* need false-color enhancement to see the fucking thing.

Now, though. Now, I want to *know*. This creature crying out across the gulf, massive as a moon, wide as a solar system, tenuous and fragile as an insect's wing: I'd gladly cash in some of my life to learn its secrets. How does it work? How can it even *live* here at the edge of absolute zero, much less think? What vast, unfathomable intellect must it possess, to see us coming from over half a light-year away, to deduce the nature of our eyes and our instruments, to send a signal we can even *detect*, much less understand?

And what happens when we punch through it at a fifth the speed of light?

I call up the latest findings on my way to bed, and the answer hasn't changed: not much. The damn thing's already full of holes. Comets, asteroids, the usual protoplanetary junk careens through this system as it does through every other. Infra picks up diffuse pockets of slow outgassing here and there around the perimeter, where the soft vaporous vacuum of the interior bleeds into the harder stuff outside. Even if we were going to tear through the dead center of the thinking part, I can't imagine this vast creature feeling so much as a pinprick. At the speed we're going we'd be through and gone far too fast to overcome even the feeble inertia of a millimeter membrane.

And yet. *Stop. Stop. Stop.*

It's not us, of course. It's what we're building. The birth of a gate is a violent, painful thing, a space-time rape that puts out almost as much gamma and X as a microquasar. Any meat within the white zone turns to ash in an instant, shielded or not. It's why *we* never slow down to take pictures.

One of the reasons, anyway.

We can't stop, of course. Even changing course isn't an option except by the barest increments. *Eri* soars like an eagle between the stars but she steers like a pig on the short haul; tweak our heading by even a tenth of a degree and you've got some serious damage at twenty percent lightspeed. Half a degree would tear us apart: the ship might torque onto the new heading but the collapsed mass in her belly would keep right on going, rip through all this surrounding superstructure without even feeling it.

Even tame singularities get set in their ways. They do not take well to change.

———

We resurrect again, and the Island has changed its tune.

It gave up asking us to *stop stop stop* the moment our laser hit its leading edge. Now it's saying something else entirely: dark hyphens flow across its skin, arrows of pigment converging toward some offstage focus like spokes pointing toward the hub of a wheel. The bullseye itself is offstage and implicit, far removed from 428's bright backdrop, but it's easy enough to extrapolate to the point of convergence six light-secs to starboard. There's something else, too: a shadow, roughly circular, moving along one of the spokes like a bead running along a string. It too migrates to starboard, falls off the edge of the Island's makeshift display, is endlessly reborn at the same initial coordinates to repeat its journey.

Those coordinates: exactly where our current trajectory will punch through the membrane in another four months. A squinting God would be able to see the gnats and girders of ongoing construction on the other side, the great piecemeal torus of the Hawking Hoop already taking shape.

The message is so obvious that even Dix sees it. "Wants us to move the gate . . ." and there is something like confusion in his voice. "But how's it know we're *building* one?"

"The vons punctured it en route," the chimp points out. "It could have sensed that. It has photopigments. It can probably see."

"Probably sees better than we do," I say. Even something as simple as a pinhole camera gets hi-res fast if you stipple a bunch of them across thirty million square kilometers.

But Dix scrunches his face, unconvinced. "So sees a bunch of vons bumping around. Loose parts—not that much even *assembled* yet. How's it know we're building something *hot*?"

Because it is very, very, smart, you stupid child. Is it so hard to believe that this, this—*organism* seems far too limiting a word—can just *imagine* how those half-built pieces fit together, glance at our sticks and stones and see exactly where this is going?

"Maybe's not the first gate it's seen," Dix suggests. "Think there's maybe another gate out here?"

I shake my head. "We'd have seen the lensing artifacts by now."

"You ever run into anyone before?"

"No." We have always been alone, through all these epochs. We have only ever run *away*.

And then always from our own children.

I crunch some numbers. "Hundred eighty-two days to insemination. If we move now, we've only got to tweak our bearing by a few mikes to redirect to the new coordinates. Well within the green. Angles get dicey the longer we wait, of course."

"We can't do that," the chimp says. "We would miss the gate by two million kilometers."

"Move the gate. Move the whole damn site. Move the refineries, move the factories, move the damn rocks. A couple hundred meters a second would be more than fast enough if we send the order now. We don't even have to suspend construction, we can keep building on the fly."

"Every one of those vectors widens the nested confidence limits of the build. It would increase the risk of error beyond allowable margins, for no payoff."

"And what about the fact that there's an intelligent being in our path?"

"I'm already allowing for the potential presence of intelligent alien life."

"Okay, first off, there's nothing *potential* about it. It's *right fucking there.* And on our current heading we run the damn thing over."

"We're staying clear of all planetary bodies in Goldilocks orbits. We've seen no local evidence of spacefaring technology. The current location of the build meets all conservation criteria."

"That's because the people who drew up your criteria *never anticipated a live Dyson sphere!*" But I'm wasting my breath, and I know it. The chimp can run its equations a million times, but if there's nowhere to put the variable, what can it do?

There was a time, back before things turned ugly, when we had clearance to reprogram those parameters. Before we discovered that one of the things the admins *had* anticipated was mutiny.

I try another tack. "Consider the threat potential."

"There's no evidence of any."

"Look at the synapse estimate! That thing's got order of mag more processing power than the whole civilization that sent us out here. You think something can be that smart, live that long, without learning how to defend itself? We're assuming it's *asking* us to move the gate. What if that's not a *request?* What if it's just giving us the chance to back off before it takes matters into its own hands?"

"Doesn't *have* hands," Dix says from the other side of the Tank, and he's not even being flippant. He's just being so stupid I want to bash his face in.

I try to keep my voice level. "Maybe it doesn't *need* any."

"What could it do, *blink* us to death? No weapons. Doesn't even control the whole membrane. Signal propagation's too slow."

"We *don't know.* That's my *point.* We haven't even tried to find out. We're a goddamn road crew; our onsite presence is a bunch of construction vons press-ganged into scientific research. We can figure out some basic physical parameters but we don't know how this thing thinks, what kind of natural defenses it might have—"

"What do you need to find out?" the chimp asks, the very voice of calm reason.

We can't find out! I want to scream. *We're stuck with what we've got! By the time the onsite vons could build what we need we're already past the point of no return! You stupid fucking machine, we're on track to kill a being smarter than all of human history and you can't even be bothered to move our highway to the vacant lot next door?*

But of course if I say that, the Island's chances of survival go from low to zero. So I grasp at the only straw that remains: maybe the data we've got in hand is enough. If acquisition is off the table, maybe analysis will do.

"I need time," I say.

"Of course," the chimp tells me. "Take all the time you need."

———

The chimp is not content to kill this creature. The chimp has to spit on it as well.

Under the pretense of assisting in my research, it tries to *deconstruct* the island, break it apart and force it to conform to grubby earthbound precedents. It tells me about earthly bacteria that thrived at 1.5 million rads and laughed at hard vacuum. It shows me pictures of unkillable little tardigrades that could curl up and snooze on the edge of absolute zero, felt equally at home in deep ocean trenches and deeper space. Given time, opportunity, a boot off the planet, who knows how far those cute little invertebrates might have gone? Might they have survived the very death of the homeworld, clung together, grown somehow colonial?

What utter bullshit.

I learn what I can. I study the alchemy by which photosynthesis transforms light and gas and electrons into living tissue. I learn the physics of the solar wind that blows the bubble taut, calculate lower metabolic limits for a life-form that filters organics from the ether. I marvel at the speed of this creature's thoughts: almost as fast as *Eri* flies, orders of mag faster than any mammalian nerve impulse. Some kind of organic superconductor perhaps, something that passes chilled electrons almost resistance-free out here in the freezing void.

I acquaint myself with phenotypic plasticity and sloppy fitness, that fortuitous evolutionary soft-focus that lets species exist in alien environments and express novel traits they never needed at home. Perhaps this is how a lifeform with no natural enemies could acquire teeth and claws and the willingness to use them. The Island's life hinges on its ability to kill us; I have to find *something* that makes it a threat.

But all I uncover is a growing suspicion that I am doomed to fail—for violence, I begin to see, is a *planetary* phenomenon.

Planets are the abusive parents of evolution. Their very surfaces promote warfare, concentrate resources into dense defensible patches that can be fought over. Gravity forces you to squander energy on vascular systems and skeletal support, stand endless watch against an endless sadistic campaign to squash you flat. Take one wrong step, off a perch too high, and all your pricey architecture shatters in an instant. And even if you beat those odds, cobble together some lumbering armored chassis to withstand the slow crawl onto land—how long before the world draws in some asteroid or comet to crash down from the heavens and reset your clock to zero? Is it any wonder we grew up believing life was a struggle, that zero-sum was God's own law and the future belonged to those who crushed the competition?

The rules are so different out here. Most of space is *tranquil*: no diel or seasonal cycles, no ice ages or global tropics, no wild pendulum swings between hot and cold, calm and tempestuous. Life's precursors abound: on comets, clinging to asteroids, suffusing nebulae a hundred light-years across. Molecular clouds glow with organic chemistry and life-giving radiation. Their vast dusty wings grow warm with infrared, filter out the hard stuff, give rise to stellar nurseries that only some stunted refugee from the bottom of a gravity well could ever call *lethal*.

Darwin's an abstraction here, an irrelevant curiosity. This Island puts the lie to everything we were ever told about the machinery of life. Sun-powered, perfectly adapted, immortal, it won no struggle for survival: where are the predators, the competitors, the parasites? All of life around 428 is one vast continuum, one grand act of symbiosis. Nature here is not red in tooth and claw. Nature, out here, is the helping hand.

Lacking the capacity for violence, the Island has outlasted worlds. Unencumbered by technology, it has out-thought civilizations. It is intelligent beyond our measure, and—

—and it is *benign*. It must be. I grow more certain of that with each passing hour. How can it even *conceive* of an enemy?

I think of the things I called it, before I knew better. *Meat balloon. Cyst.* Looking back, those words verge on blasphemy. I will not use them again.

Besides, there's another word that would fit better, if the chimp has its way: Roadkill. And the longer I look, the more I fear that that hateful machine is right.

If the Island can defend itself, I sure as shit can't see how.

———

"*Eriophora's* impossible, you know. Violates the laws of physics."

We're in one of the social alcoves off the ventral notochord, taking a break from the library. I have decided to start again from first principles.

Dix eyes me with an understandable mix of confusion and mistrust; my claim is almost too stupid to deny.

"It's true," I assure him. "Takes way too much energy to accelerate a ship with *Eri*'s mass, especially at relativistic speeds. You'd need the energy output of a whole sun. People figured if we made it to the stars at all, we'd have to do it in ships maybe the size of your thumb. Crew them with virtual personalities downloaded onto chips."

That's too nonsensical even for Dix. "*Wrong*. Don't have mass, can't fall toward anything. *Eri* wouldn't even *work* if it was that small."

"But suppose you can't displace any of that mass. No wormholes, no Higgs conduits, nothing to throw your gravitational field in the direction of travel. Your center of mass just *sits* there in, well, the center of your mass."

A spastic Dixian head-shake. "*Do* have those things!"

"Sure we do. But for the longest time, we didn't *know* it."

His foot taps an agitated tattoo on the deck.

"It's the history of the species," I explain. "We think we've worked everything out, we think we've solved all the mysteries, and then someone finds some niggling little data point that doesn't fit the paradigm. Every time we try to paper over the crack, it gets bigger, and before you know it, our whole worldview unravels. It's happened time and again. One day, mass is a constraint; the next, it's a requirement. The things we think we know—they *change*, Dix. And we have to change with them."

"But—"

"The chimp can't change. The rules it's following are ten billion years old and it's got no fucking imagination—and really that's not anyone's fault, that's just people who didn't know how else to keep the mission stable across deep time. They wanted to keep us on-track, so they built something that couldn't go off it; but they also knew that things *change*, and that's why *we're* out here, Dix. To deal with things the chimp can't."

"The alien," Dix says.

"The alien."

"Chimp deals with it just fine."

"How? By killing it?"

"Not our fault it's in the way. It's no threat—"

"I don't care whether it's a *threat* or not! It's alive, and it's intelligent, and killing it just to expand some alien empire—"

"*Human* empire. *Our* empire." Suddenly, Dix's hands have stopped twitching. Suddenly, he stands still as stone.

I snort. "What do you know about humans?"

"*Am* one."

"You're a fucking trilobite. You ever see what comes *out* of those gates once they're online?"

"Mostly nothing. " He pauses, thinking back. "Couple of—ships once, maybe."

"Well, I've seen a lot more than that, and believe me, if those things were *ever* human it was a passing phase."

"But—"

"Dix—" I take a deep breath, try to get back on message. "Look, it's not your fault. You've been getting all your info from a moron stuck on a rail. But we're not doing this for humanity, we're not doing it for Earth. Earth is *gone*, don't you understand that? The sun scorched it black a billion years after we left. Whatever we're working for, it—it won't even *talk* to us."

"Yeah? Then why do this? Why not just, just *quit*?"

He really doesn't know.

"We tried," I say.

"And?"

"And your *chimp* shut off our life support."

For once, he has nothing to say.

"It's a *machine*, Dix. Why can't you get that? It's *programmed*. It can't change."

"*We're* machines. Just built from different things. *We* change."

"Yeah? Last time I checked, you were sucking so hard on that thing's tit you couldn't even kill your cortical link."

"How I *learn*. No *reason* to change."

"How about acting like a damn *human* once in a while? How about developing a little rapport with the folks who might have to save your miserable life next time you go EVA? That enough of a *reason* for you? Because I don't mind telling you, right now I don't trust you as far as I could throw the tac Tank. I don't even know for sure who I'm talking to right now."

"*Not my fault.*" For the first time, I see something outside the usual gamut of fear, confusion, and simpleminded computation playing across his face. "That's *you*, that's *all* of you. You talk—*sideways*. *Think* sideways. You all do, and it *hurts*." Something hardens in his face. "Didn't even need you online for this," he growls. "Didn't *want* you. Could have managed the whole build myself, *told* Chimp I could do it—"

"But the chimp thought you should wake me up anyway, and you always roll over for the chimp, don't you? Because the chimp always knows best, the chimp's your *boss*, the chimp's your fucking *god*. Which is why I have to get out of bed to nursemaid some idiot savant who can't even answer a hail without being led by the nose." Something clicks in the back of my mind, but I'm on a roll. "You want a *real* role model? You want something to look up to? Forget the chimp. Forget the mission. Look out the forward scope, why don't you? Look at what your precious chimp wants to run over because it happens to be in the way. That thing is better than any of us. It's smarter, it's peaceful, it doesn't wish us any harm at—"

"How can you know that? Can't know that!"

"No, *you* can't know that, because you're fucking *stunted*. Any normal caveman would see it in a second, but *you*—"

"That's crazy," Dix hisses at me. "*You're* crazy. You're *bad*."

"*I'm* bad!" Some distant part of me hears the giddy squeak in my voice, the borderline hysteria.

"For the mission." Dix turns his back and stalks away.

My hands are hurting. I look down, surprised: my fists are clenched so tightly that my nails cut into the flesh of my palms. It takes a real effort to open them again.

I almost remember how this feels. I used to feel this way all the time. Way back when everything *mattered*; before passion faded to ritual, before rage cooled to disdain. Before Sunday Ahzmundin, eternity's warrior, settled for heaping insults on stunted children.

We were incandescent back then. Parts of this ship are still scorched and uninhabitable, even now. I remember this feeling.

This is how it feels to be awake.

———

I am awake, and I am alone, and I am sick of being outnumbered by morons. There are rules and there are risks, and you don't wake the dead on a whim, but fuck it. I'm calling reinforcements.

Dix has got to have other parents, a father at least, he didn't get that Y chromo from me. I swallow my own disquiet and check the manifest; bring up the gene sequences; cross-reference.

Huh. Only one other parent: Kai. I wonder if that's just coincidence, or if the chimp drew too many conclusions from our torrid little fuckfest back in the Cyg Rift. Doesn't matter. He's as much yours as mine, Kai, time to step up to the plate, time to—

Oh shit. Oh no. Please no.

(There are rules. And there are risks.)

Three builds back, it says. Kai and Connie. Both of them. One airlock jammed, the next too far away along *Eri*'s hull, a hail-Mary emergency crawl between. They made it back inside but not before the blue-shifted background cooked them in their suits. They kept breathing for hours afterward, talked and moved and cried as if they were still alive, while their insides broke down and bled out.

There were two others awake that shift, two others left to clean up the mess. Ishmael, and—

"Um, you said—"

"*You fucker!*" I leap up and hit my son hard in the face, ten seconds' heartbreak with ten million years' denial raging behind it. I feel teeth give way behind his lips. He goes over backward, eyes wide as telescopes, the blood already blooming on his mouth.

"*Said* I could come back—!" he squeals, scrambling backward along the deck.

"He was your fucking *father*! You *knew*, you were *there*! He died right in *front* of you and you didn't even *tell* me!"

"I—I—"

"Why didn't you tell me, you asshole? The chimp told you to lie, is that it? Did you—"

"*Thought you knew!*" he cries, "Why *wouldn't* you know?"

My rage vanishes like air through a breach. I sag back into the 'pod, face in hands.

"Right there in the log," he whimpers. "All along. Nobody hid it. How could you not know?"

"I did," I admit dully. "Or I—I mean . . ."

I mean I *didn't* know, but it's not a surprise, not really, not down deep. You just—stop looking, after a while.

There are *rules*.

"Never even *asked*," my son says softly. "How they were doing."

I raise my eyes. Dix regards me wide-eyed from across the room, backed up against the wall, too scared to risk bolting past me to the door. "What are you doing here?" I ask tiredly.

His voice catches. He has to try twice: "You said I could come back. If I burned out my link . . ."

"You burned out your link."

He gulps and nods. He wipes blood with the back of his hand.

"What did the chimp say about that?"

"He said—*it* said it was okay," Dix says, in such a transparent attempt to suck up that I actually believe, in that instant, that he might really be on his own.

"So you asked its permission." He begins to nod, but I can see the tell in his face: "Don't bullshit me, Dix."

"He—actually suggested it."

"I see."

"So we could talk," Dix adds.

"What do you want to talk about?"

He looks at the floor and shrugs.

I stand and walk toward him. He tenses but I shake my head, spread my hands. "It's okay. It's okay." I lean back against the wall and slide down until I'm beside him on the deck.

We just sit there for a while.

"It's been so long," I say at last.

He looks at me, uncomprehending. What does *long* even mean, out here?

I try again. "They say there's no such thing as altruism, you know?"

His eyes blank for an instant, and grow panicky, and I know that he's just tried to ping his link for a definition and come up blank. So we *are* alone. "Altruism," I explain. "Unselfishness. Doing something that costs *you* but helps someone else." He seems to get it. "They say every selfless act ultimately comes down to manipulation or kin-selection or reciprocity or something, but they're wrong. I could—"

I close my eyes. This is harder than I expected.

"I could have been happy just *knowing* that Kai was okay, that Connie was happy. Even if it didn't benefit me one whit, even if it *cost* me, even if there was no chance I'd ever see either of them again. Almost any price would be worth it, just to know they were okay.

"Just to *believe* they were . . ."

So you haven't seen her for the past five builds. So he hasn't drawn your shift since Sagittarius. They're just sleeping. Maybe next time.

"So you don't check," Dix says slowly. Blood bubbles on his lower lip; he doesn't seem to notice.

"We don't check." Only I did, and now they're gone. They're both gone. Except for those little cannibalized nucleotides the chimp recycled into this defective and maladapted son of mine.

We're the only warm-blooded creatures for a thousand light-years, and I am so very lonely.

"I'm sorry," I whisper, and lean forward, and lick the gore from his bruised and bloody lips.

———

Back on Earth—back when there *was* an Earth—there were these little animals called cats. I had one for a while. Sometimes I'd watch him sleep for hours: paws and whiskers and ears all twitching madly as he chased imaginary prey across whatever landscapes his sleeping brain conjured up.

My son looks like that when the chimp worms its way into his dreams.

It's almost too literal for metaphor: the cable runs into his head like some kind of parasite, feeding through old-fashioned fiber-op now that the wireless option's been burned away. Or *force*-feeding, I suppose; the poison flows into Dix's head, not out of it.

I shouldn't be here. Didn't I just throw a tantrum over the violation of my own privacy? (Just. Twelve light-days ago. Everything's relative.) And yet, I can see no privacy here for Dix to lose: no decorations on the walls, no artwork or hobbies, no wraparound console. The sex toys ubiquitous in every suite sit unused on their shelves; I'd have assumed he was on antilibinals if recent experience hadn't proven otherwise.

What am I doing? Is this some kind of perverted mothering instinct, some vestigial expression of a Pleistocene maternal subroutine? Am I that much of a robot, has my brain stem sent me here to guard my child?

To guard my *mate*?

Lover or larva, it hardly matters: his quarters are an empty shell, there's nothing of Dix in here. That's just his abandoned body lying there in the pseudopod, fingers twitching, eyes flickering beneath closed lids in vicarious response to wherever his mind has gone.

They don't know I'm here. The chimp doesn't know because we burned out its prying eyes a billion years ago, and my son doesn't know I'm here because — well, because for him, right now, there *is* no here.

What am I supposed to make of you, Dix? None of this makes sense. Even your body language looks like you grew it in a vat—but I'm far from the first human being you've seen. You grew up in good company, with people I *know*, people I trust. Trusted. How did you end up on the other side? How did they let you slip away?

And why didn't they warn me about you?

Yes, there are rules. There is the threat of enemy surveillance during long dead nights, the threat of—other losses. But this is unprecedented. Surely someone could have left something, some clue buried in a metaphor too subtle for the simpleminded to decode . . .

I'd give a lot to tap into that pipe, to see what you're seeing now. Can't risk it, of course; I'd give myself away the moment I tried to sample anything except the basic baud, and—

—Wait a second—

That baud rate's way too low. That's not even enough for hi-res graphics, let alone tactile and olfac. You're embedded in a wireframe world at best.

And yet, look at you go. The fingers, the eyes—like a cat, dreaming of mice and apple pies. Like *me*, replaying the long-lost oceans and mountaintops of Earth before I learned that living in the past was just another way of dying in the present. The bit rate says this is barely even a test pattern; the body says you're immersed in a whole other world. How has that machine tricked you into treating such thin gruel as a feast?

Why would it even want to? Data are better grasped when they *can* be grasped, and tasted, and heard; our brains are built for far richer nuance than splines and scatterplots. The driest technical briefings are more sensual than this. Why settle for stick-figures when you can paint in oils and holograms?

Why does anyone simplify anything? To reduce the variable set. To manage the unmanageable.

Kai and Connie. Now *there* were a couple of tangled, unmanageable datasets. Before the accident. Before the scenario *simplified*.

Someone should have warned me about you, Dix.

Maybe someone tried.

———

And so it comes to pass that my son leaves the nest, encases himself in a beetle carapace and goes walkabout. He is not alone; one of the chimp's teleops accompanies him out on *Eri*'s hull, lest he lose his footing and fall back into the starry past.

Maybe this will never be more than a drill, maybe this scenario—catastrophic control-systems failure, the chimp and its backups offline, all maintenance tasks suddenly thrown onto shoulders of flesh and blood—is a dress rehearsal for a crisis that never happens. But even the unlikeliest scenario approaches certainty over the life of a universe; so we go through the motions. We practice. We hold our breath and dip outside. We're on a tight deadline: even armored, moving at this speed the blueshifted background rad would cook us in hours.

Worlds have lived and died since I last used the pickup in my suite. "Chimp."

"Here as always, Sunday." Smooth, and glib, and friendly. The easy rhythm of the practiced psychopath.

"I know what you're doing."

"I don't understand."

"You think I don't see what's going on? You're building the next release. You're getting too much grief from the old guard so you're starting from scratch with people who don't remember the old days. People you've, you've *simplified*."

The chimp says nothing. The drone's feed shows Dix clambering across a jumbled terrain of basalt and metal matrix composites.

"But you can't raise a human child, not on your own." I know it tried: there's no record of Dix anywhere on the crew manifest until his mid-teens, when he just *showed up* one day and nobody asked about it because nobody *ever* . . .

"Look what you've made of him. He's great at conditional if/thens. Can't be beat on number-crunching and do loops. But he can't *think*. Can't make the simplest intuitive jumps. You're like one of those—" I remember an Earthly myth, from the days when *reading* did not seem like such an obscene waste of lifespan—"one of those wolves, trying to raise a human child. You can teach him how to move around on hands and knees, you can teach him about pack dynamics, but you can't teach him how to walk on his hind legs or talk or be *human* because you're *too fucking stupid*, Chimp, and you finally realized it. And that's why you threw him at me. You think I can fix him for you."

I take a breath, and a gambit.

"But he's nothing to me. You understand? He's *worse* than nothing, he's a liability. He's a spy, he's a spastic waste of O2. Give me one reason why I shouldn't just lock him out there until he cooks."

"You're his mother," the chimp says, because the chimp has read all about kin selection and is too stupid for nuance.

"You're an idiot."

"You love him."

"No." An icy lump forms in my chest. My mouth makes words; they come out measured and inflectionless. "I can't love anyone, you brain-dead machine. That's why I'm out here. Do you really think they'd gamble your precious never-ending mission on little glass dolls that needed to bond."

"You love him."

"I can kill him any time I want. And that's exactly what I'll do if you don't move the gate."

"I'd stop you," the chimp says mildly.

"That's easy enough. Just move the gate and we both get what we want. Or you can dig in your heels and try to reconcile your need for a mother's touch with my sworn intention of breaking the little fucker's neck. We've got a long trip ahead of us, chimp. And you might find I'm not quite as easy to cut out of the equation as Kai and Connie."

"You cannot end the mission," it says, almost gently. "You tried that already."

"This isn't about ending the mission. This is only about slowing it down a little. Your optimal scenario's off the table. The only way that gate's going to get finished now is by saving the Island, or killing your prototype. Your call."

The cost-benefit's pretty simple. The chimp could solve it in an instant. But still it says nothing. The silence stretches. It's looking for some other option, I bet. It's trying to find a workaround. It's questioning the very premises of the scenario, trying to decide if I mean what I'm saying, if all its book-learning about mother love could really be so far off-base. Maybe it's plumbing historical intrafamilial murder rates, looking for a loophole. And there may be one, for all I know. But the chimp isn't me, it's a simpler system trying to figure out a smarter one, and that gives me the edge.

"You would owe me," it says at last.

I almost burst out laughing. "*What?*"

"Or I will tell Dixon that you threatened to kill him."

"Go ahead."

"You don't want him to know."

"I don't care whether he knows or not. What, you think he'll try and kill me back? You think I'll lose his *love?*" I linger on the last word, stretch it out to show how ludicrous it is.

"You'll lose his trust. You need to trust each other out here."

"Oh, right. *Trust.* The very fucking foundation of this mission."

The chimp says nothing.

"For the sake of argument," I say, after a while, "suppose I go along with it. What would I *owe* you, exactly?"

"A favor," the chimp replies. "To be repaid in future."

My son floats innocently against the stars, his life in balance.

———

We sleep. The chimp makes grudging corrections to a myriad small trajectories. I set the alarm to wake me every couple of weeks, burn a little more of my candle in case the enemy tries to pull another fast one; but for now it seems to be behaving itself. DHF428 jumps toward us in the stop-motion increments of a life's moments, strung like beads along an infinite string. The factory floor slews to starboard in our sights: refineries, reservoirs, and nanofab plants, swarms of von Neumanns breeding and cannibalizing and recycling each other into shielding and circuitry, tugboats and spare parts. The very finest Cro Magnon technology mutates and metastasizes across the universe like armor-plated cancer.

And hanging like a curtain between *it* and *us* shimmers an iridescent life form, fragile and immortal and unthinkably alien, that reduces everything my species ever accomplished to mud and shit by the simple transcendent fact of its existence. I have never believed in gods, in universal good or absolute evil. I have only ever believed that there is what works, and what doesn't. All the rest is smoke and mirrors, trickery to manipulate grunts like me.

But I believe in the Island, because I don't *have* to. It does not need to be taken on faith: it looms ahead of us, its existence an empirical fact. I will never know its mind, I will never know the details of its origin and evolution. But I can *see* it: massive, mind boggling, so utterly inhuman that it can't *help* but be better than us, better than anything we could ever become.

I believe in the Island. I've gambled my own son to save its life. I would kill him to avenge its death.

I may yet.

In all these millions of wasted years, I have finally done something worthwhile.

Final approach.

Reticles within reticles line up before me, a mesmerizing infinite regress of bulls-eyes centering on target. Even now, mere minutes from ignition, distance reduces the unborn gate to invisibility. There will be no moment when the naked eye can trap our destination. We thread the needle far too quickly: it will be behind us before we know it.

Or, if our course corrections are off by even a hair—if our trillion-kilometer curve drifts by as much as a thousand meters—we will be dead. Before we know it.

Our instruments report that we are precisely on target. The chimp tells me that we are precisely on target. *Eriophora* falls forward, pulled endlessly through the void by her own magically-displaced mass.

I turn to the drone's-eye view relayed from up ahead. It's a window into history—even now, there's a timelag of several minutes—but past and present race closer to convergence with every corsec. The newly-minted gate looms dark and ominous against the stars, a great gaping mouth built to devour reality itself. The vons, the refineries, the assembly lines: parked to the side in vertical columns, their jobs done, their usefulness outlived, their collateral annihilation imminent. I pity them, for some reason. I always do. I wish we could scoop them up and take them with us, re-enlist them for the next build—but the rules of economics reach everywhere, and they say it's cheaper to use our tools once and throw them away.

A rule that the chimp seems to be taking more to heart than anyone expected.

At least we've spared the Island. I wish we could have stayed awhile. First contact with a truly alien intelligence, and what do we exchange? Traffic signals. What does the Island dwell upon, when not pleading for its life?

I thought of asking. I thought of waking myself when the time-lag dropped from prohibitive to merely inconvenient, of working out some pidgin that could encompass the truths and philosophies of a mind vaster than all humanity. What a childish fantasy. The Island exists too far beyond the grotesque Darwinian processes that shaped my own flesh. There can be no communion here, no meeting of minds.

Angels do not speak to ants.

Less than three minutes to ignition. I see light at the end of the tunnel. *Eri's* incidental time machine barely looks into the past anymore, I could almost hold my breath across the whole span of seconds that *then* needs to overtake *now*. Still on target, according to all sources.

Tactical beeps at us.

"Getting a signal," Dix reports, and yes: in the heart of the Tank, the sun is flickering again. My heart leaps: does the angel speak to us after all? A thank-you, perhaps? A cure for heat death?

But—

"It's *ahead* of us," Dix murmurs, as sudden realization catches in my throat.

Two minutes.

"Miscalculated somehow," Dix whispers. "Didn't move the gate far enough."

"We did," I say. We moved it exactly as far as the Island told us to.

"*Still in front of us!* Look at the *sun!*"

"Look at the *signal*," I tell him.

Because it's nothing like the painstaking traffic signs we've followed over the past three trillion kilometers. It's almost—random, somehow. It's spur-of-the-moment, it's *panicky*. It's the sudden, startled cry of something caught utterly by surprise with mere seconds left to act. And even though I have never seen this pattern of dots and swirls before, I know exactly what it must be saying.

Stop. Stop. Stop. Stop.

We do not stop. There is no force in the universe that can even slow us down. Past equals present; *Eriophora* dives through the center of the gate in a nanosecond. The unimaginable mass of her cold black heart snags some distant dimension, drags it screaming to the here and now. The booted portal erupts behind us, blossoms into a great blinding corona, every wavelength lethal to every living thing. Our aft filters clamp down tight.

The scorching wavefront chases us into the darkness as it has a thousand times before. In time, as always, the birth pangs will subside. The wormhole will settle in its collar. And just maybe, we will still be close enough to glimpse some new transcendent monstrosity emerging from that magic doorway.

I wonder if you'll notice the corpse we left behind.

"Maybe we're missing something," Dix says.

"We miss almost everything," I tell him.

DHF428 shifts red behind us. Lensing artifacts wink in our rearview; the gate has stabilized and the wormhole's online, blowing light and space and time in an iridescent bubble from its great metal mouth. We'll keep looking over our shoulders right up until we pass the Rayleigh Limit, far past the point it'll do any good.

So far, though, nothing's come out.

"Maybe our numbers were wrong," he says. "Maybe we made a mistake."

Our numbers were right. An hour doesn't pass when I don't check them again. The Island just had—enemies, I guess. Victims, anyway.

I was right about one thing, though. That fucker was *smart*. To see us coming, to figure out how to talk to us; to use us as a *weapon*, to turn a threat to its very existence into a, a . . .

I guess *flyswatter* is as good a word as any.

"Maybe there was a war," I mumble. "Maybe it wanted the real estate. Or maybe it was just some—family squabble."

"Maybe didn't *know*," Dix suggests. "Maybe thought those coordinates were empty."

Why would you think that, I wonder. *Why would you even care?* And then it dawns on me: he doesn't, not about the Island, anyway. No more than he ever did. He's not inventing these rosy alternatives for himself.

My son is trying to comfort me.

I don't need to be coddled, though. I was a fool: I let myself believe in life without conflict, in sentience without sin. For a little while, I dwelt in a dream world where life was unselfish and unmanipulative, where every living thing did not struggle to exist at the expense of other life. I deified that which I could not understand, when in the end it was all too easily understood.

But I'm better now.

It's over: another build, another benchmark, another irreplaceable slice of life that brings our task no closer to completion. It doesn't matter how successful we are. It doesn't matter how well we do our job. *Mission accomplished* is a meaningless phrase on *Eriophora*, an ironic oxymoron at best. There may one day be failure, but there is no finish line. We go on forever, crawling across the universe like ants, dragging your goddamned superhighway behind us.

I still have so much to learn.

At least my son is here to teach me.

THE ICE OWL

CAROLYN IVES GILMAN

TWICE A DAY, stillness settled over the iron city of Glory to God as the citizens turned west and waited for the world to ring. For a few moments the motionless red sun on the horizon, half-concealed by the western mountains, lit every face in the city: the just-born and the dying, the prisoners and the veiled, the devout and the profane. The sound started so low it could only be heard by the bones; but as the moments passed the metal city itself began to ring in sympathetic harmony, till the sound resolved into a note—The Note, priests said, sung by the heart of God to set creation going. Its vibratory mathematics embodied all structure; its pitch implied all scales and chords; its beauty was the ovum of all devotion and all faithlessness. Nothing more than a note was needed to extrapolate the universe.

The Note came regular as clockwork, the only timebound thing in a city of perpetual sunset.

On a ledge outside a window in the rustiest part of town, crouched one of the ominous cast-iron gargoyles fancied by the architects of Glory to God—or so it seemed until it moved. Then it resolved into an adolescent girl dressed all in black. Her face was turned west, her eyes closed in a look of private exaltation as The Note reverberated through her. It was a face that had just recently lost the chubbiness of childhood, so that the clean-boned adult was beginning to show through. Her name, also a recent development, was Thorn. She had chosen it because it evoked suffering and redemption.

As the bell tones whispered away, Thorn opened her eyes. The city before her was a composition in red and black: red of the sun and the dust-plain outside the girders of the dome; black of the shadows and the works of mankind. Glory to God was built against the cliff of an old crater and rose in stairsteps of fluted pillars and wrought arches till the towers of the Protectorate grazed the underside of the dome where it met the cliff face. Behind the distant, glowing windows of the palaces, twined with iron ivy, the priest-magistrates and executives lived unimaginable lives—though Thorn still pictured them looking down on all the rest of the city, on the smelteries and temples, the warring neighborhoods ruled by militias, the veiled women, and at the very bottom, befitting its status, the Waster enclave where unrepentent immigrants like Thorn and her mother lived, sunk in a bath of sin. The Waste was not truly of the city, except as a perennial itch in its flesh. The Godly said it was the sin, not the oxygen, that rusted everything in the Waste. A man who came home with a red smudge on his clothes might as well have been branded with the address.

Thorn's objection to her neighborhood lay not in its sin, which did not live up to its reputation, but its inauthenticity. From her rooftop perch she looked down on its twisted warrens full of coffee shops, underground publishers, money launderers, embassies, tattoo parlors, and art galleries. This was the ninth planet she had lived on in her short life, but in truth she had never left her native culture, for on every planet the Waster enclaves were the same. They were always a mother lode of contraband ideas. Everywhere, the expatriate intellectuals of the Waste were regarded as exotic and dangerous, the vectors of infectious transgalactic ideas—but lately, Thorn had begun to find them pretentious and phony. They were rooted nowhere, pieces of cultural bricolage. Nothing reached to the core; it was all veneer, just like the rust.

Outside, now—she looked past the spiked gates into Glory to God proper—there lay dark desires and age-old hatreds, belief so unexamined it permeated every tissue like a marinade. The natives had not chosen their beliefs; they had inherited them, breathed them in with the iron dust in their first breath. Their struggles were authentic ones.

Her eyes narrowed as she spotted movement near the gate. She was, after all, on lookout duty. There seemed to be more than the usual traffic this afternote, and the cluster of young men by the gate did not look furtive enough to belong. She studied them through her pocket binoculars and saw a telltale flash of white beneath one long coat. White, the color of the uncorrupted.

She slipped back through the gable window into her attic room, then down the iron spiral staircase at the core of the vertical tower apartment. Past the fifth-floor closets and the fourth-floor bedrooms she went, to the third-floor offices. There she knocked sharply on one of the molded sheet-iron doors. Within, there was a thump, and in a moment Maya cracked it open enough to show one eye.

"There's a troop of Incorruptibles by the gate," Thorn said.

Inside the office, a woman's voice gave a frightened exclamation. Thorn's mother turned and said in her fractured version of the local tongue, "Worry not yourself. We make safely go." She then said to Thorn, "Make sure the bottom door is locked. If they come, stall them."

Thorn spun down the stair like a black tornado, past the living rooms to the kitchen on street level. The door was locked, but she unlocked it to peer out. The alarm was spreading down the street. She watched signs being snatched from windows, awnings rolled up, and metal grills rumbling down across storefronts. The crowds that always pressed from curb to curb this time of day had vanished. Soon the stillness of impending storm settled over the street. Then Thorn heard the faraway chanting, like premonitory thunder. She closed and locked the door.

Maya showed up, looking rumpled, her lovely honey-gold hair in ringlets. Thorn said, "Did you get her out?" Maya nodded. One of the main appeals of this apartment had been the hidden escape route for smuggling out Maya's clients in emergencies like this.

On this planet, as on the eight before, Maya earned her living in the risky profession of providing reproductive services. Every planet was different, it seemed, except that on all of them women wanted something that was forbidden. What they wanted varied: here, it was babies. Maya did a brisk business in contraband semen and embryos for women who needed to become pregnant without their infertile husbands guessing how it had been accomplished.

The chanting grew louder, harsh male voices in unison. They watched together out the small kitchen window. Soon they could see the approaching wall of men dressed in white, marching in lockstep. The army of righteousness came even with the door, then passed by. Thorn and Maya exchanged a look of mutual congratulation and locked little fingers in their secret handshake. Once again, they had escaped.

Thorn opened the door and looked after the army. An assortment of children was tagging after them, so Maya said, "Go see what they're up to."

The Incorruptibles had passed half a dozen potential targets by now: the bank, the musical instrument store, the news service, the sex shop. They didn't pause until they came to the small park that lay in the center of an intersection. Then the phalanx lined up opposite the school. With military precision, some of them broke the bottom windows and others lit incendiary bombs and tossed them in. They waited to make sure the blaze was started, then gave a simultaneous shout and marched away, taking a different route back to the gate.

They had barely left when the Protectorate fire service came roaring down the street to put out the blaze. This was not, Thorn knew, out of respect for the school or for the Waste, which could have gone up in flame wholesale for all the authorities cared; it was simply that in a domed city, a fire anywhere was a fire everywhere. Even the palaces would have to smell the smoke and clean up soot if it were not doused quickly. Setting a fire was as much a defiance of the Protectorate as of the Wasters.

Thorn watched long enough to know that the conflagration would not spread, and then walked back home. When she arrived, three women were sitting with Maya at the kitchen table. Two of them Thorn knew: Clarity and Bick, interstellar wanderers whose paths had crossed Thorn's and Maya's on two previous planets. The first time, they had been feckless coeds; the second time, seasoned adventurers. They were past middle age now, and had become the most sensible people Thorn had ever met. She had seen them face insurrection and exile with genial good humor and a cannister of tea.

Right now their teapot was filling the kitchen with a smoky aroma, so Thorn fished a mug out of the sink to help herself. Maya said, "So what were the Incorruptibles doing?"

"Burning the school," Thorn said in a seen-it-all-before tone. She glanced at the third visitor, a stranger. The woman had a look of timeshock that gave her away as a recent arrival in Glory to God via lightbeam from another planet. She was still suffering from the temporal whiplash of waking up ten or twenty years from the time she had last drawn breath.

"Annick, this is Thorn, Maya's daughter," Clarity said. She was the talkative, energetic one of the pair; Bick was the silent, steady one.

"Hi," Thorn said. "Welcome to the site of Creation."

"Why were they burning the school?" Annick said, clearly distressed by the idea. She had pale eyes and a soft, gentle face. Thorn made a snap judgment: Annick was not going to last long here.

"Because it's a vector of degeneracy," Thorn said. She had learned the phrase from Maya's current boyfriend, Hunter.

"What has happened to this planet?" Annick said. "When I set out it was isolated, but not regressive."

They all made sympathetic noises, because everyone at the table had experienced something similar. Lightbeam travel was as fast as the universe allowed, but even the speed of light had a limit. Planets inevitably changed during transit, not always for the better. "Waster's luck," Maya said fatalistically.

Clarity said, "The Incorruptibles are actually a pretty new movement. It started among the conservative academics and their students, but they have a large following now. They stand against the graft and nepotism of the Protectorate. People in the city are really fed up with being harassed by policemen looking for bribes, and corrupt officials who make up new fees for everything. So they support a movement that promises to kick the grafters out and give them a little harsh justice. Only it's bad news for us."

"Why?" Annick said. "Wouldn't an honest government benefit everyone?"

"You'd think so. But honest governments are always more intrusive. You can buy toleration and personal freedom from a corrupt government. The Protectorate leaves this Waster enclave alone because it brings them profit. If the Incorruptibles came into power, they'd have to bow to public opinion and exile us, or make us conform. The general populace is pretty isolationist. They think our sin industry is helping keep the Protectorate in power. They're right, actually."

"What a Devil's bargain," Annick said.

They all nodded. Waster life was full of irony.

"What's Thorn going to do for schooling now?" Clarity asked Maya.

Maya clearly hadn't thought about it. "They'll figure something out," she said vaguely.

Just then Thorn heard Hunter's footsteps on the iron stairs, and she said to annoy him, "I could help Hunter."

"Help me do what?" Hunter said as he descended into the kitchen. He was a lean and angle-faced man with square glasses and a small goatee. He always dressed in black and could not speak without sounding sarcastic. Thorn thought he was a poser.

"Help you find Gmintas, of course," Thorn said. "That's what you do."

He went over to the Turkish coffee machine to brew some of the bitter, hyperstimulant liquid he was addicted to. "Why can't you go to school?" he said.

"They burned it down."

"Who did?"

"The Incorruptibles. Didn't you hear them chanting?"

"I was in my office."

He was always in his office. It was a mystery to Thorn how he was going to locate any Gminta criminals when he disdained going out and mingling with people. She had once asked Maya, "Has he ever actually caught a Gminta?" and Maya had answered, "I hope not."

All in all, though, he was an improvement over Maya's last boyfriend, who had absconded with every penny of savings they had. Hunter at least had money, though where it came from was a mystery.

"I could be your field agent," Thorn said.

"You need an education, Thorn," Clarity said.

"Yes," Hunter agreed. "If you knew something, you might be a little less annoying."

"People like you give education a bad name," Thorn retorted.

"Stop being a brat, Tuppence," Maya said.

"That's not my name anymore!"

"If you act like a baby, I'll call you by your baby name."

"You always take his side."

"You could find her a tutor," Clarity said. She was not going to give up.

"Right," Hunter said, sipping inky liquid from a tiny cup. "Why don't you ask one of those old fellows who play chess in the park?"

"They're probably all pedophiles!" Thorn said in disgust.

"On second thought, maybe it's better to keep her ignorant," Hunter said, heading up the stairs again.

"I'll ask around and see who's doing tutoring," Clarity offered.

"Sure, okay," Maya said noncommittally.

Thorn got up, glowering at their lack of respect for her independence and self-determination. "I am captain of my own destiny," she announced, then made a strategic withdrawal to her room.

The next forenote Thorn came down from her room in the face-masking veil that women of Glory to God all wore, outside the Waste. When Maya saw her, she said, "Where are you going in that getup?"

"Out," Thorn said.

In a tone diluted with real worry, Maya said, "I don't want you going into the city, Tup."

Thorn was icily silent till Maya said, "Sorry—Thorn. But I still don't want you going into the city."

"I won't," Thorn said.

"Then what are you wearing that veil for? It's a symbol of bondage."

"Bondage to God," Thorn said loftily.

"You don't believe in God."

Right then Thorn decided that she would.

When she left the house and turned toward the park, the triviality of her home and family fell away like lint. After a block, she felt transformed. Putting on the veil had started as a simple act of rebellion, but out in the street

344 | THE ICE OWL

it became far more. Catching her reflection in a shop window, she felt disguised in mystery. The veil intensified the imagined face it concealed, while exoticizing the eyes it revealed. She had become something shadowy, hidden. The Wasters all around her were obsessed with their own surfaces, with manipulating what they *seemed* to be. All depth, all that was earnest, withered in the acid of their inauthenticity. But with the veil on, Thorn *had* no surface, so she was immune. What lay behind the veil was negotiated, contingent, rendered deep by suggestion.

In the tiny triangular park in front of the blackened shell of the school, life went on as if nothing had changed. The tower fans turned lazily, creating a pleasant breeze tinged a little with soot. Under their strutwork shadows, two people walked little dogs on leashes, and the old men bent over their chessboards. Thorn scanned the scene through the slit in her veil, then walked toward a bench where an old man sat reading from an electronic slate.

She sat down on the bench. The old man did not acknowledge her presence, though a watchful twitch of his eyebrow told her he knew she was there. She had often seen him in the park, dressed impeccably in threadbare suits of a style long gone. He had an oblong, drooping face and big hands that looked as if they might once have done clever things. Thorn sat considering what to say.

"Well?" the old man said without looking up from his book. "What is it you want?"

Thorn could think of nothing intelligent to say, so she said, "Are you a historian?"

He lowered the slate. "Only in the sense that we all are, us Wasters. Why do you want to know?"

"My school burned down," Thorn said. "I need to find a tutor."

"I don't teach children," the old man said, turning back to his book.

"I'm not a child!" Thorn said, offended.

He didn't look up. "Really? I thought that's what you were trying to hide, behind that veil."

She took it off. At first he paid no attention. Then at last he glanced up indifferently, but saw something that made him frown. "You are the child that lives with the Gminta hunter."

His cold tone made her feel defensive on Hunter's behalf. "He doesn't hunt all Gmintas," she said, "just the wicked ones who committed the Holocide. The ones who deserve to be hunted."

"What do you know about the Gmintan Holocide?" the old man said with withering dismissal.

Thorn smiled triumphantly. "I was there."

He stopped pretending to read and looked at her with bristly disapproval. "How could you have been there?" he said. "It happened one hundred forty-one years ago."

"I'm one hundred forty-five years old, sequential time," Thorn said. "I was thirty-seven when I was five, and ninety-eight when I was seven, and one hundred twenty-six when I was twelve." She enjoyed shocking people with this litany.

"Why have you moved so much?"

"My mother got pregnant without my father's consent, and when she refused to have an abortion he sued her for copyright infringement. She'd made unauthorized use of his genes, you see. So she ducked out to avoid paying royalties, and we've been on the lam ever since. If he ever caught us, I could be arrested for having bootleg genes."

"Who told you that story?" he said, obviously skeptical.

"Maya did. It sounds like something one of her boyfriends would do. She has really bad taste in men. That's another reason we have to move so much."

Shaking his head slightly, he said, "I should think you would get cognitive dysplasia."

"I'm used to it," Thorn said.

"Do you like it?"

No one had ever asked her that before, as if she was capable of deciding for herself. In fact, she had known for a while that she *didn't* like it much. With every jump between planets she had grown more and more reluctant to leave sequential time behind. She said, "The worst thing is, there's no way of going back. Once you leave, the place you've stepped out of is gone forever. When I was eight I learned about pepcies, that you can use them to communicate instantaneously, and I asked Maya if we could call up my best friend on the last planet, and Maya said, 'She'll be middle-aged by now.' Everyone else had changed, and I hadn't. For a while I had dreams that the world was dissolving behind my back whenever I looked away."

The old man was listening thoughtfully, studying her. "How did you get away from Gmintagad?" he asked.

"We had Capellan passports," Thorn said. "I don't remember much about it; I was just four years old. I remember drooping cypress trees and rushing to get out. I didn't understand what was happening."

He was staring into the distance, focused on something invisible. Suddenly, he got up as if something had bitten him and started to walk away.

"Wait!" Thorn called. "What's the matter?"

He stopped, his whole body tense, then turned back. "Meet me here at four hours forenote tomorrow, if you want lessons," he said. "Bring a slate. I won't wait for you." He turned away again.

"Stop!" Thorn said. "What's your name?"

With a forbidding frown, he said, "Soren Pregaldin. You may call me Magister."

"Yes, Magister," Thorn said, trying not to let her glee show. She could hardly wait to tell Hunter that she had followed his advice, and succeeded.

What she wouldn't tell him, she decided as she watched Magister Pregaldin stalk away across the park, was her suspicion that this man knew something about the Holocide. Otherwise, how would he have known it was exactly one hundred forty-one years ago? Another person would have said one hundred forty, or something else vague. She would not mention her suspicion to Hunter until she was sure. She would investigate carefully, like a competent field agent should. Thinking about it, a thrill ran through her. What if she were able to catch a Gminta? How impressed Hunter would be! The truth was, she wanted to impress Hunter. For all his mordant manner, he was by far the smartest boyfriend Maya had ever taken up with, the only one with a profession Thorn had ever been able to admire.

She fastened the veil over her face again before going home, so no one would see her grinning.

———

Magister Pregaldin turned out to be the most demanding teacher Thorn had ever known. Always before, she had coasted through school, easily able to stay ahead of the indigenous students around her, always waiting in boredom for them to catch up. With Magister Pregaldin there was no one else to wait for, and he pushed her mercilessly to the edge of her abilities. For the first time in her life, she wondered if she were smart enough.

He was an exacting drillmaster in mathematics. Once, when she complained at how useless it was, he pointed out beyond the iron gridwork of the dome to a round black hill that was conspicuous on the red plain of the crater bed. "Tell me how far away the Creeping Ingot is."

The Creeping Ingot had first come across the horizon almost a hundred years before, slowly moving toward Glory to God. It was a near-pure lump of iron the size of a small mountain. In the Waste, the reigning theory was that it was molten underneath, and moving like a drop of water skitters across a hot frying pan. In the city above them, it was regarded as a sign of divine wrath: a visible, unstoppable Armageddon. Religious tourists came from all over the planet to see it, and its ever-shrinking distance was posted on the public sites. Thorn turned to her slate to look it up, but Magister Pregaldin made her put it down. "No," he said, "I want you to figure it out."

"How can I?" she said. "They bounce lasers off it or something to find out where it is."

"There is an easier way, using tools you already have."

"The *easiest* way is to look it up!"

"No, that is the lazy way." His face looked severe. "Relying too much on free information makes you as vulnerable as relying too much on technology. You should always know how to figure it out yourself, because information can be falsified, or taken away. You should never trust it."

So he was some sort of information survivalist. "Next you'll want me to use flint to make fire," she grumbled.

"Thinking for yourself is not obsolete. Now, how are you going to find out? I will give you a hint: you don't have enough information right now. Where are you going to get it?"

She thought a while. It had to use mathematics, because that was what they had been talking about. At last she said, "I'll need a tape measure."

"Right."

"And a protractor."

"Good. Now go do it."

It took her the rest of forenote to assemble her tools, and the first part of afternote to observe the ingot from two spots on opposite ends of the park. Then she got one of the refuse-picker children to help her measure the distance between her observation posts. Armed with two angles and a length, the trigonometry was simple. When Magister Pregaldin let her check her answer, it was more accurate than she had expected.

He didn't let on, but she could tell that he was, if anything, even more pleased with her success than she was herself. "Good," he said. "Now, if you measured more carefully and still got an answer different from the official one, you would have to ask yourself whether the Protectorate had a reason for falsifying the Ingot's distance."

She could see now what he meant.

"That old Vind must be a wizard," Hunter said when he found Thorn toiling over a math problem at the kitchen table. "He's figured out some way of motivating you."

"Why do you think he's a Vind?" Thorn said.

Hunter gave a caustic laugh. "Just look at him."

She silently added that to her mental dossier on her tutor. Not a Gminta, then. A Vind—one of the secretive race of aristocrat intellectuals who could be found in government, finance, and academic posts on almost every one of the Twenty Planets. All her life Thorn had heard whispers about a Vind conspiracy to infiltrate positions of power under the guise of public service. She had heard about the secret Vind sodality of interplanetary financiers who siphoned off the wealth of whole planets to fund their hegemony. She knew Maya scoffed at all of it. Certainly, if Magister Pregaldin was an example, the Vind conspiracy was not working very well. He seemed as penniless as any other Waster.

But being Vind did not rule out his involvement in the Holocide—it just meant he was more likely to have been a refugee than a perpetrator. Like most planets, Gmintagad had had a small, elite Vind community, regarded with suspicion by the indigenes. The massacres had targeted the Vinds as well as the Alloes. People didn't talk as much about the Vinds, perhaps because the Vinds didn't talk about it themselves.

Inevitably, Thorn's daily lessons in the park drew attention. One day they were conducting experiments in aerodynamics with paper airplanes when a man approached them. He had a braided beard strung with ceramic beads that clacked as he walked. Magister Pregaldin saw him first, and his face went blank and inscrutable.

The clatter of beads came to rest against the visitor's silk kameez. He cleared his throat. Thorn's tutor stood and touched his earlobes in respect, as people did on this planet. "Your worship's presence makes my body glad," he said formally.

The man made no effort to be courteous in return. "Do you have a license for this activity?"

"Which activity, your worship?"

"Teaching in a public place."

Magister Pregaldin hesitated. "I had no idea my conversations could be construed as teaching."

It was the wrong answer. Even Thorn, watching silently, could see that the proper response would have been to ask how much a license cost. The man was obviously fishing for a bribe. His face grew stern. "Our blessed Protectorate levies just fines on those who flout its laws."

"I obey all the laws, honorable sir. I will cease to give offense immediately."

The magister picked up his battered old electronic slate and, without a glance at Thorn, walked away. The man from the Protectorate considered Thorn, but evidently concluded he couldn't extract anything from her, and so he left.

Thorn waited till the official couldn't see her anymore, then sprinted after Magister Pregaldin. He had disappeared into Weezer Alley, a crooked passageway that Thorn ordinarily avoided because it was the epicenter of depravity in the Waste. She plunged into it now, searching for the tall, patrician silhouette of her tutor. It was still forenote, and the denizens of Weezer Alley were just beginning to rise from catering to the debaucheries of yesternote's customers. Thorn hurried past a shop where the owner was beginning to lay out an array of embarrassingly explicit sex toys; she tried not to look. A little beyond, she squeamishly skirted a spot where a shop-keeper was scattering red dirt on a half-dried pool of vomit. Several dogleg turns into the heart of the sin warren, she came to the infamous Garden of Delights, where live musicians were said to perform. No one from the Protectorate cared much about prostitution, since that was mentioned in their holy book; but music was absolutely forbidden.

The gate into the Garden of Delights was twined about with iron snakes. On either side of it stood a pedestal where dancers gyrated during open hours. Now a sleepy she-man lounged on one of them, stark naked except for a bikini that didn't hide much. Hisher smooth skin was almost completely covered with the vinelike and paisley patterns of the decorative skin fungus *mycochromoderm*. Once injected, it was impossible to remove. It grew as long as its host lived, in bright scrolls and branching patterns. It had been a Waster fad once.

The dancer regarded Thorn from lizardlike eye slits in a face forested over with green and red tendrils. "You looking for the professor?" heshe asked.

Thorn was a little shocked that her cultivated tutor was known to such an exhibitionist creature as this, but she nodded. The she-man gestured languidly at a second-story window across the street. "Tell him to come visit me," heshe said, and bared startlingly white teeth.

Thorn found the narrow doorway almost hidden behind an awning and climbed the staircase past peeling tin panels that once had shown houris carrying a huge feather fan. When she knocked on the door at the top, there was no response at first, so she called out, "Magister?"

The door flew open and Magister Pregaldin took her by the arm and yanked her in, looking to make sure she had not been followed. "What are you doing here?" he demanded.

"No one saw me," she said. "Well, except for that . . . that . . ." she gestured across the street.

Magister Pregaldin went to the window and looked out. "Oh, Ginko," he said.

"Why do you live here?" Thorn said. "There are lots better places."

The magister gave a brief, grim little smile. "Early warning system," he said. "As long as the Garden is allowed to stay in business, no one is going to care about the likes of me." He frowned sternly. "Unless you get me in trouble."

"Why didn't you bribe him? He would have gone away."

"I have to save my bribes for better causes," he said. "One can't become known to the bottom-feeders, or they get greedy." He glanced out the window again. "You have to leave now."

"Why?" she said. "All he said was you need a license to teach in public. He didn't say anything about teaching in private."

Magister Pregaldin regarded her with a complex expression, as if he were trying to quantify the risk she represented. At last he gave a nervous shrug. "You must promise not to tell anyone. I am serious. This is not a game."

"I promise," Thorn said.

She had a chance then to look around. Up to now, her impression had been of a place so cluttered that only narrow lanes were left to move about the room. Now she saw that the teetering stacks all around her were constructed of wondrous things. There were crystal globes on ormolu stands, hand-knotted silk rugs piled ten high, clocks with malachite cases stacked atop towers of leather-and-gilt books. There was a copper orrery of nested bands and onyx horses rearing on their back legs, and a theremin in a case of brushed aluminum. A cloisonné ewer as tall as Thorn occupied one corner. In the middle hung a chandelier that dripped topaz swags and bangles, positioned so that Magister Pregaldin had to duck whenever he crossed the room.

"Is all this stuff yours?" Thorn said, dazzled with so much wonder.

"Temporarily," he said. "I am an art dealer. I make sure things of beauty get from those who do not appreciate them to those who do. I am a matchmaker, in a way." As he spoke, his fingers lightly caressed a sculpture made from an ammonite fossil with a human face emerging from the shell. It was a delicate gesture, full of reverence, even love. Thorn had a sudden, vivid feeling that this was where Magister Pregaldin's soul rested—with his things of beauty.

"If you are to come here, you must never break anything," he said.

"I won't touch," Thorn said.

"No, that's not what I meant. One *must* touch things, and hold them, and work them. Mere looking is never enough. But touch them as they wish to be touched." He handed her the ammonite fossil. It was surprisingly heavy, and its curve fit perfectly in her hand. The face looked surprised when she held it up before her, and she laughed.

Most of the walls were as crowded as the floor, with paintings hung against overlapping tapestries and guidons. But one wall was empty except for a painting that hung alone, as if in a place of honor. As Thorn walked toward it, it seemed to shift and change colors with every change of angle.

It showed a young girl with long black hair and a serious expression, about Thorn's age but far more beautiful and fragile.

Seeing where she was looking, Magister Pregaldin said, "The portrait is made of butterfly wings. It is a type of artwork from Vindahar."

"Is that the home world of the Vind?"

"Yes."

"Do you know who she is?"

"Yes," he said hesitantly. "But it would mean nothing to you. She died a long time ago."

There was something in his voice—was it pain? No, Thorn decided, something less acute, like the memory of pain. It lay in the air after he stopped speaking, till even he heard it.

"That is enough art history for today," he said briskly. "We were speaking of airplanes."

———

That afternote, Hunter was out on one of his inscrutable errands. Thorn waited till Maya was talking to one of her friends and crept up to Hunter's office. He had a better library than anyone she had ever met, a necessary thing on this planet where there were almost no public sources of knowledge. Thorn was quite certain she had seen some art books in his collection. She scanned the shelves of disks and finally took down one that looked like an art encyclopedia. She inserted it into the reader and typed in "butterfly" and "Vindahar."

There was a short article from which she learned that the art of butterfly-wing painting had been highly admired, but was no longer practiced because the butterflies had gone extinct. She went on to the illustrations— and there it was. The very same painting she had seen earlier that day, except lit differently, so that the colors were far brighter and the girl's expression even sadder than it had seemed.

Portrait of Jemma Diwali, the caption said. *An acknowledged masterpiece of technique, this painting was lost in GM 862, when it was looted from one of the homes of the Diwali family. According to Almasy, the representational formalism of the subject is subtly circumvented by the transformational perspective, which creates an abstractionist counter-layer of imagery. It anticipates the "chaos art" of Dunleavy* . . . It went on about the painting as if it had no connection to anything but art theory. But all Thorn cared about was the first sentence. GM 862—the year of the Gmintan Holocide.

Jemma was staring at her gravely, as if there were some implied expectation on her mind. Thorn went back to the shelves, this time for a history of the Holocide. It seemed like there were hundreds of them. At last she

picked one almost at random and typed in "Diwali." There were unin-
formative references to the name scattered throughout the book. From the
first two, she gathered that the Diwalis had been a Vind family associated
with the government on Gmintagad. There were no mentions of Jemma.

She had left the door ajar and now heard the sounds of Hunter returning downstairs. Quickly she re-cased the books and erased her trail from
the reader. She did not want him to find out just yet. This was her mystery
to solve.

There wasn't another chance to sneak into Hunter's office before she
returned to Magister Pregaldin's apartment on Weezer Alley. She found
that he had cleared a table for them to work at, directly underneath the
stuffed head of a creature with curling copper-colored horns. As he
checked over the work she had done the note before, her eyes were drawn
irresistibly to the portrait of Jemma across the room.

At last he caught her staring at it, and their eyes met. She blurted out,
"Did you know that painting comes from Gmintagad?"

A shadow of frost crossed his face. But it passed quickly, and his voice
was low and even when he said, "Yes."

"It was looted," Thorn said. "Everyone thought it was lost."

"Yes, I know," he said.

Accusatory thoughts were bombarding her. He must have seen them,
for he said calmly, "I collect art from the Holocide."

"That's macabre," she said.

"A great deal of significant art was looted in the Holocide. In the years
after, it was scattered, and entered the black markets of a dozen planets.
Much of it was lost. I am reassembling a small portion of it, whatever I can
rescue. It is very slow work."

This explanation altered the picture Thorn had been creating in her head.
Before, she had seen him as a scavenger feeding on the remains of a tragedy.
Now he seemed more like a memorialist acting in tribute to the dead.
Regretting what she had been thinking, she said, "Where do you find it?"

"In curio shops, import stores, estate sales. Most people don't recognize
it. There are dealers who specialize in it, but I don't talk to them."

"Don't you think it should go back to the families that owned it?"

He hesitated a fraction of a second, then said, "Yes, I do." He glanced
over his shoulder at Jemma's portrait. "If one of them existed, I would give
it back."

"You mean they're all dead? Every one of them?"

"So far as I can find out."

That gave the artwork a new quality. To its delicacy, its frozen-flower beauty, was added an iron frame of absolute mortality. An entire family, vanished. Thorn got up to go look at it, unable to stay away.

"The butterflies are all gone, too," she said.

Magister Pregaldin came up behind her, looking at the painting as well. "Yes," he said. "The butterflies, the girl, the family, the world, all gone. It can never be replicated."

There was something exquisitely poignant about the painting now. The only surviving thing to prove that they had all existed. She looked up at Magister Pregaldin. "Were you there?"

He shook his head slowly. "No. It was before my time. I have always been interested in it, that's all."

"Her name was Jemma," Thorn said. "Jemma Diwali."

"How did you find that out?" he asked.

"It was in a book. A stupid book. It was all about abstractionist counter-layers and things. Nothing that really explained the painting."

"I'll show you what it was talking about," the magister said. "Stand right there." He positioned her about four feet from the painting, then took the lamp and moved it to one side. As the light moved, the image of Jemma Diwali disappeared, and in its place was an abstract design of interlocking spirals, spinning pinwheels of purple and blue.

Thorn gave an exclamation of astonishment. "How did that happen?"

"It is in the microscopic structure of the butterfly wings," Magister Pregaldin explained. "Later, I will show you one under magnification. From most angles they reflect certain wavelengths of light, but from this one, they reflect another. The skill in the painting was assembling them so they would show both images. Most people think it was just a feat of technical virtuosity, without any meaning."

She looked at him. "But that's not what you think."

"No," he said. "You have to understand, Vind art is all about hidden messages, layers of meaning, riddles to be solved. Since I have had the painting here, I have been studying it, and I have identified this pattern. It was not chosen randomly." He went to his terminal and called up a file. A simple algebraic equation flashed onto the screen. "You solve this equation using any random number for X, then take the solution and use it as X to solve the equation again, then take *that* number and use it to solve the equation again, and so forth. Then you graph all the solutions on an X and Y axis, and this is what you get." He hit a key and an empty graph appeared on the screen. As the machine started to solve the equation, little dots of blue began appearing in random locations on the screen. There appeared to be no pattern at all, and Thorn frowned in perplexity.

"I'll speed it up now," Magister Pregaldin said. The dots started appearing rapidly, like sleet against a window or sand scattered on the floor. "It is like graphing the result of a thousand dice throws, sometimes lucky, sometimes outside the limits of reality, just like the choices of a life. You spend the first years buffeted by randomness, pulled this way by parents, that way by friends, all the variables squabbling and nudging, quarreling till you can't hear your own mind. And then, patterns start to appear."

On the screen, the dots had started to show a tendency to cluster. Thorn could see the hazy outlines of spiral swirls. As more and more dots appeared in seemingly random locations, the pattern became clearer and clearer.

Magister Pregaldin said, "As the pattern fills in, you begin to see that the individual dots were actually the pointillist elements of something beautiful: a snowflake, or a spiral, or concentric ripples. There is a pattern to our lives; we just experience it out of order, and don't have enough data at first to see the design. Our path forward is determined by this invisible artwork, the creation of a lifetime of events."

"You mean, like fate?" Thorn said.

"That is the question." Her tutor nodded gravely, staring at the screen. The light made his face look planar and secretive. "Does the pattern exist before us? Is our underlying equation predetermined, or is it generated by the results of our first random choice for the value of X? I can't answer that."

The pattern on the screen was clear now; it was the same one hidden under the portrait. Thorn glanced from one to the other. "What does this have to do with Jemma?"

"Another good question," Magister Pregaldin said thoughtfully. "I don't know. Perhaps it was a message to her from the artist, or a prediction—one that never had a chance to come true, because she died before she could find her pattern."

Thorn was silent a moment, thinking of that other girl. "Did she die in the Holocide?"

"Yes."

"Did you know her?"

"I told you, I wasn't there."

She didn't believe him for a second. He *had* been there, she was sure of it now. Not only had he been there, he was still there, and would always be there.

———

Several days later Thorn stepped out of the front door on her way to classes, and instantly sensed something wrong. There was a hush; tension or expectation had stretched the air tight. Too few people were on the street, and they were casting glances up at the city. She looked up toward where the Corkscrew rose, a black sheet-iron spiral that looked poised to drill a hole through the sky. There was a low, rhythmic sound coming from around it.

"Bick!" she cried out when she saw the Waster heading home laden down with groceries, as if for a siege. "What's going on?"

"You haven't heard?" Bick said.

"No."

In a low voice, Bick said, "The Protector was assassinated last note."

"Oh. Is that good or bad?"

Bick shrugged. "It depends on who they blame."

As Bick hurried on her way, Thorn stood, balanced between going home and going on to warn Magister Pregaldin. The sound from above grew more distinct, as of slow drumming. Deciding abruptly, Thorn dashed on.

The denizens of Weezer Alley had become accustomed to the sight of Thorn passing through to her lessons. Few of them were abroad this fore-note, but she nearly collided with one coming out of the tobacco shop. It was a renegade priest from Glory to God who had adopted the Waster life-style as if it were his own. Everyone called him Father Sin.

"Ah, girl!" he exclaimed. "So eager for knowledge you knock down old men?"

"Father Sin, what's that sound?" she asked.

"They are beating the doorways of their houses in grief," he said. "It is tragic, what has happened."

She dashed on. The sound had become a ringing by the time she reached Magister Pregaldin's doorway, like an unnatural Note. She had to wait several seconds after knocking before the door opened.

"Ah, Thorn! I am glad you are here," Magister Pregaldin said when he saw her. "I have something I need to . . ." He stopped, seeing her expression. "What is wrong?"

"Haven't you heard the news, Magister?"

"What news?"

"The Protector is dead. Assassinated. That's what the ringing is about."

He listened as if noticing it for the first time, then quickly went to his terminal to look up the news. There was a stark announcement from the Protectorate, blaming "Enemies of God," but of course no news. He shut it off and stood thinking. Then he seemed to come to a decision.

"This should not alter my plans," he said. "In fact, it may help." He turned to Thorn, calm and austere as usual. "I need to make a short jour-ney. I will be away for two days, three at most. But if it takes me any longer,

I will need you to check on my apartment, and make sure everything is in order. Will you do that?"

"Of course," Thorn said. "Where are you going?"

"I'm taking the wayport to one of the other city-states." He began then to show her two plants that would need watering, and a bucket under a leaky pipe that would need to be emptied. He paused at the entrance to his bedroom, then finally gestured her in. It was just as cluttered as the other rooms. He took a rug off a box, and she saw that it was actually a small refrigerator unit with a temperature gauge on the front showing that the interior was well below freezing.

"This needs to remain cold," he said. "If the electricity should go out, it will be fine for up to three days. But if I am delayed getting back, and the inside temperature starts rising, you will need to go out and get some dry ice to cool it again. Here is the lock. Do you remember the recursive equation I showed you?"

"You mean Jemma's equation?"

He hesitated in surprise, then said, "Yes. If you take 27 for the first value of X, then solve it five times, that will give you the combination. That should be child's play for you."

"What's in it?" Thorn asked.

At first he seemed reluctant to answer, but then realized he had just given her the combination, so he knelt and pecked it out on the keypad. A light changed to green. He undid several latches and opened the top, then removed an ice pack and stood back for her to see. Thorn peered in and saw nested in ice a ball of white feathers.

"It's a bird," she said in puzzlement.

"You have seen birds, have you?"

"Yes. They don't have them here. Why are you keeping a dead bird?"

"It's not dead," he said. "It's sleeping. It is from a species they call ice owls, the only birds known to hibernate. They are native to a planet called Ping, where the winters last a century or more. The owls burrow into the ice to wait out the winter. Their bodies actually freeze solid. Then when spring comes, they revive and rise up to mate and produce the next generation."

The temperature gauge had gone yellow, so he fitted the ice pack back in place and latched the top. The refrigerator hummed, restoring the chest to its previous temperature.

"There was a . . . I suppose you would call it a fad, once, for keeping ice owls. When another person came along with a suitable owl, the owners would allow them both to thaw so they could come back to life and mate. It was a long time ago, though. I don't know whether there are still any freezer owls alive but this one."

Another thing that might be the last of its kind. This apartment was full of reminders of extinction, as if Magister Pregaldin could not free his mind of the thought.

But this one struck Thorn differently, because the final tragedy had not taken place. There was still a hope of life. "I'll keep it safe," she promised gravely.

He smiled at her. It made him look strangely sad. "You are a little like an owl yourself," he said kindly. "Older than the years you have lived."

She thought, but did not say, that he was also like an owl—frozen for one hundred forty-one years.

They left the apartment together, she heading for home and he with a backpack over his shoulder, bound for the waystation.

––––––––

Thorn did not wait two days to revisit the apartment alone to do some true detective work.

It was the day of the Protector's funeral, and Glory to God was holding its breath in pious suspension. All businesses were closed, even in the Waste, while the mourning rituals went on. Whatever repercussions would come from the assassination, they would not occur this day. Still, Thorn wore the veil when she went out, because it gave her a feeling of invisibility.

The magister's apartment was very quiet and motionless when she let herself in. She checked on the plants and emptied the pail in order to give her presence the appearance of legitimacy. She then went into the magister's bedroom, ostensibly to check the freezer, but really to look around, for she had only been in there the one time. She studied the art-encrusted walls, the shaving mirror supported by mythical beasts, the armoire full of clothes that had once been fine but now were shabby and outmoded. As she was about to leave she spotted a large box—a hexagonal column about three feet tall—on a table in a corner. It was clearly an offworld artifact because it was made of wood. Many sorts of wood, actually: the surface was an inlaid honeycomb design. But there were no drawers, no cabinets, no way inside at all. Thorn immediately realized that it must be a puzzle box—and she wanted to get inside.

She felt all around it for sliding panels, levers, or springs, but could not find any, so she brought over a lamp to study it. The surface was a parquet of hexagons, but the colors were not arranged in a regular pattern. Most tiles were made from a blond-colored wood and a reddish wood, interrupted at irregular intervals by hexagons of chocolate, caramel, and black. It gave her the strong impression of a code or diagram, but she could not imagine what sort.

It occurred to her that perhaps she was making this more complex than necessary, and the top might come off. So she tried to lift it—and indeed it shifted up, but only about an inch, enough to disengage the top row of hexagons from the ones below. In that position she found she could turn the rows below. Apparently, it was like a cylinder padlock. Each row of hexagons was a tumbler that needed to be turned and aligned correctly for the box to open. She did not have the combination, but knowing the way Magister Pregaldin's Vind mind worked, she felt sure that there would be some hint, some way to figure it out.

Once more she studied the honeycomb inlay. There were six rows. The top one was most regular—six blond hexagons followed by six red hexagons, repeating around the circumference of the box. The patterns became more colorful in the lower rows, but always included the repeating line of six blond hexagons. For a while she experimented with spinning the rows to see if she could hit on something randomly, but soon gave up. Instead, she fetched her slate from her backpack and photographed the box, shifting it on the table to get the back. When she was done, she found that the top would no longer lock down in its original position. The instant Magister Pregaldin saw it, he would know that she had raised it. It was evidently meant as a tamper detector, and she had set it off. Now she needed to solve the puzzle, or explain to him why she had been prowling his apartment looking for evidence.

She walked home preoccupied. The puzzle was clearly about sixes—six sides, six rows, six hexagons in a row. She needed to think of formulas that involved sixes. When she reached home she went to her room and started transferring the box's pattern from the photos to a diagram so she could see it better. All that afternote she worked on it, trying to find algorithms that would produce the patterns she saw. Nothing seemed to work. The thought that she would fail, and have to confess to Magister Pregaldin, made her feeling of urgency grow. The anticipation of his disappointment and lost trust kept her up long after she should have pulled the curtains against the perpetual sun and gone to bed.

At about six hours forenote a strange dream came to her. She was standing before a tree whose trunk was a hexagonal pillar, and around it was twined a snake with Magister Pregaldin's eyes. It looked at her mockingly, then took its tail in its mouth.

She woke with the dream vivid in her mind. Lying there thinking, she remembered a story he had told her, about some Capellan magister named Kekule, who had deduced the ringlike structure of benzene after dreaming of a snake. She smiled with the thought that she had just had Kekule's dream.

Then she bounded out of bed and out her door, pounding down the spiral steps to the kitchen. Hunter and Maya were eating breakfast together when she erupted into the room.

"Hunter! Do you have any books on chemistry?" she said.

He regarded her as if she were demented. "Why?"

"I need to know about benzene!"

The two adults looked at each other, mystified. "I have an encyclopedia," he said.

"Can I go borrow it?"

"No. I'll find it for you. Now try to curb your enthusiasm for aromatic hydrocarbons till I've had my coffee."

He sat there tormenting her for ten minutes till he was ready to go up to his office and find the book for her. She took the disk saying, "Thanks, you're the best!" and flew upstairs with it. As soon as she found the entry on benzene her hunch was confirmed: it was a hexagonal ring of carbon atoms with hydrogens attached at the corners. By replacing hydrogens with different molecules you could create a bewildering variety of compounds.

So perhaps the formula she should have been looking for was not a mathematical one, but a chemical one. When she saw the diagrams for toluene, xylene, and mesitylene she began to see how it might work. Each compound was constructed from a benzene ring with methyl groups attached in different positions. Perhaps, then, each ring on the box represented a different compound and the objective was to somehow align the corners as they were shown in the diagrams. But which compounds?

Then the code of the inlaid woods came clear to her. The blond-colored hexagons were carbons, the red ones were hydrogens. The other colors probably stood for elements like nitrogen or oxygen. The chemical formulae were written right on the box for all to see.

After an hour of scribbling and looking up formulae, she was racing down the steps again with her solutions in her backpack. She grabbed a pastry from the kitchen and ate it on her way, praying that Magister Pregaldin would not have returned.

He had not. The apartment still seemed to be dozing in its emptiness. She went straight to the box. As she dialed each row to line up the corners properly, her excitement grew. When the last ring slid into place, a vertical crack appeared along one edge. The sides swung open on hinges to reveal compartments inside.

There were no gold or rubies, just papers. She took one from its slot and unfolded it. It was an intricate diagram composed of spidery lines connecting geometric shapes with numbers inside, as if to show relationships or pathways. There was no key, nor even a word written on it. The next one she looked at was all words, closely written to the very edges of the paper in a tiny, obsessive hand. In some places they seemed to be telling a surreal story about angels, magic papayas, and polar magnetism; in others they disintegrated into garbled nonsense. The next document was a map of sorts, with coastlines and roads inked in, and landmarks given allegorical names like Perfidy, Imbroglio, and Redemption Denied. The next was a complex chart of concentric circles divided into sections and labeled in an alphabet she had never seen before.

Either Magister Pregaldin was a madman or he was trying to keep track of something so secret that it had to be hidden under multiple layers of code. Thorn spread out each paper on the floor and took a picture of it, then returned it to its pigeonhole so she could puzzle over them at leisure. When she was done she closed the box and spun the rings to randomize them again. Now she could push the top back down and lock it in place.

She walked home a little disappointed, but feeling as if she had learned something about her tutor. There was an obsessive and paranoid quality about the papers that ill fitted the controlled and rational magister. Clearly, there were more layers to him than she had guessed.

When she got home, she trudged up the stairs to return the encyclopedia to Hunter. As she was raising her hand to knock on his office door, she heard a profane exclamation from within. Then Hunter came rocketing out. Without a glance at Thorn he shot down the stairs to the kitchen.

Thorn followed. He was brewing coffee and pacing. She sat on the steps and said, "What's the matter?"

He glanced up, shook his head, then it boiled out: "One of the suspects I have been following was murdered last night."

"Really?" So he *did* know of Gmintas in hiding. Or had known. Thinking it over, she said, "I guess it was a good time for a murder, in the middle of the mourning."

"It didn't happen here," he said irritably. "It was in Flaming Sword of Righteousness. Damn! We were days away from moving in on him. We had all the evidence to put him on trial before the Court of a Thousand Peoples. Now all that work has gone to waste."

She watched him pour coffee, then said, "What would have happened if the Court found him guilty?"

"He would have been executed," Hunter said. "There is not the slightest doubt. He was one of the worst. We've wanted him for decades. Now we'll never have justice; all we've got is revenge."

Thorn sat quiet then, thinking about justice and revenge, and why one was so right and the other so wrong, when they brought about the same result. "Who did it?" she asked at last.

"If I knew I'd track him down," Hunter said darkly.

He started back up the stairs with his coffee, and she had to move aside for him. "Hunter, why do you care so much about such an old crime?" she asked. "There are so many bad things going on today that need fixing."

He looked at her with a tight, unyielding expression. "To forget is to condone," he said. "Evil must know it will pay. No matter how long it takes."

––––––

"He's such a phoney," she said to Magister Pregaldin the next day.

She had returned to his apartment that morning to find everything as usual, except for a half-unpacked crate of new artworks in the middle of the living room. They had sat down to resume lessons as if nothing had changed, but neither of them could concentrate on differential equations. So Thorn told him about her conversation with Hunter.

"What really made him mad was that someone beat him," Thorn said. "It's not really about justice, it's about competition. He wants the glory of having bagged a notorious Gminta. That's why it has to be public. I guess that's the difference between justice and revenge: when it's justice somebody gets the credit."

Magister Pregaldin had been listening thoughtfully; now he said, "You are far too cynical for someone your age."

"Well, people are disappointing!" Thorn said.

"Yes, but they are also complicated. I would wager there is something about him you do not know. It is the only thing we can ever say about people with absolute certainty: that we don't know the whole story."

It struck Thorn that what he said was truer of him than of Hunter.

He rose from the table and said, "I want to give you a gift, Thorn. We'll call it our lesson for the day."

Intrigued, she followed him into his bedroom. He took the rug off the freezer and checked the temperature, then unplugged it. He then took a small two-wheeled dolly from a corner and tipped the freezer onto it.

"You're giving me the ice owl?" Thorn said in astonishment.

"Yes. It is better for you to have it; you are more likely than I to meet someone else with another one. All you have to do is keep it cold. Can you do that?"

"Yes!" Thorn said eagerly. She had never owned something precious, something unique. She had never even had a pet. She was awed by the fact that Magister Pregaldin would give her something he obviously prized so much. "No one has ever trusted me like this," she said.

"Well, you have trusted me," he murmured without looking. "I need to return some of the burden."

He helped her get it down the steps. Once onto the street, she was able to wheel it by herself. But before leaving, she threw her arms giddily around her tutor and said, "Thank you, Magister! You're the best teacher I've ever had."

Wheeling the freezer through the alley, she attracted the attention of some young Wasters lounging in front of a betel parlor, who called out loudly to ask if she had a private stash of beer in there, and if they could have some. When she scowled and didn't answer they laughed and called her a lush. By the time she got home, her exaltation had been jostled aside by disgust and fury at the place where she lived. She managed to wrestle the freezer up the stoop and over the threshold into the kitchen, but when she faced the narrow spiral stair, she knew this was as far as she could get without help. The kitchen was already crowded, and the only place she could fit the freezer in was under the table. As she was shoving it against the wall, Maya came down the stairs and said, "What are you doing?"

"I have to keep this freezer here," Thorn said.

"You can't put it there. It's not convenient."

"Will you help me carry it up to my room?"

"You're kidding."

"I didn't think so. Then it's got to stay here."

Maya rolled her eyes at the irrational acts of teenagers. Now Thorn was angry at her, too. "It has to stay plugged in," Thorn said strictly. "Do you think you can remember that?"

"What's in it?"

Thorn would have enjoyed telling her if she hadn't been angry. "A science experiment," she said curtly.

"Oh, I see. None of my business, right?"

"Right."

"Okay. It's a secret," Maya said in a playful tone, as if she were talking to a child. She reached out to tousle Thorn's hair, but Thorn knocked her hand away and left, taking the stairs two at a time.

In her room, Thorn gave way to rage at her unsatisfactory life. She didn't want to be a Waster anymore. She wanted to live in a house where she could have things of her own, not squat in a boyfriend's place, always one quarrel away from eviction. She wanted a life she could control. Most of all, she wanted to leave the Waste. She went to the window and looked down at the rusty ghetto below. Cynicism hung miasmatic over it, defiling everything noble and pure. The decadent sophistication left nothing unstained.

During dinner, Maya and Hunter were cross and sarcastic with each other, and Hunter ended up storming off into his office. Thorn went to her room and studied Magister Pregaldin's secret charts till the house was silent below. Then she crept down to the kitchen to check on the freezer. The temperature gauge was reassuringly low. She sat on the brick floor with her back to it, its gentle hum soothing against her spine, feeling a kinship with the owl inside. She envied it for its isolation from the dirty world. Packed away safe in ice, it was the one thing that would never grow up, never lose its innocence. One day it would come alive and erupt in glorious joy—but only if she could protect it. Even if she couldn't protect herself, there was still something she could keep safe.

As she sat there, the Note came, filling the air full and ringing through her body like a benediction. It seemed to be answering her unfocused yearning, as if the believers were right, and there really were a force looking over her, as she looked over the owl.

———

When she next came to Magister Pregaldin's apartment, he was busy filling the crate up again with treasures. Thorn helped him wrap artworks in packing material as he told her which planet each one came from. "Where are you sending them?" she asked.

"Offworld," he answered vaguely.

Together they lifted the lid onto the crate, and only then did Thorn see the shipping label that had brought it here. It was stamped with a burning red sword—the customs mark of the city-state Flaming Sword of Righteousness. "Is that where you were?" she said.

"Yes."

She was about to blurt out that Hunter's Gminta had been murdered there when a terrible thought seized her: What if he already knew? What if it were no coincidence?

They sat down to lessons under the head of the copper-horned beast, but Thorn was distracted. She kept looking at her tutor's large hands, so gentle when he handled his art, and wondering if they could be the hands of an assassin.

That night Hunter went out and Maya barricaded herself in her room, leaving Thorn the run of the house. She instantly let herself into Hunter's office to search for a list of Gmintas killed and brought to justice over the years. When she tried to access his files, she found they were heavily protected by password and encryption—and if she knew his personality, he probably had intrusion detectors set. So she turned again to his library of books on the Holocide. The information was scattered and fragmentary, but after a few hours she had pieced together a list of seven mysterious murders on five planets that seemed to be revenge slayings.

Up in her room again, she took out her replica of one of Magister Pregaldin's charts, the one that looked most like a tracking chart. She started by assuming that the geometric shapes meant planets and the symbols represented individual Gmintas he had been following. After an hour she gave it up—not because she couldn't make it match, but because she could never prove it. A chart for tracking Gmintas would look identical to a chart for tracking artworks. It was the perfect cover story.

She was still awake when Hunter returned. As she listened to his footsteps she thought of going downstairs and telling him of her suspicions. But uncertainty kept her in bed, restless and wondering what was the right thing to do.

———

There were riots in the city the next day. In the streets far above the Waste, angry mobs flowed, a turbulent tide crashing against the Protectorate troops wherever they met. The Wasters kept close to home, looking up watchfully toward the palace, listening to the rumors that ran ratlike between the buildings. Thorn spent much of the day on the roof, a self-appointed lookout. About five hours afternote, she heard a roar from above, as of many voices raised at once. There was something elemental about the sound, as if a force of nature had broken into the domed city—a human eruption, shaking the iron framework on which all their lives depended.

She went down to the front door to see if she could catch any news. Her survival instincts were alert now, and when she spotted a little group down the street, standing on a doorstep exchanging news, she sprinted toward them to hear what they knew.

"The Incorruptibles have taken the Palace," a man told her in a low voice. "The mobs are looting it now."

"Are we safe?" she asked.

He only shrugged. "For now." They all glanced down the street toward the spike-topped gates of the Waste. The barrier had never looked flimsier.

When Thorn returned home, Maya was sitting in the kitchen looking miserable. She didn't react much to the news. Thorn sat down at the table with her, bumping her knees on the freezer underneath.

"Shouldn't we start planning to leave?" Thorn said.

"I don't want to leave," Maya said, tears coming to her already-red eyes.

"I don't either," Thorn said. "But we shouldn't wait till we don't have a choice."

"Hunter will protect us," Maya said. "He knows who to pay."

Frustrated, Thorn said, "But if the Incorruptibles take over, there won't *be* anyone to pay. That's why they call themselves incorruptible."

"It won't come to that," Maya said stubbornly. "We'll be all right. You'll see."

Thorn had heard it all before. Maya always denied that anything was wrong until everything fell apart. She acted as if planning for the worst would make it happen.

The next day the city was tense but quiet. The rumors said that the Incorruptibles were still hunting down Protectorate loyalists and throwing them in jail. The nearby streets were empty except for Wasters, so Thorn judged it safe enough to go to Weezer Alley. When she entered Magister Pregaldin's place, she was stunned at the change. The apartment had been stripped of its artworks. The carpets were rolled up, the empty walls looked dented and peeling. Only Jemma's portrait still remained. Two metal crates stood in the middle of the living room, and as Thorn was taking it all in, a pair of movers arrived to carry them off to the waystation.

"You're leaving," she said to Magister Pregaldin when he came back in from supervising the movers. She was not prepared for the disappointment she felt. All this time she had been trustworthy and kept his secrets—and he had abandoned her anyway.

"I'm sorry, Thorn," he said, reading her face. "It is becoming too dangerous here. You and your mother ought to think of leaving, as well."

"Where are you going?"

He paused. "It would be better if I didn't tell you that."

"I'm not going to tell anyone."

"Forgive me. It's a habit." He studied her for a few moments, then put his hand gently on her shoulder. "Your friendship has meant more to me than you can know," he said. "I had forgotten what it was like, to inspire such pure trust."

He didn't even know she saw through him. "You're lying to me," she said. "You've been lying all along. You're not leaving because of the Incorruptibles. You're leaving because you've finished what you came here to do."

He stood motionless, his hand still on her shoulder. "What do you mean?"

"You came here to settle an old score," she said. "That's what your life is about, isn't it? Revenge for something everyone else has forgotten and you can't let go."

He withdrew his hand. "You have made some strange mistake."

"You and Hunter—I don't understand either of you. Why can't you just stop digging up the past and move on?"

For several moments he stared at her, but his eyes were shifting as if tracking things she couldn't see. When he finally spoke, his voice was very low. "I don't *choose* to remember the past. I am compelled to—it is my punishment. Or perhaps it is a disease, or an addiction. I don't know."

Taken aback at his earnestness, Thorn said, "Punishment? For what?"

"Here, sit down," he said. "I will tell you a story before we part."

They both sat at the table where he had given her so many lessons, but before he started to speak he stood up again and paced away, his hands clenching. She waited silently, and he came back to face her, and started to speak.

————

This is a story about a young man who lived long ago. I will call him Till. He wanted badly to live up to his family's distinguished tradition. It was a prominent family, you see; for generations they had been involved in finance, banking, and insurance. The planet where they lived was relatively primitive and poor, but Till's family felt they were helping it by attracting outside investment and extending credit. Of course, they did very well by doing good.

The government of their country had been controlled by the Alloes for years. Even though the Alloes were an ethnic minority, they were a diligent people and had prospered by collaborating with Vind businessmen like Till's family. The Alloes ruled over the majority, the Gmintas, who had less of everything—less education, less money, less power. It was an unjust situation, and when there was a mutiny in the military and the Gmintas took control, the Vinds accepted the change. Especially to younger people like Till, it seemed like a righting of many historical wrongs.

Once the Gminta army officers were in power, they started borrowing heavily to build hospitals, roads, and schools for Gminta communities, and the Vind banks were happy to make the loans. It seemed like a good way to dispel many suspicions and prejudices that throve in the ignorance of the Gminta villages. Till was on the board of his family bank, and he argued for extending credit even after the other bankers became concerned about the government's reckless fiscal policies.

One day, Till was called into the offices of the government banking regulators. Alone in a small room, they accused him of money laundering and corruption. It was completely untrue, but they had forged documents that seemed to prove it. Till realized that he faced a life in prison. He would bring shame to his entire family, unless he could strike a deal. They offered him an alternative that was surprisingly generous, considering the evidence against him: he could come to work for the government, as their representative to the Vind community. He readily accepted the job, and resigned from the bank.

They gave him an office and a small staff. He had an Alloe counterpart responsible for outreach to that community; and though they never spoke about it, he suspected his colleague had been recruited with similar methods. They started out distributing informational leaflets and giving tips on broadcast shows, all quite bland. But it changed when the government decided to institute a new draft policy for military service. Every young person was to give five years' mandatory service starting at eighteen. The Vinds would not be exempt.

Now, as you may know, the Vinds are pacifists and mystics, and have never served in the military of any planet. This demand by the Gminta government was unprecedented, and caused great alarm. The Vinds gathered in the halls of their Ethical Congresses to discuss what to do. Till worked tirelessly, meeting with them and explaining the perspective of the government, reminding them of the Vind principle of obeying the local law wherever they found themselves. At the same time, he managed to get the generals to promise that no Vind would be required to serve in combat, which was utterly in violation of their beliefs. With this assurance, the Vinds reluctantly agreed. And so mothers packed bags for their children and sent them off to training, urging them to call often.

Soon after, a new land policy was announced. Estates that had always belonged to the Alloes were to be redistributed among landless Gmintas. This created quite a lot of resistance; Till and his colleague were kept busy giving interviews and explaining how the policy restored fairness to the land system. They became familiar to all as government spokespeople.

Then the decision was made to relocate whole neighborhoods of Alloes and Vinds so Gmintas could have better housing in the cities. Till could no longer argue about justice; now he could only tell people it was necessary to move in order to quiet the fears of the Gmintas and preserve peace. He was assigned to work with an officer who was in charge of setting up new housing for evacuees, but he could get no specifics about where the housing was or what would be provided.

People started to emigrate off-planet, but then the government closed down the waystations. This nearly caused a panic, and Till had to tell everyone it was merely to prevent people from taking their goods and assets offworld, thus draining the national wealth. He promised that individuals would be allowed to leave again soon, as long as they took no cash or valuables with them.

He no longer believed it himself.

It had been months since the young people had gone off to the army, and their families had heard nothing from them. Till had been telling everyone it was a period of temporary isolation, while the trainees lived in camps on the frontier to build solidarity and camaraderie. Every time he went out, he would be surrounded by anxious parents asking when they could expect to hear from their children.

Fleets of buses showed up to evacuate the Alloe and Vind families from their homes, and take them to relocation camps. Till watched his own neighborhood become a ghost town, and the certainty grew in him that the people were never coming back. One day he entered his supervisor's office unexpectedly and overheard someone saying, ". . .to the mortifactories." They stopped talking when they saw him.

You are probably thinking, 'Why didn't he speak out? Why didn't he denounce them?' Try to imagine, in many respects life still seemed quite normal, and what he suspected was so unthinkable it seemed insane. And even if he could overcome that, there was no one to speak out to. He was alone, and he was not a very courageous person. His only chance was to stay useful to the government.

Other Vinds and Alloes who had been working alongside him started to vanish. Still the Gmintas wanted him to go on reassuring people; he did it so well. He had to hide what he suspected, to fool them into thinking that he was fooled himself. Every day he lived in fear of hearing the knock on his door that would mean it was his time.

It was his Alloe colleague who finally broke. They rarely let the man go on air anymore; his nerves were too shattered. But one day he substituted for Till, and in the midst of a broadcast shouted out a warning: 'They are killing you! It is mass murder!' That was all he got out before they cut him off.

That night, well-armed and well-organized mobs broke into the remaining Alloe enclaves in the capital city. The government deplored the violence the next day, but suggested that the Alloes had incited it.

At that point they no longer had any need for Till. Once again, they were very generous. They gave him a choice: relocation or deportation. He could join his family and share their fate; or he could leave the planet. Death or life. I think I have mentioned he was not very courageous. He chose to live.

They sent him to Capella Two, a twenty-five-year journey. By the time he arrived, the entire story had traveled ahead of him by pepci, and everything was known. His own role was infamous. He was the vile collaborator who had put a benign face on the crime. He had soothed people's fears and deceived them into walking docilely to their deaths. In hindsight, it was inconceivable that he had not known what he was doing. All across the Twenty Planets, the name of Till Diwali was reviled.

He fell silent at last. Thorn sat staring at the tabletop, because she could not sort out what to think. It was all wheeling about in her mind: right and wrong, horror and sympathy, criminal and victim—all were jumbled together. Finally she said, "Was Jemma your sister?"

"I told you, I was not there," he said in a distant voice. "The man who did those things was not me."

He was sitting at the table across from her again, his hands clasped before him. Now he spoke to her directly. "Thorn, you are unitary and authentic now as you will never be again. As you pass through life, you will accumulate other selves. Always you will be a person looking back on, and separate from, the person you are now. Whenever you walk down a street, or sit on a park bench, your past selves will be sitting beside you, impossible to touch or interrogate. In the end there is a whole crowd of you wherever you go, and you feel like you will perish from the loneliness."

Thorn's whirling feelings were beginning to come to rest in a pattern, and in it horror and blame predominated. She looked up at Jemma's face and said, "She *died*. How could you do that, and walk away? It's inhuman."

He didn't react, either to admit guilt or defend his innocence. She wanted an explanation from him, and he didn't give it. "You're a monster," she said.

Still he said nothing. She got up, blind to everything but the intensity of her thoughts, and went to the door. She glanced back before leaving, and he was looking at her with an expression that was nothing like what he ought to feel—not shame, not rage, not self-loathing. Thorn slammed the door behind her and fled.

She walked around the streets of the Waste for a long time, viciously throwing stones at heaps of trash to make the rats come out. Above the buildings, the sky seemed even redder than usual, and the shadows blacker. She was furious at the magister for not being admirable. She blamed him for hiding it from her and for telling her—since, by giving her the knowledge, he had also given her a responsibility of choosing what to do.

———

When she got home the kitchen was empty, but she heard voices from the living room above. She was mounting the stairs when the voices rose in anger, and she froze. It was Hunter and Maya, and they were yelling at each other.

"Good God, what were you thinking?" Hunter demanded.

"She needed help. I couldn't say no."

"You knew it would bring the authorities down on us!"

"I had a responsibility—"

"What about your responsibility to me? You just didn't think. You never think; everything is impulse with you. You are the most immature and manipulative person I've ever met."

Maya's voice went wheedling. "Hunter, come on. It'll be okay."

"And what if it's not okay? What are you going to do then? Just pick up and leave the wreckage behind you? That's what you've been doing all your life—dragging that kid of yours from planet to planet, never thinking what it's doing to her. You never think what you're doing to anyone, do you? It's all just yourself. I never should have let you in here."

There were angry footsteps, and then Hunter was mounting the stairs.

"Hunter!" Maya cried after him.

Thorn waited a minute, then crept up into the living room. Maya was sitting there, looking tragic and beautiful.

"What did you do?" Thorn said.

"It doesn't matter," Maya said. "He'll get over it."

"I don't care about Hunter."

Mistaking what she meant, Maya smiled through her tears. "You know what? I don't care either." She came over and hugged Thorn tight. "I'm not really a bad mother, am I, Thorn?"

Cautiously, Thorn said, "No . . ."

"People just don't understand us. We're a team, right?"

Maya held out her hand for their secret finger-hook. Once it would have made Thorn smile, but she no longer felt the old solidarity against the world. She hooked fingers anyway, because she was afraid Maya would start to cry again if she didn't. Maya said, "They just don't know you. Damaged child, poppycock—you're tough as old boots. It makes me awestruck, what a survivor you are."

"I think we ought to get ready to leave," Thorn said.

Maya's face lost its false cheer. "I can't leave," she whispered.

"Why not?"

"Because I love him."

There was no sensible answer to that. So Thorn turned away to go up to her room. As she passed the closed door of Hunter's office, she paused, wondering if she should knock. Wondering if she should turn in the most notorious Gminta collaborator still alive. All those millions of dead Alloes and Vinds would get their justice, and Hunter would be famous. Then her feet continued on, even before she consciously made the decision. It was not loyalty to Magister Pregaldin, and it was not resentment of Hunter. It was because she might need that information to buy her own safety.

———

The sound of breaking glass woke her. She lay tense, listening to footsteps and raised voices below in the street. Then another window broke, and she got up to pull back the curtain. The sun was orange, as always, and she squinted in the glare, then raised her window and climbed out on the roof.

Below in the street, a mob of white-clad Incorruptibles was breaking windows as they passed; but their true target obviously lay deeper in the Waste. She watched till they were gone, then waited to see what would happen.

From somewhere beyond the tower fans of the park she could hear shouts and clanging, and once an avalanche-like roar, after which a cloud of dust rose from the direction of Weezer Alley. After that there was silence for a while. At last she heard chanting. Fleeing footsteps passed below. Then the wall of Incorruptibles appeared again. They were driving some-one before them with improvised whips made from their belts. Thorn peered over the eaves to see more clearly and recognized their victim— Ginko, the heshe from the Garden of Delights, completely naked, both breasts and genitals exposed, with a rope around hisher neck. The whips had cut into the delicate paisley of Ginko's skin, exposing slashes of red underneath.

At a spot beneath Thorn's perch, Ginko stumbled and fell. A mass of Incorruptibles gathered round. Two of them pulled Ginko's legs apart, and a third made a jerking motion with a knife. A womanlike scream made Thorn grip the edge of her rooftop, wanting to look away. They tossed the rope over a signpost and hoisted Ginko up by the neck, choking and clawing at the noose. The body still quivered as the army marched past. When they were gone, the silence was so complete Thorn could hear the patter of blood into a pool on the pavement under the body.

On hands and knees she backed away from the edge of the roof and climbed into her bedroom. It was already stripped; everything she valued or needed was in her backpack, ready to go. She threw on some clothes and went down the stairs.

Maya, dressed in a robe, stopped her halfway. She looked scattered and panicky. "Thorn, we've got to leave," she said.

"Right now?"

"Yes. He doesn't want us here anymore. He's acting as if we're some sort of danger to him."

"Where are we going?"

"I don't know. Some other planet. Some place without men." She started to cry.

"Go get dressed," Thorn told her. "I'll bring some food." Over her shoulder she added, "Pack some clothes and money."

With her backpack in hand, Thorn raced down to the kitchen.

She was just getting out the dolly for the ice owl's refrigerator when Maya came down.

"You're not taking that, are you?" Maya said.

"Yes, I am." Thorn knelt to shift the refrigerator out from under the table, and only then noticed it wasn't running. Quickly, she checked the temperature gauge. It was in the red zone, far too high. With an anguished exclamation, she punched in the lock code and opened the top. Not a breath of cool air escaped. The ice pack on top was gurgling and liquid. She lifted it to see what was underneath.

The owl was no longer nested snugly in ice. It had shifted, tried to open its wings. There were scratches on the insulation where it had tried to peck and claw its way out. Now it lay limp, its head thrown back. Thorn sank to her knees, grief-struck before the evidence of its terrifying last minutes—revived to life only to find itself trapped in a locked chest. Even in that stifling dark, it had longed for life so much it had fought to free itself. Thorn's breath came hard and her heart labored, as if she were reliving the ice owl's death.

"Hurry up, Thorn," Maya said. "We've got to go."

Then she saw what had happened. The refrigerator cord lay on the floor, no longer attached to the wall outlet. She held it up as if it were a murder weapon. "It's unplugged," she said.

"Oh, that's right," Maya said, distracted. "I had to plug in the curling iron. I must have forgotten."

Rage rose inside Thorn like a huge bubble of compressed air. "You *forgot?*"

"I'm sorry, Thorn. I didn't know it was important."

"I *told* you it was important. This was the last ice owl anywhere. You haven't just killed this one, you've killed the entire species."

"I said I was sorry. What do you want me to do?"

Maya would never change. She would always be like this, careless and irresponsible, unable to face consequences. Tears of fury came to Thorn's eyes. She dashed them away with her hand. "You're useless," she said, climbing to her feet and picking up her pack. "You can't be trusted to take care of anything. I'm done with you. Don't bother to follow me."

Out in the street, she turned in the direction she never went, to avoid having to pass what was hanging in the street. Down a narrow alley she sprinted, past piles of stinking refuse alive with roaches, till she came to a narrow side street that doglegged into the park. On the edge of the open space she paused under a portico to scan for danger; seeing none, she dashed across, past the old men's chess tables, past the bench where she had met Magister Pregaldin, to the entrance of Weezer Alley.

Signs of the Incorruptibles' passage were everywhere. Broken glass crunched underfoot and the contents of the shops were trampled under red dirt shoeprints. When Thorn reached the Garden of Delights, the entire street looked different, for the building had been demolished. Only a monstrous pile of rubble remained, with iron girders and ribs sticking up like broken bones. A few people climbed over the ruin, looking for survivors.

The other side of the street was still standing, but Magister Pregaldin's door had been ripped from its hinges and tossed aside. Thorn dashed up the familiar stairs. The apartment looked as if it had been looted—stripped bare, not a thing of value left. She walked through the empty rooms, dreading what she might find, and finding nothing. Out on the street again, she saw a man who had often winked at her when she passed by to her lessons. "Do you know what happened to Magister Pregaldin?" she asked. "Did he get away?"

"Who?" the man said.

"Magister Pregaldin. The man who lived here."

"Oh, the old Vind. No, I don't know where he is."

So he had abandoned her as well. In all the world, there was no one trustworthy. For a moment she had a dark wish that she had exposed his secret. Then she realized she was just thinking of revenge.

Hoisting her pack to her shoulder, she set out for the waystation. She was alone now, only herself to trust.

There was a crowd in the street outside the waystation. Everyone seemed to have decided to leave the planet at once, some of them with huge piles of baggage and children. Thorn pushed her way in toward the ticket station to find out what was going on. They were still selling tickets, she saw with relief; the crowd was people waiting for their turn in the translation chamber. Checking to make sure she had her copy of Maya's credit stick, she joined the ticket line. She was back among her own kind, the rootless, migrant elite.

Where was she going? She scanned the list of destinations. She had been born on Capella Two, but had heard it was a harshly competitive place, so she decided against it. Ben was just an ice-ball world, Gammadis was too far away. It was both thrilling and frightening to have control over where she went and what she did. She was still torn by indecision when she heard someone calling, "Thorn!"

Clarity was pushing through the crowd toward her. "I'm so glad we found you," she said when she drew close. "Maya was here a little while ago, looking for you."

"Where is she now?" Thorn asked, scanning the crowd.

"She left again."

"Good," Thorn said.

"Thorn, she was frantic. She was afraid you'd get separated."

"We *are* separated," Thorn said implacably. "She can do what she wants. I'm on my own now. Where are you going, Clarity?"

Bick had come up, carrying their ticket cards. Thorn caught her hand to look at the tickets. "Alananovis," she read aloud, then looked up to find it on the directory. It was only eighteen light-years distant. "Can I come with you?"

"Not without Maya," Clarity said.

"Okay, then I'll go somewhere else."

Clarity put a hand on her arm. "Thorn, you can't just go off without Maya."

"Yes, I can. I'm old enough to be on my own. I'm sick of her, and I'm sick of her boyfriends. I want control of my life." Besides, Maya had killed the ice owl; Maya ought to suffer. It was only justice.

She had reached the head of the line. Her eye caught a name on the list, and she made a snap decision. When the ticket seller said "Where to?" she answered, "Gmintagad." She would go to see where Jemma Diwali had lived—and died.

———

The translation chamber on Gmintagad was like all the others she had seen over the years: sterile and anonymous. A technician led her into a waiting room till her luggage came through by the low-resolution beam. She sat feeling cross and tired, as she always did after having her molecules reassembled out of new atoms. When at last her backpack was delivered and she went on into the customs and immigration facility, she noticed a change in the air. For the first time in years she was breathing organically manufactured oxygen. She could smell the complex and decay-laden odor of an actual ecosystem. Soon she would see sky without any dome. The thought gave her an agoraphobic thrill.

She put her identity card into the reader, and after a pause it directed her to a glass-fronted booth where an immigration official in a sand-colored uniform sat behind a desk. Unlike the air, the man looked manufactured—a face with no wrinkles, defects, or stand-out features, as if they had chosen him to match a mathematical formula for facial symmetry. His hair was neatly clipped, and so, she noticed, were his nails. When she sat opposite him, she found that her chair creaked at the slightest movement. She tried to hold perfectly still.

He regarded her information on his screen, then said, "Who is your father?"

She had been prepared to say why her mother was not with her, but her father? "I don't know," she said. "Why?"

"Your records do not state his race."

His *race*? It was an antique concept she barely understood. "He was Capellan," she said.

"Capellan is not an origin. No one evolved on Capella."

"I did," Thorn stated.

He studied her without any expression at all. She tried to meet his eyes, but it began to seem confrontational, so she looked down. Her chair creaked.

"There are certain types of people we do not allow on Gmintagad," he said.

She tried to imagine what he meant. Criminals? Disease carriers? Agitators? He could see she wasn't any of those. "Wasters, you mean?" she finally ventured.

"I mean Vinds," he said.

Relieved, she said, "Oh, well that's all right, then. I'm not Vind." Creak.

"Unless you can tell me who your father was, I cannot be sure of that," he said.

She was speechless. How could a father she had never known have any bearing on who she was?

The thought that they might not let her in made her stomach knot. Her chair sent out a barrage of telegraphic signals. "I just spent thirty-two years as a lightbeam to get here," she said. "You've got to let me stay."

"We are a sovereign principality," he said calmly. "We don't *have* to let anyone stay." He paused, his eyes still on her. "You have a Vind look. Are you willing to submit to a genetic test?"

Minutes ago, her mind had seemed like syrup. Now it bubbled with alarm. In fact, she didn't *know* her father wasn't Vind. It had never mattered, so she had never cared. But here, all the things that defined her—her interests, her aptitudes, her internal doubts—none of it counted, only her racial status. She was in a place where identity was assigned, not chosen or created.

"What happens if I fail the test?" she asked.

"You will be sent back."

"And what happens if I don't take it?"

"You will be sent back."

"Then why did you even ask?"

He gave a regulation smile. If she had measured it with a ruler, it would have been perfect. She stood up, and the chair sounded like it was laughing. "All right. Where do I go?"

They took her blood and sent her into a waiting room with two doors, neither of which had a handle. As she sat there idle, the true rashness of what she had done crept up on her. It wasn't like running away on-planet. Maya didn't know where she had gone. By now, they would be different ages. Maya could be dying, or Thorn could be older than she was, before they ever found each other. It was a permanent separation. And permanent punishment for Maya.

Thorn tried to summon up the righteous anger that had propelled her only an hour and thirty-two years before. But even that slipped from her grasp. It was replaced with a clutching feeling of her own guilt. She had known Maya's shortcomings when she took the ice owl, and never bothered to safeguard against them. She had known all the accidents the world was capable of; and still she had failed to protect a creature that could not protect itself.

Now, remorse made her bleed inside. The owl had been too innocent to meet such a terrible end. Its life should have been a joyous ascent into air, and instead it had been a hellish struggle, alone and forgotten, killed by neglect. Thorn had betrayed everyone by letting the ice owl die. Magister Pregaldin, who had trusted her with his precious possession. Even, somehow, Jemma and the other victims of Till Diwali's crime—for what had she done but re-enact his failure, as if to show that human beings had learned nothing? She felt as if caught in an iron-bound cycle of history, doomed to repeat what had gone before, as long as she was no better than her predecessors had been.

She covered her face with her hands, wanting to cry, but too demoralized even for that. It seemed like a self-indulgence she didn't deserve.

The door clicked and she started up at sight of a stern, rectangular woman in a uniform skirt, whose face held the hint of a sneer. Thorn braced for the news that she would have to waste another thirty-two years on a pointless journey back to Glory to God. But instead, the woman said, "There is someone here to see you."

Behind her was a familiar face that made Thorn exclaim in joy, "Clarity!"

Clarity came into the room, and Thorn embraced her in relief. "I thought you were going to Alananovis."

"We were," Clarity said, "but we decided we couldn't just stand by and let a disaster happen. I followed you, and Bick stayed behind to tell Maya where we were going."

"Oh, thank you, thank you!" Thorn cried. Now the tears that had refused to come before were running down her face. "But you gave up thirty-two years for a stupid reason."

"It wasn't stupid for us," Clarity said. "You were the stupid one."

"I know," Thorn said miserably.

Clarity was looking at her with an expression of understanding. "Thorn, most people your age are allowed some mistakes. But you're performing life without a net. You have to consider Maya. Somehow, you've gotten older than she is even though you've been traveling together. You're the steady one, the rock she leans on. These boyfriends, they're just entertainment for her. They drop her and she bounces back. But if you dropped her, her whole world would dissolve."

Thorn said, "That's not true."

"It *is* true," Clarity said.

Thorn pressed her lips together, feeling impossibly burdened. Why did *she* have to be the reliable one, the one who was never vulnerable or wounded? Why did Maya get to be the dependent one?

On the other hand, it was a comfort that she hadn't abandoned Maya as she had done to the ice owl. Maya was not a perfect mother, but neither was Thorn a perfect daughter. They were both just doing their best.

"I hate this," she said, but without conviction. "Why do I have to be responsible for her?"

"That's what love is all about," Clarity said.

"You're a busybody, Clarity," Thorn said.

Clarity squeezed her hand. "Yes. Aren't you lucky?"

The door clicked open again. Beyond the female guard's square shoulder, Thorn glimpsed a flash of honey-gold hair. "Maya!" she said.

When she saw Thorn, Maya's whole being seemed to blaze like the sun. Dodging in, she threw her arms around Thorn.

"Oh Thorn, thank heaven I found you! I was worried sick. I thought you were lost."

"It's okay, it's okay," Thorn kept saying as Maya wept and hugged her again. "But Maya, you have to tell me something."

"Anything. What?"

"Did you seduce a *Vind*?"

For a moment Maya didn't understand. Then a secretive smile grew on her face, making her look very pretty and pleased with herself. She touched Thorn's hair. "I've been meaning to tell you about that."

"Later," Bick said. "Right now, we all have tickets for Alananovis."

"That's wonderful," Maya said. "Where's Alananovis?"

"Only seven years away from here."

"Fine. It doesn't matter. Nothing matters as long as we're together."

She held out her finger for the secret finger-lock. Thorn did it with a little inward sigh. For a moment she felt as if her whole world were composed of vulnerable beings frozen in time, as if she were the only one who aged and changed.

"We're a team, right?" Maya said anxiously.

"Yeah," Thorn answered. "We're a team."

WEEP FOR DAY

INDRAPRAMIT DAS

I WAS EIGHT years old the first time I saw a real, living Nightmare. My parents took my brother and I on a trip from the City-of-Long-Shadows to the hills at Evening's edge, where one of my father's clients had a manse. Father was a railway contractor. He hired out labor and resources to the privateers extending the frontiers of civilization toward the frozen wilderness of the dark Behind-the-Sun. Aptly, we took a train up to the foothills of the great Penumbral Mountains.

It was the first time my brother and I had been on a train, though we'd seen them tumble through the city with their cacophonic engines, cumulous tails of smoke and steam billowing like blood over the rooftops when the red light of our sun caught them. It was also the first time we had been anywhere close to Night—Behind-the-Sun—where the Nightmares lived. Just a decade before we took that trip, it would have been impossible to go as far into Evening as we were doing with such casual comfort and ease.

Father had prodded the new glass of the train windows, pointing to the power-lines crisscrossing the sky in tandem with the gleaming lines of metal railroads silvering the hazy landscape of progress. He sat between my brother Velag and I, our heads propped against the bulk of his belly, which bulged against his rough crimson waistcoat. I clutched that coat and breathed in the sweet smell of chemlis gall that hung over him. Mother watched with a smile as she peeled indigos for us with her fingers, laying them in the lap of her skirt.

"Look at that. We've got no more reason to be afraid of the dark, do we, my tykes?" said Father, his belly humming with the sound of his booming voice.

Dutifully, Velag and I agreed there wasn't.

"Why not?" he asked us, expectant.

"Because of the Industrialization, which brings the light of Day to the darkness of Night," we chimed, a line learned both in school and home (inaccurate, as we'd never set foot in Night itself). Father laughed. I always slowed down on the word "industrialization," which caused Velag and I to say it at different times. He was just over a year older than me, though.

"And what is your father, children?" Mother asked.

"A knight of Industry and Technology, bringer of light under Church and Monarchy."

I didn't like reciting that part, because it had more than one long "y" word, and felt like a struggle to say. Father *was* actually a knight, though not a knight-errant for a while. He had been too big by then to fit into a suit of plate-armor or heft a heavy sword around, and knights had stopped doing that for many years anyway. The Industrialization had swiftly made the pageantry of adventure obsolete.

Father wheezed as we reminded him of his knighthood, as if ashamed. He put his hammy hands in our hair and rubbed. I winced through it, as usual, because he always forgot about the pins in my long hair, something my brother didn't have to worry about. Mother gave us the peeled indigos, her hands perfumed with the citrus. She was the one who taught me how to place the pins in my hair, both of us in front of the mirror looking like different sized versions of each other.

I looked out the windows of our cabin, fascinated by how everything outside slowly became bluer and darker as we moved away from the City-of-Long-Shadows, which lies between the two hemispheres of Day and Night. Condensation crawled across the corners of the double-glazed panes as the train took us farther east. Being a studious girl even at that age, I deduced from school lessons that the air outside was becoming rapidly colder as we neared Night's hemisphere, which has never seen a single ray of our sun and is theorized to be entirely frozen. The train, of course, was kept warm by the same steam and machinery that powered its tireless wheels and kept its lamps and twinkling chandeliers aglow.

"Are you excited to see the Nightmare? It was one of the first to be captured and tamed. The gentleman we're visiting is very proud to be its captor," said Father.

"Yes!" screamed Velag. "Does it still have teeth? And claws?" he asked, his eyes wide.

"I would think so." Father nodded.

"Is it going to be in chains?"

"I hope so, Velag. Otherwise it might get loose and . . ." he paused for dramatic effect. I froze in fear. Velag looked eagerly at him. "Eat you both up!" he bellowed, tickling us with his huge hands. It took all my willpower not to scream. I looked at Velag's delighted expression to keep me calm, reminding myself that these were just Father's hands jabbing my sides.

"Careful!" Mother said sharply, to my relief. "They'll get the fruit all over." The indigo segments were still in our laps, on the napkins Mother had handed to us. Father stopped tickling us, still grinning.

"Do you remember what they look like?" Velag asked, as if trying to see how many questions he could ask in as little time as possible. He had asked this one before, of course. Father had fought Nightmares, and even killed some, when he was a knight-errant.

"We never really saw them, son," said Father. He touched the window. "Out there, it's so cold you can barely feel your own fingers, even in armor."

We could see the impenetrable walls of the forests pass us by—shaggy, snarled mare-pines, their leaves black as coals and branches supposedly twisted into knots by the Nightmares to tangle the path of intruders. The high, hoary tops of the trees shimmered ever so slightly in the scarce light sneaking over the horizon, which they sucked in so hungrily. The moon was brighter here than in the City, but at its jagged crescent, a broken gemstone behind the scudding clouds. We were still in Evening, but had encroached onto the Nightmares' outer territories, marked by the forests that extended to the foothills. After the foothills, there was no more forest, because there was no more light. Inside our cabin, under bright electric lamps, sitting on velvet-lined bunks, it was hard to believe that we were actually in the land of Nightmares. I wondered if they were in the trees right now, watching our windows as we looked out.

"It's hard to see them, or anything, when you're that cold, and," Father breathed deeply, gazing at the windows. "They're very hard to see." It made me uneasy, hearing him say the same thing over and over. We were passing the very forests he travelled through as a knight-errant, escorting pioneers.

"Father's told you about this many times, dear," Mother interjected, peering at Father with worried eyes. I watched. Father smiled at her and shook his head.

"That's alright, I like telling my little tykes about my adventures. I guess you'll see what a Nightmare looks like tomorrow, eh? Out in the open. Are you excited?" he asked, perhaps forgetting that he'd already asked. Velag shouted in the affirmative again.

Father looked down at me, raising his bushy eyebrows. "What about you, Valyzia?"

I nodded and smiled.

I wasn't excited. Truth be told, I didn't want to see it at all. The idea of capturing and keeping a Nightmare seemed somehow disrespectful in my heart, though I didn't know the word then. It made me feel weak and confused, because I was and always had been so afraid of them, and had been taught to be.

I wondered if Velag had noticed that Father had once again refused to actually describe a Nightmare. Even in his most excitable retellings of his brushes with them, he never described them as more than walking shadows. There was a grainy sepia-toned photograph of him during his younger vigils as a knight-errant above the mantle of our living room fireplace. It showed him mounted on a horse, dressed in his plate-armor and fur-lined surcoat, raising his longsword to the skies (the blade was cropped from the picture by its white border). Clutched in his other plated hand was something that looked like a blot of black, as if the chemicals of the photograph had congealed into a spot, attracted by some mystery or heat. The shape appeared to bleed back into the black background.

It was, I had been told, the head of a Nightmare Father had slain. It was too dark a thing to be properly caught by whatever early photographic engine had captured his victory. The blot had no distinguishing features apart from two vague points emerging from the rest of it, like horns or ears. That head earned him a large part of the fortune he later used to start up his contracting business. We never saw it, because Nightmares' heads and bodies were burned or gibbeted by knights-errant, who didn't want to bring them into the City for fear of attracting their horde. The photograph had been a source of dizzying pride for my young self, because it meant that my father was one of the bravest people I knew. At other times, it just made me wonder why he couldn't describe something he had once beheaded, and held in his hand as a trophy.

My indigo finished, Mother took the napkin and wiped my hands with it. My brother still picked at his. A waiter brought us a silver platter filled with sugar-dusted pastries, their centers soft with warm fudge and grünberry jam. We'd already finished off supper, brought under silver domes that gushed steam when the waiters raised them with their white-gloved hands, revealing chopped fungus, meat dumplings, sour cream, and fermented salad. Mother told Velag to finish the indigo before he touched the pastries. Father ate them with as much gusto as I did. I watched him lick his powdered fingers, that had once held the severed head of a Nightmare.

When it was time for respite, the cabin lights were shut off and the ones in the corridor were dimmed. I was relieved my parents left the curtains of the windows open as we retired, because I didn't want it to be completely dark. It was dim enough outside that we could fall asleep. It felt unusual to go to bed with windows uncovered for once.

I couldn't help imagine, as I was wont to do, that as our train moved through Evening's forested fringes, the Nightmares would find a way to get on board. I wondered if they were already on the train. But the presence of my family, all softly snoring in their bunks (Velag above me, my parents opposite us); the periodic, soothing flash of way-station lights passing by outside; the sigh of the sliding doors at the end of the carriage opening and closing as porters, waiters, and passengers moved through the corridors; the sweet smell of the fresh sheets and pillow on my bunk—these things lulled me into a sleep free of bad dreams, despite my fear of seeing the creature we'd named bad dreams after, face-to-face, the next vigil.

When I was six I stopped sleeping in my parents' room, and started sleeping in the same room as my brother. At the time of this change, I was abnormally scared of the dark (and consider, reader, that this was a time when fear of the dark was as normal and acceptable as the fear of falling from a great height). So scared that I couldn't fall sleep after the maids came around and closed our sleep-shutters and drew the curtains, to block out the western light for respite.

The heavy clatter of the wooden slats being closed every respite's eve was like a note of foreboding for me. I hunkered under the blankets, rigid with anxiety as the maids filed out of the room with their lanterns drawing wild shadows on the walls. Then the last maid would close the door, and our room would be swallowed up by those shadows.

In the chill darkness that followed, I would listen to the clicking of Nightmares' claws as they walked up and down the corridors of our shuttered house. Our parents had often told me that it was just rats in the walls and ceiling, but I refused to believe it. Every respite I would imagine one of the Nightmare intruders slinking into our room, listening to its breathing as it came closer to my bed and pounced on me, not being able to scream as it sat on my chest and ran its reeking claws through my hair, winding it into knots around its long fingers and laughing softly.

Enduring the silence for what seemed like hours, I would begin to wail and cry until Velag threw pillows at me and Mother came to my side to shush me with her kisses. To solve the problem, my parents tried keeping the sleep-shutters open through the hours of respite, and moved my brother to a room on the windowless east-facing side of the house when he complained. Unfortunately, we require the very dark we fear to fall asleep. The persistent burning line of the horizon beyond the windows, while a comforting sight, left me wide awake for most of respite.

In the end Velag and I were reunited and the shutters closed once more, because Father demanded that I not be coddled when my brother had learned to sleep alone so bravely. I often heard my parents arguing about this, since Mother thought it was madness to try and force me not to be afraid. Most of my friends from school hadn't and wouldn't sleep without their parents until they were at least eleven or twelve. Father was adamant, demanding that we learn to be strong and brave in case the Nightmares ever found a way to overrun the city.

It's a strange thing, to be made to feel guilty for learning too well something that was ingrained in us from the moment we were born. Now nightmare is just a word, and it's unusual to even think that the race that we gave that name might still be alive somewhere in the world. When Velag and I were growing up, Nightmares were the enemy.

Our grandparents told us about them, as did our parents, as did our teachers, as did every book and textbook we had ever come across. Stories of a time when guns hadn't been invented, when knights-errant roved the frigid forest paths beyond the City-of-Long-Shadows to prove their manhood and loyalty to the Monarchy and its Solar Church, and to extend the borders of the city and find new resources. A time coming to a close when I was born, even as the expansion continued onward faster than ever.

I remember my school class–teacher drawing the curtains and holding a candle to a wooden globe of our planet to show us how the sun made Night and Day. She took a piece of chalk and tapped where the candlelight turned to shadow on the globe. "That's us," she said, and moved the chalk over to the shadowed side. "That's them," she said.

Nightmares have defined who we are since we crawled out of the hot lakes at the edge of fiery Day, and wrapped the steaming bloody skins of slaughtered animals around us to walk upright, east into the cooler marches of our world's Evening. We stopped at the alien darkness we had never seen before, not just because of the terrible cold that clung to the air the farther we walked, but because of what we met at Evening's end.

A race of walking shadows, circling our firelight with glittering eyes, felling our explorers with barbed spears and arrows, snatching our dead as we fled from their ambushes. Silently, these unseen, lethal guardians of Night's bitter frontier told us we could go no farther. But we couldn't go back toward Day, where the very air seems to burn under the sun's perpetual gaze.

So we built our villages where sun's light still lingers and the shadows are longest before they dissolve into Evening. Our villages grew into towns, and our towns grew into the City-of-Long-Shadows, and our City grew along the Penumbra until it reached the Seas-of-Storms to the north and the impassable crags of World's-Rim (named long before we knew this to be false) to the south. For all of history, we looked behind our shoulders at the gloaming of the eastern horizon, where the Nightmares watched our progress.

So the story went, told over and over.

We named bad dreams after them because we thought Nightmares were their source, that they sent spies into the city to infect our minds and keep us afraid of the dark, their domain. According to folklore, these spies could be glimpsed upon waking abruptly. Indeed, I'd seen them crouching malevolently in the corner of the bedroom, wreathed in the shadows that were their home, slinking away with impossible speed once I looked at them.

There are no Nightmares left alive anywhere near the City-of-Long-Shadows, but we still have bad dreams and we still see their spies sometimes when we wake. Some say they are spirits of their race, or survivors. I'm not convinced. Even though we have killed all the Nightmares, our own half-dreaming minds continue to populate our bedrooms with their ghosts, so we may remember their legacy.

To date, none of our City's buildings have windows or doors on their east-facing walls.

————

And so the train took us to the end of our civilization. There are many things I remember about Weep-for-Day, though in some respects those memories feel predictably like the shreds of a disturbing dream. Back then it was just an outpost, not a hill-station town like it is now. The most obvious thing to remember is how it sleeted or snowed all the time. I know now that it's caused by moist convective winds in the atmosphere carrying the warmth of the sun from Day to Night, their loads of fat clouds scraping up against the mountains of the Penumbra for all eternity and washing the foothills in their frozen burden. But to my young self, the constant crying of that bruised sky was just another mystery in the world, a sorcery perpetrated by the Nightmares.

I remember, of course, how dark it was. How the people of the outpost carried bobbing lanterns and acrid magenta flares that flamed even against the perpetual wind and precipitation. How everyone outside (including us) had to wear goggles and thick protective suits lined with the fur of animals to keep the numbing cold of outer Evening out. I had never seen such darkness outdoors, and it felt like being asleep while walking. To think that beyond the mountains lay an absence of light even deeper was unbelievable.

I remember the tall poles that marked turns in the curving main road, linked by the ever-present electric and telegraph wires that made such an outpost possible. The bright gold-and-red pennants of the Monarchy fluttered from those poles, dulled by lack of light. They all showed a sun that was no longer visible from there.

I remember the solar shrines—little huts by the road, with small windows that lit up every few hours as chimes rang out over the windy outpost. Through the doors you could see the altars inside; each with an electric globe, its filament flooded with enough voltage to make it look like a hot ball of fire. For a minute these shrines would burn with their tiny artificial suns, and the goggled and suited inhabitants of Weep-for-Day would huddle around them like giant flies, their shadows wavering lines on the streaks of light cast out on the muddy snow or ice. They would pray on their knees, some reaching out to rub the faded ivory crescents of sunwyrm fangs on the altars.

Beyond the road and the slanted wet roofs of Weep-for-Day, there was so little light that the slope of the hill was barely visible. The forested plain beyond was nothing but a black void that ended in the faint glow of the horizon—the last weak embers in a soot-black fireplace just doused with water.

I couldn't see our City-of-Long-Shadows, which filled me with an irrational anxiety that it was gone forever, that if we took the train back we would find the whole world filled with darkness and only Night waiting on the other side.

But these details are less than relevant. That trip changed me and changed the course of my life not because I saw what places beyond the City-of-Long-Shadows looked like, though seeing such no doubt planted the seeds of some future grit in me. It changed me because I, with my family by my side, witnessed a living Nightmare, as we were promised.

The creature was a prisoner of Vorin Tylvur, who was at the time the Consul of Weep-for-Day, a knight like Father, and an appointed privateer and mining coordinator of the Penumbral territories. Of course, he is now well remembered for his study of Nightmares in captivity, and his campaigns to expand the Monarchy's territories into Evening. The manse we stayed in was where he and his wife lived, governing the affairs of the outpost and coordinating expansion and exploration.

I do not remember much of our hosts, except that they were adults in the way all adults who aren't parents are, to little children. They were kind enough to me. I couldn't comprehend the nature of condescension at that age, but I did find the cooing manner of most adults who talked to me boring, and they were no different. Though I'm grateful for their hospitality to my family, I cannot, in retrospect, look upon them with much returned kindness.

They showed us the imprisoned Nightmare on the second vigil of our stay. It was in the deepest recesses of the manse, which was more an over-sized, glorified bunker on the hill of Weep-for-Day than anything else. We went down into a dank, dim corridor in the chilly heart of that mound of crustal rock to see the prisoner.

"I call it Shadow. A little nickname," Sir Tylvur said with a toothy smile, his huge moustache hanging from his nostrils like the dead wings of some poor misbegotten bird trapped in his head. He proved himself right then to have not only a startling lack of imagination for a man of his intelligence and inquisitiveness, but also a grotesquely inappropriate sense of levity.

It would be dramatic and untruthful to say that my fear of darkness re-ceded the moment I set eyes on the creature. But something changed in me. There, looking at this hunched and shivering thing under the smoky blaze of the flares its armored gaolers held to reveal it to its captor's guests, I saw that a phantom flayed was just another animal.

Sir Tylvur had made sure that its light-absorbent skin would not hinder our viewing of the captured enemy. There is no doubt that I feared it, even though its skin was stripped from its back to reveal its glistening red muscles, even though it was clearly broken and defeated. But my mutable young mind understood then, looking into its shining black eyes—the only visible feature in the empty dark of its face—that it knew terror just as I or any human did. The Nightmare was scared. It was a heavy epiphany for a child to bear, and I vomited on the glass observation wall of its cramped holding cell.

Velag didn't make fun of me. He shrank into Mother's arms, trying to back away from the humanoid silhouette scrabbling against the glass to escape the light it so feared; a void-like cut-out in reality but for that livid wet wound on its back revealing it to be as real as us. It couldn't, or would not, scream or vocalize in any way. Instead, we just heard the squeal of its spider-like hands splayed on the glass, claws raking the surface.

I looked at Father, standing rigid and pale, hands clutched into tight fists by his sides. The same fists that held up the severed head of one of this creature's race in triumph so many years ago. Just as in the photograph, there were the horn-like protrusions from its head, though I still couldn't tell what they were. I looked at Mother who, despite the horrific vision in front of us, despite her son clinging to her waist, reached down in concern to wipe the vomit from my mouth and chin with bare fingers, her gloves crumpled in her other hand.

As Sir Tylvur wondered what to do about his spattered glass wall, he decided to blame the Nightmare for my reaction and rapped hard on the cell with the hilt of his sheathed ceremonial sword. He barked at the prisoner, wanting to frighten it away from the glass, I suppose. The only recognizable word in between his grunts was "Shadow." But as he called it by that undignified, silly nickname, the thing stopped its frantic scrabbling. Startled, Sir Tylvur stepped back. The two armored gaolers stepped back as well, flares wavering in the gloom of the cell. I still don't know why the Nightmare stopped thrashing, and I never will know for sure. But at that moment I thought it recognized the nickname its captor had given it, and recognized that it was being displayed like a trophy. Perhaps it wanted to retain some measure of its pride.

The flarelight flickered on its eyes, which grew brighter as moisture gathered on them. It was clearly in pain from the light. I saw that it was as tall as a human, though it looked smaller because of how crouched into itself it was. It cast a shadow like any other animal, and that shadow looked like its paler twin, dancing behind its back. Chains rasped on the wet cell floor, shackled to its limbs. The illuminated wound on its back wept pus, but the rest of it remained that sucking, indescribable black that hurt the human eye.

Except something in its face. It looked at us, and out of that darkness came a glittering of wet obsidian teeth as unseen lips peeled back. I will never forget that invisible smile, whether it was a grimace of pain or a taunting leer.

"Kill it," Velag whispered. And that was when Mother took both our hands tight in hers, and pulled us away from the cell. She marched us down that dank corridor, leaving the two former knights-errant, Father and Sir Tylvur, staring into that glimmering cell at the specter of their past.

———

That night, in the tiny room we'd been given as our quarters, I asked Velag if the Nightmare had scared him.

"Why should it scare me," he said, face pale in the dim glow of the small heating furnace in the corner of the chamber. "It's in chains."

"You just looked scared. It's okay to be scared. I was too. But I think it was as well."

"Shut up. You don't know what you're saying. I'm going to sleep," he said, and turned away from me, his cot groaning. The furnace hissed and ticked.

"I think papa was scared also. He didn't want to see a Nightmare again," I said to Velag's back.

That was when my brother pounced off his cot and on top of me. I was too shocked to scream. My ingrained submission to his power as an elder male authority figure took over. I gave no resistance. Sitting on my small body, Velag took my blanket and shoved it into my mouth. Then, he snatched my pillow and held it over my face. Choking on the taste of musty cloth, I realized I couldn't breathe. I believed that my brother was about to kill me then. I truly believed it. I could feel the pressure of his hands through the pillow, and they were at that moment the hands of something inhuman. I was more terrified then than I'd ever been in my entire short life, plagued though I'd always been by fear.

He held the pillow over my head for no more than four seconds, probably less. When he raised it off my face and pulled the blanket out of my mouth he looked as shaken as I was. His eyes were wet with tears, but in a second his face was twisted in a grimace.

"Never call papa a coward. Never call papa a coward. Papa was never afraid. Do you hear me? You never had to sleep alone in the dark, you don't know. I'm going to grow up and be like papa and kill them. I'll kill them," he hissed the words into my face like a litany. I started crying, unable and probably too scared to tell him I hadn't called Father a coward. I could still barely breathe, so flooded was I with my own tears, so drunk on the air he had denied me. Velag went back to his cot and wrapped himself in his blanket, breathing heavily.

As I shuddered with stifled sobs, I decided that I would never tell my parents about this, that I would never have Velag punished for this violence. I didn't forgive him, not even close, but that is what I decided.

I was seventeen the last time I saw Velag. I went to visit him at the Royal Military Academy's boarding school. He had been there for four years already. We saw him every few moons when he came back to the City proper to visit. But I wanted to see the campus for myself. It was a lovely train ride, just a few hours from the central districts of the City-of-Long-Shadows to the scattered hamlets beyond it.

It was warmer and brighter out where the Academy was. The campus was beautiful, sown with pruned but still wild looking trees and plants that only grew farther out toward Day, their leaves a lighter shade of blue and their flowers huge, craning to the west on thick stems. The sun still peered safely behind the edge of the world, but its gaze was bright enough to wash the stately buildings of the boarding school with a fiery golden-red light, sparkling in the waxy leaves of vines winding their way around the arched windows. On every ornate, varnished door was a garish propaganda poster of the Dark Lord of Nightmares, with his cowled cloak of shadows and black sword, being struck down by our soldiers' bayoneted guns.

I sat with Velag in a cupola in the visitors' garden, which was on a gentle bluff. In the fields adjacent, his fellow student-soldiers played tackleball, their rowdy calls and whistles ringing through the air. We could see heavy banks of glowing, sunlit storm-clouds to the west where the atmosphere boiled and churned in the heat of Day, beyond miles of shimmering swamp-forests and lakes. To the east, a faint moon hung over the campus, but no stars were visible so close to Day.

Velag looked so different from the last time I saw him. His pimples were vanishing, the sallow softness of adolescence melting away to reveal the man he was to become. The military uniform, so forbidding in red and black, suited his tall form. He looked smart and handsome in it. It hurt me to see him shackled in it, but I could see that he wore it with great pride.

He held my hand and asked about my life back home, about my plans to apply to the College of Archaeology at the University of St. Kataretz. He asked about our parents. He told me how gorgeous and grown-up I looked in my dress, and said he was proud of me for becoming a "prodigy." I talked to him with a heavy ache in my chest, because I knew with such certainty that we hardly knew each other, and would get no chance to any time soon, as he would be dispatched to the frontlines of Penumbral Conquest.

As if reading my thoughts, his cheek twitched with what I thought was guilt, and he looked at the stormy horizon. Perhaps he was remembering the night on which he told me he would grow up and kill Nightmares like Father—a promise he was keeping. He squeezed my hand.

"I'll be alright, Val. Don't you worry."

I gave him a rueful smile. "It's not too late. You can opt to become a civilian after graduation and come study with me at St. Kataretz. Ma and papa would think no less of you. You could do physics again, you loved it before. We can get an apartment in Pemluth Halls, share the cost. The University's right in the middle of the City, we'd have so much fun together."

"I can't. You know that. I want this for myself. I want to be a soldier, and a knight."

"Being a knight isn't the same thing as it was in papa's time. He was independent, a privateer. Things have changed. You'll be a part of the military. Knighthoods belong to them now and they're stingy with them. They mostly give them to soldiers who are wounded or dead, Velag."

"I'm in military school, by the saints, I know what a knighthood is or isn't. Please don't be melodramatic. You're an intelligent girl."

"What's that got to do with anything?"

"I'm going. I have more faith in my abilities than you do."

"I have plenty of faith in you. But the Nightmares are angry now, Velag. We're wiping them out. They're scared and angry. They're coming out in waves up in the hills. More of our soldiers are dying than ever before. How can I not worry?"

His jaw knotted, he glared down at our intertwined hands. His grip was limp now. "Don't start with your theories about the benevolence of Nightmares. I don't want to hear it. They're not scared, they *are* fear, and we'll wipe them off the planet if need be so that you and everybody else can live without that fear."

"I'm quite happy with my life, thank you. I'd rather you be alive for ma and papa and me than have the terrible horde of the Nightmares gone forever."

He bit his lip and tightened his hand around mine again. "I know, little sister. You're sweet to worry so. But the Monarchy needs me. I'll be fine. I promise."

And that was the end of the discussion as far as he was concerned. I knew it was no point pushing him further, because it would upset him. This was his life, after all. The one he had chosen. I had no right to belittle it. I didn't want to return to the City on bad terms with him. We made what little small talk was left to make, and then we stood and kissed each other on the cheek, and I hugged him tight and watched him walk away.

What good are such promises as the one he made on our final farewell, even if one means them with all of one's heart? He was dispatched right after his graduation a few moons later, without even a ceremony because it was wartime. After six moons of excited letters from the frontlines at the Penumbral Mountains, he died with a Nightmare's spear in his chest, during a battle that earned the Monarchy yet another victory against the horde of darkness. Compared to the thousands of Nightmares slaughtered during the battle with our guns and cannons, the Monarchy's casualties were small. And yet, my parents lost their son, and I my brother.

In death, they did give Velag the knighthood he fought so hard for. Never have I hated myself so much for being right.

———

When Velag was being helped out of Mother by doctors in the city, my father had been escorting pioneers in the foothills. I see him in his armor, the smell of heated steel and cold sweat cloying under his helm, almost blind because of the visor, sword in one hand, knotted reins and a flaming torch in the other, his mount about to bolt. A new metal coal-chamber filled with glowing embers strapped to his back to keep the suit warm, making his armor creak and pop as it heated up, keeping him off-balance with its weight and hissing vents but holding the freezing cold back a little. Specks of frozen water flying through the torch-lit air like dust, biting his eyes through the visor. His fingers numb in his gloves, despite the suit. The familiar glitter of inhuman eyes beyond the torchlight, nothing to go by but reflections of fire on his foes, who are invisible in the shadows, slinking alongside the caravan like bulges in the darkness. The only thing between the Nightmares and the pioneers with their mounts and carriages weighed down by machinery and thick coils of wire and cable that will bring the light of civilization to these wilds, is him and his contingent.

How long must that journey have been to him? How long till he returned alive to see his wife and new son Velag in a warm hospital room, under the glow of a brand-new electric light?

By the time I was born, armorers had invented portable guns and integrated hollow cables in the suit lining to carry ember-heated water around armor, keeping it warmer and enabling mercenaries and knights-errant to go deeper into Evening. The pioneers followed, bringing their technology to the very tops of the foothills, infested with Nightmares. That was when Father stopped going, lest he never return. They had new tools, but the war had intensified. He had a son and daughter to think of, and a wife who wanted him home.

———

When I watched Velag's funeral pyre blaze against the light of the west on Barrow-of-Bones cremation hill, I wondered if the sparks sent up into the sky by his burning body would turn to stardust in the ether and migrate to the sun to extend its life, or whether this was his final and utter dissolution. The chanting priest from the Solar Church seemed to have no doubts on the matter. Standing there, surrounded by the fossilized stone ribs of Zhurgeith, last of the sunwyrms and heraldic angel of the Monarchy and Church (who also call it Dragon), I found myself truly unsure about what death brings for maybe the first time in my life, though I'd long practiced the cynicism that was becoming customary of my generation.

I thought with some trepidation about the possibility that if the Church was right, the dust of Velag's life might be consigned to the eternal dark of cosmic limbo instead of finding a place in the sun, because of what he'd done to me as a child. Because I'd never forgiven him, even though I told myself I had.

How our world changes.

The sun is a great sphere of burning gas, ash eventually falls down, and my dead brother remains in the universe because my family and I remember him, just as I remember my childhood, my life, the Nightmares we lived in fear of, the angel Dragon whose host was wiped out by a solar flare before we could ever witness it.

———

Outside, the wind howls so loud that I can easily imagine it is the sound of trumpets from a frozen city, peopled by the horde of darkness. Even behind the insulated metal doors and heated tunnels of the cave bunkers that make up After-Day border camp, I can see my breath and need two thick coats to keep warm. My fingers are like icicles as I write. I would die very quickly if exposed to the atmosphere outside. And yet, here I am, in the land of Nightmares.

Somewhere beyond these Penumbral Mountains, which we crossed in an airtight train, is the City-of-Long-Shadows. I have never been so far from it. Few people have. We are most indebted to those who mapped the shortest route through the mountains, built the rails through the lowest valleys, blasted new tunnels, laid the foundations for After-Day. But no one has gone beyond this point. We—I and the rest of the expeditionary team from St. Kataretz—will be the first to venture into Night. It will be a dangerous endeavor, but I have faith in us, in the brave men and women who have accompanied me here.

My dear Velag, how would you have reacted to see these beautiful caves I sit in now, to see the secret culture of your enemy? I am surrounded by what can only be called their art, the lantern-light making pale tapestries of the rock walls on which Nightmares through the millennia scratched to life the dawn of their time, the history that followed, and its end, heralded by our arrival into their world.

In this history we are the enemy, bringing the terror of blinding fire into Evening, bringing the advanced weapons that caused their genocide. On these walls we are drawn in pale white dyes, bioluminescent in the dark, a swarm of smeared light advancing on the Nightmares' striking, jagged-angled representations of themselves, drawn in black dyes mixed from blood and minerals.

In this history Nightmares were alive when the last of the sunwyrms flew into Evening to scourge the land for prey. Whether this is truth or myth we don't know, but it might mean that Nightmares were around long before us. It might explain their adaptation to the darkness of outer Evening—their light-absorbent skin ancient camouflage to hide from sunwyrms under cover of the forests of Evening. We came into Evening with our fire (which they show sunwyrms breathing) and pale skins, our banners showing Dragon and the sun, and we were like a vengeful race of ghosts come to kill on behalf of those disappeared angels of Day, whom they worshipped to the end—perhaps praying for our retreat.

In halls arched by the ribcages and spines of ancient sunwyrm skeletons I have seen burial chambers; the bones of Nightmares and their children (whom we called imps because we didn't like to think of our enemy having young) piled high. Our bones lie here too, not so different from theirs. Tooth-marks show that they ate their dead, probably because of the scarcity of food in the fragile ecosystem of Evening. It is no wonder then that they ate our dead too—as we feared. It was not out of evil, but need.

We have so much yet to learn.

Perhaps it would have given you some measure of peace, Velag, to know that the Nightmares didn't want to destroy us, only to drive us back from their home. Perhaps not.

Ilydrin tells me it is time for us to head out. She is a member of our expedition—a biologist—and my partner. To hide the simple truth of our affection seems here, amid the empty city of a race we destroyed, an obscenity. Confronted by the vast, killing beauty of our planet's second half, the stagnant moralities of our city-state appear a trifle. I adore Ilydrin, and I am glad she is here with me.

One team will stay here while ours heads out into Night. Ilydrin and I took a walk outside to test our Night-shells—armored environmental suits to protect us from the lethal cold. We trod down from the caves of After-Day and into the unknown beyond, breath blurring our glass faceplates, our head-lamps cutting broad swathes through the snow-swarmed dark. We saw nothing ahead but an endless plain of ice—perhaps a frozen sea.

No spectral spires, no black banners of Night, no horde of Nightmares waiting to attack, no Dark Lord in his distant obsidian palace (an image Ilydrin and I righteously tore down many times in the form of those Army posters, during our early College vigils). We held each others' gloved hands and returned to Camp, sweating in our cramped shells, heavy boots crunching on the snow. I thought of you, Father, bravely venturing into bitter Evening to support your family. I thought of you, Brother, nobly marching against the horde for your Monarchy. I thought of you, Mother, courageously carrying your first child alone in that empty house before it became *our* home. I thought of you, Shadow—broken, tortured prisoner, baring your teeth to your captors in silence.

Out there, I was shaking—nervous, excited, queasy. I wasn't afraid.

———

I have Father's old photograph with the Nightmare's head (he took it down from above the mantelpiece after Velag died). I have a photograph of Mother, Father, Velag and I all dressed up before our trip to Weep-for-Day. And finally, a smiling portrait of Velag in uniform before he left for the Academy, his many pimples invisible because of the monochrome softness of the image. I keep these photographs with me, in the pockets of my overcoat, and take them out sometimes when I write.

————

So it begins. I write from the claustrophobic confines of the Night-Crawler, a steam-powered vehicle our friends at the College of Engineering designed (our accompanying professors named it with them, no doubt while drunk in a bar on University-Street). It is our moving camp. We'll sleep and eat and take shelter in it, and explore farther and longer—at least a few vigils, we hope. If its engines fail, we'll have to hike back in our shells and hope for the best. The portholes are frosted over, but the team is keeping warm by stoking the furnace and singing. Ilydrin comes and tells me, her lips against my hair: "Val. Stop writing and join us." I tell her I will, in a minute. She smiles and walks back to the rest, her face flushed and soot-damp from the open furnace. I live for these moments.

I will lay down this pen now. A minute.

I don't know what we'll find out here. Maybe we *will* find the Dark Lord and his gathered horde of Nightmares. But at this point, even the military doesn't believe that, or they would have opposed the funding for this expedition or tried to hijack it.

Ilydrin says there's unlikely to be life so deep into Night—even Nightmares didn't venture beyond the mountains, despite our preconceptions. But she admits we've been wrong before. Many times. What matters is that we are somewhere new. Somewhere other than the City-of-Long-Shadows and the Penumbral territories, so marked by our history of fear. We need to see the rest of this world, to meet its other inhabitants—if there are others—with curiosity, not apprehension. And I know we will, eventually. This is our first, small step. I wish you were here with me to see it, Velag. You were but a child on this planet.

We might die here. It won't be because we ventured into evil. It will be because we sought new knowledge. And in that, I have no regrets, even if I'm dead when this is read. A new age is coming. Let this humble account be a preface to it.

SOMEDAY

JAMES PATRICK KELLY

DAYA HAD BEEN in no hurry to become a mother. In the two years since she'd reached childbearing age, she'd built a modular from parts she'd fabbed herself, thrown her boots into the volcano, and served as blood judge. The village elders all said she was one of the quickest girls they had ever seen—except when it came to choosing fathers for her firstborn. Maybe that was because she was too quick for a sleepy village like Third Landing. When her mother, Tajana, had come of age, she'd left for the blue city to find fathers for her baby. Everyone expected Tajana would stay in Halfway, but she had surprised them and returned home to raise Daya. So once Daya had grown up, everyone assumed that someday she would leave for the city like her mother, especially after Tajana had been killed in the avalanche last winter. What did Third Landing have to hold such a fierce and able woman? Daya could easily build a glittering new life in Halfway. Do great things for the colony.

But everything had changed after the scientists from space had landed on the old site across the river, and Daya had changed most of all. She kept her own counsel and was often hard to find. That spring she had told the elders that she didn't need to travel to gather the right semen. Her village was happy and prosperous. The scientists had chosen it to study and they had attracted tourists from all over the colony. There were plenty of beautiful and convenient local fathers to take to bed. Daya had sampled the ones she considered best, but never opened herself to blend their sperm. Now she would, here in the place where she had been born.

She chose just three fathers for her baby. She wanted Ganth because he was her brother and because he loved her above all others. Latif because he was a leader and would say what was true when everyone else was afraid. And Bakti because he was a master of stories and because she wanted him to tell hers someday.

She informed each of her intentions to make a love feast, although she kept the identities of the other fathers a secret, as was her right. Ganth demanded to know, of course, but she refused him. She was not asking for a favor. It would be her baby, her responsibility. The three fathers, in turn, kept her request to themselves, as was custom, in case she changed her mind about any or all of them. A real possibility—when she contemplated what she was about to do, she felt separated from herself.

That morning she climbed into the pen and spoke a kindness to her pig Bobo. The glint of the knife made him grunt with pleasure and he rolled onto his back, exposing the tumors on his belly. She hadn't harvested him in almost a week and so carved two fist-sized maroon swellings into the meat pail. She pressed strips of sponge root onto the wounds to stanch the bleeding and when it was done, she threw them into the pail as well. When she scratched under his jowls to dismiss him, Bobo squealed approval, rolled over, and trotted off for a mud bath.

She sliced the tumors thin, dipped the pieces in egg and dragged them through a mix of powdered opium, pepper, flour, and bread crumbs, then sautéed them until they were crisp. She arranged them on top of a casserole of snuro, parsnips, and sweet flag, layered with garlic and three cheeses. She harvested some of the purple blooms from the petri dish on the windowsill and flicked them on top of her love feast. The aphrodisiacs produced by the bacteria would give an erection to a corpse. She slid the casserole into the oven to bake for an hour while she bathed and dressed for babymaking.

Daya had considered the order in which she would have sex with the fathers. Last was most important, followed by first. The genes of the middle father—or fathers, since some mothers made babies with six or seven for political reasons—were less reliably expressed. She thought starting with Ganth for his sunny nature and finishing with Latif for his looks and good judgment made sense. Even though Bakti was clever, he had bad posture.

Ganth sat in front of a fuzzy black and white screen with his back to her when she nudged the door to his house open with her hip. "It's me. With a present."

He did not glance away from his show—the colony's daily news and gossip program about the scientists—but raised his forefinger in acknowledgment.

She carried the warming dish with oven mitts to the huge round table that served as his desk, kitchen counter, and sometime closet. She pushed aside some books, a belt, an empty bottle of blueberry kefir, and a Fill Jump higher action figure to set her love feast down. Like her own house, Ganth's was a single room, but his was larger, shabbier, and built of some knotty softwood.

Her brother took a deep breath, his face pale in the light of the screen. "Smells delicious." He pressed the off button; the screen winked and went dark.

"What's the occasion?" He turned to her, smiling. "*Oh*." His eyes went wide when he saw how she was dressed. "Tonight?"

"Tonight." She grinned.

Trying to cover his surprise, he pulled out the pocket watch he'd had from their mother and then shook it as if it were broken. "Why, look at the time. I totally forgot that we were grown up."

"You like?" She weaved her arms and her ribbon robe fluttered.

"I was wondering when you'd come. What if I had been out?"

She nodded at the screen in front of him. "You never miss that show."

"Has anyone else seen you?" He sneaked to the window and peered out. A knot of gawkers had gathered in the street. "What, did you parade across Founders' Square dressed like that? You'll give every father in town a hard-on." He pulled the blinds and came back to her. He surprised her by going down on one knee. "So which am I?"

"What do you think?" She lifted the cover from the casserole to show that it was steaming and uncut.

"I'm honored." He took her hand in his and kissed it. "Who else?" he said. "And you have to tell. Tomorrow everyone will know."

"Bakti. Latif last."

"Three is all a baby really needs." He rubbed his thumb across the inside of her wrist. "Our mother would approve."

Of course, Ganth had no idea of what their mother had really thought of him.

Tajana had once warned Daya that if she insisted on choosing Ganth to father her baby, she should dilute his semen with that of the best men in the village. A sweet manner is fine, she'd said, but babies need brains and a spine.

"So, dear sister, it's a sacrifice . . ." he said, standing, ". . . but I'm prepared to do my duty." He caught her in his arms.

Daya squawked in mock outrage.

"You're not surprising the others, are you?" He nuzzled her neck.

"No, they expect me."

"Then we'd better hurry. I hear that Eldest Latif goes to bed early." His whisper filled her ear. "Carrying the weight of the world on his back tires him out."

"I'll give him reason to wake up."

He slid a hand through the layers of ribbons until he found her skin. "Bakti, on the other hand, stays up late, since his stories weigh nothing at all." The flat of his hand against her belly made her shiver. "I didn't realize you knew him that well."

She tugged at the hair on the back of Ganth's head to get his attention. "Feasting first," she said, her voice husky. Daya hadn't expected to be this emotional. She opened her pack, removed the bottle of chardonnay, and poured two glasses. They saluted each other and drank, then she used the spatula she had brought—since she knew her brother wouldn't have one— to cut a square of her love feast. He watched her scoop it onto a plate like a man uncertain of his luck. She forked a bite into her mouth. The cheese was still melty—maybe a bit too much sweet flag. She chewed once, twice, and then leaned forward to kiss him. His lips parted and she let the con- tents of her mouth fall into his. He groaned and swallowed. "Again." His voice was thick. "Again and again and again."

Afterward they lay entangled on his mattress on the floor. "I'm glad you're not leaving us, Daya." He blew on the ribbons at her breast and they trembled. "I'll stay home to watch your baby," he said. "Whenever you need me. Make life so easy, you'll never want to go."

It was the worst thing he could have said; until that moment she had been able to keep from thinking that she might never see him again. He was her only family, except for the fathers her mother had kept from her. Had Tajana wanted to make it easy for her to leave Third Landing? "What if I get restless here?" Daya's voice could have fit into a thimble. "You know me."

"Okay, maybe someday you can leave." He waved the idea away. "Someday."

She glanced down his lean body at the hole in his sock and dust strings dangling from his bookshelf. He was a sweet boy and her brother, but he played harder than he worked. Ganth was content to let the future happen to him; Daya needed to make choices, no matter how hard. "It's getting late." She pressed her cheek to his. "Do me a favor and check on Bobo in the morning? Who knows when I'll get home."

By the time she kissed Ganth good-bye, it was evening. An entourage of at least twenty would-be spectators trailed her to Old Town; word had spread that the very eligible Daya was bringing a love feast to some lucky fathers. There was even a scatter of tourists, delighted to witness Third Landing's quaint mating ritual. The locals told jokes, made ribald suggestions and called out names of potential fathers. She tried to ignore them; some people in this village were so nosy.

Bakti lived in one of the barnlike stone dormitories that the settlers had built two centuries ago across the river from their landing spot. Most of these buildings were now divided into shops and apartments. When Daya finally revealed her choice by stopping at Bakti's door, the crowd buzzed. Winners of bets chirped, losers groaned. Bakti was slow to answer her knock, but when he saw the spectators, he seized her arm and drew her inside.

Ganth had been right: she and Bakti weren't particularly close. She had never been to his house, although he had visited her mother on occasion when she was growing up. She could see that he was no better a housekeeper than her brother, but at least his mess was all of a kind. The bones of his apartment had not much changed from the time the founders had used it as a dormitory; Bakti had preserved the two walls of wide shelves that they had used as bunks. Now, however, instead of sleeping refugees from Genome Crusades, they were filled with books, row upon extravagant row. This was Bakti's vice; not only did he buy cheap paper from the village stalls, he had purchased hundreds of hardcovers on his frequent trips to the blue city. They said he even owned a few print books that the founders had brought across space. There were books everywhere, open on chairs, chests, the couch, stacked in leaning towers on the floor.

"So you've come to rumple my bed?" He rearranged his worktable to make room for her love feast. "I must admit, I was surprised by your note. Have we been intimate before, Daya?"

"Just once." She set the dish down. "Don't pretend that you don't remember." When she unslung the pack from her back, the remaining bottles of wine clinked together.

"Don't pretend?" He spread his hands. "I tell stories. That's all I do."

"Glasses?" She extracted the zinfandel from her pack.

He brought two that were works of art; crystal stems twisted like vines to flutes as delicate as a skim of ice. "I recall a girl with a pansy tattooed on her back," he said.

"You're thinking of Pandi." Daya poured the wine.

"Do you sing to your lovers?"

She sniffed the bouquet. "Never."

They saluted each other and drank.

"Don't rush me now," he said. "I'm enjoying this little game." He lifted the lid of the dish and breathed in. "Your feast pleases the nose as much as you please the eye. But I see that I am not your first stop. Who else have you seen this night?"

"Ganth."

"You chose a grasshopper to be a father of your child?".

"He's my brother."

"Aha!" He snapped his fingers. "Now I have it. The garden at Tajana's place? I recall a very pleasant evening."

She had forgotten how big Bakti's nose was. "As do I." And his slouch was worse than ever. Probably from carrying too many books.

"I don't mind being the middle, you know." He took another drink of wine. "Prefer it actually—less responsibility that way. I will do my duty as a father, but I must tell you right now that I have no interest whatsoever in bringing up your baby. And her next father is?"

"Latif. Next and last."

"A man who takes fathering seriously. Good, he'll balance out poor Ganth. I will tell her stories, though. Your baby girl. That's what you hope for, am I right? A girl?"

"Yes." She hadn't realized it until he said it. A girl would make things much easier.

He paused, as if he had just remembered something. "But you're supposed to leave us, aren't you? This village is too tight a fit for someone of your abilities. You'll split seams, pop a button."

Why did everyone keep saying these things to her? "*You* didn't leave."

"No." He shook his head. "I wasn't as big as I thought I was. Besides, the books keep me here. Do you know how much they weigh?"

"It's an amazing collection." She bent to the nearest shelf and ran a finger along the spines of the outermost row. "I've heard you have some from Earth."

"Is this about looking at books or making babies, Daya?" Bakti looked crestfallen.

She straightened, embarrassed. "The baby, of course."

"No, I get it." He waved a finger at her. "I'm crooked and cranky and mothers shut their eyes tight when we kiss." He reached for the wine bottle. "Those are novels." He nodded at the shelf. "But no, nothing from Earth."

They spent the better part of an hour browsing. Bakti said Daya could borrow some if she wanted. He said reading helped pregnant mothers settle. Then he told her the story from one of them. It was about a boy named Huckleberry Flynn, who left his village on Novy Praha to see his world but then came back again. "Just like your mother did," he said. "Just like you could, if you wanted. Someday."

"Then you could tell stories about me."

"About this night," he agreed, "if I remember." His grin was seductive. "Will I?"

"Have you gotten any books from them?" She glanced out the dark window toward the river. "Maybe they'd want to trade with you?"

"Them?" he said. "You mean our visitors? Some, but digital only. They haven't got time for nostalgia. To them, my books are as quaint as scrolls and clay tablets. They asked to scan the collection, but I think they were just being polite. Their interests seem to be more sociological than literary." He smirked. "I understand you have been spending time across the river."

She shrugged. "Do you think they are telling the truth?"

"About what? Their biology? Their politics?" He gestured at his library. "I own one thousand, two hundred and forty-three claims of truth. How would I know which is right?" He slid the book about the boy Huckleberry back onto the shelf. "But look at the time! If you don't mind, I've been putting off dinner until you arrived. And then we can make a baby and a memory, yes?"

By the time Daya left him snoring on his rumpled bed, the spectators had all gone home for the night. There was still half of the love feast left but the warming dish was beginning to dry it out. She hurried down the Farview Hill to the river.

Many honors had come to Latif over the years and with them great wealth. He had first served as village eldest when he was still a young man, just thirty-two years old. In recent years, he mediated disputes for those who did not have the time or the money to submit to the magistrates of the blue city. The fees he charged had bought him this fine house of three rooms, one of which was the parlor where he received visitors. When she saw that all the windows were dark, she gave a cry of panic. It was nearly midnight and the house was nothing but a shadow against the silver waters.

On the shore beyond, the surreal bulk of the starship beckoned.

Daya didn't even bother with front door. She went around to the bedroom and stood on tiptoes to knock on his window. *Tap-tap.*

Nothing.

"Latif." *Tap-tap-tap.* "Wake up."

She heard a clatter within. "Shit!" A light came on and she stepped away as the window clattered open."

"Who's there? Go away."

"It's me, Daya."

"Do you know what time it is? Go away."

"But I have our love feast. You knew this was the night, I sent a message."

"And I waited, but you took too damn long." He growled in frustration. "Can't you see I'm asleep? Go find some middle who's awake."

"No, Latif. You're my last."

He started with a shout. "You wake me in the middle of night . . ." Then he continued in a low rasp. "Where's your sense, Daya, your manners? You expect me to be your last? You should have said something. I take fathering seriously."

Daya's throat closed. Her eyes seemed to throb.

"I told you to move to the city, didn't I? Find fathers there." Latif waited for her to answer. When she didn't, he stuck his head out the window to see her better. "So instead of taking my best advice, now you want my semen?" He waited again for a reply; she couldn't speak. "I suppose you're crying."

The only reply she could make was a sniffle.

"Come to the door then."

She reached for his arm as she entered the darkened parlor but he waved her through to the center of the room. "You are rude and selfish, Daya." He shut the door and leaned against it. "But that doesn't mean you're a bad person."

He turned the lights on and for a moment they stood blinking at each other. Latif was barefoot, wearing pants but no shirt. He had a wrestler's shoulders, long arms, hands big as dinner plates. Muscles bunched beneath his smooth, dark skin, as if he might spring at her. But if she read his eyes right, his anger was passing.

"I thought you'd be pleased." She tried a grin. It bounced off him.

"Honored, yes. Pleased, not at all. You think you can just issue commands and we jump? You have the right to ask, and I have the right to refuse. Even at the last minute."

At fifty-three, Latif was still one of the handsomest men in the village. Daya had often wondered if that was one reason why everyone trusted him. She looked for some place to put the warming dish down.

"No," he said, "don't you dare make yourself comfortable unless I tell you to. Why me?"

She didn't have to think. "Because you have always been kind to me and my mother. Because you will tell the truth, even when it's hard to hear. And because, despite your years, you are still the most beautiful man I know." This time she tried a smile on him. It stuck. "All the children you've fathered are beautiful, and if my son gets nothing but looks from you, that will still be to his lifelong advantage." Daya knew that in the right circumstance, even men like Latif would succumb to flattery.

"You want me because I tell hard truths, but when I say you should move away, you ignore me. Does that make sense?"

"Not everything needs to make sense." She extended her love feast to him. "Where should I put this?"

He glided across the parlor, kissed her forehead, and accepted the dish from her. "Do you know how many have asked me to be last father?"

"No." She followed him into the great room.

"Twenty-three," he said. "Every one spoke to me ahead of time. And of those, how many I agreed to?"

"No idea."

"Four." He set it on a round wooden table with a marble inset.

"They should've tried my ambush strategy." She shrugged out of her pack. "I've got wine." She handed him the bottle of Xino she had picked for him.

"Which you've been drinking all night, I'm sure. You know where the glasses are." He pulled the stopper. "And who have you been drinking with?"

"Ganth, first."

Latif tossed the stopper onto the table. "I'm one-fourth that boy's father . . ." He rapped on the tabletop. ". . . but I don't see any part of me in him."

"He's handsome."

"Oh, stop." He poured each of them just a splash of the Xino and offered her a glass. She raised an eyebrow at his stinginess.

"It's late and you've had enough," he said. "It is affecting your judgment. Who else?"

"Bakti."

"You surprise me." They saluted each other with their glasses. "Does he really have Earth books?"

"He says not."

"He makes too many stories up. But he's sound—you should have started with him. Ganth is a middle father at best."

Both of them ran out of things to say then. Latif was right. She had finished the first two bottles with the other fathers, and had shared a love feast with them, and had made love. She was heavy with the weight of her decisions and her desires. She felt like she was falling toward Latif. She pulled the cover off the warming dish and cut a square of her love feast into bite-sized chunks.

"Just because I'm making a baby doesn't mean I can't go away," she said.

"And leave the fathers behind?"

"That's what my mother did."

"And did that make her happy? Do you think she had an easy life?" He shook his head. "No, you are tying yourself to this village. This little, insignificant place. Why? Maybe you're lazy. Or maybe you're afraid. Here, you are a star. What would you be in the blue city?"

She wanted to tell him that he had it exactly wrong. That he was talking about himself, not her. But that would have been cruel. This beautiful, foolish man was going to be the last father of her baby. "You're right," Daya said. "It's late." She piled bits of the feast onto a plate and came around to where he was sitting. She perched on the edge of the table and gazed down at him.

He tugged at one of the ribbons of her sleeve and she felt the robe slip off her shoulder. "What is this costume anyway?" he said. "You're wrapped up like some kind of present."

She didn't reply. Instead she pushed a bit of the feast across her plate until it slid onto her fork. They watched each other as she brought it to her open mouth, placed it on her tongue. The room shrank. Clocks stopped.

He shuddered. "Feed me, then."

Latif's pants were still around his ankles when she rolled off him. The ribbon robe dangled off the headboard of his bed. Daya gazed up at the ceiling, thinking about the tangling sperm inside her. She concentrated as her mother had taught her, and she thought she felt her cervix close and her uterus contract, concentrating the semen. At least, she hoped she did. The sperm of the three fathers would smash together furiously, breaching cell walls, exchanging plasmids. The strongest conjugate would find her eggs and then . . .

"What if I leave the baby behind?" she said.

"With who?" He propped himself up on an elbow. "Your mother is dead and no . . ."

She laid a finger on his lips. "I know, Latif. But why not with a father? Ganth might do it, I think. Definitely not Bakti. Maybe even you."

He went rigid. "This is an idea you got from the scientists? Is that the way they have sex in space?"

"They don't live in space; they just travel through it." She followed a crack in the plaster of his ceiling with her eyes. "Nobody lives in space." A water stain in the corner looked like a face. A mouth. Sad eyes. "What should we do about them?"

"Do? There is nothing to be done." He fell back onto his pillow. "They're the ones the founders were trying to get away from."

"Two hundred years ago. They say things are different."

"Maybe. Maybe these particular scientists are more tolerant, but they're still dangerous."

"Why? Why are you so afraid of them?"

"*Because they're unnatural.*" The hand at her side clenched into a fist. "We're the true humans, maybe the last. But they've taken charge of evolution now, or what passes for it. We have no say in the future. All we know for sure is that they are large and still growing and we are very, very small. Maybe this lot won't force us to change. Or maybe someday they'll just make us want to become like them."

She knew this was true, even though she had spent the last few months trying not to know it. The effort had made her weary. She rolled toward Latif. When she snuggled against him, he relaxed into her embrace.

It was almost dawn when she left his house. Instead of climbing back up Farview Hill, she turned toward the river. Moments later she stepped off Mogallo's Wharf into the skiff she had built when she was a teenager.

She had been so busy pretending that this wasn't going to happen that she was surprised to find herself gliding across the river. She could never have had sex with the fathers if she had acknowledged to herself that she was going to go through with it. Certainly not with Ganth. And Latif would have guessed that something was wrong. She had the odd feeling that there were two of her in the skiff, each facing in opposite directions. The one looking back at the village was screaming at the one watching the starship grow ever larger. But there is no other Daya, she reminded herself. There is only me.

Her lover, Roberts, was waiting on the spun-carbon dock that the scientists had fabbed for river traffic. Many of the magistrates from the blue city came by boat to negotiate with the offworlders. Roberts caught the rope that Daya threw her and took it expertly around one of the cleats. She extended a hand to hoist Daya up, caught her in an embrace and pressed her lips to Daya's cheek.

"This kissing that you do," said Roberts. "I like it. Very direct." She wasn't very good at it but she was learning. Like all the scientists, she could be stiff at first. They didn't seem all that comfortable in their replaceable bodies. Roberts was small as a child, but with a woman's face. Her blonde hair was cropped short, her eyes were clear and faceted. They reminded Daya of her mother's crystal.

"It's done," said Daya.

"Yes, but are you all right?"

"I think so." She forced a grin. "We'll find out."

"We will. Don't worry, love, I am going to take good care of you. And your baby."

"And I will take care of you."

"Yes." She looked puzzled. "Of course."

Roberts was a cultural anthropologist. She had explained to Daya that all she wanted was to preserve a record of an ancient way of life. A culture in which there was still sexual reproduction.

"May I see that?"

Daya opened her pack and produced the leftover bit of the love feast. She had sealed it in a baggie that Roberts had given her. It had somehow frozen solid.

"Excellent. Now we should get you into the lab before it's too late. Put you under the scanner, take some samples." This time she kissed Daya on the mouth. Her lips parted briefly and Daya felt Roberts' tongue flick against her teeth. When Daya did not respond, she pulled back.

"I know this is hard now. You're very brave to help us this way, Daya." The scientist took her hand and squeezed. "But someday they'll thank you for what you're doing." She nodded toward the sleepy village across the river. "Someday soon."

BOTANICA VENERIS: THIRTEEN PAPERCUTS BY IDA COUNTESS RATHANGAN

IAN MCDONALD

Introduction by Maureen N. Gellard

MY MOTHER HAD firm instructions that, in case of a house fire, two things required saving: the family photograph album and the Granville-Hydes. I grew up beneath five original floral papercuts, utterly heedless of their history or their value. It was only in maturity that I came to appreciate, like so many on this and other worlds, my great-aunt's unique art.

Collectors avidly seek original Granville-Hydes on those rare occasions when they turn up at auction. Originals sell for tens of thousands of pounds (this would have amused Ida); two years ago, an exhibition at the Victoria and Albert Museum was sold out months in advance. Dozens of anthologies of prints are still in print: the *Botanica Veneris*, in particular, is in fifteen editions in twenty-three languages, some of them non-Terrene.

The last thing the world needs, it would seem, is another *Botanica Veneris*. Yet the mystery of her final (and only) visit to Venus still intrigues half a century since her disappearance. When the collected diaries, sketch books, and field notes came to me after fifty years in the possession of the Dukes of Yoo, I realized that I had a precious opportunity to tell the true story of my great-aunt's expedition—and of a forgotten chapter in my family's history. The books were in very poor condition, mildewed and blighted in Venus's humid, hot climate. Large parts were illegible or simply missing. The narrative was frustratingly incomplete. I have resisted the urge to fill in those blank spaces. It would have been easy to dramatize, fictionalize, even sensationalize. Instead I have let Ida Granville-Hyde speak. Hers is a strong, characterful, attractive voice, of a different class, age, and sensibility from ours, but it is authentic, and it is a true voice.

The papercuts, of course, speak for themselves.

> Plate 1: *V. strutio ambulans*: the Ducrot's Peripatetic Wort, known locally as Daytime Walker (Thent) or Wander-flower (Thekh).
> Cut paper, ink and card.

Such a show!

At lunch Het Oi-Kranh mentioned that a space-crosser—the *Quest for the Harvest of the Stars*, a Marsman—was due to splash down in the lagoon. I said I should like to see that—apparently I slept through it when I arrived on this world. It meant forgoing the sorbet course, but one does not come to the Inner Worlds for sorbet! Het Oi-Kranh put his spider-car at our disposal. Within moments, the Princess Latufui and I were swaying in the richly upholstered bubble beneath the six strong mechanical legs. Upward it carried us, up the vertiginous lanes and winding staircases, over the walls and balcony gardens, along the buttresses and roof walks and up the ancient iron ladder ways of Ledekh-Olkoi. The islands of the archipelago are small, their populations vast, and the only way for them to build is upward. Ledekh-Olkoi resembles Mont St. Michel vastly enlarged and coarsened. Streets have been bridged and built over into a web of tunnels quite impenetrable to non-Ledekhers. The Hets simply clamber over the homes and lives of the inferior classes in their nimble spider-cars.

We came to the belvedere atop the Starostry, the ancient pharos of Ledekh-Olkoi that once guided mariners past the reefs and atolls of the Tol Archipelago. There we clung—my companion, the Princess Latufui, was queasy—vertigo, she claimed, though it might have been the proximity of lunch—the whole of Ledekh-Olkoi beneath us in myriad levels and layers, like the folded petals of a rose.

"Should we need glasses?" my companion asked.

No need! For at the instant, the perpetual layer of grey cloud parted and a bolt of light, like a glowing lance, stabbed down from the sky. I glimpsed a dark object fall through the air, then a titanic gout of water go up like a dozen Niagaras. The sky danced with brief rainbows, my companion wrung her hands in delight—she misses the sun terribly—then the clouds closed again. Rings of waves rippled away from the hull of the space-crosser, which floated like a great whale low in the water, though this world boasts marine fauna even more prodigious than Terrene whales.

My companion clapped her hands and cried aloud in wonder.

Indeed, a very fine sight!

Already the tugs were heading out from the protecting arms of Ocean Dock to bring the ship in to berth.

But this was not the finest Ledekh-Olkoi had to offer. The custom in the archipelago is to sleep on divan-balconies, for respite from the foul exudations from the inner layers of the city. I had retired for my afternoon reviver—by my watch, though by Venusian Great Day it was still midmorning and would continue to be so for another two weeks. A movement by the leg of my divan. What's this? My heart surged. *V. strutio ambulans*: the Ambulatory Wort, blindly, blithely climbing my divan!

Through my glass, I observed its motion. The fat, succulent leaves hold reserves of water, which fuel the coiling and uncoiling of the three ambulae—surely modified roots—by hydraulic pressure. A simple mechanism, yet human minds see movement and attribute personality and motive. This was not pure hydraulics attracted to light and liquid, this was a plucky little wort on an epic journey of peril and adventure. Over two hours, I sketched the plant as it climbed my divan, crossed to the balustrade, and continued its journey up the side of Ledekh-Olkoi. I suppose at any time millions of such flowers are in constant migration across the archipelago, yet a single Ambulatory Wort was miracle enough for me.

Reviver be damned! I went to my space trunk and unrolled my scissors from their soft chamois wallet. Snip snap! When a cut demands to be made, my fingers literally itch for the blades!

———

When he learned of my intent, Gen Lahl-Khet implored me not to go down to Ledekh Port, but if I insisted (I insisted: oh, I insisted!), at least take a bodyguard or go armed. I surprised him greatly by asking the name of the best armorer his city could supply. Best Shot at the Clarecourt November shoot, ten years on the trot! Ledbekh-Teltai is most famous gunsmith in the archipelago. It is illegal to import weaponry from off-planet—an impost, I suspect, resulting from the immense popularity of hunting Ishtari janthars. The pistol they have made me is built to my hand and strength: small, as requested; powerful, as required; and so worked with spiral-and-circle Archipelagan intaglio that it is a piece of jewelry.

———

Ledekh Port was indeed a loathsome bruise of alleys and tunnels, lit by shifts of grey, watery light through high skylights. Such reeks and stenches! Still, no one ever died of a bad smell. An Earthwoman alone in an inappropriate place was a novelty, but from the nonhumanoid Venusians I drew little more than a look. In my latter years, I have been graced with a physical *presence* and a destroying stare. The Thekh, descended from Central Asian nomads abducted en masse in the eleventh century from their bracing steppe, now believe themselves the original humanity, and so consider Terrenes beneath them, and they expected no better of a subhuman Earthwoman.

I did turn heads in the bar. I was the only female—humanoid, that is. From Carfax's *Bestiary of the Inner Worlds*, I understand that among the semi-aquatic Krid, the male is a small, ineffectual symbiotic parasite lodging in the mantle of the female. The barman, a four-armed Thent, guided me to the snug where I was to meet my contact. The bar overlooked the Ocean Harbor. I watched dockworkers scurry over the vast body of the space-crosser, in and out of hatches that had opened in the skin of the ship. I did not like to see those hatches; they ruined its perfection, the precise, intact curve of its skin.

"Lady Granville-Hyde?"

What an oily man, so well lubricated I did not hear his approach.

"Stafford Grimes, at your service."

He offered to buy me a drink, but I drew the line at that unseemliness. That did not stop him ordering one for himself and sipping it—and several successors—noisily during the course of my questions. Years of Venusian light had turned his skin to wrinkled brown leather: drinker's eyes looked out from heavily hooded lids—years of squinting into the ultraviolet. His neck and hands were mottled white with pockmarks where melanomas had been frozen out. Sunburn, melancholy, and alcoholism: the classic recipe for Honorary Consuls system wide, not just on Venus.

"Thank you for agreeing to meet me. So, you met him."

"I will never forget him. Pearls of Aphrodite. Size of your head, Lady Ida. There's a fortune waiting for the man . . ."

"Or woman." I chided, and surreptitiously activated the recording ring beneath my glove.

> Plate 2: *V. flor scopulum*: The Ocean Mist Flower. The name
> is a misnomer: the Ocean Mist Flower is not a flower, but
> a coral animalcule of the aerial reefs of the Tellus Ocean.
> The seeming petals are absorption surfaces drawing mois-
> ture from the frequent ocean fogs of those latitudes. Pistils
> and stamen bear sticky palps which function in the same

fashion as Terrene spider webs trapping prey. Venus boasts an entire ecosystem of marine insects unknown on Earth.

This cut is the most three-dimensional of Lady Ida's *Botanica Veneris*. Reproductions only hint at the sculptural quality of the original. The "petals" have been curled at the edges over the blunt side of a pair of scissors. Each of the two hundred and eight palps has been sprung so that they stand proud from the black paper background.

Onion paper, hard-painted card.

The Honorary Consul's Tale

Pearls of Aphrodite. Truly, the pearl beyond price. The pearls of Starosts and Aztars. But the cloud reefs are perilous, Lady Ida. Snap a man's body clean in half, those bivalves. Crush his head like a Vulpeculan melon. Snare a hand or an ankle and drown him. Aphrodite's Pearls are blood pearls. A fortune awaits anyone, my dear, who can culture them. A charming man, Arthur Hyde—that brogue of his made anything sound like the blessing of heaven itself. Charm the avios from the trees—but natural, unaffected. It was no surprise to learn he was of aristocratic stock. Quality: you can't hide it. In those days, I owned a company—fishing trips across the archipelago. The legend of the Ourogoonta, the Island that is a Fish, was a potent draw. Imagine hooking one of those! Of course, they never did. No, I'd take them out, show them the cloud reefs, the Krid hives, the wing-fish migration, the air-jellies; get them pissed on the boat, take their photographs next to some thawed-out javelin-fish they hadn't caught. Simple, easy, honest money. Why wasn't it enough for me? I had done the trick enough times myself, drink one for the punter's two, yet I fell for it that evening in the Windward Tavern, drinking hot, spiced kashash and the night wind whistling up in the spires of the dead Krid nest-haven like the caged souls of drowned sailors. Drinking for days down the Great Twilight, his one for my two. Charming, so charming, until I had pledged my boat on his plan. He would buy a planktoneer—an old bucket of a sea skimmer with nary a straight plate or a true rivet in her. He would seed her with spores and send her north on the great circulatory current, like a maritime cloud reef. Five years that current takes to circulate the globe before it returns to the arctic waters that birthed it. Five years is also the time it takes the Clam of Aphrodite to mature—what we call pearls are no such thing. Sperm, Lady Ida. Compressed sperm. In waters, it dissolves and disperses.

Each Great Dawn the Tellus Ocean is white with it. In the air, it remains compact—the most prized of all jewels. Enough of fluids. By the time the reef ship reached the deep north, the clams would be mature and the cold water would kill them. It would be a simple task to strip the hulk with high-pressure hoses, harvest the pearls, and bank the fortune.

Five years makes a man fidgety for his investment. Arthur sent us week-ly reports from the Sea Wardens and the Krid argosies. Month on month, year on year, I began to suspect that the truth had wandered far from those chart coordinates. I was not alone. I formed a consortium with my fellow investors and chartered a 'rigible.

And there at Map 60 North, 175 East, we found the ship—or what was left of it, so overgrown was it with Clams of Aphrodite. Our investment had been lined and lashed by four Krid cantoons: as we arrived, they were in the process of stripping it with halberds and grappling hooks. Already the decks and superstructure were green with clam meat and purple with Krid blood. Arthur stood in the stern frantically waving a Cross of St. Patrick flag, gesturing for us to get out, get away.

Krid pirates were plundering our investment! Worse, Arthur was their prisoner. We were an unarmed aerial gadabout, so we turned tail and headed for the nearest Sea Warden castle to call for aid.

Charmer. Bloody buggering charmer. I know he's your flesh and blood, but . . . I should have thought! If he'd been captured by Krid pirates, they wouldn't have let him wave a bloody flag to warn us.

When we arrived with a constabulary cruiser, all we found was the cap-sized hulk of the planktoneer and a flock of avios gorging on clam offal. Duped! Pirates my arse—excuse me. Those four cantoons were laden to the gunwales with contract workers. He never had any intention of splitting the profits with us.

The last we heard of him, he had converted the lot into Bank of Ishtar Bearer Bonds—better than gold—at Yez Tok and headed in-country. That was twelve years ago.

Your brother cost me my business, Lady Granville-Hyde. It was a good business; I could have sold it, made a little pile. Bought a place on Ledekh Syant—maybe even make it back to Earth to see out my days to a decent calendar. Instead . . . Ach, what's the use? Please believe me when I say that I bear your family no ill will—only your brother. If you do succeed in finding him—and if I haven't, I very much doubt you will—remind him of that, and that he still owes me.

Plate 3: *V. lilium aphrodite*: the Archipelago sea lily. Walk-the-Water in Thekh: there is no comprehensible translation from Krid. A ubiquitous and fecund diurnal plant, it grows so aggressively in the Venerian Great Day that by Great Evening bays and harbors are clogged with blossoms and passage must be cleared by special bloom-breaker ships.

Painted paper, watermarked Venerian tissue, inks and scissor-scrolled card.

So dear, so admirable a companion, the Princess Lautfui. She knew I had been stinting with the truth in my excuse of shopping for paper, when I went to see the honorary consul down in Ledekh Port. Especially when I returned without any paper. I busied myself in the days before our sailing to Ishtaria on two cuts—the Sea Lily and the Ocean Mist Flower—even if it is not a flower, according to my Carfax's *Bestiary of the Inner Worlds*. She was not fooled by my industry and I felt soiled and venal. All Tongan women have dignity, but the princess possesses such innate nobility that the thought of lying to her offends nature itself. The moral order of the universe is upset. How can I tell her that my entire visit to this world is a tissue of fabrications?

Weather again fair, with the invariable light winds and interminable grey sky. I am of Ireland, supposedly we thrive on permanent overcast, but even I find myself pining for a glimpse of sun. Poor Latufui: she grows wan for want of light. Her skin is waxy, her hair lusterless. We have a long time to wait for a glimpse of sun: Carfax states that the sky clears partially at the dawn and sunset of Venus's Great Day. I hope to be off this world by then.

Our ship, the *Seventeen Notable Navigators*, is a well-built, swift Krid *jaicoona*—among the Krid the females are the seafarers, but they equal the males of my world in the richness and fecundity of their taxonomy of ships. A *jaicoona*, it seems, is a fast catamaran steam packet, built for the archipelago trade. I have no sea legs, but the *Seventeen Notable Navigators* was the only option that would get us to Ishtaria in reasonable time. Princess Latufui tells me it is a fine and sturdy craft though built to alien dimensions: she has banged her head most painfully several times. Captain Highly-Able-at-Forecasting, recognizing a sister seafarer, engages the princess in lengthy conversations of an island-hopping, archipelagan nature, which remind Latufui greatly of her home islands. The other humans aboard are a lofty Thekh, and Hugo Von Trachtenberg, a German in very high regard of himself, of that feckless type who think themselves gentleman adventurers but are little more than grandiose fraudsters. Nevertheless, he speaks Krid (as truly as any Terrene can) and acts as translator between princess and captain. It is a Venerian truth universally recognized that two unaccompanied women travelers must be in need of a male protector. The dreary hours Herr von Trachtenberg fills with his notion of gay chitchat! And in the evenings, the interminable games of Barrington. Von Trachtenberg claims to have gambled the game professionally in the cloud casinos: I let him win enough for the sensation to go to his head, then take him game after game. Ten times champion of the County Kildare mixed bridge championships is more than enough to beat his hide at Barrington. Still he does not get the message—yes, I am a wealthy widow but I have no interest in jejune Prussians. Thus I retire to my cabin to begin my studies for the *crescite dolium* cut.

————

Has this world a more splendid sight than the harbor of Yez Tok? It is a city most perpendicular, of pillars and towers, masts and spires. The tall funnels of the ships, bright with the heraldry of the Krid maritime families, blend with god-poles and lighthouse and customs towers and cranes of the harbor, which in turn yield to the tower houses and campaniles of the Bourse, the whole rising to merge with the trees of the Ishtarian Littoral Forest—pierced here and there by the comical roofs of the estancias of the Thent *zavars* and the gilded figures of the star gods on their minarets. That forest also rises, a cloth of green, to break into the rocky palisades of the Exx Palisades. And there—oh how thrilling!—glimpsed through mountain passes unimaginably high, a glittering glimpse of the snows of the altiplano. Snow. Cold. Bliss!

It is only now, after reams of purple prose, that I realize what I was trying to say of Yez Tok: simply, it is city as botany—stems and trunks, boles and bracts, root and branch!

And out there, in the city-that-is-a-forest, is the man who will guide me farther in my brother's footsteps: Mr. Daniel Okiring.

> Plate 4: *V. crescite dolium*: the Gourd of Plenty. A ubiquitous climbing plant of the Ishtari littoral, the Gourd of Plenty is so well adapted to urban environments that it would be considered a weed, but for the gourds, which contains a nectar prized as a delicacy among the coastal Thents. It is toxic to both Krid and humans.
>
> The papercut bears a note on the true scale, written in gold ink.

The Hunter's Tale

Have you seen a janthar? Really seen a janthar? Bloody magnificent, in the same way that a hurricane or an exploding volcano is magnificent. Magnificent and appalling. The films can never capture the sense of scale. Imagine a house, with fangs. And tusks. And spines. A house that can hit forty miles per hour. The films can never get the sheer sense of mass and speed—or the elegance and grace—that something so huge can be so nimble, so agile. And what the films can never, ever capture is the smell. They smell of curry. Vindaloo curry. Venerian body chemistry. But that's why you never, ever eat curry on *Asjan*. Out in the Stalva, the grass is tall enough to hide even a janthar. The smell is the only warning you get. You catch a whiff of vindaloo, you run.

You always run. When you hunt janthar, there will always be a moment when it turns, and the janthar hunts you. You run. If you're lucky, you'll draw it on to the gun line. If not . . . The 'thones of the Stalva have been hunting them this way for centuries. Coming-of-age thing. Like my own Maasai people. They give you a spear and point you in the general direction of a lion. Yes, I've killed a lion. I've also killed janthar—and run from even more.

The 'thones have a word for it: the *pnem*. The fool who runs.

That's how I met your brother. He applied to be a pnem for Okiring *Asjans*. Claimed experience over at Hunderewe with Costa's hunting company. I didn't need to call Costa to know he was a bullshitter. But I liked the fellow—he had charm and didn't take himself too seriously. I knew he'd never last five minutes as a pnem. Took him on as a camp steward. They like the personal service, the hunting types. If you can afford to fly yourself and your friends on a jolly to Venus, you expect to have someone to wipe your arse for you. Charm works on these bastards. He'd wheedle his way into their affections and get them drinking. They'd invite him and before you knew it he was getting their life-stories—and a lot more beside—out of them. He was a careful cove too—he'd always stay one drink behind them and be up early and sharp-eyed as a hawk the next morning. Bring them their bed tea. Fluff up their pillows. Always came back with the fattest tip. I knew what he was doing, but he did it so well—I'd taken him on, hadn't I? So, an aristocrat. Why am I not surprised? Within three trips, I'd made him Maître de la Chasse. Heard he'd made and lost one fortune already . . . is that true? A jewel thief? Why am I not surprised by that either?

The Thirtieth Earl of Mar fancied himself as a sporting type. Booked a three-month Grand *Asjan*; he and five friends, shooting their way up the

Great Littoral to the Stalva. Wives, husbands, lovers, personal servants, twenty Thent *asjanis* and a caravan of forty *graapa* to carry their bags and baggage. They had one *graap* just for the champagne—they'd shipped every last drop of it from Earth. Made so much noise we cleared the forest for ten miles around. Bloody brutes—we'd set up hides at waterholes so they could blast away from point blank range. That's not hunting. Every day they'd send a dozen bearers back with hides and trophies. I'm surprised there was anything left, the amount of metal they pumped into those poor beasts. The stench of rot . . . God! The sky was black with carrion avios.

Your brother excelled himself: suave, in control, charming, witty, the soul of attention. Oh, most attentive. Especially to the Lady Mar . . . She was no kack-hand with the guns, but I think she tired of the boys-club antics of the gents. Or maybe it was just the sheer relentless slaughter. Either way, she increasingly remained in camp. Where your brother attended to her. Aristocrats—they sniff each other out.

So Arthur poled the Lady Mar while we blasted our bloody, brutal, bestial way up onto the High Stalva. Nothing would do the thirtieth earl but to go after janthar. Three out of five *asanjis* never even come across a janthar. Ten percent of hunters who go for janthar don't come back. Only ten percent! He liked those odds.

Twenty-five sleeps we were up there, while Great Day turned to Great Evening. I wasn't staying for night on the Stalva. It's not just a different season, it's a different world. Things come out of sleep, out of dens, out of the ground. No, not for all the fortune of the earls of Mar would I spend night on the Stalva.

By then, we had abandoned the main camp. We carried bare rations, sleeping out beside our mounts with one ear tuned to the radio. Then the call came: Janthar sign! An *asjani* had seen a fresh path through a spear grass meadow five miles to the north of us. In a moment, we were mounted and tearing through the high Stalva. The earl rode like a madman, whipping his *graap* to reckless speed. Damn fool: of all the Stalva's many grasslands, the tall pike grass meadows were the most dangerous. A janthar could be right next to you and you wouldn't see it. And the pike grass disorients, reflects sounds, turns you around. There was no advising the Earl of Mar and his chums, though. His wife hung back—she claimed her mount had picked up a little lameness. Why did I not say something when Arthur went back to accompany the Lady Mar! But my concern was how to get everyone out of the pike grass alive.

Then the earl stabbed his shock goad into the flank of his *graap* and before I could do anything he was off. My radio crackled—form a gun line! The mad fool was going to run the janthar himself. Aristocrats! Your pardon, ma'am. Moments later, his *graap* came crashing back through the pike grass to find its herd mates. My only hope was to form a gun line and hope—and pray—that he would lead the janthar right into our crossfire. It takes a lot of ordnance to stop a janthar. And in this kind of tall-grass terrain, where you can hardly see your hand in front of your face, I had to set the firing positions just right so the idiots wouldn't blow each other to bits.

I got them into some semblance of position. I held the center—the *lakoo.* Your brother and the Lady Mar I ordered to take *jeft* and *garoon*—the last two positions of the left wing of the gun line. Finally, I got them all to radio silence. The 'thones teach you how to be still, and how to listen, and how to know what is safe and what is death. Silence, then a sustained crashing. My spotter called me, but I did not need her to tell me: that was the sound of death. I could only hope that the earl remembered to run in a straight line, and not to trip over anything, and that the gun line would fire in time . . . a hundred hopes. A hundred ways to die.

Most terrifying sound in the world, a janthar in full pursuit! It sounds like its coming from everywhere at once. I yelled to the gun line; steady there, steady. Hold your fire! Then I smelled it. Clear, sharp: unmistakable. Curry. I put up the cry: Vindaloo! Vindaloo! And there was the mad earl, breaking out of the cane. Madman! What was he thinking! He was in the wrong place, headed in the wrong direction. The only ones who could cover him were Arthur and Lady Mar. And there, behind him: the janthar. Bigger than any I had ever seen. The Mother of All Janthar. The Queen of the High Stalva. I froze. We all froze. We might as well try to kill a mountain. I yelled to Arthur and Lady Mar. Shoot! Shoot now! Nothing. Shoot for the love of all the stars! Nothing. Shoot! Why didn't they shoot?

The 'thones found the Thirtieth Earl of Mar spread over a hundred yards.

They hadn't shot because they weren't there. They were at it like dogs—your brother and the Lady Mar, back where they had left the party. They hadn't even heard the janthar.

Strange woman, the Lady Mar. Her face barely moved when she learned of her husband's terrible death. Like it was no surprise to her. Of course, she became immensely rich when the will went through. There was no question of your brother's ever working for me again. Shame. I liked him. But I can't help thinking that he was as much used as user in that sordid little affair. Did the Lady of Mar murder her husband? Too much left to chance. Yet it was a very convenient accident. And I can't help but think that the thirtieth earl knew what his lady was up to; and a surfeit of cuckoldry drove him to prove he was a man.

The janthar haunted the highlands for years. Became a legend. Every aristo idiot on the Inner Worlds who fancied himself a Great Terrene Hunter went after it. None of them ever got it though it claimed five more lives. The Human-Slayer of the Selva. In the end it stumbled into a 'thone clutch trap and died on a pungi stake, eaten away by gangrene. So we all pass. No final run, no gun line, no trophies.

Your brother—as I said, I liked him though I never trusted him. He left when the scandal broke—went up-country, over the Stalva into the Palisade country. I heard a rumor he'd joined a mercenary *javrost* unit, fighting up on the altiplano.

Botany, is it? Safer business than Big Game.

Plate 5: *V. trifex aculeatum*: Stannage's Bird-Eating Trifid. Native of the Great Littoral Forest of Ishtaria. Carnivorous in its habits; it lures smaller, nectar-feeding avios with its sweet exudate, then stings them to death with its whiplike style and sticky, poisoned stigma.

Cut paper, inks, folded tissue.

The princess is brushing her hair. This she does every night, whether in Tonga or Ireland, on Earth, or aboard a space-crosser, or on Venus. The ritual is invariable. She kneels, unpins, and uncoils her tight bun and lets her hair fall to its natural length, which is to the waist. Then she takes two silver-backed brushes, and, with great and vigorous strokes, brushes her hair from the crown of her head to the tips. One hundred strokes, which she counts in a Tongan rhyme that I very much love to hear.

When she is done, she cleans the brushes, returns them to the baize-lined case, then takes a bottle of coconut oil and works it through her hair. The air is suffused with the sweet smell of coconut. It reminds me so much of the whin flowers of home, in the spring. She works patiently and painstakingly, and when she has finished, she rolls her hair back into its bun and pins it. A simple, dedicated, repetitive task, but it moves me almost to tears.

Her beautiful hair! How dearly I love my friend Latufui!

We are sleeping at a hohvandha, a Thent roadside inn, on the Grand North Road in Canton Hoa in the Great Littoral Forest. Tree branches scratch at my window shutters. The heat, the humidity, the animal noise are all overpowering. We are far from the cooling breezes of the Vestal Sea. I wilt, though Latufui relishes the warmth. The arboreal creatures of this forest are deeper voiced than in Ireland; bellings and honkings and deep booms. How I wish we could spend the night here—Great Night—for my Carfax tells me that the Ishtarian Littoral Forest contains this world's greatest concentration of luminous creatures—fungi, plants, animals, and those peculiarly Venerian phyla in between. It is almost as bright as day. I have made some daytime studies of the Star Flower—no Venerian Botanica can be complete without it—but for it to succeed, I must hope that there is a supply of luminous paint at Loogaza; where we embark for the crossing of the Stalva.

My dear Latufui has finished now and closed away her brushes in their green baize-lined box. So faithful and true a friend! We met in Nuku'alofa on the Tongan leg of my Botanica of the South Pacific. The king, her father, had issued the invitation—he was a keen collector—and at the reception I was introduced to his very large family, including Latufui, and was immediately charmed by her sense, dignity, and vivacity. She invited me to tea the following day—a very grand affair—where she confessed that as a minor princess, her only hope of fulfilment was in marrying well—an institution in which she had no interest. I replied that I had visited the South Pacific as a time apart from Lord Rathangan—it had been clear for some years that he had no interest in me (nor I in him). We were two noble ladies of compatible needs and temperaments, and there and then we became firmest friends and inseparable companions. When Patrick shot himself and Rathangan passed into my possession, it was only natural that the princess move in with me.

I cannot conceive of life without Latufui; yet I am deeply ashamed that I have not been totally honest in my motivations for this Venerian expedition. Why can I not trust? Oh secrets! Oh simulations!

Plate 6: *V. stellafloris noctecandentis*: the Venerian Starflower. Its name is the same in Thent, Thekh, and Krid. Now a popular Terrestrial garden plant, where it is known as glow berry, though the name is a misnomer. Its appearance is a bunch of night-luminous white berries, though the berries are in fact globular bracts, with the bioluminous flower at the center. Selective strains of this flower traditionally provide illumination in Venerian settlements during the Great Night.

Paper, luminous paint (not reproduced). The original papercut is mildly radioactive.

By high train to Camahoo.

We have our own carriage. It is of aged gothar wood, still fragrant and spicy. The hammocks do not suit me at all. Indeed, the whole train has a rocking, swaying lollop that makes me seasick. In the caravanserai at Loogaza, the contraption looked both ridiculous and impractical. But here, in the high grass, its ingenuity reveals itself. The twenty-foot-high wheels carry us high above the grass, though I am in fear of grass fires—the steam tractor at the head of the train does throw off the most ferocious pother of soot and embers.

I am quite content to remain in my carriage and work on my Stalva-grass study—I think this may be most sculptural. The swaying makes for many a slip with the scissor, but I think I have caught the feathery, almost downy nature of the flower heads. Of a maritime people, the princess is at home in this rolling ocean of grass and spends much of her time on the observation balcony, watching the patterns the wind draws across the grasslands.

It was there that she fell into conversation with the Honorable Cormac de Buitlear, a fellow Irishman. Inevitably, he ingratiated himself and within minutes was taking tea in our carriage. The Inner Worlds are infested with young men claiming to be the junior sons of minor Irish gentry, but a few minutes' gentle questioning revealed not only that he was indeed the Honorable Cormac—of the Bagenalstown De Buitlears—but a relative, close enough to know of my husband's demise, and the scandal of the Blue Empress.

Our conversation went like this.

HIMSELF: The Grangegorman Hydes. My father used to knock around with your elder brother—what was he called?

MYSELF: Richard.

HIMSELF: The younger brother—wasn't he a bit of a black sheep? I remember there was this tremendous scandal. Some jewel—a sapphire as big as a thrush's egg. Yes—that was the expression they used in the papers. A thrush's egg. What was it called?

MYSELF: The Blue Empress.

HIMSELF: Yes! That was it. Your grandfather was presented it by some Martian princess. Services rendered.

MYSELF: He helped her escape across the Tharsis steppe in the revolution of '11, then organized the White Brigades to help her regain the Jasper Throne.

HIMSELF: Your brother, not the old boy. You woke up one morning to find the stone gone and him vanished. Stolen.

I could see that Princess Latufui found The Honorable Cormac's blunt-ness distressing, but if one claims the privileges of a noble family, one must also claim the shames.

MYSELF: It was never proved that Arthur stole the Blue Empress.

HIMSELF: No, no. But you know how tongues wag in the country. And his disappearance was, you must admit, *timely*. How long ago was that now? God, I must have been a wee gossoon.

MYSELF: Fifteen years.

HIMSELF: Fifteen years! And not a word? Do you know if he's even alive?

MYSELF: We believe he fled to the Inner Worlds. Every few years we hear of a sighting, but most of them are so contrary, we dismiss them. He made his choice. As for the Blue Empress; broken up and sold long ago, I don't doubt.

HIMSELF: And here I find you on a jaunt across one of the Inner Worlds.

MYSELF: I am creating a new album of papercuts. The *Botanica Veneris*.

HIMSELF: Of course. If I might make so bold, Lady Rathangan: the Blue Empress: do you believe Arthur took it?

And I made him no verbal answer but gave the smallest shake of my head.

Princess Latufui had been restless all this evening—the time before sleep, that is: Great Evening was still many Terrene days off. Can we ever truly adapt to the monstrous Venerian calendar? Arthur has been on this world for fifteen years—has he drifted not just to another world, but another clock, another calendar? I worked on my Stalva-grass cut—I find that curv-ing the leaf-bearing nodes gives the necessary three-dimensionality—but my heart was not in it. Latufui sipped at tea and fumbled at stitching and pushed newspapers around until eventually she threw open the cabin door in frustration and demanded that I join her on the balcony.

The rolling travel of the high train made me grip the rail for dear life, but the high plain was as sharp and fresh as if starched, and there, a long line on the horizon beyond the belching smokestack and pumping pistons of the tractor, were the Palisades of Exx: a grey wall from one horizon to the other. Clouds hid the peaks, like a curtain lowered from the sky.

Dark against the grey mountains, I saw the spires of the observatories of Camahoo. This was the Thent homeland; and I was apprehensive, for among those towers and minarets is a *hoondahvi*, a Thent opium den, owned by the person who might be able to tell me the next part of my brother's story—a story increasingly disturbing and dark. A person who is not human.

"Ida, dear friend. There is a thing I must ask you."

"Anything, dear Latufui."

"I must tell you, it is not a thing that can be asked softly."

My heart turned over in my chest. I knew what Latufui would ask.

"Ida: have you come to this world to look for your brother?"

She did me the courtesy of a direct question. No preamble, no preliminary sifting through her doubts and evidences. I owed it a direct answer.

"Yes," I said. "I have come to find Arthur."

"I thought so."

"For how long?"

"Since Ledekh-Olkoi. Ah, I cannot say the words right. When you went to get papers and gum and returned empty-handed."

"I went to see a Mr. Stafford Grimes. I had information that he had met my brother soon after his arrival on this world. He directed me to Mr. Okiring, a retired *asjan*-hunter in Yez Tok."

"And Cama-oo? Is this another link in the chain?"

"It is. But the Botanica is no sham. I have an obligation to my backers— you know the state of my finances as well as I, Latufui. The late Count Rathangan was a profligate man. He ran the estate into the ground."

"I could wish you had trusted me. All those weeks of planning and organizing. The maps, the itineraries, the tickets, the transplanetary calls to agents and factors. I was so excited! A journey to another world! But for you, there was always something else. None of that was the whole truth. None of it was honest."

"Oh, my dear Latufui . . ." But how could I say that I had not told her because I feared what Arthur might have become. Fears that seemed to be borne out by every ruined life that had touched his. What would I find? Did anything remain of the wild, carefree boy I remembered chasing old Bunty the dog across the summer lawns of Grangegorman? Would I recognize him? Worse, would he listen to me? "There is a wrong to right. An old debt to be cancelled. It's a family thing."

"I live in your house but not in your family," Princess Latufui said. Her words were barbed with truth. They tore me. "We would not do that in Tonga. Your ways are different. And I thought I was more than a companion."

"Oh, my dear Latufui." I took her hands in mine. "My dear dear Latufui. You are far far more to me than a companion. You are my life. But you of all people should understand my family. We are on another world, but we are not so far from Rathangan, I think. I am seeking Arthur, and I do not know what I will find, but I promise you, what he says to me, I will tell to you. Everything."

Now she laid her hands over mine, and there we stood, cupping hands on the balcony rail, watching the needle spires of Camahoo rise from the grass spears of the Stalva.

> Plate 7: *V. vallumque foenum*: Stalva Pike Grass. Another non-Terrene that is finding favor in Terrestrial ornamental gardens. Earth never receives sufficient sunlight for it to attain its full Stalva height. *Yetten* in the Stalva Thent dialect.
>
> Card, onionskin paper, corrugated paper, paint. This papercut is unique in that it unfolds into three parts. The original, in the Chester Beatty Library in Dublin, is always displayed unfolded.

The Mercenary's Tale

In the name of the Leader of the Starry Skies and the Ever-Circling Spiritual Family, welcome to my *hoondahvi*. May *apsas* speak; may *gavanda* sing, may the *thoo* impart their secrets!

I understand completely that you have not come to drink. But the greeting is standard. We pride ourselves on being the most traditional *hoondahvi* in Exxaa Canton.

Is the music annoying? No? Most Terrenes find it aggravating. It's an essential part of the *hoondahvi* experience, I am afraid.

Your brother, yes. How could I forget him? I owe him my life.

He fought like a man who hated fighting. Up on the altiplano, when we smashed open the potteries and set the Porcelain Towns afire up and down the Valley of the Kilns, there were those who blazed with love and joy at the slaughter and those whose faces were so dark it was as if their souls were clogged with soot. Your brother was one of those. Human expressions are hard for us to read—your faces are wood, like masks. But I saw his face and knew that he loathed what he did. That was what made him the best of *javrosts*. I am an old career soldier; I have seen many many come to our band. The ones in love with violence: unless they can take discipline, we turn them away. But when a mercenary hates what he does for his silver, there must be a greater darkness driving him. There is a thing they hate more than the violence they do.

Are you sure the music is tolerable? Our harmonies and chord patterns apparently create unpleasant electrical resonance in the human brain. Like small seizures. We find it most reassuring. Like the rhythm of the kittening womb.

Your brother came to us in the dawn of Great Day 6817. He could ride a *graap*, bivouac, cook, and was handy with both bolt and blade. We never ask questions of our *javrosts*—in time they answer them all themselves—but rumors blow on the wind like *thagoon* down. He was a minor aristocrat, he was a gambler; he was thief, he was a murderer; he was a seducer, he was a traitor. Nothing to disqualify him. Sufficient to recommend him.

In Old Days the Duke of Yoo disputed mightily with her neighbor the Duke of Hetteten over who rightly ruled the altiplano and its profitable potteries. From time immemorial, it had been a place beyond: independently minded and stubborn of spirit, with little respect for gods or dukes. Wars were fought down generations, laying waste to fames and fortunes, and when in the end the House of Yoo prevailed, the peoples of the plateau had forgotten they ever had lords and mistresses and debts of fealty. It is a law of earth and stars alike that people should be well governed, obedient, and quiet in their ways, so the Duke of Yoo embarked on a campaign of civil discipline. Her house corps had been decimated in the Porcelain Wars, so House Yoo hired mercenaries. Among them, my former unit, Gellet's *Javrosts*.

They speak of us still, up on the plateau. We are the monsters of their Great Nights, the haunters of their children's dreams. We are legend. We are Gellet's *Javrosts*. We are the new demons.

For one Great Day and Great Night, we ran free. We torched the topless star shrines of Javapanda and watched then burn like chimneys. We smashed the funerary jars and trampled the bones of the illustrious dead of Toohren. We overturned the houses of the holy, burned elders and kits in their homes. We lassoed rebels and dragged them behind our *graapa*, round and round the village, until all that remained was a bloody rope. We forced whole communities from their homes, driving them across the altiplano until the snow heaped their bodies. And Arthur was at my side. We were not friends—there is too much history on this world for human and Thent ever to be that. He was my *badoon*. You do not have a concept for it, let alone a word. A passionate colleague. A brother who is not related. A fellow devotee . . .

We killed and we killed and we killed. And in our wake came the Duke of Yoo's soldiers—restoring order, rebuilding towns, offering defense against the murderous renegades. It was all strategy. The Duke of Yoo knew the plateauneers would never love her, but she could be their savior.

Therefore, a campaign of final outrages was planned. Such vileness! We were ordered to Glehenta, a pottery town at the head of Valley of the Kilns. There we would enter the *glotoonas*—the birthing crèches—and slaughter every infant down to the last kit. We rode, Arthur at my side, and though human emotions are strange and distant to me, I knew them well enough to read the storm in his heart. Night snow was falling as we entered Glehenta, lit by ten thousand starflowers. The people locked their doors and cowered from us. Through the heart of town we rode; past the great conical kilns, to the *glotoonas*. Matres flung themselves before our *graapa*—we rode them down. Arthur's face was darker than the Great Midnight. He broke formation and rode up to Gellet himself. I went to him. I saw words between your brother and our commander. I did not hear them. Then Arthur drew his blasket and in single shot blew the entire top of Gellet's body to ash. In the fracas, I shot down three of our troop; then we were racing through the glowing streets, our hooves clattering on the porcelain cobbles, the erstwhile Gellet's *Javrosts* behind us.

And so we saved them. For the Duke of Yoo had arranged it so that her Ducal Guard would fall upon us even as we attacked, annihilate us, and achieve two notable victories: presenting themselves as the saviors of Glehenta and destroying any evidence of their scheme. Your brother and I sprung the trap. But we did not know until leagues and months later, far from the altiplano. At the foot of the Ten Thousand Steps, we parted—we thought it safer. We never saw each other again, though I heard he had gone back up the stairs, to the Pelerines. And if you do find him, please don't tell him what became of me. This is a shameful place.

And I am ashamed that I have told you such dark and bloody truths about your brother. But at the end, he was honorable. He was right. That he saved the guilty—an unintended consequence. Our lives are made up of such.

Certainly, we can continue outside on the *hoondahvi* porch. I did warn you that the music was irritating to human sensibilities.

Plate 8: *V. lucerna vesperum*; Schaefferia: the Evening Candle. A solitary tree of the foothills of the Exx Palisades of Ishtaria, the Schaefferia is noted for its many upright, luminous blossoms, which flower in Venerian Great Evening and Great Dawn.

Only the blossoms are reproduced. Card, folded and cut tissue, luminous paint (not reproduced). The original is also slightly radioactive.

A cog railway runs from Camahoo Terminus to the Convent of the Starry Pelerines. The Starsview Special takes pilgrims to see the stars and planets. Our carriage is small, luxurious, intricate, and ingenious in that typically Thent fashion, and terribly tedious. The track has been constructed in a helix inside Awk Mountain, so our journey consists of interminable, noisy spells inside the tunnel, punctuated by brief, blinding moments of clarity as we emerge onto the open face of the mountain. Not for the vertiginous!

Thus, hour upon hour, we spiral our way up Mount Awk.

Princess Latufui and I play endless games of Moon Whist, but our minds are not in it. My forebodings have darkened after my conversation with the Thent *hoondahvi* owner in Camahoo. The princess is troubled by my anxiety. Finally, she can bear it no more.

"Tell me about the Blue Empress. Tell me everything."

———

I grew up with two injunctions in case of fire: save the dogs and the Blue Empress. For almost all my life, the jewel was a ghost stone—present but unseen, haunting Grangegorman and the lives it held. I have a memory from earliest childhood of seeing the stone—never touching it—but I do not trust the memory. Imaginings too easily become memories, memories imaginings.

We are not free in so many things, we of the landed class. Richard would inherit, Arthur would make a way in the worlds, and I would marry as well as I could—land to land. The Barony of Rathangan was considered one of the most desirable in Kildare, despite Patrick's seeming determination to drag it to the bankruptcy court. A match was made, and he was charming and bold; a fine sportsman and a very handsome man. It was an equal match: snide comments from both halves of the county. The Blue Empress was part of my treasure—on the strict understanding that it remain in the custody of my lawyers. Patrick argued—and it was there that I first got an inkling of his true character—and the wedding was off the wedding was on the wedding was off the wedding was on again and the banns posted. A viewing was arranged, for his people to itemize and value the Hyde treasure. For the first time in long memory, the Blue Empress was taken from its safe and displayed to human view. Blue as the wide Atlantic it was, and as boundless and clear. You could lose yourself forever in the light inside that gem. And yes, it was the size of a thrush's egg.

And then the moment that all the stories agree on: the lights failed. Not so unusual at Grangegorman—the same grandfather who brought back the Blue Empress installed the hydro plant—and when they came back on again; the sapphire was gone: baize and case and everything.

We called upon the honor of all present, ladies and gentlemen alike. The lights would be put out for five minutes, and when they were switched back on, the Blue Empress would be back in the Hyde treasure. It was not. Our people demanded we call the police, Patrick's people, mindful of their client's attraction to scandal, were less insistent. We would make a further appeal to honor: if the Blue Empress was not back by morning, then we would call the guards.

Not only was the Blue Empress still missing, so was Arthur.

We called the Garda Siochana. The last we heard was that Arthur had left for the Inner Worlds.

The wedding went ahead. It would have been a greater scandal to call it off. We were two families alike in notoriety. Patrick could not let it go: he went to his grave believing Arthur and I had conspired to keep the Blue Empress out of his hands. I have no doubt that Patrick would have found a way of forcing me to sign over possession of the gem to him and would have sold it. Wastrel.

As for the Blue Empress: I feel I am very near to Arthur now. One cannot run forever. We will meet, and the truth will be told.

———

Then light flooded our carriage as the train emerged from the tunnel on to the final ramp and there, before us, its spires and domes dusted with snow blown from the high peaks, was the Convent of the Starry Pelerines.

> Plate 9: *V. aquilonis vitis visionum*: the Northern Littoral, or Ghost Vine. A common climber of the forests of the southern slopes of the Ishtari altiplano, domesticated and widely grown in Thent garden terraces. Its white, trumpet-shaped flowers are attractive, but the plant is revered for its berries. When crushed, the infused liquor known as *pula* creates powerful auditory hallucinations in Venerian physiology and forms the basis of the Thent mystical *hoondahvi* cult. In Terrenes, it produces a strong euphoria and a sense of omnipotence.
>
> Alkaloid-infused paper. Ida Granville-Hyde used Thent Ghost-Vine liquor to tint and infuse the paper in this cut. It is reported to be still mildly hallucinogenic.

The Pilgrim's Tale

You'll come out on to the belvedere? It's supposed to be off-limits to Terrenes—technically blasphemy—sacred space and all that—but the pelerines turn a blind eye. Do excuse the cough . . . ghastly, isn't it? Sounds like a bag of bloody loose change. I don't suppose the cold air does much for my dear old alveoli, but at this stage it's a matter of damn.

That's Gloaming Peak there. You won't see it until the cloud clears. Every Great Evening, every Great Dawn, for a few Earth-days at a time, the cloud breaks. It goes up, oh so much farther than you could ever imagine. You look up, and up, and up—and beyond it, you see the stars. That's why the pelerines came here. Such a sensible religion. The stars are gods. One star, one god. Simple. No faith, no heaven, no punishment, no sin. Just look up and wonder. The Blue Pearl: that's what they call our Earth. I wonder if that's why they care for us. Because we're descended from divinity? If only they knew! They really are very kind.

Excuse me. Bloody marvelous stuff, this Thent brew. I'm in no pain at all. I find it quite reassuring that I shall slip from this too too rancid flesh swaddled in a blanket of beatific thoughts and analgesic glow. They're very kind, the pelerines. Very kind.

Now, look to your right. There. Do you see? That staircase, cut into the rock, winding up up up. The Ten Thousand Steps. That's the old way to the altiplano. Everything went up and down those steps: people, animals, goods, palanquins and stick-stick men, traders and pilgrims and armies. Your brother. I watched him go, from this very belvedere. Three years ago, or was it five? You never really get used to the Great Day. Time blurs.

We were tremendous friends, the way that addicts are. You wouldn't have come this far without realizing some truths about your brother. Our degradation unites us. Dear thing. How we'd set the world to rights, over flask after flask of this stuff! He realized the truth of this place early on. It's the way to the stars. God's waiting room. And we, this choir of shambling wrecks, wander through it, dazzled by our glimpses of the stars. But he was a dear friend, a dear dear friend. Dear Arthur.

We're all darkened souls here, but he was haunted. Things done and things left undone, like the prayer book says. My father was a vicar—can't you tell? Arthur never spoke completely about his time with the *javrosts*. He hinted—I think he wanted to tell me, very much, but was afraid of giving me his nightmares. That old saw about a problem shared being a problem halved? Damnable lie. A problem shared is a problem doubled. But I would find him up here all times of the Great Day and Night, watching the staircase and the caravans and stick convoys going up and down. Altiplano porcelain, he'd say. Finest in all the worlds. So fine you can read the Bible through it. Every cup, every plate, every vase and bowl, was portered down those stairs on the shoulders of a stickman. You know he served up on the altiplano, in the Duke of Yoo's Pacification. I wasn't here then, but Aggers was, and he said you could see the smoke going up—endless plumes of smoke, so thick the sky didn't clear and the pelerines went for a whole Great Day without seeing the stars. All Arthur would say about it was, that'll make some fine china. That's what made porcelain from the Valley of the Kilns so fine: bones—the bones of the dead, ground up into powder. He would never drink from a Valley cup—he said it was drinking from a skull.

Here's another thing about addicts—you never get rid of it. All you do is replace one addiction with another. The best you can hope for is that it's a better addiction. Some become god addicts, some throw themselves into worthy deeds, or self-improvement, or fine thoughts, or helping others, God help us all. Me, my lovely little vice is sloth—I really am an idle little bugger. It's so easy, letting the seasons slip away; slothful days and indolent nights, coughing my life up one chunk at a time. For Arthur, it was the visions. Arthur saw wonders and horrors, angels and demons, hopes and fears. True visions—the things that drive men to glory or death. Visionary visions. It lay up on the altiplano, beyond the twists and turns of the Ten Thousand Steps. I could never comprehend what it was, but it drove him. Devoured him. Ate his sleep, ate his appetite, ate his body and his soul and his sanity.

It was worse in the Great Night . . . Everything's worse in the Great Night. The snow would come swirling down the staircase and he saw things in it—faces—heard voices. The faces and voices of the people who had died, up there on the altiplano. He had to follow them, go up, into the Valley of the Kilns, where he would ask the people to forgive him—or kill him.

And he went. I couldn't stop him—I didn't want to stop him. Can you understand that? I watched him from this very belvedere. The pelerines are not our warders, any of us is free to leave at any time though I've seen anyone leave but Arthur. He left in the evening, with the lilac light catching Gloaming Peak. He never looked back. Not a glance to me. I watched him climb the steps to that bend there. That's where I lost sight of him. I never saw or heard of him again. But stories come down the stairs with the stickmen and they make their way even to this little aerie; stories of a seer—a visionary. I look and I imagine I see smoke rising, up there on the altiplano.

It's a pity you won't be here to see the clouds break around the Gloaming, or look at the stars.

Plate 10: *V. genetric nives*: Mother-of-snows (direct translation from Thent). Ground-cover hi-alpine of the Exx Palisades. The plant forms extensive carpets of thousands of minute white blossoms.

The most intricate papercut in the *Botanica Veneris*. Each floret is three millimeters in diameter. Paper, ink, gouache.

A high-stepping spider-car took me up the Ten Thousand Steps, past caravans of stickmen, spines bent, shoulders warped beneath brutal loads of finest porcelain.

The twelve cuts of the *Botanica Veneris* I have given to the princess, along with descriptions and botanical notes. She would not let me leave, clung to me, wracked with great sobs of loss and fear. It was dangerous; a sullen land with Great Night coming. I could not convince her of my reason for heading up the stairs alone, for they did not convince even me. The one, true reason I could not tell her. Oh, I have been despicable to her! My dearest friend, my love. But worse even than that, false.

She stood watching my spider-car climb the steps until a curve in the staircase took me out of her sight. Must the currency of truth always be falsehood?

Now I think of her spreading her long hair out, and brushing it, firmly, directly, beautifully, and the pen falls from my fingers . . .

———

Egayhazy is a closed city; hunched, hiding, tight. Its streets are narrow, its buildings lean toward one another; their gables so festooned with starflower that it looks like a perpetual festival. Nothing could be further from the truth: Egayhazy is an angry city, aggressive and cowed: sullen. I keep my Ledbekh-Teltai in my bag. But the anger is not directed at me, though from the story I heard at the Camahoo *hoondahvi*, my fellow humans on this world have not graced our species. It is the anger of a country under occupation. On walls and doors, the proclamations of the Duke of Yoo are plastered layer upon layer: her pennant, emblazoned with the four white hands of House Yoo, flies from public buildings, the radio-station mast, tower tops and the gallows. Her *javrosts* patrol streets so narrow that their *graapa* can barely squeeze through them. At their passage, the citizens of Egayhazy flash jagged glares, mutter altiplano oaths. And there is another sigil: an eight-petaled flower; a blue so deep it seems almost to shine. I see it stenciled hastily on walls and doors and the occupation-force posters. I see it in little badges sewn to the quilted jackets of the Egayhazians; and in tiny glass jars in low-set windows. In the market of Yent, I witnessed *javrosts* overturn and smash a vegetable stall that dared to offer a few posies of this blue bloom.

The staff at my hotel were suspicious when they saw me working up some sketches from memory of this blue flower of dissent. I explained my work and showed some photographs and asked, what was this flower? A common plant of the high altiplano, they said. It grows up under the breath of the high snow; small and tough and stubborn. Its most remarkable feature is that it blooms when no other flower does—in the dead of the Great Night. The Midnight Glory was one name though it had another, newer, which entered common use since the occupation: The Blue Empress.

I knew there and then that I had found Arthur.

A pall of sulfurous smoke hangs permanently over the Valley of Kilns, lit with hellish tints from the glow of the kilns below. A major ceramics center on a high, treeless plateau? How are the kilns fueled? Volcanic vents do the firing, but they turn this long defile in the flank of Mount Tooloowera into a little hell of clay, bones, smashed porcelain, sand, slag and throat-searing sulfur. Glehenta is the last of the Porcelain Towns, wedged into the head of the valley, where the river Iddis still carries a memory of freshness and cleanliness. The pottery houses, like upturned vases, lean toward each other like companionable women.

And there is the house to which my questions guided me: as my informants described; not the greatest but perhaps the meanest; not the foremost but perhaps the most prominent, tucked away in an alley. From its roof flies a flag, and my breath caught: not the Four White Hands of Yoo—never that, but neither the Blue Empress. The smoggy wind tugged at the hand-and-dagger of the Hydes of Grangegorman.

Swift action: to hesitate would be to falter and fail, to turn and walk away, back down the Valley of the Kilns and the Ten Thousand Steps. I rattle the ceramic chimes. From inside, a huff and sigh. Then a voice: worn ragged, stretched and tired, but unmistakable.

"Come on in. I've been expecting you."

> Plate 11: *V. crepitant movebitvolutans.* Wescott's Wandering Star. A wind-mobile vine, native of the Ishtari altiplano, that grows into a tight spherical web of vines which, in the Venerian Great Day, becomes detached from an atrophied

root stock and rolls cross-country, carried on the wind. A central calyx contains woody nuts that produce a pleasant rattling sound as the Wandering Star is in motion.

Cut paper, painted, layered and gummed. Perhaps the most intricate of the Venerian papercuts.

The Seer's Story

Tea?

I have it sent up from Camahoo when the stickmen make the return trip. Proper tea. Irish breakfast. It's very hard to get the water hot enough at this altitude, but it's my little ritual. I should have asked you to bring some. I've known you were looking for me from the moment you set out from Loogaza. You think anyone can wander blithely into Glehenta?

Tea.

You look well. The years have been kind to you. I look like shit. Don't deny it. I know it. I have an excuse. I'm dying, you know. The liquor of the vine—it takes as much as it gives. And this world is hard on humans. The Great Days—you never completely adjust—and the climate: if it's not the thin air up here, it's the molds and fungi and spores down there. And the ultraviolet. It dries you out, withers you up. The town healer must have frozen twenty melanomas off me. No, I'm dying. Rotten inside. A leather bag of mush and bones. But you look very well, Ida. So, Patrick shot himself. Fifteen years too late, says I. He could have spared all of us . . . enough of that. But I'm glad you're happy. I'm glad you have someone who cares, to treat you the way you should be treated.

I am the Merciful One, the Seer, the Prophet of the Blue Pearl, the Earth Man, and I am dying.

I walked down that same street you walked down. I didn't ride, I walked, right through the center of town. I didn't know what to expect. Silence. A mob. Stones. Bullets. To walk right through and out the other side without a door opening to me. I almost did. At the very last house, the door opened and an old man came out and stood in front of me so that I could not pass. "I know you." He pointed at me. "You came the night of the *javrosts*." I was certain then that I would die, and that seemed not so bad a thing to me. "You were the merciful one, the one who spared our young." And he went into the house and brought me a porcelain cup of water and I drank it down, and here I remain. The Merciful One.

They have decided that I am to lead them to glory, or, more likely, to death. It's justice, I suppose. I have visions you see—*pula* flashbacks. It works differently on Terrenes than Thents. Oh, they're hardheaded enough not to believe in divine inspiration or any of that rubbish. They need a figurehead—the repentant mercenary is a good role, and the odd bit of mumbo jumbo from the inside of my addled head doesn't go amiss.

Is your tea all right? It's very hard to get the water hot enough this high. Have I said that before? Ignore me—the flashbacks. Did I tell you I'm dying? But it's good to see you; oh, how long is it?

And Richard? The children? And Grangegorman? And is Ireland . . . of course. What I would give for an eyeful of green, for a glimpse of summer sun, a blue sky.

So, I have been a conman and a lover, a soldier and an addict, and now I end my time as a revolutionary. It is surprisingly easy. The Group of Seven Altiplano Peoples' Liberation Army do the work: I release gnomic pronouncements that run like grassfire from here to Egayhazy. I did come up with the Blue Empress motif: the Midnight Glory: blooming in the dark, under the breath of the high snows. Apt. They're not the most poetic of people, these potters. We drove the Duke of Yoo from the Valley of the Kilns and the Ishtar Plain: she is resisted everywhere, but she will not relinquish her claim on the altiplano so lightly. You've been in Egayhazy—you've seen the forces she's moving up here. Armies are mustering and my agents report 'rigibles coming through the passes in the Palisades. An assault will come. The Duke has an alliance with House Shorth—some agreement to divide the altiplano up between them. We're outnumbered. Outmaneuvered and outsupplied, and we have nowhere to run. They'll be at each other's throats within a Great Day, but that's a matter of damn for us. The Duke may spare the kilns—they're the source of wealth. Matter of damn to me. I'll not see it, one way or other. You should leave, Ida. *Pula* and local wars—never get sucked into them.

Ah. Unh. Another flashback. They're getting briefer, but more intense.

Ida, you are in danger. Leave before night—they'll attack in the night. I have to stay. The Merciful One, the Seer, the Prophet of the Blue Pearl can't abandon his people. But it was good, so good of you to come. This is a terrible place. I should never have come here. The best traps are the slowest. In you walk, through all the places and all the lives and all the years, never thinking that you are already in the trap, then you go to turn around, and it has closed behind you. Ida, go as soon as you can . . . go right now. You should never have come. But . . . oh, how I hate the thought of dying up here on this terrible plain! To see Ireland again . . .

Plate 12: *V. volanti musco*: Altiplano Air-moss. The papercut shows part of a symbiotic lighter-than-air creature of the

Ishtari altiplano. The plant part consists of curtains of extremely light hanging moss that gather water from the air and low clouds. The animal part is not reproduced.

Shredded paper, gum.

He came to the door of his porcelain house, leaning heavily on a stick, a handkerchief pressed to mouth and nose against the volcanic fumes. I had tried to plead with him to leave, but whatever else he has become, he is a Hyde of Grangegorman, and stubborn as an old donkey. There is a wish for death in him; something old and strangling and relentless with the gentlest eyes.

"I have something for you," I said, and I gave him the box without ceremony.

His eyebrows rose when he opened it.

"Ah."

"I stole the Blue Empress."

"I know."

"I had to keep it out of Patrick's hands. He would have broken and wasted it, like he broke and wasted everything." Then my slow mind, so intent on saying this confession right, that I had practiced on the space-crosser, and in every room and every mode of conveyance on my journey across this world, flower to flower, story to story: my middle-aged mind tripped over Arthur's two words. "You knew?"

"All along."

"You never thought maybe Richard, maybe Father, or Mammy, or one of the staff had taken it?"

"I had no doubt that it was you, for those very reasons you said. I chose to keep your secret, and I have."

"Arthur, Patrick is dead, Rathangan is mine. You can come home now."

"Ah, if it were so easy!"

"I have a great forgiveness to ask from you, Arthur."

"No need. I did it freely. And do you know what, I don't regret what I did. I was notorious—the Honorable Arthur Hyde, jewel thief and scoundrel. That has currency out in the worlds. It speaks reams that none of the people I used it on asked to see the jewel, or the fortune I presumably had earned from selling it. Not one. Everything I have done, I have done on reputation alone. It's an achievement. No, I won't go home, Ida. Don't ask me to. Don't raise that phantom before me. Fields of green and soft Kildare mornings. I'm valued here. The people are very kind. I'm accepted. I have virtues. I'm not the minor son of Irish gentry with no land and the arse hanging out of his pants. I am the Merciful One, the Prophet of the Blue Pearl."

"Arthur, I want you to have the jewel."

He recoiled as if I had offered him a scorpion.

"I will not have it. I will not touch it. It's an ill-favored thing. Unlucky. There are no sapphires on this world. You can never touch the Blue Pearl. Take it back to the place it came from."

For a moment, I wondered if he was suffering from another one of his hallucinating seizures. His eyes, his voice were firm.

"You should go Ida. Leave me. This is my place now. People have tremendous ideas of family—loyalty and undying love and affection: tremendous expectations and ideals that drive them across worlds to confess and receive forgiveness. Families are whatever works. Thank you for coming. I'm sorry I wasn't what you wanted me to be. I forgive you—though as I said there is nothing to forgive. There. Does that make us a family now? The Duke of Yoo is coming, Ida. Be away from here before that. Go. The townspeople will help you."

And with a wave of his handkerchief, he turned and closed his door to me.

I wrote that last over a bowl of altiplano mate at the stickmen's caravanserai in Yelta, the last town in the Valley of the Kilns. I recalled every word, clearly and precisely. Then I had an idea; as clear and precise as my recall of that sad, unresolved conversation with Arthur. I turned to my valise of papers, took out my scissors and a sheet of the deepest indigo and carefully, from memory, began to cut. The stickmen watched curiously, then with wonder. The clean precision of the scissors, so fine and intricate, the difficulty and accuracy of the cut, absorbed me entirely. Doubts fell from me: why had I come to this world? Why had I ventured alone into this noisome valley? Why had Arthur's casual acceptance of what I had done, the act that shaped both his life and mine, so disappointed me? What had I expected from him? Snip went the scissors, fine curls of indigo paper fell from them onto the table. It had always been the scissors I turned to when the ways of men grew too much. It was simple cut. I had the heart of it right away, no false starts, no new beginnings. Pure and simple. My onlookers hummed in appreciation. Then I folded the cut into my diary, gathered up my valises, and went out to the waiting spider-car. The eternal clouds seem lower today, like a storm front rolling in. Evening is coming.

I write quickly, briefly.

Those are no clouds. Those are the 'rigibles of the Duke of Yoo. The way is shut. Armies are camped across the altiplano. Thousands of soldiers and

436 | BOTANICA VENERIS

javrosts. I am trapped here. What am I to do? If I retreat to Glehenta, I will meet the same fate as Arthur and the Valley people—if they even allow me to do that. They might think that I was trying to carry a warning. I might be captured as a spy. I do not want to imagine how the Duke of Yoo treats spies. I do not imagine my Terrene identity will protect me. And the sister of the Seer, the Blue Empress! Do I hide in Yelta and hope that they will pass me by? But how could I live with myself knowing that I had abandoned Arthur?

There is no way forward, no way back, no way around.

I am an aristocrat. A minor one, but of stock. I understand the rules of class, and breeding. The Duke is vastly more powerful than I, but we are of a class. I can speak with her, gentry to gentry. We can communicate as equals.

I must persuade her to call off the attack.

Impossible! A middle-aged Irish widow, armed only with a pair of scissors. What can she do? Kill an army with gum and tissue? The death of a thousand papercuts?

Perhaps I could buy her off. A prize beyond prize: a jewel from the stars, from their goddess itself. Arthur said that sapphires are unknown on this world. A stone beyond compare.

I am writing as fast as I am thinking now.

I must go and face the Duke of Yoo, female to female. I am of Ireland, a citizen of no mean nation. We confront the powerful, we defeat empires. I will go to her and name myself and I shall offer her the Blue Empress. The true Blue Empress. Beyond that, I cannot say. But I must do it and do it now.

I cannot make the driver of my spider-car take me into the camp of the enemy. I have asked her to leave me and make her own way back to Yelta. I am writing this with a stub of pencil. I am alone on the high altiplano. Above the shield wall, the cloud layer is breaking up. Enormous shafts of dazzling light spread across the high plain. Two mounted figures have broken from the line and ride toward me. I am afraid—and yet I am calm. I take the Blue Empress from its box and grasp it tight in my gloved hand. Hard to write now. No more diary. They are here.

Plate 13: *V. Gloria medianocte*: The Midnight Glory, or Blue Empress.

Card, paper, ink.

JONAS AND THE FOX

RICH LARSON

For Grandma

A FLYER THUNDERS overhead through the pale purple sky, rippling the crops and blowing Jonas's hair back off his face. Fox has no hair to blow back: his scalp is shaven and still swathed in cling bandages from the operation. He knows the jagged black hunter drones, the ones people in the village called crows, would never recognize him now. He still ducks his head, still feels a spike of fear as the shadow passes over them.

Only a cargo carrier. He straightens up. Jonas, who gave the flyer a raised salute like a good little child of the revolution, looks back at him just long enough for Fox to see the scorn curling his lip. Then he's eyes-forward again, moving quickly through the rustling field of genemod wheat and canola. He doesn't like looking at Fox, at the body Fox now inhabits, any longer than he has to. It's becoming a problem.

"You need to talk to me when we're in the village," Fox says. "When we're around other people. Out here, it doesn't matter. But when we're in the village, you need to talk to me how you talked to Damjan."

Jonas's response is to speed up. He's tall for twelve years old. Long-legged, pale-skinned, with a determined jaw and a mess of tangled black hair. Fox can see the resemblance between Jonas and his father. More than he sees it in Damjan's face when he inspects his reflection in streaked windows, in the burnished metal blades of the harvester. But Damjan's face is still bruised and puffy and there is a new person behind it, besides.

Fox lengthens his stride. He's clumsy, still adjusting to his little-boy limbs. "It looks strange if you don't," he says. "You understand that, don't you? You have to act natural, or all of this was for nothing."

Jonas mumbles something he can't pick up. Fox feels a flash of irritation. It would've been better if Jonas hadn't known about the upload at all. His parents could have told him his brother had recovered from the fall, but with brain damage that made him move differently, act differently. But they told him the truth. They even let him watch the operation.

"What did you say?" Fox demands. His voice is still deep in his head, but it comes out shrill now, a little boy's voice.

Jonas turns back with a livid red mark on his forehead. "You aren't natural," he says shakily. "You're a digital demon."

Fox narrows his eyes. "Is that what the teachers are telling you, now?" he asks. "Digital storage isn't witchcraft, Jonas. It's technology. Same as the pad you use at school."

Jonas keeps walking, and Fox trails after him like he really is his little brother. The village parents let their children wander in the fields and play until dusk—it seems like negligence to Fox, who grew up in cities with a puffy white AI nanny to lead him from home to lessons and back. Keeping an eye on Jonas is probably the least Fox can do, after everything the family has done to keep him safe. Everything that happened since he rapped at their window in the middle of the night, covered in dry blood and wet mud, fleeing for his life.

They pass the godtree, the towering trunk and thick tubular branches that scrape against a darkening sky. Genetically derived from the baobobs on Old Earth, re-engineered for the colder climes of the colony. Fox has noticed Jonas doesn't like to look at the tree, either, not since his little brother tumbled out of it.

The godtree marks the edge of the fields and the children don't go past it, but today Jonas keeps walking and Fox can only follow. Beyond the tree the soil turns pale and thick with clay, not yet fully terraformed. The ruins of a quickcrete granary are backlit red by the setting sun. Fox saw it on his way in, evaluated it as a possible hiding place. But the shadows had spooked him, and in the end he'd pressed on toward the lights, toward the house on the very edge of the village he knew belonged to his distant cousin.

"Time to go back, Jonas," Fox says. "It'll be dark soon."

Jonas's lip curls again, and he darts toward the abandoned granary. He turns to give a defiant look before he slips through the crumbling doorway. Fox feels a flare of anger. The little shit knows he can't force him to do anything. He's taller than him by a head now.

"Do you think I like this?" Fox hisses under his breath. "Do you think I like having stubby little legs and a flaccid little good-for-nothing cock?" He follows after Jonas. A glass bottle crunches under his foot and makes him flinch. "Do you think I like everything tasting like fucking sand because that patched-up autosurgeon almost botched the upload?" he mutters, starting forward again. "I was someone six months ago, I drew crowds, and now I'm a little shit chasing another little shit around in the country and . . ."

A sharp yelp from inside the granary. Fox freezes. If Jonas has put an old nail through his foot, or turned his ankle, he knows Damjan's little arms aren't strong enough to drag him all the way home. Worse, if the ruin is occupied by a squatter, someone on the run like Fox who can't afford witnesses, things could go badly very quickly. Fox has never been imposing even in his own body.

With his heart rapping hard at his ribs, he picks up the broken bottle by the stem, turning the jagged edge outward. Maybe it's nothing. "Jonas?" he calls, stepping toward the dark doorway. "Are you alright?"

No answer. Fox hesitates, thinking maybe it would be better to run. Maybe some desperate refugee from the revolution has already put a shiv through Jonas's stomach and is waiting for the next little boy to wander in.

"Come and look," comes Jonas's voice from inside, faint-sounding. Fox drops the bottle in the dirt. He exhales. Curses himself for his overactive imagination. He goes into the granary, ready to scold Jonas for not responding, ready to tell him they are leaving right now, but all of that dies in his throat when he sees what captured Jonas's attention.

Roughly oblong, dark composite hull with red running lights that now wink to life in response to their presence, opening like predatory eyes. The craft is skeletal, stripped down to an engine and a passenger pod and hardly anything else. Small enough to slip the blockade, Fox realizes. So why had it been hidden here instead of used?

Fox blinks in the gloom, raking his eyes over and around the pod, and catches sight of a metallic-gloved hand flopped out from behind the craft's conical nose. His eyes are sharper now. He supposes that's one good thing. Jonas hasn't noticed it yet, too entranced by the red running lights and sleek shape. He's even forgotten his anger for the moment.

"Is it a ship?" he asks, voice layered with awe.

Fox snorts. "Barely."

He's paying more attention to the flight glove, studying the puffy fingers and silvery streaks of metal running through the palm. It's not a glove. Bile scrapes up his throat. Fox swallows it back down and steps around the nose of the craft.

The dead man tore off most of his clothing before the end. His exposed skin is dark and puffy with pooled blood, and silver tendrils skim underneath it like the gnarled roots of a tree, spreading from his left shoulder across his whole body. Fox recognizes the ugly work of a nanite dart. The man might have been clipped days or even weeks ago without knowing it. He was this close to escaping before it ruptured his organs.

"What's that?" Jonas murmurs, standing behind him now.

"Disgusting," Fox says.

But there's no time to mourn for the dead when the living are trying to stay that way. A month hiding in the family cellar, then Damjan's accident, the tearful arguments, the bloody operation by black-market autosurgeon. Uploading to the body of a braindead little boy while his own was incinerated to ash and cracked bone to keep the sniffers away. It was all for nothing.

His chance at escape had been waiting for him here in the ruins all along.

"You can't tell anyone about this, Jonas," Fox says. "None of your friends. Nobody at school."

Jonas's nostrils flares. His mouth opens to protest.

"If you tell anyone about this, I'll tell everyone who I really am," Fox cuts him off. He feels a dim guilt and pushes through it. This is his chance to get off-world, maybe his only chance. He can't let anyone ruin it. He needs to put a scare into the boy. "Your parents will be taken away to prison for helping me," he says. "They'll torture them. Do you want that, Jonas?"

Jonas shakes his dark head. His defiant eyes look suddenly scared.

"Don't tell anyone," Fox repeats. "Come on. Time to go home."

Fox thought himself brave once, but he is realizing more and more that he is a coward. He leads the way back through the rustling fields, past the twisting godtree, as dusk shrouds the sky overhead.

———

Don't tell anyone. It's the refrain Jonas has heard ever since the morning he came into the kitchen to find all the windows shuttered, their one pane of smart glass turned opaque, and a strange man sitting at the table, picking splinters from the wood. When he looked up and saw Jonas, he flinched. That, and the fact that his mother was scrubbing her hands in the sink as if nothing was out of the ordinary, made Jonas brave enough to stare.

The man was tall and slim and his hands on the table were soft-looking with deep blue veins. There were dark circles under his eyes and the tuft of hair that wasn't hidden away under the hood of father's stormcoat was a fiery orange Jonas had never seen before. Everyone in the village had dark hair.

Damjan, who had followed him from his bunk how he always did, jostled Jonas from behind, curious. Jonas fed him an elbow back.

Their mother looked up. She dried her scalded red hands in her apron. "Jonas, Damjan, this is your uncle who's visiting," she said, in a clipped voice. But this uncle looked nothing like the boisterous ones with bristly black beards who helped his father repair the thresher and drank bacteria beer and sometimes leg-wrestled when they drank enough of it.

"Pleased to meet you, what's your name?" Jonas asked.

The man tugged at the hood again, pulling it further down his face. He gave a raspy laugh. "My name is nobody," he said, but Jonas knew that wasn't a real name.

"What's uncle's name?" he asked his mother.

"Better you don't know," she said, still twisting her fingers in her apron. "And you can't tell anyone uncle is visiting us. Same for you, Damjan."

But Damjan hardly ever spoke anyways, and when he did he stammered badly. Jonas was going to tell his new uncle this when the front door banged open. His uncle flinched and his mother did, too, cursing under her breath how Jonas wasn't allowed to. He didn't know what they were scared of, since it was only father back from the yard. He stank like smoke.

"Burned everything," he said. "The gloves too, I'll need new ones." His eyes flicked over to Jonas and Damjan, slightly bloodshot, slightly wild. "Good morning, my beautiful sons," he said, crossing the room in his long bouncing stride to ruffle Jonas's hair how he always did, to kiss Damjan on his flat forehead.

"Wash first!" Jonas's mother hissed. "Damn it. Wash first, you hear?"

Father's face went white. He swallowed, nodded, then went to the basin and washed. "You've met your uncle, yes, boys?" he asked, slowly rinsing his hands. "You've said hello?"

Jonas nodded, and Damjan nodded to copy him. "Is uncle here because of the revolution?" he asked.

Lately all things had to do with the revolution. Ever since the flickery blue holo-footage, broadcast from a pirate satellite, that had been projected on the back wall of old Derozan's shop one night. The whole village had crowded around to watch as the rebels, moving like ghosts, took the far-off capital and dragged the aristos out from their towers. Jonas had cheered along with everyone else.

"He is," father said, exchanging a look with Jonas's mother. "Yes. He is. A lot of people had to leave the cities, after the revolution. Do you remember when the soldiers came?"

Jonas remembered. They came in a roaring hover to hand out speaka-loud pamphlets and tell the village they were Liberated, now. That they could keep the whole harvest, other than a small token of support to the new government of Liberated People.

"Some of them were looking for your uncle," father said. "If anyone finds out he's here, he'll be killed. So don't talk about him. Don't even think about him. Pretend he's not here."

Jonas's new uncle had no expression on his gaunt face, but on top of the wooden table his hands clenched so hard that the knuckles throbbed white.

———

After supper is over and Jonas goes to bed, Fox stays behind to speak to his parents. There is a new batch of bacteria beer ready and Petar pours each of them a tin cup full. It's dark and foamy and the smell makes Fox's stomach turn, but he takes it between his small hands. His cousin Petar is tall and handsome in a way Fox never was, but he has aged a decade in the weeks since Damjan fell. There are streaks of gray at his temples and his eyes are bagged. He slumps when he sits.

His wife Blanka conceals it better. She is the same mixture of cheery and sharp-tongued as she was before. In public she holds to Fox's hand and scolds and smiles as if he really is Damjan, so realistic Fox worried for her mind at first. But he knows now it's only that she's a better actor than her husband, and more viscerally aware of what will happen if someone discovers the truth: that Damjan's brain-dead body is inhabited by a fugitive poet and enemy of the revolution. She drinks the stinking bacteria beer every night, even when Petar doesn't.

"Jonas and I found something in the field today," Fox says, hating how his voice comes shrill and high when he's trying to speak of something so important. "A ship."

Petar was using his thumb to wipe the foam off the top of his cup, but now he looks up. "What kind of ship?" he asks.

"Just a dinghy," Fox says. "Small. One pod. But everything's operational. It only needs a refuel." He takes a swallow of beer too big for his child's throat, and nearly chokes. "Someone was going to use it to break the blockade before a nanodart finished them off," he says. "Now that someone could be me. If you help me again. With this one last thing."

His chest is tight with hope and fear. Petar looks to Blanka.

"You would leave," Blanka says. "In Damjan's body."

Fox nods his bandaged head. "The transfer was a near thing," he said. "Even if we could find that bastard with the autosurgeon again, trying to extract could wipe me completely."

That isn't true, not strictly true. He would probably survive, but missing memories and parts of his personality, the digital copy lacerated and corrupted. That might be worse than getting wiped.

"So, we would have another funeral," Petar says. "Another funeral for Damjan, but this time with all the village watching and with no body to bury."

"You can tell people it was a blood clot," Fox says. "An aftereffect from the fall. And the casket can stay closed."

Petar and Blanka look at each other again, stone-faced. People are different out here in the villages. Hard to read. It makes Fox anxious.

"Then you can be at peace," he says. "You don't have to see . . . This." He encompasses his body with one waving hand. "You just have to help me one more time. It might be the best shot I'll ever have at getting off-world."

"Maybe the ship was put there as a trap," Blanka says. "Did you think of that, poet? To draw you or other aristos out of hiding."

Fox hadn't thought of that, but he shakes his head. "They wouldn't go to that much trouble," he says. "Not for me or anyone else that's left. All the important people digicast out before the capital fell." He leans forward, toes barely scraping the floor. "I'll never forget what your family has done for me."

"Family helps family," Petar mutters. "Family over everything." He looks up from his beer and Fox sees his eyes are wet. "I'll need to see the ship," he says. "You've been safe like this, in Damjan's body. Maybe now you can escape and be safe forever. Maybe that is why Damjan fell. His life for your life."

His shoulders begin to shake, and Blanka puts her arm across them. She pulls Fox's beer away and pours it slowly into her empty cup. "It's time for you to go to bed," she tells him, not looking into his eyes—into Damjan's eyes.

Fox goes. The room he shares with Jonas is tiny, barely big enough to fit the two quickfab slabs that serve as beds. Jonas isn't asleep, though. He's sitting upright with his blanket bunched around his waist.

"You're going to take the ship, aren't you?" he says. "You're going to go up into space and visit the other worlds and see all the stars up close. That's what aristos do." The penultimate word is loaded with disdain.

"I'm going to get away from the people who want me executed," Fox says.

Jonas slides down into his bed, turned away facing the wall. "Aristos go up and we sit in the mud, teacher says. Aristo bellies are full of our blood."

"Your teacher spouts whatever the propaganda machine sends him," Fox says wearily. *"Bellies bloated with the blood of the masses.* That was my line. Bet your teacher didn't tell you that."

Jonas doesn't reply.

Fox undresses himself and climbs into bed. He tries, and fails, to sleep.

————

Jonas doesn't sleep right away either. He's wary of bad dreams since the day he climbed the godtree. The day they learned, in school, about the smooth white storage cone embedded in the backs of the aristos' soft-skinned necks.

Their new teacher was a tall stern man dressed all in black, replacing the chirping AI that had taught them songs and games, but everyone got brand new digipads so they didn't mind. All the lessons were about the revolution, about the aristos who'd kept their boot on the throat of the people for too long and now were reaping the harvest, which made no sense to Jonas because the teacher also said aristos were weak and lazy and didn't know how to work in the fields.

One day the teacher projected a picture on the wall that showed a man without skin or muscles, showing his gray skeleton, and a white knob sunk into the base of the skull.

"This is where aristos keep a copy of themselves," the teacher said, pointing with his long skinny finger. "This is what lets them steal young healthy bodies when their old ones die. It's what lets them cross the stars, going from world to world, body to body, like a disease. Like digital de-mons."

Jonas thought of his uncle who stayed in the basement, the hood he al-ways wore. That, and his soft hands, his way of speaking that swallowed no sounds, made it obvious.

He was an aristo. It made Jonas frightened and excited at the same time. Had he lived in a sky-scraping tower in the city and eaten meat and put his boot on the throat of the good simple people? Had he skipped through the stars and been to other worlds?

When Jonas came home from school, he tried to ask his father, but his father shook his head.

"Whatever he was, he's family," he said. "Family over everything. So you can't talk about him. Don't even think about him. Promise me, Jonas."

But it was hard to not think about. Especially hard to not think about the stars and the other worlds. Jonas knew the branches of the godtree were the best place to watch the stars from. To dream from. Sometimes they looked close enough to touch, if he could only climb high enough and stretch out his arms. Jonas was a good climber. Feeling electric with new excitement, he dodged his mother's chores that day and went out to the fields.

He barely noticed Damjan following, how he always followed.

Fox is waiting outside the small quickcrete cube of a building that serves as the village school. The pocked gray walls are painted over with a mural, a cheery yellow sun and blooming flowers. All the children streamed out a few minutes ago, chattering, laughing. Some of them came over to touch Fox gingerly on the head and ask if he was better yet. Fox encounters this question often and finds it easiest to nod and smile vaguely. He knows Damjan was never much of a talker.

But the last of the children have gone home now, and Jonas still hasn't come out. It's making Fox anxious. He stands up from his squat—he can squat for ages now, Damjan's small wiry legs are used to it more than they are to chairs—and walks around the edge of the building, toward the window. The smart glass is dimmed, and scratched, besides, but when he stands on tip-toe he can see silhouettes. One is Jonas and the other a tall, straight-backed teacher with his arms folded across his chest. The conversation is muffled.

Fear prickles in Fox's stomach again, the fear that's threatened to envelop him ever since a friend woke him in the middle of the night and showed him his face on the blacklist, declared an enemy of the Liberated People. The new government isn't stupid. They know to start with the children. Jonas's head is full of the vitriol Fox helped spark not so long ago, back when he'd fooled himself into thinking the violence of the revolution would be brief and justified.

Fox's heart pounds now. He sees Jonas's silhouette turn to leave, and he quickly darts back to his usual waiting place outside the main door. The boy comes out with a scowl on his face that falters, then deepens, when he catches sight of Fox. He gives only the slightest jerk of his head as acknowledgement, then goes to walk past.

Fox doesn't let him. "What did you tell him?" he demands in a whisper, seizing Jonas's arm.

Jonas wrests it away. His expression turns hard to read, like his parents'. Then a hesitant smirk appears on his face.

Fox feels the panic welling up. "What did you do?" he demands, grabbing for him again.

Jonas grabs back, pinching his hand hard with his nails. "Come on, Damjan," he says with a fake cheeriness, tugging him along. "Home time, Damjan."

"You stupid little shit," Fox rasps, barely able to speak through the tightness in his chest. "They'll take your parents, you know that? They'll take them away for helping me. You'll never see them again." He can already hear the whine of a hunter drone, the stamp of soldiers' boots. His head spins. "The fall wasn't my fault," he says, with no aim now but lashing out like a cornered animal. "It was yours."

Jonas's face goes white. His hand leaps off Fox's like it's been burnt. "He followed me," Jonas says. "I told him to wait on the low branch. But he didn't." He's gone still as a statue. A sob shudders through him. "I didn't tell teacher anything."

"What?" Fox feels a wave of relief, then shame.

"I didn't tell teacher about you," Jonas hiccups, and then his eyes narrow. "I should have. I should tell him. If I tell him, they'll forgive my parents. They aren't aristos. They're good. They're Liberated People."

Suddenly, Jonas is turning back toward the school, his jaw set like his father's. The red mark on his forehead is back.

"Wait," Fox pleads. "Jonas. Let me explain myself."

Jonas stops, turns. Giving him a chance.

Fox's mind whirls through possibilities. "The fall wasn't your fault," he says slowly. "And Damjan knows that."

"Damjan is dead," Jonas says through clenched teeth. "His brain had no electric in it."

"But when they did the transfer," Fox says. "You remember that, yes? The surgery? When they put my storage cone into Damjan's brainstem, I got to see his memories. Just for a moment."

Jonas's eyes narrow again, but he stays where he is. He wipes his nose, smearing snot across the heel of his hand.

"I saw Damjan wanted to follow you up the tree," Fox says slowly, feeling his way into the lie. "Because he always wanted to be like you. He knew you were strong and brave and honest. He was trying to be like you, even though he knew he should have waited on the lower branch. And when he fell, he didn't want you to feel bad. He didn't want you to feel guilty." Fox taps the back of his bandaged head, where the storage cone is concealed. "That was the last thing Damjan thought."

Tears are flowing freely down Jonas's cheeks now. "I wanted to go higher," he says. "When I go high enough, it feels like I can touch the sky."

Fox reaches up and puts his hand on Jonas's shoulder, softly this time. His panic is receding. He has Jonas solved now. There's a bit of guilt in his gut, but he's told worse lies. He would tell a dozen more to make sure nothing goes wrong, not now that Petar has seen the ship and agrees it will fly. Not now that he's so close to escaping.

————

Jonas's father has forbidden him to go near the granary again, but he still goes out to the fields the next day. He has always bored quickly of the games the other children play, even though he can throw the rubber ball as hard as anyone and dodges even better. He's always preferred to wander.

His nameless uncle is with him. It's still hard to look at Damjan's face and know Damjan is not behind it, but talking comes a little easier since what happened yesterday. When his uncle asks why he was kept behind after school by the teacher, Jonas tells him the truth.

"We're learning about the revolution," he says. "About the heroes. Stanko was my favorite. He took the capital with a hundred fighters and he's got an eye surgery to see in the dark. But yesterday the lesson changed on my pad." He motions with his hand, trying to capture how the text all dissolved and then reformed, so quick he barely noticed it. "Now it says General Bjelica took the capital. It says Stanko was a traitor and they had to execute him. So I told teacher it wasn't right."

Damjan's face screws up how it does before he cries, but no tears come out, and Jonas knows it's because grown-ups don't cry. "I met Stanislav once," his uncle says. "He was a good man. Maybe too good. An idealist."

"You met Stanko?" Jonas demands. "What did his eyes look like?"

His uncle blinks. "Bright," he says. "Like miniature suns."

Jonas stops where he is, the tall grass rustling against his legs, as he envisions Stanko tall and strong with eyes blazing. "Like stars," he murmurs.

His uncle nods. "Maybe he got away," he says. "There's a lot of false reports. Maybe he's in hiding somewhere."

Jonas asks the question, then, the one that has been bubbling in the back of his mind for days. "The revolution is good," he says. "Isn't it?"

His uncle gives a laugh with no happiness in it. "I thought it was," he says. "Until the bloodshed. Until cynics and thugs like Bjelica took over. After everything I did for their cause—all the rallies, all the writing—they turned on me. Ungrateful bastards."

"Why did you want the revolution if you're an aristo?" Jonas asks plainly.

"Because there weren't meant to be aristocrats or underclass after the revolution," his uncle says, with a trace of anger in Damjan's shrill voice. "Everyone was meant to be equal. But history is a wheel and we always make the same mistakes. The only difference is who gets crushed into the mud." He picks anxiously at a stalk. "The ruling families were bad," he says. "The famines, and all that. But this is worse."

Jonas considers it. The teacher told them that there would be no famines anymore. They would keep their whole crop, except for a small token of support to the government of Liberated People. "Did you lose many in the famine?" he asks, because it's a grown-up question. "I had a little sister who died. And that's why Damjan is different. Was different. Because mother couldn't feed him well enough."

Damjan's mouth twists. For a moment his uncle doesn't respond. "No," he finally says. "Not many." Damjan's face is red, and Jonas realizes his uncle is ashamed of something, though what he can't guess. "I wrote a poem series about the famine," he says. "Years ago. I still remember it. Do you want to hear some of it, maybe?"

Jonas hesitates. He doesn't know if he likes poetry. But maybe if he listens to the poetry, he can ask more questions about Stanko and the capital, and then about the stars and the other worlds his uncle will soon go to.

"Alright," he agrees. "If it's not really long."

———

The week passes at two speeds for Fox, agonizingly slow and terrifyingly fast. Petar has spread word that the old granary past the edge of the terraform has broken glass and an old leaking oil drum inside it, to ensure the other parents keep their children away. Fox's nights are spent poring over schematics with Blanka or else sneaking out to the ship itself with Petar.

During the day, he spends most of his time with Jonas. The boy is bright and never runs dry of questions, and ever since Fox's first recitation he's been devouring poetry. Not necessarily Fox's—he prefers it when Fox recites the older masters, the bolder and more rhythmic styles. He has even started scribbling his own poem using charcoal on the wall of their bedroom, which made Petar and then Blanka both shake their heads.

He reminds Fox a little bit of himself as a child. Too clever to get along with the other children, too brash and too stubborn, worryingly so. But Fox has other concerns. The ship is tuned and refueled and finally ready to fly, and the village's weather probe predicts a rolling storm in a fortnight. That's when Fox will launch, while the thunder and lightning masks the take-off. His days in the village, his days in Damjan's body, are finally numbered.

Fox is in the cramped bedroom, laboring with a piece of Jonas's charcoal. The boy's favorite poem is a short one, but even so it takes a long time for Fox to transcribe it onto the clear stretch of wall. He's only halfway finished the memento, his small hands smeared black, when he hears Jonas arrive home from the school. A moment later, he hears a shriek from Blanka.

Fox goes stiff and scared, ears strained for the thump of soldiers' boots, but there's nothing but Blanka's angry voice and Jonas's near-inaudible reply. He wipes his hands on his trousers and goes to the kitchen.

Jonas is standing sullenly with his shirt knotted in his hands. Blanka is in a rage, and Fox realizes why as soon as he sees the bruises on Jonas's bare back.

"That spindly bastard, I'll snap him in halves," she's snarling. "What happened, Jonas? What happened, my beautiful boy?"

Jonas lifts his head. "Teacher switched me," he says. "For telling lies." He turns as he says it, and his eyes catch on Fox. He gives a smile that fills Fox with pure dread. Fox knows, somehow, what's coming. "We learned about enemies of the revolution today," Jonas says. "There was one aristo who tried to convince the Liberated People to let all the aristos go without getting punished. They called him the Fox because he had red hair."

"Oh, no," Blanka murmurs. "Oh, Jonas. What did you say?"

"I said he helped the revolution," Jonas says defiantly, looking Fox in the eye. "I said he wrote the poem, the one about aristo bellies full of our blood."

"You should not have done that, Jonas," Fox says, surprised he can speak at all. "That was dangerous. That was very dangerous." His panic is welling up again, numbing him all over. "They have gene records. They know that I'm a cousin to your father."

Jonas bites at his lip, but his eyes are still defiant. "I wanted to be brave," he says. "Strong and brave and honest. Like Damjan thought I am."

Fox feels adrift. He knows Jonas, no matter how sharp he seems, is still a child. There's no way he can understand what he's just done. Maybe it's Fox's own fault, for filling his head with all the poems.

Maybe they'll be lucky, and the teacher will keep Jonas's transgression to himself. Fox has been lucky before.

———

When father comes home mother tells him what happened, and his whole body seems to sink a little. Jonas feels the disappointment like he feels the welts on his back, and worse, he can tell that his father is scared. There is a brutal silence that lasts all evening until he goes to bed, lying on his stomach with a bit of medgel spread over his back. He knows he made a mistake. Even though he didn't say his uncle was with them, he said too much.

Jonas tries to apologize to his uncle, who is lying very straight and very still, staring up at the ceiling, and Damjan's voice mutters something about everything being fine and not to worry about anything. It doesn't sound like he believes it. Between the aches in his back and the thoughts in his head, Jonas takes a very long time to fall asleep. Halfway through a bad dream, his mother's hands shake him awake.

"Up, Jonas. You, too, Damjan."

Jonas wrenches his eyes open. It's still dark through the window and he hears a high whining noise he recognizes coming from outside. A hover. Jonas feels a spike of cold fear go all the way through him.

"I need to pee," he says.

"Later," mother says. "There are some men here to speak with your father. To look around the house." Her voice is strained. "If they ask you anything, think three times before you say anything back. Remember that uncle was never here."

Then she's gone again, leaving Jonas alone with his uncle. In the light leaking from the hall, Jonas can see Damjan's small round face is etched with terror, so much that he almost wants to take his hand and squeeze it. As if he really is Damjan, and not the Fox. Jonas listens hard to the unfamiliar voices conversing with his father. One of them sounds angry.

Loud stomping steps in the hall, then the door opens all the way and two soldiers come in with mother and father close behind. They are not as tall as father but their black coats and bristling weapons make them seem bigger, more frightening, like flying black hunter drones that have turned into men.

"Good morning, children," one of them says, even though it is the middle of the night. He gives a small smile that doesn't crinkle his eyes and raises one fist in the salute of the Liberated People.

Jonas returns it, and shoots his uncle a meaningful look, but Damjan's little fists are stuck to his sides. Fortunately, the soldier is focused on him, not his uncle.

"You must be the older," he says. "Jonas, isn't it? You told our friend the teacher something very strange today, Jonas. What did you tell him?"

Jonas's mouth is dry, dry. He looks to mother, who is framed between the men's broad shoulders, and she starts to speak but the second soldier puts a warning finger to his lips.

"We want to hear from Jonas, not from you," the first one says. "What did you tell your teacher, Jonas?"

Jonas knows it is time to be brave, but not honest. "I said that the Fox helped the revolution," he says. "I was confused. I thought he was Lazar. Lazar makes the songs for the satellite to play." He looks at both the soldiers, trying to gauge if they believe him. He lifts his nightshirt and turns so he won't have to look them in the eye. "Teacher was mad and didn't let me explain," he says. "He just started to switch me. Look how bad he switched me."

"A few stripes never killed anyone," the soldier says. "It'll make you look tough. Your little girlfriends will like that, right? Turn around."

Jonas drops his shirt and turns back, ready to meet the soldiers' gaze again. His uncle gives an encouraging nod where they can't see him.

"Did you know that this Fox, this enemy of the revolution, is a relative of yours?" the soldier asks. "A cousin to your father?"

"Yes," Jonas says. "But we don't know him. He's never come here."

The other soldier, who hasn't spoken yet, barks a short and angry laugh. "We'll see about that," he says, in a voice like gravel. "We'll have a sniff." He pulls something from his jacket and fits it over his mouth and nose like a bulbous black snout.

Jonas has heard of sniffer masks—his uncle explained them when they were in the field one day, how each person born had a different odor, because of their genes and their bacteria, and you could program a sniffer mask to find even the tiniest trace of it—but he has never seen one before now. It makes the soldier look like a kind of animal. When he inhales, the sound is magnified and crackling and makes Jonas shudder.

Behind the soldiers, mother has her hands tucked tight under her armpits. Her face is blank, but Jonas imagines she is thinking of all the scrubbing, all the chemicals she used anywhere uncle sat or ate. But uncle's old body has been gone for weeks now, and the smells would be too, wouldn't they?

As the sniffer moves around the room, the first soldier leans in close to the wall to look at the charcoal lettering. "What's this?" he asks. "Lessons?"

"Yes," Jonas says quietly.

"Good," the soldier says, and Jonas sees his eyes moving right to left on it, instead of left to right, and realizes he's like most of the older people in the village who can't read. It gives him a small sense of relief.

That only lasts until he looks over and sees the sniffer has stopped beside his uncle. "What happened to the boy's head?" the sniffer asks, voice distorted and grating.

"He fell," father says from the doorway. "A few weeks ago. He isn't healed in the brain yet. He's a little slow."

"Are you, boy?" the sniffer demands.

Jonas clenches his thumbs inside his fists. There is no part of uncle's body left in Damjan's, only his digital copy, his soul, but Jonas wonders if the sniffer might somehow be able to detect that, too.

His uncle looks up with a confused smile and reaches to touch the sniffer mask. The sniffer jerks back, then pushes him toward the door, more gently than Jonas would have expected, and continues searching the room. Jonas releases a breath he didn't know he was holding.

The sniffer works through the rest of the house, too, and Jonas and his family drift slowly along with him to open doors and cupboards, to make sure there are no traps or surprises. The horrible sucking sound of the sniffer mask sets Jonas's teeth on edge. It feels like a strange dream, a bad one. His eyes are sore and his bladder is squeezing him.

When they finally finish with the cellar, the sniffer looks irritated but the other soldier is relieved. "We'll be off, then," he says. "Remember, if he ever contacts you in any way, it's your duty to report him. He's not one of us. He cut ties with you and with all decent people the day he had his storage cone implanted."

Father nods, his mouth clenched shut, and shows the soldiers out. Jonas follows, because he wants to make sure, really sure, that the nightmare is over. Father doesn't send him back in. The soldiers are out the door and past the bushes when the sniffer suddenly stops. His mask is still on, and the sucking noise comes loud in the still night air.

Jonas remembers that the last charred bits of uncle's old skeleton are buried underneath the bushes. His father is not breathing, only staring. The sniffer lingers.

Jonas braces himself. He reminds himself that he is brave. Then he darts away from the door before father can pull him back, jogging up behind the sniffer and tugging his arm. "Can I see the hover?" he asks loudly.

The sniffer whirls and shoves him backward. Jonas squeals, loud and shrill how mother hates it, and he lets his piss go in a long hot stream that soaks his legs, splatters the bushes and the soldier's boots. It's very satisfying. Especially when the sniffer yanks his mask down and curses.

"I thought the other boy was the slow one," he says.

"He's frightened," father says, coming and gripping Jonas by the arm. "You frightened him. Please, just go."

As Jonas watches, the soldiers climb into their hover. They go.

————

The instant the whine of the hover fades away into the distance, Fox tells Petar and Blanka that it has to be tonight. His heart is still pounding away at his tiny ribcage, so hard he imagines the bones splintering. He's sweating all over.

"That was too close," he says. "Too close. I have to launch tonight."

Everyone is in the kitchen. Blanka is wetting a rag for Jonas to clean himself; Petar is standing behind a chair and gripping it tightly, rocking it back and forth on its legs. They all turn their heads to look at Fox.

"There's no storm tonight," Blanka says, handing Jonas the rag. "Someone will see the exhaust burn. It'll be loud, too."

Fox shakes his head. "Nobody around here knows what a launch looks or sounds like," he says. "And Petar, you told everyone there was oil in the granary, didn't you?"

His cousin blinks. "Yes." He pauses, then looks to his wife. "We could set fire to the granary. That should be enough to cover the noise and the light so long as he goes up dark."

Blanka slowly nods. "Alright. Alright. You'll need help moving the ship out. I'll come as well."

"I want to come," Jonas says, wide-eyed, wringing the rag between his hands. Fox realizes he never did finish the poem on the wall.

"Bring Jonas, too," he says. "To say goodbye."

Bare minutes later, they are dressed and out the door, moving quickly through the crop field. The night air is cold enough to sting Fox's cheeks. Fear and anticipation speed his short legs and he manages to keep pace with Petar and Blanka, who are lugging the gas. Jonas skips ahead and then back, electric with excitement, already forgetting the fear.

"I pissed on a soldier," he whispers.

"I saw from the window," Fox grunts. "But a sniffer can't read DNA from ashes and bone. He had nothing."

"Oh." Jonas's face reddens a bit. "I'll do it again, though. I hate the soldiers as bad as the aristos. I want everyone equal, like you said."

Blanka puts a finger to her lips, and Jonas falls silent. Fox is glad to save his breath. They pass under the godtree, its twisted branches reaching up toward a black sky sewn with glittering stars. For a moment Fox dares to imagine the future. Slipping through the blockade and into the waiting arms of civilization. Telling his tale of survival against all odds. Maybe he'll be famous on other worlds how he so briefly was here.

And he'll be leaving Jonas's family to suffer through whatever comes next. The thought gnaws at him so he shoves it away. He reminds himself that Petar and Blanka are clever people. They know how to keep their heads down. They know how to keep silent and survive.

At the entrance to the abandoned granary, Fox switches on the small lantern he brought from the kitchen and lights the way for Petar and Blanka. They haul the tiny ship out on wooden sledges Petar made for it a day ago. Jonas puts his small shoulder into it and pushes from behind.

Fox checks everything he remembers, moving from the nosecone to the exhaust, then yanks the release. The ship shutters open, revealing the waiting passenger pod. Its life support status lights glow a soft blue in the dark. Ready. In the corner of his eye Fox sees Jonas staring up at the stars.

The ones who survive will be the ones who can keep their heads down. Fox knows it from history; he knows in his gut it's happening here. Jonas isn't one of those. Maybe he'll learn to be, but Fox doesn't think so.

Before he can stop himself, he turns to Blanka. "Jonas should go," he says. "Not me."

454 | JONAS AND THE FOX

Jonas's head snaps around, but Fox doesn't look at him. He watches Blanka's face. She doesn't look shocked, the way he thought she would, but maybe it's just that people are different in the village. Harder to read.

"What do you mean?" Petar demands.

"Jonas should take the ship," Fox says, because why else would he have told them to bring Jonas? He must have known, in the back of his mind, that this was what he needed to do. One brave thing, and then he can go back to being a coward. "He's already pissed off the teacher and pissed on a soldier," Fox continues. "He's going to keep putting himself in danger here. And the two of you, as well."

"You're the one who put us in danger," Petar snaps. "You would take another son from me now, cousin?"

"He's never fit right here, Petar," Blanka says, and for the first time Fox sees tears in her eyes. "He's always had his head up in the sky. We used to say that, remember?"

"He would be safer somewhere else," Fox says. "Let him take the ship. It's all automated from here on in." He pauses. Breathes. "Let him take the ship, then you can burn down the granary and say he was playing in it. You can use what's left of my bones if you need proof."

Petar looks at his son. "Is this what you want to do, then, Jonas?" he asks hoarsely.

Jonas chews his lip. Turns to Fox. "Could I come back? Will I be able to come back?"

"Not soon," Fox says. He knows there are still too many factions scrabbling in the power vacuum, knows things will get worse before they get better. "But some day. When things stabilize. Yes." He can feel himself losing his nerve. He almost hopes Jonas will refuse.

"I want to go," Jonas says solemnly. Petar gives a ragged cry and wraps him in his arms. Blanka hugs him from behind, putting her cheek against his cheek. Fox feels ashamed for watching. He looks away.

"What about uncle?" Jonas asks, his voice muffled by the embrace. "Will he be Damjan forever?"

Fox swallows as his cousin straightens up, and tries to look him in the eye. "You could say I was in the fire, too," he says. "That Damjan was in there. And I could leave again. Try my luck going north. You wouldn't have to look at me and remember all the time."

Petar looks sideways to Blanka. Slowly, they both shake their heads. "You can never be Damjan and you can never be Jonas," Blanka says. "But you are family. We've kept you safe this long, haven't we?"

Fox dares to imagine the future again, this time in the village, slowly growing again in Damjan's body. He did used to dream of retiring to the countryside one day. And he's learned how to keep his head down. Soon the bandages will be off and his storage cone, shaved down and covered over with a flap of skin by the autosurgeon, will be undetectable.

Maybe the violence will be over in a few years' time. Maybe Damjan will become a poet, a better one than Fox ever was.

"Thank you," he says. "All of you."

He stands aside while Jonas's parents say their goodbyes. Jonas does his best to be sad, but Fox sees his eyes go to the ship over and over again, an excited smile curling his lips. He hugs his mother fiercely, then his father, then comes to Fox.

"You can have my bed," he says. "It's bigger." He raises his arms. Pauses. He sticks out one hand instead to shake.

Fox clasps it tight. "I'll do that," he says.

Then Jonas is clambering into the pod, the restraints webbing over him to hold him in place during launch, and it's too late for Fox to take it all back even if he wanted to. The ship folds shut. The smell of gas prickles Fox's nose and he realizes Petar is dousing one side of the granary to ensure it burns. When he's finished, Blanka takes his gas-slicked hand in hers, and takes Fox's with the other. They walk the agreed-upon distance with a few steps extra to be safe.

The ship squats on the pale soil, rumbling through its launch protocols, and then the engine ignites. Fox feels it in his chest, vibrating through his bones. Riding a bonfire of smelting orange flame, the ship begins to rise, one fiery tongue catching the roof of the granary on the way up. The engine burns even brighter, stamping itself onto Fox's retinas, and by the time he blinks them clear the ship is only a pinpoint of light disappearing into the sky.

The crackling flames leap high, consuming the granary and making it hard to see the stars. Fox can imagine them, though. He can imagine Jonas slipping through the blockade to freedom. In the corner of his eye, Petar lifts his hand high, but open, not the clenched fist of the soldiers.

Fox raises his arm. He does the same.

Extracurricular Activities

Yoon Ha Lee

For Sonya Taaffe

WHEN SHUOS JEDAO walked into his temporary quarters on Station Muru 5 and spotted the box, he assumed someone was attempting to assassinate him. It had happened before. Considering his first career, there was even a certain justice to it.

He ducked back around the doorway, although even with his reflexes, he would have been too late if it'd been a proper bomb. The air currents in the room would have wafted his biochemical signature to the box and caused it to trigger. Or someone could have set up the bomb to go off as soon as the door opened, regardless of who stepped in. Or something even less sophisticated.

Jedao retreated back down the hallway and waited one minute. Two. Nothing.

It could just be a package, he thought—paperwork that he had forgotten?—but old habits died hard.

He entered again and approached the desk, light-footed. The box, made of eye-searing green plastic, stood out against the bland earth tones of the walls and desk. It measured approximately half a meter in all directions. Its nearest face prominently displayed the gold seal that indicated that station security had cleared it. He didn't trust it for a moment. Spoofing a seal wasn't that difficult; he'd done it himself.

He inspected the box's other visible sides without touching it, then spotted a letter pouch affixed to one side and froze. He recognized the handwriting. The address was written in spidery high language, while the name of the recipient—one Garach Jedao Shkan—was written both in the high language and his birth tongue, Shparoi, for good measure.

Oh, Mom, Jedao thought. No one else called him by that name anymore, not even the rest of his family. More importantly, how had his mother gotten his address? He'd just received his transfer orders last week, and he hadn't written home about it because his mission was classified. He had no idea what his new general wanted him to do; she would tell him tomorrow morning when he reported in.

Jedao opened the box, which released a puff of cold air. Inside rested a tub labeled KEEP REFRIGERATED in both the high language and Shparoi. The tub itself contained a pale, waxy-looking solid substance. *Is this what I think it is?*

Time for the letter:

> *Hello, Jedao!*
> *Congratulations on your promotion. I hope you enjoy your new command moth and that it has a more pronounceable name than the last one.*

One: What promotion? Did she know something he didn't? (Scratch that question. She always knew something he didn't.) Two: Trust his mother to rate warmoths not by their armaments or the efficacy of their stardrives but by their *names*. Then again, she'd made no secret that she'd hoped he'd wind up a musician like his sire. It had not helped when he pointed out that when he attempted to sing in academy, his fellow cadets had threatened to dump grapefruit soup over his head.

> *Since I expect your eating options will be limited, I have sent you goose fat rendered from the great-great-great-etc.-grandgosling of your pet goose when you were a child. (She was delicious, by the way.) Let me know if you run out and I'll send more.*
> *Love,*
> *Mom*

So he was right: the tub contained goose fat. Jedao had never figured out why his mother sent food items when her idea of cooking was to gussy up instant noodles with an egg and some chopped green onions. All the cooking Jedao knew, he had learned either from his older brother or, on occasion, those of his mother's research assistants who took pity on her kids.

What am I supposed to do with this? he wondered. As a cadet, he could have based a prank around it. But as a warmoth commander, he had standards to uphold.

More importantly, how could he compose a suitably filial letter of appreciation without, foxes forbid, encouraging her to escalate? (Baked goods: fine. Goose fat: less fine.) Especially when she wasn't supposed to know he was here in the first place? Some people's families sent them care packages of useful things, like liquor, pornography, or really nice cosmetics. Just his luck.

At least the mission gave him an excuse to delay writing back until his location was unclassified, even if she knew it anyway.

———

Jedao had heard a number of rumors about his new commanding officer, Brigadier General Kel Essier. Some of them, like the ones about her junior wife's lovers, were none of his business. Others, like Essier's taste in plum wine, weren't relevant, but could come in handy if he needed to scare up a bribe someday. What had really caught his notice was her service record. She had fewer decorations than anyone else who'd served at her rank for a comparable time.

Either Essier was a political appointee—the Kel military denied the practice, but everyone knew better—or she was sitting on a cache of classified medals. Jedao had a number of those himself. (Did his mother know about those too?) Although Station Muru 5 was a secondary military base, Jedao had his suspicions about any "secondary" base that had a general in residence, even temporarily. That, or Essier was disgraced and Kel Command couldn't think of anywhere else to dump her.

Jedao had a standard method for dealing with new commanders, which was to research them as if he planned to assassinate them. Needless to say, he never expressed it in those terms to his comrades.

He'd come up with two promising ways to get rid of Essier. First, she collected meditation foci made of staggeringly luxurious materials. One of her officers had let slip that her latest obsession was antique lacquerware. Planting a bomb or toxin in a collector-grade item wouldn't be risky so much as *expensive*. He'd spent a couple hours last night brainstorming ways to steal one, just for the hell of it; lucky that he didn't have to follow through.

The other method took advantage of the poorly planned location of the firing range on this level relative to the general's office, and involved shooting her through several walls and a door with a high-powered rifle and burrower ammunition. Jedao hated burrower ammunition, not because it didn't work but because it did. He had a lot of ugly scars on his torso from the times burrowers had almost killed him. That being said, he also believed in using the appropriate tool for the job.

No one had upgraded Muru 5 for the past few decades. Its computer grid ran on outdated hardware, making it easy for him to pull copies of all the maps he pleased. He'd also hacked into the security cameras long enough to check the layout of the general's office. The setup made him despair of the architects who had designed the whole wretched thing. On top of that, Essier had set up her desk so a visitor would see it framed beautifully by the doorway, with her chair perfectly centered. Great for impressing visitors, less great for making yourself a difficult target. Then again, attending to Essier's safety wasn't his job.

Jedao showed up at Essier's office seven minutes before the appointed time. "Whiskey?" said her aide.

If only, Jedao thought; he recognized it as one he couldn't afford. "No, thank you," he said with the appropriate amount of regret. He didn't trust special treatment.

"Your loss," said the aide. After another two minutes, she checked her slate. "Go on in. The general is waiting for you."

As Jedao had predicted, General Essier sat dead center behind her desk, framed by the doorway and two statuettes on either side of the desk, gilded ashhawks carved from onyx. Essier had dark skin and close-shaven hair, and the height and fine-spun bones of someone who had grown up in low gravity. The black-and-gold Kel uniform suited her. Her gloved hands rested on the desk in perfect symmetry. Jedao bet she looked great in propaganda videos.

Jedao saluted, fist to shoulder. "Commander Shuos Jedao reporting as ordered, sir."

"Have a seat," Essier said. He did. "You're wondering why you don't have a warmoth assignment yet."

"The thought had crossed my mind, yes."

Essier smiled. The smile was like the rest of her: beautiful and calculated and not a little deadly. "I have good news and bad news for you, Commander. The good news is that you're due a promotion."

Jedao's first reaction was not gratitude or pride, but *How did my mother—?* Fortunately, a lifetime of *How did my mother—?* enabled him to keep his expression smooth and instead say, "And the bad news?"

"Is it true what they say about your battle record?"

This always came up. "You have my profile."

"You're good at winning."

"I wasn't under the impression that the Kel military found this objectionable, sir."

"Quite right," she said. "The situation is this. I have a mission in mind for you, but it will take advantage of your unique background."

"Unique background" was a euphemism for *we don't have many commanders who can double as emergency special forces.* Most Kel with training in special ops stayed in the infantry instead of seeking command in the space forces. Jedao made an inquiring noise.

"Perform well, and you'll be given the fangmoth *Sieve of Glass,* which heads my third tactical group."

A bribe, albeit one that might cause trouble. Essier had six tactical groups. A newly-minted group tactical commander being assigned third instead of sixth? Had she had a problem with her former third-position commander?

"My former third took early retirement," Essier said in answer to his unspoken question. "They were caught with a small collection of trophies."

"Let me guess," Jedao said. "Trophies taken from heretics."

"Just so. Third tactical is badly shaken. Fourth has excellent rapport with her group and I don't want to promote her out of it. But it's an opportunity for you."

"And the mission?"

Essier leaned back. "You attended Shuos Academy with Shuos Meng."

"I did," Jedao said. They'd gone by Zhei Meng as a cadet. "We've been in touch on and off." Meng had joined a marriage some years back. Jedao had commissioned a painting of five foxes, one for each person in the marriage, and sent it along with his best wishes. Meng wrote regularly about their kids—they couldn't be made to shut up about them—and Jedao sent gifts on cue, everything from hand-bound volumes of Kel jokes to fancy gardening tools (at least, they'd been sold to him as gardening tools; they looked suspiciously like they could double for heavy-duty surgical work). "Why, what has Meng been up to?"

"Under the name Ahun Gerav, they've been in command of the merchanter *Moonsweet Blossom.*"

Jedao cocked an eyebrow at Essier. "That's not a Shuos vessel." It did, however, sound like an Andan one. The Andan faction liked naming their trademoths after flowers. "By 'merchanter,' do you mean 'spy'?"

"Yes," Essier said with charming directness. "Twenty-six days ago, one of the *Blossom*'s crew sent a code red to Shuos Intelligence. This is all she was able to tell us."

Essier retrieved a slate from within the desk and tilted it to show him a video. She needn't have bothered; the combination of poor lighting, camera jitter, and static made it impossible to watch. The audio was little better: ". . . *Blossom,* code red to Overwatch . . . Gerav's in . . ." Frustratingly, the

static made the next few words unintelligible. "Du Station. You'd better——"
The report of a gun, then another, then silence.

"Your task is to investigate the situation at Du Station in the Gwa Reality, and see if the crew and any of the intelligence they've gathered can be recovered. The Shuos heptarch suggested that you would be an ideal candidate for the mission. Kel Command was amenable."

I just bet, Jedao thought. He had once worked directly under his heptarch, and while he'd been one of her better assassins, he didn't miss those days. "Is this the only incident with the Gwa Reality that has taken place recently, or are there others?"

"The Gwa-an are approaching one of their regularly scheduled regime upheavals," Essier said. "According to the diplomats, there's a good chance that the next elected government will be less amenable to heptarchate interests. We want to go in, find out what happened, and get out before things turn topsy-turvy."

"All right," Jedao said, "so taking a warmoth in would be inflammatory. What resources will I have instead?"

"Well, that's the bad news," Essier said, entirely too cheerfully. "Tell me, Commander, have you ever wanted to own a merchant troop?"

———

The troop consisted of eight trademoths, named *Carp 1* to *Carp 4*, then *Carp 7* to *Carp 10*. They occupied one of the station's docking bays. Someone had painted each vessel with distended carp-figures in orange and white. It did not improve their appearance.

The usual commander of the troop introduced herself as Churioi Haval, not her real name. She was portly, had a squint, and wore gaudy gilt jewelry, all excellent ways to convince people that she was an ordinary merchant and not, say, Kel special ops. It hadn't escaped his attention that she frowned ever so slightly when she spotted his sidearm, a Patterner 52, which wasn't standard Kel issue. "You're not bringing that, are you?" she said.

"No, I'd hate to lose it on the other side of the border," Jedao said. "Besides, I don't have a plausible explanation for why a boring communications tech is running around with a Shuos handgun."

"I could always hold on to it for you."

Jedao wondered if he'd ever get the Patterner back if he took her up on the offer. It hadn't come cheap. "That's kind of you, but I'll have the station store it for me. By the way, what happened to *Carps 5* and *6*?"

"Beats me," Haval said. "Before my time. The Gwa-an authorities have never hassled us about it. They're already used to, paraphrase, 'odd heptarchate numerological superstitions.'" She eyed Jedao critically, which

462 | Extracurricular Activities

made her look squintier. "Begging your pardon, but do you *have* undercover experience?"

What a refreshing question. Everyone knew the Shuos for their spies, saboteurs, and assassins, even though the analysts, administrators, and cryptologists did most of the real work. (One of his instructors had explained that "You will spend hours in front of a terminal developing posture problems" was far less effective at recruiting potential cadets than "Join the Shuos for an exciting future as a secret agent, assuming your classmates don't kill you before you graduate.") Most people who met Jedao assumed he'd killed an improbable number of people as Shuos infantry. Never mind that he'd been responsible for far more deaths since joining the regular military.

"You'd be surprised at the things I know how to do," Jedao said.

"Well, I hope you're good with cover identities," Haval said. "No offense, but you have a distinctive name."

That was a tactful way of saying that the Kel didn't tolerate many Shuos line officers; most Shuos seconded to the Kel worked in Intelligence. Jedao had a reputation for, as one of his former aides had put it, being expendable enough to send into no-win situations but too stubborn to die. Jedao smiled at Haval and said, "I have a good memory."

The rest of his crew also had civilian cover names. A tall, muscular man strolled up to them. Jedao surreptitiously admired him. The gold-mesh tattoo over the right side of his face contrasted handsomely with his dark skin. Too bad he was almost certainly Kel and therefore off-limits.

"This is Rhi Teshet," Haval said. "When he isn't watching horrible melodramas—"

"You have no sense of culture," Teshet said.

"—he's the lieutenant colonel in charge of our infantry."

Damn. Definitely Kel, then, and in his chain of command, at that. "A pleasure, Colonel," Jedao said.

Teshet's returning smile was slow and wicked and completely unprofessional. "Get out of the habit of using ranks," he said. "Just Teshet, please. I hear you like whiskey?"

Off-limits, Jedao reminded himself, despite the quickening of his pulse. Best to be direct. "I'd rather not get you in trouble."

Haval was looking to the side with a "where have I seen this dance before" expression. Teshet laughed. "The fastest way to get us caught is to behave like you have the Kel code of conduct tattooed across your forehead. *No one* will suspect you of being a hotshot commander if you're sleeping with one of your crew."

"I don't fuck people deadlier than I am, sorry," Jedao said demurely.

"Wrong answer," Haval said, still not looking at either of them. "Now he's going to think of you as a challenge."

"Also, I know your reputation," Teshet said to Jedao. "Your kill count has got to be higher than mine by an order of magnitude."

Jedao ignored that. "How often do you make trade runs into the Gwa Reality?"

"Two or three times a year," Haval said. "The majority of the runs are to maintain the fiction. The question is, do *you* have a plan?"

He didn't blame her for her skepticism. "Tell me again how much cargo space we have."

Haval told him.

"We sometimes take approved cultural goods," Teshet said, "in a data storage format negotiated during the Second Treaty of—"

"Don't bore him," Haval said. "The 'trade' is *our* job. He's just here for the explodey bits."

"No, I'm interested," Jedao said. "The Second Treaty of Mwe Enh, am I right?"

Haval blinked. "You have remarkably good pronunciation. Most people can't manage the tones. Do you speak Tlen Gwa?"

"Regrettably not. I'm only fluent in four languages, and that's not one of them." Of the four, Shparoi was only spoken on his birth planet, making it useless for career purposes. Which reminded him that he was still procrastinating on writing back to his mother. Surely being sent on an undercover mission counted as an acceptable reason for being late with your correspondence home?

"If you have some Shuos notion of sneaking in a virus amid all the lectures on flower-arranging and the dueling tournament videos and the plays, forget it," Teshet said. "Their operating systems are so different from ours that you'd have better luck getting a magpie and a turnip to have a baby."

"Oh, not at all," Jedao said. "How odd would it look if you brought in a shipment of goose fat?"

Haval's mouth opened, closed.

Teshet said, "Excuse me?"

"Not literally goose fat," Jedao conceded. "I don't have enough for that and I don't imagine the novelty would enable you to run a sufficient profit. I assume you have to at least appear to be trying to make a profit."

"They like real profits even better," Haval said.

Diverted, Teshet said, "You have goose fat? Whatever for?"

"Long story," Jedao said. "But instead of goose fat, I'd like to run some of that variable-coefficient lubricant."

Haval rubbed her chin. "I don't think you could get approval to trade the formula or the associated manufacturing processes."

"Not that," Jedao said, "actual canisters of lubricant. Is there someone in the Gwa Reality on the way to our luckless Shuos friend who might be willing to pay for it?"

Haval and Teshet exchanged baffled glances. Jedao could tell what they were thinking: *Are we the victims of some weird bet our commander has going on the side?* "There's no need to get creative," Haval said in a commendably diplomatic voice. "Cultural goods are quite reliable."

You think this *is creativity,* Jedao thought. "It's not that. Two battles ago, my fangmoth was almost blown in two because our antimissile defenses glitched. If we hadn't used the lubricant as a stopgap sealant, we wouldn't have made it." That much was even true. "Even if you can't offload all of it, I'll find another use for it."

"You do know you can't cook with lubricant?" Teshet said. "Although I wonder if it's good for—"

Haval stomped on his toe. "You already have plenty of the medically approved stuff," she said crushingly, "no need to risk getting your private parts cemented into place."

"Hey," Teshet said, "you never know when you'll need to improvise."

Jedao was getting the impression that Essier had not assigned him the best of her undercover teams. Certainly they were the least disciplined Kel he'd run into in a while, but he supposed long periods undercover had made them more casual about regulations. No matter, he'd been dealt worse hands. "I've let you know what I want done, and I've already checked that the station has enough lubricant to supply us. Make it happen."

"If you insist," Haval said. "Meanwhile, don't forget to get your immunizations."

"Will do," Jedao said, and strode off to Medical.

Jedao spent the first part of the voyage alternately learning basic Tlen Gwa, memorizing his cover identity, and studying up on the Gwa Reality. The Tlen Gwa course suffered some oddities. He couldn't see the use of some of the vocabulary items, like the one for "navel." But he couldn't manage to *un*learn it, either, so there it was, taking up space in his brain.

As for the cover identity, he'd had better ones, but he supposed the Kel could only do so much on short notice. He was now Arioi Sren, one of Haval's distant cousins by marriage. He had three spouses, with whom he had quarreled recently over a point of interior decoration. ("I don't know anything about interior decoration," Jedao had said, to which Haval retorted, "That's probably what caused the argument.")

The documents had included loving photographs of the domicile in question, an apartment in a dome city floating in the upper reaches of a very pretty gas giant. Jedao had memorized them before destroying them. While he couldn't say how well the decor coordinated, he was good at layouts and kill zones. In any case, Sren was on "vacation" to escape the squabbling. Teshet had suggested that a guilt-inducing affair would round out the cover identity. Jedao said he'd think about it.

Jedao was using spray-on temporary skin, plus a high-collared shirt, to conceal multiple scars, including the wide one at the base of his neck. The temporary skin itched, which couldn't be helped. He hoped no one would strip-search him, but in case someone did, he didn't want to have to explain his old gunshot wounds. Teshet had also suggested that he stop shaving—the Kel disliked beards—but Jedao could only deal with so much itching.

The hardest part was not the daily skinseal regimen, but getting used to wearing civilian clothes. The Kel uniform included gloves, and Jedao felt exposed going around with naked hands. But keeping his gloves would have been a dead giveaway, so he'd just have to live with it.

The Gwa-an fascinated him most of all. Heptarchate diplomats called their realm the Gwa Reality. Linguists differed on just what the word rendered as "Reality" meant. The majority agreed that it referred to the Gwa-an belief that all dreams took place in the same noosphere, connecting the dreamers, and that even inanimate objects dreamed.

Gwa-an protocols permitted traders to dock at designated stations. Haval quizzed Jedao endlessly on the relevant etiquette. Most of it consisted of keeping his mouth shut and letting Haval talk, which suited him fine. While the Gwa-an provided interpreters, Haval said cultural differences were the real problem. "Above all," she added, "if anyone challenges you to a duel, don't. Just don't. Look blank and plead ignorance."

"Duel?" Jedao said, interested.

"I knew we were going to have to have this conversation," Haval said glumly. "They don't use swords, so get that idea out of your head."

"I didn't bring my dueling sword anyway, and Sren wouldn't know how," Jedao said. "Guns?"

"Oh no," she said. "They use *pathogens*. Designer pathogens. Besides the fact that their duels can go on for years, I've never heard that you had a clue about genetic engineering."

"No," Jedao said, "that would be my mother." Maybe next time he could suggest to Essier that his mother be sent in his place. His mother would adore the chance to talk shop. Of course, then he'd be out of a job. "Besides, I'd rather avoid bringing a plague back home."

"They *claim* they have an excellent safety record."

Of course they would. "How fast can they culture the things?"

"That was one of the things we were trying to gather data on."

"If they're good at diseasing up humans, they may be just as good at manufacturing critters that like to eat synthetics."

"While true of their tech base in general," Haval said, "they won't have top-grade labs at Du Station."

"Good to know," Jedao said.

Jedao and Teshet also went over the intelligence on Du Station. "It's nice that you're taking a personal interest," Teshet said, "but if you think we're taking the place by storm, you've been watching too many dramas."

"If Kel special forces aren't up for it," Jedao said, very dryly, "you could always send me. One of me won't do much good, though."

"Don't be absurd," Teshet said. "Essier would have my head if you got hurt. How many people *did* you assassinate?"

"Classified," Jedao said.

Teshet gave a can't-blame-me-for-trying shrug. "Not to say I wouldn't love to see you in action, but it isn't your job to run around doing the boring infantry work. How do you mean to get the crew out? Assuming they survived, which is a big *if*."

Jedao tapped his slate and brought up the schematics for one of their cargo shuttles. "Five per trader," he said musingly.

"Du Station won't let us land the shuttles however we please."

"Did I say anything about landing them?" Before Teshet could say anything further, Jedao added, "You might have to cross the hard way, with suits and webcord. How often have your people drilled that?"

"We've done plenty of extravehicular," Teshet said, "but we're going to need *some* form of cover."

"I'm aware of that," Jedao said. He brought up a calculator and did some figures. "That will do nicely."

"Sren?"

Jedao grinned at Teshet. "I want those shuttles emptied out, everything but propulsion and navigation. Get rid of suits, seats, all of it."

"Even life support?"

"Everything. And it'll have to be done in the next seventeen days, so the Gwa-an can't catch us at it."

"What do we do with the innards?"

"Dump them. I'll take full responsibility."

Teshet's eyes crinkled. "I knew I was going to like you."

Uh-oh, Jedao thought, but he kept that to himself.

"What are *you* going to be doing?" Teshet asked.

"Going over the dossiers before we have to wipe them," Jedao said. Meng's in particular. He'd believed in Meng's fundamental competence even back in academy, before they'd learned confidence in themselves. What had gone wrong?

———

Jedao had first met Shuos Meng, then Zhei Meng, during an exercise at Shuos Academy. The instructor had assigned them to work together. Meng was chubby and had a vine-and-compass tattoo on the back of their left hand, identifying them as coming from a merchanter lineage.

Today, the class of twenty-nine cadets met not in the usual classroom but a windowless room with a metal table in the front and rows of two-person desks with benches that looked like they'd been scrubbed clean of graffiti multiple times. ("Wars come and go, but graffiti is forever," as one of Jedao's lovers liked to say.) Besides the door leading out into the hall, there were two other doors, neither of which had a sign indicating where they led. Tangles of pipes led up the walls and storage bins were piled beside them. Jedao had the impression that the room had been pressed into service at short notice.

Jedao and Meng sat at their assigned seats and hurriedly whispered introductions to each other while the instructor read off the rest of the pairs.

"Zhei Meng," they said. "I should warn you I barely passed the weapons qualifications. But I'm good with languages." Then a quick grin: "And hacking. I figured you'd make a good partner."

"Garach Jedao," he said. "I can handle guns." Understatement; he was third in the class in Weapons. And if Meng had, as they implied, shuffled the assignments, that meant they were one of the better hackers. "Why did you join up?"

"I want to have kids," Meng said.

"Come again?"

"I want to marry into a rich lineage," Meng said. "That means making myself more respectable. When the recruiters showed up, I said what the hell."

The instructor smiled coolly at the two of them, and they shut up. She said, "If you're here, it's because you've indicated an interest in fieldwork. Like you, we want to find out if it's something you have any aptitude for, and if not, what better use we can make of your skills." *You'd better have some skills* went unsaid. "You may have expected you'd be dropped off in the woods or some such nonsense. We don't try to weed out first-years quite that early. No; this initial exercise will take place right here."

The instructor's smile widened. "There's a photobomb in this room. It won't cause any permanent damage, but if you don't disarm it, you're all going to be walking around wearing ridiculous dark lenses for a week. At least one cadet knows where the bomb is. If they keep its location a secret from the rest of you, they win. Of course, they'll also go around with ridiculous dark lenses, but you can't have everything. On the other hand, if someone can persuade someone to give up the secret, everyone wins. So to speak."

The rows of cadets stared at her. Jedao leaned back in his chair and considered the situation. Like several others in the class, he had a riflery exam in three days and preferred to take it with undamaged vision.

"You have four hours," the instructor said. "There's one restroom." She pointed to one of the doors. "I expect it to be in impeccable condition at the end of the four hours." She put her slate down on the table at the head of the room. "Call me with this if you figure it out. Good luck." With that, she walked out of the room. The door whooshed shut behind her.

"We're screwed," Meng said. "Just because I'm on the leaderboard in *Elite Thundersnake 9000* doesn't mean I could disarm *real* bombs if you yanked out my toenails."

"Don't give people ideas," Jedao said. Meng didn't appear to find the joke funny. "This is about people, not explosives."

Two pairs of cadets had gotten up and were beginning a search of the room. A few were talking to each other in hushed, tense voices. Still others were looking around at their fellows with hard, suspicious eyes.

Meng said in Shparoi, "Do *you* know where the bomb is?"

Jedao blinked. He hadn't expected anyone at the Academy to know his birth tongue. Of course, by speaking in an obscure low language, Meng was drawing attention to them. Jedao shook his head.

Meng looked around, hands bunching the fabric of their pants. "What do you recommend we do?"

In the high language, Jedao said, "You can do whatever you want." He retrieved a deck of jeng-zai cards—he always had one in his pocket—and shuffled them. "Do you play?"

"You realize we're being graded on this, right? Hell, they've got cameras on us. They're watching the whole thing."

"Exactly," Jedao said. "I don't see any point in panicking."

"You're out of your mind," Meng said. They stood up, met the other cadets' appraising stares, then sat down again. "Too bad hacking the instructor's slate won't get us anywhere. I doubt she left the answer key in an unencrypted file on it."

Jedao gave Meng a quizzical look, wondering if there was anything more behind the remark—but no, Meng had put their chin in their hands and was brooding. *If only you knew*, he thought, dealing out a game of solitaire. It was going to be a very dull game, because he had stacked the deck, but he needed to focus on the people around him, not the game. The cards were just to give his hands something to do. He had considered taking up crochet, but thanks to an incident earlier in the term, crochet hooks, knitting needles, and fountain pens were no longer permitted in class. While this was a stupid restriction, considering that most of the cadets were learning unarmed combat, he wasn't responsible for the administration's foibles.

"Jedao," Meng said, "maybe you've got high enough marks that you can blow off this exercise, but—"

Since *I'm not blowing it off* was unlikely to be believed, Jedao flipped over a card—three of Doors, just as he'd arranged—and smiled at Meng. So Meng had had their pick of partners and had chosen him? Well, he might as well do something to justify the other cadet's faith in him. After all, despite their earlier remark, weapons weren't the only things that Jedao was good at. "Do me a favor and we can get this sorted," he said. "You want to win? I'll show you winning."

Now Jedao was attracting some of the hostile stares as well. Good. It took the heat off Meng, who didn't have great tolerance for pressure. *Stay out of wetwork*, he thought; but they could have that chat later. Or one of the instructors would.

Meng fidgeted; caught themselves. "Yeah?"

"Get me the slate."

"You mean the instructor's slate? You can't possibly have figured it out already. Unless—" Meng's eyes narrowed.

"Less thinking, more acting," Jedao said, and got up to retrieve the slate himself.

A pair of cadets, a girl and a boy, blocked his way. "You know something," said the girl. "Spill." Jedao knew them from Analysis; the two were often paired there, too. The girl's name was Noe Irin. The boy had five names and went by Veller. Jedao wondered if Veller wanted to join a faction so he could trim things down to a nice, compact two-part name. Shuos Veller: much less of a mouthful. Then again, Jedao had a three-part name, also unusual, if less unwieldy, so he shouldn't criticize.

"Just a hunch," Jedao said.

Irin bared her teeth. "He *always* says it's a hunch," she said to no one in particular. "I *hate* that."

470 | Extracurricular Activities

"It was only twice," Jedao said, which didn't help his case. He backed away from the instructor's desk and sat down, careful not to jostle the solitaire spread. "Take the slate apart. The photobomb's there."

Irin's lip curled. "If this is one of your fucking clever *tricks*, Jay—"

Meng blinked at the nickname. "You two sleeping together, Jedao?" they asked, *sotto voce*.

Not *sotto* enough. "*No*," said Jedao and Irin at the same time.

Veller ignored the byplay and went straight for the tablet. He bent to inspect the tablet without touching it. Jedao respected that. Veller had the physique of a tiger-wrestler (now *there* was someone he wouldn't mind being caught in bed with), a broad face, and a habitually bland, dreamy expression. Jedao wasn't fooled. Veller was almost as smart as Irin, had already been tracked into bomb disposal, and was less prone to flights of temper.

"Is there a tool closet in here?" Veller said. "I need a screwdriver."

"You don't carry your own anymore?" Jedao said.

"I told him he should," Irin said, "but he said they were too similar to knitting needles. As if anyone in their right mind would knit with a pair of screwdrivers."

"I think he meant that they're stabby things that can be driven into people's eyes," Jedao said.

"I didn't ask for your opinion, Jay."

Jedao put his hands up in a conciliatory gesture and shut up. He liked Irin and didn't want to antagonize her any more than necessary. The last time they'd been paired together, they'd done quite well. She would come around; she just needed time to work through the implications of what the instructor had said. She was one of those people who preferred to think about things without being interrupted.

One of the other cadets wordlessly handed Veller a set of screwdrivers. Veller mumbled his thanks and got to work. The class watched, breathless.

"There," Veller said at last. "See that there, all hooked in? Don't know what the timer is, but there it is."

"I find it very suspicious that you gave up your chance to show up everyone else in this exercise," Irin said to Jedao. "Is there anyone else who knew?"

"Irin," Jedao said, "I don't think the instructor told *anyone* where she'd left the photobomb. She just stuck it in the slate because that was the last place we'd look. The test was meant to reveal which of us would backstab each other, but honestly, that's so counterproductive. I say we disarm the damn thing and skip to the end."

Irin's eyes crossed and her lips moved as she recited the instructor's words under her breath. That was another thing Jedao liked about her. Irin

YOON HA LEE | 471

had a *great* memory. Admittedly, that made it difficult to cheat her at cards, as he'd found out the hard way. He'd spent three hours doing her kitchen duties for her the one time he'd tried. He *liked* people who could beat him at cards. "It's possible," she said grudgingly after she'd reviewed the assignment's instructions.

"Disarmed," Veller said shortly after that. He pulled out the photo-bomb and left it on the desk, then set about reassembling the slate.

Jedao glanced over at Meng. For a moment, his partner's expression had no anxiety in it, but a raptor's intent focus. Interesting: what were they watching for?

"I hope I get a nice quiet posting at a desk somewhere," Meng said.

"Then why'd you join up?" Irin said.

Jedao put his hand over Meng's, even though he was sure that they had just lied. "Don't mind her," he said. "You'll do fine."

Meng nodded and smiled up at him.

Why do I have the feeling that I'm not remotely the most dangerous person in the room? Jedao thought. But he returned Meng's smile, all the same. It never hurt to have allies.

————

A Gwa patrol ship greeted them as they neared Du Station. Haval had assured Jedao that this was standard practice and obligingly matched velocities.

Jedao listened in on Haval speaking with the Gwa authority, who spoke flawless high language. "They don't call it 'high language,' of course," Haval had explained to Jedao earlier. "They call it 'mongrel language.'" Jedao had expressed that he didn't care what they called it.

Haval didn't trust Jedao to keep his mouth shut, so she'd stashed him in the business office with Teshet to keep an eye on him. Teshet had brought a wooden box that opened up to reveal an astonishing collection of jewelry. Jedao watched out of the corner of his eye as Teshet made himself comfortable in the largest chair, dumped the box's contents on the desk, and began sorting it according to criteria known only to him.

Jedao was watching videos of the command center and the communications channel, and tried to concentrate on reading the authority's body language, made difficult by her heavy zigzag cosmetics and the layers of robes that cloaked her figure. Meanwhile, Teshet put earrings, bracelets, and mysterious hooked and jeweled items in piles, and alternated helpful glosses of Gwa-an gestures with borderline insubordinate, not to say lewd, suggestions for things he could do with Jedao. Jedao was grateful that his ability to blush, like his ability to be tickled, had been burned out of him in

Academy. *Note to self, suggest to General Essier that Teshet is wasted in special ops and maybe reassign him to Recreation?*

Jedao mentioned this to Teshet while Haval was discussing the cargo manifest with the authority. Teshet lowered his lashes and looked sideways at Jedao. "You don't think I'm good at my job?" he asked.

"You have an excellent record," Jedao said.

Teshet sighed, and his face became serious. "You're used to regular Kel, I see."

Jedao waited.

"I end up in a lot of situations where if people get the notion that I'm a Kel officer, I may end up locked up and tortured. While that could be fun in its own right, it makes career advancement difficult."

"You could get a medal out of it."

"Oh, is *that* how you got promoted so—"

Jedao held up his hand, and Teshet stopped. On the monitor, Haval was saying, in a greasy voice, "I'm glad to hear of your interest, madam. We would have been happy to start hauling the lubricant earlier, except we had to persuade our people that—"

The authority's face grew even more imperturbable. "You had to figure out whom to bribe."

"We understand there are fees—"

Jedao listened to Haval negotiating her bribe to the authority with half an ear. "Don't tell me all that jewelry's genuine?"

"The gems are mostly synthetics," Teshet said. He held up a long earring with a rose quartz at the end. "No, this won't do. I bought it for myself, but you're too light-skinned for it to look good on you."

"I'm wearing jewelry?"

"Unless you brought your own—scratch that, I bet everything you own is in red and gold."

"Yes."

Teshet tossed the rose quartz earring aside and selected a vivid emerald earstud. "This will look nice on you."

"I don't get a say?"

"How much do you know about merchanter fashion trends out in this march?"

Jedao conceded the point.

The private line crackled to life. "You two still in there?" said Haval's voice.

"Yes, what's the issue?" Teshet said.

"They're boarding us to check for contraband. You haven't messed with the drugs cabinet, have you?"

Teshet made an affronted sound. "You thought I was going to get Sren high?"

"I don't make assumptions when it comes to you, Teshet. Get the hell out of there."

Teshet thrust the emerald earstud and two bracelets at Jedao. "Put those on," he said. "If anyone asks you where the third bracelet is, say you had to pawn it to make good on a gambling debt."

Under other circumstances, Jedao would have found this offensive—he was *good* at gambling—but presumably Sren had different talents. As he put on the earring, he said, "What do I need to know about these drugs?"

Teshet was stuffing the rest of the jewelry back in the box. "Don't look at me like that. They're illegal both in the heptarchate and the Gwa Reality, but people run them anyway. They make useful cover. The Gwa-an search us for contraband, they find the contraband, they confiscate the contraband, we pay them a bribe to keep quiet about it, they go away happy."

Impatient with Jedao fumbling with the clasp of the second bracelet, he fastened it for him, then turned Jedao's hand over and studied the scar at the base of his palm. "You should have skinsealed that one too, but never mind."

"I'm bad at peeling vegetables?" Jedao suggested. Close enough to "knife fight," right? And much easier to explain away than bullet scars.

"Are you two *done*?" Haval's voice demanded.

"We're coming, we're coming," Teshet said.

Jedao took up his post in the command center. Teshet himself disappeared in the direction of the airlock. Jedao wasn't aware that anything had gone wrong until Haval returned to the command center, flanked by two personages in bright orange space suits. Both wielded guns of a type Jedao had never seen before, which made him irrationally happy. While most of his collection was at home with his mother, he relished adding new items. Teshet was nowhere in sight.

Haval's pilot spoke before the intruders had a chance to say anything. "Commander, what's going on?"

The broader of the two arrivals spoke in Tlen Gwa, then kicked Haval in the shin. "Guess what," Haval said with a macabre grin. "Those aren't the real authorities we ran into. They're pirates."

Oh, for the love of fox and hound, Jedao thought. In truth, he wasn't surprised, just resigned. He never trusted it when an operation went too smoothly.

The broader pirate spoke again. Haval sighed deeply, then said, "Hand over all weapons or they start shooting."

Where's Teshet? Jedao wondered. As if in answer, he heard a gunshot, then the ricochet. More gunshots. He was sure at least one of the shooters was Teshet, or one of Teshet's operatives: they carried Stinger 40s and he recognized the whine of the reports.

Presumably Teshet was occupied, which left matters here up to him. Some of Haval's crew went armed. Jedao did not—they had agreed that Sren wouldn't know how to use a gun—but that didn't mean he wasn't dangerous. While the other crew set down their guns, Jedao flung himself at the narrower intruder's feet.

The pirates did not like this. But Jedao had always been blessed, or per-haps cursed, with extraordinarily quick reflexes. He dropped his weight on one arm and leg and kicked the narrow pirate's feet from under them with the other leg. The pirate discharged their gun, and the bullet whined over Jedao and banged into one of the status displays, causing it to spark and sputter out. Haval yelped.

Jedao had already sprung back to his feet—damn the twinge in his knees, he should have that looked into—and twisted the gun out of the nar-row pirate's grip. They had the stunned expression that Jedao was used to seeing on people who did not deal with professionals very often. He shot them, but thanks to their loose-limbed flailing, the first bullet took them in the shoulder. The second one made an ugly hole in their forehead, and they dropped.

The broader pirate had more presence of mind, but chose the wrong target. Jedao smashed her wrist aside with the knife edge of his hand just as she fired at Haval—five shots, in rapid succession. Her hands trembled visibly, and four of the shots went wide. Haval had had the sense to duck, but Jedao smelled blood and suspected she'd been hit. Hopefully nowhere fatal.

Jedao shot the broad pirate in the side of the head just as she pivoted to target him next. Her pistol clattered to the floor as she dropped. By reflex, he flung himself to the side in case it discharged, but it didn't.

Once he had assured himself that both pirates were dead, he knelt at Haval's side and checked the wound. She had been very lucky. The single bullet had gone through her side, missing the major organs. She started shouting at him for going up unarmed against people with guns.

"I'm getting the medical kit," Jedao said, too loudly, to get her to shut up. His hands were utterly steady as he opened the cabinet and brought the kit back to Haval, who at least had the good sense not to try to stand up.

Haval scowled, but accepted the painkiller tabs he handed her. She held still while he cut away her shirt and inspected the entry and exit wounds.

YOON HA LEE | 475

At least the bullet wasn't a burrower or she wouldn't have a lung anymore. He got to work with the sterilizer.

By the time Teshet and two other soldiers entered the command center, Jedao had sterilized and sealed the wounds. Teshet crossed the threshold with rapid strides. When Haval's head came up, Teshet signed sharply for her to be quiet. Curious, Jedao also kept silent.

Teshet drew his combat knife, then knelt next to the larger corpse. With a deft stroke, he cut into the pirate's neck, then yanked out a device and its wires. Blood dripped down and obscured the metal. He repeated the operation for the other corpse, then crushed both devices under his heel. "All right," he said. "It should be safe to talk now."

Jedao raised his eyebrows, inviting explanation.

"Not pirates," Teshet said. "Those were Gwa-an special ops."

Hmm. "Then odds were they were waiting for someone to show up to rescue the *Moonsweet Blossom*," Jedao said.

"I don't disagree." Teshet glanced at Haval, then back at the corpses. "That wasn't you, was it?"

Haval's eyes were glazed, side-effect of the painkiller, but she wasn't entirely out of it. "Idiot here risked his life. We could have handled it."

"I wasn't the one in danger," Jedao said, remembering the pirates' guns pointed at her. Haval might not be particularly respectful, as subordinates went, cover identity or not, but she *was* his subordinate, and he was responsible for her. To Teshet: "Your people?"

"Two down," Teshet said grimly, and gave him the names. "They died bravely."

"I'm sorry," Jedao said; two more names to add to the long litany of those he'd lost. He was thinking about how to proceed, though. "The *real* Gwa-an patrols won't be likely to know about this. It's how I'd run the op—the fewer people who are aware of the truth, the better. I bet *their* orders are to take in any surviving 'pirates' for processing, and then the authorities will release and debrief the operatives from there. What do you normally do in case of *actual* pirates?"

"Report the incident," Haval said. Her voice sounded thready. "Formal complaint if we're feeling particularly annoying."

"All right." Jedao calmly began taking off the jewelry and his clothes. "That one's about my size," he said, nodding at the smaller of the two corpses. The suit would be tight across the shoulders, but that couldn't be helped. "Congratulations, not two but three of your crew died heroically, but you captured a pirate in the process."

Teshet made a wistful sound. "That temporary skin stuff obscures your musculature, you know." But he helpfully began stripping the indicated corpse.

"I'll make it up to you some other time," Jedao said recklessly. "Haval, make that formal complaint and demand that you want your captive tried appropriately. Since the nearest station is Du, that will get me inserted so I can investigate."

"You're just lucky some of the Gwa-an are as sallow as you are," Haval said as Jedao changed clothes.

"I will be disappointed in you if you don't have restraints," Jedao said to Teshet.

Teshet's eyes lit.

Jedao rummaged in the medical kit until he found the eyedrops he was looking for. They were meant to counteract tear gas, but they had a side effect of pupil dilation, which was what interested him. It would help him feign concussion.

"We're running short on time, so listen closely," Jedao said. "Turn me over to the Gwa-an. Don't worry about me; I can handle myself."

"Je—Sren, I don't care how much you've studied the station's schematics, you'll be outnumbered thousands to one *on foreign territory*."

"Sometime over drinks I'll tell you about the time I infiltrated a ring-city where I didn't speak any of the local languages," Jedao said. "Turn me in. I'll locate the crew, spring them, and signal when I'm ready. You won't be able to mistake it."

Haval's brow creased. Jedao kept speaking. "After you've done that, load all the shuttles full of lubricant canisters. Program the lubricant to go from zero-coefficient flow to harden completely in response to the radio signal. You're going to put the shuttles on autopilot. When you see my signal, launch the shuttles' contents toward the station's turret levels. That should gum them up and buy us cover."

"*All* our shuttles?" Haval said faintly.

"Haval," Jedao said, "stop thinking about profit margins and repeat my orders back to me."

She did.

"Splendid," Jedao said. "Don't disappoint me."

The Gwa-an took Jedao into custody without comment. Jedao feigned concussion, saving him from having to sound coherent in a language he barely spoke. The Gwa-an official responsible for him looked concerned, which was considerate of him. Jedao hoped to avoid killing him or the guard they'd assigned to him. Only one, thankfully; they assumed he was too injured to be a threat.

The first thing Jedao noticed about the Gwa-an shuttle was how roomy it was, with wastefully widely-spaced seats. He hadn't noticed that the Gwa-an were, on average, that much larger than the heptarchate's citizens. (Not that this said much. Both nations contained a staggering variety of ethnic groups and their associated phenotypes. Jedao himself was on the short side of average for a heptarchate manform.) At least being "concussed" meant he didn't have to figure out how the hell the safety restraints worked, because while he could figure it out with enough fumbling, it would look damned suspicious that he didn't already know. Instead, the official strapped him in while saying things in a soothing voice. The guard limited themselves to a scowl.

Instead of the smell of disinfectant that Jedao associated with shuttles, the Gwa-an shuttle was pervaded by a light, almost effervescent fragrance. He hoped it wasn't intoxicating. Or rather, part of him hoped it was, because he didn't often have good excuses to screw around with new and exciting recreational drugs, but it would impede his effectiveness. Maybe all Gwa-an disinfectants smelled this good? He should steal the formula. Voidmoth crews everywhere would thank him.

Even more unnervingly, the shuttle played music on the way to the station. At least, while it didn't resemble any music he'd heard before, it had a recognizable beat and some sort of flute in it. From the others' reactions, this was normal and possibly even boring. Too bad he was about as musical as a pair of boots.

The shuttle docked smoothly. Jedao affected not to know what was going on and allowed the official to chirp at him. Eventually a stretcher arrived and they put him on it. They emerged into the lights of the shuttle bay. Jedao's temples twinged with the beginning of a headache. At least it meant the eyedrops were still doing their job.

The journey to Du Station's version of Medical took forever. Jedao was especially eager to escape based on what he'd learned of Gwa-an medical therapies, which involved too many genetically engineered critters for his comfort. (He had read up on the topic after Haval told him about the dueling.) He did consider that he could make his mother happy by stealing her some pretty little microbes, but with his luck they'd turn his testicles inside out.

When the medic took him into an examination room, Jedao whipped up and downed her with a blow to the side of the neck. The guard was slow to react, and Jedao grasped their throat and grappled with them, waiting the interminable seconds until they slumped unconscious. He had a bad moment when he heard footsteps passing by; luckily, the guard's wheeze didn't attract attention. Jedao wasn't modest about his combat skills, but they wouldn't save him if he was sufficiently outnumbered.

Too bad he couldn't steal the guard's uniform, but it wouldn't fit him. So it would have to be the medic's clothes. Good: the medic's clothes were robes instead of something more form-fitting. Bad: even though the garments would fit him, more or less, they were in the style for women.

I will just have to improvise, Jedao thought. At least he'd kept up the habit of shaving, and the Gwa-an appeared to permit a variety of haircuts in all genders, so his short hair and bangs wouldn't be too much of a problem. As long as he moved quickly and didn't get stopped for conversation—

Jedao changed, then slipped out and took a few moments to observe how people walked and interacted so he could fit in more easily. The Gwa-an were terrible about eye contact and, interestingly for station-dwellers, preferred to keep each other at a distance. He could work with that.

His eyes still ached, since Du Station had abominably bright lighting, but he'd just have to prevent people from looking too closely at him. It helped that he had dark brown eyes to begin with, so the dilated pupils wouldn't be obvious from a distance. He was walking briskly toward the lifts when he heard a raised voice. He kept walking. The voice called again, more insistently.

Damn. He turned around, hoping that someone hadn't recognized his outfit from behind. A woman in extravagant layers of green, lilac, and pink spoke to him in strident tones. Jedao approached her rapidly, wincing at her voice, and hooked her into an embrace. Maybe he could take advantage of this yet.

"You're not—" she began to say.

"I'm too busy," he said over her, guessing at how best to deploy the Tlen Gwa phrases he knew. "I'll see you for tea at thirteen. I like your coat."

The woman's face turned an ugly mottled red. "You like my *what?*" At least, he thought that was what she had said. She stepped back from him, pulling what looked like a small perfume bottle from among her layers of clothes.

He tensed, not wanting to fight her in full view of passersby. She spritzed him with a moist vapor, then smiled coolly at him before spinning on her heel and walking away.

Shit. Just how fast-acting were Gwa-an duels, anyway? He missed the sensible kind with swords; his chances would have been much better. He hoped the symptoms wouldn't be disabling, but then, the woman couldn't possibly have had a chance to tailor the infectious agent to his system, and maybe the immunizations would keep him from falling over sick until he had found Meng and their crew.

How had he offended her, anyway? Had he gotten the word for "coat" wrong? Now that he thought about it, the word for "coat" differed from the word for "navel" only by its tones, and—hells and foxes, he'd messed up the tone sandhi, hadn't he? He kept walking, hoping that she'd be content with getting him sick and wouldn't call security on him.

At last he made it to the lifts. While stealing the medic's uniform had also involved stealing their keycard, he preferred not to use it. Rather, he'd swapped the medic's keycard for the loud woman's. She had carried hers on a braided lanyard with a clip. It would do nicely if he had to garrote anyone in a hurry. The garrote wasn't one of his specialties, but as his girl-friend the first year of Shuos Academy had always been telling him, it paid to keep your options open.

At least the lift's controls were less perilous than figuring out how to correctly pronounce items of clothing. Jedao had by no means achieved reading fluency in Tlen Gwa, but the language had a wonderfully tidy writing system, with symbols representing syllables and odd little curlicue diacritics that changed what vowel you used. He had also theoretically memorized the numbers from 1 to 9,999. Fortunately, Du Station had fewer than 9,999 levels.

Two of the other people on the lift stared openly at Jedao. He fussed with his hair on the grounds that it would look like ordinary embarrassment and not *Hello! I am a cross-dressing enemy agent, pleased to make your acquaintance.* Come to that, Gwa-an women's clothes were comfortable, and all the layers meant that he could, in principle, hide useful items like garrotes in them. He wondered if he could keep them as a souvenir. Start a fashion back home. He bet his mother would approve.

Intelligence had given him a good guess for where Meng and their crew might be held. At least, Jedao hoped that Du Station's higher-ups hadn't faked him out by stowing them in the lower-security cells. He was betting a lot on the guess that the Gwa-an were still in the process of interrogating the lot rather than executing them out of hand.

The layout wasn't the hard part, but Jedao reflected on the mysteries of the Gwa Reality's penal code. For example, prostitution was a major offense. They didn't even fine the offenders, but sent them to remedial counseling, which surely *cost* the state money. In the heptarchate, they did the sensible thing by enforcing licenses for health and safety reasons and taxing the whole enterprise. On the other hand, the Gwa-an had a refreshingly casual attitude toward heresy. They believed that public debate about

Poetics (their version of Doctrine) strengthened the polity. If you put forth that idea anywhere in the heptarchate, you could expect to get arrested.

So it was that Jedao headed for the cellblocks where one might find unlucky prostitutes and not the ones where overly enthusiastic heretics might be locked up overnight to cool off. He kept attracting horrified looks and wondered if he'd done something offensive with his hair. Was it wrong to part it on the left, and if so, why hadn't Haval warned him? How many ways could you get hair wrong anyway?

The Gwa-an also had peculiarly humanitarian ideas about the surroundings that offenders should be kept in. Level 37, where he expected to find Meng, abounded with fountains. Not cursory fountains, but glorious cascading arches of silvery water interspersed with elongated humanoid statues in various uncomfortable-looking poses. Teshet had mentioned that this had to do with Gwa-an notions of ritual purity.

While "security" was one of the words that Jedao had memorized, he did not read Tlen Gwa especially quickly, which made figuring out the signs a chore. At least the Gwa-an believed in signs, a boon to foreign infiltrators everywhere. Fortunately, the Gwa-an hadn't made a secret of the Security office's location, even if getting to it was complicated by the fact that the fountains had been rearranged since the last available intel and he preferred not to show up soaking wet. The fountains themselves formed a labyrinth and, upon inspection, it appeared that different portions could be turned on or off to change the labyrinth's twisty little passages.

Unfortunately, the water's splashing also made it difficult to hear people coming, and he had decided that creeping about would not only slow him down, but make him look more conspicuous, especially with that issue with his hair (or whatever it was that made people stare at him with such affront). He rounded a corner and almost crashed into a sentinel, recognizable by Security's spear-and-shield badge.

In retrospect, a simple collision might have worked out better. Instead, Jedao dropped immediately into a fighting stance, and the sentinel's eyes narrowed. *Dammit,* Jedao thought, exasperated with himself, *and this is why my handlers preferred me doing the sniper bits rather than the infiltration bits.* Since he'd blown the opportunity to bluff his way past the sentinel, he swept the man's feet out from under him and knocked him out. After the man was unconscious, Jedao stashed him behind one of the statues, taking care so the spray from the fountains wouldn't interfere too much with his breathing. He had the distinct impression that "dead body" was much worse from a ritual purity standpoint than "merely unconscious," if he had to negotiate with someone later.

He ran into no other sentinels on the way to the office, but as it so happened, a woman sentinel was leaving just as he got there. Jedao put on an expression he had learned from the scariest battlefield medic of his acquaintance, back when he'd been a lowly infantry captain, and marched straight up to Security. He didn't need to be convincing for long, he just needed a moment's hesitation.

By the time the sentinel figured out that the "medic" was anything but, Jedao had taken her gun and broken both her arms. "I want to talk to your leader," he said, another of those useful canned phrases.

The sentinel left off swearing (he was sure it was swearing) and repeated the word for "leader" in an incredulous voice.

Whoops. Was he missing some connotational nuance? He tried the word for "superior officer," to which the response was even more incredulous. *Hey Mom*, Jedao thought, *you know how you always said I should join the diplomatic corps on account of my always talking my way out of trouble as a kid? Were you ever wrong. I am the worst diplomat ever.* Admittedly, maybe starting off by breaking the woman's arms was where he'd gone wrong, but the sentinel didn't sound upset about *that*. The Gwa-an were very confusing people.

After a crescendo of agitation (hers) and desperate rummaging about for people nouns (his), it emerged that the term he wanted was the one for "head priest." Which was something the language lessons ought to have noted. He planned on dropping in on whoever had written the course and having a spirited talk with them.

Just as well that the word for "why" was more straightforward. The sentinel wanted to know why he wanted to talk to the head priest. He wanted to know why someone who'd had both her arms broken was more concerned with propriety (his best guess) than alerting the rest of the station that they had an intruder. He had other matters to attend to, though. Too bad he couldn't recruit her for her sangfroid, but that was outside his purview.

What convinced the sentinel to comply, in the end, was not the threat of more violence, which he imagined would have been futile. Instead, he mentioned that he'd left one of her comrades unconscious amid the fountains and the man would need medical care. He liked the woman's concern for her fellow sentinel.

Jedao and the sentinel walked together to the head priest's office. The head priest came out. She had an extremely elaborate coiffure, held in place by multiple hairpins featuring elongated figures like the statues. She froze when Jedao pointed the gun at her, then said several phrases in what sounded like different languages.

"Mongrel language," Jedao said in Tlen Gwa, remembering what Haval had told him.

"What do you want?" the high priest said in awkward but comprehensible high language.

Jedao explained that he was here for Ahun Gerav, in case the priest only knew Meng by their cover name. "Release them and their crew, and this can end with minimal bloodshed."

The priest wheezed. Jedao wondered if she was allergic to assassins. He'd never heard of such a thing, but he wasn't under any illusions that he knew everything about Gwa-an immune systems. Then he realized she was laughing.

"Feel free to share," Jedao said, very pleasantly. The sentinel was sweating.

The priest stopped laughing. "You're too late," she said. "You're too late by thirteen years."

Jedao did the math: eight years since he and Meng had graduated from Shuos Academy. Of course, the two of them had attended for the usual five years. "They've been a double agent since they were a cadet?"

The priest's smile was just this side of smug.

Jedao knocked the sentinel unconscious and let her spill to the floor. The priest's smile didn't falter, which made him think less of her. Didn't she care about her subordinate? If nothing else, he'd had a few concussions in his time (real ones) and they were no joke.

"The crew," Jedao said.

"Gerav attempted to persuade them to turn coat as well," the priest said. "When they were less than amenable, well—" She shrugged. "We had no further use for them."

I will not forgive this, Jedao thought. "Take me to Gerav."

She shrugged again. "Unfortunate for them," she said. "But to be frank, I don't value their life over my own."

"How very pragmatic of you," Jedao said.

She shut up and led the way.

Du Station had provided Meng with a luxurious suite by heptarchate standards. The head priest bowed with an ironic smile as she opened the door for Jedao. He shoved her in and scanned the room.

The first thing he noticed was the overwhelming smell of—what *was* that smell? Jedao had thought he had reasonably cosmopolitan tastes, but the platters with their stacks of thin-sliced meat drowned in rich gravies and sauces almost made him gag. Who needed that much meat in their diet? The suite's occupant seemed to agree, judging by how little the meat had been touched. And why wasn't the meat cut into decently small pieces so as to make for easy eating? The bowls of succulent fruit were either for show or the suite's occupant disliked fruit, too. The flatbreads, on the other hand, had been torn into. One, not entirely eaten, rested on a meat platter and was dissolving into the gravy. Several different-sized bottles were partly empty, and once he adjusted to all the meat, he could also detect the sweet reek of wine.

Most fascinatingly, instead of chopsticks and spoons, the various plates and platters sported two-tined forks (Haval had explained to him about forks) and knives. Maybe this was how they trained assassins. Jedao liked knives, although not as much as he liked guns. He wondered if he could persuade the Kel to import the custom. It would make for some lively high tables.

Meng glided out, resplendent in brocade Gwa-an robes, then gaped. Jedao wasn't making any attempt to hide his gun.

"Foxfucking hounds," Meng slurred as they sat down heavily, "*you*. Is that really you, Jedao?"

"You know each other?" the priest said.

Jedao ignored her question, although he kept her in his peripheral vision in case he needed to kill her or knock her out. "You graduated from Shuos Academy with high marks," Jedao said. "You even married rich, the way you always talked about. Four beautiful kids. Why, Meng? Was it nothing more than a cover story?"

Meng reached for a fork. Jedao's trigger finger shifted. Meng withdrew their hand.

"The Gwa-an paid stupendously well," Meng said quietly. "It mattered a lot more, once. Of course, hiding the money was getting harder and harder. What good is money if you can't spend it? And the Shuos were about to catch on anyway. So I had to run."

"And your crew?"

Meng's mouth twisted, but they met Jedao's eyes steadfastly. "I didn't want things to end the way they did."

"Cold comfort to their families."

"It's done now," Meng said, resigned. They looked at the largest platter of meat with sudden loathing. Jedao tensed, wondering if it was going to be flung at him, but all Meng did was shove it away from them. Some gravy slopped over the side.

Jedao smiled sardonically. "If you come home, you might at least get a decent bowl of rice instead of this weird bread stuff."

"Jedao, if I come home, they'll *torture me for high treason*, unless our heptarch's policies have changed drastically. You can't stop me from killing myself."

"Rather than going home?" Jedao shrugged. Meng probably did have a suicide failsafe, although if they were serious they'd have used it already. He couldn't imagine the Gwa-an would have neglected to provide them with one if the Shuos hadn't.

Still, he wasn't done. "If you do something so crass, I'm going to visit each one of your children *personally*. I'm going to take them out to a nice dinner with actual food that you eat with actual chopsticks and spoons. And I'm going to explain to them in exquisite detail how their Shuos parent is a traitor."

Meng bit their lip.

More softly, Jedao said, "When did the happy family stop being a cover story and start being real?"

"I don't know," Meng said, wretched. "I can't—do you know how my spouses would look at me if they found out that I'd been lying to them all this time? I wasn't even particularly interested in other people's kids when this all began. But watching them grow up—" They fell silent.

"I have to bring you back," Jedao said. He remembered the staticky voice of the unnamed woman playing in Essier's office, Meng's *crew*, who'd tried and failed to get a warning out. She and her comrades deserved justice. But he also remembered all the gifts he'd sent to Meng's children down the years, the occasional awkwardly written thank-you note. It wasn't as if any good would be achieved by telling them the awful truth. "But I can pull a few strings. Make sure your family never finds out."

Meng hesitated for a long moment. Then they nodded. "It's fair. Better than fair."

To the priest, Jedao said, "You'd better take us to the *Moonsweet Blossom*, assuming you haven't disassembled it already."

The priest's mouth twisted. "You're in luck."

———

Du Station had ensconced the *Moonsweet Blossom* in a bay on Level 62. The Gwa-an they passed gawped at them. The priest sailed past without giving any explanation. Jedao wondered whether the issue was his hair or some other inexplicable Gwa-an cultural foible.

"I hope you can pilot while drunk," Jedao said to Meng.

Meng drew themself up to their full height. "I didn't drink *that* much."

Jedao had his doubts, but he would take his chances. "Get in."

The priest's sudden tension alerted him that she was about to try something. Jedao shoved Meng toward the trademoth, then grabbed the priest in an armlock. What was the point of putting a priest in charge of security if the priest couldn't *fight?*

Jedao said to her, "You're going to instruct your underlings to get the hell out of our way and open the airlock so we can leave."

"And why would I do that?" the priest said.

He reached up and snatched out half her hairpins. Too bad he didn't have a third hand; his grip on the gun was precarious enough as it was. She growled, which he interpreted as "fuck you and all your little foxes."

"I could get creative," Jedao said.

"I was warned that the heptarchate was full of barbarians," the priest said.

At least the incomprehensible Gwa-an fixation on hairstyles meant that he didn't have to resort to more disagreeable threats, like shooting her subordinates in front of her. Given her reaction when he had knocked out the sentinel, he wasn't convinced that would faze her anyway. He adjusted his grip and forced her to the floor.

"Give the order," he said. "If you don't play any tricks, you'll even get the hairpins back without my shoving them through your eardrums." They were very nice hairpins, despite the creepiness of the elongated humanoid figures, and he bet they were real gold.

Since he had her facing the floor, the priest couldn't glare at him. The venom in her voice was unmistakable, however. "As you require." She started speaking in Tlen Gwa.

The workers in the area hurried to comply. Jedao had familiarized himself with the control systems of the airlock and was satisfied they weren't doing anything underhanded. "Thank you," he said, to which the priest hissed something venomous. He flung the hairpins away from him and let her go. She cried out at the sound of their clattering and scrambled after them with a devotion he reserved for weapons. Perhaps, to a Gwa-an priest, they were equivalent.

One of the workers, braver or more foolish than the others, reached for her own gun. Jedao shot her in the hand on the way up the hatch. It bought him enough time to get the rest of the way up the ramp and slam the hatch shut after him. Surely Meng couldn't accuse him of showing off if they hadn't seen the feat of marksmanship; and he hoped the worker would appreciate that he could just as easily have put a hole in her head.

The telltale rumble of the *Blossom*'s maneuver drive assured him that Meng, at least, was following directions. This boded well for Meng's health. Jedao hurried forward, wondering how many more rounds the Gwa-an handgun contained, and started webbing himself into the gunner's seat.

"You wouldn't consider putting that thing away, would you?" Meng said. "It's hard for me to think when I'm ready to piss myself."

"If you think *I'm* the scariest person in your future, Meng, you haven't been paying attention."

"One, I don't think you know yourself very well, and two, I liked you much better when we were on the same side."

"I'm going to let you meditate on that second bit some other time. In the meantime, let's get out of here."

Meng swallowed. "They'll shoot us down the moment we get clear of the doors, you know."

"Just *go*, Meng. I've got friends. Or did you think I teleported onto this station?"

"At this point I wouldn't put anything past you. Okay, you're webbed in, I'm webbed in, here goes nothing."

The maneuver drive grumbled as the *Moonsweet Blossom* blasted its way out of the bay. No one attempted to close the first set of doors on them. Jedao wondered if the priest was still scrabbling after her hairpins, or if it had to do with the more pragmatic desire to avoid costly repairs to the station.

The *Moonsweet Blossom* had few armaments, mostly intended for dealing with high-velocity debris, which was more of a danger than pirates if one kept to the better-policed trade routes. They wouldn't do any good against Du Station's defenses. As *signals*, on the other hand—

Using the lasers, Jedao flashed, HERE WE COME in the merchanter signal code. With any luck, Haval was paying attention.

———

At this point, several things happened.

Haval kicked Teshet in the shin to get him to stop watching a mildly pornographic and not very well-acted drama about a famous courtesan from 192 years ago. ("It's historical, so it's educational!" he protested. "One, we've got our signal, and two, I wish you would take care of your *urgent needs* in your own quarters," Haval said.)

Carp 1 through *Carp 4* and *7* through *10* launched all their shuttles. Said shuttles were, as Jedao had instructed, full of variable-coefficient lubricant programmed to its liquid form. The shuttles flew toward Du Station, then opened their holds and burned their retro thrusters for all they were worth. The lubricant, carried forward by momentum, continued toward Du Station's turret levels.

Du Station recognized an attack when it saw one, but its defenses consisted of a combination of high-powered lasers, which could only vaporize small portions of the lubricant and were useless for altering the momentum of quantities of the stuff, and railguns, whose projectiles punched through the mass without effect. Once the lubricant had clogged up the defensive emplacements, *Carp 1* transmitted an encrypted radio signal that caused the lubricant to harden in place.

The *Moonsweet Blossom* linked up with Haval's merchant troop. At this point, the *Blossom* only contained two people, trivial compared to the amount of mass it had been designed to haul. The merchant troop, of course, had just divested itself of its cargo. The nine heptarchate vessels proceeded to hightail it out of there at highly non-freighter accelerations.

————

Jedao and Meng swept the *Moonsweet Blossom* for bugs and other unwelcome devices, an exhausting but necessary task. Then, at what Jedao judged to be a safe distance from Du Station, he ordered Meng to slave it to *Carp 1*.

The *Carp 1* and *Moonsweet Blossom* matched velocities, and Jedao and Meng made the crossing to the former. There was a bad moment when Jedao thought Meng was going to unhook their tether and drift off into the smothering dark rather than face their fate. But whatever temptations were running through their head, Meng resisted them.

Haval and Teshet greeted them on the *Carp 1*. After Jedao and Meng had shed the suits and checked them for needed repairs, Haval ushered them all into the business office. "I didn't expect you to spring the trademoth as well as our Shuos friend," Haval said.

Meng wouldn't meet her eyes.

"What about the rest of the crew?" Teshet said.

"They didn't make it," Jedao said, and sneezed. He explained about Meng's extracurricular activities over the past thirteen years. Then he sneezed again.

Haval grumbled under her breath. "Whatever the hell you did on Du, Sren, did it involve duels?"

"'Sren'?" Meng said.

"You don't think I came into the Gwa Reality under my own"—sneeze—"name, did you?" Jedao said. "Anyway, there might have been an incident . . ."

Meng groaned. "Just how good is your Tlen Gwa?"

"Sort of not, apparently," Jedao said. "I *really* need to have a word with whoever wrote the Tlen Gwa course. I thought I was all right with languages at the basic phrase level, but was the proofreader asleep the day they approved it?"

Meng had the grace to look embarrassed. "I may have hacked it."

"You what?"

"If I'd realized *you'd* be using it, I wouldn't have bothered. Botching the language doesn't seem to have slowed you down any."

Wordlessly, Teshet handed Jedao a handkerchief, and Jedao promptly sneezed into it. Maybe he'd be able to give his mother a gift of a petri dish with a lovely culture of Gwa-an germs after all. He'd have to ask the medic about it later.

Teshet then produced a set of restraints from his pockets and gestured at Meng. Meng sighed deeply and submitted to being trussed up.

"Don't look so disappointed," Teshet said into Jedao's ear. "I've another set just for you." Then he and Meng marched off to the brig.

Haval cleared her throat. "Off to the medic with you," she said to Jedao. "We'd better figure out why your vaccinations aren't working and if everyone's going to need to be quarantined."

"Not arguing," Jedao said meekly.

———

Some days later, Jedao was rewatching one of Teshet's pornography dramas while in bed. At least, he thought it was pornography. The costuming made it difficult to tell, and the dialogue had made *more* sense when he was still running a fever.

The medic had kept him in isolation until they declared him no longer contagious. Whether due to this precaution or pure luck, no one else came down with the duel disease. They'd given him a clean bill of health this morning, but Haval had insisted that he rest a little longer.

The door opened. Jedao looked up in surprise.

Teshet entered with a fresh supply of handkerchiefs. "Well, Jedao, we'll re-enter heptarchate space in two days, high calendar. Any particular orders you want me to relay to Haval?" He obligingly handed over a slate so Jedao could look over Haval's painstaking, not to say excruciatingly detailed, reports on their current status.

"Haval's doing a fine job," Jedao said, glad that his voice no longer came out as a croak. "I won't get in her way." He returned the slate to Teshet.

"Sounds good." Teshet turned his back and departed. Jedao admired the view, wishing in spite of himself that the other man would linger.

Teshet returned half an hour later with two clear vials full of unidentified substances. "First or second?" he said, holding them up to the light one by one.

"I'm sorry," Jedao said, "first or second what?"

"You look like you need cheering up," Teshet said hopefully. "You want on top? You want me on top? I'm flexible."

Jedao blinked, trying to parse this. "On top of wh—?" *Oh.* "What's *in* those vials?"

"You have your choice of variable-coefficient lubricant or goose fat," Teshet said. "Assuming you were telling the truth when you said it was goose fat. And don't yell at Haval for letting me into your refrigerator; I did it all on my own. I admit I can't tell the difference. As Haval will attest, I'm a *dreadful* cook, so I didn't want to fry up some scallion pancakes just to taste the goose fat."

Jedao's mouth went dry, which had less to do with Teshet's eccentric choice of lubricants than the fact that he had sat down on the edge of Jedao's bed. "You don't have anything more, ah, conventional?" He realized that was a mistake as soon as the words left his mouth; he'd essentially accepted Teshet's proposition.

For the first time, Jedao glimpsed uncertainty in Teshet's eyes. "We don't have a lot of time before we're back to heptarchate space and you have to go back to being a commander and I have to go back to being responsible," he said softly. "Or as responsible as I ever get, anyway. Want to make the most of it? Because I get the impression that you don't allow yourself much of a personal life."

"Use the goose fat," Jedao said, because as much as he liked Teshet, he did not relish the thought of being *cemented* to Teshet.

It would distract Teshet from continuing to analyze his psyche, and, yes, the man was damnably attractive. What the hell, with any luck his mother was never, ever, *ever* hearing of this. (He could imagine the conversation now: "Garach Jedao Shkan, are you meaning to tell me you finally found a nice young man and you're *still* not planning on settling down and providing me more grandchildren?" And then she would send him *more goose fat.*)

Teshet brightened. "You won't regret this," he purred, and proceeded to help Jedao undress.

BY THE WARMTH OF THEIR CALCULUS

TOBIAS S. BUCKELL

THREE SHIPS HUNG in the void. One sleek and metallic, festooned with jagged sensors and the melted remains of powerful weapons, all of it pitted by a millennium of hard radiation and micro-impacts. The other two, each to either side, were hand-fashioned balls of ice and rock, flesh and blood, vegetation and animal, cratered from battles and long orbits through the Ring Archipelago where the dust had long battered their muddy hulls.

Koki-Fiana fe Sese hung in the air inside a great bauble of polished, clear ice in the underbelly of her dustship, and looked out at the ancient seedship as the sun's angry red light glinted across nozzles and apparatus the purpose of which she could only guess.

There was the void between the two ships. And when she looked past that, she could see the small sparks of light that were the outer planets where her people could not reach as they were far out of the dust plane. And then beyond the outer planet came the stars, where the priests said people traveled from on their seedships. Though artificiers could believe that, as it would have taken millennia to cross distances that vast, and seedships were just fragile metal buckets.

And angry, dark things waited in the dark between the stars.

Then she saw something that chilled her more than the ice just an arm's length away, or the void beyond it: a sequence of lights, some flickering and dying away, appeared all down the center of the ancient ship's hull.

Another, lone light began winking furiously on the hull of the seedship. It was battle language. Fiana pushed away from the clear, window-like ice and grabbed a handhold near the airlock. There was a speaking tube there.

She smacked the switch for Operations. There was a hiss, and a click as pneumatic tubes reconfigured.

"Mother here," she said quickly. "I see incoming communication."

Fiana didn't have the common words and their sequences memorized anymore. It had been twenty years since she'd had her eyes glued to a telescope, watching for incoming while hoping she wouldn't have to page through a slim dictionary floating from a belt. She was the Mother Superior now, the heart of the ship.

She wished she still had the aptitude, waiting for the message to get passed on was taking too damn long.

"Mother Superior!" The response was tinny, and they weren't following their training to throw their voice well. "Sortie Leader Two says the Belshin Historians tried to recover data from the seedship. They turned on a subsystem, and that triggered another power up somewhere else."

Ancient circuits were coming online just across the void.

"Floating shit," Fiana whispered.

"Please repeat?" Ops sounded terrified. Their voice had cracked.

They were all floating next to a giant beacon. They were like a raw hunk of meat hanging outside at sunset back on Sese, and the sawflies would be coming to chew them apart any second now.

"Call for all riggers to stand by the sail tubes," Fiana ordered. "Every available pair of eyes not in Figures and Orbits needs to be on a telescope, and if we run out of scopes, stand next to someone with one. Cancel all watches, muster all minds. Sound the alarm, Ops."

A moment later a plaintive wail filled the rocky corridors of the dustship. Commands were shouted, echoed, and hands slapped against rails as people rushed to their posts.

"Tell F&O to begin plotting possible escape vectors," Fiana added. "All possibilities need to be in the air for us to consider."

"Urgent from Sortie Two: they're under attack."

"Attack? From what?" Fiana looked back at the ice, but all she could see was the silver metal of ancients. She could see the wink wink wink of communication, but nothing else betrayed what was happening.

She felt helpless.

The other dustship's hull rippled, as if something inside was pushing at the skin from the inside to get out. Then the Belshin ship cracked open. It vomited water and air slowly into the void as Fiana watched in horror.

"Sortie Two have warned us not to signal back," Ops said.

"Is there an F&O rep there?" Fiana asked. "If so, put her on, now."

"Heai-Lily here," came a strong voice.

"I want full sails out, and a vector away from here. Pick the first one out."

Lily hesitated. "There are Hunter-Killer exhaust signs reported. We're plotting them against known objects in this plane. We need to work the figures, but, most of F&O is guessing we're surrounded."

"It was a trap."

"Yes, Mother."

"We can't deploy the sails, they'll spot the anomaly."

"I think so, Mother."

They should have swung by and left the ship alone when they found the Belshin dustship arriving at the same time. Archipelago treaty rules gave them both genetic exploration rights, and Fiana had wanted to get in and pull material out. She'd assumed the Belshin were after the same thing. It wouldn't have been the first time multiple dustships from opposing peoples had to work on an artifact together. There were rules for this sort of thing.

But the Belshin had been greedy and violated those rules.

The Hunter-Killers had left something in the seedship for them. And now Belshin were paying the price. And Fiana's entire ship might well pay it as well.

"Ops is telling me to tell you that Sortie Two is free of the hull and re-turning."

The team would be jumping free of the seedship, eyeballing their own trajectories back to the netting on that side of the dustship. They'd pull it in after them. They wanted nothing that looked made by intelligence on the outside of the dustship.

"Lock down all heat exchangers and airlocks once they're in. We're running tight from here on out."

Fiana wanted to curl up into a ball near the speaking tube, but instead she forced herself to kick away, grab a corner, and flip into the corridor. She flew her way down the center, using her fingertips to adjust her course.

Ops, the hub deep in the ship, was packed with off-watch specialists, their eyes wide with fear but plugging away at tasks and doing their best to pitch in. Everyone hung from footholds, making Ops feel like a literal hive of busy humanity.

There was an "up" to the sphere that was Ops, but many of the stations were triplicated throughout. This was so that the crew could let the ship orient however it needed, and also to give engineering two failsafe command stations for every primary. Watches rotated station placements to make sure everything was in good order.

But in an all-call situation like this, everyone was at a station. Once Fiana had an acceleration vector ordered, if it became safe to do it, they'd reorganize Ops so that everyone was at a station on the "down" part.

For now, they were drifting slowly away from the seedship. But with Hunter-Killers arrowing in toward them, she doubted they would get far enough away to not be of interest when the damn things arrived.

––––––––

Sortie Two gave their report right away. The all-male team floated nervously in a ready room in front of Fiana and Odetta-Audra fe Enna, one of the Secondary Mothers.

"There were two Hunter-Killers on board," Sim, the sortie leader said. "They lit up the moment the Belshin Historians got the engine room powered up. I think it was a mistake though, they were just trying to get the ancient screens to talk to them."

"Treaty breakers," Audra spat. She'd been simmering with fury since Fiana first saw her in Ops. She was concealing her fear, Fiana knew, covering it up with anger to fuel herself. Most times, it made her a fast, decisive leader, though it often led to intimidation and some distance between Audra and the folk she needed to lead. Right now, it was making the sortie men nervous.

They'd been in a dangerous situation and their nerves were already rattled, so Fiana gently tapped Audra's wrist. A warning to let her Mother Superior lead the questions for now. They'd worked together long enough for Audra to get the signal.

"It's a temptation all librarians and historians struggle with," Fiana said. "Particularly peoples on the far side of the Archipelago. A wealth of knowledge from the ancients and their golden age of machinery. A piece of that could give them the ability to draw even with us."

Nations had, after all, been built on the success of daring raids on old ships, with historians writing down what they saw in ancient script as fast as they could before making a dash for it. Only one of ten missions would make it out alive, though.

"We asked them to wait until we were done with the collection mission," Sim said. "But one of their team told us they were low on consumables because they were so far from home. We focused on doing what we came to do as quickly as we could and getting away. We did not think the historians already knew a power-up sequence or we wouldn't have stayed."

They had thought they had time to work on carefully cracking the glass pods open enough to slip a needle through without triggering any of the seedship's alarms.

But Sim had kept his head and captured what they could. Seven samples, ancient DNA that would be uncorrupted by radiation and genetic drift or the tight bloodlines of the small worldlets of the Archipelago.

The Great Mothers of the worlds wouldn't invest in these missions without that payoff. When their ancestors built the Archipelago, they'd suspected that background radiation and cosmic rays would wreak havoc over time. Whatever the world was like that people fled from, it was well shielded, and the people who ran before the Hunter-Killers hadn't had time to invent a biological solution.

So these missions, these long loops out of the safety of the great dust planes to the drifting seedships for their frozen, protected heritage, were necessary for her people to continue to survive. These ships had shielding they did not understand and could not replicate. Not without the kind of industry that would bring the Hunter-Killers screaming toward them.

"Did you see—" Fiana started.

"Yes." Sim looked down and shivered slightly. "It looked like a spider. When we heard the alarm, we did as trained. Stripped down, no artificial fibers, no clothes, no tools, no weapons. We let it come."

"That couldn't have been easy." Fiana reached out and squeezed Sim's hand, the poor thing was shivering as he thought back to what happened on the seedship they were still within jumping distance of.

"It ran past us to the Belshin. They had weapons. They fought it. They died. It broke out the airlock they came through and went for their ship."

And Fiana had seen what came next. The Hunter-Killer had detonated itself, destroying the Belshin world ship.

———

Heai-Lily came with a bundle of flexies two hours later. Her strong hair joyously sprung out around her head, as if holding compressed energy inside like springs. Her eyes, though, were tired and red.

She carefully hung the transparent sheets in the air of the ready room around Fiana.

"We have trajectories," she said. The clear rectangles had been marked up with known objects in small, careful dots from one of the navigation templates.

In red, nine X marks with arrows denoted velocities and directions. From where Fiana hung, she could get a sense of the three-dimensional situation they were in.

"They're converging on us." Fiana had suspected as much but hearing it from Lily still made her stomach roil slightly. "With options for covering any chances at escape if we run."

"So you have no solutions for me?"

"Right now, we have a far side that is hidden from their instruments. We could vent consumables that would match the profile of an icy rock getting heated up. It'd be suspicious, but not completely outside of the realm of naturally occurrent activity."

"That'll get us up to a walking pace away from the seedship," Fiana said.

"Over time. We'll have to randomize the jets, and it'll eat into our water and air."

And that would be dangerous, as right now they needed to drift in place to avoid attention.

"What does that drift get us?" Fiana asked.

"Further above the dust planes," Lily said. "Until we re-intersect."

"That's not good." They would be unable to maneuver with sails. The hundreds of dust rings around the Greater World, separated by bands and layers, would be too far away for them to shoot their sails out into. Fiana's dustship had hundreds of miles of cable they could use to guide a sail far out into a pocket of faster or slower moving dust, or even to grapple with a larger object. But above it all, they would be helpless until they'd swung all the way back around the Greater World and hit the dust planes again.

"We have a good library of discovered objects and their trajectories. If we can swing out and back in, there's a collision zone we can disguise our trajectory with."

It just meant weeks above the dust. Above everything they were comfortable with.

But what was the alternative? Stay put and wait for the Hunter-Killers? Fiana wasn't a historian, but even she knew that the Hunter-Killers tore apart everything in an area that registered electrical activity.

Her ancestors had tall, black steles scattered around their world with old pictograms carved into their sides that warned them about the Hunter-Killers. Told stories about how the alien machines followed shouts into the stellar night to their source and destroyed them. And despite those proscriptions, Hulin the Wise had experimented with crystal radio devices in the polar north of Sese. An asteroid impact had cracked the world, almost revealing the hollow interior her people had hidden inside since the ancestors first arrived. Those had been years of children dying as air fouled, and great engineering projects struggled to do the impossible: fix a cracked world.

"How fast can we get out of here?"

"Using consumables, it's dangerous, Mother. We need to coordinate with Ops. The margin will be thin, if we want to get out of here before the Hunter-Killers."

Fiana swept the transparent sheets around her away. "I'll get Ops ready to follow your commands."

To stay put would be to wait passively for death, and she wasn't ready to welcome the Hunter-Killers onto her ship.

Within the hour, the far side of the dustship was venting gases as crew warmed the material up (but not too much, or the heat signature would be suspicious and hint at some kind of unnatural process), compressed the water and hydrogen in airlocks through conduits of muscular tubes that grew throughout the ship, and blasted it out in timed dumps at F&O's orders.

Slowly, faster than the natural differential drift already there, Fiana's dustship began to move away from the seedship. It trailed a tail behind, gleaming like a comet.

———

The dustship was a living organism. Its massive hearts pumped ichor around webs of veins that exchanged heat generated by the living things inside the rock and ice hull, both human and engineered. The great lungs heaved, and the air inside moved about. Its bowels gurgled with waste, and its stomach fermented grain to feed the people.

Sese's people had worked hard to create a biological, living shell that could move through the rings around the Greater World. And they had found the other worlds the ancients had created, some of them dead hulks. Because the Hunter-Killers were ever on the prowl and not just myths to scare children with that had been passed down through the mists of prehistory.

Figures and Orbits, down in their calculatorium, worked away at the reports of Hunter-Killer movements, tracking them as they arrowed in toward the seedship. And other telescopists watched as the seedship dwindled away, until it became a glint among the other points of light in the busy sky.

And Fiana hung in Ops, watching as the activity of the ship passed on through the watch stations and crew.

It was tense, the first few full rotations. No one slept. There were tears that hung in the air. Salty fear, exhaustion, tension. The idea that the killers of the Ancients were chasing them could unnerve anyone.

Yes, they'd escaped the initial trap, but that didn't mean they were safe yet.

Fiana broke the tension when she ordered watches to resume a standard staggered watch rotation again. Even if she wasn't so sure she wouldn't need all-call, she needed the crew to function. Any more than three shifts and a person could not function under a constant press of fear, watchfulness, and readiness.

So she took the pressure for herself.

———

Fiana was inspecting the crew shaving ice from the outer walls, using one of the many burrowed tunnels in the hull, when Lily caught up to her.

"May I have a moment, Mother?" she asked softly.

"They keep sending you to brief me," Fiana noted. "You are a subordinate, not a superior. Why is your team doing this?"

"The more experienced calculating seniors need to be in the calculatorium at all times. We are at capacity, Mother, and this is not a time for anyone who needs work verified."

Lily wouldn't meet her eyes.

Well, she was either ashamed to admit she was the weakest calculator in the ship, or the F&O mothers were using her as a firewall in case Fiana got angry with them.

Or, if the F&O mothers were smart, and they were the elite of void-faring peoples, the answer could be both things at the same time. Maybe it didn't hurt that Fiana would be less likely to be angry with a young, nervous Lily. And maybe they needed the best to stay in the room and work the problem.

"What's the emergency, Lily?"

"We're moving slower than expected, Mother. It has orbital and schedule implications. We can't vent heat because we didn't quite get where we thought we'd be to have cover of several larger rocky objects blocking us from Hunter-Killer view."

Fiana batted aside ice shavings and tried to focus over the hammering of pickaxes and scrape of shovels.

"F&O made a mistake?" she asked. This could cost lives. No wonder they'd sent the almost childlike Lily to stare over at her with wide eyes. "Are you sure? The signal crew could have made a sighting mistake."

A bunch of boys with astrolabes at the telescopes doing their best astronomical sightings. F&O took the averages of repeated sightings.

"The math is strong," Lily protested, her voice firm with trust in her colleagues. "And junior F&O took sightings to confirm. The signal crew were accurate."

"But we're off track?" There was no room for that kind of error. If they didn't arrive at the right place at the right time, they wouldn't be able to tether off the right large rock, or hit the right dust plane to adjust their path.

They'd end up running out of air, or water, slowly dying, out of reach of any other dust ship or world that could lend aid.

Lily gave her a summary report, written in small and careful handwriting, filled with diagrams and area maps. Fiana would have to crawl over the details later in her quarters, poring over the equations and running checks with her own slide rule. A Mother Superior of a dust ship was required to know the math, Fiana had been an F&O staffer herself in her youth.

But it was going to be slow work to make sure she understood everything in the report.

Tight was the crown of leadership, Fiana knew. It would be a headache she had to bear.

Fiana cursorily looked through the report until she found the summary. She bit her lip. "F&O thinks there's more mass than we accounted for?"

"About sixty chipstones worth of mass."

Sixty chipstones. About ten people's worth of mass. Had they known their audit was off, they could have thrown out non-essential material from the inside to balance the ship. They could have hidden it away in the ice and consumables they'd blown.

It shouldn't have been off, though. They'd based their lives on the audit run before maneuvers.

"There was an audit," Fiana said. And everyone on board knew how important an audit was before a maneuver.

"F&O is not accusing anyone of anything, we are merely reporting the math. It doesn't lie, Mother. You can check it yourself."

She would. But for now, Fiana was not going to assume her specialists were wrong. She had to trust that her team was doing their best work. "I will check it, but I will wager it agrees with you. I'll call another mass audit. Something isn't right. We'll see if we can solve for the mystery yet."

Even though she hung in the air, Lily visibly relaxed as tension drained from her body.

"Of course, Mother. We will put our second shift at your disposal and keep only a core team running calculations."

————

The heat began to build. Crew took to wearing just simple wraps when off shift, and then Fiana gave permission for everyone to strip to just undergarments.

Globes of salty sweat hung in the stultifying air and sunken eyes made everyone look like tired ghosts.

The ship's Surgeon, Lla-Je fe Sese kicked his foot against the door to the captain's quarters in the middle of an off-watch. Fiana was startled to find him hanging in place, face flushed and worried.

"Mother, we are all in danger of heat stroke," Je said, without apologizing for waking her. The red emergency light in the doorway glimmered off his shaved scalp. It was the way of the surgeons to shave, though Je was male and used to shaving. For surgeons it was ritual demonstration of control of a razor, a tradition hundreds of years old. A surgeon with a nick on her body was not to be trusted, or so the saying went. Je said it was actually done for hygiene, but it helped that men were expected to be fastidious about it as well. Fiana always imagined it must have been weirder for the regular surgeons to hew to the tradition, given expectations. "How much longer will we be containing our waste heat?"

They'd been drifting for days now, moving further away from the seed-ship. The thick wall of ice around the hull that they mined for air and water had been scraped down, warmed, and vented. In some parts, the hull was down to only rock and mud.

"Fifteen full shifts before we reintersect with the dust fields." One orbit around the Greater World. They would have to deploy full sails on return, but the higher orbit would let the area the Hunter-Killers were infesting move ahead under them. They would plunge back into a different part of the Archipelago with barely any water and air left.

"Crew will be dying from the heat long before then," Je said somberly.

"What should we look for?" Fiana asked wearily. Die of heat now, or miss their chance to get to safety when they reintersected with the dust planes and the Archipelago. Floating diarrhea, those choices.

"Confusion, irritability—" Like Fiana's irritability at being woken? Though, to be fair, she'd been sleeping slightly, dozing as she bumped from the wall to the hammock. "Dry skin, vomiting, panting, and flushed faces."

"We're out in the void, Je. The Hunter-Killers can move out here without needing sails or tethers, but we're helpless until we intersect with the dust rings again."

"Then all that our people will find will be a ghost ship," Je said seriously. "If they are able to find us at all."

He was so serious. Always worried. And it wasn't his place to look this long in the face. It was Fiana's. But Je had always been high-minded. He wouldn't have fought so hard for a place in the Surgeons' Academy without a certain amount of hard pushiness.

"What do you recommend, my surgeon?"

"Daily internal thermometer checks for every crewmember," Je said.

"Internal? Is that what I think you mean?"

"It is."

"Je . . ." Fiana trailed off. Then she took a deep breath. "I can't have your team sticking tubes up everyone's ass once a day."

Particularly not if some male surgeon was doing it. Her team of commanding mothers trusted that Fiana valued Je, but a lot of them were old-fashioned and uncomfortable with having large, awkward hands on the handle of a blade.

"Then draw up a list of essential crew that you can't afford to lose, and they will be tested once a day. We're risking lives, understand?"

"I'll have the list drawn up, but we don't start taking temperatures until people start passing out," Fiana said. "The DNA samples are in lead cases in the ice rooms with our food. We can put anyone in danger there for now."

But it would be a temporary solution.

It was enough to mollify Je. For now.

But the decisions would become tougher as this went on.

———

The mass audit came back from a sweaty, tired Audra, who tracked Fiana down in the galley hall. The Secondary Mother had sheaves of clear flexies filled with accounting tables.

"There's unaccounted for mass. We did the audit. We tested the ship's acceleration profile. The amount of mass they estimated is dead-on: there's sixty chipstone worth of something *somewhere*. Manifests can't account for it. We've checked everything we can think of."

Fiana offered her a pocket of cooled water, which Audra took and sucked on gratefully. Fiana used that as a moment to capture her own thoughts and continue nibbling at a basket of grapes.

"We're going to have to search everyone's cabins, verify personal allowances," Audra said, before Fiana could even speak.

"No." Fiana shook her head. "There are just over a hundred crew. And yes, split, that could be enough." And when they sailed out from Sese, they did not have to consider how true their mass was, they just deployed sails into the appropriate dust plane until they had the speed and vectors needed.

"We only did a rough manifest and mass account before leaving," Audra noted.

"I've sailed the dust planes of the Greater World all my life, Audra. I've been F&O, then Secondary Mother, and now Mother. I'd sense it in my bones the moment we left if the sails were straining, our vessel heavy," Fiana said. "No, this has only been a problem since that seedship."

Audra, her legs looped around an air-chair, straightened. "What are you thinking?"

"Take the survey teams, the men, out onto the hull. Use airlocks facing away from the dust to keep cover. Full Encounter rules. Do you understand what I am asking you? Can you do that?"

Audra looked past Fiana, out into a personal darkness and into fear as she considered her own death. Fiana was asking her to go out an airlock, seal it with ice and rock once the team was out, and then they would search the hull.

If they encountered Hunter-Killers, they would jump off into the vacuum and scatter to their deaths. They would not, under any circumstance, return to any known airlock, lest they lead the enemy inside. Maybe the Hunter-Killers wouldn't buy that. Maybe they would. It was still a hard thing to ask of a person.

Audra would know that if she turned this down, Fiana would honor her choice. But it would be a blow to her standing.

"I will lead a team," Audra said in a low, determined voice. "We need to find out what may have killed us."

Fiana held her hand and squeezed it. Such bravery. She had no doubt in Audra. It's why she had chosen the strong mind from her old F&O cohort to join her when the World Mothers had given Fiana a command of her own.

For an entire watch, the ship went about its business in a pre-funereal silence, with crew jumping at every bang and creak in the empty air.

Je came to report on two crewmembers who had passed out. An older F&O calculator and one of the survey men. He had given them fluids and put them in a freezer to let them cool down.

"The ship is suffering too," he told her. The ship's heart had an infection, he judged. Some kind of pericarditis inflaming the sac around the great muscle. They were pumping it full of antibiotics and hoping for the best.

"We can't dump heat, not yet," Fiana told him.

"I know," Je said, softly. "I know."

The warble of airlock alarms echoed. Je twisted in the air to look down the corridor. "They're coming back inside."

Crew streamed through the air toward the doors. They weren't carrying weapons. There was nothing that would stop a Hunter-Killer, there was no point.

But they still came, determination on their faces, fists clenched. They would have thrown their bodies against the deadly machines to buy their sisters another minute of life, Fiana knew, with a tight knot in her stomach.

Voidsuits came through instead of gleaming, spidery balls of death. Fiana relaxed slightly.

And then more suits struggled through.

And more.

Despite herself, Fiana said aloud, "There are too many of them!"
Ten other suits that hadn't piled into the airlock on the way out.
Ten.
That could be sixty chipstones. If they were . . .
They removed their helmets, and the confused crew gasped.
Belshin men. Ten Belshin men.

————

Ten Belshin males had maybe doomed them all. It was something that Fiana kept rolling around her head for all its strangeness as she stared at the ten foreign faces hovering before her.

It was the math. The simple math. The massive ball of rock and ice looked substantial, but orbital mechanics were precise and unforgiving. Their weight had slowed them down enough to throw off the maneuver.

Fiana pointed at them. "You activated the seedship, you unleashed the Hunter-Killers on us all, and then you fled to our hull to hide! You have the audacity to hide on *my* ship?"

"They don't speak Undak," Je said. "Do you want me to translate? They're expecting that you will throw them out of the airlock. They're terrified."

Fiana saw it on their faces. Resignation, fear, some defiance.

Audra crossed her arms. "We should slice off their balls, put them in the fridge with the seedship DNA, and then shove the floating shits out the airlock."

"Don't translate that," Fiana said to Je.

"Engage the Lineage Protocol," Audra said. "We need to initiate it now. While we still have some sort of chance."

Fiana could hear Je suck in his breath. She looked over at Audra. "We're not going to talk about the Protocol right now. These are human lives you're talking about."

Audra glanced at Je. "Mother, he knew the risks when he agreed to join the ship."

"Lives," Fiana said. "All of the lives on this ship are important."

Je was only half listening. Several of the newcomers were chattering to him.

"They know you're angry," Je reported, cutting Audra off. "They're expecting you to kill them. They're gastric plumbers. Belshin slaves. They fled when their ship was attacked."

"We cannot afford the increase in consumables," Audra hissed. "We're far out into the void. We're off orbit and schedule. You know what needs to be done, and it needs to be done quickly. Your crew is depending on you."

Fiana raised a finger. "Audra—"

Audra pushed herself back away from the room. "As one of your secondaries, I have to remind you: every moment those males remain on board is a moment stolen from our own future. It's math. It means cold, hard decisions. But that is what leaders do: they make the hard choices."

———

Fiana took Lily into one of the observation ice bowls.

"I wanted to show you something," Fiana said, drifting out toward the polished ice.

The young F&O calculator hung next to her. "Mother?"

Fiana pointed out at the dark. "Look out there, Lily. All those small points of light. That's something few, if any people from the Archipelago ever get to see."

From here, they could see the entirety of the dust plane. The multitudes of the rings, the rocky moons.

Lily held up a thumb. "All of our people out there. Hiding away from Hunter-Killers."

They stared at the dust band for a long while.

Lily cleared her throat. "Even if you sacrifice the Belshin, we can't fix the orbit."

"I spent two whole nights running the figures," Fiana said. "Audra ran them as well. Fifty people can survive a full braking maneuver and a loop by object IF-547, then 893, and a second all-sails slow that you and F&O have given me."

"So, it's Lineage Protocol." Lily turned her back to the dust plane. "They tell you in the Academy not to get too attached to the men aboard."

"People I trust are all telling me it's time." Fiana rubbed her forehead. The headaches were getting more and more intense. "We only have enough for fifty people to survive until we reintercept the dust plane."

Protocol said it was time to take donations from all the men, store the material, and then ask them all to do the honorable thing. The *noble* thing. If they balked, then it was the Mother Superior's job to enforce the choice.

Only women could bear the next generation. Fiana needed to act to secure futures.

And yet . . .

"The ideas that fix this situation, they won't come from just one person dictating them. It's going to have to come from everyone working the math. And being cross-checked."

Lily's eyes widened. "You're not going to engage the protocol?"

504 | By the Warmth of Their Calculus

504 | By the Warmth of Their Calculus

"Hard choices. The other mothers keep telling me to make hard choices." Fiana pushed away. "But the people who tell me that don't have to bear the consequences of those choices, and don't see the whole community, just the part of it that they identify with. It's easy to make a 'hard' choice when the price is paid by someone else."

"This won't be a popular decision," Lily said. "And I won't tell Audra you called her unimaginative."

"Thank you." Fiana patted her shoulder. "I need you to work the problem, talk to anyone who might have ideas, and to lean on your peers."

"We'll keep running ideas through the team," Lily promised. "There are things the engineers have proposed in the past. More non-essential mass that could be jettisoned. It could help."

Because there was math. And then there was *math*. Math was a tool, wasn't it? A tool to be wielded or mastered.

And Fiana wasn't going to give it blood.

Four crew passed out and were found floating in the corridors. Je came to Fiana, his face pinched and ruddy, to give her an update.

"Mother, we should have off-duty crew switch to a three-person cross-check system so that no one ends up alone."

"I'll send out orders." Fiana was hooked into the "top" of her room, which was laced with foot-webbing. She'd been holding a position in front of an air vent, letting the rush of air bob her back and forth.

"And I need to check you over," Je said.

Fiana waved a hand. "I am fine. There are others who need your attention, Je."

"You are the Mother Superior," Je insisted.

Fiana wiped a fat bead of sweat collecting behind her ear. The air was getting so thick she felt like she couldn't breathe anymore. They'd stopped venting and the heat, the moisture from shaving the ice, and the dust in the air had turned the ship into a swamp.

"I will endure," Fiana said. "If I feel I'm at risk I'll let you know."

Je didn't look happy, but he couldn't really do anything about it, so he nodded. He had floated his way back to the entryway, and he paused there, hands and feet in an X and gripping the door's lip.

"Mother, may I ask you something?"

His voice had softened, and Fiana could hear the worry.

"Lineage Protocol?" she asked him.

"Such a dry name for something so horrific," Je said as he nodded.

"F&O is working hard on a solution. I've asked all for ideas. But, in a nutshell, we need to breathe less, surgeon. We used too much as a simple rocket to get us away from the Hunter-Killer area. The math is simple and hard to escape. We only have so much air and we know how many people are onboard."

"The equation is simple," Je said. "So we change the assumed inputs. The air-use rate is based on an assumption created by surgeons for average crew with average activity."

Je had her complete attention.

"Can you actually get the crew to breathe less?"

"The more you move, the more you breathe. So, we freeze crew shifts. Everyone bound to their room and webbed in. No one moves until rescue. The command room shift stays in place and sleeps in place."

"You're asking the entire crew to stay in bed for twelve full shift rotations?"

"And to focus on breathing slowly and deeply. And that is not all. We have drugs for surgeries. The larger ones that use more air, we will need to drug them."

"And what will that get us, Je? Will that get us to the dust plane? Will that halve the air we use?"

"This isn't math, it's biology. Messy, imprecise," Je said.

"Give me an estimate," Fiana ordered. Because she couldn't risk lives based on messiness.

"I think we can reduce our air usage to two thirds. Maybe to a half. We won't know until we start the experiment and monitor the impact."

Two thirds still left a ghost ship. A third was an unblinking gulf that still couldn't be crossed.

But it would mean fewer lives that needed chosen for sacrifice.

"Ready the drugs," Fiana said. "We'll run the experiment and get a shift's worth of data." It wouldn't get them there by itself. It wasn't the solution. But it was something they could test.

Audra appeared at the door and shoved Je aside. She had a bandolier strapped tight across her chest and had changed into her dark black sortie uniform. Her pistol was in its forearm holster.

"Mother, we have a mutiny!" Audra said. "The men heard that Lineage Protocol will be called for. Some of them released the Belshin prisoners and broke into the armory."

———

The mutiny spread quickly. Panicked men took weapons into common areas which they barricaded with decoration panels ripped from the walls.

Many of them were on sortie parties, so were familiar with in-ship combat and knew where to find the weapons.

"We have the numbers," Audra said. Few could match her well-trained cadre. "My sisters are fast and are the best hall-grapplers in the fleet."

Audra and her team would fight bitterly. They were Sortie Three, rarely sent to other ships, but trained to protect this one. They were backed up by members of engineering and women from the stays and tether teams, with their arms muscled from handling spider-silk ropes.

They raced down corridors to the heart of the mutiny where the chanting men were making their demands heard.

"Stop here!" Another woman in black held out a hand near a turn in the rock-ice corridor. "Mother, they're shooting anyone who tries to approach the barricade."

They all grabbed rails and stopped. Fiana listened to the shouts, the men trying to keep each other roused to bravery with their too deep voices. No raising them to neutral-sounding tones now because they were speaking to mothers or sisters around the ship.

"We should have expected this," Audra said, acid in her voice.

Je said nothing but shrank back as if trying to hide against the wall.

Fiana looked around again at the nervous, but anticipatory sortie crew all watching Audra, waiting for the command. Then, she quickly peeked around the corner.

"Mother!"

The men shouted at her but didn't shoot. Fiana took that as a good sign and stopped to look at the crudely hammered together door leading to the common rooms and the forms that she could see through the gaps nervously flitting around.

"Get Lily from F&O," Fiana ordered.

"And?" Audra also looked ready to go.

"It's the heat," Fiana said. She was panting from the race over here. "It's affecting our minds. Leading us to mistakes."

"My mind is tempered well," Audra hissed. "They are traitors to Sese, and foreign agitators from the other side of the Archipelago."

"What are their demands?" Fiana couldn't tell from all the yelling.

"They want the chance to live through lottery," one of the tether women with a simple club in her hands said.

"That's treason," Audra said. She leaned forward. "If we fight them, we can take care of the dilemma we face."

"Death makes traitors of many," Fiana said. "And the heat addles their minds. All our minds. Wouldn't you say, surgeon?"

Je did not look happy about being addressed. "Mother . . ."

But Fiana saw Lily coasting toward them and waved her over. "My calculator! We have a tricky situation."

Fiana pulled the last of her wrap off, stripping herself naked, and then gently tapped the wall so that she would float out into the center of the corridor before Audra could react.

She could hear the sudden murmurs of surprise, the repeated low whispers of "Mother."

They began to shout their demands through the barricade, but she held up a hand.

"It is too hot for a fight, but if we have to, you are outnumbered. And you know this. So we are going to talk about this instead, because I did not come out here into the void to do the Hunter-Killers' work for them. Not when our ancestors risked so much to create the Archipelago and dust planes for our survival. I will not spit on their memories."

They quieted.

"I don't have the answer to our situation. But we, together, do. Come out to me, Je, Lily. Tell them what you've been telling me."

Fiana looked back. She gestured at them both.

Slowly, the surgeon and the F&O calculator bobbled out to join her.

"F&O found our mass problem. They saved us from the Hunter-Killers. Je is keeping us alive as best as he can in this heat. I don't have the solution to how we make it back to the dust plane alive, but the two of them, with all of our help, might. There is no one answer here, but if we piece all of their ideas together, and add in some new ones, they could add up to enough to get us back home."

Lily stared at the men, then bit her lip. "We need to shed mass once we're at the apoapsis. Everything we can imagine we can do without and things we can't. We need to pare the ice and rock to the bare minimum, down to nothing but air, sails, and our own bodies."

"And the rest of us must strap in and not move until rescue. The biggest among us must be drugged," Je said.

The men protested. That would surely impact them the most.

But Je argued with them. "These are the realities," he insisted. "We have to breathe less . . . or not at all."

"We could thin the air more," one of the male voices on the other side suggested. "I'm in gastric, we can change the recirculation mixes."

As the suggestions continued, Fiana relaxed.

"We are not separate from the civilization that birthed us," she said to Audra. "We do not have to fall into murder and blood. Not this time."

The great dustship calved at apoapsis, the very height of its orbit. Fiana would have liked to have seen it and the entire dust plane glinting its encirclement of their Greater World. But she had to be in her cabin. No one moved about, not even her. Surgeon's orders.

It was not unusual for objects to break apart. Hopefully, anything watching would assume it was a normal event, a weakened body splitting apart and becoming two.

Now they would begin to gain speed, to dump off heat and more consumables to alter their trajectory *just* enough. They were speeding up, every tick as they dropped lower and lower.

"Why would you want to go back out there?" Je had once asked her, when they were on Sese's interior walking through the botanical gardens. He raised a hand to encompass the whole world in all its lushness. She had been trying to recruit him as surgeon. The first male surgeon to fly the Archipelago void. "Why not stay and enjoy this world?"

"The only difference between them is scale, Je. Come see all the worlds. It reveals us for who we really are, to go out there."

Fiana lay strapped to her webbing, in a drugged stupor, breathing slowly. There were many more full shifts ahead to endure before they would come screaming back into the dust and throw out the sails to chatter and bite and shake.

But they would get home, she thought dimly.

The math was there.